Thomas Dunham Whitaker

An History of the Original Parish of Whalley and Honor of Clitheroe

Vol. 1

Anatiposi

Thomas Dunham Whitaker

An History of the Original Parish of Whalley and Honor of Clitheroe

Vol. 1

Reprint of the original, first published in 1872.

1st Edition 2023 | ISBN: 978-3-38212-901-9

Anatiposi Verlag is an imprint of Outlook Verlagsgesellschaft mbH.

Verlag (Publisher): Outlook Verlag GmbH, Zeilweg 44, 60439 Frankfurt, Deutschland
Vertretungsberechtigt (Authorized to represent): E. Roepke, Zeilweg 44, 60439 Frankfurt, Deutschland
Druck (Print): Books on Demand GmbH, In de Tarpen 42, 22848 Norderstedt, Deutschland

AN HISTORY

OF THE

ORIGINAL PARISH OF WHALLEY,

AND

HONOR OF CLITHEROE.

TO WHICH IS SUBJOINED

AN ACCOUNT OF THE PARISH OF CARTMELL.

BY

THOMAS DUNHAM WHITAKER, LL.D., F.S.A.

VICAR OF WHALLEY.

THE FOURTH EDITION, REVISED AND ENLARGED,

BY

JOHN GOUGH NICHOLS, F.S.A.

AND THE REV. PONSONBY A. LYONS, B.A.

VOLUME I.

"Antiquities, or remnants of history, are 'tanquam tabula naufragii,' when industrious persons, by an exact and scrupulous diligence and observation, out of monuments, names, words, proverbs, traditions, private records and evidences, fragments of stories, passages of books that concern not story, and the like, do save and recover somewhat from the deluge of time. In these kinds of imperfect histories I do assign no deficience, for they are 'tanquam imperfecta mista,' and therefore any deficience in them is but their nature."—LORD BACON, *Advancement of Learning*, book ii.

LONDON: GEORGE ROUTLEDGE AND SONS, THE BROADWAY, LUDGATE.

MANCHESTER: L. C. GENT.

1872.

CONTENTS OF THE FIRST VOLUME.

BOOK III.

LIST OF PLATES.

PREFACE TO THE PRESENT EDITION.

THE History of Whalley on its first appearance, in the year 1801, was hailed with general approbation. A scholar and a man of genius had condescended to irradiate with his learning and his eloquence a department of literature that of late had been mainly characterised by tedious details relating to the descent of property, and dry deductions of genealogy. Books of Topography had hitherto been books for reference only, but here was one that could be perused with gratification and delight.

The Author had great advantages in the field of his inquiries. A country of extraordinary natural magnificence and beauty, yet of the utmost wildness in its pristine condition, had become the thriving dwelling-place of a teeming and busy population: offering the most wonderful contrasts, and presenting for observation and comment continual changes in social progress. A Roman city yielded up a rich store of its buried treasures. A wealthy monastery unfolded ample records of its former grandeur and influence, and all the curious details of its internal discipline. The ancient lords of the territory had been historical personages, acting their busy parts in life among the highest of the ancient nobility, and merging at last in princes of the blood royal. Here were some of those forests which provided certain of their wants, and a large proportion of their pleasures, but under laws and customs very different to those of modern use. These were interesting subjects, and the materials for illustrating them were fortunately abundant. When such subjects and materials were treated not only with intelligence and taste, but with all those embellishments that were the fruit of brilliant talents and well-directed scholarship, the result was such as to persuade the world that a new era had arrived in Topography. The success which the author achieved encouraged him to pursue his inquiries in other neighbouring districts, and to produce a series of works, of which some account will be found in the ensuing biography.

The History of Whalley was reprinted in the year 1818 as a Third Edition; the Second Edition, dated 1806, not having been an entire reprint, but formed by many cancellings, additions, and supplements. And this course of procedure constitutes, in fact, the chief defect of the Third Edition, as well as of the Second, and even, it must be admitted, of Dr. Whitaker's whole method, or want of method, as a local historian. The *limæ labor* was not a task in which he was disposed to engage. He took no pains to amend his original text,[1] but continually corrected it by supplementary statements, reverting to preceding passages, perhaps from memory only, and expecting the reader to do the same. Thus, in the course of the present work, he will often be found to introduce a subject for a second time,[2] amplify and elucidate his former statements, and sometimes, from a lapse of his really powerful memory, to which he too much trusted, actually to some extent repeat them.[3]

Many subjects are thus dislocated and divided, or discussed in several places, an arrangement which, if intentional, would show that the Author not merely expected that his book should be read throughout, but that the reader should retain in his mind all he had previously perused, as in other historical works of the highest class. Remembering, however, the more ordinary character of works of this kind, and the more ordinary uses to which they are generally applied, as books for occasional consultation, the present Editors have considered it desirable to make cross-references in such cases, and the book when completed will be rendered still further useful and available by an adequate Index, a very necessary feature in which it has hitherto been miserably defective.

Another matter to which in the revision of this Edition especial attention has been paid is the collation of documents, and the verification of quotations and references, many of which, it may be fairly declared, Dr. Whitaker had put forth with "all the carelessness of genius;" and this is said advisedly, not overlooking the claim to "correct and authentic transcripts," which, with singular self-deception, he makes in his first Preface. For the records the present Editors have had recourse to the original manuscripts, wherever they were accessible, and in such cases it may be asserted that, with scarcely an exception, they have now the satisfaction to present a more accurate and often much fuller text. For

[1] The reader will find a very extraordinary instance of this noticed in p. 31. Dr. Whitaker never withdrew (in any of his three editions) his hope expressed in 1796 (in his *manuscript* copy) that Mr. Towneley would write on the Roman Antiquities discovered at Ribchester, although Mr. Towneley had actually addressed the Society of Antiquaries on the subject in 1798, and the Society had published his memoir in 1799. Yet in another place, at p. 486, Dr. Whitaker mentioned the Dissertation on the Ribchester Helmet, printed in the Vetusta Monumenta, as the only literary essay that Mr. Towneley ever gave to the public.

[2] The most serious instance of this is Clitheroe, the history of which is given partly in Chapter IV. of Book III. and partly in Chapter II. of Book IV. The latter will fall in the Second Volume of the present Edition.

[3] Among several other *repetitions* in the Third Edition, the same document regarding the Chapelries of the Classis of Blackburn that is printed in full in the note at p. 160 is afterwards given in abstract in the text at p. 416.

such blemishes as, they are sensible, may after all have escaped their notice they still solicit a candid indulgence.

In justice to themselves, and to the Publishers who are at the expense of this Edition, the Editors think it proper to specify further the extent of their additions. They must first remark, by way of anticipation, that they do not undertake to continue the recent history of the ancient Parish of Whalley during the last half-century. That would not only have enlarged the work to too great an extent, but it would have diluted its historical character, and have in fact made it a totally different book. The modern history of the district has been in part published in Baines's History of Lancashire, and more recently, to a certain extent, in Newbigging's History of the Forest of Rossendale. It may hereafter be written, more in detail, on a consistent and well-considered plan.

But in respect to the descent of great properties, and the correction and continuation of the lists of incumbents of the older churches, and the masters of the grammar schools, this edition will be rendered as complete as possible.

More particularly it is intended that the Pedigrees of the principal resident families, being brought down in all particulars to the present time, should impart a character to this edition which will deserve and insure a lasting reputation.

In every case, when such information is obtained as the Author would have probably been disposed to employ had it been available to him, the occasion is taken to improve the text and to add valuable information in the notes. Altogether this First Volume has received an accession of more than one-fourth of new matter: which the reader will readily distinguish by its being marked throughout with [ ].

The chapter on the Roman Antiquities of Ribchester is enlarged by the addition of fresh information and additional engravings to the extent of more than seventeen pages, including a description of Dr. Whitaker's own plates, which was hitherto wholly omitted.

To the documents illustrative of the history of the Abbey there are important accessions, from various sources, and especially from the singular commonplace-book or miscellany kept by the monks (and now preserved in the British Museum,) from which Dr. Whitaker himself made many extracts. Among these are the two political Poems in pp. 155, 156, only partly and incorrectly printed by Dr. Whitaker, but now rendered complete. The exceedingly curious Lectionary in pp. 193-199 is a new feature, and a document of which the Editors know of no parallel belonging to any English monastery.

The Seals engraved by Dr. Whitaker are now for the first time described, and the Seal of the Abbey itself has been found, and is engraved for the first time.

Among the documents relating to the Forests very large additions are inserted; and, generally speaking, considerable use has been made of the records of the Duchy of Lancaster, which have become accessible in the Public Record Office. The various *compoti*, and more particularly that relating to the Royal *equitium*, or haras, at Ightenhill Park, will be found to unfold many particulars of a character hitherto little understood. The lists of Foresters, Parkers, and Officers of Clitheroe Castle are now first compiled.

The Customs of the Honor of Clitheroe, at p. 292, are also introduced for the first time into this Edition.

An account of the principal records and other archives upon which this History is chiefly founded, (promised at p. 149,) it is proposed to prefix to the Second Volume.

The Author's own copy of the last Edition being now the property of the Publishers, his latest marginal notes have been available for use; and others made by his amanuensis the late Rev. Samuel J. Allen, M.A. in a copy still belonging to his son the Rev. George Samuel Allen, M.A. of Manchester, have contributed a considerable amount of information; whilst Mr. G. D. Tomlinson of Huddersfield has kindly communicated various manuscript corrections made in the first and second editions by Dr. Whitaker's antiquarian friend and coadjutor Mr. Beaumont of Whitley and Little Mitton. To Ralph F. Ainsworth, esq., M.D., of Manchester, the Editors are indebted for the loan of the copy of the First Edition formerly belonging to Matthew Gregson, F.S.A.

The Rev. Robert Nowell Whitaker, M.A. the present Vicar of Whalley, has, with the utmost kindness, answered the various inquiries with which the Editors have found it necessary to trouble him; and many important communications have been received from the Rev. F. R. Raines, M.A., F.S.A. Vicar of Milnrow, and Hon. Canon of Manchester; from William Langton, esq. of Manchester; William Beamont, esq. of Orford Hall, Warrington, F.R.A.S.; Mr. Dixon Robinson, of Clitheroe Castle; Mr. Alderman Wilkinson, of Burnley; Mr. William Haworth, of Burnley; and other gentlemen. In architectural matters, Mr. William Angelo Waddington, author of *Architectural Sketches on the Calder and Ribble, in and around Whalley*, has earned their especial thanks, and particularly for his careful ground-plan of Whalley Abbey.

BIOGRAPHICAL MEMOIRS

OF

THOMAS DUNHAM WHITAKER,

LL.D. F.R.S. F.S.A.

AT the close of the account, given in this Work, of his predecessors in the Vicarage of Whalley, Dr. Whitaker introduced the following biographical notices of himself, which it has been thought desirable to transfer to the present more prominent position, and to append to them some additional particulars, and an account of his literary performances:

"Thomas Dunham Whitaker, the author of this Work, was born June 8th, 1759, in the parsonage-house of Rainham, Norfolk, which is the subject of a singular story, recorded by Sir Henry Spelman.[1] The writer's father was, in 1759, Curate of that parish; but, his elder brother dying unmarried in the beginning of the following year, he came, Oct. 3, 1760, to reside at his paternal house at Holme,[2] which had never been out of the occupation of the family from the reign of Henry VI.

"In November, 1766, the writer of this was placed under the care of the Rev. John Shaw, of Rochdale, an excellent grammarian and teacher. In 1771 he became sickly, and apparently declined, so as to be incapable of any attention to books till the year 1774, when he was placed in the family of the Rev. William Sheepshanks,[3] at Grassington, in Craven, an airy and healthful situation.

"In November of that year he was admitted of St. John's College, Cambridge, where he

[1] "In the reign of Charles I. Sir Roger Townshend, purposing to rebuild his house at Rainham, conveyed a large quantity of stones for the purpose from the ruins of Coxford Abbey in the neighbourhood. These stones, as often as any attempt was made to build them up in this unhallowed edifice, obstinately gave way. The owner next tried them in the construction of a bridge; the arch of which, in like manner, suddenly shrunk. He then piously determined to apply them to the rebuilding of the parsonage-house, where they quietly remained till about the year 1764, when they were once more removed by the late Viscount, afterwards Marquess Townshend, to another place, and the site of the original manse, of which the foundations are still visible north-west from the church, was taken into the park. The strange wanderings of this *Casa Santa* are now, probably, at an end."

[2] The Rev. William Whitaker, our Author's father, died in 1782, aged 51: see under Holme (in vol. II.) the Latin epitaph which was erected there to his memory, and to that of his widow, (Lucy, daughter of Mr. Robert Dunham of Sedgford in Norfolk,) who died in 1788, at the age of 64.

[3] Dr. Whitaker has left a biography of Mr. Sheepshanks in his History of Craven, second edit. p. 474, and afterwards published his portrait in the Supplement (1821) to *Loidis and Elmete*.—"At the village of Grassington he received into his house a limited number of pupils, among whom, in the years 1774 and 1775, was the writer of this article."

went to reside Oct. 3, 1775. In November 1781 he took the degree of LL.B. intending to pursue the profession of the Civil Law, which he studied, for two years, with great attention. But in June 1782, his father having died, after a week's illness, he settled upon his paternal estate, which for thirty years he has continued to improve and adorn, by successive plantations.

"In August 1785 he was ordained deacon at Rose Castle by Dr. John Law, Bishop of Clonfert [and afterwards of Elphin, eldest son of Dr. Edmund Law, then Bishop of Carlisle]; and in July the following year received the order of priesthood from the same prelate, both without title.

"In 1788, having previously recovered, by a donation of 400*l.*, the patronage of the Chapel of Holme, which had been founded by one of his ancestors, with the aid of some liberal subscriptions, but at an expense of 470*l.* to himself, he rebuilt it, the old edifice being mean and dilapidated. In 1797, he was licensed to the perpetual curacy of Holme, on his own nomination.

"In July, 1799, he qualified as a magistrate for the county of Lancaster; and, in the next year but one, for the West Riding of the county of York.

"At the Cambridge Commencement, 1801, he completed the degree of LL.D.

"In the month of January, 1809, he was presented, by the present Archbishop of Canterbury (Manners Sutton), to the Vicarage of Whalley, the great object of his wishes.[1] For this favour, besides his Grace's own generous disposition to reward a stranger who had written the History of the Parish, he was also indebted to the recommendation of that learned and excellent prelate, Dr. Cleaver, formerly his diocesan, and then Bishop of Ban-

[1] "Accept my sincere thanks for your most kind and friendly congratulations upon my attainment of an object which has long been very near my heart, and which after all will in a pecuniary view be, for some time at least, the gaining of a loss. For the vicarage house is in a sad dilapidated state, and I find that I am in hands from which little can be wrung without ligitation. Then there is a tenant in the house who, after having given voluntary notice to quit at Easter, now threatens to hold over, when all the materials are prepared for the repairs.

"I feel a pleasure and a pride in improving and adorning so favourite a spot, where I mean to reside as much, especially in winter, as I conveniently can, though I scarcely know how I can pack my large family within the walls. For this intention, however, I have several reasons. And first, a sense of duty,—that I may be found as much as possible at my post. Secondly, that I may be nearer my friends than at Holme, though at Whalley I must receive them *presso lare*, which I trust will be overlooked if the receiver be also *dulcis amicis*. A third, and I hope a still inferior motive, is my health, as I am persuaded that the mild air of Whalley in early spring will better agree with my lungs than the harsh unkindly blasts that sweep our eastern moors.

"Whalley also is a more central situation than this for my clerical excursions through the parish; for it is my wish to preach annually in every church and chapel within it, and you, I trust, will have no objection to accept my services in course at Clitheroe and Downham. Will you do me the favour to mention the same subject to Mr. Clarke with respect to Whitewell? As I am a wretched horseman, I propose to economise distances by taking two neighbouring churches every Sunday. I hope this plan will neither be unuseful nor disagreeable in the parish. It will at least bring me acquainted with the parishioners, and *noscere exercitus, nosci exercitui* may be applied to a parish minister as well as an officer. Dr. Coulthurst [the Vicar of Halifax] and Mr. Haddon [the Vicar of Leeds] have found great satisfaction in pursuing this plan in their respective parishes." (Letter to the Rev. Thomas Wilson, from Holme, March 23 1809. The living of Whalley, at this time, was worth little more than 100*l.*, and Holme about 50*l.* per annum.

gor, whose many instances of friendly attention he remembers with gratitude, and whose recent death he deeply deplores."

On the 14th Jan. 1813, Dr. Whitaker was presented by Thomas Clarkson, then a minor, to the rectory of Heysham near Lancaster, but at that place he never resided; and he resigned the benefice in 1819, Mr. Clarkson being then qualified to present himself to it.

On the 7th Nov. 1818, Archbishop Manners Sutton presented Dr. Whitaker to the vicarage of Blackburn, which he retained, together with Whalley, until his death.[1]

Such were the main events of Dr. Whitaker's progress in life; and we may now endeavour to recall some of the associations from which they arose, or to which they led. It is evident that his early course was much influenced by his attachment to his tutor Mr. Sheepshanks, who had been a Fellow and Tutor of St. John's college, Cambridge, the contemporary of Bishop John Law (named in the opposite page) and of Archdeacon Paley, and the tutor of many distinguished pupils, among whom were Edward Law (younger brother of John,) afterwards Chief Justice of the King's Bench and Lord Ellenborough, and John Pretyman, afterwards Tomline, successively Bishop of Lincoln and Winchester. Whitaker, by the advice of Mr. Sheepshanks, went to the same college, where one of his contemporaries and most intimate friends was Herbert Marsh, afterwards Bishop of Peterborough.

Subsequently, when having succeeded to his ancestral property, and become resident in the country, he paused in his legal studies, and determined to make the Church his profession, it was to Bishop Law that he had recourse for ordination, and his earliest efforts in the pulpit were exerted at Leeds,[2] where his friend Mr. Sheepshanks became

[1] "Since he was presented to the vicarage of the populous and extensive parish of Blackburn, he has resided in that town the greater part of the year, and takes his full share along with the Curates in performing three services every Sunday, in a large church, and to a crowded congregation. In Dr. Whitaker's church Divine Service is performed, and a Sermon preached, on the Sunday night. I mention this, because I consider that Dr. Whitaker's approbation of a measure the tendency of which has sometimes been questioned, is of very great importance." (Part of a Letter signed Clericus Lancastriensis, and dated Bury, Lancashire, Oct. 2, 1820, written "by one who is totally unknown to him," and printed in the Gentleman's Magazine, xc. ii. 402.)

[2] A list is here appended of Dr. Whitaker's published Sermons :—

Religion and Loyalty connected : being the substance of a Discourse (on 1 Tim. ii. 1—3) preached in St. John's Church, Leeds, on the General Fast Day, February 28, 1794, and published at the request of the Congregation.

A Sermon preached at the Consecration of the Chapel of Holme in Lancashire, July 19, 1794.

A Sermon (on Isaiah x. 25, 26), preached in St. John's Church, Leeds, on the General Fast Day, Feb. 25, 1795.

A Sermon (on Revelations, xxii. 2) preached in Trinity Church, Leeds, on Sunday, October 3, 1796, for the benefit of the General Infirmary in that town.

A Sermon preached at the Consecration of the Chapel of Salesbury, in Lancashire, September 8, 1807. ("I entirely agree with you in the sentiments and feelings which our friend W.'s excellent Consecration Sermon has produced; it is certainly a very masterly performance." The Rev. Thomas Starkie, Vicar of Blackburn, to the Rev. Thomas Wilson, Dec. 21, 1807.)

A Sermon preached at the Primary Visitation of the Lord Bishop of Chester (George Henry Law), 1814.

A Sermon on the Consecration of Whitewell Chapel, 1818. ("A memorable Sermon, preached in troublous times, from the words, Sound an Alarm," Joel, ii. 1. *Not. Cestriensis*, ii. 346.)

resident in 1777, and Vicar of St. John's church in 1783. On the 13th January in the latter year (two years before his ordination) Whitaker had married Lucy, daughter of Mr. Thomas Thoresby a merchant in Leeds,[1] and in the same town his two elder children were born in 1785 and 1787.[2]

When settled in his ancestral mansion at Holme, being desirous to bring the neighbouring clergy together for social and religious intercourse, Whitaker instituted a sort of literary club, consisting of half a dozen members, whose tastes were congenial, and who dined together at each other's houses once a month for several years. The Rev. Thomas Starkie the Vicar of Blackburn, the Rev. William Barton (M. D.) the Incumbent of Harwood and Samlesbury, the Rev. Robert Smith the Incumbent of Waddington, and the Rev. Thomas Wilson the Master of Clitheroe School, were amongst the regular members. The Rev. Henry William Coulthurst, D.D. the Vicar of Halifax, the Rev. Rowland Ingram the Vicar of Giggleswick, Mr. John Dawson the learned mathematician of Sedbergh, and Mr. William Cockin of Milnthorpe, who had been writing-master and accountant of the grammar school at Lancaster, were occasionally welcome guests. At these meetings there was much sympathy of moral and religious feeling, elegant hospitality, pleasurable conversation, and quiet enjoyment. The subjects discussed—previously announced—were of a general and miscellaneous description, embracing matters affecting the Church, literature, and politics, and rendered especially attractive by the playful humour of Wilson, the mechanical listlessness of Starkie, the meditative tenderness of Barton, and the masculine freshness and warmth of Whitaker.[3]

At this period, his studies were principally devoted to the works of the early Fathers

A Sermon preached in the parish church of Blackburn on Sunday July 11, 1819, on occasion of a late seditious meeting held in that town. This was published in a cheap form, pp. 20, for circulation among the operatives. It is a noble piece of oratory, and did great good in bringing the middle classes to a sense of the dangers which at that time surrounded them.

A Sermon preached for the relief of the Poor in the Town of Blackburn, Jan. 30, 1820. 8vo.

The Mourning of Hadad Rimmon, a Sermon preached on the evening of His late Majesty's Interment, Feb. 16, 1820. 8vo.

[1] At p. xv of his Life of Ralph Thoresby, prefixed to the *Ducatus Leodiensis*, 1816, Dr. Whitaker gives some account of that collateral branch of the family of Thursby or Thorsby from which his own wife was descended. Thomas Thoresby was living in Leeds in the reign of Charles the Second, and "Thus much is certain, that this person and Ralph were contemporaries in Leeds 41 years, and lived together on the footing of relations." Thomas was father of another Thomas, and "This second Thomas had a son of the same name, who, with a stronger and more original mind than Ralph, had a great bias to antiquarian pursuits, and bore a striking resemblance in the features of his countenance to the portrait of his celebrated relative. His oldest daughter married the Editor of this Work, who continued the name in the baptismal appellative of his oldest son." Just before it had been stated that "The name (excepting that it has been engrafted into another family by baptism) is now reduced to a single individual, without issue, and unmarried." This is believed to refer to Mrs. Whitaker's younger sister.

[2] For further information in regard to Dr. Whitaker's family see the Pedigree under Holme in Volume II.

[3] Memoirs of the Rev. Thomas Wilson, B. D., by the Rev. Mr. Canon Raines, prefixed to Miscellanies, &c. (Chetham Soc. vol. xlv.) p. lvi.

of the Church, and to the Greek and Roman historians of the same period.[1] To the antiquities of his own locality and neighbourhood he was first earnestly directed by the perusal in Dugdale's Monasticon of the *Status de Blackburnshire*,[2] a very interesting relic of that class of historical composition which was most in favour in the monasteries. As this unfolded to his view a very extraordinary picture of the pristine ecclesiastical arrangements of the district in which he resided,[3] he was led by the curiosity thus excited to further investigation, and to pursue the history of the church and parish of Whalley in other records of its early ages.

It was during the three closing years of the last century that the composition of the History of Whalley was seriously undertaken. The first portion of it was committed to the press early in 1800;[4] and was published during that year, with the Dedication to Mr. Townley, and the Preface, which are reprinted in the ensuing pages.[5] "PART THE SECOND," which bears date 1801, commenced at page 217 of the first edition, and closed with page 408, supplemented by many additions and corrections. PART THE THIRD commenced with page 411, and closed at p. 483, followed by further supplementary pages. A Title-page was then printed for the whole volume, with the date M.D.CCCI.

Dr. Whitaker was very fortunate in the assistance he received from his friends towards the expense of the engravings of this work. Both the plates of Roman antiquities were

[1] See his own statement to this effect, quoted hereafter in p. xxii.

[2] See his allusion to "this germ of the *History of Whalley*," in p. 96 of the present volume.

[3] The results appear in the Chapter on the Ecclesiastical History of the Parish (Book II. chapter i.) See pp. 66 *et seq.* of the present Edition, where a more accurate text is given of the narrative of the *Status de Blackburnshire* than has previously been published.

[4] On the 6th Feb. 1800, in a letter to the Rev. Thomas Wilson, the Master of Clitheroe School, Whitaker mentions that he had then just sent to Hemingway, his printer at Blackburn, the manuscript of the First Book of the History of Whalley, "some parts of which will exercise both his optics and his sagacity." This letter further contains a remarkable anecdote of "Turner, the draftsman," who was "showing all the irritability of youthful genius." See this passage hereafter at Gawthorp, to which place it relates.

[5] It may be interesting to notice that the History of Whalley was on its first appearance cordially reviewed by Mr. Gough the Editor of Camden, in the *Gentleman's Magazine* (January 1802), at the unusual length of fourteen pages. The article, however, is rather a long series of extracts than anything more, for the critical observations are few; but it concludes with this passage: "We flatter ourselves our readers will not be displeased with this extended review of a work whose author has shewn himself master of all that general knowledge which Cicero's friend Crassus requires in an orator, and qualified to discuss more at large the various topics which he has handled so judiciously on a smaller scale." Again, in the Magazine for December, 1805, the History of Craven was run through in like manner to the extent of nearly seventeen pages.

The History of Whalley was reviewed in the *British Critic*, xxi. 101–108, and 229–236.

An article in the *Monthly Review*, vol. xxxviii. criticised the History of Whalley with more freedom, and was not forgotten by its author when he published his subsequent work: "I understood that some of the Reviews had been sufficiently civil to *The History of Craven*; if the *Monthly* gentry are otherwise, unless they are guilty of some very gross misrepresentations, I have determined to treat them with silent contempt." Letter to the Rev. Thomas Wilson, March 1, 1808.

presented to him by Mr. Townley,[1] as were the views of Gawthorp and Townley Hall. Of the three plates of Whalley Abbey, one was certainly presented by Lady Howe (for it is so acknowledged in the inscription), another probably by Lord Curzon, and the third not improbably by Mr. Beaumont of Whitley. Mr. Beaumont was certainly the contributor of the large plate of Little Mitton Hall, and of all the portraits of the Beaumonts. Mr. Lister Parker gave the two plates of Browsholme, and the use of several etchings which had been made for him by Mr. John Chessell Buckler. The view of Read Hall was contributed by the author's cousin, Alexander Nowell, esq.

It is worthy of especial remark that most of the drawings for these plates were early works (in water-colours) of the great painter, Joseph Mallord William Turner, R. A., though they bear his name under the simple designation of "Wm. Turner, A." It was only in the year 1800, at the time when Turner, then five and twenty, was employed for "Whalley," that he was elected an Associate of the Royal Academy,—an Academician in 1802. The landscapes that he subsequently drew for Dr. Whitaker's Richmondshire rank among the finest of his works.

A distant view of Clitheroe, from Eadisford Bridge, was dedicated to Lord Ribblesdale, and the plate probably engraved at his expense. It is the subject in the present work most characteristic of the painter's future excellence, and one upon which the engraver bestowed correspondent pains.[2]

After the History of Whalley was completed, and had been received with very general approbation, Dr. Whitaker was encouraged, particularly at the suggestion of the Rev. William Carr, of Bolton Abbey,[3] to direct the same attention to the adjoining district of

[1] Dr. Whitaker to Mr. Wilson of Clitheroe, Feb. 6, 1800. "If Mr. T.'s delicacy will allow, I propose the following inscription for one of the plates of Roman Antiquities which he gives me :—

CAROLO TOWNLEY, Arm. S. S. A. artium et elegantiarum arbitro eximio hanc Tabulam sumptibus ejus ære incisam in animi grati testimonium D. D. D. T. D. W."

This inscription first appeared in the *Wilson Correspondence*, p. 169: for both the plates of Roman Antiquities, it will be seen, are dedicated (in the same words) to the Society of Antiquaries; but under the plate of Townley hall will be found a Latin dedication to Mr. Townley, and under the distant view of Townley an inscription to his memory, including the encomiastic designation proposed in 1800,—artium et elegantiarum arbitro eximio. Dr. Whitaker's Dedication to Mr. Townley of the First Edition of this Work is reprinted hereafter.

Some explanation perhaps is required of the orthography of this name, now so generally known from Mr. Charles Towneley's collections at the British Museum, as well as other reasons. Dr. Whitaker usually wrote and spelt it Townley, and his spelling has been left unaltered in several places of this volume. It appears that the middle *e* was adopted, *i.e.* resumed, during Mr. Towneley's time.

[2] "Mr. Basire is now at work on the plate of Clitheroe, which he says will deserve twenty-five guineas." Dr. Whitaker to Mr. Wilson, Feb. 6, 1800.

[3] "His highly-esteemed friend the Reverend William Carr, B.D. Minister of Bolton Abbey, and late Fellow of Magdalen College, Oxford, as he first suggested the idea of the present work, has continued to urge it on, through every part of its progress, with a zeal and activity which merit his warmest thanks." Preface to the First Edition of the History of Craven, 1805.

Craven. His plans were matured at the close of 1802, when he issued a Prospectus[1] in which the scope of the proposed work was thus developed:—

Prospectus of a HISTORY of the DEANERY of CRAVEN and WAPONTAKE of STAINCLIFFE in the County of York, in six Books, intended as a continuation of the History of Whalley. By THOMAS DUNHAM WHITAKER, LL.D., F.S.A.

The Introduction will contain a general Outline of the subject, together with Remarks on the Soil, Climate, Mineralogy, and Scenery of the country.

BOOK 1st. Will consist of the British and Roman Antiquities of Craven, particularly the Station of Olicana and other Encampments, a Roman Villa, Roads, &c. together with the Discoveries belonging to those two Periods, which, at different times, have been made within that District.

BOOK 2nd. Will embrace Monastic Antiquities, including an ample Account of the Monasteries of Salley and Bernoldswick (*i. e.* Kirkstall) and the Priory of Bolton. Observations on the Monastic Life and Manners, the State of Religion in the 12th and 13th Centuries, &c. Several interesting Epistles and other Remains of the Abbots of Kirkstall and Salley, hitherto unpublished. Also many original Epistles and other curious Particulars of the first Abbots of Whalley, from a MS. communicated to the Author since the Publication of the History of that Parish.[2]

BOOK 3rd. Will give a general Survey of the State of Property in Craven from the Æra of Domesday Book, together with an Account of the Origin, Descents, and final Union of the two great Fees of Percy and Clifford, intended as an Introduction to the three following Books.

BOOK 4th. RIBBLESDALE, or a Survey of the respective Parishes in Craven, contiguous to the Ribble, including an Account of the ancient and present State of the several Churches, their Dedications, Endowments, Appropriations, Monumental Inscriptions, Incumbents, Patrons, testamentary Burials, &c. from very early Times: as also the several Manors and their Descents; Pedigrees of the principal Families, whether existing or extinct, State of their Mansions, armorial Bearings, &c.

BOOK 5th. AREDALE, containing, in addition to the particulars enumerated above, an Account of the Castle and Honour of Skipton nearly from the Conquest to the present Time, together with Memoirs of the noble Families of Romilly, Albemarle, and Clifford. This Book will also contain an Investigation of the Sources of the Are and a Description of the Romantic Environs of Malham.

BOOK 6th. WHARFDALE, containing a similar Survey to the two former; and, in addition, a particular Representation of the Scenery of Bolton, Bardon, Kilnsey, and the whole course of the River Wharf upwards to its Source.

The Collections for this Work in general, and particularly for the Monastic Part, have been made from personal observation, and, with a few exceptions, from original or at least from MSS. Authorities.

[1] This Prospectus is now reprinted from the Author's original Manuscript, which has fortunately been preserved. It was sent to Mr. Nichols in a letter (dated Holme, Nov. 3, 1802), which commences thus: "Sir,—I am now engaged in a History of the Deanery of Craven, which will form a kind of Sequel to the History of Whalley, and as I have suffered many inconveniences from Country Printers, I feel myself directed, by many considerations, to yourself, and especially as a Brother Antiquary and Topographer." The plan detailed above was not eventually adopted in every respect, for the History of Craven follows the more ordinary arrangement of Parishes, and the monasteries and antiquities are placed under their respective localities.

[2] These were afterwards reserved for the Second Edition of the History of Whalley.

The whole will be comprised in one Volume large Quarto, illustrated with numerous engravings. Price to subscribers 2*l.* 2*s.* 0*d.* Subscriptions received by Mr. Hatchard, No. 190, Piccadilly, Mr. Edwards, Pall Mall, and Messrs. Edwards, Halifax, Yorkshire.

Dr. Whitaker was at this period addressed by the Editor of Camden with congratulations and proffers of assistance, and it is with great pleasure that the present writer finds himself able to insert in this place the cordial reply that was immediately returned:—

The Rev. Dr. Whitaker to Richard Gough, Esq.

Holme, Feb. 16, 1803.

Sir,—I have this day received the favour of your letter, and hasten to acknowledge with many thanks the pleasure with which I perused it.

I am not possessed of your Edition of the Britannia,[1] tho' I have read the greater part of it and hope to have an opportunity of consulting it once more in the course of a few days, when if any thing occurs with respect to Craven I will avail myself of your most obliging offer.

However contemptible the account given by the Monthly Reviewers[2] of the History of Whalley may be in itself, it has been far from contemptible in its effects either upon my Interest or Reputation, at least in the Country, where few Readers are either able or willing to judge for themselves, but indolently acquiesce in every thing they are told by the Periodical Retailers of what they call Criticism.

It is however no small consolation to be assured by such judges as Mr. Gough that their opinion is neither general nor his own.

One circumstance with respect to that work I owe it to myself to account for. The work, as you cannot but have observed, abounds with errors of the press, the history of which was this, that having been persuaded to print the book in a neighbouring town I committed the care of the press to a respected friend the Vicar of the place,[3] who discharged his trust very faithfully. But we have since discovered that when the foul copy was struck off and sent to him for correction the workmen without waiting for the return of it struck off the whole impression, and when this operation was over, in order to impose upon him, corrected the types according to his emendations and returned a clean copy, the only one which was ever printed.

With respect to the History of Craven I have every assistance which the Gentlemen of that Country (excepting the two noble Representatives of the Cliffords) can afford. I have not overlooked the celebrated Family Picture at Skipton, and if the Monthly Review do not ruin my Subscription, which I am certain they will greatly injure, I mean to put a copy of it into the hands of Mr. Basire, who will undoubtedly do justice to it.

In the course of a few days I expect to be summoned to a very interesting scene. The vault of the Cliffords which has been closed many years is about to be opened in order to repair one of the tombs which has given way and which stands immediately above it, and a friend upon the spot has promised to give me timely instruction of the day when the process will begin.[4]

[1] It is very pleasing to find in Dr. Whitaker's review of the *Magna Britannia* of Lysons, in the Quarterly Review the following tribute to the Editor of the earlier *Britannia*:—

"Of the name of Mr. Gough we wish to speak with reverence; he was the father of English Antiquaries in his day; he generously patronized rising merit in others; he devoted his own life and ample fortune to the pursuit of antiquities, and he still lives in the affections of many surviving friends." (vol. v. p. 332.)

In his life of Thoresby (p. xiv.) Whitaker quotes Gough's "candid and moderate estimate of Thoresby's merits as an antiquary," as that of "a great Master of English Topography."

[2] See note in p. xvii.

[3] The Rev. Thomas Starkie, M.A.

[4] It took place in the chancel of Skipton church, on the 29th March 1803, and Dr. Whitaker has described the results in the History of Craven, (second edit.) p. 355.

It is almost impossible to procure franks in a situation like this, otherwise I should not have put you to the expence of postage[1] for the inclosed sheet, of which I beg your acceptance.

My Pedigree of the Radcliff Family being unavoidably incorrect and defective from want of authoritative materials when that part of the work was printed, and much good information being communicated afterwards, I compiled a second which I think is as nearly complete as any existing documents can make it. But of this I only struck off fifty copies which I intended as presents to the friends of the Work, and of which this is the last. I am, with Sincere Respect, Sir, Your much obliged and obedient Servant,

T. D. WHITAKER.

Richard Gough, Esq., Enfield, Middlesex.

The History of the Deanery of Craven, comprising twenty-five parishes, was published in 1805, in a quarto volume, not very different in general appearance from the History of Whalley. It was dedicated to the Duke of Devonshire and Lord Ribblesdale,[2] to the former (the fifth Duke, who died in 1811,) as Lord of the Percy Fee in Craven, and representative of the last male line of the Cliffords Earls of Cumberland; "yet not more distinguished for his ancient descent than for the ancient virtues of an English nobleman,—disinterestedness, liberality, and attention to the happiness of his numerous dependants:" the latter, the first Lord Ribblesdale (who died in 1826), "whose loyalty and patriotism have twice assembled under his standard the Gentry and Yeomanry of Craven, now constituting one of the finest provincial corps in the Kingdom." The Duke gave to the work all the engravings of Bolton and Bardon, together with one of the great family picture of the Cliffords; Lord Ribblesdale contributed seven plates, and twelve other plates were presented by Stephen Tempest, esq. of Broughton, James Hamerton, esq. Pudsay Dawson, esq. the Rev. William Roundell, Danson Richardson Currer, esq. the Rev. Thomas Sheepshanks, and Richard Heber, esq. of Marton. A still more important favour conferred on the author was the communication of the collections that had been made by John Richardson Currer for a History of Craven, which included transcripts of those of Dodsworth, and John Charles Brooke, Somerset herald.

"The Townley MSS." as in the author's former work, "continued to pour out their inexhaustible stores on every part of the present subject;" and, while making this acknowledgment, he took the opportunity to append a tribute to the memory of Mr. Towneley, then recently deceased, which may well claim admission here in the character of a biographical reminiscence of both the eminent men to whom it relates, more particularly as it did not reappear when the book was reprinted.

Here let me for a moment, and in my own person, give way to feelings which will not easily be

[1] It will be admitted, in the present days of cheap postage, that this apology was not wholly unnecessary, when the charge of 4*s*. 2*d*. is found marked on the cover, the weight being 1¼ oz.

[2] The Second Edition of the History of Craven is dedicated only to the sixth Duke of Devonshire (1812-58): "To his Grace William Spencer, Duke of Devonshire, Marquis of Hartington, Lord of the Percy Fee, &c. in Craven, and representative in the male line of the illustrious House of Clifford, this Work is respectfully inscribed, with an earnest wish that the favoured portion of his domains which constitutes the principal subject of it, may continue to receive from him the same attention and regard with which his good taste has honoured it in early life."

suppressed. My last research in that library, where I had spent so many happy hours, was in company with its late excellent and accomplished owner. So completely at that time did the vigour of his understanding and the vivacity of his spirits appear to buoy up a sinking constitution, that I little foresaw how soon I should be called to attend his remains to the tomb of his ancestors. A monument is preparing to his memory, which I doubt not will be worthy of his taste and virtues, but the best monument of Mr. Towneley will be fixed in the hearts of those who knew him—"non quod intercedendum putem imaginibus quæ marmore finguntur, sed ut vultus hominum, ita simulacra vultûs fluxa ac fragilia sunt, forma mentis æterna, quam tenere et exprimere non per alienam materiam et artem, sed tuis ipse moribus posses." TACITUS.

The History of Craven was reviewed in the *British Critic* for December 1805, which pronounced the volume to be "full of interest, information, and amusement;" adding, that "in no place, nor any subject, do the writer's industry of investigation fail, or his vivacity of remark relax."

Another critic, in the *Eclectic Review* for April, 1806, made further amends to Dr. Whitaker for the indignities which he had suffered from the Monthly Reviewer of his History of Whalley. It was predicted that the History of Craven would not preserve that unmolested enjoyment of *otium cum dignitate* upon the shelf of the library which was the usual reward of Topography. "It is so much enlivened by picturesque descriptions, by judicious remarks, by sketches of biography, and by natural delineations of life and manners in different periods, that we lay it aside, for the present, with little weariness, in the hope of resuming it with renewed satisfaction." . . . . "The author has succeeded in rendering the History of Craven one of the most complete and valuable pieces of topography that have come within our observation."

The History of Craven being accomplished, its author proceeded in the summer of 1805[1] to form the Second Edition of the *History of Whalley*. This was completed, with eight additional engravings,[2] in September 1806.

The Second Edition of the *History of Craven* was published in 1812. Unlike the History of Whalley, it was entirely reprinted, and was now embellished with fifty-five plates, of which fifteen were accessions to this edition.[3]

It may be thought an omission if we do not mention, among the works of Dr.

[1] In a letter dated July 10, 1805, he states that 150 copies of the History of Whalley then remained unsold, that he wished to cancel several sheets, and to insert much additional matter which had fallen into his hands since the first publication of the work. "By this means a kind of Second Edition will be made up."

[2] The "Advertisement" (as reprinted hereafter in p. lxvi) says "four" only. These were those which had been engraved specially for this Edition: 1, the view of Whitewell; 2, the portrait of Parker the Bowbearer of Bowland, and other objects at Browsholme; 3, the view of Read hall; and 4, the distant view of Townley hall and park, bearing the Latin inscription to Mr. Townley's memory. But, besides these, Mr. Beaumont gave the three Beaumont portraits, and, further, a folio engraving by H. Meyer of a portrait of Henry Tilson, painter, by himself. This last, however, is not found in all copies, and, as well as the Beaumont portraits (see vol. ii. p. 24 of the present Edition), is not even mentioned by the Author. See all the plates carefully set forth in Upcott's "Bibliographical Account of the principal Works relating to English Topography," 1818, p. 473.

[3] See all technically described in Upcott's English Topography, pp. 1394-8. In the folio copies of the History of

Whitaker, the *Description of Browsholme Hall*, 1815, 4to, which is usually named in the list of his works. That book however (which is noticed at p. 337 of the present volume) was rather the compilation of Mr. Lister Parker himself, though the leading features of its descriptive portions were drawn from the History of Whalley. To these were appended a variety of historical papers, from the originals at Browsholme, edited without note or comment. The clever etchings by Mr. John Chessell Buckler added great interest to the book, of which only 100 copies were printed.

The Third Edition of the *History of Whalley* followed in 1818. Dr. Whitaker had been desirous to reprint this work for many years before the intention was carried out. In a letter to Mr. Nichols dated so early as the 16th June, 1810, he writes:—

> The remaining copies of the History of Whalley, which were disposed of by me to Mr. Edwards at 1*l.* 10*s.* each, have been nearly sold by him at 7 or 8 guineas per copy.
>
> I have ample and valuable materials for another Edition: particularly an account of the Abbey of Lamb-spring,[1] communicated to me by one of the ex-monks; and the Journal [2]—a most curious one—of a Gentleman of the Parish in the year 1617. My predecessor (not my immediate one)[3] left also some valuable papers, which have fallen into my hands. With these and other helps I propose to print 250 copies uniformly with Craven, discarding a great deal of trifling stuff which I was compelled to admit before in order to make a Book. With this wholesome severity the whole in the type and page I have mentioned will be reduced to 320 pages.

He mentions again in May 1811 that he was then "extremely desirous to see the History of Whalley reprinted;" and again in Nov. 1813:—

> I am now at leisure to attend to another Edition of the History of Whalley, and sincerely wish that Mr. Edwards[4] would authorise you to set about it.
>
> My *History of Lonsdale* will I trust be ready to send to press by May next.

But it was not until July 1818 that the Third Edition of "Whalley" was completed. It has this brief Dedication to Archbishop Manners Sutton:

> To the Most Reverend CHARLES, LORD ARCHBISHOP OF CANTERBURY, Primate of all England, and Metropolitan, this Work is inscribed, by his Grace's most obliged and devoted servant, the Author.

It was embellished with fifty-one plates, twenty of which had not been in the previous editions.[5] The price was six guineas in royal quarto, and twelve guineas in folio.

It was the Doctor's intention, in the same year, to produce a new edition of the *History of Manchester*, by his namesake the Rev. John Whitaker, which had been published in the year 1773. This appears from the following letter to Mr. Nichols:

Craven, published at Fifteen Guineas, there are duplicate impressions of the aquatinted plates by S. Alken, worked in colours. The price of the copies in Royal Quarto was Five Guineas.

[1] In Westphalia; see Third Edition, p. 547.

[2] That of Nicholas Assheton.

[3] The Rev. William Johnson: see these papers described in p. 215 of this volume.

[4] Mr. Edwards, of Halifax, supplied the necessary paper for Dr. Whitaker's works.

[5] Several of these were merely borrowed from Churton's Life of Dean Nowell. It is stated in Boyle's *Yorkshire Library* that the number of copies printed of the third edition of the History of Whalley was only 25 on large paper and 100 on small; but the writer was misinformed, for the numbers were 150 large and 250 small.

Holme, March 25th, 1818.

Dear Sir,—On my way through Manchester yesterday I took an accurate survey of the Collegiate Church and College, and have also well considered the amount of the additions which will be required. The result is that I think that the whole of Mr. Whitaker's text, together with my own additions, notes, &c. may be included in one quarto of the same type with your reprint of the History of Whalley, with which I should wish it to be uniform. Three or four engravings and not more will be required.

If you would like to undertake the publishing as well as printing of this work, I will thank you to inform me what plan you would recommend. I think it may be made an interesting undertaking.

I am, Dear Sir, Very sincerely yours, T. D. Whitaker.

Will you be so obliging as to forward a copy of Whalley to Adam Cottam, Esq. Whalley, near Blackburn, Lancashire, and place it to my account with Mr. Edwards.

But, besides this History of Manchester, there was another work at one time proposed to range with the Histories of Whalley and Craven. The reader will have already remarked the Doctor's mention of a *History of Lonsdale*, undertaken before Nov. 1813, and proposed to be published in the course of the ensuing twelvemonths. As it is unknown under that name, it is satisfactory to be able to give the complete account of its design which is furnished by the following (undated) Prospectus.

Preparing for the Press, in one volume quarto, illustrated with numerous engravings, **Alauna Setantiorum**, or a History of the Vale of Lune; containing Accounts of the *Setantiorum Portus* of the Romans, the Castle, Dutchy, Priory, Parish, and Friary of Lancaster, the Saxon antiquities of Heysham, the chain of Danish forts on the Lune, the Castle, Honour, and Priory of Hornby, the Roman *Bremetonacæ*, or Overborough, the Castle of Thurland Tunstall, the Environs of Ingleborough and Kirkby Lonsdale, and lastly the Parish and School of Sedbergh, with a Catalogue and short Biographical notices of eminent persons educated in that seminary. By Thomas Dunham Whitaker, LL.D. F.S.A. Vicar of Whalley, and Rector of Heysham, in Lancashire. London: Printed by Nichols, Son, and Bentley, for John Murray, 50, Albemarle Street.

This was evidently intended to form a volume correspondent with the Histories of Whalley and Craven. The materials collected for it were eventually added to the book now called the History of Richmondshire. But before we proceed to the circumstances which led to the latter work, we have to recur to the author's sentiments at an earlier period, when, during the winter of 1810-11, he experienced a serious failure of health,[1] and consequent depression of spirits, whereby he was induced to take leave of the History of Craven in the following terms:

On these "Cold Keld Heads" we have reached some of the highest ground in the Island; and, looking southward as far as the confines of the Peak, survey beneath our feet the three valleys of Craven, with all their boundaries of rock and fell, their scattered villages, rich pastures, and diversified landscapes. Further, in the same direction, stretch the brown hills of "the ancient parish of Whalley," with their populous towns, descried through smoke, and their uniting streams gradually expanded into one great æstuary, and mingling

[1] "The truth is that my constitution is greatly broken within the last six months, and I can have no great expectation of surviving many winters like the last. . . . My health requiring change of air, I am going in a few days to a friend's house in Cumberland." Letter to Mr. Nichols, May 28, 1811.

with the sea. These ample districts have now been exhausted in two successive Works, by the labours of the same Topographer. The point on which now he stands, the elevation, and almost unbounded prospect, are inspiring. He now turns his eye in another direction, and the valleys and plains of Richmondshire stretch like a map before him.

To the left is the Roman *Bracchium*, with its elevated summer camp. Beneath appear the grey towers of Nappay; while, bounding over the cataracts of Aysgarth, the Eure conducts him to another Bolton, pregnant with facts and recollections. Immediately beyond rise the proud towers of the Nevilles at Middleham, and far to the north-east the Norman keep of Richmond, begirt with its monastic accompaniments. In that vale to the east the arches of Coverham distinctly present themselves. In those fertile meadows beneath appear the fragments of Joreval, and Tanfield beyond, in whose church repose, beneath magnificent tombs, the Marmions of *real* History. Turning to the south-west the "troublous Skell" leads him to the mighty carcase of Fountains, and to the more ancient and venerable foundation of Wilfred.

Time has been when such a scene might have inspired and dictated another Work. But the recollection of increasing years and declining health, together with the demands of duty in a most serious and important charge, checks at once the unseasonable impulse, and compels him to resign an *History of Richmondshire*[1] to some younger and more vigorous Antiquary, on whom, were it in his power, he would willingly bestow whatever portion he may possess of two qualifications henceforward of little value to himself, but indispensable to a true Topographer, namely, Perseverance and Enthusiasm.

These feelings, however, were transient. We have seen already that Whitaker did not at all abandon either his love for topography or the literary composition to which it led; but in his latter years he was drawn into a different line of procedure by the liberal offers which were made to him by publishers. His series of works in quarto, whether accomplished or projected, have been purposely reviewed in succession; and we now proceed to the more magnificent series in folio.

A new edition of the *Ducatus Leodiensis, or History of Leedes*, by Ralph Thoresby, first published in 1715, was undertaken on a sumptuous scale by Messrs. Robinson, Son, and Holdsworth of Leeds, and Mr. John Hurst of Wakefield. Dr. Whitaker made copious additions, and inserted a memoir of the author. The book was published in a very large folio; and in a corresponding volume, having the same date in its title-page, 1816, both being richly embellished with excellent engravings, appeared Dr. Whitaker's "*Loidis and Elmete*; or, an attempt to illustrate the Districts described in those words by Bede, and supposed to embrace the lower portions of Aredale and Wharfdale, together with the entire Vale of Calder in the County of York." The former book was dedicated to the Duke of Leeds, and the latter to the Archbishop of York, Dr. Venables-Vernon. Subsequently, in 1821, there was added "An Appendix to *Loidis and Elmete*," consisting of 88 pages, with four plates, one of which—Gledhow, by J. M. W. Turner, engraved by George Cooke, is a landscape that is scarcely surpassed by those in the "Richmondshire."

Dr. Whitaker had now arrived at the height of his success and of his enthusiasm as a topographical historian. Whilst still engaged in the *Loidis and Elmete*, he continued his collections for the History of Lonsdale, and was tempted, by the offers held out to

[1] Which has been suggested to the author. From some future undertaking of a much less laborious nature, if life and leisure permit, he means not to preclude himself. (*Note by Dr. Whitaker.*)

him by some London publishers then distinguished for the magnificent scale of their transactions, to form visions of a work hitherto unexampled.[1] The Prospectus of this undertaking, which was issued in Feb. 1816, is here reproduced, for, as displaying the extended scope of a design of which he was eventually able to accomplish but a small portion, it may certainly be regarded as one of the most remarkable effusions that ever proceeded either from the pen of Dr. Whitaker or from any other literary projector, however confident and ambitious :—

Prospectus of A GENERAL HISTORY of the COUNTY of YORK. BY THOMAS DUNHAM WHITAKER, LL.D. F.S.A. Vicar of Whalley, and Rector of Heysham, in Lancashire.

THE History of Craven, together with the republication of Thoresby's Ducatus Leodiensis, and the supplementary volume which accompanies it, having already embraced more than one fourth part of this great county, both in extent and population, the Author of two of these works, and the Editor of the other, has been induced to submit to the Public, and especially to the Nobility, Gentry, and Clergy of Yorkshire, such an extension of the plan, as will gradually comprehend the whole.

With respect to the limits of such an undertaking it is impossible to speak with precision: an unexpected redundancy of materials in one part, and an equally unforeseen deficiency in a second, may frequently occur, and yet be very far from balancing each other; but, as a conjecture, rather than an assertion, it may be stated that seven folio volumes, of about five hundred pages each, and of the same type with the supplementary volume to Thoresby's Ducatus, will probably complete the work. To render this limitation, with respect to the treatment of a subject so extensive and multifarious, the more credible, the Author wishes it to be understood that his great objects in the use of the materials to be committed to him will be selection and compression. Subjects which are really important, either in point of picturesque beauty, of antiquity, or of their connexion with historical facts, will be treated of in detail: those, on the contrary, which have none of these recommendations, will, as far as it may appear consistent with accuracy, be thrown into the shade, in order to give relief and prominence to the others.

The Author's researches, besides a personal application to original authorities existing in public libraries, and, where he may be permitted, in private collections also, will extend to an exact survey of every parish: thankful as he shall always be for previous directions to objects of curiosity, he will take nothing upon trust. He will see every thing with his own eyes; he will make minutes upon the spot. In order to the attainment of the same accuracy in those parts of his subject which depend upon written evidence, he most respectfully desires the representatives of ancient and noble families, who may be induced to encourage the projected work, to consider what a stamp of authenticity is impressed upon the whole by a general opinion of its having been

[1] It will be remembered that the *Magna Britannia* of the brothers Daniel and Samuel Lysons, a really sound, substantial, and comprehensive, if less brilliant, work, was actually in progress at the same time, though unfortunately lingering in its laborious course. The counties were taken alphabetically, and published,—Bedfordshire, Berkshire, and Buckinghamshire, 1806; Cambridgeshire, 1808; Cheshire, 1810; Cornwall, 1814; Cumberland, 1816; Derbyshire, 1818; Devonshire, 1822. There this excellent work stopped. It must also be borne in mind that at a time when Whitaker had not yet conceived his own magnificent scheme, he had done ample justice to the *Magna Britannia* in the *Quarterly Review* for May 1811: "On the whole, considering the laborious work of Messrs. Lysons as a series of volumes for the purposes of reference, ... we think it entitled to much and general commendation. The arrangement also is clear and the style perspicuous and unaffected. These are praises which belong to the authors; the defects of the work arise out of the plan itself—perpetual abridgement where detail was loudly called for, and mortifying transitions from one subject to another at the moment when interest and anxiety were beginning to be excited." The apology for which limitations must always be *Est quodam prodire tenus si non datur ultra.*

compiled from original authorities. In more than one topographical work, already before the public, it has been, with very few exceptions, the happiness of the Author to have drawn from the first fountains of information. In this age of general intelligence and liberal communication little, it may be hoped, remains of that absurd jealousy, by which the ancient stores of families were supposed to contain unknown and unsuspected secrets, which might shake the titles to estates. The most superficial knowledge of the law of England, as it exists at present, must in a moment remove every such apprehension. Discovery, while it is the most animating object of a topographer, can alone give an interest in the minds of real judges to a topographical work. What, for example, would have been the feelings of the writer, what the loss and disappointment of his readers, had he been debarred from access to the stores of the Cliffords, in their two surviving branches at Skipton and Bolton? And can it be supposed that in a county, which for several centuries has been the principal residence of so many noble families, distinguished for their activity and exertions in war and peace, the grantees also of so many religious houses, there should neither have been curiosity to collect, nor care to preserve, the evidences, which from time to time had fallen into their hand?

Antiquarian research, and even poetry itself, have of late been turned to the elucidation of ancient manners: and the pursuit is a decisive proof of the superior intelligence and curiosity which belong to modern times. Heretofore, when an antiquary had given a tolerable view of the ruins of a religious house, the name of the founder, the date of the foundation, with the manors and carucates which it possessed, in faithful and dull detail, his office was performed, and his readers were satisfied. Meanwhile it never occurred to the one or the other that all this was the body only, not the soul of monastic history; that monkish manners, a system of life not only picturesque and magnificent, but combined in some degree both with piety and usefulness, was a study for philosophers; that all its varieties are yet accessible, and what is better, accessible not by means of direct and formal narrative, but through the medium of inference and induction (one of the most delightful exercises of an intelligent antiquary) in the compotuses of the religious houses. To the stores of this nature which are reposited in the libraries of ancient families, and still perhaps unexplored, the Author looks with anxious expectations: but in the Harleian and Cotton libraries, and above all, in the indigested, but almost inexhaustible, collections of Dodsworth, he reckons with certainty on much original intelligence.

Besides those objects of research which are already pointed out in other topographical works, he is aware that throughout the progress of a personal survey he must be indebted to the original information of respectable persons resident on the spot for a knowledge of many interesting objects hitherto unnoticed, and of discoveries which have lately taken place. On this subject he respectfully addresses himself to his brethren the parochial clergy, whose local knowledge of their respective districts, as well as intimate acquaintance with their own parish registers, and the antiquities of their churches, renders them peculiarly qualified to communicate hints and directions to an inquisitive stranger. Such communications the Author will always receive with gratitude.

For a continuation of the catalogues of incumbents from the time of Charles II. when Mr. Torre's collections cease, the author will feel himself much indebted to their living successors.

To add materials to a history of manners as well as of places, any intelligence with respect to the birth-places of eminent persons, as subjects for short biographical memoirs, and any account of curious and ancient customs, will best be derived from the same respectable and intelligent authorities.

Architecture, ancient and modern, civil, military, and ecclesiastic, will always be regarded in this work with peculiar attention; and the magnificent seats of the nobility and gentry, with which this great county abounds, together with the distinguished specimens of art in painting and sculpture with which they are severally adorned, will not fail to receive a due tribute of respect.

Picturesque natural scenery, as well as the efforts of modern taste in the production of scenery which rivals nature, will in no instance be passed over without attention.

The entire text of Domesday, Leland's Itinerary, and many portions of that of Camden will be incorporated with the work. The late returns of population will also be subjoined to the account of every parish.

A work of this nature would be extremely imperfect without genealogical accounts of the principal and ancient families of the county; yet of all branches of antiquarian literature, none has remained to the present time in such a state of error and confusion, especially with respect to the earlier descents, as genealogies. On this subject, however, the author is quite at ease, as no pedigree will be inserted in the following work which has not been either compiled, or at least revised and corrected, by one of the most skilful genealogists in the kingdom, William Radclyffe, esq. Rouge Croix, so that each may be considered as having received the stamp of official authority. Much more amusing and instructive memorials however of the ancient nobility and gentry of Yorkshire will be given at the close of their respective genealogies, in original letters and other curious documents, principally referring to their services on the Scottish border, from the reign of Henry VIII. to that of Elizabeth. To these, of which a very large and valuable collection has been entrusted to the author, will be added facsimiles of the autographs.

As a proper accompaniment to genealogies, the armorial blazonings, which once adorned the windows of almost every church in Yorkshire, though the greater part of them are now no more, having been preserved by the care of Glover and Dugdale, in their respective visitations, will be enumerated, and many of them engraved.

Nearly allied to the subject of genealogies is that of epitaphs, with respect to which a system of very strict selection will be observed. The bulk of this work will never be purposely swelled by prolix and tumid panegyrics on inconsiderable persons; and it may sometimes happen, according to the merit or demerit of each, that a monument will be given without an epitaph, or an epitaph without a monument. Elegance in the composition, or distinguished merit in the subject of a monumental inscription, will alone ensure its insertion.

Subsidiary to the Author's department in this laborious work are those of the draftsman and the engraver, concerning which the public have a right to be informed that no expense will be spared to render the History of Yorkshire what, in the present state of the national taste, can alone procure for it a favourable reception—truly magnificent. To this end distinct but superior artists will be engaged for subjects of landscape and architecture.

It is sufficient to name J. M. W. Turner, esq. R. A. in the former of these departments, and Mr. Buckler in the latter.

One species of ornament will be peculiar to the present work.

It was the complaint of Stukeley, an excellent draftsman, that the Roman antiquities of Britain had never been drawn. Even in Horsley's Britannia Romana, the inscriptions are represented by miserable scratches of mere outlines. In the History of Yorkshire they will be engraved from finished drawings, in all the softness of mouldering antiquity.

The engravings will of course be numerous, as no object of real beauty or importance will be omitted; but in the outset of the plan it is no more possible to conjecture what will be the number of these embellishments, than to pronounce with tolerable accuracy on the quantity of letter-press. It is obvious, however, from the character of the different districts into which the county of York is divided, that the number of plates must vary greatly in different volumes.

The work will commence with an account of the portion of the North Riding popularly called the County of Richmond, together with those parts of Lonsdale and Eweeross which are included in the Everwicschire of Domesday.

This part, which is already in considerable forwardness, will be put to press in the course of a few months.

It will naturally be asked, what use is intended to be made in the ensuing work of the well-known publications by which the county of York has already been partially illustrated. Of these, perhaps, the most celebrated, Thoresby's Ducatus, has been completely reprinted in conformity with a plan which had been partially executed before the undertaking now proposed was thought of. But the example will not be followed in other instances. Drake's Eboracum, for instance, though a work of great merit, contains too much matter of a sort purely local to be incorporated, in its present state, with a general history of the county. Its contents will therefore be melted down into a general mass; the less interesting portions will be rejected; and an uniform text, with respect to the city of York, will be formed out of that and such other authorities as may be accessible to the author. Minor works of the same nature, all of which, however useful within the respective districts of which they treat, are liable to the same objection as parts of a more extensive undertaking, may, it is hoped, be brought to undergo the same process, and to endure the transfusion of their better and brighter parts into the projected volumes without a murmur.

Such is the general outline of a work, undertaken, as the author freely confesses, at too late a period of life, but under the cheering influence of some encouragements and expectations with which he could not have flattered himself earlier. In the course of three months, however, will appear what may properly be regarded as a more extended prospectus, or rather specimen, of a general History of Yorkshire; that is, the Supplemental Volume to Thoresby's Ducatus, executed precisely according to the Sketch which has been traced on the present sheet.

In order to remove a doubt which has been suggested, the Subscribers to the present volumes are requested to observe that they will form integral parts of the general work, and that they (the Subscribers) will be entitled at a fair price to all the supplemental matter and engravings which it may be judged expedient to insert in the correspondent parts of the general work when reprinted.

The work will be handsomely printed in folio, on fine demy paper, and the large-paper copies on super-royal drawing paper, and will be delivered to the subscribers in Parts, price *2l. 2s.* each, or on large paper, with proof impressions of the plates, price *4l. 4s.* each Part.

The impressions of the plates will be delivered in the exact order they are subscribed for.

Subscriptions to be received by Messrs. LONGMAN, HURST, REES, ORME, and BROWN, Paternoster Row, London; Messrs. ROBINSON, SON, and HOLDSWORTH, Leeds; Mr. JOHN HURST, Wakefield; and by all the other Booksellers in the county.

The printing of the work will commence as soon as 500 copies, or as many as will cover the expenses, are subscribed for.

February, 1816.

[This Prospectus is followed by a list of Subscribers for 57 copies on Large Paper, and 81 on Small Paper.]

This Prospectus was issued at a period when, commercially speaking, costly literature had attained its summit of favour, and flourished not only in works of high pictorial art, such as Turner's *Liber Studiorum*, and his Picturesque Views on the Southern Coast, Sir Walter Scott's Antiquities of the Scottish Border, and Lodge's Illustrious Portraits, but also in certain antiquarian works, as the enlarged editions of Dugdale's Monasticon and Dugdale's History of St. Paul's, and Stothard's Monumental Effigies,—all published periodically in numbers, or in detached volumes, as were the county histories then in progress, by Ormerod, Surtees, Clutterbuck, Baker, &c. Thus even an antiquarian author, if so eminent as Dr. Whitaker, was enabled to share in the literary extravagance of the time, and we find that the meed awarded to the Historian of Richmondshire was at the handsome rate of One Pound for every page,[1] whether the page was occupied with his own writing, or with epitaphs and documentary evidence, or even with vignettes and "blank spaces."

[1] "By the contract, it is to be printed uniformly with the Additions to Thoresby's Ducatus, and the Author is to

The sentiments with which Dr. Whitaker had closed the second edition of his History of Craven, in the year 1811, have been already extracted. Subsequently he described those passages as a lingering and reluctant leave-taking of Topography, that had been provoked by sickness, and its natural concomitant despondency.[1]

Six years later, when he buckled on his harness for the History of Richmondshire, he was sufficiently sanguine to adopt a very different tone. He now declared that, "by a singular blessing of Providence, the strength and spirits of the Author have been renewed, and his whole constitution has undergone a kind of rejuvenescence. Imagination, curiosity, and the spirit of research have, in his breast, become as active as ever. Locomotion and change of scene relieve the tedium, and remove the inconveniences, of uninterrupted study; the assistance of skilful artists at once excites and gratifies the writer; and instead of shrinking, as he once did, from the toil of a History of Richmondshire, considered as a whole, he now dares to regard it as the auspicious commencement of a still greater undertaking, as an opening to more extended research, and more copious illustration."

At the same time he distinctly renounced all responsibility for genealogies, his repugnance to which he had always confessed,[2] and prominently asserted this freedom in the following

Advertisement to the Reader.

The Author of the History of Richmondshire has the sincere pleasure of stating, that the genealogical parts of the work are from other hands, much more conversant with subjects of this nature than himself. Those with the initials (or his name) have been furnished by William Radclyffe, Esq. Rouge Croix.[3] He can now, therefore, no longer give offence by presuming to hint, that since the deluge it has not been usual for three generations of the human race to survive more than three centuries, or by declining to accept without animadversion whatever either dulness or design may have obtruded upon the genealogies of ancient families.

But it is due to the present College of Arms to say, that, although much remains upon their records in the earlier descents of many lines to which a critical test has never been applied, a diligence of inquiry and accuracy of reasoning now prevail in the compilation of pedigrees, which, as they result even in these trifles from the general intelligence of the age, were certainly not equalled in any other period.

Subsequently, in the same History, the Author expresses himself still more strongly, when introducing the pedigree of Tunstall. "In this work I am happy to be emancipated from the slavery of compiling genealogies; but in defiance of family prejudice and bigotry, of which I have had sufficient experience, I shall never knowingly adopt errors, nor conceal truth." (vol. ii. p. 270.)

receive the same price, viz. 4*l.* per sheet; in which the blank spaces at the beginning and end of every Parish, spaces for vignettes &c., are to be included." (These particulars are copied from an autograph letter of Dr. Whitaker, dated July 22, 1817.)

[1] History of Richmondshire, vol. i. p. 1.

[2] In his edition of the *Ducatus Leodiensis*, Dr. Whitaker had inserted (at the back of the Dedication) a notice that "For the Continuation of the Pedigrees the Editor desires it to be understood that he is principally indebted to Mr. Christopher Bolland, who has executed the task with great Fidelity and Exactness."

[3] Radclyffe was also a valuable assistant to Mr. Surtees in his History of Durham. See his letters, ranging from 1805 to 1819, in the Life of Surtees, by Taylor and Raine, pp. 327, 362, 387; and the lines in p. 211, commencing "*Rouge Croix* is the monarch of heralds," &c. His professional career was closed under a cloud.

It was not however until 1819 that the First Part of the proposed "General History of the County of York" was given to the world.[1] The work was continued under that title until Dr. Whitaker's death, which ensued at the close of 1821. When that event happened, only eight Parts out of the ten had been published. He had left, however, certain collections prepared for the remaining parishes of Richmondshire, together with the more matured materials for Lonsdale that have been already described. The History of Richmondshire extends to nearly the middle of the second volume; its remainder is occupied by "An History of Lonsdale, Ewecross, and Amunderness, parts of the Everwicschire of Domesday, now included in the counties of York, Lancaster, and Westmoreland." The work was announced as completed in the spring of 1823, in two volumes folio. Its price on demy paper was 25*l.* 4*s.*, and on super-royal drawing paper, with Indian proof impressions of the plates, 50*l.* 8*s.*[2] Its plates from the landscapes of J. M. W. Turner were of beauty unsurpassed; and the architectural views from the pencil of John Buckler were excellent in their way; whilst many embellishments were boldly and effectively engraved on wood.[3] The Dedication was addressed to a native of Lancashire, the Rev. James Wood, D.D. Master, and to the Fellows of St. John's college, Cambridge,—the foundation of Margaret Countess of Richmond, and the place of the Author's academical education. What editorial charge was taken of the work after the Author's decease[4] does not appear, nor was any other notice of the circumstance inserted than in a few lines placed at the close of a table of errata of almost unprecedented length.[5]

On the whole the judicious were greatly disappointed,[6] and not without reason, in the

[1] Quarterly Review, vol. xxi. p. 567.

[2] Quarterly Review, vol. xxix. p. 282.

[3] A full bibliographical account of the History of Richmondshire, its embellishments and sheet pedigrees, has been published in *The Yorkshire Library,* by William Boyne, F.S.A. 4to. 1869, pp. 175-180.

[4] In Lonsdale, pp. 316-323, occurs the parish of Heysham, of which Whitaker was for some years Rector; but the list of Incumbents, p. 321, does not include his name!

[5] "The Publishers trust that the peculiar circumstances in which the Work has been placed, in consequence of the illness and death of its lamented Author, and the unavoidable disadvantages of a residence distant from the press, will apologise for the numerous errata here pointed out, as well as for any others which may be discovered."

[6] No one was better qualified to appreciate Whitaker's real merits than the Historian of Durham, Robert Surtees, and it was equally impossible for him to be blind to the deficiencies of the History of Richmondshire. In a letter to the late Rev. James Raine, D.C.L. the Historian of North Durham, written on the 22nd Feb. 1822, Mr. Surtees remarks: "I lament that Whitaker's last work on such a gallant subject is so meagre. The desideratum is a History of noble Richmondshire, on a new flation and fashion, carefully preserving every glowing gem and fragment of sparkling mica which the magician has flung from his rich mines so carelessly over the surface, fusing in the same furnace the grosser ores which he threw aside, and following up the numerous rich veins which he neglected to pursue. And who should be the subtle alchymist? who but C. Clarkson, whose industry and fidelity are on record in his substantial sterling quarto, [a History of the Town of Richmond, published in 4to. 1821,] which will be a book of reference and authority as long as Swale washes the castled cliffs of Richmond; but I fear too much has been done to expect this, and Whitaker will at least stop the way for years against any regular and ample historian. To correct merely the errata of *Richmondshire* would be a tedious task; to fix where additional information and illustration should terminate is still less easy. A mere account of parochial churches and fonts, with scattered touches of landscapes, and reflections here and there *pro re nata,* which recall the best days of Whitaker to mind, compose the whole work, and to render it complete

result of this abortive attempt at a "General History of the County of York;" and a recent critic, after paying a just tribute to Whitaker's scholarship and taste, the liveliness of his fancy, and the vigorous beauty of his style, has plainly pronounced his last work to be at once the most pretentious and the most defective of all the county histories ever published.[1]

We have still to mention another scheme of Dr. Whitaker's latter years, to which he had evidently been persuaded to assent at the solicitation of his publishers, but for which he probably did no more than write the following Prospectus, which we reprint without hesitation as eminently characteristic of the writer, as well as being one of his latest compositions:

Proposals for publishing by Subscription, an Historical and Descriptive Account of the ABBEYS AND CASTLES IN YORKSHIRE, BY THOMAS DUNHAM WHITAKER, LL.D. F.R.S. F.S.A. illustrated by a series of views, drawn and engraved by W. Westall, A.R.A. and F. Mackenzie.

The existing remains of monastic antiquity in the County of York are beyond all comparison the most interesting and magnificent in the kingdom.

The peculiarly durable materials with which they were constructed have hitherto resisted the operation of atmospheric causes; the remote situation in which many of them were placed has afforded no inducement to their removal; and modern taste has in many instances prompted their owners to preserve them with due care and veneration.

With all their durability, however, they must finally, though slowly, perish; and walls constructed with all the skill, and united by the most durable cement of the middle ages, can have no pretensions to survive the art of the graver and the multiplying powers of the press.

Much, it may be said, has already been done to rescue from oblivion these precious and slowly perishing remnants of ancient wealth, elegance, and devotion.

a sturdy detail should be given of the descent of property and blood." See the rest of this letter, in which the writer proceeds to urge his friend Raine to give up his school and undertake this task, in the *Memoir of Surtees*, by Taylor and Raine, (Surtees Society, 1852,) p. 404. Of Mr. Surtees's own work it was very justly remarked by a critic in the *Retrospective Review* (ix. 229) that it "constitutes one of the best and most perfect specimens of County History that it has been our fortune to meet with, blending together, in very happy proportions, the severer labours of the genealogist and antiquary, and the more congenial reflections and illustrations of the man of taste and feeling."

The article here quoted appeared in the *Retrospective Review* in 1824. It is a general retrospect of the more important works of English Topography, in which those of Whitaker receive particular attention, and it is remarked that "No work of County History has hitherto issued from the press (not excepting even Sir Richard Hoare's magnificent Wiltshire) so splendid in respect both of typography and graphic illustrations as Dr. Whitaker's Richmondshire; and yet, with all the author's high reputation and acknowledged talent, few (we believe) have fallen so short of the expectations formed by readers of real science and desirous of substantial information, principally in those very points in which we have represented Mr. Baker [in his *History of Northamptonshire*] as far excelling. That the causes of this failure are to be met with in the ill-directed spirit of enterprise evinced by the publishers, rather than in any defect of judgment on the part of the author, is an inference due, perhaps, to this eminent character; but it is not to be the less lamented that he surrendered his judgment to those who, with all their skill in what constitutes the external attractions, are so much less competent judges as to the essential requisite of works of learning and science. The imaginative faculty, and enthusiastic spirit of the genuine antiquary, are however displayed in almost every page of his History."

[1] The Rev. James Raine, M.A. Canon of York, on the Materials for the Topography of the Wapentake of Agbrigg, 23 Jan. 1868, published in the Yorkshire Archæological and Topographical Journal, i. 14.

To say nothing of the rude attempts which, in the comparative infancy of drawing and sculpture, were made to perpetuate the monastic ruins of this great county, elaborate drawings, and even paintings, have at a late period been employed to represent them; but the best of these have not only never been engraved, but were never intended either to be multiplied or even copied; while such representations, as they possess the value, have also the instability and insecurity of manuscripts, besides that they partake of the same difficulty of access.

Nay, even in those partial attempts which have hitherto been made to perpetuate these remains by engraving united with verbal description, the former mode of representation has too often failed from want of skill, or where skill has not been wanting, from want of multiplicity in the points for representation under the same general subject. One or two of these have generally been thought sufficient for the satisfaction of general curiosity, whereas on nicer and more judicious inspection, or by the adoption of plans more liberal and comprehensive, points in the highest degree interesting and beautiful, even within the compass of the same ruin, may be multiplied with success, while additional lights are thrown on the specific uses and destination of different apartments in monastic edifices, highly illustrative of the habits of their ancient inhabitants.

With these impressions strongly operating on their minds, the projectors of the present undertaking presume to lay this Prospectus before the Public, pledging themselves to present to them a series of Engravings from drawings of monastic remains in the County of York, more numerous, and more correct, at least, than have ever been attempted in any former instance.

These Engravings will be accompanied by verbal descriptions annexed to each article, which, although they aspire not to the elaborate research or minute details of works purely and locally devoted to the illustration of single objects or confined districts, will be found equally remote from the trite repetitions, the slight and shallow descriptions, and, above all, the copied and multiplied errors in nomenclature, chronology, and even facts, which have usually disgraced the flimsy narratives of those who were content to have the author considered as merely subsidiary to the engraver, and, without the labour of investigation or even the exercise of reflection, to tread the same paths of indolent and unthinking error, which their predecessors in the same walk have, with servile deference to authorities of no value, been willing to tread before them.

Conditions. The Work will be divided into distinct portions, each portion to be complete in itself. The first will consist of Rivaulx and Byland Abbeys and Helmsley Castle, in eleven Numbers.

The first Number to appear in November, 1819, and to be published Monthly, each Number to contain three Plates, with descriptive Letterpress, price 10*s*. 6*d*.

The Work to correspond with the "Views of the Caves in Yorkshire;" a few Copies will be taken off on large paper, with proof impressions of the plates, to illustrate "Dr. Whitaker's History of Yorkshire."

London: Printed for Hurst, Robinson, and Co. (late Boydell's), 90, Cheapside. Subscriptions received by Robinson and Co. Leeds; Whitley, Halifax; Wolstenholme and Todd, York; and Wilson and Rodford, Hull.

It is believed that the design thus announced was not pursued at the time,[1] either under the care of Dr. Whitaker or any other editor. The previous work on the Caves of Yorkshire,[2] to which the advertisement refers, was a thin volume that had been produced in 1818 by William Westall, A.R.A.

[1] At a subsequent date a portion of its design has been carried out in *The Monastic Ruins of Yorkshire*, sixty plates from drawings by William Richardson, architect, in two vols. folio, 1843-1855. The descriptions, however, by the Rev. Edward Churton, M.A. do not fulfil Dr. Whitaker's intention, if we accept the criticism passed upon them in Boyne's *Yorkshire Library*, p. 25.

[2] "Views of the Caves near Ingleton, Gordale Scar, and Malham Cove, in Yorkshire. Drawn and engraved by

Having now reviewed the whole of Dr. Whitaker's labours in topography, it remains for us to notice his other literary efforts. When he had completed the History of Craven, in the spring of 1806, his thoughts recurred to a project which he had entertained in early life, and which he thus described in a letter to his friend Mr. Wilson of Clitheroe :—

I am now meditating a new work, but of such magnitude and importance, that I fear you will seriously advise me to consider

——————— quid ferre recusent,
Quid valeant humeri.

In short, it is no less than a History of the Roman Empire connected with that of the Christian Church, upon a new plan. For this, however, I have large materials. The first fifteen years of my residence here (at Holme) after leaving college was principally devoted to the study of the Greek and Latin Historians of this period, together with select works of the Fathers.

The great objection is the fame and splendour of Mr. Gibbon's History. This, however, will be acknowledged in its utmost extent; and the work will be given to the public merely as one which the pious may read without a sigh, and the modest without a blush, neither of which can be said to be the case with respect to that great but depraved and mischievous performance.

It will require, I think, the unremitting attention of ten years, which at forty-seven, or indeed at any age, it would be presumptuous for a man to promise himself with any certainty; but with me to be employed is to be happy, and if I die in harness, I shall at least have the satisfaction of dying innocently and perhaps usefully employed.

We have already seen that during the years which followed the date of this letter Dr. Whitaker was occupied by literary engagements that left no room for the great design which is here sketched out: at the same time it is obvious how well these studies must have armed him for the article on Gibbon which (it will be found hereafter) he contributed to the Quarterly Review in 1814.

Another important literary project which Whitaker entertained was a new edition of Horsley's *Britannia Romana*. It is mentioned thus in his letter to Mr. Nichols of the 16th June, 1810, already in part quoted :—

I many years ago projected an edition of Horsley's *Britannia Romana*, but was deterred from prosecuting it by the expense of the plates, as the old ones could not be found. For this Work I have very ample materials by me, and as I now find that the engravings, being mere scratches, could scarcely double the expense of the copper, I should think no bookseller, either of enterprise or opulence would feel that circumstance any objection to undertaking it. If liberal offers were made me so as to indemnify me for the expense of journeys, &c. I would engage to keep the press employed from this time, and to make the work a perfect Sylloge of Roman Inscriptions discovered in Britain to the present day.

Horsley's work, which was published in 1732, has never been reprinted; but many portions of its materials have been reproduced, in a very superior style, in the publications of Samuel Lysons, Dr. Collingwood Bruce, and others. The work[1] of the Society of

William Westall, A.R.A. F.L.S. London: published by John Murray, Albemarle Street, 1818." Small folio and 4to. pp. 8. Twelve plates, aquatinted. This work has been overlooked by Mr. Boyne, who has described other books on the same subject in his *Yorkshire Library*, pp. 124, 125.

[1] *Lapidarium Septentrionale:* or, a Description of the Monuments of Roman Rule in the North of England.

Antiquaries of Newcastle (mentioned at p. 25 of the present volume) realises Dr. Whitaker's proposals so far as the North of England is concerned; whilst the more comprehensive *Corpus Inscriptionum Latinarum*, undertaken by the Royal Prussian Academy in 1863, promises to extend to the province of *Britannia* as complete a sylloge of its Roman inscriptions as it has already provided for *Hispania*,[1] and under the care of the same laborious editor, Æmilius Hübner.

Dr. Whitaker's constant study of Tacitus directed him to a minor effort, which was undertaken rather as an amusement than a task. It was a treatise, in the language and style of his favourite Latin author, on the Rebellion of 1745. For the materials of this he almost wholly relied on the History of that period by John Home, first published in 1802. It is entitled "De Motu per Britanniam Civico, Annis MDCCXLV. et MDCCXLVI. Liber Unicus, 1809." 12mo. pp. 145. Only 250 copies were printed. It was dedicated to his old college friend, Dr. Herbert Marsh, then Lady Margaret's Professor, and afterwards Bishop of Llandaff and Peterborough, and reviewed[2] very carefully by a critic no less competent than Mr. (afterwards Bishop) Copleston[3] in the Quarterly Review, February 1811, vol. v. p. 84.

In 1810 Dr. Whitaker edited "The Life and Original Correspondence of Sir George Radcliffe, Knt. LL.D. the friend of the Earl of Strafford," in 4to. pp. 296. Of this volume 600 copies were printed, of which 100 were on royal paper. Its materials were derived from original papers which had remained in an old chest at Overthorpe near Dewsbury, the residence of Sir George Radcliffe;[4] for access to which the Editor was indebted to "the friendship and curiosity of Mr. Beaumont," and Dr. Whitaker took this opportunity to acknowlege the favours which he had previously received from the same hand in the Histories of Whalley and Craven. The volume was inscribed "To Richard Henry Beaumont, Esq. of Whitley Beaumont in Yorkshire, F.S.A. as a memorial of the uninterrupted and pleasing intercourse on antiquarian subjects which has long subsisted between

Published by the Society of Antiquaries of Newcastle-upon-Tyne. In small folio. Part I. 1870. Part II. 1871. A third part will complete the work.

[1] The second volume of the Imperial *Corpus Inscriptionum Latinarum*, published in 1869, consists of *Inscriptiones Hispaniæ Latinæ edidit Æmilius Hübner*.

[2] More briefly, but less favourably, in the Monthly Review for September 1810. Also in the Gentleman's Magazine for April 1809. By a note written in Essex Street, January 24, 1809, Dr. Whitaker directed presentation copies of this little book to be sent to—"John Towneley, Esq. 7, Park Street, Westminster; the Rev. Thomas Sheepshanks, Wimpole, near Royston; the Rev. Dr. Marsh, Cambridge; Richard Heber, Esq. near Elliott's Brewery, Westminster; the Rev. Reginald Heber; the Bishop of Chester (Dr. Majendie), Amen Corner;" and one to Mr. Nichols himself.

[3] Mr. Copleston writes to his father, 13th Jan. 1811: "The employments which have detained me here are various. One of them is that which you guess—a contribution to the *Quarterly Review*. Much communication has passed between me and the editor (Gifford) on that subject." See the rest of this letter in the *Memoir of Edward Copleston, D.D., Bishop of Llandaff*, 1851, p. 40, and at p. 347 the list of the Bishop's contributions to the Quarterly Review, of which this was the first.

[4] "Dr. Whitaker has the pleasure of informing Mr. Nichols that having now obtained most of Sir George Radcliffe's original papers he can say with something like accuracy, that the work will afford matter for a thin Quarto about the size of Dr. Zouche's *Life of Sir Philip Sidney*, and in the same type." (Letter from Holme, October 14, 1808.)

himself and the compiler, and as an acknowledgement of the many literary obligations conferred by him upon the latter, during the progress of two laborious works,[1] already in the possession of the public."

"On the whole, this volume may be considered as a sequel to the Collection of Lord Strafford's Letters (1739), to the Editor of which (W. Knowler) the contents of it were evidently unknown; and for that reason, had the quantity of matter permitted, it would have been expanded into a thin folio, in order to bind up uniformly with that magnificent work. By means, indeed, of Carte's Life of Ormond, and Thurloe's State Papers, this object might still have been accomplished, had not an aversion to the modern art of book-making long since determined me, in every collection I might lay before the public, to confine myself to original matter." Preface, p. vi.

[1] Namely, the History of Whalley and the History of Craven. In the Preface to the Second Edition of the latter, Dr. Whitaker introduced the following passages:

"Scarcely had Mr. Beaumont, whose latest correspondence with the Author was on the subject of the present volume (the Second Edition of the History of Craven) received from him a public testimony of grateful friendship, in the Dedication to the Life and Correspondence of Sir George Radcliffe, when he also was no more. On this occasion the writer waited till those who stood nearer, or were more obliged than himself, had time to discover that talents for panegyric are best directed to living objects. This silence, however, far better than ill-judged flattery, has left space for fact and truth. Let it now therefore be told, without offence, that his peculiarities were great, and his prejudices strong; he had a clear understanding and a tenacious memory, which, after his return from Italy, were devoted principally to the study of English History and Antiquities. Inheriting a fine estate, and having never married, he became, through the ardour of this pursuit, an hermit in a palace; for such was his house at Whitley. At his other mansion of Little Mitton, in which he took great delight, he was wont to say, that he contended with the owls for possession. His apartments were not merely strewed, but piled, with books and papers of his own transcribing. No man living had taken the same pains with Dodsworth's MSS. or was so well qualified to make an Index to that confused but valuable collection. As a Magistrate, he was skilful and upright, but very irascible, and altogether irreconcilable to everything which he thought improper in the conduct of his brethren. He was a warm and faithful friend, and more especially a literary friend; but subject to fits of resentment, which, if he thought well of the objects of them on the whole, were easily appeased. To his indigent acquaintance the large sums which he professed to lend were eventually given. His liberality to his immediate relatives knew no bounds but the extent of his means, and scarcely even that. With an income of little less than 10,000*l.* per annum and no personal expense (for he was remarkably inattentive both to his own comforts and to external appearance), his estate was left somewhat in debt. He had all the pride of ancient descent, and with it an high sense of honour, which, together with his good understanding, would not permit him to be either duped or flattered by the ascription of alliances to which he had no claim. He knew and despised all the tricks of pedigree-mongers, and when some herald, whom he employed to marshal the bearings of his family, had officiously inserted that of the Viscounts and Barons Beaumont, he struck the quartering out with his own hand, saying to the writer of the present article,—'These are honourable bearings, but they belong not to me.' [There is a large folio plate of the arms and quarterings, the latter twenty-eight in number, of Beaumont of Whitley Beaumont, in the *History of Leeds*, p. 338.] His eye, when an object could be brought within its short focus, was perfectly microscopical; and he was perhaps the best reader of ancient charters in his time. For the same reason he was an excellent judge of forgeries. Such were the mixed qualities, such the head and heart, of this singular man, delineated at a distance of time sufficient to allow the first feelings of surviving friendship to cool; without partiality therefore, but not without affection. He died November 22, 1810, aged 61, and was interred in the family chapel within the church of Kirk Heaton."

I have judged it not inappropriate to transplant this from the Preface to the History of Craven, where few would think of looking for it, to the present place, after having in vol. ii. p. 25 of the present volume extracted the slighter tribute to the memory of Mr. Beaumont which I found under Whitley in the *Loidis and Elmete.* (J. G. N.)

Whilst inquiring into the History of Lonsdale, the attention of Dr. Whitaker was directed to the works of Archbishop Sandys, a native of Hawkshead in Furness, which led him to re-edit, in 1812, "The Sermons of Dr. Edwin Sandys, formerly Archbishop of York; with a Life of the Author," in 8vo.[1]

At the same time Dr. Whitaker was engaged upon the works of an old poet, from whose graphic and caustic lines he has made frequent quotations in the course of the present volume.[2] The History of Craven had introduced him to the family of Heber,[3] and that circumstance had further introduced him to an intimate acquaintance with the works of William Langland, "the first English satirist,"[4] of which Mr. Richard Heber placed two MS. copies at his service.[5] These poems had been printed shortly after the Reformation, in the years 1550 and 1561, but at no later date, and when Dr. Whitaker devoted his attention to them they were known chiefly from the comments of Tyrwhitt and Warton. Dr. Whitaker determined to follow for his text one of the MSS. lent him by Mr. Heber, which he was disposed to regard as a monument of "the true Mercian language, as far as it remained uncorrupted by additions since the Conquest:[6]" affirming, further,[7] "that the orthography and dialect in which this MS. is written approach very near to that semi-Saxon jargon, in the midst of which he was brought up, and which, notwithstanding some

[1] The previous editions of these Sermons had been in 1585 (during the Archbishop's life), and in 1616. More recently they have been republished in 1841, by the Parker Society, under the superintendence of the Rev. John Eyre, M.A.; who, strange to say, neither recognises Dr. Whitaker's edition nor his biographical memoir. But the latter is "generally followed" (xxvii. 136) by Alexander Chalmers in his *Biographical Dictionary* 1816: see also the *Athenæ Cantabrigienses*, by Cooper, ii. 24.

[2] See pp. 102, 122, 126, 137. It is asserted in Lowndes' *Bibliographer's Manual*, that "The value of the old editions is not at all lessened by the reprint of Dr. Whitaker, as he has carefully suppressed all the passages relating to the indecent lives and practices of the Romish Clergy;" and this statement, having been adopted by Mr. Grenville, is repeated in the Catalogue of the Grenville Library. But what can have suggested this imputation upon Whitaker's editorial fidelity it is difficult to conceive. His quotations made in *The History of Whalley* have rather the opposite tendency; and I learn from Mr. Skeat that any omissions of lines in Dr. Whitaker's edition are evidently accidental, arising from editorial oversight and not from intention.

[3] "Richard Heber, of Marton, esq. a name familiar to every scholar, has obligingly communicated all that was of importance in the evidences of his family, together with a plate of Marton Hall; and his brother Thomas Heber, esq. of Brazennose College, Oxford, has kindly transcribed several curious particulars from the MSS. of Dodsworth and Ashmole. It is not the least useful or pleasing circumstance attending such undertakings that they introduce their author to the acquaintance of men whose virtues and accomplishments he could otherwise have known only through the medium of general reputation." Preface to the History of Craven, 1805.

[4] Dr. Whitaker dedicated "To Richard Heber, esq. of Hodnet, co. Salop, this edition of the first English satirist, his old and spirited countryman,"—adopting the statement of Bale that Langland was a native of Shropshire. The designation was borrowed from Bishop Hall, who, in his own satires, claimed to be the second English satirist, referring to the author of Piers Ploughman as his predecessor.

[5] Both Mr. Heber's MSS. passed into the collection of the late Sir Thomas Phillipps, Bart., of Middlehill and Cheltenham. That from which Dr. Whitaker printed is now the MS. Phillipps 8231, formerly Heber 973. Of the other, MS. Phillipps 8252, formerly Heber 1088, he made but little use, nor of a MS. which was lent him from Oriel College, by the favour of Mr. Copleston (afterwards Bishop of Llandaff). But a full description of the last will be found in Mr. Skeat's Preface to his B. text, pp. xvi—xx.

[6] Introduction, p. xxxii.

[7] Ibid.

inroads within the last half-century upon its archaisms, he continues to hear daily spoken on the confines of Lancashire, and the West Riding of the county of York."

Dr. Whitaker had made arrangements for this work with Mr. John Murray the publisher, then of Fleet Street, and soon after of Albemarle Street, before the close of the year 1810;[1] but the book was not produced until 1813, when it appeared under the following title:

Visio Will'i de Petro Plouhman, Item Visiones ejusdem de Dowel, Dobet, et Dobest, or, The Vision of William concerning Piers Plouhman, and The Visions of the same concerning the Origin, Progress, and Perfection of the Christian Life. Ascribed to Robert Langland, a secular priest of the County of Salop; and written in, or immediately after, the year MCCCLXII. Printed from a MS. contemporary with the Author, collated with two others of great antiquity, and exhibiting the original Text; together with an Introductory Discourse, a Perpetual Commentary, Annotations, and a Glossary. By THOMAS DUNHAM WHITAKER, LL.D. F.S.A. Vicar of Whalley, and Rector of Heysham, in Lancashire. London: printed for John Murray, Albemarle Street, MDCCCXIII.

The dissertation which is prefixed to this volume may, for the elegance of its style and language, if not for the accuracy of all its conclusions, be still read with pleasure and advantage: but as a critical work this edition of Piers Plowman has been completely superseded by the labours of subsequent editors,[2] and the more exact scholarship in the

[1] "Mr. Murray, the bookseller in Fleet Street, has undertaken to publish for me an edition of Peirce Plowman's Visions, which I mean to print from two original MSS. with a Commentary, Notes, Glossary and preliminary Dissertation. I have made it a condition that you should print it if you thought proper, as also a new edition of the History of Whalley. With respect to the first book, Mr. Murray wishes it to be a large Octavo. I should certainly prefer a Quarto, especially as I doubt whether one octavo volume will contain the Text, Notes, &c., but I shall not vehemently contend about it. Booksellers are the best judges of the mechanical parts of authorship . . . As Mr. Murray is your neighbour, may I beg the favour of you to confer with him on these subjects, and inform me of the result." (Letter to Mr. Nichols, Dec. 20, 1810.) Eventually the book was printed by Mr. Joseph Harding, of St. John's Square, London. It is printed in black letter, with many rubrications, and decorated with woodcut head and tail pieces, and is said to have cost 400*l*. The price at which it was published was eight guineas.

[2] Mr. Thomas Wright, M.A. F.S.A. has published two popular editions, in 1843, and 1856; and more recently the Rev. Walter W. Skeat, M.A., besides producing a manual edition of the first seven Passus of the Visions in the Clarendon Press Series, 1869, has bestowed, and is still bestowing, the most persevering attention on the writings of this great mediæval poet in the series of the Early English Text Society. There Mr. Skeat's labours are in five divisions: 1. Parallel extracts from twenty-nine manuscripts of Piers Plowman, 1866. (Mr. Skeat has now, May 1872, traced as many as forty-two MSS.) 2. The Vision of William concerning Piers Plowman, together with *Vita de Dowel, Dobet, et Dobest, secundum Wit et Resoun*, by William Langland, Part I. the text (written about 1362) from the Vernon MS. in the Bodleian Library. 1867. 3. Part II. the text (circ. 1377), from a Laud MS. in the Bodleian Library, being nearly identical with that printed by Crowley in 1550. 1869. 4. Part III., the text (circ. 1390), from MS. Phillipps 8231, being the same as that edited by Dr. Whitaker, but with many hundred emendations and collations from several other MSS. This will be accompanied by a revised edition of Langland's very striking poem on the Deposition of Richard II. of which only one MS. has been found, but which has been twice edited by Mr. Wright, first for the Camden Society and afterwards in his *Political Poems*, in the Master of the Rolls' Series. 5. A General Preface, Notes, and a Glossary to all the three texts. The two latter volumes have still to appear. An essay by Mr. Skeat, on the life and writings of William Langland, may also be found in Hazlitt's Edition of Warton's History of English Poetry, 1871, vol. ii. p. 244.

ancient forms of the English language which has since been cultivated; indeed, Dr. Whitaker felt himself bound to make many apologies for "the languor of bad health," and his want of leisure, in excuse for faults that might possibly have been attributed to the indolence and carelessness of the Editor,[1] and many of which he himself admitted in a very long list of Corrigenda.

But even his title-page contains several errors. The author's name was really William Langland, not Robert, though this misnomer is as old as his earliest biographer, John Bale. There is no proof that he was a secular priest of the county of Salop; and though his Visions were first written in 1362, or immediately after, the version edited by Dr. Whitaker is of a considerably later date (circ. 1390). Langland had nothing to do with the North of England: but all the localities he mentions are towards the South, and most of his allusions are to London. In the prologue to his Visions he imagines himself dreaming on the Malvern hills; but his presumed connection with the county of Salop rests only upon the unsupported assertion of Bale that he was born at Cleobury Mortimer; whereas another account states that his father was a gentleman at Shipton under Wichwood in Oxfordshire,[2] and, though he styles himself a clerk, he could scarcely have been either a secular priest or a monk, as he mentions both Kitte his wife and his daughter Calotte.[3] In regard to language Dr. Whitaker's text is not that peculiar to his own district, but rather a West Midland dialect with admixture of Southern forms: and he was very much mistaken in regarding it as the "original" text of the poet.[4]

In 1814 Dr. Whitaker edited "*Pierce the Ploughman's Crede*,"[5] uniformly with his edition of the Visions, but reprinted from its first edition in 1553, for he was not aware of

[1] Preface, pp. xl. xli.

[2] "Memorandum quod Stacy de Rokayle, pater Willielmi de Langlond, qui Stacius fuit generosus, et morabatur in Schiptone under Whicwode, tenens domini le Spenser in comitatu Oxon. qui prædictus Willielmus fecit librum qui vocatur Piers Ploughman." (MS. in Trin. Coll. Dublin.) This may account for his naming the neighbouring abbey of Abingdon as the representative of monastic institutions in general, in that remarkable passage which in the opinion of some of his admirers has raised him almost to the dignity of a prophet.

> And thanne shal the Abbot of Abyndoun and alle his issu for evere
> Have a knokke of a Kynge and incurable the wounde.
>
> Passus x. 326.

[3] Whether the author adopted this as a blind may perhaps be a question, but Mr. Skeat is disposed to understand him as speaking literally and truly. Kitte is mentioned twice at least. See Mr. Skeat's observations on the author's name and life in the Preface to his Part I. of the Vision, p. xxxiv: also the catalogue of the poet's allusions to himself, to places, and to circumstances, in Mr. Skeat's Preface to Part II. p. xl.

[4] I state this as the conclusion formed by Mr. Skeat, who remarks, further, "Of course there are certain words which also occur in the Lancashire dialect, and quite enough similarity to the Lancashire dialect to have led Dr. Whitaker to his opinion; but the true locality of the version is more towards Worcestershire, Herefordshire, or Shropshire." The author's own language is thought to be most faithfully represented in the Laud MS., from which Mr. Skeat's B-Text (in his Part II.) has been edited; and that MS. is possibly an autograph of Langland. Mr. Wright's text is substantially the same.

[5] The title is: "Pierce the Ploughman's Crede. London: Reprinted by T. Bensley, Bolt Court, Fleet Street, for Lackington, Allen and Co. Finsbury Square, and Robert Triphook, St. James's Street, 1814." It was published at *1l. 11s. 6d.*

the existence of any manuscript copies.[1] He wrote only a single page of introduction, dated April 20, 1814.

The relish which Dr. Whitaker had always possessed for philological inquiries was sharpened by the study of Piers Plowman, which impelled him to take a still deeper interest than before in the vernacular speech of his humble neighbours. John Collier, a schoolmaster at Milnrow, near Rochdale, had during the last century set forth with much dexterity and mother-wit some specimens of that vernacular, under the assumed character of "Tim Bobbin," which soon attained an extended popularity that has endured to the present day. The Historian of Whalley, in a note which will be found at p. 234 of the present volume, has expressed an enthusiastic commendation of Collier's compositions; and in a letter to the late J. H. Markland, esq. D.C.L. F.R.S. and F.S.A. (dated Holme, Aug. 20, 1818), Whitaker writes:—"Were there not something indecorous in my undertaking the office of Editor to such a performance, I should undoubtedly do it; and perhaps, after striking out a few passages, I may even now venture upon it, though anonymously. In that event I will ask the favour of the use of your copy, in order to enable me to give an account of the insertion."

The MS. alluded to, possessed by Mr. Markland, was an autograph of Collier, of eleven octavo pages, being the episode which is printed in Bamford's edition (1850) of the *Lancashire Dialect*, but with many remarkable variations.[2] It was wholly in Collier's handwriting, though Dr. Whitaker had been inclined to attribute it in part to some clever imitator of Tim Bobbin's compositions.[3]

At an early stage of *The Quarterly Review* Dr. Whitaker was invited to take a part in it: he consented, and for many years was one of its most constant contributors. The following list of his articles, though probably not complete, is so far as it goes authentic,[4] and is sufficient to show the range of subjects upon which he undertook to write. :—

[1] It had been appended to the Vision by Owen Rogers in 1561, but does not occur in all his copies. It also accompanies the Visions in Mr. Wright's editions. Mr. Skeat has edited it separately, as No. xxx. of the Works of the Early English Text Society, and has appended to it *God spede the Plough*, a short poem written about A.D. 1500. Mr. Skeat has availed himself of two MSS. of the Crede, which furnish many improvements upon the old printed copies. The Crede was not composed by the same author as the Visions, but by one who imitated his metre and satirical tone, about A.D. 1394. The later writer was an avowed Wycliffite. There is nothing to show that Langland was a follower of Wycliffe, though he may have regarded his teaching with complacency. The author of the Crede is unknown, but Mr. Skeat attributes to his pen *The Complaint of the Ploughman*, one of the poems formerly assigned to Chaucer. (Preface, pp. xi. xiv.)

[2] In the same letter he thanks Mr. Markland for a copy of his "elegant and curious edition of the *Chester Mysteries*, (printed for the *Roxburghe Club*,) which exhibit a singular and interesting picture of ancient manners in the combination of religion, grossness, and buffoonery." I quote from a transcript made by Mr. Markland for Mr. Canon Raines in 1855.

[3] For further particulars on this subject reference should be made to the essays on the South Lancashire Dialect by the late Thomas Heywood, esq. F. S. A., published in the third volume of the *Chetham Miscellanies;* the second of which is particularly on "*Tim Bobbin* and its author."

[4] It is formed from two lists kindly furnished by James Crossley, esq. F. S. A. of Manchester, one of which was given by Bishop Heber to the Doctor's widow. See also the list of writers in the Quarterly given in the Gentleman's

1809	Aug.	Vol. II.	page 75	Sermons by Dr. Paley, and Meadley's Life of Paley.[1]
	Nov.	———	310	Bawdwen's Translation of the Record called Domesday.
		———	401	Bishop Warburton's Letters.
1810	Feb.	Vol. III.	111	Churton's Life of Dean Nowell.
	May	———	347	Milner's History of Winchester.
		———	398	Bishop Horsley's Sermons, vols. I. and II.
	Aug.	Vol. IV.	93	Wordsworth's Ecclesiastical Biography.
	Nov.	Vol. V.	342	Chalmers's Caledonia.
1811	Feb.	———	111	Sir R. Colt Hoare's Ancient Wiltshire, Part I.
	May	———	332	Lysons's Magna Britannia.
	Oct.	Vol. VI.	62	Milner's Ecclesiastical Architecture.
		———	98	Churton's Life of Archdeacon Townson.
	Dec.	———	440	Hoare's Ancient Wiltshire, Part II.
			448	Buchanan's Christian Researches in Asia.
1812	March	Vol. VII.	92	Lingard's Antiquities of the Saxon Church.
	June	———	382	Hurd's Edition of Warburton's Works.[2]
	Sept.	Vol. VIII.	163	Galt's Life of Cardinal Wolsey.
	Dec.	———	422	Belsham's Memoirs of the Rev. Theophilus Lindsay.
1813	March	Vol. IX.	30	Bishop Horsley's Sermons, vol. III.
	July	———	418	MacCrie's Life of John Knox.
1814	July	Vol. XI.	304	Gray's Works, by Mathias.
1815	Jan.	Vol. XII.	369	Gibbon's Miscellaneous Works, edited by Lord Sheffield.
	Oct.	Vol. XIV.	201	Wordsworth's Poems.[3]
		———	236	Cox's Life of Melancthon, and Bonney's Life of Jeremy Taylor.
1816	July	Vol. XV.	376	The Works of Mason.
1817	July	Vol. XVII.	451	Chalmers on the Christian Revelation.
	Oct.	Vol. XVIII.	229	The Life of Richard Watson, Bishop of Landaff.
1819	Jan.	Vol. XXI.	41	Gisborne's Natural Theology.

During the prevalence of that system of publication which issued books at very high prices, but for which the number of purchasers was necessarily limited, the stipulation of the Copyright Act by which so many as eleven copies were required to be supplied gratuitously to the universities and other public libraries, was felt to be a very severe tax

Magazine, Feb. 1844. From the present Mr. Murray I have received confirmation as to the authorship of the articles on Jeremy Taylor, Mason, and Gisborne; but he possesses no list of the writers before No. xxiii.

[1] "The estimation of Paley's talents (in this article, remarks Dr. Dibdin, in his *Library Companion*, p. 88,) seems to me to be a little unworthy of that great man's name;" but in a note attention is directed to Dr. Whitaker's subsequent article on Gisborne, in which Paley is termed an "admirable writer—wherever he turned his eyes, the prospect was illuminated by bright skies and cloudless sunshine." And in the *History of Craven*, p. 129, he says "if any earthly object can render extreme old age desirable (as in the case of Dr. Paley's parents) it must be to see a beloved son risen to great literary reputation and advanced by his own merit to wealth and dignities in the church."

[2] "The review of Warburton's Works (supposed to have been written by the late Rev. Dr. Whitaker) is perhaps one of the most perfect specimens of acute analysis and impassioned eloquence that the pages of modern criticism record." Dibdin's *Library Companion*, 1824, p. 88.

[3] A previous article on Wordsworth in vol. xii. was by Charles Lamb; "but so mercilessly mangled by Mr. Gifford the Editor that I entreated Wordsworth not to read it."—Charles Lamb's Letters, p. 323.

by publishers and authors. One of the Petitions that were from time to time presented to the House of Commons for the redress of this grievance, bears the name of Dr. Whitaker as the first of its numerous signatures, and possibly the petition itself was in whole, or in part, drawn by him.[1]

In the composition of Latin Inscriptions he had much taste and skill. Besides those to his own family at Holme, others will be found in this work to the memory of Dr. Holmes at Haslingden, and Mr. Wilson at Clitheroe. The epitaph of Mr. Charles Towneley at Burnley has been attributed[2] to his pen; but the terms in which he introduces it at the close of his memoir of Mr. Towneley makes this very doubtful. Two inscriptions which he wrote, for the tomb of Archdeacon Paley, and for an intended monument to Ralph Thoresby the historian, are preserved only upon paper.[3]

The peace of Dr. Whitaker's latter years, and his literary leisure, if not his health also, were considerably disturbed by the public commotions of the times, with which his residence at Blackburn, and his determination to fulfil all the duties of an acting magistrate, brought him directly into contact. It was remarked by one of his intimate friends, the Rev. William Parker,[4] that, "Though possessing a delicate frame, no violence of the Jacobinical mob, however malignant, no threatenings however diabolical, excited his fears, or prevented him from discharging the most laborious and dangerous office of a magistrate in the disaffected district of Lancashire where he resided." Ordinarily (according to the same writer) "his eloquence was rarely exerted on political occasions. A friend of mine expressed his utmost astonishment when Dr. Whitaker addressed the meeting at Blackburn convened by the magistrates in order to support the arm of Government, and to check the nefarious designs of the lower ranks. The hall was crowded to excess, particularly by the Radicals. When the Doctor unexpectedly rose to address the meeting, he instantly poured forth such a torrent of eloquence, that the higher ranks were completely electrified, and the disaffected sneaked out one by one, overpowered by his arguments, or convicted by their consciences."

[1] On further examination I have no doubt that this petition was prepared by Mr. Sharon Turner, F.S.A., a solicitor in Red Lion Square, and the well-known historian, whose signature is last of the "65 authors of the first respectability," from whom it proceeded, as Dr. Whitaker's is the first. It was presented to the House of Commons April 6, 1818. My attention has been directed to it by its being entered under Dr. Whitaker's name in the Catalogue of the British Museum Library, where it forms part of a very curious volume (shelf-mark 515 l. 20) consisting of pamphlets and other documents on the Copyright question, collected by the Rev. Rogers Ruding, B.D., F.S.A., Vicar of Maldon in Surrey. This gentleman individually petitioned Parliament upon the same subject, stating that in his *Annals of the Coinage of Great Britain*, the value of the eleven copies taken was 154*l.*, and that if he attempted a second edition, with any improvements, which he could not deliver separately, he must deliver eleven copies again. At the same time the loss arising from this cause on Dr. Whitaker's Leeds was reckoned as 161*l.* 14*s.*; on Mr. Omerod's Cheshire 238*l.* 10*s.*

[2] Baines, History of Lancashire, 1836, iii. 258; 1870, ii. 38; and Wilkinson's History of Burnley Church, 1869, p. 11. It seems unlikely that Dr. Whitaker would describe his own composition as "*chosen for its classical purity and elegance.*" History of Whalley, Third edit., p. 487.

[3] See the former in *Wilson's Miscellanies*, p. 187 (its place in Carlisle Cathedral is occupied by a very few words in English,) and the latter in Mr. Hunter's preface to Thoresby's Diary, 1830, p. viii.

[4] Under the signature P. W. in the *Leeds Intelligencer*, shortly after Dr. Whitaker's death.

It was considered desirable to confirm the impression made by Dr. Whitaker's efforts on this occasion by the publication of his address, which was printed as "The substance of a Speech delivered at a meeting of the Magistrates, Clergy, and other inhabitants of the Hundred of Blackburn, convened in order to enter into certain Resolutions, tending to support the Laws and Constitution of England. Blackburn, 1817." 8vo. This was also inserted in the Gentleman's Magazine, vol. lxxxvii. i. 213.

On other occasions in the years which ensued there were further demands on Dr. Whitaker's energies as a magistrate; as is still remembered by some living witnesses. Mr. Canon Raines, now Vicar of Milnrow, was present at Burnley, when during Henry Hunt's political disturbances in 1819 the Riot Act was read by Dr. Whitaker; whose fine voice, dignified bearing, and haughty independence of manner, as displayed on that occasion, he has never forgotten.

Scarcely a year before his death there was a turn-out of the colliers of Altham, Padiham, and Hapton, who assembled in large numbers at Padiham, threatening to march riotously into Burnley. Many parties recommended that they should not be allowed to approach the town, but that they should be dispersed by the military. Dr. Whitaker, although an invalid, drove into Burnley on the day when the colliers were expected, and declared that he would not order the military out, until he had tried, in person, to persuade the mob to return. Accordingly he met them near Gannow, a mile out of the town, in a post-chaise; he was there helped into the driver's seat, from whence he harangued them so successfully that they agreed to go home quietly; and such was the respect paid to him when he had finished, that the strong rough men lifted him down, like a child, and told him, "Doctor, put your foot here; we will take care that you shall not be hurt."

When the political atmosphere had somewhat cleared, it was resolved that a public testimonial should be offered to Dr. Whitaker for these patriotic services; and, upon the arrangements being completed, this was presented to him at a dinner held in the Assembly Room at Blackburn on St. George's day, April 23, 1821. The chair was filled by William Feilden, esq. (afterwards Sir William Feilden, bart.) of Feniscowles; and John Hargreaves, esq. John Hornby, esq. and William Maude, esq. acted as Vice-Presidents. The offering consisted of a silver soup tureen, and four corner dishes, upon each of which was engraved the following inscription, with the armorial shield of Whitaker:

THOMAE · DVNHAM · WHITAKER · I · C · D · A · S · ATQVE · R · S · SODALI.
BLACKBVRNIAE · ET · WALLEIAE · SVAE · VICARIO.
QVI · IN · MOTV · CIVILI · COERCENDO · MAGISTRATVM · GERENS ·
OPTIME · DE · PATRIA · MERITVS · EST ·
ANIMIS · GRATIS · EX · AMICIS · NONVLLI · ET · VICINIS ·
D · D · D ·
ANNO · SACRO · M · D · C · C · C · X · X · I.

The Chairman, in his address to Dr. Whitaker, desired his acceptance of this testimony of the esteem which the subscribers entertained for him "as a Man and a Christian, and as a token of their approbation of the great services he had afforded to the town and neighbourhood in his capacity of a Magistrate, during the late most awful and perilous times of Radicalism."

Dr. Whitaker replied in the following speech :—

Mr. CHAIRMAN,—Permit me to return to yourself and to the Gentlemen now assembled, my heartfelt acknowlegements for the magnificent present which you have offered to my acceptance.

While I reflect upon the short and inconsiderable services rendered by me as a Magistrate in the town and neighbourhood of Blackburn, I cannot but be filled with confusion, when compelled to institute a comparison between two objects so incommensurate as those services and the splendid recompense which has been offered for them. Much rather therefore do I receive that recompense as a stimulus to future activity, an inducement to future usefulness. Never blessed however with a robust constitution, and shattered of late by attacks of actual disease, I feel my hopes and anticipations considerably damped, and the alliance almost inevitable between sickness and approaching age cannot, to the reflecting mind, but draw a dark cloud over the prospect. From one circumstance, however, I derive great encouragement,—the struggle of the last years we hope is over for ever; the people, too long wrought up by their deceivers, are returning to a better understanding; our persons and our houses are no longer threatened, and the great body of the inferior orders, long misled, are beginning to perceive and to feel the difference between real friends and artful seducers.

The most powerful medicines are perhaps the most distasteful; and the exertions of a Magistrate who seeks not the praise of man are the same; but the favourable opinions expressed by spontaneous offerings of the wise, the wealthy, and the good, while they are not unfrequently wanted, countervail very far all the irritation excited by the waywardness of others, and leave the object of them flattered at least by the assurance that his endeavours however imperfect, however unskilful, have not wholly been disapproved.

My connexion with you, though not of long continuance, has in many respects to myself been eminently delightful. How long it may be continued, and whether usefulness may not depart before life, it is impossible for you or for me to predict; but of one fact I feel assured, that if, in the close of life, bodily debility should leave any portion of mental energy, its last aspirations will be directed to the best interests, present and future, of the Parishes of Blackburn and Whalley.

After many months of impaired health Dr. Whitaker died at his vicarage in Blackburn on the 18th of December, 1821, in the 63rd year of his age. His funeral took place on the following Monday the 24th of December, when his body was conveyed for interment to his ancestral chapel at Holme. Many of the townsmen of Blackburn accompanied the procession, and others from Burnley and its neighbourhood testified their respect by joining it at that place.

Mr. Allen, who had long acted as Dr. Whitaker's amanuensis, had at this period determined to enter the ministry of the Church, and it is remarkable that his ordination took place in the interval between the death and funeral of his revered master. The following letter (partly published at the time in the Gentleman's Magazine) may now be printed as it was written.

The Rev. S. J. Allen to Mr. Nichols.

Blackburn, December 26, 1821.

MY DEAR SIR,

I presume you have long before now received the sad tidings of our friend Dr. Whitaker's death. They were communicated to me on the Bishop of Chester's threshold just as I was entering to encounter his examination, and you may readily imagine what kind of a preparation they would be for that trial. I did however pass through without difficulty, was ordained on Sunday, and entered this Town on the day following, where the first sound I heard was that of the passing bell which announced that the grave had closed on all that was mortal of that excellent man, on whose loss I believe I cannot utter a sentiment in which you will not cordially unite.

It is impossible to describe what I felt at the sound; every incident of the three happy weeks we spent together in Richmondshire, our journeys from Heysham, and indeed every circumstance of my intercourse with him at Holme and elsewhere, arose as vividly on my recollection as if they were but now transacting, and when I recalled to mind the fire of his eye, his eloquence and energy of manner, with his animated and venerable form, I could hardly persuade myself it was possible he could be dead.

You will I believe give me credit when I assert that the blasting of the small expectations I might have entertained of his patronage seemed the least part of my loss. The advice and countenance of such a man, the fund of information to be derived from his conversation, and the constant resource I should have had in his friendship, in a place where I knew nobody beside, seemed far more irreparable privations, and I still consider them so, though I have been received here in a very friendly manner, and have every prospect of comfort during my stay.

I was at first disposed to regret deeply that I had not arrived in time to get a last glance of him living or dead, but from Mrs. Whitaker and family I received such information as much to diminish any regret on this account. He had never fully recovered the attack of paralysis he had last year, brought on by constant alarm and fatigue during the Radical disturbances: it terminated in a nervous asthma from which, after experiencing incessant sufferings for some months, he was relieved by dropsy, the sure harbinger of dissolution. His mind also had suffered, and the fine imagination, retentive memory, and other faculties, at whose fancied decay we used to smile, were indeed in ruins before the body decayed, though intervals occurred to the last, in which, like the remains of those venerable structures he has so nobly described, his former brilliance seemed to return as an arch or a column erect amidst desolation, to tell how magnificent the structure had been. He was himself long conscious of the manner in which his disorder must terminate; and before he left the Holme for the last time, he who had shivered to cross a stream, or descend a hill, for fear of death, walked calmly into his woods, and setting his back against a master tree of his own planting, compared its bulk with his own, and ordered it to be cut down and hollowed to form his coffin, which was done accordingly. In this he lies interred in the Holme Chapel, attended to the grave by all the Clergy and most of the Gentry of Blackburn, Whalley, and the neighbourhood.

The King has not living a more true and loyal subject, the Church a more useful and zealous minister, or the literary world a more distinguished ornament.

Yours sincerely,

S. J. A.

At the invitation of Mr. Nichols, the same gentleman undertook to compose, for insertion in the Gentleman's Magazine, a more extended memorial of his deceased patron, and, as no contemporary writer appears to have performed the task better, we will now avail ourselves of some of his remarks upon one whose manners and character he enjoyed so much opportunity to observe.

As a literary man, in which character he is most generally, though perhaps not most deservedly, known, he was distinguished not less for industry and acuteness in research, accuracy of reasoning, and extent of knowledge, than warmth of imagination and vigour of style. To the study of English Antiquities, which the lovers of Greek and Roman lore too often affect to despise as barbarous and uninteresting, he brought a rich store of classical information, and, what is of much rarer occurrence, a correct and classical taste; and when to these we add the knowledge of such modern languages as throw most light on the subject, an intimate acquaintance with the Anglo-Saxon and Gothic dialects, on which our own is chiefly founded, and the habit of close attention to those numerous traces they have left in the rude tongue of the people around him, it may be admitted that few champions have appeared in the arena of antiquarian warfare more completely armed for the field.

* * * * * *

To him we are chiefly indebted, if it has, in modern times, been discovered, that Topography may be united with the keenest relish for natural beauty, with the most devoted attachment to the Fine Arts, with the grave contemplation of the Moralist, the edifying labours of the Biographer, and the loftiest flights of the Bard.

* * * * * *

In the fields of verse he never rambled, though no man could better appreciate the merits of poetry,[1] or more readily transfuse its chief graces into his own compositions. His style was nervous, yet elegant; concise, yet fluent; averse to the modern barbarisms and affectation which degrade the English tongue, but never hesitating to naturalize a foreign word, so it were of respectable origin, and would conform to the usages of its adopted country. In the use of simile and quotation he was remarkably happy; but, above all, excelled in the faculty of painting (if it may be so called) the object before him—of seizing at once the chief features, whether of scenery, architecture, or human character, and, by a few well-chosen epithets, or by one masterly stroke, conveying a rapid but finished picture to the mind. In this respect he strongly resembled Camden; and, had the custom of publishing in a learned language prevailed now, as it did in the Elizabethan age, we have reason to suppose, from his little work, "De Motu per Britanniam Civico," &c., that he would not have fallen short of that great Master in his Latin style.[2] To his characteristic warmth, however, the defects as well as the merits of his works may be mainly ascribed; nor is it to be wondered, that, though for the most part no less accurate than vivid in his ideas, his rapidity should now and then have overlooked an object worthy of notice, or represented it in a manner which a second glance would infallibly have corrected; that in his opposition to principle, he should occasionally have appeared somewhat too unsparing of persons; and that his zeal, when counteracted by those with whom reason and authority had about equal weight, should sometimes have defeated its own object, where partial concession, and a more conciliatory tone, might have prevailed.

[1] Mr. Mitford in his Preface (p. xxi.) to the *Correspondence of Gray and Mason*, remarks that Dr. Whitaker "added to great acquirements much of the elegance and enthusiasm of the poetic mind." Gibbon, in a note to his History, had lamented "that Gray, instead of compiling tables of chronology and natural history, did not apply the powers of his genius to finish the philosophical poem of which he left so exquisite a specimen,"—but a later writer, Dr. Whitaker, (remarks Mr. Mitford,) in his admiration of Gray's genius, has far exceeded the cautious language and the moderate desires of the Historian, and has regretted to behold "that fatal gulf of pertinacious industry in which the fire and genius of Gray were swallowed up, and which perhaps extinguished in its first conception *some great epic work* which would have placed the author on the level which he was entitled to ascend—that of Spenser or Tasso." (Quarterly Review, xi. 306: Whitaker's own words are now given, which the printer of Mr. Mitford's Preface, doubtless in consequence of his very bad manuscript, has materially altered.)

[2] The admiration which Whitaker entertained of Camden's style of composition may be perceived, not only in his review of the *Britannia* of Lysons, (Quarterly Review, May, 1811,) but in that he wrote upon Chalmers's *Caledonia* (November 1810). Of the latter work he says, "Written in a very inferior language, it will notwithstanding be allowed to rank with the immortal *Britannia* of Camden, which it as much surpasses in industry of research and accumulation of matter, as it falls short of it in purity and elegance of style." Of the first edition of the *Britannia* he adds, "The information which it contained was of course superficial, but the matter was well arranged, the style good the reasoning clear, and the whole work classical."

His Theological Works were confined to the publication of occasional Sermons, but he had the enviable art of making every literary undertaking subservient to the great interests of religion and morality, without violating the proprieties of the subject in hand ; an object which certainly no Clergyman should ever suffer to escape his view, whatever be the lighter studies or amusements he may think proper to indulge.

In this character, indeed, Dr. Whitaker was most exemplary. Placed in situations which gave him a sort of episcopal superintendance over a district no less than thirty miles in extreme length, nearly the same in breadth, containing twenty-four dependant chapelries, and occupied by more than 100,000 inhabitants, he exercised this important influence in a manner which might well have become a still wider sphere of labour. In his appointments to the chapels which came under his own immediate patronage, he was ever actuated by the purest and most disinterested motives; nor could any practicable scheme for promoting the temporal or spiritual welfare of his parishioners be proposed to him, which did not meet his ready concurrence, and active co-operation. More frequently, indeed, these plans originated with himself; and while he was thus enabled to place around him a body of zealous and useful clergy, his own conduct in the discharge of his more personal functions furnished an excellent model to all. To this part of his character such ample justice was done him by one of the correspondents to the Gentleman's Magazine,[1] during his life-time, that I need not dwell on it in this work.

His discourses partook largely of the peculiarities already noticed in his other works: they had the same fire, the same strength and fluency of language, the same acuteness of reasoning and originality of illustration, the same happy use of ornament; but they were also so perfectly simple, and intelligible to the humblest of his auditors, and delivered with eloquence so natural and impressive, that, though far from courting popularity, he never failed to attract overflowing congregations.

But the principles which regulated his whole conduct as a Clergyman cannot be better expressed than in his own words: "The dispensation of the Gospel has been committed to me within a certain district, and under certain forms and limitations. I owe, under the most solemn obligations, obedience to my immediate superiors in the Church, and conformity to all its established rules: here I have no option; I eat my bread on that condition; if I transgress it, I am a dishonest man. I see, indeed, the genuine doctrines of my own Church entirely neglected by some of its ministers, and mingled with fanaticism, democracy, and other poisonous combinations, by others; nevertheless, I know them to be the word of truth. I will, by God's grace, not reject, but separate them from these admixtures; preach them boldly, yet rationally; and if, in so doing, my motives are mistaken, my principals decried, and myself am classed with a sect to which I do not belong, I will bear my cross in patience." These observations occur in a note to the History of Whalley, p. 389, the whole of which is well deserving the attention of all friends of the Establishment, and merits a more general circulation than the particular object of the work is likely to afford. It has, I believe, seldom happened, that men so gifted for the pulpit and the press, have as successfully interchanged the retirement of the study for the more active walks of life; but with all the aversion to minute calculation, and the detail of mechanical arrangement, which the most abstracted student could have expressed, no man could more practically weigh the merits of an extended plan; and with nerves that shrunk at the very shadow of trivial and imaginary danger, none could more firmly encounter its real form, when duty led the way. Composition, also, with him required little or no effort; and while he could dictate his most finished descriptions on the spot, or lay up in the solitude of a morning walk abundant employment for the too tardy pen, many a tract was recovered from the encroachments of time, which his activity never allowed to remain long uncultured. Hence he was no less busily employed in the preservation of old and the erection of new churches, throughout his parishes, than in providing for the furtherance of the great objects to which they were dedicated; nor

[1] See the Gentleman's Magazine, 1820, vol. xc. part ii. p. 402. The more remarkable passages have been already extracted in p. xv.

could the trustees of the parliamentary fund, lately applied to those purposes, have selected a more active and useful associate. Blessed early in life with the possession of a patrimonial estate, to which he was ever enthusiastically attached, he became a planter and improver on no narrow scale, and in this profitable and patriotic pursuit received the gold medal of the Society of Arts, while more than half a million of trees, rising gradually beneath his hand, gave grace and dignity to the rugged scenery around him. To watch their growth and beauty was the frequent solace of his lighter hours; and when, at his last visit to the Holme, declining health admonished him that he should see them no more, he calmly selected one of the comeliest of his own planting to be the depositary of his mortal remains.

In a district where the non-residence or extinction of the ancient gentry had much weakened the civilizing influence of polished manners on the humbler classes of society, and even the restraints of law were but feebly exerted, the office of a magistrate, for which his education and pursuits had so well qualified him, was accepted as a duty, and at Holme might have been exercised with unmixed pleasure to himself, and advantage to others; but, transplanted into the midst of a manufacturing population, at a time when sedition and blasphemy were unusually prevalent, and the poison of a system, whose evils he had from the first foretold and resisted, was fermented to its utmost height of malignity, the conscientious discharge of his duty, rewarded as it was by the approbation of his sovereign, and the warm thanks of his neighbours and countrymen, was attended with sacrifices which his friends and the lovers of literature may be excused for thinking almost too great even in the best of causes—the suspension of those calmer studies in which he delighted; and, as it may be feared, the introduction of that distressing disorder to which he fell a victim.

Adorned with these accomplishments, as an author, a clergyman, a subject, a man, and endowed by nature and age with a commanding person, a venerable and expressive countenance, and a peculiarly animated eye, he seemed to possess the faculty of impressing his own image on the mind no less vividly than the features of landscape were depicted by his pen. An image which no one who has once beheld him in the pulpit, amidst the trophies of antiquity, or the peaceful seclusion of domestic life, will ever be able to efface from recollection.

One material feature of Dr. Whitaker's manners Mr. Allen has omitted. This is supplied by his friend the Rev. William Parker, the Vicar of Waddington, in a tribute to Dr. Whitaker's memory (under the signature P. W.) communicated to the *Leeds Intelligencer*. After remarking that "Among strangers Dr. Whitaker was silent and reserved," Mr. Parker afterwards adds, "In the company of a few select friends, his conversation was of a very superior cast; full of acute remarks, of argument, or of anecdote. *Modo tristi, sæpe jocoso.* To affectation, to disguise, or hypocrisy his heart was a stranger. He was sometimes accused of severity. But piety and modest worth ever found in him a protector and a friend. The vanity of ignorance, or the presumption of the upstart, he held in equal contempt. If he were severe, he was, to use his own words, *sola in vitia asper.*"

I have great pleasure in being allowed to add in this place the following interesting reminiscences of the historian's daily habits, from the authentic information of his son the present Vicar of Whalley. "Dr. Whitaker was an early riser: he breakfasted before eight o'clock, and immediately went into his study, where he at once occupied himself in writing. The study at Holme was a pleasant room up-stairs, and the window near which he wrote looked directly upon a noble yew-tree, called Dean Nowell's Yew, because it was traditionally said to have been planted by the Dean in his boyhood. Dr. Whitaker always wrote upon a volume of Tacitus, resting upon an easel or stand of yew. He scarcely ever omitted to read a page or two of Tacitus every day, excepting on a Saturday, when he read one of the Fathers, preferring Chrysostom; this was preparatory to his extempore sermon on the following day,[1] when one of the great charms of his discourse would be the introduction of historical notices and anecdotes taken from the Fathers. But Tacitus in prose, Juvenal in verse, were his favourite authors. He remained in the study writing, or arranging papers to be copied by his amanuensis Mr. Allen, who sat in a room below, until he went out about noon to his workmen in the woods, and it was among his favourite plantations that the most admired and beautiful portions of his writings were composed, for subsequent transference to paper. The great delight of his life was planting, and the beautiful woods and demesnes at the Holme are the result of his wise expenditure and forethought. He came into the possession of a tree-denuded estate, when there were not above six or seven acres of wood upon it, and he left it covered with thriving plantations of all sizes, and trees of various growth. It was the finest larch in the Old Clough, planted by himself, that was felled to form his coffin, which was hewn out from its bulk like a canoe, according to his own directions given to his bailiff William Edmundson.[2] Addison asserts, in his *Spectator*,

[1] "His extempore eloquence in the pulpit was rapid, energetic and impressive. His language was so terse, so correct, and, at the same time, so elegant, that the most learned and polished audience could not but admire it." Rev. William Parker, (P. W.) in the Leeds Intelligencer.

[2] By the kindness of Mrs. Crossley of Scaitcliffe, I am able to append the following letter addressed to her late husband's father.

Mr. William Edmundson to John Crossley, Esq. F.S.A.

SIR, Knowing you have a valuable collection of ancient and curious documents, and an anxious desire to extend the same, I beg leave to hand you a few very memorable particulars of the last days of the learned Thomas Dunham Whitaker, LL.D. which will be the more esteemed by you, because of your particular friendship with the Doctor.

On the 21st August, 1821, the Doctor sent for me from the hay-field, to go with him into the wood—and when we got there, he walked to the side of a larch tree, and said, "William, I planted this tree with my own hands, and intend to have my coffin made of it; have you your two-foot in your pocket?" I said I had, "Then (says he,) measure it." Afterwards he turned his back to the said tree, closed his arms up, and said, "Will it hold my body when it is hollowed out of the solid?" I replied, "It will be little enough;" and he immediately observed,—"The tree is growing bigger, and I am growing less."

On the 17th of October following, he sent his servant with a letter, (sealed with black wax, and with his own seal of arms,) directed to me, as follows:

"Mr. W. EDMUNDSON, Cliviger.

"To be opened and read as soon as I am dead. T. D. W."

A copy of which Letter I also beg to hand you, viz.

"I, Thomas Dunham Whitaker, Clerk, LL.D. do hereby direct my body to be interred in the Chapel under the old pulpit, as it now stands, and on the north side of the body of my father; and I also direct that as soon as I am dead two graves, one beneath the other, be made for the reception of my own body and that of my dear wife, both bricked, and each covered and bottomed with flags, one upon the other.

"And as soon as I am dead, I also direct, that a Larch Tree planted by me A.D. 1786, and now standing at the entrance of the Old Clough, be cut down and be hollowed out into one excavation for my body, after which it is to be lined with lead for my interment; and I desire these directions may be fully and literally complied with.

"T. D. WHITAKER."

This larch tree had been planted about 35 years, and was 63 feet long, and contained 31½ feet of wood, and

that 'The love of woods, of fields, of flowers, of rivers, and waterfalls seems to be a passion implanted in our nature the most early of any, and is one not unbecoming of serious thought.' This Whitaker fully enjoyed. The waterfalls in Dodbottom and at the Earl's Bower,—a spot which he has noticed in his description of Cliviger, attracted him by their beauty. Among these woods he remained with his workmen until three o'clock, and he liked to have two greyhounds with him, as he was fond of dogs, and they were as fond of him, and awaited his coming out in the morning. Neither the distinguished honour with which the first edition of his History of Whalley was received by the public, nor the complimentary letters addressed to him by his literary contemporaries and friends,—by Marsh, Bishop of Peterborough, his old and intimate friend at St. John's; by Richard Heber of Hodnet; by Archdeacon Churton; or George Law, Bishop of Chester, and others; not even his appointment to his favourite church of Whalley so flatteringly made by Archbishop Manners Sutton, none of them carried with them half the delight that he derived from the love of his plantations, and walks in them, and the improvements which he was continually making in them. He received the gold medal of the Society of Arts[1] (which is now at the Holme,) for the greatest number of larch trees planted in one year; and his example and that set on a still larger scale by Mr. Towneley, were afterwards followed by many of his friends, to the great benefit of their estates, in the vallies of the Calder and Ribble,—by Mr. Taylor of Moreton, by Colonel Hargreaves of Ormerod, by Colonel Clayton of Carr Hall, by Mr. Lister Parker, and others.

"He returned from his walks to dinner at three; and from dinner to six, or half-past, he did little. At that time we had tea; after which, he went up to the study, and read or wrote, until half past seven. His family then joined him, and one of his sons read aloud, whilst the ladies worked, from such authors as Clarendon, Robertson, Southey, &c. and, above all, each of Sir Walter Scott's novels, as they came out, which were sent by Mr. Murray, in the box with books to be reviewed in the Quarterly. One evening, while we were so engaged, he was called down stairs to see a gold chain, which it was said the ploughman had just found. The plough had turned over, but not broken, a very beautiful gold torques on his own land. The gold glittered in the furrow, and hence it was discovered; and it remains at the house still, the celebrated Holme Torques."

after 22 inches of the bottom of the tree was cut off, a proper length was obtained for his coffin. The piece presented to you was cut off the same tree about 14 feet from the bottom, which I cut off myself with a handsaw, on the 13th April 1822.

I am, Sir, &c. &c.

WILLIAM EDMUNDSON.

Cliviger, April 15, 1822.

[1] It was in their Session of 1794 that the Society of Arts adjudged their Gold Medal to the Rev. Thomas Dunham Whitaker, of Holme, in Cliviger, in Lancashire, for having planted 64,135 larches between June 1790 and June 1791; and at the same time their Silver Medal to Mr. Thomas Gaitskell, of Little Braithwait, in Cumberland, for having planted 43,300 larches between 1st February and 1st April 1791.

To these anecdotes may be added one which appeared first in the Gentleman's Magazine for Feb. 1822: "In the year 1809, on the occasion of the consecration of Grindleton Chapel, a party consisting of the Rev. Thomas Starkie, the Rev. Thomas Wilson, Dr. Watson the Bishop of Landaff, and Dr. Whitaker, met at Browsholme Hall, the hospitable seat of Thomas Lister Parker, esq. The Bishop, whose powers of conversation and retentive memory were conspicuous on all occasions, was so forcibly struck with Dr. Whitaker's profound learning in divinity, that he afterwards observed to Mr. Parker: 'Though I have so long filled the Professor's chair, yet I was obliged yesterday to go to my fourth, nay even to my fifth shelf, to cope with the Doctor's knowledge of the old and learned authors in Divinity.'"

Another writer, signing P. W., and who we have reason to know was Mr. Lister Parker's brother, the Rev. William Parker before named, soon after[1] made some comments on this anecdote, to the following effect:

Not long after this visit, Dr. Whitaker gave me a particular account of the conversation which he had with Bishop Watson. His Lordship having advanced some doctrine a little heterodoxical, the Doctor thought himself bound to confute his assertion, by adducing various passages from the Fathers and Orthodox Divines of the Church of England. So forcible and appropriate were the Doctor's arguments, that the Bishop was absolutely *posed*, and though he might have recourse to the *fourth or fifth shelf*, he was unable to *cope* with the Doctor, but gently took him by the hand, and jocosely though artfully waved the argument by saying, "My good friend, when you come to see me at Calgarth I shall be happy to resume the subject." Notwithstanding Dr. Watson's excessive vanity, he was a most pleasant companion. I will now, said Dr. Whitaker, give you one example of it. "I never," remarked his Lordship, "expect to rise higher in the Church, *though all the world knows it is not for want of abilities.*"

In accordance with directions left by Dr. Whitaker in his will, a vault was formed for the reception of his coffin, and that of his wife, in his own pew in the chapel at Holme, "as nearly as possible under the place where the old pulpit now stands," and, also by his testamentary desire, a slab of black Kendal marble was placed over the spot bearing this inscription:

DEPOSITUM
THOMÆ D. WHITAKER, LL. D. S. R. ET S. A.
VICARII DE WHALLEY ET BLACKBURN
QUI DIEM OBIIT SUPREMUM
XV CAL. JAN. A. S. MDCCCXXI.
IN SPE BEATÆ RESURRECTIONIS
PER SOLA CHRISTI MERITA.
NECNON LUCIÆ CONJUGIS
FORMÆ PARITER AC INDOLIS ELEGANTISSIMÆ
IV NON. FEB. MDCCCXXXVII.
QUORUM E PROGENIE DORMUERUNT IN XTO
MARIA CARALOTA XIII CAL. MA. MDCCCXVI.

[1] Gentleman's Magazine, April 1822, p. 312.

THOS. THORESBEIUS M. A. IV CAL. SEP. MDCCCXVII.
GULIELMUS IX ID. AUG. MDCCCXXXV.
LUCIA XVI CAL. JUN. MDCCCXXXVIII.
CONSORS THO^s STARKEI A. M. DE TWISDEN (*i.e.* TWISTON)
CONSILIAR. DOM. REG. AD LEGEM
ET COL. DOWN. CANTAB. LEGUM PROFESS.
JOHANNES RICHARDUS VII NO. AP. MDCCCXL.

There are two Portraits of Dr. Whitaker: one by W. D. Fryer of Knaresborough,[1] from which the engraving prefixed to this work is taken; the other (at the age of 56) by John Northcote, R.A.[2] of which there is an engraving (W. Holl *sc.*) in the *Loidis and Elmete*, and a smaller copy (P. Audinet *sc.*) in the *Gentleman's Magazine* for Feb. 1822, and also in Nichols's *Literary Illustrations of the Eighteenth Century*. The former is preferred by his family as being the most characteristic likeness, for Northcote's is heavy and wants animation.

A monument to the memory of Dr. Whitaker was prepared by subscription of his friends, and placed on the north side of the chancel at Whalley in the year 1842. It was designed by Anthony Salvin, esq. F.S.A. and is of Caen stone, in the form of an altar-tomb, upon which rests a cumbent effigy of the deceased, from the chisel of Mr. C. Smith of London.

The following inscription was supplied by the Rev. Dr. Cardwell, Principal of St. Alban's hall, Oxford, and Camden Professor of Ancient History:

THOMAS DUNHAM WHITAKER, LL.D., R.S. et A.S. Sodalis,
Parœchiarum de Whalley et Blackburn Vicarius,
ex antiqua litteratorum hominum stirpe oriundus,
ipse litteratissimus,
vixit annos LXII—menses VI—dies X.
et mortuus est decimo quinto cal. Januar.
anno sacro MDCCCXXII.
Inerant in hoc viro sensus
ad excogitandum acris et subtilis, ad ornandum ferax et profluens,
ingenium doctrinarum capax atque avidum,
animique ardor vehemens ille quidem sed assiduus et indefessus.
Huc accesserunt
in omni litterarum genere copiosa et limata eruditio,
in explorandis historiæ et philosophiæ fontibus,

[1] Of this there is one painting at the Holme, and another in the possession of Mrs. Power, Dr. Whitaker's grand-daughter, at Dublin. The name of "Mr. Fryer, Portrait Painter, Knaresborough," is in the list of Subscribers to the History of Craven 1805, and he is noticed in the Preface to that volume as "a rising artist in Knaresborough, of whom it is sufficient praise to say that he drew the wild cattle at Gisburne Park" engraved in two plates in the same volume. His name is also attached to the views of Sallay Abbey, Hallifield Peel, and Broughton Hall, and to some plates of monuments.

[2] Northcote's picture is at the Vicarage, Whalley.

quam in artem se penitus demittebat,
curiosa sollertia,
et mirifica tum in loquendo tum in orando tum in scribendo eloquentia,
qua nihil enucleatius, nihil gravius aut distinctius,
nihil autem ubertate ac splendore speciosius.
Præcipue vero in eo elucebant
indoles quasi ruris et nemorum dulcedine perfusa,
voluntas ad instituta majorum propensissima,
mores intimo gravitatis et sanctitatis studio firmati,
sincera erga Ecclesiam Anglicanam pietas,
fides unice in Christo posita,
quæque omnibus animi motibus erat eadem origo et terminus,
summa Dei veneratio.
Ut in iis potissimum locis,
quos eruditis cujusque famæ scriptis commendaverat,
et oratione et exemplo impleverat ipse mira sui reverentia,
tanti viri consisteret atque commoraretur memoria,
hoc monumentum collata pecunia posuerunt amici ejus superstites.

The likeness of Dr. Whitaker in his sepulchral effigy is considered to be excellent. The features were derived from a bust by Macdonald (which is now at the Holme), with some advice from his surviving relatives.

Dr. Whitaker's library was sold by Mr. Sotheby in a sale of three days, Jan. 23—25, 1823, and produced the sum of 814*l.* From the priced Catalogue (now preserved in the British Museum) the following items may be extracted as more immediately connected with his own studies :

85 Crosley's Funeral Discourse on the Death of L. Britliffe, 1743, with an interesting MS. note by Dr. Whitaker: bought by Mr. Ormerod for 8*s.*

87 Dallaway on English Architecture, 1806, with MS. notes by Dr. Whitaker. 16*s.* (Priestley and Weale.)

164 Evelyn's Sylva, printed at York, 1776, with numerous MS. notes by Dr. Whitaker. 7*l.* 7*s.* (Heber.)

233 Lord Clarendon's History of the Rebellion, 1707, illustrated with drawings and engravings, in 3 vols large paper. 17*l.* 6*s.* 6*d.* (J. Taylor.)

253 Examinations, &c. of persons concerned in the noted Plot at Farnley Wood;[1] transcribed from the originals by Thomas Wilson. 3*l.* 10*s.* (Triphook.)

266 Gisborne's Moral Philosophy, 1789, with MS. notes by Dr. Whitaker. 6*s.* 6*d.* (Burn.)

235 Milton's Poems, edited by Thomas Warton, 1785, with MS. notes by Dr. Whitaker. 13*s.* (Burn.)

378 Gray's Poems, and Memoirs by Mason, 1775, with MS. notes by Dr. Whitaker. (Heber.)

391 Home's History of the Rebellion, in 1745, 4to 1802, with MS. notes by Dr. Whitaker. 1*l.* 13*s.* (Heber.)

413 Mason's English Garden, Goldsmith's Deserted Village, with other Poems, in 1 volume, some of them containing MS. notes by Dr. Whitaker. 1*l.* 4*s.* (Heber.)

[1] An attempt in favour of the restoration of King James II. See *Loidis and Elmete*, pp. 106—113. Mr. Thomas Wilson, F.S.A., was master of the Charity School at Leeds, a very industrious historical collector, many of whose MSS. are preserved in Leeds Library : see Taylor's *Biographia Loidiensis*, p. 587, where it is suggested that Whitaker (in his Life of Thoresby, p. ix.) too hastily condemned Wilson of ingratitude towards Thoresby, with whom there is no evidence that he had personal acquaintance.

435 Richard Greenham's Works, by H. Holland, 1612, with MS. notes by Dr. Whitaker. 15s. (Heber.)

461 Horsley's Britannia Romana, 1732, with MS. notes and several documents. *7l. 5s.* (Heber.)

588 Survey of the County of York, from Domesday Book, a MS. transcribed by T. Wilson, in two volumes, 1768. *4l. 5s.* (Rodd.)

624 West's Antiquities of Furness, by Close, Ulverstone, 1813, with MS. notes. 13s. (Rodd.)

663 Stukeley's Account of Richard of Cirencester, 1757, with MS. notes by Dr. Whitaker. *3l.* 5s. (Heber.)

677 Vision of Piers Plowman, edited by Dr. Whitaker. 1831. *4l.* 12s. (Rodd.)

682 Isaac Walton's Lives of Donne, Wotton, &c. York, 1796, with numerous MS. notes by Dr. Whitaker. *4l.* (S——.)

683 Bishop Warburton's Works, 1788, 7 vols., with MS. notes by Dr. Whitaker. *10l.* 10s. (Thorpe.)

685 Watson's History of Halifax, 1775, with numerous notes by Dr. Whitaker. *2l.* 10s. (Rodd.)—This volume, with several others in this list, is now in the possession of James Crossley, esq. F.S.A., the President of the Chetham Society.

686 Watson's Memoirs of the ancient Earls of Warren and Surrey, 1782, with additional plates and MS. notes. *3l. 19s.* (Rodd.)

691 J. Whitaker's History of Manchester, in 2 vols. 1771, with numerous MS. notes by Dr. Whitaker. *5l. 10s.* (Heber.)

692 Dr. Whitaker's Life of Sir G. Radcliffe, 1810, with letters from Mr. Bindley, Mr. R. H. Beaumont, and Mr. Joseph Hunter. *1l. 10s.* (Rodd.)

711 Saxton's Maps of England, 1642, with autograph of H. Bradshawe and MS. notes by Dr. Whitaker. *6l. 15s.* (R. Jones.)

771 Dr. Whitaker's History of Craven, 1812, large paper, with several illustrative documents, and two letters from the Duke of Devonshire and Dr. Paley. *13l. 5s.* (Rodd.)

772 The History of Whalley, 1818, large paper, illustrated with MS. documents, drawings, and marginal notes. *17l. 17s.* (Rodd.)

These last two volumes were resold, January 21, 1864, for *77l.* (Boyne's *Yorkshire Library*, p. 133.)

In Second Sale, Jan. 1824:

75 Boscobel; with MS. notes by Dr. Whitaker. *1l. 2s.* (Dodd.)

78 Shakespeare's Plays; with MS. notes by Dr. Whitaker. (Starkie.)

Dr. Whitaker's collection of Greek, Roman, and English Coins, Roman Antiquities, Prints, and Drawings, together with a few remaining Books, were sold at the same place on the 14th January, 1824. Their total produce was *175l. 14s. 6d.*; of which the Coins amounted to *58l. 4s.* and the Armour to *46l. 15s. 6d.* Among the Drawings were several of those which were engraved to illustrate the Histories of Whalley and Craven.

The Antiquities which appeared at this sale were:—

A curious ancient Ring, probably that described in p. 30 of the present volume. *2l. 14s.* (Starkie.)

Eight fossil bones. *1l. 2s.* (Jarman.)

Fourteen Roman Antiquities, consisting of belts, spear-heads, &c., &c., found at Ribchester and other places in Yorkshire. *4l. 19s.* (Cuerton.)

The Torques found at Holme. *5l.* (Starkie.)

Silver Arm of Victory [see p. 45 of the present volume] *2l. 4s.* (Starkie.)

The first and two last, being purchased by Mr. Starkie, the Doctor's son-in-law, were restored to Holme.

Among the Drawings were the following, the first seven by Turner :—

Ancient Seals. 14*s.* (White.)

Crosses and Inscriptions (drawn for the Plate at p. 69 of this Volume.) 12*s.* (White.)

Townley Hall (for Plate in Volume II.) 3*l.* 7*s.* (Colnaghi.)

Stonyhurst (for Plate in Volume II.) 4*l.* 7*s.* (Colnaghi.)

Whalley Abbey (Plate at p. 83 of this volume.) 3*l.* 3*s.* (Colnaghi.)

Nearer view of the Ruins (Plate at p. 139.) 4*l.* 4*s.* (Colnaghi.)

Inside of Mitton Church (Plate in Volume II.) 2*l.* 19*s.* (Colnaghi.)

Inside of Mitton Hall, by W. Craig (for the large Plate in Volume II.) 1*l.* 10*s.* (Triphook.)

Radcliffe Tower Hall, by the same (for the Plate in Volume II.) 8*s.* (Dodd.)

Shipping near Newcastle-on-Tyne, by Clennell. 4*l.* 4*s.* (White).

Ancient steelyards found at Ribchester, a Roman vessel by Lowe, ground-plan of Ravensworth Castle by Bradley, and a stone Font (four drawings.) 3*s.* 6*d.* (Dodd.)

Views in Yorkshire, by Dr. Griffith, Master of University College, engraved for the *History of Craven* (eleven in number.) 1*l.* 9*s.* (Graves.)

An inside View of the Chapter-house of Cockersand Abbey, now the burial-place of the Daltons of Thurnham, by Taylor the architect (sold for 4*s.* 6*d.* to Mr. Bentham,) was probably connected one of the latest of Dr. Whitaker's productions; see his account of the parish of Cockerham, in Lonsdale, inserted with starred pages 325*—335*, in vol. ii of the *Richmondshire*, but unaccompanied by engravings.

Some more important Roman Antiquities were bequeathed to St. John's College, Cambridge, by the following clause of his will :—

"I also give and bequeath to the Master, Fellows, and Scholars of St. John's College, Cambridge, all my Roman Altars and Inscriptions on Stone, to be placed by them in the Bow Window of the College Library, with this inscription in a small Tablet of Marble, at the expense of my Executors: Legatum Thomæ Dunham Whitaker, LL.D. hujus Collegii." The Will is dated Blackburn, March 10, 1818.

One of the most remarkable of the altars from Ribchester now stands at the New Bridge of St. John's College, with the inscription printed hereafter, at p. 29.

Among the curiosities collected by the late John Crossley, esq., F.S.A. and now preserved at Scaitcliffe, near Todmorden, are several relics of Dr. Whitaker; among them, the bands he wore, sent by Mrs. Whitaker; part of the larch tree out of which his coffin was hewn (already mentioned in William Edmundson's letter), and the MS. of his first sermon preached at Blackburn. A large 4to Commonplace Book kept by Dr. Whitaker at Cambridge is now in the possession of Mr. Canon Raines, at Milnrow. It contains the lectures which he heard whilst at the University, "on the Roman, Civil, and Canon Laws, and their authority in England;" also critical annotations on the Gospels; Latin themes; two Latin letters to Mr. Sheepshanks; an ode by Mason whilst an undergraduate at St. John's, from a copy in the possession of Dr. Balguy, &c. Mr. Crossley preserves some of the proof-sheets of the History of Leeds, which are chiefly curious from little notes to the printer, evincing the Editor's disgust when a pedigree came in his way.

Of his literary correspondence but little has hitherto been published; none indeed, but the few letters addressed to Mr. Wilson of Clitheroe, ranging in date from 1800 to 1809, which are contained in the *Wilson Miscellanies*, (edited by Mr. Canon Raines for the Chetham Society, vol. xlv.), and the few others which have been introduced into the present memoir. But many of his letters must still be preserved that are sure to be deemed hereafter of sufficient interest to deserve publication, and among them are known to be some addressed to his intimate friend James Maden of Greens, near Bacup, esq. who was nominated one of his executors, together with Mr. Starkie (the testator's son-in-law), and Adam Cottam, esq. of Whalley. The great bulk of the letters of his friends, many of them written by men of eminence not inferior to his own, and which would now have been of the highest literary value, was unfortunately destroyed by Mrs. Whitaker shortly after his death, and it is believed that whatever literary essays or unpublished collections then remained in his study shared the same disastrous fate.

In reference to this circumstance, and to the MS. volume in the possession of Mr. Canon Raines already described, I add the following extract from a letter addressed to that gentleman by the Rev. S. J. Allen, dated from Easingwold, June 6, 1852:—

> I imagine few authors who wrote so much and so well [as Dr. W.] have left so little for posterity, in addition to his printed works. I have a vague recollection of having some time seen such a volume [as the Common Place Book], but never examined it. The notes of Lectures on Civil Law in 1777 I conclude are of a course by Bishop Hallifax, of whom Dr. W. thought very highly. The Doctor was once a candidate for that Professorship at Cambridge, but he did not succeed in his application. Your MS. book is a great rarity.

JOHN GOUGH NICHOLS.

TO

CHARLES TOWNLEY,

OF

TOWNLEY, ESQ. F.R.S. F.S.A.

AND

ONE OF THE TRUSTEES OF THE BRITISH MUSEUM.

SIR,

HAD it been as unusual, as it is the contrary, to prefix to works of this description the amulet of a distinguished name, I might have been tempted to trespass upon the rules of literary decorum, in inscribing the HISTORY OF WHALLEY to yourself.—For, in truth, your personal and hereditary connection with the subject, and the many obligations both of the work and the author to you, would have justified some deviation from the common forms of prefatory address.

The subject of this history in each of its great divisions will be found to possess one excellence, which few works of so local and circumscribed a nature can pretend to, and that is unity; so that, in a large tract of country, now broken into many subordinate districts, ecclesiastical and civil, we are enabled to trace a very numerous and ramified church establishment to one benefice of a singular constitution, and of an antiquity almost beyond example in the history of the English church: that we are empowered also, at a later period, to contemplate the local effects of the Norman conquest in consolidating more than thirty primitive manors into a single barony, which under various tenures, and in different degrees of dependence, now forms one common centre of property within its ample bounds.

The fortunes of these, with their several dependencies, constitute the principal subject of this volume: one, however, has long been dissolved,—and the other, after various changes of fortune, has merged in the Crown; but a clear and connected chain of evidence will conduct us to the period when your ancestors in the male or female line were possessed of both: in the latter it will direct our inquiries to the house of Lacy, the foundaries of monasteries, and the heroes of crusades; and, in the former, it will carry them up to an æra of high Saxon antiquity, in which another branch of this distinguished race is found in the hereditary exercise of ecclesiastical jurisdiction within the same limits.

In comparison of this duration, every other name and interest in the original parish of Whalley, however dignified by rank and titles, is but of yesterday.

But, from the period at which this peculiar function became extinct, a period beyond which no authentic memorials of any other family within the compass of this history can be proved to extend, the posterity of the Deans of *Whalley*, seated upon the *villa de Tunlay*, by their descents and alliances, their activity and usefulness,* their devotion and munificence, their loyalty and sufferings, appear for several centuries principal actors in the scene before us.

In later days, however, when motives respectable in every cause removed them in a great measure from the scene of active life, superior intelligence and love of literature have been propagated through the line by a kind of hereditary descent, till they are become characteristic of the family—*Vigebat in illâ domo patrius mos et disciplina.*

* In his "Additional Corrections to Part I." the author directed the words *activity and usefulness* to be altered to *public spirit.*

Traduction of character, like that of countenance, after a long interval of cessation, is one of the best attested though least explicable facts in the history of human nature, and if example and early habit, domestic intercourse with living talents, or an affectionate remembrance of recent and departed excellence, might in your instance account for an eager and successful application to general literature, yet we must have recourse to the former principle to discover the source of that ardent love and critical knowledge of ancient art, which, more than a century ago, shone with so much lustre in your maternal ancestor the great Earl of Arundel, and which now preside over a museum that he would have beheld with admiration.

To an eye, therefore, exercised in contemplating the fairest forms of Grecian sculpture, it may be deemed a misplaced and preposterous expression of respect, to hold up the coarse though picturesque efforts of Gothic art, or to obtrude upon a mind familiarized with the scenery and manners of classical antiquity a rude survey of a remote district, or a barbarous detail of obscure families, most of which are distinguished for little but having long been rooted, like their own hereditary oaks, to their own paternal acres.

But, after all, there is a charm in contrast, and as the palate, satiated by habitual indulgence, sometimes feels itself stimulated by the coarsest fare, so it is possible that in the *intervalla ac spiramenta temporum*, which long literary indulgence may be compelled to resort to, an homely and frugal repast upon domestic history may not want its relish.

Yet I will not affect to suppose you indifferent to a place which your taste has so much contributed to adorn, or to a subject which your exertions have been so actively employed to elucidate. That place, at least, has been endeared to you by early possession, by temporary absence, by a system of progressive and successful improvement, and, above all, by the consciousness of much happiness produced, in a long course of years, and among a numerous body of dependants.

That the same habits of beneficence, together with the reflections which ever accompany them, will continue to spread a calm and sunshine over your later days, I persuade myself not only from general observation of the effects of conduct upon happiness, but from the authority of a great master in the science of manners—*artes exercitationesque virtutum, cum diu multumque vixeris, mirificos efferunt fructus, non solum quia nunquam deserunt, ne in extremo quidem tempore ætatis, verum etiam quia multorum bene factorum recordatio jucundissima est.—Est etiam quiete et eleganter actæ ætatis placida ac lenis senectus.*—Cicero in Cat. Maj.

In a species of playful divination long in exercise among men of letters, the *sortes Tullianæ* have often been resorted to; but that the last words of this citation, as now applied, may be seriously prophetic, is the sincere and affectionate wish of,

Sir,

Your most obliged

And most faithful servant,

T. D. WHITAKER.

PREFACE TO THE FIRST EDITION, IN 1800.

It is now more than seventy years since a writer,* whose eminence, in his later days, confers some degree of importance even upon the crude and hasty dogmas of his youth, was pleased to lament the decay of our national taste for genuine historical composition, and the growing prevalence of a vicious appetite in its stead, by which *any uninformed, senseless heap of rubbish, under the name of an history of a town, society, college, or province, have long since taken from us the very idea of a genuine composition;* and, to give authority to his opinion, he has cited a critical edict of *Boccalini*, in which that lively writer *expressly prohibits, on pain of perpetual infamy, any attempts, in future, to write an history, of which the subject is inferior in dignity to the metropolis of a kingdom, or, at least, a considerable province.*†

Our countrymen, however, in the genuine spirit of English freedom, seem to have resisted the introduction of foreign laws in criticism, as well as civil polity; and the promulgation of this formidable edict amongst us is so far from having checked the evil against which it was directed, that the practice has ever since been increasing, and, having called in the charms of sculpture to its aid, is now become more prevalent than ever.

But in this long period of topographical improvement, the taste and spirit of genuine history have revived, and, though modern times have produced nothing like the spirit and originality of *Clarendon*, in any great writer who had the fortune to bear a dignified part in the transactions which he records, yet the present age has raised up one English historian,‡ who, had the purity and sincerity of his mind been in any degree comparable to his acuteness and erudition, would have equalled the greatest of his predecessors, and two, who in elegance and correctness have surpassed them all.§

And henceforward, the muse of History‖ having come forth once more in her native dignity and vigour, Topography, though little disposed to withdraw from her own station at the mandate of a capricious foreigner, has no higher claim than to be considered as the humble handmaid of the other, and to be permitted to glean after her those less important, but interesting and amusing, facts, which she, in her rapid and comprehensive views of antiquity, must necessarily overlook.

With these inferior pretensions, however, Topography has charms for a writer, and those too resulting even from her want of dignity and of distance: to exalt scenes of daily observation into subjects of literary inquiry, to account for striking but obscure appearances in his own vicinity, to reconcile apparent contradictions in ancient dates or facts, of which the objects are familiar; to trace some neighbouring work of ancient art, which is now magnificent in decay, to its perfection or its commencement; to compare some great revolution of a kingdom with its effects upon private property, provincial dialect, or domestic manners; to develope the progress of parochial endowments, in which himself has an interest; to trace the origin and alliances, the advancement or decline of families, with whom he is connected; and to combine them all with

* *Bp. Warburton's* Critical Inquiry into the causes of Prodigies as related by Historians, published in 1727.

† Di piu, sotto la pena della perpetua infamia expressamente prohibiamo il potersi per l'avenire scrivere historie particolare di citta alcuna, se ella non sarà metropoli d'Imperio, di Regno, o di provincia grande.

‡ *Gibbon.*

§ *Hume* and *Robertson.*

‖ *Warburton's* account of the malady into which the historic muse had fallen is too coarse to be transcribed, and too well known, perhaps, to need transcribing.

objects endeared by early habit and long association, cannot but afford a mingled exercise, to the powers of reason and fancy, of observation and memory, gratifying, in an high degree, to the topographical *writer*.

But if there be no radical defect in the powers of the writer, or in the feelings and faculties of his readers, topography will not be without an interest in *them*: ingenuous curiosity, indeed, is rarely united to sordid tempers, or to mean understandings, but there are few, perhaps, exempted from those disqualifications, who have not felt what, however, it is difficult to describe, namely, the power of mere representation, in exciting a lively attention to scenery which we have been accustomed to contemplate without emotion, or to manners in which we have mingled even with disgust.

But inhabitants of remote districts, especially where they are marked with any peculiarities of dialect or manners, are addicted to a singular species of local partiality, not perhaps illaudable in itself, which, from a quick perception, even of fancied contempt, and something of the spirit of opposition resulting from it, strongly disposes them to magnify the importance, to admire the beauty, or to pride themselves in the antiquity of their native province; and, when the aspect of their country is also wild and picturesque, this feeling is also heightened to a pitch of enthusiasm, which seems to have been intended by Providence to counterbalance the power of interest, the love of society, and the advantages of climate, in order to prevent the desertion of tracts, which, without such a fascination, would be abandoned to beasts, or to the meanest of mankind.

But, supposing the particular object of topographical inquiry to have no such attractions, the subject itself deserves somewhat better treatment than the severe interdict of the Italian critic: it is very true, that readers, as well as writers, may addict themselves in this walk of literature as well as others to an habit of laborious trifling, which will debar them from the intercourse, and disqualify them for the duties of life;—for such indolent and useless pedantry I am not concerned to apologize: but no ingenuous mind can conceive itself to be disgraced, nay, I will venture to add, no serious mind ought to fear itself to be misemployed, in devoting a few hours of relaxation to a subject, which is in fact history upon a narrower and therefore a more useful scale, in which the scenery is familiar, the examples are domestic, in which the topics of praise and censure are drawn from instances in common life, and accessible ranks in society.—Thus much for the uses of topography, when written upon proper principles, to the serious and the conscientious mind.

And, as an occasional exercise of the understanding, to an ingenuous and cultivated reader, to attend to a series of transactions which involved all the interests, and agitated almost all the passions, of our immediate countrymen, from the earliest period, cannot but lead to some discovery of what every such inquirer would previously have wished to learn—some solution of present appearances for which he has heretofore inquired in vain—some recovery of facts hitherto forgotten, which are rendered interesting by the intervention perhaps of a venerated ancestor, or their effects on property and manners.

A severe censor, however, may urge that no part of this apology, either for the writers or readers of topographical works, applies to the author of the work now before him. By such an estimator of the value of time, and the application of talents, it may be said that, for a man occupied in the active discharge of a serious and important profession, to have devoted somewhat more than the leisure hours of three whole years, to an employment which scarcely deserves a gentler name than solemn and elaborate trifling, even if it have never interfered with the calls of duty, must at least infer an idle curiosity, and an unbecoming levity of mind: to this accusation he is willing to concede, that, without any consciousness of diminished attention to the duties of his profession, he has however felt and lamented the interruption which the present work has occasioned in his professional studies; but an early and ardent propensity to these pursuits, an enthusiastic attachment to a country endeared to him by long residence and many family considerations, the possession of many valuable documents which several fortunate coincidences had thrown into his hands, and an unwillingness that much local information, accumulated by the inquiries of many years, should perish with himself; all these motives, and another which will soon be mentioned, induced him to undertake the present work, and, that resolution once formed, a strong sense of the value of time, and, may he be allowed to add, his own constitution and temper, impelled him to pursue it in the spirit and for the reason of the preacher, *Whatsoever thine hand findeth to do, do it with thy might, for there is no work, nor device, nor knowledge, nor wisdom in the grave, whither thou goest.**

But the lightest effusions of a serious mind ought to be directed to *the use of edifying;* and while histories and novels, works the most popular in their nature, and the most extensive in their circulation, were daily issuing from a licentious press as the vehicles of impiety and sedition, he does not wish to dissemble, that he entered upon the present work with a deliberate purpose, which the ensuing pages, it is hoped, will prove that he has not forgotten, of giving a contrary and perhaps a new direction to topography, that is, of vindicating the present constitution of England, and of serving the interests of religion, by the occasional introduction of such remarks as appeared to arise out of the subject.

After an apology for so much egotism, it may be necessary to add a few observations on the conduct of the present work—

With respect to the British and Roman periods, it will be remarked that the subject has been treated in a short and cursory manner: and for a very obvious reason: the author having been forestalled in that part of his work by a writer who, to all the stores of erudition, adds an ardour of spirit which no difficulties can discourage, a penetration which no obscurity can baffle, and a splendour, yet perhaps a wildness of imagination, which, if it throws over the page of historical antiquity somewhat of the air of romance, seldom fails to delight, where it is impossible that it should convince: and if a calm investigation of facts and appearances have sometimes led the historian of *Whalley* to differ very widely in his conclusions from the historian of *Manchester*, if in particular, after much reflection, he has been compelled to reject the authority of an Itinerary, which, as it seconded the great antiquary's impetuous spirit of topographical discovery, was adopted by him with too little investigation of the evidences on which it rested, he has endeavoured at least to bear in mind that the eccentricities of genius, like the extravagances of virtue, are to be touched with a tender and respectful hand.

The following periods afford however abundant scope for new and original information, and after the *Status de Blackburnshire*, an authentic and singular memoir, happily preserved in the Monasticon, had sketched an outline of our early ecclesiastical history, and the labours of *Dugdale* and Sir *Peter Leycester* had retrieved with some degree of exactness a genealogical account of the house of Lacy, nothing either remained, or, indeed, was wanted to the completion of the present work, but the evidence of written authorities, from which, with these two exceptions, it has been principally compiled.

To detail these authorities will be the more grateful to the writer, as it will afford an opportunity of commemorating those benefactors by whose kindness he has obtained access, as he persuades himself, to all the authentic and important information which now exists upon the subject.

His first and warmest acknowledgments then are due to *Charles Townley*, of *Townley*, Esq. not only for a most zealous and indefatigable patronage of this work in general, but for the liberal communication of the Townley MSS. so often referred to in the history.

These are contained in sixteen folio volumes, the labour of *Christopher Townley*, son of Richard Townley, Esq. who, uniting indefatigable industry to a fair, though singular hand-writing, in pursuance of a great plan, carried on in concert with his illustrious friends *Dugdale* and *Dodsworth*, occupied a long life of leisure, part of which was spent in the troublesome times of the last century, in the painful but useful task of transcribing all the charters and ancient evidences of the parish and neighbourhood.

From these he compiled, besides, two large volumes of pedigrees, in which, if he does not appear to have fully availed himself of his own materials, he has at least afforded the means to those who come after him, of supplying casual omissions, especially in the more ancient times. A transcript of these was made by Mr. *John Hopkinson* of *Lofthouse*, a laborious disciple of the same school, who, from his official situation, was

* Eccles. xi. 10.

enabled to retrieve many valuable documents, relating to the Lacies, from the castle of Pontefract, immediately before its demolition. The originals of these are now in the library of Bierley near Bradford, but copies were taken from them about forty years ago by the late *Thomas Wilson* of *Leeds*, F.S.A. a man of obscure and blundering diligence.

To the Right Hon. *Assheton* Lord *Curzon*, and the Right Hon. Baroness *Howe*, the author is indebted for unlimited access to the Coucher-book of Whalley, which is a fair and handsome transcript of the last century, from the original chartulary of abbot Lyndlay, now, it is to be feared, irreparably lost. By favour of the same noble personages the author has been enabled to make many important discoveries, from a vast collection of original evidences, now filling two large chests at Whalley, and consisting of a series of original authorities, from the foundation of the abbey of Stanlaw to the dissolution of Whalley, and afterwards, during the possession of the Assheton family, nearly to the close of the last century. From these, together with some other original charters which fell, at the dissolution, into the hands of the Braddylls, and have been communicated by the kindness of Mr. *Cottam* of *Whalley*, together with many scattered memorials in the Cotton and Harleian libraries, the history of the Abbey of Whalley has been principally compiled.

By *Thomas Lister Parker*, Esq. Bowbearer of *Bowland*, he has been gratified with the perusal of some valuable MS. collections made by his ancestors, and now in the library at *Browsholme;* and he is happy in this opportunity of acknowledging, that he has received many other kindnesses in the progress of this work from the same young and zealous benefactor.

From *William Assheton* of *Downham* and *Kuerdale*, Esq. he has received several valuable drawings and other important communications relating to the manor of *Downham* and the family of *Assheton.* A similar acknowledgment is due to *Legendre Piers Starkie*, Esq. of *Huntroyd*, for having imparted several evidences to elucidate the later passages of the manor of *Merlay.*

He has also to acknowledge his obligations to *Richard Henry Beaumont*, Esq. F.S.A. of *Whitley Beaumont* and *Little Mitton*, for many evidences relating to the *Holts* of *Grislehurst* and *Mitton;* and for many valuable extracts from Dodsworth's MSS.

To his learned and excellent friends the Rev. *Thomas Starkie*, A.M. vicar of *Blackburn*, the Rev. *Thomas Wilson*, of *Clitheroe*, B.D. and the Rev. *William Barton*, of *Whalley*, M.D. he is indebted for innumerable instances of friendly assistance; and to the first especially for his indefatigable attention to a country press, working upon an half-legible manuscript.

The Rev. Dr. *Drake*, vicar of *Rochdale*, has made several communications; the Rev. Mr. *Adamson*, of *Padiham*, has furnished much useful matter with respect to his own church, together with that of *Colne;* and the clergy of the parish in general have been extremely liberal in imparting the use of their registers.

But in this catalogue of benefactors few have contributed more effectually to the History of Whalley than *Henry Greenwood* of *Burnley*, Esq. who, with much information upon this subject, and a very accurate knowledge of the original sources whence it may be derived, has, with great industry, arranged, abstracted, and communicated many evidences relating to the neighbourhood of *Burnley*, a large collection of which is now in the possession of *Nicholas Halsted*, of *Rowley*, Esq. who has withheld no information which was in his power to impart.

From these collections, which altogether consist of unnumbered and almost innumerable charters, besides the local and personal information which they afford, a few general conclusions have been drawn, for the insertion of which a preface seems the proper place.

By those who have attended to the chronology of charters, it is well known that dates do not generally occur till the reign of Henry III. or even his son. But among those which relate to the subject of this work, one bears date 22d Henry II. and another the 6th of John. Our oldest charters are Latin; the earliest of Henry I.; no remains of legal transactions in the Saxon language having descended to us, if they ever existed. The reigns of Henry III. and Edward I. were seasons of great activity in grants and transfers of lands: about this time instances of subinfeudation were common,—a practice which, whenever it occurs in an undated charter, fixes its æra to a period before the statute of *Quia Emptores*, or 18 Edward I. Henceforward, and to the reign of Edward III. they gradually diminish in number. French charters commence in the reign of Edward I. and terminate in that of Richard II. Of the reign of Henry IV. out of a miscellaneous collection which may be estimated at more than 20,000 charters, not more than 10 occur; * a fact which I barely mention without pretending to account for it. The number in Henry the Fifth's reign is also inconsiderable. In that of his son the English language was first used in our legal transactions. At the same period the titles of esquyer and gentleman first occur, knights having been designed by their proper distinction from the earliest times. In the reign of Henry VIII. parties first appear subscribing at the bottom of deeds in their own hands, and witnesses upon the back. In awards of the same period, arbitrators and parties are sometimes found subscribing together.

The clergy were much in the confidence of families, and therefore perpetually occur in trusts, but rectors and vicars only are mentioned with the addition of their churches, chaplains being simply entitled capellani, which is the reason that, though many names of these inferior ecclesiastics occur, we are able to assign very few to their proper chapels or altars,—a very great desideratum in writing the history of an establishment in which these small foundations were so numerous.

But to return,

In assistance so flattering, in materials so copious and original, a compiler may be allowed to take pleasure, yet this sensation is far from being unmixed, for with advantages such as have fallen perhaps to the lot of few topographers, he is appalled by the reflection that his own responsibility is increased in proportion; and having seen few objects through the obscure or distorting medium of printed books, having written in general with original charters before him, and where they failed, having always been able to avail himself of correct and authentic transcripts, he feels how seldom the charge of incorrectness can be transferred to careless epitomizers, or unfaithful reporters of ancient evidence, who have gone before him. With respect, however, to any inaccuracies which may be discovered in facts or dates (and in so long a work what author shall promise himself a total exemption from them?) deliberate fraud, he hopes, will not be imputed to him; a want of ordinary care he cannot impute to himself; some faults, after all his own vigilance, and that of his friends, will still adhere to the press; and, for what remains, he has to claim the general indulgence due from man to man, for mere incogitancy and involuntary error.

But in a subject, of which the very essence is conjecture, working upon remote facts, and often upon uncertain chronology, † he has to remind, at least one class of readers, that his conclusions are only to be tried by laws which belong to them, namely, by the laws of probable evidence, and of literary honor;—that in the investigations of an antiquary he reasons well who guesses happily,—and he, perhaps, best of all, who neither to support an hypothesis, nor to indulge in the exercise of intellectual playfulness, will ever undertake to establish a fact, however trifling or indifferent, when he does not believe it to be probable, in the same degree of which he would persuade his reader.

For, even in these lighter exercises of the understanding, so much is due to the sanctity of truth, that where no other possible evil can follow from misleading, a dealer in probabilities ought to make it a matter of conscience never to mislead.

With these views of his subject, and with a consciousness of many imperfections in himself, yet remembering that what is amiss will not be amended by apologies, and what is otherwise does not require them, the author now commits his work to the candor of a discerning public.

* The Townley MSS. and the same deficiency occurs in other collections.

† It must be remembered that our oldest charters are without date, and their æras can therefore be ascertained only from circumstances, and particularly from the names of witnesses, which are themselves liable to much uncertainty.

SUBSCRIBERS TO THE HISTORY OF WHALLEY, 1802-1806.

A.

REV. J. Adamson, Minister of Padiham
Rev. R. Assheton, D.D. Warden of Manchester
W. Assheton, Esq. Cuerdale Lodge, 2 copies
H. Aspinall, Esq. Reedley
J. Aspinall, Esq. London
T. Astle, Esq. F.R.S. F.S.A. Battersea Rise
J. Addison, Esq. Preston

B.

The Hon. Lady Bromley
Rt. Hon. Sir J. Banks, Bart. &c. &c.
Sir J. Beaumont, Bt. South Audley-street
J. Blackburne, Esq. M.P. Park-street, Westminster
Major-General Barnard, Heaton Lodge
R. H. Beaumont, Esq. F.S.A. Whitley, 2 copies
Wade Browne, Esq. Leeds
F. S. Brydges, Esq. Little Horton
T. Browne, Esq. Grassington
Rev. W. Breithwaite, D.D. Archdeacon of Richmond
Miss Brownes, Leeds
Mr. Bolton, Attorney at Law, Colne
R. Birley, Esq. Blackburn
Mr. J. Birley, do.
Mr. H. H. Birley, do.
Rev. W. Barton, M.D. Whalley
J F. Butler, Esq. Pleasington
Rev. Mr. Bellas, A.M. Rector of Holdenby
E. Ball, Esq. Wardleworth
Rev. Mr. Balme
W. Bray, Esq. Russell-street, Bloomsbury
Rev. R. C. Bernard, B.D. Rector of Withersfield
Book Society, Colne
Mrs. Wilbraham Bootle, Latham House
Subscription Library, Blackburn
W. Bentham, Esq. Lincoln's Inn
Book Society at Newchurch, in Rossendale
—— Boddenham, Esq. Rotherwas, Herefordshire
H. Blundell, Esq. Ince Blundell

C.

The Rt. Rev. William, Lord Bishop of Chester
Rt. Hon Lord Curzon
Hon. G. A. Curzon
Hon. Miss Curzon
Major Clayton, Little Harwood
Rev. W. Henry Coulthurst, D.D. Vicar of Halifax
Rev. T. Collins, D.D. Minister of Burnley
Rev. W. Carr, B.D. Fellow of the Magdalen College, Oxford
H. O. Cunliffe, Esq. Wycoller
R. Cross, Esq. Burgh Hall
J. Calverley, Esq. Leeds
Capt. Cable, Isle of Man
R. Cardwell, Esq. Blackburn
Mr. A. Cottam, Whalley
W. Cubbin, Esq. Liverpool
Elijah Cobham, Esq. Everton
Miss Crosley, Halifax
Dr. Chew, Billington
Major Clarke, Waddow
Mr. Clarke, Bond-street
Governors of Clitheroe School

D.

The Hon. and Rt. Rev. the Lord Bishop of Durham
Rev. T. Drake, D.D. Vicar of Rochdale
R. Drummond, Esq. Cleveland-row, St. James's
Pudsey Dawson, Esq. Liverpool
Rev. W. Drake, Horley Green
J. Dearden, Esq. Rochdale
Mr. Dent, Barrowford

E.

J. Entwistle, Esq. Foxholes
T. Eccleston, Esq. Scarisbrick

F.

Rev. J. Fawcett, B.D. Norrisian Professor in the University of Cambridge
Rev. G. S. Faber, A.M. Fellow of Lincoln College, Oxford
Mr. J. Fawcett, Leeds
H. Feilden, Esq. Blackburn
W. Feilden, Esq. do.
Rev. R. Formby, Formby Hall
Mr. Fox, Manchester
Miss Foulds, Trawden
Mr. J. Foulds, Trawden

G.

Rt. Hon. Lord Grey de Wilton
Sir J. W. S. Gardiner, Bart. Clerk Hill
R. Gough, Esq. F.S.A. London
B. Gott, Esq. Mayor of Leeds
N. Grimshaw, Esq. Preston
Mr. C. Grimshaw, Burnley
H. Greenwood, Esq. do.
J. Greenwood, Esq. do.
W. Greenwood, Esq. Leeds
Mr. Grundy, Bury
Mr. Greaves, Preston Bank
Mr. Gore, Rochdale
Mr. Golds, Wardleworth
Mr. Gregg, James's-street, Buckingham Gate

H.

His Grace the Duke of Hamilton, Grosvenor-square
Rt. Hon Baroness Howe
Sir H. P. Houghton, Bart. Walton Hall
Sir T. Hesketh, Bart. Rufford
J. Horrocks, Esq. Preston
Rev. Mr. Harrison, Grimsargh
W. Hill, Esq. Blyth Hall
Rev. R. Harris, B.D. Preston
Mr. N. Halsted, Burnley
Hemingway and Crook, Blackburn
J. F. Hindle, Esq. do.
Mr. J. Hargreaves, Clitheroe
Mr. George Howarth, Rossendale
Mr. J. Hamer, Rochdale
Rev. J. H. Hall, Risley Hall
J. Hilton, Esq Pennington
Mr. Hargreaves, Newchurch, Rossendale
W. Harper, Esq. Everton
Rev. J. Hargreaves, Bank-top, Burnley
Mr. J. Holgate, Burnley
Mr. J. Hitchen, London
W. Hornby, Esq. Kirkham
E. Howarth, Esq Turton
C. Hornyold, Esq. Lombard-street
T. Hornyold, Esq. Blackmore Park

J.

W. Jones, Esq. Banker, Manchester, 2 copies
Mrs. Jackson, Preston
M. Jones, Esq. Lancaster

K.

E. King, Esq. Vice-Chancellor of the Dutchy of Lancaster, Lincoln's Inn
R. P. Knight, Esq. M.P. Downton, Ludlow

L.

Circulating Library, Preston
The Circulating Library, Manchester
The Library of St. John's College, Cambridge
The Heralds' College Library
The Circulating Library, Leeds
R. G. Lomax, Esq. Clayton Hall
Lt.-Colonel Lloyd, Horsorth
T. Lloyd, Bashall
T. Lowe, M.D Preston
W. Langton, Esq. Kirkham
Mr. H. Lord, Rossendale
Mr. J. Lord, Rossendale
Mr. R. Lonsdale, Haslingden

M.

W. Middleton, Esq. Middleton Lodge
E. Markland, Esq. Leeds
B. Markland, Esq. Blackburn
Mr. Maden, jun. Rossendale
Mr Moon, Attorney at Law, Colne
Mr. Milne, Attorney at Law, Rochdale
Rev. T. Moss, A.M. Liverpool
Mr. W. Marriot, Clare Green, Colne
Mrs. Meadows, Preston
Mr. Marshall, Leeds
Rev. S. Master, A.M. Rector of Croston
Rev. W. Master, A.M. Rector of Chorley

N.

His Grace the Duke of Norfolk
L. Nihill, M.D. Leicester-place, Leicester-square
Miss Nowell, Linton, Craven
A. Nowell, Esq. Turhoot, Bengal, 3 copies
R. Nowell, Esq. Essex-street, Strand, 3 copies

O.

T. Oakes, Esq. Liverpool
Miss Ormerod, of Ormerod
Rev. R. Ormerod, A.M. Vicar of Kensington
H. Ormerod, M.D. Rochdale
G. Ormerod, Greensnook
Mr. J. Ormerod, Solicitor at Law, Rochdale
P. Ormerod, Esq. Rosegrove
Mr. J. Ormerod, Rossendale
Mr. O. Ormerod, Foxstones

P.

Sir G. O. Paul, Bart. Rodborough, Gloucestershire
T. Lister Parker, Esq. Bowbearer of the Forest of Bowland, 2 copies
T. Parker, Esq. Alkincoates
Rev. R. Parke, A.M. Wavertree
W. Pole, Esq. Liverpool
Mr. R. Peele, Accrington
Mr. T. Peele, Sawley
Mr. W. Peele, Burnley
Mr. J. Parr, Colne
Rev. W. Prescot, M.A. Vicar of Long Preston
E. Pedder, Esq. Cuerden Hall
Mr. R. Prince, Manchester

Q.

Rev. J. Quartley, A.M. Vicar of Ribchester

R.

Rt. Hon. Lord Ribblesdale, Gisburn Park
J. Robinson, Esq. Chatburn
W. H. C. Roundell, Esq. Gledston House
R. H. Roundell, Esq. do.
W Rawson, Esq. Mill House, Halifax
Rev. R. H. Roughsedge, A.M. Rector of Liverpool
L. Rawstorne, Esq. Preston
Colonel Ratcliffe, Milnes Bridge
Miss Richardson, Gargreave
Rev. Mr. Raws, Burnley

S.

Rt. Hon. Earl Spencer, &c. &c.
Sir R. Sutton, Bart. Hanover-square
L. P. Starkie, Esq. Huntroid, 2 copies
Rt. Hon. Lord Stanley
Rev. T. Starkie, A.M. Vicar of Blackburn
R. T. Sullivan, Esq. Thames Ditton, Surrey
T. Staniforth, Esq. Liverpool
S. Staniforth, Esq do.
T. Shuttleworth, Esq. Attorney at Law, Preston
R. Shuttleworth, Esq. Gawthorpe
Mr. R. Shuttleworth, Attorney at Law, Rochdale
Rev. Mr. Smalley, Darwen
Rev. W. Sheepshanks, A.M. Prebendary of Carlisle and Minister of St John's, Leeds
Rev. T. Sheepshanks, A M. Rector of Wimpole and Aspenden, 2 copies
Rev. Mr. Shorrock, A.M. Minister of Newchurch in Rossendale
Rev. J. Sheepshanks, A.M. Fellow of Trinity College, Cambridge
For the late Dr. Shepherd's Library, Preston
W. St. Clair, M.D. Preston
Literary Society, Settle
E. Standish, Esq. Standish Hall
T. A. Smyth, Esq. Berkeley-street, Portman-square
Mr. W. Sutcliffe, Field Head
Mr J. Swinglehurst, Parkhill, Rossendale
E. Stephenson, Esq. Queen-square, Bloomsbury

T.

Hon Baron Thomson, Bedford-square
C. Townley, Esq. F.R.S. F.S.A. Townley
J. Townley, Esq. F.R.S. F.S.A. Devonshire-place
Peregrine Townley, Esq. Cleveland-row, St. James's
H. Taylor, Esq. Palace House and Rock House, 3 copies
J. Taylor, Esq. Read, 2 copies
J. Tarleton, Esq. Finch House
Mr. Tatham, Duxbury
—— Talbot, Esq.
Mr. J. Thursby, Leeds
Mr. J. Tickle, Padiham
Miss Thursby, Leeds

V.

Rev. J. Vause, A.M. Fellow of King's College, Cambridge
Mr. Varley, Strangeways Hall
G. Venables, Esq. Mount Vernon
Mr. S. Veevers, Coal-clough

W.

Rt. Hon. Sir R. Worsley, Bart. Pall Mall
R. Wilbraham, Esq. St. James's-place
M. Wilson, Esq. Manor House, Otley
Rev. T. Wilson, B.D. Minister of Clitheroe
Rev. R. Roe Walton, Marsden
Rev. Mr Wade, Tottington
Rev. H. Wigglesworth, A.M. Rector of Slaidburn
Mr. J. Whitaker, Broadclough
G. Walmesley, Esq. Rochdale
R. Walmesley, Esq. Showley
T. W. Whalley, Esq. Roche Court, Hampshire
W. Whalley, Esq. Orrel
Colonel Wright, Roefield
Rev. F. Wilkinson, A.M. Vicar of Bardsey
Mr. H. Winterbottom, Goodshaw Chapel
G. Wilbraham, Esq. Seymour-place

ADVERTISEMENT TO THE SECOND EDITION, 1806.

MUCH additional matter having come to the Author's hands since the Publication of this Work, it has been judged expedient to incorporate the substance of it with the remaining Copies, as well as to make several Corrections. Four Engravings are also added.

ADVERTISEMENT TO THE THIRD EDITION, 1818.

IN this Volume the Author of the History of Whalley presents his first Work, for the last time, to a judicious Public.

As the production of a young and zealous Antiquary, prone, from local attachment, to ascribe to some objects a degree of importance to which they were not entitled, he is fully aware of the imperfections with which it once abounded, and has never been inattentive to the admonitions which he has received on the subject, with whatever temper, or in whatever style, they may have been expressed.

Nineteen years, however, which have elapsed since the first publication, might perhaps have converted enthusiasm into indifference, had not the bounty of a great Prelate placed the Writer in a situation, which, as it closely connected him with the principal subject of the Work, not only endeared to him that and the whole parish beyond the feelings of local attachment and early zeal, but presented to him many opportunities of information which he had not before enjoyed.

At the same time unremitted inquiry into other topographical subjects incidentally threw in his way numerous particulars relating to the parish of Whalley, of which he has in no instance neglected to avail himself.

Many mistakes which had been discovered in the former edition have in consequence been rectified, many facts which were there hypothetically stated have been reduced to certainty, and an ample fund of original matter has been introduced.

Conscious, therefore, that nothing on the subject but a few gleanings could possibly remain for future investigation to supply, he was on the point of ushering into the world, with unmixed satisfaction, discoveries connected with that ancient Church and delightful Residence, where, for the last eight years, in society endeared to him by every tie of nature and affection, he had passed so many happy and edifying days.

But the light and sunshine of the scene are now overcast by a gloom never to be dispelled. His constant companion in public duties and private society, the Son, the Pupil, and the Friend, has been snatched away by a momentary and awful stroke,* while in the possession of every domestic comfort, and in the exercise of every domestic virtue; and henceforward a place once so dear can only serve to revive the painful recollection of past happiness too great to continue, and embitter sensations of present dereliction too deep to be effaced.

Yet all feelings are not absorbed in one, however intense or abiding; and it is even now with lively and affectionate regard that this Volume, the memorial of a connexion which he rejoices in transmitting to posterity, is bequeathed as a legacy to the parishioners of Whalley, by their Minister and Friend.

February 26, 1818.

* The Rev. Thomas Thoresby Whitaker, M.A., who was killed by a fall from his horse, August 28, 1817. See the Latin epitaph, by his father, at Holme.

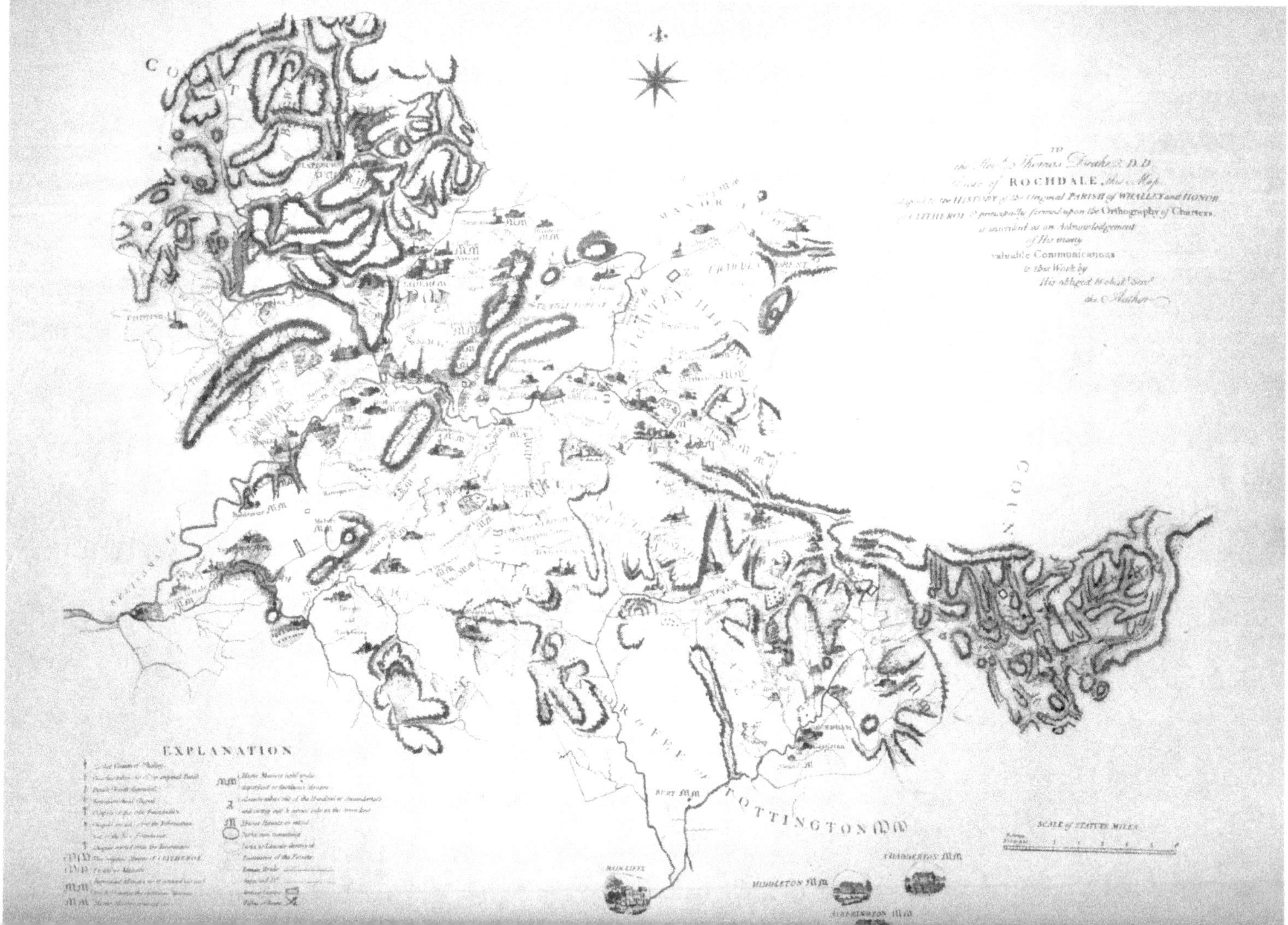
TO
ROCHDALE
HISTORY
PARISH of WHALLEY and HONOR
formed upon the Orthography of Charters
as an Acknowledgement
of His many
valuable Communications
to this Work by
the Author
EXPLANATION
SCALE of STATUTE MILES
TOTTINGTON
BURY
RADCLIFFE
MIDDLETON
CHADDERTON

HISTORY OF WHALLEY.

BOOK I.

CHAPTER THE FIRST.

AMONG the native tribes of Britain, the *Brigantes* were the most numerous and powerful: they stretched from sea to sea in one direction from the shore of Humber to that of Tyne, and from the æstuary of Mersey to that of Eden on the other. But, within these ample confines were comprehended other inferior clans, of whom one, denominated by Ptolemy the *Setontii*, or rather the *Segantii*,[1] are placed by that geographer in the mountainous tract usually termed the *British Apennine*, which divides the island in a longitudinal ridge, and from which the rivers fall, in a long and gentle course, to the German Ocean, but with a short and precipitate descent to the Irish Sea. Their other boundaries may be conjectured to have been the bay of Moricambe to the north, and the copious æstuary of the Mersey to the south. Thus situated, on an elevated level, along the sources of numerous brooks and of some considerable rivers, their name may be referred to the great characteristic feature of their country, *Se cond uï*[2]—the Head of the Waters.[3]—Out of this wild and dreary tract, and contiguous only to its eastern boundary, arose in much later times that district, ecclesiastical and civil, which I have undertaken to describe. It comprehends, within the original boundaries of the Saxon parish of Whalley, the present extensive vicarage of that name, together with those of Rochdale and Blackburn, the rectory of Slaidburn, the vicarages of Mitton, Chipping, and Ribchester, with their

[1] This is the reading of the Palatine MS. The anonymous Ravennas calls them *Sistuntiaci*, more probably *Seguntiaci*. *Vide* Baxter *in voce*.

[2] See again the excellent British etymologist Baxter *in voce*.

[3] Richard of Cirencester has thought proper to make us a present of the *Voluntii*, an Irish tribe, whom, as they have no legal claim upon us, we will take leave to remove to their original place of settlement. Stukeley's edition of Ric. Corinensis.

several dependencies.[1] The features of the country are uniform, and rarely striking: never expanding into spacious plains, and never soaring into bold and majestic mountains, they swell into a tiresome succession of long and dreary ridges, sometimes, indeed, intersected by the pleasing scenery of deep and woody valleys, but often separated by tame and unbroken slopes, brown and cheerless, from which the wearied eye flies alike for refreshment to the bolder features of nature and to the lively hues of cultivation.

One charming accompaniment of mountain scenery has been denied to the valleys of our Apennine—for we have no lakes or considerable pools, which in fact rarely appear but in countries where the hills are bolder and more precipitous, where they tower into bulky cones, or are broken into sharp and serrated ridges. Thus the fells of Furness, of Westmerland, and Cumberland, to the north, no sooner assume either of these striking forms, than their feet begin to be washed in the cool and translucent gatherings of their own torrents; and thus the soft and swelling hills of Denbighshire to the south have no other accompaniment of water than their own descending streams, while the naked cliffs of *Snowdonia*, often sharpened into ridges without a surface, are reflected on every side by the expanse of llyns and pools to which nature has denied an immediate outlet.

The reason of a fact so general that I recollect only two or three exceptions to it, seems to be this—that, in countries truly alpine, vast masses of rock are often pitched across the valleys, and thus become dams and ramparts which no force of torrents, or weight of congregated waters, can ever move;[2] while the fells above, composed of slate or quartz, transmit their streams charged with few or no earthy particles to choke the pools beneath by gradual accumulation, whereas the loose and ill-compacted banks casually thrown athwart our spongy bottoms still appear in many instances to have been broken by the first pressure of floods,[3] or the hollows above them to have been filled by gradual deposits of earth and rubbish, which every little swell brings down in vast quantities, from the sides of mountains composed of clay, schistus, or other loose materials.

A decomposition also of these or other minerals, almost all akin to coal or iron, forms the basis of our vegetable mould; and thus, as every species of native soil is attended with a concomitant train of indigenous plants, while the granite of bolder fells is clad with the glowing purple of heath, and the mamillary swells of limestone are enlivened by the cheerful green of their native grasses—the long and barn-like ridges of these hills are thatched with an uninteresting covering of pale and meagre bent.[4]

[1] Status de Blackburnshire.

[2] See Stukeley's Iter Boreale, p. 48.

[3] It is an ingenious and probable conjecture of Mr. Mitford, that the deluges of Ogyges and Deucalion were occasioned by the bursting of lakes in the vales of Thessaly and Bœotia while the crust of the earth was yet tender and unsettled, after the general deluge.—History of Greece.

[4] The *Agrostis capillaris*. [*The Agrostis capillaris* of Leers. *A. alba*, Linn. *A. vulgaris* and *A. alba*, Engl. Bot. *A. alba* (Bentham, Handbook of the Brit. Flora). "*A. capillaris*, Linn. Sp. pl. 93, Sm. pl. Ic. t. 54, is a totally different plant found in Portugal," Eng. Flora, vol. i. p. 93. "Some species (of Agrostis) are commonly called *bents* in some parts of the country, a name given by others more especially to the crested dogstail" (*Cynosurus cristatus*), Bentham, ib. p. 961. The herbage of these hills, however, chiefly consists of the root-leaves of the heath rush (*Juncus squarrosus*), which is far more abundant than the bent, although the flowering stems are not nearly so conspicuous.—P. A. L.]

Neither is the climate of this tract much more favourable than its general aspect. Presenting the broad and bulky masses of its hills to those copious exhalations which, rising in the Irish Sea, or even in the Atlantic, are driven by the continual prevalence of western winds against their sides, its summers are too often ungenial, its autumns lost in fogs, its grain damp and musty, its fruits crude and unmellowed.

In a state of nature, however, another cause, which is now at least partially done away, contributed to augment the evil. Our vales, which are now drained by the hand of cultivation, were then steaming and unwholesome swamps; and our mountains, which even yet condense immense quantities of vapour by their chilling contact, then attracted, in a much larger proportion, the humidity of the atmosphere, by the projection of their native woods, which at the same time checked the wholesome influence of evaporation by their impenetrable umbrage.

This was the character given by the historian to the climate of Britain in general; but it applies with peculiar propriety to our Apennines—ἐξ ὧν [ἑλῶν] τῆς ἀναθυμιάσεως καὶ παχυτῆτος ὁ κατ' ἐκείνην τὴν χώραν ἀὴρ ζοφώδης ἀεὶ φαίνεται.[1]

In this state, however, peopled by the wild boar and the wolf, and by their natural prey, the moose deer, the stag, the wild bull, these wastes were traversed, rather than occupied, by their first human inhabitants; and these were probably not only few in numbers, but inferior to their southern neighbours in arts and civilization. Hence it is that they have left, in a tract of great extent, only one remain[2] of those gigantic fortifications which, under all the disadvantages of mechanical inexpertness, mark the toil and perseverance of savages—that they have left few specimens of their skill in working metals, or of their art in shaping instruments of stone—that they have erected none of those circular monuments, or rude columnar shafts, or well-poised rocking stones, which antiquarian uncertainty has agreed to term druidical.[3]

But of their flexible and expressive language they have left many striking remains in the names of permanent objects, such as rivers and mountains. These may best be considered if we first divide the whole district into those great portions which the hand of

[1] Herodian, lib. iii. cap. 14, § 15. So also Tacitus (Agricola, c. 12), "cœlum crebris imbribus ac nebulis fœdum." And again, "multus humor terrarum cœlique."

[2] *Vide* ROSSENDALE.

[3] In the contiguous parish of Halifax, Mr. Watson, the historian of that place, has found or fancied several of these remains; but since the publication of his book a very considerable discovery was made, an account of which may be allowed to supply the deficiency of similar information in our own parish. A countryman digging peat upon Mixenden Moor turned up the following instruments: 1st. A very fine celt of brass, but so white as to appear to have been alloyed by tin; 2nd. A small battle-axe of beautiful green pebble veined with white; 3rd. An instrument of grey stone resembling a carpenter's gouge, and probably intended for the purpose of excavating wood; 4th. A whetstone of a black basaltic appearance; 5th. Four arrow-heads of flint. These are now in my possession. [Besides the entrenchment of Broadclough here referred to, the following may be enumerated as British remains belonging to the ancient parish of Whalley. They will be more fully noticed under their respective localities:—Sepulchral urns found at Over Darwen. Rock basins on Pendle and the hills about Burnley. Stone mallet found at Newchurch-in-Pendle. Celts found at Waddington, Read, and Clitheroe. Fibula found at Waddington. Beaded torc found near Rochdale. Gold torc brought to Dr. Whitaker on the evening after he had finished the last edition of Whalley.]

nature has marked out, and which have materially affected its civil and ecclesiastical distribution in later times.

In this survey it is not intended to pursue the boundaries of parishes with the servile accuracy of a perambulation; but with a freer and bolder hand to trace those great original objects which Providence seems to have interposed, as dykes and ramparts, for the purpose of ascertaining the claims or of restraining the hostility of neighbouring and contending tribes in after ages.[1]

If we take, therefore, an extended view of the whole tract which is intended, either briefly or in detail, to constitute the subject of this work, it will appear to have been thus originally distributed into nine different portions, of which some are principally defined by the course of rivers; but the greater part are deep and winding excavations, bounded by the long and irregular outline of the surrounding hills, and all are strongly marked by natural features on every side, excepting the eastern boundary of Bowland, the western extremity of the parishes of Chipping and Ribchester, and the south-western limit of the parish of Rochdale, in all which the original parish declines towards the adjoining plains, and partakes of their tamer and less definite character.

This general survey will assist the reader in forming a distinct conception of the natural characters of the country. It will bring together in one view such relics of the British language as still subsist in the names of our rivers and mountains; and it will show what influence the hand of nature has had upon the subsequent arrangements of civil society.

Natural Districts.	British Names.	Modern Distribution, Civil and Ecclesiastical.
First, of these natural districts to the north, is the tract interposed between the Ribble, the Hodder, and the fells of Totteredge, Trough Scar, Goodgreave, Ravish Castle, and Bowland Knots. The eastern boundary not strongly marked.	Ribble, Hodder.	Forest and country of Bowland. Parishes of Mitton and Sladeburn.
Secondly, the tract bounded by Ribble, Hodder, and Fairsnape Fell. The boundary towards the Filde country not strongly defined.	As before.	Parishes of Chipping and Ribchester.
Third, the tract lying betwixt Pendle and Ribble.	Pendle, Cliderhow.	Chapelries of Cliderhow and Downham.
Fourth, the great excavation between Pendle, Pinhow, Bulswerd,[2] Hameldon, Cliviger Pike, and Hameldon in Hapton.	Pinhow, Hameldon, Calder, Colne.	Whalley, with its immediately dependent townships, the chapelries of Burnley and Colne, and the forests of Pendle and Trawden.

[1] "Mutuo metu et montibus separantur." Tacitus de Mor. Germ.

[2] The orthography of these names is principally that of ancient charters, often very different from the modern.

Natural Districts.	British Names.	Modern Distribution, Civil and Ecclesiastical.
Fifth, the country lying betwixt Hameldon, Criddon, Musbury, and the rivers Calder and Hyndeburne.	Criddon.	Chapelries of Church, Altham, Accrington, Haslingden.
Sixth, the tract bounded by Ribble, Derwent, and Hyndeburne.	Derwent.	Parish of Blackburn.
Seventh, Country bounded by Cliviger Moor, Hameldon, Criddon, Musbury, Copelaw, Gorsithlache.	Rossendale.	Forest of Rossendale.
Eighth, the valleys of Roch and Spodden, with their several acclivities, to Gorsithlache, Flourscar, Blackstonedge, and the hills of Butterworth. The south-west boundary not strongly marked.	Roch, Biel.	Parish of Rochdale within Lancashire.
Ninth, the tract bounded by Blackstonedge, Stanedge, Goodgreave, Walstonedge, &c. terminating the original parish of Whalley to the south on the confines of Cheshire, and the Peak of Derby.[1]	Withins, Diggles, Chaw, Tame.	Saddleworth, a member of the same parish, but in Yorkshire.

First, and most celebrated in this catalogue of British names, is the Ribble, which by the general consent of our antiquaries has been understood to be the *Belisama* of Ptolemy. And this hypothesis is supported by the resemblance and the etymology of the two words, as well as by the bearings and distances laid down by that geographer. A late antiquary,[2] however, of great talents and learning, having a favourite hypothesis to support, has thought proper to transfer *Belisama* to the Mersey, and to leave the more distinguished river nameless and unnoticed. In order to understand the grounds of this controversy, it will, in the first place, be necessary to state and to explain Ptolemy's chart of the British coast from the *Setcia* to the *Moricambe*.

Moricambe Æstuarium	17	30	——	58	20
Segantiorum Portus	17	29	——	57	45
Belisama Æstuarium	17	30	——	57	20
Setcia Æstuarium	17	—	——	57	—

Moricambe (the great curvature) and *Setcia* are here given quantities, one of which is allowed to be the deep and spacious bay formed by the æstuaries of *Ken* and *Leven*, and the other is as plainly the Dee.[3] But in the interval between these are three principal

[1] Tottington is not included in this survey, because, though a member of the honor of Clitheroe, it forms no part of the original parish of Whalley.

[2] Mr. Whitaker, Hist. Manc. b. i. c. 5.

[3] *Se* is the British prefix, or præpositive article; and *Teia* is the true Welsh pronunciation of *Deia*, or *Deva*.

rivers, the Lune, the Ribble, and the Mersey, of which two only are noticed by the geographer. Now, prior to all reasoning upon the chart itself, there is an antecedent probability, that, as Ptolemy is known to have taken his accounts of our British coasts from the observations of mariners, those æstuaries which had no celebrated ports upon them would be omitted in those observations. But the Mersey was exactly in this predicament, whereas the Ribble and Lune had considerable harbours and stations upon their banks, which would of course be resorted to by sailors, and therefore noted in their charts.

However, in order to do justice to Mr. Whitaker's argument in support of his position that *Belisama* is the Mersey, we will state it in his own words:[1] "From the *Seteia*, advancing 20 miles to the north, Ptolemy goes 30 to the east—to the æstuary *Belisama*. This is plainly the Mersey, because *Belisama* is at the distance of the Mersey from the Dee, and because such a considerable object as the Mersey could not be overlooked any more than the Dee. And thus far we are certain of the conclusions. The former is evidently too southerly for it, and the latter is as evidently too northerly. But the geographer, ranging along the coast for 25 miles from the Mersey, turns with the turning shore, and goes ten miles to the west, to the harbour of the *Sistuntii*. This sufficiently argues the harbour not to be at the mouth of the Mersey. And this equally argues it not to be at the mouth of the Lune. Twenty-five miles to the north of the Mersey can carry us only to one place convenient for an harbour—the mouth of the Ribble."

Let us now examine this representation distinctly and by parts: First, then, "So considerable an object as the Mersey could not be overlooked." But one considerable river betwixt the *Seteia* and *Moricambe* is actually overlooked by Ptolemy, and I have already assigned a reason why the Mersey should be overlooked rather than the Ribble. Secondly, we are told, that "advancing twenty miles to the north, and turning thirty miles east from the mouth of Dee, we shall find ourselves at the mouth of the Mersey." Let the reader cast his eye on a common map of Lancashire and Cheshire, and say whether the mouth of Mersey is even ten miles north and five miles east from that of Dee. But if we stretch from the mouth of Dee twenty miles northward, according to the geographer's directions, we shall find ourselves out at sea indeed, but in a latitude exactly corresponding with the mouth of Ribble, and, turning thence at a right angle to the east for thirty miles, we shall stretch a little further inward than Mr. Whitaker's supposed station (which, however, was certainly not the *Setantiorum Portus*) near the *Neb* of the *Nese*. Again, the geographer ranges indeed twenty-five miles to the north, but only one to the west, if the figures in Bertius's Ptolemy be right. Supposing ourselves therefore to be stationed on the æstuary near Freckleton, we are southward from Lancaster about twenty-one English, or twenty-five of Ptolemy's miles, and westward about two English miles—so clearly do the geographer's data lead us to seek for *Belisama* in the Ribble, and the *Setantiorum Portus* in Lancaster. But Mr. Whitaker had an unfortunate theory to support: he had implicitly addicted himself to the dreams of a monk, before whose unsupported conjectures

[1] Hist. Manc. b. i. c. 5.

the contemporary[1] and decisive authorities of Antonine and Ptolemy were equally to give way—for him the *Coccium* of the one was to be removed to Blackrod, and the *Rigodunum* of the other to be merged in his misplaced *Rerigonium;*[2] and, to give some appearance of consistency to this strange hypothesis, the *Setantiorum Portus* was to be removed to the mouth of Ribble, that celebrated stream left without a name, and *Belisama*, which is obviously represented in the modern word, violently transferred to the Mersey;[3] while Ptolemy's bearings and distances unanimously concurred in supporting the truth of the old hypothesis, and in demonstrating the impossibility of the new one.

After having established the real site of *Belisama*, we are next to ascertain the etymology of the word, and to prove its identity with the modern Ribble.[4] *Bel is am*, or in the plural *amon*, in the British language signifies Head of the Waters, an appellation peculiarly adapted to the Ribble, which unites, and carries down with it to the sea, numbers of tributary streams. Again, in the same language, *Rhiu bel*, from which the present name is obviously formed, has exactly the same meaning, namely, the Head River. Of the word *Am*, as it occurs in the composition of this word, we shall have frequent occasion to make use hereafter, and it may therefore be worth while to remark the various forms in which it appears in the composition of the names of rivers. *V* and *M* are convertible in the British language. We have, therefore, the same radical in the twofold form of *Av* and *Am;* and, with the prepositive letters, *Tam* and *Sam—Tav* and *Sav;* from whence come the Avon, the Thames, the Tay, the Towy; and in our own country the Tame, the Chaw, the Savok.[5]

This beautiful stream, intersecting in its sinuous course the whole county of Lancaster, receives near Mitton the Hodder, which, coming down from Cross of Grete, for several of

[1] Not with each other; for Ptolemy flourished under the first Antonines, and the compiler of the Itinerary was probably Antoninus Caracalla—but contemporary with the actual existence of the two names in question, and therefore original authorities.

[2] See the next chapter.

[3] The word *Mersey* is evidently neither British nor Roman, but pure Saxon, which powerfully argues the obscurity of the river so denominated in the Roman era. If we adopt the hypothesis that it was, at the time when it received its appellation, the boundary of the Mercian and Northumbrian kingdoms, its etymology will plainly be Ꝺepre-ea, the Mercian Water; if otherwise, Ꝺepeſ-ea will sufficiently describe a river which, through the intervention of the Dane, the Fulbrook, and the Wever, is fed by nearly twenty large *Meres*, in the county of Chester. After all, it is a bold conjecture, but strongly supported by natural appearances, that the *æstuary* of Mersey did not exist in the Roman period, but that its waters, after passing the promontory of Frodsham, expanded over the flat and sandy tract of Wirral, and found an uncertain and irregular outlet into the Dee. The word is not even mentioned in the Saxon Chronicle, but is, perhaps, first met with in the "Terra inter Ripam (Ribble) et Merseiam" of Domesday, though Ric. of Cirencester assigns to Merseia fl. a place in what he styles Mappa Britanniæ faciei Romanæ.

[4] "Ribil riseth in Ribilsdale abowte Sallay Abbay, and so to Sawlley. A IIII miles beneth Sawley it reseyvith Calder that cummeth by Walley, and after receyvith a nother water cawllid Oder. Walley a x miles from Preston; Sawlley a . . . . miles or more." Leland's Itinerary, vol. vii. part 1, fol. 58, Blackburnshire.

[5] *Savok*, qu. *Is av uch*, the High Stream, as it has its source in Longridge. To these may be added two genuine British names of brooks injuriously omitted in modern maps, *Short Taud and Dartow Small, two little country maids* (Drayton's Polyolbion, Song 27), of which the former is the uncompounded radical word, and the first syllable of the latter is descriptive of its ancient accompaniment, *Dar-taw*, the Stream of Oaks.

the last miles forms the boundary of Yorkshire and Lancashire, as it must originally have done between two British tribes, the word *Odre* in that language signifying a limit or bound.[1]

Our next great natural object, indeed the most distinguished and well-known feature of the whole district, is Pendle, which, though it wants the bold conical form of its northern rivals Penigent and Ingleborough,[2] and is, in fact, nothing more than a longitudinal ridge like its immediate neighbours, yet from its superior height and bulk, as well as insulated situation, presents on every side, and especially on the north, a bold and striking figure. Of this word the first syllable is pure British, and enters into the composition of many Celtic names—the *PENnine* Alps, *APENnines*, &c. *Ben*, in the Gaelic dialect, with the slight difference in the two labials which marks the distinction between the pronunciation of South Britain and Caledonia, is the same word. The composition of the modern word is an instance, of which several others will occur in the course of this work, in which a name once significant, but become unintelligible by change of language, has had an explanatory syllable attached to it: thus the British *Pen*, or Head, became in the Saxon era *Penhull*; and this continued to be the orthography of the word till long after the Conquest: afterwards, however, the second syllable was melted down into the insignificant *dle*, and required another explanatory addition, altogether constituting the modern *Pendle Hill*. Of its two rivals mentioned above, one retains its genuine British appellation *Pen gwyn*, the White Head, or *Pen gwynt*, the Head of Winds: the latter, whatever it was, is lost in the Saxon *Ingleborough*.[3]

For Clitheroe, of which the two first syllables are apparently British, see the conjectures which will be offered under that place.[4]

Next is Pinhow, an high and heathy ridge, dividing the parish of Whalley on the north from those of Carlton and Kildwick. This local name is compounded on similar principles to the former, of *Pin*, the same word, with a slight dialectic variation, and the Saxon *How*.

With respect to the etymology of Hameldon, which twice occurs in this circuit, I can only offer the following conjecture, after premising that, at all events, and after repeated attempts to discover something Saxon in its composition, I can only refer it to the original language of Britain, *Am ael don, ad supercilium montis*.

For Calder and Colne, the latter of which it must be remembered denoted the river and not the town, I can acquiesce either in Baxter's etymology *Calai dwr, aqua lutosa*, or Mr. Whitaker's *Coldwr*, Narrow Water, for the former; and for the latter, *Colaun*, of the same meaning with the word immediately preceding, seems to be the true orthography.

[1] Thus the Rother is *Yr Odre*, the same word with a prepositive article.

[2] ["Horum libentius meminerim, quod in Apennino nostro sunt eminentissimi, unde vulgò usurpatur,

Ingleborrow, Pendle, and Penigent
Are the highest hills between Scotland and Trent."—*Camden, Brit.* 1586, p. 430.]

[3] See a good account of this mountain and the beacon upon it, whence its present name, in Rauthmell's Bremetonacæ.

[4] I am now convinced that the word is Danish, from *klettur* a crag, and *how* an hill.

Criddon, a bold and lofty hill upon the confines of Rossendale, and commanding an extended prospect southward over the plains of Lancashire, is pretty obviously *Keiru don*, the Hill of Stags. It is precisely such an elevation as that animal affects during the heat of summer, while the fallow deer graze on the plains or slopes beneath; and it might continue to merit an appellation acquired in the remotest ages of antiquity till within less than three centuries of the present time.

Derwent is the only remnant of the British language which has occurred to me in the parish of Blackburn, a district singularly deficient in striking natural objects. Billinge, which is also the name of a mountain in Airedale, and of a third in the south of Lancashire, may have indeed some pretensions, but I am unable to assign any meaning to the word in our aboriginal tongue.

Derwent, however, is evidently *Dwr-gwyn* or *gwent*, the White (or clear) Water, a quality in which, though superior in some degree to the Blakeburn or yellow[1] stream which denominates the parish, it has little claim to rival its beautiful namesake in Cumberland, the full, deep, translucent inlet of Derwent Lake.

For Rossendale, see the etymology of the word, under the Forest of that name, where it will also be proved that the Irwell has no pretensions to a British origin.

The parish of Rochdale affords nothing of a British sound excepting the *Roch* and the *Beil*.

The former of these, which is the latinized *Rhæus* of Harrison,[2] is in ancient charters generally spelt *Rache*, but sometimes, and that in the most ancient, *Rached*;[3] and it is apparently formed by a slight metathesis from *Rhi esk*, *tractus aquæ*. The latter orthography is formed by the addition of *Head*, the *Rach-head*; and from this word was evidently derived the ancient and genuine name of the town itself, *Reced-ham*.[4]

The name of *Beyle* or *Beil* is now nearly or altogether obsolete; but by this appellation our old topographer Harrison describes the stream which rises from two principal sources, one in the root of Coldgreave, and the other within the township of Crompton, unites near Butterworth Hall, passes by Belfield to which it gives name, and falls into the Roch near Wardleworth. This word is the simple British monosyllable *Bel*, or Head, and it may refer to the high and remote sources of the rivulet which it denotes.

In the dreary and late reclaimed district of Saddleworth are more remains of the original language than in those where the general use of it was early superseded by the Saxon. For within the space of a few miles are three streams, which still retain their significant British names: these are, the Diggles, the Tame, the Chaw. The first of these is evidently the same word with the Douglas of Lower Lancashire, recorded by Nennius for one of the victories of Arthur, and with the Douglas of Scotland, memorable for having given name to

[1] See the reasons assigned for this etymology under Blackburn.

[2] Description of Britain A.D. 1577, p. 65.

[3] Townley MSS.

[4] This is the orthography of Domesday Book, and of all the charters for two centuries. See further under Rochdale.

the most illustrious family in that kingdom. And it is no less evidently compounded of *Dhuglas, atro-cæruleus.*[1]

Tame (*vide supra*) is nothing more than the general appellation *av* or *am* with one of the prepositive letters.

Chaw is the same, though it may be difficult to assign a meaning or origin to the singular prefix. *Kég* seems to approximate nearer to it than any other word, and *Kégaw* would be *gutter aquæ.*

One mountain which overlooks this dreary tract on the side of Blackstonedge is the Green Withins; opposite to which is the Withins Mouth; and the Coucher Book of Whalley mentions a third, within the township of Whitworth, from its elevation called Hore Withins.[2] We are not to suppose that these lofty ridges, so remote from each other, so uniform in their relative situation, should have received their appellation from the contemptible withy or sallow, which never grew in such situations, but rather from a circumstance more general, and which at an early period may be proved to have been common to them all—*Gueithiu,* or the Woods.

Akin to this word are the Goodgraves of Saddleworth and of Bowland, two fells at the distance of forty miles from each other. The common English adjective *good* in this connexion is perfectly insignificant; but the real word is one which occurs much oftener in the composition of local names than we are aware of—this is, the British *coed,* a wood, which is reflected in Coitmore, Cadbeeston, Chatmoss, Catlow, and many others.

The latter syllable *grave* is purely Saxon, from the word ᵹꞃæꝼan *fodere,* and, whether singly as it sometimes occurs, or in composition as it is more frequently found, denotes one of those deep and naked gullies which in the forests and on the sides of the hills we see excavated by torrents in the schistus and other minerals. But this by the bye.

Such are the remains of our aboriginal language, which may be traced in local names through this widely-extended district—names which, after the lapse of so many centuries, and the shock of so many revolutions, still subsist, and may probably continue as long as the objects which they denote.

We now hasten forward from a period of extreme barbarism, barren alike of facts and of remains, to a partial and temporary scene of activity, civilization, and elegance.

[1] Drayton, who is often learned as well as accurate in his epithets, calls the former "Swart Douglas."

[2] A fourth, and that in a similar situation, has since occurred to me in Erringden.

CHAPTER THE SECOND.

ROMAN HISTORY.

THE History of Roman Britain, when connected with remote and provincial topography, has an interest peculiar to itself.

To combine names and facts, which had exercised the fancy in our happiest days of classical study, with the obscure but romantic scenery in which those days were passed; to confirm and particularise the general evidence of ancient history by contemporary remains; to bring home, for instance, the narrative of Tacitus, and the operations of Agricola, to our own villages; is a process of the mind which can dignify what else were mean, or endear what were indifferent.

This charm, difficult as it may be to analyse, yet appears to be composed of two principal ingredients—opposition and harmony: of opposition between familiar locality and distant greatness, between uncertainty of place produced by a long lapse of ages and existing remains which have defied their power:—of harmony between historical truth and local appearances, at once so remote as to exercise the understanding in comparing, so clear as to produce conviction, and so interesting as to fill the imagination when once compared.

For, overwhelmed, as every curious mind must be, on first visiting the ancient Mistress of the World, by the vastness of the objects and by the recollections which must accompany them, yet what ingenuous native of the district which we are describing would be equally affected by the image of Hadrian walking in the gardens of his own villa, or marching on foot and bareheaded over the fells of Lancashire—by Constantine and Severus under their own triumphal arches, or leading the long file of their legions along the crest of Watling-street—by Agricola receiving triumphal ornaments at Rome,[1] or choosing with judicious eye the future site of Coccium? In one situation they are expected and at home—the splendour of the place is suited to the rank of its inhabitants; in the other we are astonished to find the masters of the world, at the distance of nearly two thousand miles, traversing districts which are now scarcely visited but by a solitary sportsman or shepherd, and reposing in villages which will now scarcely accommodate a single traveller.

Such are the feelings with which we enter upon the present chapter, and upon the 10th Iter of Antonine, which, passing in a direction nearly North and South through the original parish of Whalley for the space of more than 20 miles, will conduct us, about the middle of the line, to one of the most illustrious scenes of antiquity in Roman Britain.

[1] Tac. Vit. Agr. c. 40.

This road, which has been distinctly traced by Mr. Whitaker[1] through the parishes of Prestwich, Ratcliffe, and Bury, at the northern extremity of the last enters upon the parish of Whalley, where, in a perambulation of the manor of Tottington, A.D. 1686, I find that it constituted the N.W. boundary of the lordship, which was said to extend in that direction *usque le Watling-streate.* It then entered Musbury, crossed the top of Haslingden Grain, ascended the opposite acclivity, where however no remains of it appear at present, and entered upon the wild wastes of Oswaldtwisle, where, before the late inclosure, its agger was everywhere conspicuous, as it is now at intervals, particularly in the fields near Knusden; thence it disappears once more in the cultivated grounds of Little Harwood, and, having gained the summit of the hill, descends through the township of Clayton-le-Dale to the Roman ford above Ribchester.

Of this station, the *Rigodunum* of Camden,[2] the *Coccium* of Horsley, and the *Rerigonium* of Mr. Whitaker,[3] how, after the disagreement of such men shall a fourth antiquary presume to fix the appellation? There is however the less presumption in this attempt, as the two former opinions are capable of being reconciled to each other, though the radical identity of the names never occurred to either of those great men; but the third must stand or fall on the unsupported authority of Richard the Monk, to whose frauds or errors our ingenious and learned contemporary has unhappily done too much honour.

[1] Hist. Manc. vol. i. p. 121. See also Phil. Transactions, vol. xlvii. p. 228.

[2] ["Ex his *(the inscriptions)* nihil plane luminis ad priscum hujus loci nomen eruendum, de quo ambigitur, nisi subinde nomen mutarit, quod non nunquam usu venit. Hoc enim situ Ptolemæus RIGODVNVM, si pro RIBODVNUM a *Ribbechester* non omnino abludit." *Camden Brit.* (ed. 1586) p. 431. In edition 1607 he continues, "et ad hanc a Mancunio distantiam, videlicet xviii miliarium COCCIVM, quod et Goccium in nonnullis legitur exemplaribus, locat Antoninus."]

[3] I give Mr. Whitaker ample credit for the diligence of his inquiries and the accuracy of his representations with respect to the existence of a Roman road from Mancunium to Blackrod, and of the remains of a Roman fortress at that place. In his conclusion, however, that this obscure place was the *Coccium* of Antonine, and the *Rigodunum* of Ptolemy, I am compelled to differ from him, for the following reasons:—1st. A continuation of the road from Blackrod, through the Filde, to Lancaster, and thence to Bremetonacæ, has, since Mr. W.'s inquiries, been distinctly traced. Now, had this been the 10th Iter of Antonine, an intermediate station, of the importance of Lancaster, could never have been unnoticed. In the next place, the discovery of a miliary stone near Ashton, inscribed with the name of the Emperor Philip, renders it highly probable that this was a diversion of the great North-Western Iter to the frontier of Caledonia, made at that time for the two-fold purpose of taking Lancaster in the way to Bremetonacæ, and of avoiding the rugged and difficult line from Ribchester over Longridge, through Bowland, and by Cross of Greet, to Bentham. Once more: the direct line pursued by the road from Mancunium through Ribchester to Bremetonacæ, and the firm and durable manner in which it was constructed, prove it to have been one of the great and original works of the Upper Empire; whereas the line which leads from Manchester to Lancaster has been ascertained to consist of small stones, like a modern turnpike-road, and to have been constructed in a more slight and perfunctory manner.— Lastly, the indubitable remains of the Higher Empire at Ribchester, the coins of the first Cæsars, the residence of the entire Twentieth Legion there, ascertained by an inscription which from internal evidence appears to be coeval with the earliest in Britain, and the restoration of a temple decayed by time in the reign of Alexander Severus, all concur to prove that it was one of the first foundations of that people among the Brigantes; while the superior magnificence of its public works proves it to have been a place of much more importance than an ordinary provincial station. Lancaster also bears almost equal marks of antiquity and splendour in the Roman æra; yet, with these superior claims, according to Mr. Whitaker's hypothesis, neither Lancaster nor Ribchester is noticed in the Itinerary of Antonine, while an obscure baiting-place, a mere post-house, of which the remains are scarcely visible, is exalted into the *Coccium* of Antonine and the *Rigodunum* of Ptolemy.

Without repeating reasons so lately adduced for restoring the Ribble to its ancient name of *Belisama*, I shall now assume the point as proved, at least with the degree of evidence which such investigations admit of; and shall merely state, that upon this river Ptolemy places his *Rigodunum;* and upon this river the Itinerary of Antonine, if the line of the 10th Iter and the two given stations between which it is interposed, together with the incontrovertible evidence of remains,[1] be allowed to interpret, has fixed the station of *Coccium.*[2] Yet no concurrence of roads, no discovered remains, lead to the supposition that two[3] stations or towns of eminence in the age of Ptolemy or of Caracalla were planted on the banks of the Ribble.[4] How then is this apparent difficulty to be solved? A little attention to British etymology and to the obvious appearances of the place will remove every doubt. In the first place, let the name, as it stands in Ptolemy, be stripped of the Roman termination *dunum;* and, with a British aspirate at the end, it becomes *Rigoch.* In the next place, cut off from the itinerary name its Roman generic termination, and we have *Cochiu.* G and C are convertible; some MSS. of the Itinerary read *Goccium*, and the radical syllable *Coch*, or *Goch*, is the same in both. *Goch*, in the British language is red—*Rhigoch*, Red River; and *Gochui*, or *Cochui*, Red Water. And accordingly the stone, the sand, the soil, of Ribchester, are alike distinguished by this very colour, which would naturally arrest the attention of the first inhabitants, and occasion a name peculiarly significant and proper.

This hypothesis, which goes far towards proving the identity of the place designed by both these appellations, relieves the antiquary from an embarrassment which he has never yet been able to shake off—namely, that of having a STATION TOO MUCH—an embarrassment

[1] I draw no argument from the numbers, which, upon every hypothesis, are allowed to be corrupt.

[2] ["*Mancunium* occurs but in two Itinera of Antoninus, the Second and the Tenth." The second goes through York to the Roman Vallum. Ribchester cannot then be on this line. "The Tenth Iter, which passes from the north through Cumberland, Westmerland, and the whole length of Lancashire, and is identical with the line now under consideration, gives *Coccium* as the name of the station nearest to Manchester. As there are no remains of a station on the line of Antonine's Tenth Iter from Ribchester to Manchester, and as the remains of the Roman military road are easily traceable throughout the whole space between these two places, Ribchester can be the site of no other Roman station than the *Coccium* of Antoninus." On Roman Ribchester, by John Just, Esq. and John Harland, Esq. Journal of the Archæological Association, vol. vi. p. 299. 1851.]

[3] I agree, however, with Mr. Whitaker, that there has been a Roman port about Freckleton, towards which the Watling-street, as it is called, first discovered by Dr. Leith upon Fullwood Moor, evidently tends. But this is entirely out of the question with respect to the present Iter; and, moreover, it has been already proved not to be the *Setantiorum Portus.*

[4] [" A *second* station has nevertheless been found on this river, near to Walton le Dale; and its discoverer, Mr. Charles Hardwick, has given a full account of it in vol. viii. pp. 127—140, of the Transactions of the Historic Society of Lancashire and Cheshire, and again in pp. 39—46 of his valuable *History of Preston.* A fall of earth at this place has recently disclosed a very fine portion of Roman pavement, probably forming part of the military road from Walton to Lancaster. The pavement lay about 30 inches below the present surface of the soil; it was nearly ten yards wide, and was composed of boulder stones, sand, and gravel, very firmly set. Since then a well-preserved coin of Germanicus has been found on the site of the new station; and these, together with numerous fragments of pottery, &c. abundantly prove that the Romans certainly had a *second* permanent station on the Ribble not far from the present town of Preston."—From a paper *On the Roman Topography of East Lancashire*, by T. T. Wilkinson, F.R.A.S. &c. read before the Historic Society of Lancashire and Cheshire, March 16, 1865.]

which has driven Camden to seek for *Coccium* at Cockley,[1] and Mr. Whitaker to place it at Blackrod; while, on the other hand, it has compelled Horsley, who saw with his usual sagacity the real situation of *Coccium*, to remove *Rigodunum* to Warrington, as he had previously confounded *Belisama* with the Mersey.

Of Mr. Whitaker's *Rerigonium* it is difficult to speak without a few previous observations on the character and credit of his favourite guide, Richard of Cirencester, the monk who, I fear, has led him, with a *friar's lantern*,[2] into many devious paths, through many a bog and brake, in his bold and excursive wanderings over the Sistuntian Monarchy. That the Itinerary published by Dr. Stukeley, under the name of Richard of Cirencester, is really genuine, by which I mean that it is the work of him whose name it bears, there seems no reason to doubt.[3] But a work may be indubitably genuine, yet of little or no

1 ["Bury, another market town not less considerable, near which, as I was seeking eagerly for *Coccium* mentioned by Antoninus, I saw Cockley, a wooden chapel among trees, Turton chapel among precipices and wastes," &c. Camden (edit. Gough), iii. 127. "Mancunio in Antonini Itinerario succedit Coccivm, quod at Cockly sacellum fuisse juxta Bury credam ego donec dies certiora dederit." The same sentence is in Camden, Brit. (ed. 1586), p. 429, but not in the edition of 1607, from which it might seem that Camden abandoned this idea.—P. A. L.]

2 "And he by friar's lantern led."—Milton's *L'Allegro*.

3 [The authenticity of this Itinerary, which Dr. Whitaker had the sagacity to doubt, but could not summon sufficient confidence to deny, has now been decidedly determined in the negative of that long debated question, after it had, since his time, very much divided the opinions of those who have studied the Roman antiquities of Britain. The Itinerary of Richard is not only as Dr. Whitaker asserts of no authority; it is a modern forgery of which the MS. has never been seen by any one. Nor was the work quoted before the middle of the last century. In the preface to *Ricardi de Cirencestria Speculum Historiale de Gestis Regum Angliæ*, edited by John E. B. Mayor, M.A. Fellow of St. John's college, Cambridge, and published in the historical series of the Master of the Rolls, 1869, the *De Situ*, with its accompanying "diaphragmata" or itineraries, has been distinctly manifested to have been the fabrication of Dr. Charles Julius Bertram, Professor of English in the Marine School at Copenhagen, who first communicated it to Dr. Stukeley in the year 1747. Stukeley, one of the most credulous of antiquaries, innocently helped his correspondent to the name of Richard of Cirencester, who was a monk of Westminster, after Bertram had at first named his pretended author "Richard of Westminster." Though some other writings have been attributed to Richard of Cirencester, Mr. Mayor shows that the *Speculum Historiale* is really his sole extant work. It is true that the genuineness of the Roman itineraries thus palmed upon antiquaries has been much suspected by others beside Dr. Whitaker, and questioned more particularly by Gough, by Reynolds the author of *Iter Britanniarum*, by John Hodgson the historian of Northumberland, by Joseph Hunter the historian of South Yorkshire, by Raine the historian of North Durham, latterly by our historical antiquaries Stevenson and Sir Thomas Duffus Hardy, and by the learned foreigners Wex and Böcker: whilst Dr. Wellbeloved, in his *Eburacum*, as plainly indicated his unbelief by discreetly ignoring Richard of Cirencester altogether. But the great crowd of our county-historians and topographers during the last and present centuries had been deceived: in the foremost place, Whitaker of Manchester; the county historians Hutchins, Nash, Hutchinson, Collinson, Polwhele, Shaw, Warner, Duncumb, Jones of Brecon, Fosbrooke, Hoare, Bray, Clutterbuck, Dallaway, Ormerod, Surtees, Horsfield, Brayley, and lastly Baines in his Lancashire; together with a series of minor topographers that might be enumerated to as long if not longer extent; and, in addition, the more general authors on our national and local antiquities, the brothers Lysons, George Chalmers in his *Caledonia*, Pinkerton, Thomas Wright, Roach Smith, and Beale Poste (until 1853, when he pronounced it apocryphal); the special writers on Roman roads, Major-General Roy, Leman, Bishop Bennett, and others; and Robert Stuart, in his *Caledonia Romana*; not to mention Richard of Cirencester's devoted editor and champion Henry Hatcher, and Hatcher's biographer John Britton, with Dr. Giles a subsequent editor; whilst the list of very learned though uninquiring believers is swollen by the great names of Gibbon, of Lappenberg, and Dr. Lingard. Even such recent and important works as Mr. Mac-

authority. And such appears to be the case in the instance before us. This monk, who lived in the beginning of the fifteenth century, was undoubtedly a man of curiosity and diligence, worthy of a better age. He travelled, he collated MSS., he drew maps, and he drew conclusions; but these conclusions, unhappily, though the author of them has no claim to any other regard than a modern antiquary, and in some instances even less, have been erected by the zeal of his disciples, Dr. Stukeley and Mr. Whitaker, into original and independent authorities. Yet he may be proved to have had no ancient materials which we have not, and he wanted some which we possess. The *Fragmenta quædam à Duce quodam Romano consignata* appear to have been the Itinerary of Antonine; the basis of his map was that of Ptolemy, whom he expressly mentions; and his general divisions of Roman Britain were taken from the *Notitia*. To have adjusted all these, and to have formed an account of Roman Britain from the result, would have required a judicious and faithful hand. This last the Monk had not: on the contrary, he was possessed with the general spirit of his profession in the middle ages—something between bold conjecture and inventive fraud. He laid out new itinera: he imagined colonies, towns invested with the

lauchlan's survey of the Watling Street executed for the late Duke of Northumberland, Mr. C. C. Babington's map of Roman Cambridgeshire, the school and college maps of Roman Britain published by the Useful Knowledge Society, and the text of *Ancient Geography* superintended by Dr. William Smith, are all vitiated by the use of "Richard of Cirencester" as an authority. At the same time it will be only just to mention, in addition to the judicious critics already named, that some recent writers have set themselves earnestly and determinedly to work to stem the tide of error: more particularly Mr. Daniel Wilson in *The Archæology and Prehistoric Annals of Scotland*, Dr. Edwin Guest in the Archæological Journal, the Rev. Arthur Hussey in the Gentleman's Magazine 1853 and 1851, and the late Mr. B. B. Woodward, F.S.A. in the Gentleman's Magazine 1866 and 1867. But the true mode of dealing with this unexampled deception was that contemplated, but not performed, by the Rev. J. J. Conybeare, who "was confident that the work was a modern forgery, and meditated a paper on the subject for the Archæologia. He considered the Latinity of Richard as not that of the fourteenth or fifteenth century, but of the preface-writers of the eighteenth." (Nichols, *Literary Illustrations of the Eighteenth Century*, vi. 430, 440.) This efficient process has at length been thoroughly accomplished by Mr. Mayor; who has devoted nearly 150 pages of his Preface prefixed to Richard of Cirencester's genuine work to a thorough analysis and dissection of the whole composition of the *De Situ*, both in its language (which differs in style, orthography, and the names of places from those of the *Speculum*,) and in its statements, which he proves are borrowed, not only from such authors as Tacitus, Cæsar, Ptolemy, Dio, Solinus, Isodorus, &c. from Beda, Gildas, and the mediævalists, but even from their commentators and scholiasts; from Camden, Baxter, and Horsley, and other comparatively modern materials. The Itinerary, Mr. Mayor states, as the result of his investigations, is in the main from Antoninus, but routes are broken, combined, and reversed. Where a town has two names, the name given by Antoninus is always replaced by its synonym. Nine-tenths of the names in Antoninus re-appear, with additions from Ptolemy, the *Notitia*, Ravennas, the *Tabula Peutingerana*, as well as from Camden's, Baxter's, and Bertram's guesses and imagination. The preposition *ad*, with the name of a mountain or river [this is exemplified in the Lancastrian *ad Alpes Peninos*,] or with the number of a milestone, supplies many stations; *in medio*, *ad fines*, [*Ad fines* is "a common name for Bertram's stations: see Iter v. and xviii. It is also common in Antoninus, but no example occurs in Britain." Mayor, p. lxxxv.] and the like innocent fictions, supply more. Sometimes we have a station without a number, sometimes a number without a station. Everywhere artifice is apparent. At the same time the carelessness displayed is only less astonishing than the credulity which has been so blind to it. * * * * Bertram's success is a signal reproach on the historical inquirers of the last 120 years." In the sixth part of the library of Richard Heber there was a copy of Stukeley's *Account of Richard of Cirencester*, with notes by Dr. T. D. Whitaker. It was sold for 10*s*. (Lowndes, by Bohn, 2541 b.) Mr. Mayor justly remarks, "These notes would be of interest;" but he has not traced their present possessor.—J. G. N.]

Jus Latii, and others merely stipendiary, long after those distinctions were abolished; he inserted some names, which, though real, were posterior to the Roman empire in Britain, and some which may safely be affirmed to have been fabricated by himself. This is not a place for entering further into the controversy; otherwise, I am prepared to support all these assertions by irrefragable proofs, having had occasion to attend particularly to the subject when engaged in another work.

We shall now be prepared to attend to the seventh Iter of Richard, with all due respect and reverence.

[I here introduce Mr. Mayor's marginal analysis of the sources from which Bertram made up this Iter.—J. G. N. 1870.]

A PORTU SISTUNTIORUM *Eboracum usque sic* —		The Sistuntiaci in Anonym. Ravenn. (Petrie, xxv b.), the harbour of the Segantii (Ptol. ibid. xii b.), the mouth of the Ribble (Horsley, 376-7).
Rerigonio m. p. - -	XXIII.	Ptol. xii a, xiii b. (Rerigonium bay and Rerigonium town, both in Galloway, Horsley, 375.)
Ad Alpes Peninos -	VIII.	See Bertram (Havniæ, 1758), i. 6, § 53.
Alicana - - - - - -	X.	In Bertram, i. 6, § 31, and in map and index, *Olicana*, which occurs next to York in Ptol. xiii a. Ilkley according to Horsley, 373.
Isurio - - - - - -	XVIII.	Antonin. 468, [after *Cataractone*,] Isurium xxiiii.
Eboraco - - - - -	XVI.	Eburacum xvii.

Of this Iter, the three first stations alone are to be taken on the credit of the Monk; as the fourth rests on the authority of Ptolemy, and fifth and sixth on that of Antonine.

Now that the *Portus Setantiorum* was upon the æstuary of Ribble, cannot be proved even to be a conclusion of the Monk. Dr. Stukeley certainly supposed him to mean the Lune; and, for the road which Mr. Whitaker has so distinctly traced from the Neb of the Nese to Ribchester, though I give entire credit both to the accuracy of his research and the fidelity of his representation, I must beg leave to remind him, that these appearances prove nothing as to any particular station, but merely that a station or port in general existed at the former place.

The word *Rerigonium* is either an involuntary error of Richard for the *Rigodunum* of Ptolemy, or it is a rash and arbitrary substitution, for the latter word is evidently suppressed to make way for the former. I am inclined to the second hypothesis, and for these reasons:—The genuine *Rerigonium* and *Sinus Rerigonius* of the geographer evidently lay on the æstuary of the Clyde, and upon the coast of Galloway. But the word[1] was written in some MSS. *Berigonium*, which the Monk adopted, and very properly, in its real situation, but seems to have imagined that when written with the initial R it denoted another place; and, looking out for something, however distantly, resembling it in sound, unhappily fell upon *Rigodunum*, which he rashly and unwarrantably displaced. To these

[1] Vide Baxter, *in voce*.

conjectures I have only to add, that the Monk, not aware of the identity of *Coccium* and *Rigodunum*, like all succeeding antiquaries, has had a station upon his hands, which he chose to dispose of at random, in a situation[1] which evidently led Mr. Whitaker[2] to seek it at Blackrod.

The names of *Coccium* and of *Rigodunum* are now equally forgotten, and are not even faintly echoed in the more recent name of this place—the *Ribelcastre* of Domesday and the modern *Ribchester*. Hence it may be conjectured that there was an interval of time, after the Romans withdrew from Britain, when it ceased to be inhabited and to have a name; after which the first Saxon colonists of Northumbria found it, though abandoned, yet conspicuous in decay; and from the remains of its fortifications, united with the circumstance of its site, gave it the appellation by which it is still distinguished.[3]

This celebrated station was placed, with the peculiar judgment which marks Agricola's encampments (for to him unquestionably it must be referred), on the northern bank of the river, and flanked by the deep channel of a brook on the east; corresponding to which, on the west, is a large sluice or channel, to which tradition has assigned an use confirmed by many nautical relics, namely, that of a dock or slip for vessels. That the tides once rose so high as to waft vessels of considerable burden to the quays of *Coccium*, there can be little doubt; nor is it necessary to resort to the violent expedient of an earthquake, in order to account for their recess. A gradual aggestion of sands, aided by strong westerly winds, and not sufficiently repelled by floods from the land, will abundantly account for an appearance so frequent that we have almost ceased to inquire into its causes. And that the high precipitous banks which now border this valley, at a considerable distance from the stream, were once washed by the tides, while the sandy plain beneath formed a broad and irregular æstuary, is also credible: but the level of Ribchester[4] itself, little elevated above the plain, and still more that of the Roman town, which, from the appear-

[1] Vide Richard's map of Britain, prefixed to Dr. Stukeley's edition of his Itinerary.

[2] Vide Chap. I.

[3] Even at the time of the Domesday survey, among sixty-one villages in Amunderness (to which hundred Ribchester then belonged) sixteen are described as inhabited by a few persons, and the rest lay waste.

[4] "It flouith and ebbith in Ribyl most communely more than half way up betuixt Prestun and Ribcestre, and at ragis of spring-tydes farther."—Leland, vol. iv. part i. fol. 39.

I now think it impossible [adds Dr. Whitaker, after "the observations of fourteen years,"] that Ribchester should ever have been a Port, for the following reasons:—The Roman Road from that place to the Neb of the Nese proves the general level of the flat country to have been the same in the Roman æra and at present. Yet the ascent of the tides to the level of Ribchester, to say nothing of the bars of rock, which must have obstructed it, would at high tides have inundated the Filde, by which means the Roman road to Lancaster would also have been rendered impassable. The nautical remains, such as anchors, boat-nails, &c., discovered at Ribchester, are sufficiently accounted for by the supposition of a manufactory in iron carried on there, and by the use of a boat for the *trajectus* of the Ribble, which was probably moored in the western foss of the station where it united with the Ribble. [Our author subsequently remarked, "All the nautical remains discovered about Anchor Hill prove nothing more than the existence of a ferry, which the Romans must have had, and which our English ancestors also enjoyed as late as Edw. III.; and, with respect to the disclosure of an anchor, I know of nothing to negative the opinion, that, as the Calder arises in a valley abounding with iron, the ore might be transported to Ribchester, and manufactured there for the use of their port below."—*Richmondshire*, ii. 458. 1823.]

ances of floors, &c., appears to have lain from two to three feet beneath the present surface, seem to indicate that even then the sea had begun to recede, and that these appearances belong to an earlier period in the history of the earth.

Many of the Roman stations in Britain seem to have been little more than military posts; and, of those which also appear to have been cities or populous towns, many form the basis of our modern provincial capitals. But Ribchester is an exception to this rule, as tradition and discoveries concur in proving it to have been a place of considerable magnitude and wealth,[1] though now reduced to an inconsiderable village. It seems also to have had a large manufactory in brass, which the scattered remains of various utensils and ornaments wrought in that metal, and, above all, innumerable metallic fragments, resembling sweepings of shops, which are picked up on the shelving bank of the Ribble, serve to evince.

It is pleasing to imagine the revolutions which seventeen centuries have produced in the environs of this place; where, after the Roman conquest, a curious observer, placed upon a commanding point of Ribblesdale, might have surveyed the windings of the vale, covered perhaps to the summits of the fells with native oak, birch, pine, ash, and alder: its woods pierced only by the long line of Watling-street,[2] or by another way from East and West: the *Belisama*, a noble stream, deep and broad, agitated by tides and diversified by sails; on its northern bank the walls and towers of *Coccium*, surmounted by roofs of temples or cupolas of baths; within, the noise of industry and the tumult of military preparation; and without, the naked and painted forms of the *Setantii*, sometimes advancing with the irresistible impulse of barbarous curiosity to behold the operations of these new intruders, and then retreating, with the swiftness of wild beasts, to their cabins in the woods. From the same point he might now contemplate the Ribble, shrunk and shallow; the woods either decayed by the silent operation of natural causes, or destroyed by tasteless and improvident avarice; the tower of a Christian church lifting its plain but venerable head over the buried remnants of paganism; and the once naked salt-marshes, now become firm and fertile soil, smiling under the hand of cultivation.

It appears from the *Notitia*, that the mere stations which had been planted in the interior of Britain, to secure the yet recent conquest of the island, were generally abandoned in the time of the second Theodosius; but *Coccium*, not being a military establishment only, but a flourishing and probably a manufacturing town, appears from the barbarous style of an inscription, which will be given below, to have subsisted to the latest period of the Roman power amongst us. Destroyed, probably, by no violent assault, succeeded by no Saxon town, and even in the reign of the Conqueror remaining in a state

[[1] "Ubi tot Romanæ vetustatis vestigia, statuæ, numismata, columnæ, columnarum bases, epistylia, aræ, marmora, inscriptiones subinde effodiuntur, ut non abs re fuisse videatur, quod incolæ claudicante rythmo dictitant,

It is written upon a wall in Rome
Ribchester was as rich as any Toune in Christendome.

Camden Brit. (ed. 1586) p. 431.]

[2] The word *Watling-street* is used, throughout this book, in its local and popular sense.

approaching to desolation, its firm and durable walls must long have defied the ravages of time, and long have presented a noble monument of Roman greatness. Something, perhaps, like the state of Silchester and Caergwent at present, might have been its appearance at the last of these periods; that is, a spacious parallelogram, surrounded with vast walls of excellent masonry, strengthened with herring-bone work within, and laced at intervals with courses of different dimensions, or variegated by lozenge and chequer-work without. Within must have appeared the slender remains of Roman habitations in their last period of decay; while the massy temple might still have all its columns erect and vaults unbroken, its dedication legible, and even its altars upon their bases. So at this day appear some of the cities of Magna Græcia, in which the remains of private houses have so nearly perished, and the religious edifices are so entire, that a traveller is inclined to ask whether they were intended only for habitations of the gods.

After another interval of more than four centuries, Ribchester was visited by Leland, the first person, so far as we know, who beheld it with antiquarian eyes;[1] and his description

[1] The genius of Dr. Stukeley, after a rapid survey of a few hours, gave at once the most circumstantial and entertaining account of this place which has ever been communicated to the world. The few mistakes are very excusable in a stranger and a journalist. As the "Itinerarium Curiosum" * is become very scarce, I shall subjoin the whole, verbatim.

"RIBLECHESTER.

"I went to view this old Station: it is prettily seated on a rising knoll upon the river; at some distance all round inclosed with higher ground, well clothed with wood and hedge-rows: beyond which the barren mountains, or fells as they generally call them here, from the Cimbric *fiâl*. The soil hereabouts is gravel, with clay and sand by spots. The river Rible is very broad at this place, rapid and sonorous, running over the pebbles, and, what is much to be lamented, over innumerable Roman antiquities; for in this long tract of time it has eaten away a third part of the city. I traced out the old ground plot, and where the wall and ditch went round it; it lay in length, east and west, along the north side of the river, upon its brink, 800 feet long, 500 broad:† originally, I apprehend, two streets ran along its length, and three crossed them on its breadth. This place has long been famous for old monuments found therein; and some fragments still remaining I had a sight of. At the door of the Red Lion ale-house I saw the base of a pillar, and a most noble shaft, seven foot long, handsomely turned, which was fished out of the river: it is undoubtedly Roman originally, though the base has, I guess, been used as the stump of a later cross, in which this country abounds: there is a scotia and two torus's ‡ at the bottom, though not very elegantly formed; perhaps it was never finished; the whole piece is 2½ feet high, 22 inches in diameter. The *frustum* of the column lay in the ale-house yard, where the weather, and other accidents, have obliterated an inscription consisting of three or four lines, towards the top; it is 17 inches diameter at top. One corner of this house is a Roman partition-wall, built of pebbles and hard mortar, as usual. This house now is by the brink of the river, leaving only a scanty road between; but within memory a great many houses opposite, and among them the chief inn of the town, were washed away. Farther on, down the river, a great part of an orchard fell down last year; and the apple-trees still grow in their own soil at bottom. Viewing the breach of the bank exposed thereby, I saw the joists and boards of a floor of oak, four feet under the present surface, with

* Dr. Stukeley published his Itinerarium Curiosum in 1724. In 1725 he "travelled over the western and northern part of England" with Mr. Roger Gale, son of Dr. Gale, Dean of York, the celebrated antiquary. They visited on their way to the north Chester, Liverpool, Ribchester, and Lancaster. After Stukeley's death, 3 March, 1765, his account of this journey was published in 1776 in the 2nd edition of the Iter Curiosum, under the title of "Iter Boreale."—P. A. L.

† I have not had an opportunity of verifying this measurement, which will give an area of nearly 10 acres for the city within the walls. [See the admeasurement hereafter, p. 39.]

‡ Exactly the same with the base of the column and the anta lately discovered in the churchyard; the diameters also agree.

proves the remains to have been then very conspicuous, in comparison of its present state, in which even a curious and practised eye can discover no outward vestige of its former greatness, but the base of a single column, two or three half-legible inscriptions, and a few

many bits of Roman bricks, potshreds, and the like, and such floors are to be seen along the whole bank, whence most antiquities are found in the river. The late minister of this place, Mr. Ogden [ob. 1706], collected all the coins, intaglios, and other antiquities, found here in great quantities, but his widow, as far as I could learn, disposed of them to Mr. Prescot of Chester. I was shown the top of a great two-handled *amphora*, or wine-jar, taken out of the river, of whitish clay;* I saw another like fragment, and, among antiquities, he took up a very large piece of *corallium tubulatum*, bigger than a man's head; an admirable curiosity of nature. By symmetry I find the whole channel of the river, at present, lies within the precincts of the old city; the original channel on the other side being filled up with the city walls and rubbish; for it bends with a great elbow toward the city. The eastern limit of the city, or that upward of the river, lies against a brook there falling in, and the two streams, playing against that angle, have carried it away, and still threaten them. At the western end of the city, or down the stream, a whole road, and some houses too, by a barn, are absorbed, and great quantity of ashler, the remains of the wall, has been carried off for building: much remains in the ground, and on the edge of the stream. Farther up the land, and all along the west side of the church wall, the ditch is perfect, and the rampire where the wall stood pretty high, and the foundation of the wall a little apparent. They tell me the ashler-stone still lies its whole length. They call this Anchor-hill; and, when digging by the house that stands upon part of it, they found anchors, and great quantities of iron pins, of all sizes, for ships or barges, for they say this river was navigable so high formerly, at least for smaller vessels. The north-west angle of the city is manifest, and where the northern wall turned down the north side of the church: a little way down a lane at that angle, a great bank runs westward, made of stone, like a Roman road. There is a lane goes down north of the city to the brook called the Strand, which confirms their having some sort of navigation here. At the end of this lane is the street which is the Roman road, running directly northward up the fell, called Green gate: it passes over Langridge, a great mountain so named from it, so through Bowland forest: it appears green to the eye. In this street, over against the Strand, is an old white house, where they say Oliver Cromwell lay when going to Preston in pursuit of the Scots, after the battle of Marston-moor.† The eastern wall over the brook stood likewise on a sort of precipice. I saw a large coin of Domitian, of yellow brass, very fair, found in the river; *Imp. cæs. domit. aug. germ. cos. xvi. cens. per pp.* reverse, Jupiter sitting in a curule chair, the *hasta pura* in his left, an eagle on his right hand, Jovi Victori; exergue, S. C. Another pedestal of a pillar found in the river. Just under the Red Lion a subterraneous canal comes into the river, so high that one may walk upright in it, paved at the bottom. Many urns have been found hereabouts, but all lost and disregarded since Mr. Ogden died, who collected such things. They know the track of the Roman road all the way over the hills. In a garden by the Unicorn's Head, a gold finger was found, and another brass finger as large as a man's; two intaglia's of Mercury, with wings on his feet, the *caduceus*, &c. found near Anchor hill: much ashes and bones found about the city. Up the river, eight miles off, is Pendle hill, a vast black mountain, which is the morning weather-glass of the country people: upon it grows the cloudberry plant.

"Digging in the churchyard, silver coins have been frequently turned up. The river hither open and deep, but

* [Afterwards in the possession of the Rev. Samuel J. Allen, as would appear by the following passages :—

"What other pieces of sculpture, &c. I had were at the same time sent to T. H. Whitaker, esq. of the Holme, near Burnley, in whose possession they now are. They were not of great interest. The first was, I believe, the top of the great two-handled amphora mentioned by Stukeldy, the mouth six inches in diameter, and the whole fragment about one foot and a half in height. [But perhaps one of the great amphoræ found in the ruins of the temple in 1813, p. 35.] The second had for some time been used as a stand for milk at Salesbury Hall, and seemed from the mouldings to have been part of a building. It bore faintly traced a patera, or sacrificial implement of some kind. The third was a portion of a cylindrical column, with a capital and remains of foliage, having a rude resemblance to the Corinthian style. I could not quite satisfy myself whether it was Roman or of later date, and cannot put my hand on any delineation of it, though I think I made one before I parted with it. I found it at a cottage in Salesbury, and have a clear recollection of having seen one with similar foliage at Salesbury Hall, both probably brought from Ribchester. These were all the Ribchester antiquities which were ever in my possession."—Letter published by Messrs. Just and Harland in Journal of Archæological Association, vol. vi. p. 245.]

† A strange mistake, since at Marston-moor Cromwell and the Scots fought on the same side. Cromwell certainly passed through Ribchester, and might probably sleep at this house, on his way to fight the Duke of Hamilton, in 1648.

uninscribed stones, wrought after Roman mouldings.—But "Ribchester," says our ancient topographer, "is now a poore thing: it hath beene an Auncient Towne. Great squarid stones, voultes, and antique coynes be found ther: and ther is a place wher that the people fable[1] wher that the Jues had a temple."[2]—Leland, Itinerary, iv. fol. 39. The edifice, we see, had now disappeared, but the name had been continued by tradition; and the inhabitants, whose ideas of a temple were all fetched from that of Solomon, assigned it, of course, to that well-known and detested people.

The collections of Leland, though he was a classical scholar of the first rank, are very

at Salesbury, a mile higher, rocks begin: therefore it is likely this place was chosen by the Romans because at the extent of navigation. Half of one longitudinal street, and of two latitudinals, are consumed. Horses and carriages frequently fall down the steep from the street, because it is narrow, and but factitious ground.

"Panstones, up the hill, by the Green-moor lane, or Roman road, is a place much talked of; but they know not for what. I suppose it is either some Roman building, or a road eastward, or some *terminus*. They told me of an altar thereabouts, with an inscription, axes, and the like carved on it: it is on Duttonley, by Panstones. Haughton tower is within view, a great castle; upon a precipitous hill.

"Many are the inscriptions found here from time to time: Dr. Leigh has seen them all. Now they are removed, lost, or spoiled: one great altar they told me was carried to Dunkin hall, the seat of Lady Petre, with an inscription, a ram, and a knife: many taken away by the family of Warrens, living lately at Salesbury hall. I saw the fragment of a stone in a corner of a house by the mill, cut with very fair large letters: under the next house is the *frustum* of a pillar 20 inches diameter, made into a horse-block. I saw another flat stone at the town's end, laid over a gutter, with a monumental moulding upon it.

"Above the town half a mile is a noble bridge of four very large arches, built lately by the country: over this I went to Salesbury; but all the inscriptions are carried away, probably to Mr. Warren's other seat, near Stockport in Cheshire. I found a large stone in the corner of the house, which has been a Roman monumental stone, foolishly placed there for the sake of the carving: there are three large figures upon it, sweetly performed; and good drapery, though half worn away by time; a man and a woman holding hands, both half naked; somewhat roundish in the woman's hand: at the end is Apollo resting on his harp, his head leaning on his hand, as melancholy for the loss of a votary; for such we may guess the deceased, either a poet, physician, or musician: probably there was more carving on those sides within the wall.* This has been a very large seat, with a park. They told me there were some carved stones at Dinkley, another seat of Mr. Warren's, a mile farther; but I found they were all carried elsewhere, save two altars, both obliterated, but well cut: one stood in a grass-plot in the garden, covered over with moss and weeds; another used in the house as a cheese-press.† This is a romantic place, hanging over the river purling across the rocky falls, and covered with wood. The late Mr. Warren was very careful of these learned remnants. They told me Ribchester was destroyed by the Scots.‡ These are all the memoirs I could pick up in about five hours I staid there, *et antiquum tenuerunt flumina nomen*. Ovid, Met. [xiii. 897]." *Itinerarium Curiosum*, vol. ii. p. 36-38.

[1] There is the same tradition at Leicester, and probably from the same cause. [Those who know the history of Leicester best, suppose that the Jewry Wall there, really the West-gate of the Roman city, derived its name from contiguity to the Jews' quarter, as in the case of the Old Jewry in London.—J. G. N.]

[2] So faithful is tradition to the transmission of facts through a period of eleven or twelve centuries. The remains of this temple have now been traced.

---

* This is the identical altar of Apollo Apoxus; now, by favour of Lord Bulkeley, in my possession.

† That seen by Camden, No. IV. in p. 27 hereafter.

‡ The tradition was right. For in the *Inquisitio Nonarum*, lately published [1807], Ribchester is expressly returned as laid waste by the Scots, in their destructive expedition of 1322 [et etiam dicta parochia destructa est apud Scottos, Inq. Non. p. 38. Eccl'ia de Rybleester' com. Lanc. Inq. capta apud Lanc. 15 Edw. III.]. They never crossed the Ribble, at least so as to do any considerable mischief.

defective in point of information on the subject of Roman antiquity: he glanced over our stations with an hasty eye: he scarcely transcribed an inscription. But about fifty years after (A.D. 1582) Ribchester was first visited by the great Camden, to whom we are indebted for an account of several valuable remains of this station, which are now no more.

From him, from Leigh,[1] from Horsley, and from later discoveries, is collected the following sylloge of inscriptions discovered here, which I believe to be complete:—

The first seems to have been very obscure, and may be supposed to have been transcribed incorrectly. It stands, however, in Camden as follows:

I. SEOESAM
ROLNASON
OSALVEDN
AL Q. Q. SAR
BREVENM
BEDIANIS
ANTONI
VS MEG VI
IC DOMV
ELITER

We are told by Camden that the stone with this inscription was in a wall at Salesbury Hall, with a portraiture of a Cupid and another little image. I strongly suspect this to have been the stone yet remaining there, and engraved by Leigh, on which, however, the principal figure is an Apollo Pharetratus, which occasioned the mistake; and this may afford some support to the conjectural reading which I am about to offer. Camden fairly acknowledges, that after much study he could make no sense of it. Leigh foolishly mistook the third line for the Saxon name of *Osbaldiston;* and the cautious and accurate Horsley, who seldom ventured far into the regions of conjecture, threw little further light upon the subject. After the despair of two great men (for Leigh was childishly ignorant of the subject), will it be deemed presumption to offer a conjectural reading of the whole?

[It is unnecessary to reprint Dr. Whitaker's arguments in support of his first conjectural reading, which was thus, Deo sancto soli invicto socio ob salutem Domini nostri (the Emperor's name crased) ala Equitum Sarmatarum cui præest Ventidius . . . . . . Antoninus, Centurio Legionis sextæ Victricis, Domu Eliberi. In his last edition of this work, and in his Richmondshire, ii. 462, it was amended as follows:]

It is not without some satisfaction that I find my conjecture to have been substantially right. In the summer of the year 1814, by the favour of Lord Bulkeley, I was permitted to detach this fine sculpture from the wall, of which, for more than two centuries, it had formed a corner stone, when, on the third side, appeared the inscription which had been so unskilfully transcribed for Camden, and which, without correction, has found its

[1] [Leigh visited Ribchester in 1699. (*Nat. Hist. Lanc.* bk. 3, p. 6.)]

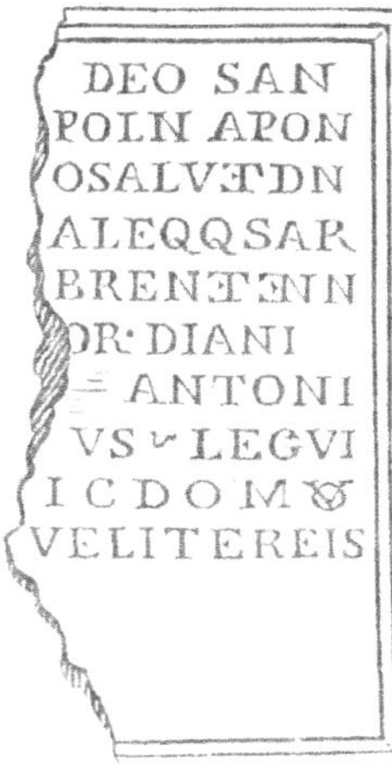

way into Gruter, Horsley, and Leigh. After the most attentive consideration, I now think that the inscription is to be read:

"Deo Sancto Apollini Apono, pro salute Domini nostri, Ala equitum Sarmatarum, Brennetennorum, Dianius Antonius, Centurio Legionis Sextæ Victricis, Domo (*or* Domu) Velitris."

There is space for four lines, which appear to have been worn away, at the bottom of the stone, and which would probably have explained the connection of a Centurion of Roman foot with an Ala of Sarmatian horse. I suspect the word which follows Sarmatarum to express a subordinate tribe of that vast and widely-spread nation, the Sarmatæ Brennetenni: at least, I can assign no other meaning to it. There is an instance of a similar combination in Horsley's Northumberland, cviii. "Equites Cæsarienses Corionatæ;" of which the meaning of the last word is equally unknown.

It is remarkable that the engraver, uncertain about the proper termination of the ablative of Domus, cut both the letters V and O, the one over the other, so that it is impossible to discover which was his last determination. The *formula* is common. Thus we have *Domo Samosata* on one of the Chester altars engraved by Leigh.

Still, there is an apparent impropriety in placing a Centurion of the sixth legion over an Ala of Sarmatian horse, but this objection is done away by the following authority (see Horsley, Pl. 49, and p. 280), *Marcus Censorius Cornelianus centurio legionis decimæ Fretensis, præfectus coh. primæ Hispanorum.*

On the front side is a basso-relievo of Apollo reposing upon his lyre, better designed than any work of a Roman-British artist which I have ever seen. On a second are the figures of two priests in long robes, holding the head of some horned animal between them; on the third is the inscription; the fourth is rough, having been originally attached to a wall. The stone is so large, that it appears to have had a distinct base and capital, which accounts for there being no appearance of a focus.

It now turns out to be a dedication to Apollo Aponus, or the indolent Apollo, the god of medicine, who restores health by relaxation or repose,[1] on behalf of an emperor who

[1] The classical reader will scarcely deem his attention too severely taxed by the length of the following remarks, much less by that of their attendant citations, when he is told that, according to the most probable conjecture, the *Fons Aponi* was the birthplace of Livy, and that this is the only inscription ever discovered to the Apollo Aponus. That warm springs were usually dedicated to the Sun our own *Aquæ Solis*, the modern Bath, affords one example, supported by many others. The Fount of Aponus is, I believe, first mentioned by Suetonius, in the Life of Tiberius; and mentioned not for its healing, but its oracular powers:—"Quum Illyricum petens juxta Patavium adisset Geryonis Oraculum, sorte tractâ, quâ monebatur, ut de consultationibus in Aponi fontem talos aureos jaceret, evenit, ut summum numerum jactu ab eo ostenderent; hodieque sub aqua visuntur hi tali."—(Tiber. c. xiv.)

The Piscina Neroniana (which appears to have been the name of one of the baths at this place) proves it to have been frequented by that Emperor; and his contemporary Lucan describes a hill in the Euganean country:—"Aponus

unfortunately is not mentioned. This accounts for the reposing attitude of the principal figure. But, as watering-places are the scenes where such cures are generally effected, the

terris ubi fumifer exit."—(Phars. l. vii. l. 193.) By Martial these fountains are described as "Fontes Aponi rudes puellis."—(L. vi. Epigr. xlii.)

A long and elegant Idyllium of Claudian, entitled "Aponus," proves that these salutary springs were equally celebrated in the time of Honorius; and the following lines are a direct address to Apollo, the tutelar Deity:

"Salve, Pæoniæ largitor nobilis undæ;
 Dardanii, salve, gloria magna soli,
Publica morborum requies, commune medentum
 Auxilium, præsens numen, inempta salus.—l. 67 to 70.
Felices, proprium qui te meruere, coloni,
 Fas quibus est Aponon juris habere sui."—l. 89, 90. (Idyll. vi.)

But, as the human constitution is the same under every change of religion and manners, the fountain of Aponus continued to be equally celebrated under the Gothic kings; and a tumid and half-barbarous Epistle of Theodoric describes the place and its accommodations in a very curious and lively manner. I shall abridge the passage, for it is very long, as much as is consistent with the sense:—

"Delectat enim salutiferi Aponi meminisse potentiam. Cæruleum fontem vidimus in formam dolii concavis hiatibus æstuantem. Ore plenissimo, in sphæræ similitudinem, supra terminos suos aquarum dorsa turgescunt [37 words omitted]. Unde latex tantà quiete defluit, tantâ quasi stabilitate decurrit, ut eum non putes crescere nisi quia inde aliquid rauco murmure sentis exire [17 lines omitted]. A cautibus unda descendens et aera suâ qualitate succendit et tactu fit habilis, quum recepta fuerit in lavacris: unde non tantum deliciosa voluptas acquiritur, quantum blanda medicina confertur. *Scilicet sine tormento cura, sine horrore remedia, sanitas impunita balnea contra diversos dolores corporis attributa.* Quæ ideo Aponum, Græcâ linguâ, beneficialis nominavit antiquitas * [19 words omitted]. Illud quoque stupendum esse didicimus, quod una fluentorum natura diversis ministeriis videatur accommoda. Nam protinus saxo suscipiente collisa, inhalat primæ cellulæ sudatoriam qualitatem; deinde in solum mitigata descendens, minaci ardore deposito, suavi temperatione mollescit [11 words omitted]; postremò, ipso quoque tepore derelicto, in Piscinam Neronianam frigida tantum efficitur quantum prius ferbuisse sentitur [23 words omitted]. Sed ut ipsum quoque lavacrum mundius redderetur, stupendâ quâdam continentiæ disciplinâ, in undam, quâ viri recreantur, si mulier descendat inceditur."—Does this explain the *rudes puellis* of Martial? This *continentiæ exemplum* was very like a Christian superstition of the age of Theodoric, but very unlike one of the second century, and under the *tutela* of Apollo, who was *non usque adeo rudis puellis.*

The description now becomes more turgid and tedious; but the passage ends with an order to repair a place so salutary and delightful:—"Palatium longâ senectute quassatum reparatione assiduâ corrobora." (Cassiodorus, in Variar. l. ii. epist. xxxix.) Aloisio Architecto Theodoricus Rex.

I learn, from Cluver's Ital. Antiq. v. i. p. 148-153, together with much of what has here been given, that in his time, about two centuries ago, these fountains were not deserted.

Such, then, is the *Fons Aponi*, the subject of this curious and singular Dedication. From the classical style of the sculpture, this altar must be referred to one of the earliest Emperors, who bore the style of Dominus Noster; in other words, to the beginning of the Lower Empire.

---

* This explains the word Aponus: "Health restored, without pain or effort." Compare this with Claudian's lines on the same subject:

"Quod si forte malus membris exuberat humor,
 Languida vel nimio viscera felle virent,
Non venas reserant, nec vulnere vulnera sanant,
 Pocula nec tristi gramine mista bibunt,
Amissum lymphis reparant impune vigorem,
 Pacaturque ægro luxuriante dolor."—Idyl. vi. 95-100.

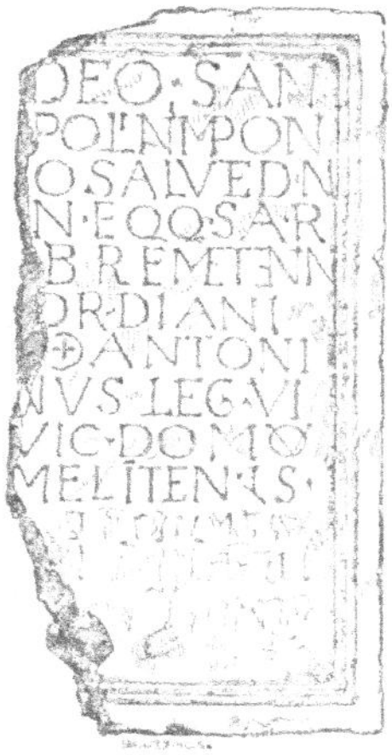

god of health was the Apollo Aponi as well as Aponus, and some highly salubrious warm springs in the neighbourhood of Padua, long frequented by the Romans under the name of Fontes Aponi, and still retaining the denomination of Poni, were unquestionably the waters from which a cure was supplicated on behalf of this unknown emperor.

[Dr. Whitaker published some further remarks on this inscription in his Richmondshire, vol. ii. p. 461; but the investigations of subsequent antiquaries have given it another interpretation. The altar[1] was bequeathed by Dr. Whitaker to St. John's college, Cambridge, where it is now preserved; and when the Archæological Institute met at that university in 1854, it received the attentive consideration of Dr. Bruce, the experienced historian of the Roman Wall, who remarks that "it is without doubt the most elaborately carved altar which the Romans resident in Britain have left us." Dr. Bruce came to the conclusion that, "Instead of APONO, which Dr. Whitaker conceived to be an epithet of Apollo, MAPONO is probably the true reading. We nowhere else meet with Aponus (indolent) as an epithet of this deity.' At Plumpton, in Cumberland, an altar has been found which is inscribed: DEO MAPONO ET N. AVG., &c. (Lysons, Cumberland, p. clv.) To Mr. Roach Smith I am indebted for the reading now suggested, as well as for the idea that Maponus may be the British name of Apollo, as Belatucader is of Mars. It is nothing uncommon to address a god both by his classical and local name. The first letter in the fourth line appears to be N (*numerus*) rather than A (*ala*); both designations, as applied to a troop of cavalry, are common. * * * The chief value of the inscription depends upon the fifth line. Mr. Hodgson Hinde, in a paper read before the Society of Antiquaries

[1] [For the loan of these engravings the publishers are indebted to the Rev. Dr. J. Collingwood Bruce, the historian of the Roman Wall, who is now, at the instance of the Society of Antiquaries of Newcastle, preparing a corpus of all the Roman inscriptions found in the north of England.]

of Newcastle-upon-Tyne, and published in their Transactions,[1] conjectured (without having seen the altar) that Dr. Whitaker's reading of Bre*n*eten. should be Bre*m*eten. Such, as is shown in the woodcut, appears to be the fact. He further argues that the station (Ribchester) at which the Sarmatian cavalry were located was the *Bremetenracum* of the Notitia. He does so upon the same principle that High Rochester is conceded to be *Bremenium*, and Risingham *Habitancum*.

"The Emperor for whose welfare this altar was erected does not appear; but, judging from the excellence of the design of the altar, and from the clearness of its lettering, he must have been one of the earlier series.

"Besides the inscription, the altar is sculptured upon two of its sides. The subject of one of these carvings is the youthful Apollo resting upon his lyre. The figure, notwithstanding the hard usage it has met with in the course of centuries, exhibits considerable grace. Two females, the one fully draped, the other only partially so, are shown on the other side of the altar. They hold some object between them which is so much injured as to be undistinguishable; it may have been a basket of fruit or an offering of flowers. Dr. Whitaker is surely wrong in describing these figures as two priests holding in their hands the head of a victim." (*Archæological Journal*, vol. xii. p. 226. 1855.)

This altar is now at St. John's college, Cambridge, standing at the entrance to the New Bridge, fixed on a pedestal which bears this inscription: "Apollinis aram, prope Coccium in agro Lancastriensi repertam, testamento legavit Thomas Dunham Whitaker, LL.D. hujus Collegii alumnus."]

II. [On "a votive altar to Mars Pacifer:"—Horsley, p. 303:]

PACIFE
RO MARTI
ELEGAVR
BA POS
VIT. EX VO
TO.

["We meet with Mars Pacifer in several coins of the lower emperors."—Horsley.] The word *Elegaurba* is very ingeniously read, by Professor Ward, ap. Horsley, p. 303, *Elegans Aurelius Bassus*.[2]

III. [On the pedestal of a pillar seen by Camden at Salesbury Hall]:

DEO
MARTI ET
VICTORIAE
DD AVGG
ET CC NN.

Here were two *Augusti* and two *Cæsars* at the same time, which corresponds with Dioclesian and Maximian, Augg. and Constantine and Galerius, Cæss.

[1] Archæologia Æliana, vol. iv. p. 109.

[2] [Elegans is not known as a prænomen. It occurs three times in Gruter and twice in Kellermann's Vigiles, but always as a cognomen or agnomen.—P. A. L.]

IV. Camden's second visit to Ribchester, in 1603,[1] was rewarded by the discovery of "a very fair altar," with this inscription :

DEIS MATRIBVS
M. INGENVI
VS. ASIATICVS
DEC. AL. AST.
SS. LL. M.

The *Asti*, or *Astæ*, were a people of Thrace, 'Αστοι Θρακων ἔθνος, Strabo, l. 7. Steph. Bizan. 'Ασται ἔθνος Θρακικον. *Deis*, instead of *Deabus*, is held to be pure Latin, where there is another word expressive of the sex. (Vossius de Anal. 2, 4.)

[Dr. Whitaker is here mistaken. The inscription plainly relates to the Astures, a people of the north-west of Hispania Tarraconensis (whence the well-known royal title in Spain of Prince of the Asturias), several of whose inscriptions have occurred at the stations on the Roman Wall.[2]

[1] ["When I was here again in 1603, I met with the largest and fairest altar I ever saw, with this inscription, in the house of Thomas Rhodes." The engraving here inserted is from a drawing made in 1850, and lent to this work by the British Archæological Association.]

[2] [See Bruce's *Roman Wall*, 3rd edit. pp. 64, 109, 159, 235. One, like that at Whalley, is to the *Deæ Matres*: "Matribus Campestribus et Genio Alæ Primæ Hispanorum Astur[um]," &c. Another, a monumental stone : "Aventino Curatori Alæ II. Asturum." A third, this remarkable record of the rebuilding of a barn: "Imp. Cæs. M. Aur. Severus Alexander Pii F. Aug. Horreum conlabsum Coh. II. Asturum S[everianæ] A[lexandrianæ] a solo restituerunt," &c.]

The altar now stands in the garden at Stonyhurst, having been removed thither about 1822 from Dinkley, where it served for a cheese-press, as before mentioned from Stukeley (p. 22). "It is 33 inches high by 22 broad; the inscription has become obliterated from exposure to the weather."—*Baines*.]

[V. "Here was also lately dug up a stone, on which was carved a naked figure on horseback without saddle or bridle, brandishing a spear in both hands, and insulting over a naked man on the ground holding in his hand something square.[1] Between the horse and the prostrate figure are D. M.; under the figure GAL SARMATA. The rest of the many letters are so decayed as not to be read, nor can I form any conjecture about them." (Camden, edit. Gough.)]

VI. The last of Camden's inscriptions, which he transcribed out of the papers of Lambard, who had most probably received it from his friend Lawrence Nowell, is in a very peculiar style, and has been justly conjectured, by Mr. Ward, to belong to a very low period in the Empire.

HIS. TERRIS. TEGITVR
AEL. MATRONA. QV . . . .
VIX. AN. XXVIII. M. II. D. VIII.
ET M. IVLIVS. MAXIMVS. FIL.
VIX. AN. VI. M. III. D. XX. ET. CAM
PANIA. DVBBA. MATER
VIX. AN. L. IVL. MAXIMVS
. . . . ALAE. SAR. CONIVX
CONIVGI. INCOMPARABILI
ET. FILIO. PATRI. PIENTIS
SIMO. ET. SOCERAE. TENA
CISSIMAE MEMORIAE. P.

Here the words *mater* and *socera* intimate the same person in two relations; *pientissimo patri*, for *in patrem*, is very barbarous; and *tenacissimæ memoriæ*, in a passive sense, is altogether unauthorised. But the style of this inscription is not only late, but deformed by provincial barbarisms. Antiquaries, while they employ their time and talents in elucidating monuments of fifteen hundred years old, are apt to forget that the objects of their criticism are often compositions of no higher rank than the frail memorials of our own churchyards, "with uncouth rhymes and shapeless sculpture deckt."[2]

[1] [This monument, noticed by Camden in 1607, was accidentally omitted by Dr. Whitaker. It presented a bas-relief of not unfrequent occurrence as the sepulchral memorial of a Roman knight or cavalry soldier. Two such found at Littlemoor near Cirencester in 1835 and 1836 were shortly after engraved in the *Gentleman's Magazine*, and again represented in *History and Antiquities of Cirencester*, T. P. Baily, 1842, 12mo. p. 201. Another, found at Stanwix, will be seen in Bruce's *Roman Wall*, p. 292.]

[2] Doctor Leigh, the historian of Lancashire, was not content with republishing these inscriptions, but, in pure compassion to the unlearned, favoured them with his own translations, of which I select the following as a specimen: "*Aæl*, a matron who lived 28 years two months and eight days, in this earth lies entombed; and *Marcus Julius*

VII. The foregoing are from Camden: the next was, I believe, first copied by Leigh (book iii. p. 8), and from him transcribed [and modified] by Dr. Gale, who made one happy conjecture concerning the etymology of *Coccium,* but proposed it with a degree of diffidence which a visit to the place would certainly have removed, as it must have convinced him that he was in the right. I had long since made the same guess, and was happy to find it confirmed by the authority of so great a man.

DEO MARTI ET
VICTORIAE DEC
ASIATIC. AL. SARMAT.
SLLMIЗCCNN.

This is reasonably conjectured by Horsley to have been compounded, by misapprehension, of Nos. III. and IV.

VIII. This imperfect votive stone was first transcribed by Horsley (Lancashire, ii.) and

IMP . CA
IMP . CA
VEX . LEC
SVB . SEX

is now remaining (though the letters are more than half effaced) in a garden wall within the village. Who the two emperors were to whom it was inscribed it is now impossible to discover, but the form of the letters seems to point at Severus and Caracalla.

[IX. A rude miliary stone, engraved by Horsley (Lancashire, iii.)

[At its head these three lines:

IMP CAES
MA . . . .
CO . . . .

[At its foot these three:

OM
C . GA
SEIFL.

"The form of this looks somewhat like a miliary pillar. It was lying in a garden at the west end of the town, and near the river. So much of the inscription is quite effaced as makes it hard to guess at the meaning of the whole." (Horsley, p. 302.)

Maximus her son, who lived six years three months and twenty days; and *Campania Dubba,* her mother, who lived 50 years. *Julius Maximus,* and *Alæ,* a Sarmatian, wife to her incomparable husband, erects this to perpetuate the memory of *Simo,* the son of a pious father, and his father-in-law."—Book iii. p. 5. The following are a few more flowers of his criticism:—*Coccium* from *Coccius Nerva;* CCNN. *Coccio Nervæ;* IETCCNN. *imperatori triumphanti Cæsari Coccio Nervæ,* for *Imperatori et Cæsaribus nostris.* Had this Doctor filled his whole book, as he has done nearly one half of it, with medical cases, it might have been of some use; but how, with all possible allowances for the blindness and self-partiality of human nature, a man should have thought himself qualified to write and to publish critical remarks on a subject of which he understood not the elementary principles, it is really difficult to conceive. After all, his errors might have slept with himself, had not his vanity and petulance been at least equal to his want of literature.

X. LEG XX V V.
FECIT.

This has been the corner-stone of a building, and is now remaining in an outhouse near the church.[1] It has two sides exposed, and on the second is a rude figure of a boar, the well-known cognizance of the Twentieth legion, which, though usually stationed at Chester, might be quartered here at intervals.[2] It has never been published before.

Beside inscriptions,[3] the smaller antiquities discovered here are innumerable. The coins, of which many are found of the large brass, are generally so much corroded as to be scarcely legible. Denarii of the upper empire are not uncommon. A very pretty intaglio ["of Mars"] in a ruby is engraved by Leigh (Tab. I. fig. i.); and I have a gold ring, found here some years since, set with a cornelian of many faces, with a dove in the centre, and round it the words AVE MEA VITA,—the present, as it should seem, of a lover to his mistress. Tradition also records a singular discovery at Ribchester, viz. the skull of an ox, covered with some remains of leather, and studded with gold. It is very possible that such a preparation might have been used for some sacrificial purpose, and it was an idea not likely to occur to an inventor.[4]

[1] It has since been removed to Browsholme, [and thence to Holme. It is the same which is represented in the miscellaneous plate introduced where the former place occurs in a subsequent page, and again in the *History of Richmondshire*, ii. 462.]

[2] [The Twentieth Roman Legion, *Legio XX Valeria Victrix*, is first heard of in Illyria A.D. 6, when Valerius Messalinus defeated with it, though much under its full strength (*semiplena*), more than 20,000 enemies. (*Velleius Paterc.* ii. 112.) There can be no doubt, as Pauly says (*Real Encycl.* iv. p. 897), that it thence won the name Valeria Victrix. After the defeat of Varus it was sent to Germany. Its winter quarters were at Bonn; where it joined, on the death of Augustus, in the mutiny of the German legions which was appeased by Germanicus, under whom it afterwards took part in the campaigns against the Germans, and has left many inscriptions in Lower Germany. Under Claudius the legion came to Britain and fought under Suetonius Paulinus. After the death of Nero their *vexillarii* formed part of the army which accompanied Vitellius to Rome. Vespasian made Agricola legate of the legion. Its head-quarters were in Chester; but inscriptions in Scotland, Northumberland, Cumberland, and Durham, &c. show the presence of detachments throughout the North of Britain, and tombstones of its members have been found at Bath and London. As it is not mentioned in the Notitia Imperii there is reason to suppose that when that work was compiled it had just been withdrawn from Britain. (Pauly, *Real Encyc.* art. *Legio* (Geschichte). Hübner, *Die römischen Heeresabtheilungen in Britannien in Rheinisches Museum für Philologie*, Neue Folge, Jahr. ii. 1856.) Sculptures representing the boar (usually running) as the device of the Twentieth Legion have been found at various places in this country, as at Chesterholm, High Rochester, Lanchester, and Maryport, on the Roman Wall (see Bruce, pp. 217, 327, 347, 369); in Scotland (No. v.) and Durham (No. xvi.) as engraved by Horsley. Near Great Chesters in Northumberland has been found a very curious sculpture without inscription, representing in relief two winged genii, two eagles with wings spread, settled on the branches of trees, and two boars, running, facing each other. (Horsley, Northumberland, lxiii.)]

[3] [We should perhaps not wholly pass unnoticed the circumstance that Mr. Thomas Wright, in his *Celt, Roman, and Saxon* (second edit. p. 299, followed by Mr. H. Godwin, in his *Archæological Handbook*), has asserted that among the altars found at Ribchester was one to the goddess Jalouna. This is altogether a misapprehension. An altar inscribed DEO JALONO, a male deity, supposed to personify the River Lune, was found at Lancaster, and is described by Dr. Whitaker in his *Richmondshire*, i. 214. Mr. Wright also states (*ubi supra*) that an inscription DEO HERCVLENTI occurs at Ribchester, which is an error for Riechester, in Northumberland; see Horsley, p. 241.]

[4] It was most probably one of the ancient *encarpia*. There is also in the possession of Dr. St. Clare, of Preston, a Roman *cyathus* or *diota* of silver, found at Ribchester, not inelegantly embossed, and containing about half a gill.

But the noblest discovery ever made here, or perhaps in Britain, was in the year 1796, when the shelving bank of the Ribble exposed the following remains, which seemed to have been deposited in an excavation of the earth, filled up with soil of a different quality.[1] These were, 1st, a large flat earthen vessel, extremely thick, with the potter's stamp very distinct, "BORIEDOF, Boriedi Officina." 2nd. An entire patera of copper, about six inches diameter, with a handle. 3rd. The imperfect remains of a similar vessel. 4th. A *colum*, or colander, of the same size and metal. 5th. Several concave and circular plates of copper, with loops behind, which had evidently been intended to fasten them perpendicularly against a shaft, in order to form a Roman vexillum: such are frequent upon ancient monuments, but, for a particular illustration, the reader is referred to a monument of Lucius Duccius, *Signifer*[2] of the ninth legion, in Horsley. (Yorkshire, VIII.) 6th. A very fine helmet (of which the crest was a sphinx, afterwards unfortunately lost[3]), the head-piece enriched with a *basso relievo* of armed men skirmishing with swords, and a visor consisting of an entire and beautiful female face, with orifices at the eyes, mouth, and nostrils.

From the style of the head-piece it is conjectured by the best judges not to be prior to the age of Severus; but the vizor is a much more delicate and exquisite piece of workmanship, and is supposed not only to be Grecian, but, from the boldness of its lines, to belong to a period somewhat anterior to the last perfection of the arts in that wonderful country.

All these remains are now in the museum of Charles Townley, esq. who, it is hoped, will one day gratify the public with a comment on the symbolical figures in front of the helmet.[4]

"A Roman *cyathus* or *diota*, the instrument, no doubt, of much ancient conviviality at Coccium, was found here, and is now in the possession of Dr. St.Clare, of Preston."—(*Richmondshire*, ii. p. 462.)

[1] [The site of this remarkable discovery is described by Mr. Townley as "a hollow that had been made in the waste land at the side of the road leading to the church, and near the bend of the river. The boy, about thirteen years old (son of Joseph Walton), being at play in that hollow, rubbed accidentally upon the helmet, at the depth of about nine feet from the surface of the ground. When the helmet was extracted the other articles were found with it, deposited in a heap of red sand, which formed a cube of three feet. They are much defaced by the effect of the sand. Joseph Walton dug them out, and sold them to C. T. 8 Dec. 1797."]

[2] There is now at Standen, near Clitheroe, a sepulchral stone removed from Ribchester by the late Mr. Serjeant Aspinall, without inscription, but with a figure in high relief of a Roman standard-bearer of the lower empire, with the labarum in his hand.

[3] ["In the summer of the year 1796, Mr. Wilson, of Clitheroe, and myself saw a bronze helmet and other remains of Roman antiquity, then recently discovered at Ribchester, and I now distinctly recollect that, besides the pieces in Mr. Townley's possession, there was a sphinx of bronze, which, from the remains of solder on its lower side, and also from its curvature, appeared to have been attached to some convex surface, probably to the top of the helmet. And on September 19th, 1798, on a second visit to this celebrated station, I learned that a piece of brass (to use the man's own words) having the body of a lion, and the face of a woman, and which was found along with the helmet, &c. had been for some time in the possession of Laurence Walton, brother of Joseph Walton, from whom Mr. Townley purchased the other remains, but that, as it was carelessly left on the chimney-piece of his cottage, it was, as he supposes, carried away by his children, and irretrievably lost."—T. D. Whitaker, Sept. 19, 1798, in *Vetusta Monumenta*, vol. iv. p. 12.]

[4] [This passage occurs in the first edition of the History of Whalley, at p. 23, and appears to have been written very shortly after the discovery was made in 1796. It is almost as unaccountable that it should have appeared in the first edition (published in 1800) as that it should not afterwards have been removed or altered: for Mr. Townley's

[The course of the discoveries made at Ribchester is pursued in Dr. Whitaker's own words in the History of Richmondshire, where he resumed the subject (correcting the account given in the notes to the third edition of this work, p. 17) :—

"In the month of July, 1811, some workmen, in securing the same bank (where the

"Account of Antiquities discovered at Ribchester" was addressed to the Secretary of the Society of Antiquaries on the 17th Jan. 1798, and it was published in their *Vetusta Monumenta*, accompanied by four Plates, on the 23rd April, 1799. The first and second of these Plates represent the bronze helmet in its actual size as seen in profile and front; Plate II. its scull-piece expanded so as to show the whole of the figures of warriors in relief upon it; and Plate IV. represents several of the minor antiquities which also occur upon Dr. Whitaker's plates.

Of those two Plates the present Editors now attempt to supply the explanation which has hitherto been deficient.

Plate I. 1. Four circular plates, considered by Dr. Whitaker to have formed a Vexillum. They are also engraved in *Vetusta Monumenta*, IV. pl. iv. figs. 1, 2, 3, 4, with the reversès of two, that have four rings or loops; but they are *all of one size*, viz. 4 inc. diam. Mr. Townley thus describes them: "Four circular plates, 4 inc. in diameter, with a moulding at the border. They are gently hollowed, and in every respect resemble the form of the patera without a handle; they had also no doubt the usual protuberance in the centre, as the nail, or the hole of the nail, that held something which is wanting, remains in the centre of each of them. On the back of these plates are loops for fastening them occasionally to whatever they were applied, by strings or straps. Their resemblance to the pateræ which formed one kind of Roman military standards, and their being found together with a helmet in a Roman military station, are sufficient grounds to decide that they served for that purpose. Upon the Trajan Column, engraved by Bartoli in plates xxxviii., xli., and xliii., where standards of this kind appear, the pateræ are of the same form, and bear the same proportion in size to the human heads, as these do."

2. The back and front of another circular plate. There were three of these, which Mr. Townley thus describes: "Three circular plates, about $1\frac{1}{2}$ inc. diam., of the same form as those last mentioned, but from their small size, and the addition of a hinge, with the remains of a tongue, they appear to have been fibulæ, or buckles to fasten the toga, the paludamentum, or the chlamys at the shoulder. Such kinds of fibulæ are often seen upon ancient busts and statues. See Gori, *Museum Etruscum*, i. tab. 140." Engraved in Vetusta Monumenta, fig. 7.

3. The bronze helmet, back and front. Upon this subject Mr. Townley's dissertation is of great length, occupying seven large folio pages. He describes it, "A helmet, divided into two pieces, one of which is the skull part, ornamented with figures of eleven combatants on foot and six on horseback; the other part is the mask or vizor to cover the face, which has very effeminate features, and joins exactly to the skull part. to which it was fastened by rings and studs, some of which still remain. The beauty of the features, the excellent work of the figures in relief, and more particularly the sharp edges and lines with which the eyebrows, eyelids, and lips are marked after the manner of Grecian art preceding the Cæsars, denote this mask to have been executed some centuries before the headpiece, the coarse and heavy work of which corresponds with that of the artists employed in the reign of Severus, and particularly with the sculptures upon his arch at Rome. The mask measures $10\frac{1}{2}$ inches from the skull-piece to the bottom under the chin. On a row of small locks of hair a little above the eyes rests the bottom of a diadem or *tutulus*, $2\frac{1}{4}$ inches high at the centre and $1\frac{1}{8}$ inches at the ends. The lower part represents a wall divided into seven parts by projecting turrets, with openings for weapons. In the middle division are two arched doors, and one in each of the end divisions. The upper part of the diadem had seven embossed figures under seven arches, the abutments of which are heads of genii. The central arch and its figure are destroyed, but the other six arches are filled by a repetition of the following three groups: a Venus sitting upon a marine monster, before her a draped figure with wings bearing a wreath and a palm branch, and behind her a triton, whose lower parts terminate in tails of fish. Two serpents are represented on each side of the face near the ears, their bodies surrounding each cheek and joining under the chin." This mask Mr. Townley believes to represent the goddess Isis, who, according to Apuleius and other ancient writers, comprehends all the female deities, in her generating, preserving, and destroying capacities as the Dea Triformis. The first is referred to by Venus attended as usual by marine deities, the second by the walls and turrets, and the third by the face of the Gorgon Medusa, who held among the three Gorgons the same malefic character as Hecate among the three Dianas, and is often represented as handsome and even joyous. A helmet thus composed in honour of the Magna Mater was a proper appendant in Roman

PL. I.

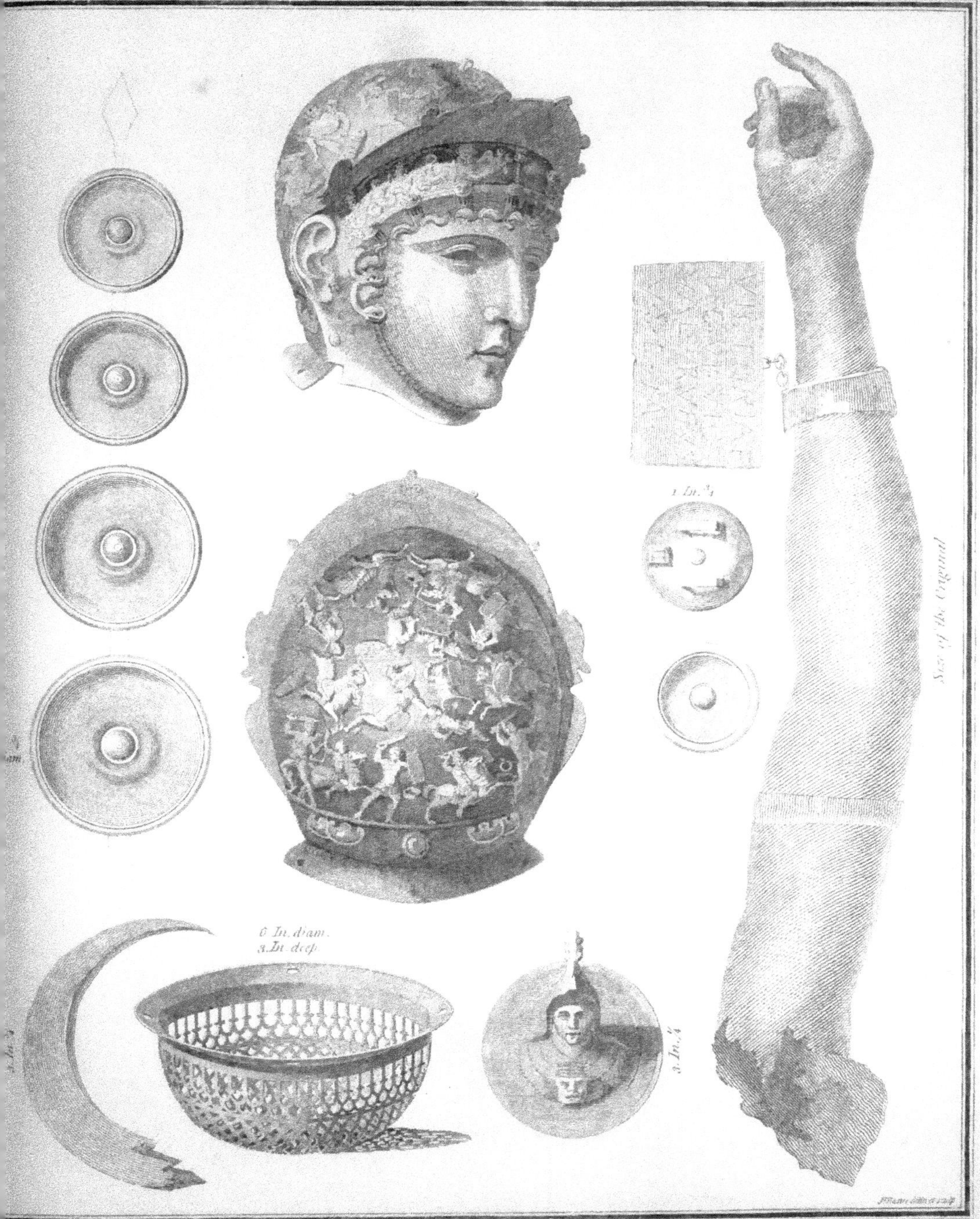

...iam hanc exhibentem quasdam Romanæ vetustatis reliquias magna ex parte inter rudera Coccii repertas et in Musæo Caroli Towneley Arm: ...servatas Societati Antiquariorum Londinensi honoris et observantiæ testandæ gratiâ dicat Sodalis obsequentissimus T.D. Whitaker.

helmet was found) from the depredations of the Ribble, at the distance of forty or fifty yards below, and almost opposite to the parish church of Ribchester (at about a yard beneath the surface), several fragments of flagstone, each containing Roman characters. This led to further investigation, and when all the pieces were put together, like a dissected map, they produced this fine but very difficult and still mutilated inscription :—

camps, which, as well as the Circensian games, were placed under her particular protection. She is even called, on the medals of the elder Faustina, the Mater Castrorum. The altar found at Ribchester dedicated to the Deæ Matres, who are supposed to be Juno, Cybele, and Ceres, shows this to be only another of the many names of the trinity comprised in Isis.

Another theory, however, was advanced by the Rev. Stephen Weston, B.D. F.S.A. in a paper on this helmet addressed to the Society of Antiquaries, and printed in the Archæologia, vol. xii. He considers that the mask or visor was intended to represent Bacchus, who was called *διφύης* and *διμόρφος*, partaking of both sexes, and remarks that it accords more perfectly with a head of Bacchus on a coin of Thasos, than with Cybele or Isis, or even Medusa.

When perfect this helmet must have been equal in beauty to those in the museum at Portici, which are considered the finest known, and Mr. Townley believes that it is the only ancient example having a vizor imitating so exactly the human features. He is of opinion that it was not destined for actual wear, but only for a trophy erected at military festivals or carried in processions. Such trophies are seen on medals; and Dionysius of Halicarnassus, comparing the styles of Demosthenes and Plato, says that they differ as much *as arms made for war do from those made for processions* (De vi dicend. in Dem. § 22), which proves that arms of the latter sort were lighter and more ornamented than the former, like this helmet, which is exceedingly ornamented and too flimsy for defence. There seems, says Mr. Townley, to be nothing remarkable in the combatants on the skull-piece. At the time of the Antonines, the Romans had adopted in addition to their original oval and oblong-square shields, the oblong-hexagonal used by the Parthians and other barbarous nations. The armour and caparisons are the same as the Roman of the second and third centuries.

4. A sickle-shaped fragment, not described by Mr. Townley.

5. A *colum*, or colander, which Mr. Townley describes as "about six inches in diameter, and near four in depth; in good preservation, with its perforations unusually large and of an elaborate design." There were also parts of two others, exactly alike. Engraved, in its real size, Vet. Mon. pl. iv. fig. 8.

To explain this in order: the characters IS. DN. ET CASTR. SV. can have no other meaning than Matris Domini Nostri et Castrorum suorum. Now the empresses this distinguished were, the elder Faustina, Julia Pia the wife of Severus, Julia Mammæa, and Julia Otacilia the wife of the elder Philip. For the first of these the character of this inscription is far too modern, besides that IVLI are visible upon the stone. It must therefore be one of the Julias. Julia Mœsa was described as Mater CCNN. et Castrorum, in reference to Caracalla and Geta. For Julia Mammæa, written at length, I find, upon another trial with compasses, that there is not room on the black space, where a fragment has been lost. The last, though her son was for a short time Augustus, would probably have been described as the wife, not mother, of the reigning emperor. Julia Pia, or Domna, the wife of Severus, alone remains, for whose addition there is exactly space enough on the stone.

I have now therefore to retract my conjecture made in a former work,[1] that this Mater Castrorum was Julia Mammæa, and consequently that the title of the emperor, Dominus

6. "A bust of Minerva, attached to a circular disk, three inches in diam. with the remains of the nails and cramps which served to fasten it, as an ornament, probably of a *lectisternium* or tripod. It is of coarse work. An ornament of this kind is engraved in Caylus, *Recueil d'Antiquités*, vol. i. pl. lxxi." Engraved in Vet. Mon. fig. 5.

All these antiquities are now preserved in the British Museum.

The silver Arm, also represented in this Plate, is described hereafter in p. 45.

PLATE II. The vessel at the head of this plate is thus described by Mr. Townley: "An ansated patera 5½ inc. diam. and 1 inch deep, well preserved. The borders, inside and outside, are ornamented with parallel and perpendicular lines, which at the first had the appearance of letters."

The "bronze patera, 7½ inc. diam." at the foot of the Plate, is *restored*, for the greater part of its basin was wanting. There was also the rim and the handle of a third patera, 6½ inc. diam. of which the basin was destroyed. Five bronze vessels of the same kind were found at the Castle Howard estate in Yorkshire in 1856, and are engraved in the *Archæologia*, vol. xli. pl. xv. accompanied by a memoir by Edmund Oldfield, esq. M.A. F.S.A. who considers that they were used for measuring out wine. Two others found in 1841 in the parish of Masham, co. York, are preserved in the museum at Swinton Park, and were exhibited to the Archæological Institute at York in 1846, on which occasion they were described as "two patellæ, or skillets, of bronze, the inner side tinned, supposed to have been culinary vessels. They have flat handles, perforated at the extremity for suspension. The bottom is of considerable thickness, and ornamented with deeply-cut concentric hollows and raised mouldings, formed by the lathe." These were somewhat smaller than those found at Ribchester: and on the handle of one is an impressed pattern, composed of a thyrsus, vine-leaves, and tendrils. (These ornaments favour Mr. Oldfield's view of the use of such vessels.) A fine example, found at Prickwillow in the Isle of Ely, is figured in the Archæologia, vol. xi. pl. viii.; a pair, found near Dumfries, in vol. xi. pl. viii.; and another, of silver, found near Capheaton, Northumberland (and now in the British Museum), in vol. xv. pl. xxiii. See also Montfaucon, tom. iii. pl. lxiv.

The basin of bronze resembles some engraved in Gori, *Museum Etruscum*, vol. i. pl. xii. and xiii. It was not so perfect as it is represented.

The next is the earthen vessel which Dr. Whitaker has described in the text. The part lightly shaded is intended to show where the edge is lowered in order to afford a spout in pouring out liquid. A similar vessel with a different potter's mark is engraved in the *Archæologia*, vol. xii. pl. li.

The vase is a restoration of a vessel of which the only remains were the bottom and part of its sides. "It appears (writes Mr. Townley) to have been about 10 inc. in diameter and 15 in height; was highly finished, the polish still remaining in the inside, and the metal has a line of silver, similar to that of which the ancient mirrors were made."

The Celt, found at Read in Lancashire, which is the last article in the Plate, is also in the British Museum.]

[1] [*i.e.* the 3rd edition of the History of Whalley, at p. 18.]

Tabulam hanc, exhibentem quasdam Romanæ vetustatis reliquias magna ex parte inter rudera Coccii repertas et in Museo Caroli Townley Arm. conservatas, Societati Antiquariorum Londinensi, honoris et observantiæ pergrandis gratiâ, dicat Sodalis obsequentissimus T. D. Whitaker.

Noster, referred to Alexander Severus. Another reason is this: a fragment of the uppermost line, excepting that containing the name of the divinity to whom the whole was dedicated, still remains. Now this must have contained the name of the emperor; but in this precise situation, instead of any distinct characters, there appear to be some slight vestiges of letters industriously erased. These must surely have been part of M. Aurel. Antoninus Aug. If, in the next place, any antiquary should doubt whether Caracalla was ever entitled Dominus Noster, I must tell him that the question has been satisfactorily answered in the affirmative by Horsley (p. 350. Cumberland 44).

The next difficulty occurs on the violent contraction of PRAEPN̄. ET REG., after a most attentive consideration of which, I can assign no other sense to the words than *præpotenti numini et reginæ*. And here again I expect to be met with the objection that Regina generally, if not exclusively, applies to Juno. But when the discovery of the brazen head of Minerva,[1] almost under the wall of this temple, is taken into the account, and that Luna or Diana is also styled Regna by Horace, I think it will be admitted that, while there is no analogy against it, circumstances are so strongly in favour of a dedication to Minerva, as hardly to admit of any other rational interpretation. With these explanations, therefore, the inscription may be read as follows:

DEAE MINERVAE
PRO SALVTE IMP M AVREL ANTONINI AVG ET
IVLI PIAE MATRIS DN ET CASTR SVOR ET
VAL CRESCENTIS FVLVIANI LEG EIVS PP PR PR
T FLORIDVS NATALIS LEG PRAEP N̄ ET REGINAE
TEMPLVM A SOLO EX RESPONSV RE-
STITVIT ET DEDICAVIT.

Or more at length,

Deæ Minervæ—Pro Salute Imperatoris Marci Aurelii Antonini Augusti et Juliæ Piæ matris domini nostri et castrorum suorum, et Valerii Crescentis Fulviani Legati, provinciæ præsidis, proprætore, Titus Floridus Natalis legatus præpotenti numini et reginæ templum a solo ex responsu restituit et dedicavit.

On the whole this inscription is extremely valuable, as it adds one if not two names (for Natalis was probably the successor of Fulvianus in the province) to the catalogue of Imperial Legates in Britain. There is, however, before the second LEG. something like a centurial mark, which would have reduced Natalis to a very inferior rank, had it not been turned the wrong way, and that the name of the legion is omitted. In addition to these remarks, I have only to observe the superstitious fondness of the Romans for names of good omen: Valerius Crescentius in the first designation, and Titus Floridus Natalis in the second, being all adopted with an anxious regard to that circumstance.

But to return. This sufficiently proved the existence of a temple, of which the inscription must have formed the tympanum. Accordingly, in the summer of 1813, leave having been obtained to dig into the adjoining gardens, betwixt the river and the church-

[1] [Dr. Whitaker here applies this description to the helmet.]

yard, the first appearances, at the depth of about three feet, were a stratum of charcoal, evidently formed by the conflagration of the roof, and nearly in the centre a cavity in the earth had been made, by the uniting of the ends of the beams at their fall, large enough to contain a man sitting. Beneath this was a confused mass of large amphoræ, some almost entire at first,[1] and many beautiful remnants of pateræ in the red Samian ware, mingled with which lay several human skeletons, all of the largest size, in every direction. Every appearance about the place indicated that it had been taken by storm, and that the defenders had been buried in the ruins of the roof; but the absence of tiles or slates seemed to prove that the outer covering of the building had been previously stripped by the assailants. Here too was found a very curious Roman *statera*, or steel-yard, very exactly graduated, and a singular bodkin of polished stone.

The progress of discovery was now once more suspended, till (a few months afterwards) the sexton, digging a grave where no interment had taken place before, on the left hand of the entrance of the churchyard, found the base of a column and an *anta* or square-moulded corner of the *naos* itself, upright and in their original situations. Measurements were now accurately made from the place where the inscription was found, which must have been the front of the building, to the base of the column. This gave the entire length, excepting one intercolumniation, for the whole had evidently had a peristyle. The distance of the *anta* from the column, by the rules of architecture, gave the distance also between column and column; by which data, with the help of a very conspicuous line of mortar, about forty-five feet westward in the churchyard, the site of the west wall was ascertained; a ground plan of the building was laid down; after which, by the well-known proportions of Doric architecture, a complete elevation was obtained. From remains not originally more promising than these Palladio has restored, in the most satisfactory and convincing manner, several ancient temples. But every appearance about this work (for unlike those beautiful specimens of ancient art which that great architect had the happiness to retrieve) indicated, at once, provincial barbarism, and a declining age in art. For the column was ill wrought, and the different diameters so varied from each other as to show that it had never been struck from a centre.

Let all these be laid together, and it will scarcely be doubted that this was a temple of Minerva, restored by command of Caracalla; that the helmeted head of brass was that of the goddess; that the temple had been stormed and burnt in some irruption of the Caledonians, during the last period of the Roman power in Britain; and that the precious object of worship itself had been carefully deposited in the earth, on the approach of the threatened danger, in a situation from which the depositor never lived to disinter it.

I have only to add to this account that within a few yards of the east wall of the temple was disclosed the statue of a lion of tolerable workmanship, which, from the rudeness of one side, must have been an architectural ornament;[2] and that in August, 1818, the writer of this, examining the contents of a dilapidated chimney, immediately adjoining

[1] ["Two handles of amphoræ, stamped CVRVS, are to be seen at the vicarage."—Just and Harland, 1850.]

[2] [This, it is believed, is still preserved at Holme.]

to the west side of the peristyle, discovered the lower half of an altar,[1] on which unfortunately nothing remained but the letters CVM SVIS V S L M.

[So far from Dr. Whitaker in his History of Richmondshire.]

[In 1819 an altar was found in the cellar of the White Bull Inn, in Ribchester. "This will probably still be found at the White Bull, where I saw it some years ago, as also the base of a column in the street, nearly opposite the front of the house, and another in the vicarage yard." (Rev. S. J. Allen to Messrs. Just and Harland 1850, in Journal of British Archæological Association, vi. 246.)

In Jan. 1829 two Roman coins, a Saxon styca of Keanred thirteenth King of Northumbria, and fragments of a Saxon cross, about a foot and a half high, were found together at the Anchor Hill. One of these coins had *obv.* CRISPVS CON.; *rev.* within a wreath, VOL. X.; and around it, CÆSARVM ICON AVORVM. The other, *obv.* MARCVS AVRELIVS AVG.; *rev.* a standing female figure, with the cornucopia, and the legend ABUNDANTIA AVG.

On the 28th Feb. 1833 a fine Roman altar, $2\frac{1}{2}$ feet in height, 1 foot 10 inches in breadth, and 1 foot 7 inches in depth, was dug up in the churchyard; and is now placed in the entrance-hall of the vicarage. The sides are ornamented with vine-branches, and the front bears this inscription:

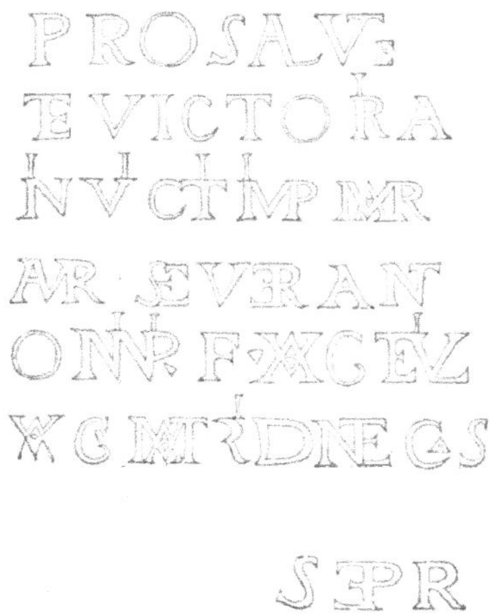

[1] [The accompanying engraving is lent by the British Archæological Association, from their Journal, vol. vi.]

This careful copy was communicated to Baines's History of Lancashire by the late Rev. Samuel J. Allen, of Salesbury, with the following remarks: "A difficulty arises in the construction of the fifth line. If the conjecture be correct that this was an altar erected in honour of Caracalla, I think this reading of it (if supported by other inscriptions of a contemporary date) would not be an improbable one: 'Pro Salute et Victoria invicti Imperatoris Marci Aurelii Severi Antonini Pii filii Augusti et Juliæ Augustæ matris Domnæ et Castrorum suorum . . . . . . Senatus et Populus Romanus.' I cannot, however, quite reconcile the inscription with this interpretation of it, unless we may, in the sixth line, supply the letter s to MATRI, and alter it from the dative to the genitive case, and thus dedicate the altar to the emperor, the son of Augustus and of Julia Augusta Domna, and for the safety of the Camp. The seventh line has been erased, though not with much care, as some remains of letters still appear, but so imperfectly as to render their construction unintelligible.

"Besides the altar, a small fibula and ring of brass, a bulla, apparently inscribed with some characters but now illegible, and three brass coins were found, one of which was of Trajan, and another of Valerian, *rev.* FELICITAS AUG.

"To the south-west of the church, about midway between the chancel and the churchyard wall, five steps were discovered at the same time with this altar, each 4 feet in length, 1 foot 4 inches in width, and 4 inches in depth. The altar was discovered about 12 yards westward from the spot where the remains of the temple were excavated in 1813, surrounded by the appearances of burning soot, &c. which have usually attended such disclosures at Ribchester. Near one of the stiles to the churchyard (I think to the east) is a stone resembling a low-backed seat, 2½ feet in height, 1 foot 10 inches in breadth at the front, and 1 foot 5 inches at the sides; perhaps it may be the corner *anta* described by Dr. Whitaker [see p. 35]." (Rev. S. J. Allen to Messrs. Just and Harland, 1850.)

In March 1834 a beautiful and perfect fibula of bronze was discovered, 1¾ mile SSW. of Ribchester, in the grounds of Harwood Fold, Clayton le Dale, through which the Roman road from Manchester to Ribchester passed (see p. 12). "It is or was in the possession of J. Eccles, Esq. of Leyland, near Chorley." (Ibid. p. 246.)

A small oval intaglio, engraved on onyx, found here at some forgotten date, is now in the possession of James Fenton, Esq. of Norton hall, Gloucestershire, who has had it set in a ring. It represents a man standing, and holding in his right hand a hare by its heels,[1] and in his left some smaller object, apparently a brace of birds suspended from a stick.

In 1840, in the extreme north-eastern angle of the station, a Roman bath was opened; the tiles, stones, &c. were taken away, but the floor was left untouched, and covered up again. Some of the stone props of the tiles are yet to be seen in the garden of a resident surgeon (Mr. Patchett).

[1] ["Evidently the signet of some Roman-British sportsman. Cupid similarly employed is a frequent subject for signets: one such was formerly in my own possession."—Rev. C. W. King, author of the Handbook of Engraved Gems, and other more elaborate works on that subject, to J. G. N. July 6, 1870.]

In 18—, on a piece of land close to the town belonging to Lord de Tabley (but which is now the property of Joseph Fenton, Esq.), another Roman bath was discovered; and the pottery and other relics there found were taken to Tabley Hall.

"The excavations lately undertaken, with the view of obtaining information for the congress (of the *British Archæological Association* in 1850,) have laid bare the outer wall to its foundation on the western side. Unlike the foundations of the walls of the ramparts at Borrow Bridge, Melandra Castle, &c. it consists of loose stones, without mortar, or the cement grouting common to such foundations. On the opposite side, in the angle between the river and the junction of the brook, a large quantity of Roman pottery was found, consisting of numerous fragments of Samian ware, chiefly of pateræ, many marked with the potter's name; one ampulla with both hands perfect, and others broken; fragments of glass, of common pottery, nails, bones of animals, in which were tusks of boars and swine; five Roman coins, three of which are of silver, but much corroded; two appear to be coins of Vespasian and Titus, the third of Vitellius; two of copper, much corroded, but apparently of the same period, &c."—(Just and Harland.)

Roman coins have been repeatedly found at all times, but usually in a state of considerable decay. Leigh says, "The Roman coins I met there, which are discovered as the hill shelves into the river, were one of them *Augustus Cæsar's*: the rest *Titus, Vespasian, Dioclesian, Coccius Nerva* (from whom it is likely the place was by some called *Coccium*,[1]) *Domitian, Trajan, Adrian, Severus, Commodus, Marcus Antoninus*, and *Julia*, some in copper and some in a mixed metal, in which last the letters are very legible; likewise one Saxon coin, and that in silver."—(Natural History, B. III. p. 7.)

Besides many others which have been already incidentally noticed, the following isolated discoveries have occurred:

COINS IN GOLD.

In Jan. 1837 a small gold coin is said to have been found not far from the river, bearing the head of NERO CAESAR AVGVSTVS. *Rev.* a female (?) seated, IVPPITER CVSTOS. It came to the hands of John Swarbrick, living in Clayton's Court, Preston.—(Newspaper paragraph.)

VESPASIAN. *Obv.* His profile: VESPASIANVS . . . . . . *Rev.* An ox, COS. VII. Now in the possession of Joseph Fenton, Esq. of Bamford Hall.

TRAJAN. Head of the Emperor, TRAJANO AVG. GER. DAC. P. M. TR. P. *Rev.* V. P.P. S. P. Q. R. OPTIMO PRINCIPI. The Emperor in the toga, and two small figures to whom he is distributing food. *Exerg.* ALIMON. ITAL. (In the possession of James Fenton, Esq. of Norton Hall, co. Glouc.)

FAUSTINA. In Dec. 1831 the same John Swarbrick above-mentioned is said to have found, on the bank of the river, about 150 yards above the church, a small gold coin of this empress, bearing on the *Obverse* her head, DIVA FAVSTINA. *Rer.* a full-length female figure holding in her right hand, with extended and elevated arm, a bowl (probably a globe), and having a ring or circle (perhaps a veil) pendant above the elbow of the left

[1] [Dr. Whitaker's ridicule of this idea has already appeared in p. 29.]

arm.[1] Legend AETERNITAS. This was in high relief and excellent preservation.—(Note by the Rev. S. J. Allen.)

COINS IN SILVER.

TRAJAN. In 1830, in digging up the bowling-green, a silver coin was found,—*Obv.* IMP. CAES. NERVA TRAIAN. AVG. GERM.; *Rev.* P.M. TR. P. COS. II. P.P. with a sitting figure, in her right hand a garland, in her left a cornucopia.—(Just and Harland, p. 245.)

HADRIAN. In June 1840 a small silver coin of debased metal and workmanship, bearing on the obverse, HADRIANVS AVG. COS. III. P.P.; on the reverse a figure of Romulus bearing spoils, with the legend ROMVLO CONDITORI.—(See a letter in the *Blackburn Standard* signed S. dated Blackburn, June 13, 1840.)

SEPTIMIVS SEVERVS. About 1834, on the bank of the Ribble, opposite Ribchester, L. SEP. SEVER. AVG.—(Rev. S. J. Allen.)

Writing in 1850, Messrs. Just and Harland gave the following account of the state of Roman Ribchester:—"At present the river Ribble has encroached vastly upon the area of the station. Taking the extent of the fosse on the western side as a complete side of the station, and, from the angle close to the river at the southern extremity, making a straight line perpendicular to this side, we find that the other angle to complete the rectangle would be on the other side of the river, just over the fence of the field, and directly opposite to the brook which forms the boundary of the station on the east. At an estimate by the eye there may have been one-fourth of the area of the station washed away by the river; burying within its sandy bed Roman treasures and relics, probably for ever. In a line with this, or nearly so, the fishermen state that the Roman wall of the rampart extends into the river, and that at low water they can stand, about middle deep, on the sunken remains; when off the remains, on each side, the water is beyond their depth. The northern rampart has run from the angle at Anchor Hill, along the fence of the field north of the church, in a direct line through the town to the brook, at the eastern side of the town. This has constituted the longer side of the rectangular area on which the station stood, and measured about 300 yards. The shorter side measures about 130 or 140 yards.[2] Most of the relics discovered have been washed bare by the encroachments of the river. Little remains of Roman antiquity above ground. The bases of the shafts of two Roman pillars are within the vicarage-yard. Four smaller ones, taken out of the river, form the front of the doorway of the White Bull inn, within the town, but outside the station N.E. about 70 yards.

"The walls of the rampart around the station have wholly disappeared. Most of the houses of the town have been built out of their remains. Besides, these have been robbed to build up the greater portions of Salesbury Hall and Osbaldeston Hall in the neighbour-

[1] [See the numerous varieties of Æternitas on the brass coins of Faustina in Hobler's *Records of Roman History*, 1860, 4to. p. 480, *et seq.*]

[2] [According to the Ordnance six-inch map the station measures 850 by 390 feet. The Roman city of York was of a rectangular form, of about 650 yards by about 550. (Wellbeloved, *Eburacum*, p. 53.) It was therefore nearly ten times the size of Ribchester. York contained 357,500 square yards; Ribchester, 36,700. P. A. L.]

hood, though nothing Roman is now to be seen at the modernized buildings, but a quern at Salesbury, and perchance some short pillars in the bee-house in the garden."]

From Ribchester our Watling-street takes a northern course over Longridge Fell, and is distinguished as a long stripe of green intersecting the brown heath of the mountain. Having reached the summit of the hill it takes a turn towards the north; then descends again, is very conspicuous at intervals, has a broad and high ridge in the inclosures of the townships of Thornley and Chargeley, enters Bowland a little below Dowford Bridge, passes about half a mile west from Browsholme, traverses in a direct line the high grounds to the north of that house, and then passes to the north of Newton and Sladeburn, and traces the Hodder to its source at Cross of Greet, which is the northern boundary of the original parish of Whalley.[1]

A portion of this way, about 330 yards in length, was laid open by the cultivation of a morassy piece of ground, and is described by Rauthmell,[2] the sensible and observing antiquary of Overborough, to have consisted of a substratum of large pebbly gravel spread on the surface of the morass, and covered with large flat paving-stones above. This method of constructing military ways was copied and continued by our immediate ancestors, though upon a smaller scale, in those durable causeways which, imitating in this also the Roman fashion, they carried in right lines through bogs and over fells, and which have been superseded within the last forty years only by turnpike roads. These well-planned but ill-executed works have indeed opened the scenery of valleys, and added warmth and shelter to expedition; but, after flattering the traveller for a few years by their compact and even surface, have left him for the most part little reason to triumph in the change of rugged but durable pavements, and of the ἄναντα and κάταντα of the hills, for a road sinking once more into the subjected bog, or worn down to the shelving surface of its parent rock.

The course of this great military way from north to south being thus traced, and the existence of another in this direction of east and west, from the Neb of the Nese, assumed on the authority of Mr. Whitaker and of Dr. Leigh, who observed it upon Fulwood Moor, we have next the assertion of Camden himself for its elongation to the east of Ribchester. Its line must then have been conspicuous, when vast tracts of land, now inclosed, lay in common, and the plough, the great destroyer of such remains, had never passed upon them.

1 ["If any of my hearers is desirous of seeing the perfect formation of a Roman road, he has only to visit the lower portion of Hardle, where, if he traces it through the present bridle-gate over the railroad, he will find that it was lately opened out for a considerable distance in repairing the occupation road leading north up to Standen. Coming south from this, the Roman road crosses Hardle and the Milton road about 50 yards nearer Whalley Moor than Barker's farmhouse in the hollow." (*Lecture of the Rev. R. N. Whitaker, Vicar of Whalley, delivered in* 1866.)

[In Mr. Just's paper on the Roman Roads in Lancashire in the Transactions of the Historic Society of Lancashire and Cheshire, is a description of that portion of this road then exposed at Pendleton brook, below Standen hall, now covered by a young plantation.]

2 [The work quoted by Dr. Whitaker is "*Antiquitates Bremetonacences*, or the Roman Antiquities of Overborough; wherein Overborough is proved the Bremetonacæ of Antoninus. 1746," 4to. The dedication to Robert Fenwick, Esq. is signed Richard Rauthmell, and dated Bolland, March 24, 1738-9; see further in Upcott's Catalogue of British Topography, p. 476. Dr. Whitaker has reviewed the Roman antiquities of Overborough in his *Richmondshire*, ii. 265-270, and gives a biographical note upon Rauthmell (see hereafter under Whitewell.)

The course of this road is well ascertained. It passed the Calder at Potterford; forms the boundary of the townships of Whalley and Little Mitton; traverses Chatburn and Worston by Standen, where it was anciently denominated the *Brede* (or *Broad*) Street; has been lately cut through near Downham Hall; and, passing through *Olicana* and *Burgodurum*, or *Adel*, joins the great Eastern Iter near Castleford.

But on this line, or another, of which I have little doubt that it traversed the eastern skirts of Pendle, whether at the distance of eight, or of eighteen, or of twenty-eight miles from *Rerigonium*, the seventh Iter of Richard calls upon us to look out for his station *ad Alpes Peninos*.[1]

Whalley, which is nearly at the first distance, has nothing Roman.[2] Burnley, which exhibits now and then some evidence of a Roman settlement, is too remote from Pendle or Pinhow; Broughton, however, where it has been fixed by Mr. Whitaker, may be thought to have a very plausible claim. But it is irksome to seek for a nonentity, as the fact really seems to have been that in laying-out one of his new and arbitrary "diaphragmata," the monk, having fixed in right positions *Rigodunum* (though mis-written by him *Rerigonium*) on one side of the mountains, and *Alicana*, or *Olicana*, on the other, and having very properly interposed between them on his map the *Alpes Peninos Montes*, saw the distance of the other two to require an intermediate station, and boldly invented this plausible and ingenious name. But had he seen the anonymous Ravennas, his honesty would not have been put to the test, and that unknown topographer, obscure and corrupt as he is, would have furnished him with a genuine station in the very position which he wanted, a station of which the summer-camp remains at Castercliff, and the name is echoed in Colne.

This was *Calunio*, the fourth name in an Iter (if, in an assemblage of names so ill-arranged, any number of mere local words can deserve the appellation,) which appears to have taken a circuitous route, unlike the regular and rectilinear Itinera of Antonine and the Notitia, from Manchester to Ribchester. The names which precede and follow the first and last words of this route appear to be unconnected with them, and indeed are absolutely unintelligible. Thus insulated, therefore, it will stand as follows:

MANTIO.
ALUNNA.
CAMULODUNO.
CALUNIO.
GALLUNIO.
MODIBOGDO.

Of the first and third of these names, *Mantio* and *Camuloduno*, there can be no doubt but that they are intended for the *Mancunium* and *Cambodunum* of Antonine, of which the former has been fixed at Manchester, by the unanimous suffrage of our antiquaries, and the latter has been removed from Almonbury to Slack, by the diligent investigation of Mr.

[1] That is, supposing the Monk's name *ad Alpes Peninos* to be of any authority. [See before, p. 16.]

[2] [This assertion of Dr. Whitaker in his first edition will be in some degree contradicted by what will be found hereafter, under Whalley.]

Watson, and by the decisive reasonings of Mr. Whitaker. The second, *Alunna*, is uncertain; if, however, we are to suppose, with Mr. Percival and Mr. Watson, that it is rightly placed between the other two, Castleshaw may have a fair claim to it, and Littleborough, from its situation on the infant stream of the Roach, a still fairer, for it is certainly no argument, or at least a very feeble one, against the existence of a station in the fifth century, that it was unnoticed by Antonine two centuries before, and as there are existing remains upon the two lines (for such I deem them to have been) which led from Manchester to Slack, it seems but fair to assign this hitherto unappropriated name either to the one or the other. If it be misplaced, as undoubtedly many names in this irregular catalogue are misplaced, it may be corrupted from *Alauna*,[1] or from *Alione*; it may have denoted Lancaster or Whitley Castle, but at all events the Iter proceeds from Manchester to Slack.

Next appear *Calunio* and *Gallunio*, of which the latter has been placed by Dr. Gale, and afterwards by Mr. Horsley, at Whalley, though the etymology of that word is purely Saxon, and though there is not a vestige of Roman antiquity about the place. But the probability is (and here I adopt, with pleasure, Mr. Whitaker's conjecture,) that by a very frequent error in the hurry and oscitancy of transcription, the name was repeated in one copy, the orthography altered in another, and by that means two stations produced out of one.

Again, taking it for granted that the barbarous word *Modibogdo* is corrupted from *Rigoduno*, we are next to ascertain the site of a station interposed betwixt Slack and Ribchester. Now the route of this Iter is confessedly circuitous, and the Vale of Calder, which would have formed the direct line of communication between these two points, has no remains considerable enough to claim our regard. But a few miles to the north, and in the very line too betwixt *Coccium* and *Olicana*, the name of Colne, and the remains of Castercliff, plainly indicate the real site of *Calunio*.

It seems probable that the exact spot occupied by this station was in some of the low grounds beneath the present town, and on the banks of the river, where all remains of it have been effaced by cultivation,[2] for Castercliff itself, placed upon a bleak but commanding elevation, which overlooks a large expanse of Craven to the north, and many miles of the vale of Calder to the west, has plainly been the *Castra Æstiva* only of *Calunio*. Hither, however, points the Roman road mentioned by Mr. Whitaker, which, long after, intersecting the Roman way from Manchester to Ilkley, may be traced in a broken causeway over the wild moors above Heptonstall; and hence appears to have issued another vicinal way pointing directly towards Ilkley, of which there are remains in the upper part of Trawden. Neither of these, however, are marked by the high bold rampart of the greater Itinera, or are distinguished from the old English causeways of the country, otherwise than

[1] The name *Al aun* indicates the situation of this obscure place to have been on the bank of a stream.

[2] Hist. Manc. vol. i. p. 134. Perhaps the real site is now irretrievable, but there are two lingulæ of land betwixt Colne and Barrowford (a name indicating something of antiquity) on the north side of Colne water, and formed by the influx of the two inconsiderable brooks, which have equal pretensions. The modern town of Colne has certainly none. It is much too elevated and too far from the water.

by the direction which they evidently pursue towards objects which have become obscure and uninteresting, ever since the Romans abandoned Britain.

The area of Castercliff has been a parallelogram of about 120 yards by 110, though somewhat rounded off at the angles. It has been surrounded by a double vallum and foss; and all the stones about it bear marks of fire.

I have lately inspected this camp more accurately, and have procured a sketch of it. The area within the trenches amounts to four acres thirty perches statute measure, and appears to have been levelled with great exactness. It has had a double wall and foss. The larger stones of the wall have from time to time been removed; but the smaller ones, which remain, universally bear marks of fire. The north and east sides are rectilinear, but those on the south and west have followed the line of two very precipitous banks, which have added greatly to the strength of the place. Immediately at the foot of the western rampart is a line of springs. The site of this work was admirably calculated for a camp of observation, as it commands the Vale of Calder, a considerable tract of Ribblesdale, all the high grounds towards Accrington and Haslingden, and the wildest parts of Pendle Forest.—(From Addenda to edit. of 1811.)

Great numbers of Roman silver coins have formerly been discovered in the long ascending lane which leads from Colne Water to Castercliff; but nothing Roman, so far as I have been able to learn, has been turned up within the area of the camp itself. It is singular, however, that an iron cannon-ball, weighing six pounds, was lately found at this place,[1] a circumstance of which no probable account can be given, but that in the civil wars of the last century the works were still so entire as to constitute a strong post, which was defended by one party and battered by the other.

The environs of Colne appear to have been populous in the Roman times, as great numbers of their coins have been discovered in the neighbourhood, particularly at Wheatley Lane, and near Emmet, where a large silver cup filled with them was turned up by the plough in the latter end of the last century.[2]

Another Iter from *Mancunium* has crossed a portion of the ancient parish of Whalley from south-west to north-east. The existence of this has been very clearly proved, and its course very accurately laid down by Mr. Whitaker; but from its direction it appears to have pointed immediately at *Cambodunum*, and to have united with the road from thence to Ilkley, which would form a communication with the latter station. At the foot of Blackstonedge, at a proper distance from both the greater stations, and in a commodious

[1] It is now in my possession.

[2] See a very sensible letter of Mr. Hargreave, rector of Brandsburton and a native of Colne, in Leigh, B. iii. p. 10. Notwithstanding which, that author, "stiff in opinion, always in the wrong," determines that Colne was not a Roman station. The first application of *Calunio* to Colne is owing to the learned Dr. Gale. The orthography of this word, in the most ancient charter we have, viz. of Henry the First's time, is *Calna*. [For the name in the Itinerary, as that document is written in the dative case, we should more strictly read *Calunium*. J. G. N.]

[Exhibited, Hist. Soc. Lancashire and Cheshire, 18 Dec. 1856, a donation from T. T. Wilkinson, F.R.A.S. Two stones from Castercliff near Colne; one specimen completely vitrified from intense heat, the other partially burnt through.]

site for refreshing the soldiers after their toilsome marches over those inhospitable mountains, appears to have been a subordinate fort, still denominated the Castle, and within half a mile of the modern Littleborough, to which it is thought [1] to have given its name. Whether both the lines of communication between these two stations were contemporary, or one was abandoned for the other, it is now difficult to ascertain. But a discovery made some years since at Castlemere, in the neighbourhood of Rochdale, and very near the line of this Iter, consisting of several coins of the middle brass and of the higher empire, one, if I am not mistaken (for I am compelled to write from recollection), as early as Claudius, seems to prove that the Blackstonedge line was at least as early as the other. About two miles north-east from the last-mentioned place,[2] and, like that near the line of the Roman road, was dug up in the year 1793 a very singular and noble remain of Roman antiquity. This was the right arm of a silver statue of Victory (represented in Plate I. of Roman Antiquities), of which the length was ten inches, and its weight nearly six ounces. The hand was a cast, and solid; the arm hollow, and formed apparently by having been beaten upon a model of wood; the anatomy and proportions good; and on the inside of the thumb a piece of solder which remained may be conjectured to have held a chaplet or palm branch. There was, besides, a loose armilla about the wrist, and another united to the arm above the elbow, to the former of which was appended a plate of silver with the following inscription, formed by the pointed strokes of a drill:

VICTORIAE
LEG VI VIC
VAL RVFVS
VSLM

Valerius Rufus, whose name occurs nowhere else among the inscriptions of Roman Britain, may be supposed to have been an officer of rank in the sixth legion,[4] and the arm of this vote has in all probability been broken off and lost in one of their marches from York, their stated quarters, to Manchester, where the altar to Fortune [5] proves them to

[1] "The castrum at Littleborough must have given denomination to the village." Hist. Manc. vol. i. p. 170.

[2] [This discovery was made in a slate quarry at Butterworth, near Rochdale. It was also engraved in the Gentleman's Magazine for May 1801, communicated by a correspondent signing PHILARGUROS, who is believed to have been Charles Chadwick of Healey Hall, Esq. F.S.A.]

[4] [Dr. Smith, in his Dictionary of Greek and Roman Mythology, has enumerated more than fifty *cognomina* of the Valeria Gens, but Rufus does not occur among them. There was a C. Valgius Rufus, a poet and grammarian, and a friend of Horace; he was Consul suffectus B.C. 13.]

[5] [FORTVNI CONSERVATRICI L. SENECIANIVS MARTIUS CENTURIO Ↄ LEG. VI. VICT. Found at Aldport near the Medlock in 1612.—Horsley, p. 301. This, which is said by Gough, Additions to Camden, iii. 135, to be preserved in Lady Bland's garden at Holme about a mile from Manchester, has now disappeared. Baines, *Lanc.* ii. 154.]

have been occasionally stationed. Gruter (565, ii.) has a funeral inscription for Valerius Rufus, a soldier of the seventh legion, at Tarraco, in Spain, but a vote of this importance must have exceeded the ability and the ambition of a private soldier.

These images of Victory were frequently of gold, and in great military processions (ἐν θέαις καὶ πόμπαις) were borne by a boy elevated on the shoulders of men. The statue to which this arm belonged must have been about two feet high, and therefore of a proper size for the purpose which has been described. Any misfortune which befel these palladia of the camp was held to be extremely ominous, and the loss of this arm and label[1] must have spread consternation through the whole legion to which it belonged. An accident of this kind preceded, and probably contributed to the defeat and death of Cassius: λέγεται δὲ καὶ πρότερον (says Plutarch) ἐν θέᾳ τινὶ καὶ πομπῇ, χρυσῆν Κασσίου ΝΙΚΗΝ διαφερομένην πεσεῖν, ὀλισθόντος τοῦ φέροντος. Brutus, c. 39. See also Dion Cassius, l. 47, c. 40.

It was impolitic and dangerous to call in superstition to the aid of military enthusiasm, a quality no less open to the impressions of terror than those of hope or resolution from external accidents and appearances.

The editors of 1870 take the opportunity to append to this chapter the following references to dissertations illustrating the Roman and Primæval antiquities of the ancient parish of Whalley, which have appeared since the days of the author of this work:—

In the Archæologia of the Society of Antiquaries of London.

Vol. XXX. 1844. Discovery of a Roman Urn near Burnley in Lancashire.

In the Archæological Journal of the Royal Archæological Institute.

Vol. VIII. 1851. Notices of Roman Ornaments connected with the Worship of the Deæ Matres, and purchased for the British Museum. By Edward Hawkins, F.R.S. and F.S.A. 35-45.

Vol. IX.—X. 1852. British Antiquities in the British Museum. By Augustus W. Franks, F.S.A. pp. 9-15.

Vol. X. 1853. On some of the relations of Archæology to Physical Geography in the North of England. By John Phillips, F.R.S.

Vol. XII. 1855. On Roman Antiquities from the North of England in the Libraries of Trinity and St. John's colleges, Cambridge. By the Rev. John Collingwood Bruce, LL.D. F.S.A. pp. 23-28.

In the Journal of the British Archæological Association.

Vol. II. 1846. On certain Mythic Personages mentioned on Roman Altars found in England and on the Rhine. By Thomas Wright, F.S.A. pp. 239-255.

Vol. V. 1850. Notes on Roman Remains at Chester. By C. Roach Smith, F.S.A. pp. 207-233.

Vol. VI. 1851. On Roman Ribchester. By John Just, Esq. and John Harland, Esq. pp. 229-251.

Vol. VIII. 1853. On the Tenth Iter of Antoninus. By John Just, Esq. pp. 35-43.

Vol. XII. 1856. Account of the Discovery of Roman coins at Hooleywood. By Mr. Harland. pp. 236-238.

---

[1] This valuable relic is in the possession of the author. [It is now (1870) at the residence of the historian's grand-daughter, Mrs. Kate Blanche Guthrie, Twiston Manor-house, near Clitheroe. It may here be mentioned that the late lord of the manor of Rochdale, James Dearden, Esq. F.S.A. obtained Miss Starkie's permission to have a fac-simile (in silver) made of the arm. This, we believe, was given by his son to Mr. George Shaw of Saddleworth.]

Vol. XX. 1864. On the Roman Roads intersecting the parish of Halifax. By F. A. Leyland, Esq. pp. 205-219.

In the Rheinisches Museum für Philologie, herausgegeben Von F. G. Welche und F. Ritschl. Neue Folge.

Jahrgang 11, 1856. Die römischen Heeresabtheilungen in Britannien. Von G. Hübner. pp. 1-57.

Jahrg. 12, 1857. Die römischen Legaten in Britannien. Von G. Hübner. pp. 46-83.

Jahrg. 12, 1857. Nachträge und Berichtigungen zu dem Aufsatz über die römischen Heeresabtheilungen in Britannien. Von G. Hübner. pp. 84-87.

In the Proceedings and Papers of the Historic Society of Lancashire and Cheshire.

Vol. I. pp. 68-76. On the Roman Roads in Lancashire, with a particular account of the Tenth Iter of Antoninus. By J. Just, of the Grammar School, Bury.

Vol. II. pp. 35-38. On the Roman station Condate. By J. Robson, Esq. Warrington.

Vol. III. pp. 3-10. Roman Roads of Lancashire, Part II. On the Seventh Iter of Richard of Cirencester. By J. Just.

Vol. III. p. 57. Remarks on the Evidences of Roman Occupation in the Fylde District. By Rev. William Thornber of Blackpool. (See pp. 26, 113.)

Vol. III. p. 85. On the Nomenclature of British Tribes. By Dr. Bell.

Vol. IV. p. 100. Traces of the Britons, Saxons, and Danes in the Foreland of the Fylde. By Rev. William Thornber.

Vol. V. p. 199. The materials for the History of the two Counties, and the mode of using them.

Vol. VIII. p. 1. On the State of the ancient kingdom of Northumberland down to the period of the Norman Conquest, especially pp. 135-140 on Ribchester, Coccium, &c.

Vol. VIII. pp. 127-140. On Roman Remains at Walton-le-dale—*Coccium*. By Charles Hardwick. Important.

Vol. IX. p. 1. The Battle of Brunanburgh and the probable locality of the conflict. By T. T. Wilkinson. Fought at Burnley—description of Castercliff, &c. Roman roads. A very important paper.

Vol. IX. pp. 61-76. The Castle Hill at Penwortham. By Rev. William Thornber.

Vol. X. p. 198. Supposed elevation of the bed of the Ribble.

Vol. V. p. 1. (New Series.) On the Druidical Rock Basins in the neighbourhood of Burnley. By T. T. Wilkinson.

Vol. V. p. 262. (New Series.) On the Roman topography of East Lancashire. By T. T. Wilkinson.

Vol. VI. p. 273. (New Series.) Ancient British Remains at Over Darwen. By Charles Hardwick.

Vol. VII. p. 13. (New Series.) Historical Sketches of the Forest of Rossendale. By Thos. Newbiggin.

Vol. VIII. (New Series.) pp. 16-32. On the Ancient Castle at Bury. By Charles Hardwick.

Vol. X. (New Series.) Operations at Wilderspool, near Warrington; the *Condate* of Antoninus. By Dr. Kendrick.

In the Memoirs of the Manchester Literary and Philosophical Society.

Vol. V. Part II., (Old Series,) p. 527. Account of some Antiquities found in the River Ribble. By Thomas Barritt.

Vol. VI. (New Series.) pp. 409-425. An Essay on the Roman Road in the vicinity of Bury, Lancashire. By John Just.

Vol. VII. (New Series.) pp. 1-21. On the Roman Military Road between Manchester and Ribchester. With Map of District and Road. By John Just.

Vol. VII. (New Series.) pp. 368-390. On the Leteia and Belisama of Ptolemy. By J. Black, M.D.

Vol. VII. (New Series) pp. 528-558. An Account of the Roman Road from Manchester to Wigan. With Map. By Rev. Edmund Sibson.

CHAPTER THE THIRD.

MEMORIALS OF THE PARISH DURING THE SAXON ÆRA.

THESE are more considerable than might have been expected from the obscure situation of the place, and the meagre accounts which have been transmitted to us of that barbarous and uninteresting period.

The deplorable state of weakness and barbarism into which the Britons lapsed after the final desertion of their country by the Romans, is the true cause of that total revolution in language, laws, manners, and property, which took place after the Saxon Conquest. Unlike the operation of those irruptions which rude but vigorous tribes sometimes make upon their more polished and feeble neighbours, in which, though property for the most part changes hands, the conquerors themselves are gradually subdued to the habits, the arts, and the language of their captives, these invasions found the miserable remnant of the native inhabitants unable to solicit their subduers by the blandishments of Roman luxury, to refine them by the cultivation of Roman arts, or to enlighten them by the institution of Roman laws. All these themselves had successively learned and lost; and with them they had nearly lost a greater treasure, which is never found to endure a state of second barbarism; namely, Christianity itself: so that, from the middle of the fifth to that of the sixth century, they are accused by Gildas and by Bede of having lost not only the power of religion, but the external form, of having abolished, except in a few instances, the order of priesthood and the distinctions of civil society.[1]

The Saxons, therefore, were at full liberty to institute an order of things altogether original: they parcelled out the country upon their own plan, *called the lands by their own names*,[2] and transmitted to their posterity a local nomenclature and a fundamental system of legal usages, which sustained the shock of the Norman Conquest, and even subsist at present.

Above the rest of Britain the name of *Deira*, or Deoꞃalonꝺ, which marked the whole

[1] Bede, l. 1, ch. 22. Gildas de excidio Brit. S. xxvi.

[2] This was remarkably the case, almost all local names among the Saxons being formed from those of their first possessors. After the Conquest a contrary process took place, and men were generally denominated from places.

tract of country interposed between the Tine, the Ribble, and the Humber, leads to the idea of depopulation and decay, from which the Saxons themselves never completely reclaimed it; for, while the map of all their other kingdoms in this island is thickly strewn with towns and cities, *Bernicia* and *Deira* together supply not more than twenty names, among which stands distinguished, on the south-western confines of Deoꞃalonð, the Ƿalalæᵹ of Simeon of Durham, the Ƿꞃællæᵹ[1] of the Saxon Chronicle, and the modern Whalley.

Having now arrived at the word which denominates the subject of this History, it remains that we inquire whether the Saxon language, from which it is obviously deduced, will furnish a proper and descriptive etymology. In that language ƿeall is a well, from ƿeallan, *scaturire;* and this diphthong was undoubtedly pronounced broad, like the Dutch *Wall*, which is, in fact, the same word. In the neighbouring parish of Rochdale, the true Saxon pronunciation of the word remains to the present day: there they have *Cold Wall* and *Wall Head*, to denote two remarkable springs.—Dr. Plot, *History of Staffordshire*, p. 47, mentions a spring called *Hungerwall*,[2] and one of the fountains of Whalley itself is still denominated the *High Wall Well*.[3]

(Highwall Well appears to have been the cold bath of the Abbey, for which purpose it is singularly well contrived. It is walled with excellent hewn stone, about four feet and a half deep, and is contracted, step by step, as follows: first, are two circles, the lower much narrower than the higher; then a square, inscribed within the last circle; and beneath all, a rhombus, inscribed within the last square. The convenience of this contrivance, for the purpose of going in and getting out, as well as for immersion, is obvious. *Addenda*, 1818.)

Ƿalalæᵹ, therefore, is the *Field of Wells*, and a term more strikingly descriptive could not have been chosen: for, situated as Whalley is, upon the skirts of Pendle, and upon the face of those half-inverted mineral beds popularly denominated the *Rearing Mine*, the earth, if not drained, bleeds almost at every pore; and there are no less than six considerable springs within the immediate precincts of the village.

The first occasion in which the name occurs, in civil history, is in the year DCCXCVIII. Ƿeꞃ (says the Saxon Chronicle) ƿæꞅ mẏcel ᵹeꝼeoht on Noꞃðhẏmbꞃa lanðe on lenᵹꞃene on iv. non. Aꝑꞃ. æt Ƿꞃaellæᵹe, ⁊ þæꞃ man ofꞅloh Alꞃic Heaꞃbeꞃteꞅ ꞅunu ⁊ oðꞃe mæniᵹe mið him.

The account of this event by Simeon of Durham, from some more ancient authority

[1] In our oldest charters the Saxon aspirate is retained. The Deans sometimes signed themselves *Dec. de Hwall.* and somethings *Quallay.*

[2] ["Near Ashwood bridge, in the parish of King's Swinford, and not far from Swyndon. Commonly called *Hunger-wall*, because it is usually either quite *dry* or at most *stagnates*, and runs not at all (but, as the vulgar will have it, against a *dearth* of *Corne*) which how true it may be I shall not here dispute, but most certain it is it does not always *run;* and when it does, it sometimes they say comes forth with such a *noise* that it has frightened people that have then happen'd to be near it, as particularly they will tell you it did some *rabbit-stealers* that were not far off when it once thus happen'd to burst out."—The Natural History of Staffordshire, by Robert Plot, LL.D. &c. Oxford, 1686, folio, p. 47, 48.]

[3] So also *Walshaw* is a wood, and *Walsden*, a valley, abounding with springs.

than that of the Chronicle, is much more interesting and circumstantial. His words are these:—"Anno D. 798. Conjuratione facta ab interfectoribus Ethelredi regis, Wada Dux in illa conjuratione cum eis bellum inivit contra Eardwlphum regem in loco qui appellatur ab Anglis *Billangahoth* juxta Walalege, et, ex utraque parte plurimis interfectis, Wada Dux cum suis in fugam versus est et Eardwlfus rex victoriam regaliter sumpsit ab inimicis."

Billange, or *Billinge*, I suppose to have been at that time the name of the whole ridge extending from the mountain near Blackburn, now bearing that appellation, to Whalley. *Billangaton*, therefore, will be the original orthography of *Billington;* and *Billangahoh*, or the low hill by Billinge, will leave, after cutting off the first syllable, the modern village of Langho. Of this great battle there are, however, no remains, unless a large tumulus near Hacking Hall, and in the immediate vicinity of Langho, be supposed to cover the remains of Alric, or some other chieftain, among the slain.

This tumulus is called the Loe Hill, and is nearly 120 yards in circumference at the base, more conical than sepulchral tumuli usually are, but less so than Saxon keeps when entire. At a small distance are the remains of a large cairn of stones. In the summer of the year 1815 I obtained leave to dig into the Loe Hill, which appeared to be evidently artificial, as no part of it was stratified. On the contrary, the whole, as far as the investigation proceeded, was made up of large water gravel, mixed with exceedingly tough marle, of which there is a bed by the river side. The labour and expense of removing such materials was found so great, that we were compelled to desist before we had arrived at the centre, so that unfortunately nothing was found. I must not omit to add, that on a point of high woody ground washed by the Calder, and where it formerly united with the Ribble, is a very deep trench, consisting of about two-thirds of an oval. The rest has been carried away by the current. As I have little doubt that Loe Hill is either the sepulchral tumulus, or at least a memorial, of Alric, I think it highly probable that this was a fortified post, made use of in the engagement, when he was slain.

But though tradition itself, the faithful preserver of events even more remote than this, be silent on the subject, a few local names in the neighbourhood, which are evidently Saxon, appear to have a reference to some circumstances relating to it. Thus Wadhow, a beautiful swelling hill, four miles higher up the Ribble, may be the hill of *Wada*, perhaps the site of his camp before the engagement. Waddington, in Domesday *Wadelon,* the town of *Wada.* Edisforth, or Eaδigisforð,[1] the *Nobleman's Ford;* and Wiswall, which is much nearer to the field of battle, Ƿigasƿælla, or the *Hero's Well.*

Considered as an obscure village, in a remote province, this testimony is honourable to Whalley. Few even of our large provincial towns, excepting those which lay claim to Roman antiquity, have any earlier record than the great register of Domesday; but our story reaches nearly three centuries backward into the Saxon æra, is connected in its origin

[1] Eaδig, which means *vir nobilis, beatus, locuples*, is never used as a proper name but in composition. Ƿiga signifies *heros, semideus*, and is melted into the first syllable of *Wiswall*, as from *Begastown* comes *Beeston.* See Wiswall.

with an important national event, and attested by no private register, but by the annals of the Northumbrian kingdom.

Domesday itself, however, by referring to the tenures in the Confessor's reign, contains the last memorial of the state of property during the Saxon period: and, being perpetually interwoven with representations of the great change produced by the Norman Conquest, has, in a local history, peculiar claims to our attention. The entire district between the Ribble and Mersey appears to have been surveyed by the same commissioners, and bears marks of the same peculiarities. I have therefore subjoined the whole, together with a Commentary, and some previous observations with respect to the situation of the *Terra inter Ripam et Mersham,* under the Heptarchy.[1]

A question has arisen among antiquaries, whether, in the æra of the Heptarchy, the tract of country interposed between the Mersey and Ribble, and consequently the parish of Whalley, were a portion of the Northumbrian or the Mercian kingdom.[2] The town of Ꝺanıᵹ-ceaꞅꞇꞃe, indeed, which was repaired by Edward the Elder, is, in the Saxon Chronicle, expressly said to be in Northumberland. The Council of *Calcluith,* though under the control of Offa, King of Mercia, is said to have been held in the same kingdom; and it has been powerfully contended, that *Calcluith*[3] is no other than an obscure place called *Culcheth,* near Manchester.

The note beneath will, I trust, have removed all claims on the part of *Calcluith* to a place in Northumbria; and with respect to the little evidence which can be adduced in favour of this tract having once formed a part of *Northumbria,* it refers to periods subse-

[1] In Delaval's charter, about 50 years after Domesday, Whalley is expressly said to be in Cestershyriâ.

[2] See History of Craven, 2d. edit. 1812, p. 493; since the publication of which, I scruple not to acknowledge that I have changed my opinion on the subject.

[3] It is strange, indeed, that the attention of no antiquary has been directed to Checkley, in Staffordshire, as the real scene of this quarrelsome and opprobrious assembly. But, upon every hypothesis, Checkley was far within the limits of Mercia; and it is highly improbable that a Council, in the decrees of which so powerful and spirited a prince as Offa had so near an interest, would be permitted to assemble anywhere but in his own territories. Let us see, however, on what grounds the evidence in favour of Checkley rests. 1st. The initial *c*, in Saxon, was pronounced as *ch* in church. Thus *Ceadde* was altered in the orthography only to *Chad; Calcluith,* then, would be pronounced as *Chalcluith,* and the last consonants very indistinctly; invert the two letters *c* and *l*, in the middle of the word, and we have *Chacli,* or *Checkley.*

This, however, would be a wild hypothesis, were it not supported by positive evidence. But at Checkley, in the time of Dr. Plot, were remaining three crosses, of which the constant tradition of the place recorded, that they were erected on the following occasion:—Speaking of "tall pyramidal stones" in churchyards, which he supposes to be sepulchral, the Doctor adds (Hist. Staffordshire, p. 432), that there are "three close together at Checkley, ... and probably funeral monuments of the dead, which agrees with the tradition of theirs at Checkley, the inhabitants reporting them the memorials of three bishops slain in a battle fought here, about a quarter of a mile E.N.E. from the church." Compare these circumstances with the character of that Council which is called by the Saxon Chronicle * ᵹeꞅlıꞇꞅullıc (a word yet retained in the Lancashire dialect, which would literally translate it "fliting,") † and the violence with which it is known to have been conducted, and there can be no doubt but that the tradition is an exaggerated account of that event; whence it must follow, that *Calcluith* is Checkley.

* Anno DCCLXXXV. † [The Cotton. MS. Tib. B. I. reads ᵹeꞅlıꞇ ⁊ ꞅullıc, *i. e.* strife and base synod. P. A. L.]

quent to the extinction of the Heptarchy, and when an union of dominion rendered accuracy in adhering to the ancient boundaries a matter of comparative indifference. Thus nothing is more common, in the South of England, than to denominate all persons Yorkshiremen, who have been born on the north side of the Trent.

But, on the other hand, there are two most cogent arguments, the one historical, the other etymological, to prove that this district, under the Heptarchy, formed a portion, not of *Northumbria*, but of the Mercian kingdom; and that, with respect to the present County of Lancaster, the Ribble was the actual boundary. First, then, we have the authority of the *Status de Blackburnshire*, to prove that the parish of Whalley was, from the earliest times, a portion of the diocese of Lichfield; and it is very certain that this diocese, founded as it was by the earlier Mercian kings, never passed the limit of their territories. But, secondly, the peculiar dialect of the Northumbrian kingdom, which, with many subordinate varieties, prevails from the confines of the Highlands of Scotland to the southern verge of Yorkshire, including, that is, the whole of the ancient *Bernicia* to the north and *Deira* to the south, immediately and strikingly ceases on the confines of the present parish of Whalley, so as plainly to indicate that on that bounding line it has been met and repelled by the language of another tribe. Were it worth while to illustrate this position by a general comparison between the language of Craven and of Whalley, I could prove this position in the most satisfactory manner. But the following comparative table of the names of local objects, which severally prevail in these two adjoining districts, and are in a very small degree common to both, will surely suffice for the purpose.

Northumbria.	Mercia.
Fell—occurs to the Northern bank of the Ribble, never to the South.	Edge—as Blackstonedge, Stonedge, &c.
Scar	Scout.
Beck	Brook—Burn; the last common to both, but more rare to the South.
Tarn	Mere.
Dub	Lumb, a deep pool in a river.
Mire	Halgh.[1]
Carr	Leach, a Plash.
How	Know, knoll.

Northumbria.	Mercia.
Thwait . . .	Riding, Ridding, Rode, or Royde.
Ings . . .	Eases—Holmes, common to both.
Thorp . . .	Wick, comparatively rare to the N. of Ribble. Thorp never occurs to the South.
Hope	Greave.
Gill	Clough.
Skell	Well.
Scrogg	Shaw—Scholes.
Sike	Rindle.
Wath	Ford.
	Twisle.

[1] *Halgh.* This is the Scottish *Haugh*, a flat spungy piece of ground. We have three instances in which it is compounded with personal names, as Dunken-halgh, Pout-halgh, Hesmond-halgh; and three others in which the local word united with it plainly indicates its meaning, as Aspen-halgh, the Halgh of Aspens, Ridy-holgh, the Halgh of Reeds, and Becks-halgh, the Halgh by the Brooks; the last immediately north of Ribble, which accounts for its combination from Beck. Greenhalgh is another combination, which may be referred to the same cause.

Northumbria.	Mercia.	Northumbria.	Mercia.
Scale	Rake.	Stank . .	Wham, a bog.
Dale[1]	Dene, or Dean, sometimes, however, occurring in Craven.	Hope.[2]	
		Busk.	
Toft	Holt, a tuft of Trees.	Ergh, Er, or Argh, in composition.[3]	
	Hurst — Hag — Holgh, a wood.		

If we try, by the same rule, the hypothesis which fixes the Mersey as the boundary of the two kingdoms, the result will be widely different. Between natives of the northern and southern bank of that river there is scarcely a perceptible difference of language: they are evidently descendants, in common, from the same parental stock.

On the whole, I am persuaded that the outline of the parish of Whalley, as far as it extends along the Ribble, and afterwards as far as it coincides with the limit of the West Riding of Yorkshire, is the ancient national line of separation between these two great kingdoms of the Heptarchy. A single merestone (an immense natural block), called the Wolf-stone, the property of the writer, marks at once the confine of the townships of Cliviger and Stansfield; the parishes of Whalley and Halifax; the counties of Lancaster and York; the ancient diocese of Lichfield (now Chester), and the diocese of York; the provinces of York and Canterbury; and lastly, the kingdoms of Deira and Mercia.

Domesday Book for Lancashire, south of the Ribble.

INTER RIPAM ET MERSHAM.

Terram infra Scriptam Tenuit Rogerius Pictavensis.

Inter Ripam et Mersham. In Derbei Hvndreto.

Ibi habuit Rex Edwardus unum Manerium Derbei nominatum, cum vi. Bereuuichis. Ibi iiii hidæ. Terra est xv carucatæ. Foresta ii leuuis longa, et una lata, et aira accipitris.

Vetredus tenebat vi Maneria, Rabil, Chenulueslei, Cherchebi, Crosebi, Magele, Achetun. Ibi ii hidæ. Silvæ ii leuuis longæ et latæ, et ii airæ accipitris.

Dot tenebat Hitune et Torboc. Ibi i hida quieta ab omni consuetudine præter geldum. Terra est iiii carucatæ. Valebat xx solidos.

[1] This appellative occurs precisely on the confines, as Bleasdale, Whitendale, Lothersdale; but in Rossendale only south of Ribble.

[2] A small valley running up to a point among hills. We have nothing exactly to oppose to it. It is frequent in the hilly parts of the West Riding, and occurs in the Peak of Derby. It is, indeed, a curious fact, that in and adjoining to the Peak of Derbyshire, almost in the heart of the Mercian kingdom, many striking vestiges of the Northumbrian dialect appear.

[3] This is a singular word, which occurs, however, both to the north and south of Ribble, though much more frequently to the north. To the south I know not that it occurs, but in Angles-ark and Brett-ergh. To the north are Batarghes (Butterax), Ergh-holme, Stras-ergh, Siz-ergh, Feiz-er, Goosen-ergh. In all the Teutonic dialects I meet with nothing resembling this word, excepting the Swedish ARF, *terra* (*vide* Ihre *in voce*), which, if the last letter be pronounced gutturally, is precisely the same with *argh*.

Bernulf tenebat Stochestede.[1] Ibi I uirgata terræ, et dimidia carucata terræ. Reddebant IIII solidos.

Stainulf tenebat Stochestede. Ibi I virgata terræ, et dimidia carucata terræ. Valebant IIII solidos.

Quinque taini tenebant Sextone.[2] Ibi I hida. Valebat XVI solidos.

Vetredus tenebat Chirchedele.[3] Ibi dimidia hida quieta ab omni consuetudine, præter geldum. Valebat X solidos.

Winestan tenebat WALETONE. Ibi II carucatæ terræ, et III bovatæ. Valebant VIII solidos.

Elmær tenebat Liderlant. Ibi dimidia hida. Valebant VIII solidos.

Tres taini tenebant Hinne[4] pro III Maneriis. Ibi dimidia hida. Valebat VIII solidos.

Aseha tenebat Torentun. Ibi dimidia hida. Valebat VIII solidos.

Tres taini tenebant MELE pro III maneriis. Ibi dimidia hida. Valebat VIII solidos.

Vetred tenebat Vluentune.[5] Ibi II carucatæ terræ, et dimidia leuua silvæ. Valebant LXIIII denarios.

Edelmundus tenebat ESMEDVNE. Ibi una carucata terræ. Valebat XXXII denarios.

Tres taini tenebant Alretune pro III Maneriis. Ibi dimidia hida. Valebat VIII solidos.

Vetred tenebat Spec. Ibi II carucatæ terræ. Valebant LXIIII denarios.

Quatuor radmans tenebant CILDEUUELLE pro IIII Maneriis. Ibi dimidia hida. Valebat VIII solidos. Ibi presbyter erat habens dimidiam carucatam terræ elemosinam.

Vlbert tenebat Wibaldeslei. Ibi II carucatæ terræ. Valebant LXIIII denarios.

Duo taini tenebant Vuetone, pro II Maneriis. Ibi I carucata terræ. Valebat XXX denarios.

Leuingus tenebat Wauretreu. Ibi II carucatæ terræ. Valebant LXIIII denarios.

Quatuor taini tenebant Boltelai pro IIII Maneriis. Ibi II carucatæ terræ. Valebant LXIIII denarios. Presbyter habebat I carucatam terræ, ad ecclesiam Waletone.

Vetred tenebat Achetun. Ibi I carucata terræ. Valebat XXXII denarios.

Tres taini tenebant Fornebei pro III Maneriis. Ibi IIII carucatæ terræ. Valebant X solidos.

Tres taini tenebant Emuluesdel. Ibi II carucatæ terræ. Valebant LXIIII denarios.

Steinulf tenebat Hoiland. Ibi II carucatæ terræ. Valebant LXIIII denarios.

Vetred tenebat Daltone. Ibi I carucata terræ. Valebat XXXII denarios.

Isdem Vetred SCHEMERESDELE. Ibi I carucata terræ. Valebat XXXII denarios.

Isdem Vetred tenebat Literland. Ibi I carucata terræ. Valebat XXXII denarios.

Wilbertus tenebat ERENGERMELES. Ibi II carucatæ terræ. Valebant VIII solidos. Hæc terra quieta fuit præter geldum.

Quinque taini tenebant Otegrimele. Ibi dimidia hida. Valebat X solidos.

Vetredus tenebat LATONE cum I bereuuicha. Ibi dimidia hida. Silua I leuua longa et dimidia lata. Valebant X solidos et VIII denarios.

Vetred tenebat Hirletun, et dimidium Merretun. Ibi dimidia hida. Valebat X solidos et VIII denarios.

Godeue tenebat Melinge. Ibi II carucatæ terræ. Silua I leuua longa et dimidia lata. Valebat X solidos.

Vetred tenebat Leiate.[6] Ibi VI bovatæ terræ. Silua I leuua longa, et II quarentenis lata. Valebat LXIIII denarios.

Duo taini tenebant VI bovatas terræ, pro II Maneriis, in Holand. Valebant II solidos.

Vetred tenebat Acrer. Ibi dimidia carucata terræ. Wasta fuit.

Teos tenebat Bartune. Ibi I carucata terræ. Valebat XXXII denarios.

Chetel tenebat Heleshale.[7] Ibi II carucata terræ. Valebant VIII solidos.

Omnis hæc terra geldabilis, et XV Maneria nil reddebant, nisi geldum Regi Edwardo.

Hoc Manerium Derbei cum his supradictis hidis reddebant Regi Edwardo de firma XXVI libras et II

1 Toxteth. 2 Sephton. 3 Kirkdale. 4 Ince.
5 Wolton. 6 Lidyate. 7 Halsbal.

solidos. Ex his III hidæ erant liberæ. Quarum censum perdonavit teinis qui eas tenebant. Istæ reddebant IIII libras et XIIII solidos et VIII denarios.

Omnes isti taini habuerunt consuetudinem reddendi II oras denariorum de unaquaque carucata terræ, et faciebant per consuetudinem domos regis et quæ ibi pertinebant sicut uillani, et piscarias et in silva haias et stabilituras, et qui ad hæc non ibat quando debebat, II solidis emendabat, et postea ad opus ueniebat, et operabatur donec perfectum erat. Vnusquisque eorum, uno die in Augusto, mittebat messores suos secare segetes regis. Si non, per II solidos emendabat.

Si quis liber homo faceret furtum, aut forestel, aut heinfara, aut pacem regis infringebat, XL solidos emendabat.

Si quis faciebat sanguinem aut raptum de femina, uel qui remanebat de siremot sine rationabili excusatione, per X solidos emendabat. Si de hundreto remanebat, aut non ibat ad placitum ubi prepositus iubebat, per V solidos emendabat.

Si cui iubebat in suum servitium ire et non ibat, IIII solidos emendabat.

Si quis de terra Regis recedere uolebat, dabat XL solidos et ibat quo uolebat.

Si quis terram patris sui mortui habere uolebat, XL solidos releuabat.

Qui nolebat, et terram et omnem pecuniam patris mortui Rex habebat.

Vetredus tenuit Crosebi, et Chirchedele, pro I hida, et erat quieta ab omni consuetudine præter has VI. pace infracta, forestel, heinfara, et pugna que post sacramentum factum remanebat, et si constrictus iusticia præpositi alicui debitum soluebat, et si terminum a præposito datum non attendebat, hoc per XL solidos emendabat. Geldum uero Regis, sicut homines patriæ solvebant.

In Otringimele et Hirleshalla et Hiretun erant III hidæ quietæ a geldo carucatarum terræ, et a forisfactura sanguinis, et fœminæ uiolentia. Alias uero consuetudines reddebant omnes.

De isto manerio DERBEI tenent modo, dono Rogeri Pictaviensis, hi homines terram. Goiffridus II hidas et dimidiam carucatam, Rogerius I hidam et dimidiam, Willelmus unam hidam et dimidiam, Warinus dimidiam hidam, Goiffridus I hidam, Tetbaldus hidam et dimidiam, Robertus II carucatas terræ, Gislebertus I carucatam terræ.

Hi habent in dominio IIII carucatas, et XLVI uillanes et I radman, et LXII bordarios, et II seruos, et III ancillas. Inter omnes habent XXIIII carucatas.

Silua eorum III leuuis et dimidia longa, et I leuua et dimidia et XL perticæ latitudine, et ibi III airæ accipitrum.

Totum ualet VIII libras et XII solidos. In unaquaque hida sunt VI carucatæ terræ.

Dominium uero huius Manerii, quod tenebat Rogerius, valebat VIII libras. Sunt ibi modo in dominio III carucatæ, et VI bovarii, et unus radman, et VII villani.

IN NEWTONO HUNDRETO.

In NEWTONO Tempore Regis Edwardi fuerunt V hidæ. Ex his una erat in dominio. Ecclesia ipsius Manerii habebat II carucatam terræ, et Sanctus Osuuoldus de ipsa uilla II carucatas terræ habebat quietas per omnia.

Huius Manerii aliam terram XV homines quos drenchs vocabant pro XV Maneriis tenebant, sed huius Manerii bereuuichæ erant, et inter homines XXX solidos reddebant.

Silua ibi X leuuis longa, et VI leuuis et II quarentenis lata, et ibi airæ accipitrum.

Huius hundredi homines liberi præter duos erant in eadem consuetudine qua homines Derberiæ, et plus illis II diebus in Augusto metebant in culturis Regis.

Illi duo habebant V carucatas terræ, et forisfacturam sanguinis et fœminæ uiolentiam passæ, et pasnagium suorum hominum. Alias habebat Rex.

Totum hoc manerium reddebat de firma Regi X libras et X solidos.

Modo sunt ibi VI drenghs, et XII villani, et IIII bordarii. Inter omnes, IX carucatas habent. Valet IIII libras hoc dominium.

IN WALINTVN HVNDRETO.

Rex Edwardus tenuit WALINTONE cum III bereuuichis. Ibi I hida.

Ad ipsium Manerium pertinebant XXXIIII drenghs, et totidem Maneria habebant. In quibus erant XLII carucatæ terræ, et una hida et dimidia.

Sanctus Elfin tenebat I carucatam terræ quietam de omni consuetudine præter geldum.

Totum Manerium cum HUNDRETO reddebat regi de firma XV libras II solidis minus. Modo sunt in dominio II carucatæ, et VIII homines cum I carucata.

Homines isti tenebant ibi terram, Rogerus I carucatam terræ, Tetbaldus I carucatam et dimidiam, Warinus I carucatam, Radulfus V carucatas, Willelmus II hidas et IIII carucatas terræ, Adelardus I hidam et dimidiam carucatam, Osmundus I carucatam terræ.

Valet hoc totum IIII libras et X solidos. Dominium ualet III libras et X solidos.

IN BLACHEBVRN HVNDRETO.

Rex Edwardus tenuit BLACHEBVRNE. Ibi II hidæ et II carucatæ terræ. Ecclesia habebat II bouatas de hac terra, et ecclesia Sanctæ Mariæ habebat in Wallei II carucatas terræ quietas ab omni consuetudine.

In eodem Manerio, silva I leuua longa, et tantundem lata, et ibi aira accipitris.

Ad hoc Manerium vel HVNDRETUM adiacebant XXVIII liberi homines, tenentes V hidas et dimidiam et XL carucatas terræ, pro XXVIII Maneriis. Silua ibi VI leuuis longa et IIII leuuis lata, et erant in supradictis consuetudinibus.

In eodem HUNDRETO habebat rex Edwardus, HUNNICOT de II carucatis terræ, et WALETUNE de carucatis terræ, et PENILTUNE de dimidia hida.

Totum Manerium cum HUNDRETO reddebat regi de firma XXXII libras et II solidos. Hanc terram totam dedit Rogerius Pictauensis Rogerio de Busli et Alberto Greslet, et ibi sunt tot homines, qui habent XI carucatas et dimidiam, quos ipsi concesserunt esse quietos usque ad III annos, et ideo non appreciantur modo.

IN SALFORD HVNDRETO.

Rex Edwardus tenuit SALFORD. Ibi III hidæ et XII carucatæ terræ wastæ, et foresta III leuuis longa, et tantundem lata, et ibi plures haiæ et aira accipitris.

RADECLIUE tenebat rex Edwardus pro Manerio. Ibi I hida et alia hida pertinens ad Salford.

Ecclesia Sanctæ Mariæ et ecclesia Sancti Michaelis tenebant in Mamecestre unam carucatam terræ, quietam ab omni consuetudine præter geldum.

Ad hoc Manerium uel HUNDRETUM pertinebant XXI bereuuichæ, quas tenebant totidem taini pro totidem Maneriis, in quibus erant XI hidæ et dimidia, et X carucatæ terræ et dimidia.

Silua ibi IX leuuis et dimidia longa, et V leuuis et una quarentena lata.

Vnus eorum Gamel, tenens II hidas in Recedham,[1] habebat suas consuetudines quietas, præter VI has, furtum, heinfare, forestel, pacem regis infractam, terminum fractum a præposito stabilitum, pugnam post sacramentum factum remanentem. Hæc emendabat XL solidis. Aliquæ harum terrarum erant quietæ ab omni consuetudine præter geldum, et aliquotæ a geldo sunt quietæ.

Totum Manerium SALFORD CUM HUNDRETO reddebat XXXVII libras et IIII solidos. Modo sunt in Manerio in dominio II carucatæ, et VIII serui, et II uillani cum I carucata. Valeto C solidos hoc dominium.

[1] Rochdale.

De hac terra hujus Manerii tenent milites dono Rogeri Pictauiensis, Nigellus III hidas et dimidiam carucatam terræ, Warinus II carucatas terræ, et alter Warinus I carucatam et dimidiam, Goiffridus I carucatam terræ, Gamel II carucatas terræ. In his sunt III taini et XXX uillani, et IX bordarii, et presbyter, et X serui. Inter omnes habent XXII carucatas. Valet VII libras.

In Lailand Hundreto.

Rex Edwardus tenuit Lailand. Ibi I hida et II carucatæ terræ. Silua II leuuis longa, et una lata, et aira accipitris.

Ad hoc Manerium pertinebant XII carucatæ terræ, quas tenebant XII homines liberi pro totidem Maneriis. In his VI hidæ et VIII carucatæ terræ.

Silua ibi VI leuuis longa et III leuuis et una quarentena lata.

Homines huius Manerii et de Salford non operabantur per consuetudinem ad aulam regis, neque metebant in Augusto. Tantummodo I haiam in silva faciebant, et habebant sanguinis forisfacturum, et fœminæ passæ violentiam.

De aliis consuetudinibus aliorum superiorum Maneriorum erant consortes.

Totum Manerium Lailand cum HUNDRETO reddebat de firma regi XIX libras et XVIII solidos et II denarios.

De hac terra huius Manerii tenet Girardus hidam et dimidiam, Robertus III carucatas terræ, Radulfus II carucatas terræ, Rogerius II carucatas terræ, Walterus I carucatam terræ. Ibi sunt IIII radmans, presbyter, et XIIII uillani et VI bordarii et II bovarii. Inter omnes habent VIII carucatas. Silua III leuuis longa et II leuuis lata, et ibi IIII airæ accipitrum. Valet totum L solidos. Et parta est Wasta.

Rex Edwardus tenuit Peneverdant. Ibi II carucatæ terræ, et reddebant X denarios. Modo est ibi castellum, et II carucatæ sunt in dominio, et VI burgenses et III radmans et VIII uillani et IIII bouarii. Inter omnes habent IIII carucatas. Ibi dimidia piscaria. Silva et airæ accipitrum, sicut tempore Regis Edwardi. Valet III libras.

In his VI HUNDRETIS, Derbie, Neutone, Walintune, Blacheburne, Salford, et Lailand, sunt C quater XX et octo Manerii. In quibus sunt quater XX hidæ geldabiles, una minus.

Tempore Regis Edwardi ualebant CXLV libras et II solidos et II denarios.

Quando Rogerius Pictauensis de Rege recepit, valebat CXX libras. Modo tenet Rex, et habet in dominio XII carucatas et IX milites feudum tenentes. Inter eos et eorum homines sunt CXV carucatæ et III boues. Dominium quod tenuit Rogerius appreciatur XXIII libris et X solidis. Quod dedit militibus, XX libris et XI solidis appreciatur.

It is not easy to treat with distinctness of the origin and ramifications of property in Blackburn hundred otherwise than by connecting it with the rest of the county of Lancaster, which lies south of Ribble. At the period of the Domesday Survey, [finished A.D. 1086,] this extensive and most fertile part of the present county belonged to none, but was separately surveyed under the title of the country *Inter Ripam et Mersham*.

In the time of King Edward, the whole of this district was the property of the Crown. It had been granted soon after the Conquest (a vast donation) to Roger of Poitou: at the time of Domesday, with the exception of the grants made by Roger, it had been taken in exchange or resumed by the Conqueror, and, excepting certain knight's fees previously granted by him, it remained in the Crown.

This Survey has many peculiarities and many difficulties. Among them one of the most remarkable is the use of the word Hide, which, in every other instance with which I am acquainted, is commensurate with carucate: yet in the Hundred of Derby, and I think evidently in the rest of the district, "In unaquaque hida sunt sex carucatæ terræ." Another general distinction appears to be that where hides and carucates are mentioned under the same manor, the latter appears to denote (and especially when combined with the word "terræ,") land actually or anciently under the plough: I add "anciently," for there are "carucatæ terræ vastæ." And when an hide is defined as consisting of six carucates, it must be understood to mean as much land as, if thrown into cultivation, would employ so many ploughs drawn by eight oxen, for such was the ancient Caruca. The term Hide also excludes meadows, woods, and commons. It is therefore land fit for the plough, but never actually cultivated: in other words, native pasture land, properly so called.

It must also be observed that the measure of woodland in every hundred, however the woods might be dispersed, is added together and reduced to square miles; a mode which, however compendious, is obviously very inaccurate.

The word Manor, in its more extended sense, denoted the whole hundred.

The hundred of West Darby (at what period I do not know) has swallowed up those of Newton and Warrington.

The hundred of West Darby had two churches, Walton and Childwall. That of Newton had one church belonging to the hundred, and a separate endowment of Saint Oswald, belonging to the town of Winwick; but as the whole hundred extended over Newton and Winwick alone, it is not probable that there was more than one place of worship. The church of St. Elphin (a dedication now lost) at Warrington was the only church of that hundred. Blackburn hundred had two churches, Whalley and Blackburn. Salford had those of St. Mary and St. Michael in Manchester, with one endowment only; and Lailand had one Presbytery, whose particular situation, by the inaccuracy of the surveyors, is not ascertained.

Of these Winwick had an endowment of three carucates; Whalley of two; (to each of which [churches] was annexed the manor of the town); Walton, Manchester, and Warrington, a carucate each; Childwall, half a carucate; Blackburn two oxgangs; and of the Presbyter of Leyland hundred, we know not what or where was his provision.[1]

Such was the ecclesiastical establishment of South Lancashire, at the time of Domesday; an establishment adequate to the slender population of that period, and under which there was probably a greater proportion of ministers to people than at present, but attended with this inconvenience, that many villages were at the distance of fifteen or twenty miles from their parish church, and without the convenience of chapels, which, in the great parishes, they enjoy at present. What increase in the number of parishes had taken place in 1292, when Pope Nicholas's Valor was made, and to what number they have been further augmented at present, will be noticed in its proper place.

[1] Presbyters, in Domesday, are frequently mentioned without churches.

In the whole of this district (the "Terra inter Ripam et Mersham") the Survey of the hundred of West Derby alone, excluding those of Newton and Warrington, which now constitute parts of it, has the advantage of having its manors and vills enumerated by name. In the other hundreds they are grouped together, unless where some peculiarity of custom or tenure rendered it necessary to specify the places so differing from their neighbours. In this and in all the other hundreds, however, within this insulated district, the same method is pursued. It begins with the town from which the hundred (or manor, in its most extended sense) received its denomination; gives a particular survey of that and its immediate dependencies or berewicks, specifying the measurement of wood and forest within the same, separately, from the general measurement of similar grounds within the rest of the hundred; then enumerates the several vills and manors, with their respective owners, customs, tenures, and rents, as they had existed under the Confessor; and lastly recapitulates the same as then subsisting under the great change of property occasioned by the Conquest. There were under King Edward sixty-seven vills or manors (I presume that every vill was at least a manor, though some are divided into two, three, or four manors), subject to the geld.

The grantees of Roger of Poitou held of these 8½ hides (each hide consisting of 6 carucates,) and 3½ carucates. These several persons held in demesne 4 carucates, besides which there were on the rest of their estates 46 villans, 1 radman, 62 bordarii, 3 slaves, and 2 female slaves. On the part not granted out by Roger there were 3 carucates in demesne, besides which the rest of the estate was occupied by 6 bovarii or herdsmen, 1 radman, and 7 villans.

The whole of the land included under hides and carucates when reduced to carucates amounts to 85½, and, as even slaves male and female are enumerated, it may be inferred that the whole population is stated, viz. 136 families; a number very inadequate either to the cultivation of the ground, or to the consumption of its produce. The whole, consisting of at least 8,500 acres, was estimated at 16*l.* 12*s.* which, supposing money to be 100 times its present value, amounts to no more than 1,660*l.* or little more than 4*s.* per acre; a mere quit-rent, which proves how advantageous was then the condition of a tenant.

The customs of these manors, which extended, with little variation, over the other hundreds within the district, will be explained here. Under the old Saxon government the Thanes or Mesne Lords of the highest order paid two oræ or thirty-two pence for every carucate; and they were equally bound with the villains to repair the King's houses and fish-ponds, and in the forests the haiæ (hedges or ditches by which they were surrounded), and the buckstalls. For neglecting the performance of these services each defaulter paid two shillings, and was bound after payment of the penalty to finish the work. Each of these also was bound to send his reapers to cut the King's corn one day in August.

With respect to the penal code—if any freeman committed theft, or was guilty of forestalling, enticing away a slave, or breaking the King's peace, he incurred a penalty of forty shillings. It was a crude system of jurisprudence which classed together felonies and breaches of the peace; but the heavy penalty upon the last offence, equal at least to 200*l.* at present, proves our Saxon ancestors to have been a very turbulent and refractory race. In the next place, if any one committed rape or manslaughter, or absented himself from the Siremot, that is, the general assembly of the county, without reasonable excuse, he incurred a penalty of ten shillings. As this district belonged to no county, it may be doubted where the Siremot was held; but the next article plainly distinguishes the hundred court. If any man stayed away from the assembly of the hundred, and did not attend the pleas of the same when summoned by the præpositus, or chief constable, he forfeited five shillings. If when the chief constable summoned anyone to assist him in the discharge of his office such person refused, the penalty was four shillings. If anyone wished to leave the King's lands and inhabit elsewhere he paid forty shillings, and migrated whither he would. Everyone paid a relief of forty shillings for entering upon his father's land after his decease. Strange as it may seem there appears, to have been no difference in this respect between the smallest and the largest estates. Besides these are mentioned three distinct obligations, the breach of each of which incurred a penalty of forty shillings: 1st. "Pugna, quæ post sacramentum factum remanebat," by which, I suppose, is meant a breach of the peace after having entered into recognizances to keep it. 2ndly, "Si constrictus justitia præpositi alicui debitum solvebat," which seems to mean, if a man paid any private debt after his goods had been pledged to the præpositus for a sum due to the hundred. And, 3rdly, "Si terminum a præposito datum non attendebat," *i. e.* if, having been bound by the same to attend on a certain day, he did not appear.

Such were the laws and customs of South Lancashire before the Conquest.

Newton Hundret.

Whether it were that the remaining hundreds of this district were surveyed by less able and accurate commissioners, or from whatever cause, there is, henceforth, no distinct enumeration of vills and manors as in West Derby. The first peculiarity under Newton hundred is that there was a church belonging to the whole hundred, as well as the church of St. Oswald belonging to the town of Winwick, if indeed these were not different parts of the same church. Each, however, had a distinct endowment. The quantity of wood or forest land in this hundred (an area of more that sixty square miles) is remarkable. The customs, excepting that the freeholders received pannage of hogs (a valuable payment where there were so many woods) varied little from those of the neighbouring hundred. The number of free men under King Edward is not enumerated; but there were fifteen drenghes, who held as many manors. At the time of the Survey the cultivated land was reduced from at least 22 to 9 carucates; and, in consequence, from a rent of 10*l.* 10*s.* to 4*l.* At that period it was possessed by six drenghs, 12 villans, and 4 bordarii. Of these the drenghs appear to have been military vassals of the next inferior order to thanes: the villans were evidently freemen, who held by rustic services. The bordarii, who were the lowest rank of landowners, appear to have been such as held cottages and small portions of ground by the service of cultivating the bord or demesne lands of the mesne lord, or who made their payments in kind for the use of his table.

Walintune (now Warrington) Hundret.

Walintune itself consisted of one hide, and had three dependent berewicks; but to the hundred itself appertained 34 manors, consisting of 1½ hide and 42 carucates. St. Elfin, the church of the hundred, had the usual endowment of one carucate.

This appears to have been a cultivated tract, as there is no return of wood-land. Here is, unfortunately, no distinct account of the population subordinate to the drenghs, or mesne lords, excepting that there were seven homines, who held a large tract of land within the same. The word *homines* appears to be studiously opposed to *liberi homines*, who embrace the taini, the villani (as the word is used in its ancient and proper sense), and the bordarii; and therefore appears to mean those who, in later times, were called villans, or held lands in villanage. But the feudal senses of the word *homo* are so various that it is not easy to ascertain the precise meaning of it in this and similar passages of Domesday.

The hundred of Warrington appears to have been depreciated more than one-half since the time of the Confessor.

In Blacheburn Hundret.

It appears that at the original institution of hundreds Blackburn was become a considerable place, otherwise it would not have superseded Whalley in giving denomination to the wapentake. This preference, however, may have been occasioned as much by the extent of the township as the populousness of the town, as there were within the place two hides and two carucates of land. Two oxgangs (the only instance in which that fractional measure is mentioned in this Survey,) are specified as the glebe of the church, and 16 acres are the extent of the glebe at present. Yet I would not infer that an oxgang amounted to 23 acres (as Mr. Whitaker has perhaps somewhat too hastily concluded with respect to Kirkmanshulme, the ancient carucate belonging to the church of Manchester, that, because it now consists of 246 statute acres, that was precisely the extent of the carucate). Both the one and the other have probably been extended by inclosures; for there was no township without common, and no common which has not, either wholly or in part, been inclosed. The church of Whalley held its two carucates free from every custom, even from geld, which, besides itself, was the privilege of Winwick only. This hundred, south of Ribble, (for the parishes of Ribchester and Chipping then belonged to Amunderness,) consists of about 300 square miles: of these 25 miles are returned as covered by wood.

The forests, which are wholly unnoticed, occupied at least sixty more. If we continue to understand the hide as consisting of six carucates,[1] and average every carucate at 100 acres Lancashire measure, there was, in corn-land and pasture, 9,150 acres, or nearly 20 square miles: there remain, therefore, little less than two-thirds of the whole extent for wastes and commons appropriated to the several townships or manors. Of these King Edward held in demesne Blackburne, Huncot, Walton, and Pendleton, which are therefore specifically mentioned in the Survey. But besides these, by that unhappy inattention which mocks curiosity and baffles inquiry, throughout the survey of every hundred within this district, excepting Derbei, 28 manors, without name or designation, are generally mentioned as having been held, under the former æra, by as many freemen. Neither will this general enumeration give the number of villages or townships, at the time of the Survey, since we are left in uncertainty whether, as in Derbei, single vills might not contain more manors than one. The whole of this hundred, however, had been given to Roger de Busli and Albert Greslet, who at the time of the Survey had re-granted, to certain "homines," eleven carucates and an half, which were not charged, as the grantors had acquitted them of all burdens for the term of three years. And here again, by the same inattention which marks almost every feature of the Survey as it relates to Blackburn hundred, no return whatever is made of the part which these grantees retained, amounting to eight-ninths of the whole, as to the mode of occupation, the value, or any other circumstance.

In Salford Hundret.

In the manor of Salford, which denominated the hundred, were three hides and 12 carucates of land. Radcliff alone had been the immediate property of King Edward: over the rest of the hundred, as over the whole of this district, he was only lord paramount.

In Manchester were two churches, respectively dedicated to St. Mary and St. Michael, holding one carucate between them (we are not told whether in common), liable to the geld only. In this hundred were somewhat more than 45 miles of native wood. To this hundred, also, in King Edward's time, appertained 21 berewicks, held each by a Saxon thane, for so many manors. They consisted of 11½ hides and 10½ carucates; or, according to the account given of the hide in Derbei hundred, about 700 acres each. One of these thanes, named Gamel, who held two hides in *Recedham* (certainly Rochdale) had certain peculiarities in his customs which have been already explained. Nothing is said of the castle, which, as it gave denomination to Castleton, must have existed before this time, but was now probably in decay; yet seems to have been afterwards restored, as the burgesses of a decayed castle here are mentioned as late as the reign of Edward II. The quantity of land held by Gamel will, I think, warrant the conclusion, that he was thane of the four townships into which that parish is divided.

[1] See under Derbei Hundred.

At the time of Domesday a great revolution had taken place in the state of property here. There remained in demesne two carucates, cultivated by eight slaves and two villans, who occupied one carucate between them.

Of the rest of the hundred Roger of Poitou had already granted out, to be held by military service, to one Nigel (*qu.* De Greslet ?) three hides and half a carucate; to Warin, two carucates; another Warin, $1\frac{1}{2}$ carucate; Goiffrid, one carucate (all Norman names); and to Gamel, perhaps the old lord of *Recedham*, two carucates. These were occupied by three thanes, 39 villans, eight bordarii, one presbyter, and eight slaves, holding in all 22 carucates. Here let it be observed that three hides and seven carucates are described as equal to 22 carucates; therefore, the hide, *here*, consisted of five carucates; the demesne consisted of three carucates. But this is far from accounting for the quantity of land enumerated above, which amounts, at the same rate, to 93 carucates: this will be explained by the difference in the rental. Under King Edward the hundred of Salford yielded 37*l.* 4*s.* At the time of the Survey it was reduced (undoubtedly by depopulation and neglect) to 12*l.*

It is very difficult to conceive the statement here given of the inhabitants to be meant of the entire population; yet how can any enumeration descend lower than slaves? and even comprehending these, only 63 families are accounted for in the hundred of Salford; and how should these consume the produce of 2,500 acres; or how indeed cultivate the ground, of which a large portion must have been under tillage?

In Lailand Hundret.

The reader is, by this time, so well acquainted with the general style and arrangement of the Domesday Survey, as applied to this district, that, under Leyland, I shall only notice one or two peculiarities.

First, though there was a presbyter within this hundred, there was no church. It may be inquired, where did this ecclesiastic officiate? I have long been persuaded that there existed many unendowed chapels,[1] some of which afterwards became parish churches: Leyland may have been one of these. But the absence of a church, in this hundred alone, leads to a conclusion, which Mr. Whitaker had already adopted, that Leyland hundred had, at no long period before the Confessor's time, been separated from that of Blackburn. But a real difficulty remains. For whereas it is said, that in King Edward's time there were 12 carucates held by five men, for so many manors, it is next stated that these same 12 carucates consisted of six hides and eight carucates; which, even supposing the identity of the hide and carucate here, produces the absurdity of saying that 12 are equal to 14. This, however, is easily removed, by supposing that the first 12 has been miswritten by the transcriber for 40; for, in the old numerals, the mistake would be very easy, as XII might catch an hasty eye, and be confounded by XL; which will make the hide in this

[1] This is not inconsistent with what has been said on the subject, p. 58. I only suppose chapels in hundreds where there are no churches.

hundred consist of something between six hides, which it was in Derby hundred, and five as it was in Salford.

Penwortham, the only place in this district which had a castle, was a considerable town, having 21 families; and, as no slaves are mentioned, it had probably many more inhabitants in the whole.

Only 32 families are accounted for in the rest of the hundred, which was partly waste. The reduction in point of value in consequence of devastation which must have taken place since the Confessor's reign is striking. It then yielded 19*l.* 18*s.* 2*d.*; in the latter end of the Conqueror's reign it was reduced to 5*l.* 10*s.* It is thus that tyranny cuts the nerves of its own power.

BOOK II.

CHAPTER THE FIRST.

ECCLESIASTICAL HISTORY.

THE origin of parishes is justly accounted one of the *opprobria* of English topography. Too local and obscure to be recorded in the general histories of the times, and too ancient, for the most part, to be preserved in any episcopal registers now extant, these subdivisions of the ancient diocesan *parœchiæ* usually commenced at an uncertain as well as an early period. It is therefore a circumstance not the least interesting in this history, that it will afford materials for tracing, with considerable exactness, the origin of the church of Whalley nearly to the first preaching of Christianity in the North of England, and also for ascertaining that of its dependent churches and chapels, some of which claim an antiquity higher than the Norman Conquest.

The great extent of the original parish, upwards of 50 miles in length, and containing more than 400 superficial miles, is a proof of its high antiquity. The beauty and fertility of Whalley itself would point it out as an object of prime occupancy in the first re-population of the country after its abandonment by the Romans; and it is pleasing to contemplate the descendants of the first settlers gradually diverging from their first seat, as from a centre, pursuing the course of the valleys which unite near the place, and planting in succession the numerous villages whose names still indicate their Saxon origin. The present parish, from the summit of Little Bowland north to the extremity of Cliviger south, is 30 miles in length, and from the verge of the chapelry of Colne east to the Hyndeburn west, 15 miles. That portion of it which lies south of Ribble has been ascertained to consist of 161 square miles. Little Bowland may be estimated at 10 miles, and the scattered and insulated portions of it which lie intermixed with the parish of Slaidburn, in Yorkshire, at as much more. The county of Lancaster, south of Ribble, measures 1003 square miles; that on the north 616; in all 1619 miles; estimating, therefore, the present parish of Whalley at 180 miles, it is nearly equal to one ninth part of the county of Lancaster, or to 115,200 acres.[1] Though a mere village, the parish which it denominates con-

[1] [According to the Ordnance Survey the area of the present parish of Whalley, including the forests, is 116,909 acres and 38 perches, nearly 183 miles, of which 5,465 acres 1 rood and 6 perches are in Yorkshire. The area of Lancashire, including the foreshore, 119,665 acres, is 1,327,258 acres 3 roods and 2 perches, or nearly 2,043 square miles, not including the foreshore.]

tains within its limits four market-towns, of which one is a borough; and the church has under it 16 existing chapels, besides several which are dilapidated. It is also the mother of seven parish churches, with their several dependent chapels.

Of the foundation of the parent church we will first relate a naked traditional account, preserved in that curious memoir the *Status de Blackburnshire;* [1] and afterwards endeavour to appreciate the value of that account, and to confirm its veracity by such external evidences as can be adduced in its support.

The story is shortly this:

That in the time of Ethelbert King of Kent, who began his reign A.D. 596, Augustine the monk was sent to preach the gospel in England by Gregory Bishop of Rome: that, in the course of his mission, he travelled into Northumbria, and preached at Whalley: in memory of which event certain crosses were erected, which, after more than seven centuries, continued to be called the crosses of Augustine. That, at the same time, a parish church was erected, dedicated to All Saints,[2] and denominated WHITE CHURCH UNDER THE LEIGH;—that the rectors of this church were also lords of the town, and married men, who held it not by presentation from any other patron, but as their own patrimonial estate, receiving institution, however, from the bishops of Lichfield as ordinaries of the place. That these incumbents wrote themselves and were usually styled not rectors but deans; of which the reason is supposed to be, that, on account of the remote and almost

[1] [The best text of the Status de Blackburnshire will be derived from the original edition of the Monasticon of Dugdale, who printed it *Ex authenticis nuper penes Radulfum Assheton Baronettum.*

DE STATU BLAGBORNESHIRE.

Ecclesiæ de Whalleya prima fundatio per Augustinum archiepiscopum Dorovernniæ, aliarumque ecclesiarum infra limites de Blagburneshire. Successio decanorum in eadem. Ejusdem appropriationem et concessio monachorum de Staulawe per Johannem de Lascy comitem Lincolniæ cum multis nato dignissimis.

Memorandum quod tempore Ethelberti Regis Anglorum qui cœpit regnare A.D. DXCVI.—eo videlicet tempore Beatus Augustinus Anglorum Apostolus missus per beatum Gregorium Papam, tertio papatus anno, ad instantiam et rogatum dicti Regis prædicavit in Anglia, et fidem docuit Christianam,—fuit apud Whalley in Blagbornshire Ecclesia quædam parochialis constructa in honore Omnium Sanctorum, in cujus quidem Ecclesiæ cimeterio erant cruces quædam lapideæ tunc erectæ et vocatæ a populo *Cruces beati Augustini*, quæ sub eodem nomine usque hodie ibi durant, appellataque erat, tempore illo, ecclesia supradicta *Alba Ecclesia subtus Legh.* Infra fines autem et limites parochiæ ejusdem Ecclesiæ continebantur tunc temporis tota Blagburnshire et tota Boland, et sic annis plurimis perdurabant. Post hæc autem, crescente fidelium devotione, numeroque credentium augmentato in partibus illis, constructæ fuerunt aliæ tres ecclesiæ infra Blagbornshire; videlicet Ecclesia de Blagborne, Ecclesia de Chepyn, et Ecclesia de Riblechester; parochiæ Ecclesiarum earundem ab invicem distinctæ, et certis undique limitibus designatæ, prout in præsens usque continue perseverant et apud omnes partibus illis innotescunt. His autem temporibus, dum dictæ Ecclesiæ taliter fuerant ordinatæ, non erat in Blagbornshire, apud Clyderhowe, vel alibi, castrum ædificatum, neque capella quæcunque prætre Ecclesias supradictas, nec dominus aliquis qui patrocinium dictarum Ecclesiarum vel alicujus earundem ullatenus vendicaret, sed rector quilibet terram et villam in qua Ecclesia sua fuerat situata, tanquam dotem Ecclesiæ suæ, tenuit et possedit; ipsamque Ecclesiam suam sic dotatam tanquam patrimonium suum et hæreditatem propriam gubernavit; successoremque sibi de filiis vel amicis suis libere subrogavit, interveniente duntaxat acceptatione seu institutione

[2] There is reason to think this account strictly correct; for though it is called in Domesday *Ecclesia S'cæ Mariæ in Wallei*, yet in a charter almost two centuries later (Townley MS.) it is styled *Ecclesia Sanctæ Mariæ et Omnium Sanctorum.*

inaccessible situation of the place, entangled with woods and over-run with wild beasts, the bishops of Lichfield devolved upon them a large portion of ecclesiastical jurisdiction, reserving only to themselves the decision of certain difficult and important cases: that this constitution remained for 470 years before the Conquest; after which period, when the lordship of Blackburnshire fell into the hands of one grantee from the Crown, the absolute independence of this benefice was so far intrenched upon, that, though the order of hereditary succession was still preserved, upon every avoidance commendatory letters to the ordinary were granted by the lords, which *they* seemed to consider as partaking of the nature of a presentation, and the clerks affected to accept merely as a testimonial of their birth and family.

Episcopi Lichefeldiencis; fueruntque dicti rectores de Whalley et de Blagborn, præcipue, homines uxorati, et domini villarum. Et quidam de Whalley *Decani*, non personæ, fuerunt appellati. Cujus causa verisimilis estimatur, quod tempore fundationis ejusdem Ecclesiæ, et per tempora diu postmodum subsequentia, populus illarum partium tam rarus fuerit, tamque indomitus et silvestris, tanta insuper vulpium et ferarum nocivarum ibidem existerat multitudo, necnon locus quasi hominibus inaccessibilis adeo videbatur, quod tam Episcopi ejusdem loci qui pro tempore fuerant quam ipsorum officiales totam jurisdictionem ordinariorum parochiæ supradictæ, pertinentem ad officium communium Decanorum, præfatis rectoribus propter incommoditates prælibatas penitus reliquerunt, et quasi jugiter commiserunt, causis difficilioribus et arduis duntaxat Episcopo reservatis. Unde ex hujus decanatus officio quod successivè et continuè exercebant, non Rectores, sed Decani à populo vocabantur. Ac per hunc modum ordinabantur Ecclesiæ usque ad tempus Regis Willielmi Conquestoris; scilicet per CCCCLXX annos, et post tempus ejusdem Regis Willielmi Conquestoris, usque ad concilium Lateranense (1215), prout ex antiquis et veracibus Cronicis satis liquet. Quis autem dominium de Blagbornshire tenebat ante tempus dicti Regis Willielmi, sub certo in Cronicis non habetur. Vulgaris opinio tenet et asserit quod quot fuerant villæ vel mansæ, seu maneria hominum, tot fuerunt Domini, nedum in Blagbornshire, verum etiam in Rachdale, Tottington, et Boland, et toto convicinio adjacente, quorum nullus de alio tenebat, sed omnes in capite de ipso domino Rege. Memorandum, quod rectores de Whalley ab antiquo fuerunt uxorati, et *Decani* vocabantur, non rectores aut personæ; tenebantque dictam Ecclesiam, una cum Ecclesia de Rachedale, jure quodam hæreditario. Ita quod semper filius patri, vel frater fratri, aut alius parens proximior in jure, possessione dictarum ecclesiarum hæreditariè succedebat; sic videlicet, quod defuncto quocunque Decano de Whalley, statim filius ejus, aut frater, aut alius parens ad quem jus hæreditarium dictarum ecclesiarum pertinebat, offerret se Domino de Blagbornshire tanquam hæredem proximum earum Ecclesiarum, et, acceptis ipsius Domini litteris hoc testantibus, ad episcopum loci ordinarium, presbyteros aliquos, in prædictis ecclesiis, et, earum capellis, servituros, ad eundem Episcopum cum suis et præfati domini litteris transmitteret pro cura parochianorum subeunda, vel saltem pro licentia et potestate ministrandi ecclesiastica sacramenta in eisdem Ecclesiis et Capellis. Et per istum modum regebantur Ecclesiæ supradictæ usque ad Concilium prædictum Lateranense.

Èt sciendum quod primus rector, sive Decanus ecclesiæ de Whalley, de quo, in registro Diocesanorum Lichefeldiensium mentio reperitur, vel cujus nominis est memoria in Chronicis, vel apud plebem, vocabatur Spartlingus, vocabatur Decanus de Whalley, cui successit Liwlphus Cutwolfe filius suus et hæres, Decanus ejusdem Ecclesiæ appellatus. Post hunc successit Cudwolfus ejusdem Ecclesiæ Decanus. Huic etiam successit Henricus senior hæres, similiter ejusdem Ecclesiæ Decanus. Post quem Robertus filius suus et ejusdem Ecclesiæ Decanus; et huic successit Henricus junior, filius et hæres, ejusdem Ecclesiæ Decanus. Cui successit Willielmus Decanus. Post hunc successit Galfridus senior, ejusdem Ecclesiæ similiter Decanus. Iste Galfridus senior desponsavit filiam domini Rogeri de Lascy tunc Domini de Blagbornshire. Huic etiam Galfrido successit Galfridus junior, filius suus et hæres, ejusdem ecclesiæ Decanus; cui successit Rogerus filius etiam suus et hæres, qui ultimus ejusdem Ecclesiæ Decanus existit nominatus, nec ex tunc permittebatur successio hæreditaria in Decanatu, vel in possessione ecclesiæ supradictæ, quæ per homines uxoratos, et successione hæreditaria, ut præmittitur, solebat antiquitùs occupari, obstante Concilio Lateranensi tunc temporis celebrato, clericis quibuslibet, et ecclesiarum rectoribus, continentiam imponente.

With this change of constitution the deanery of Whalley subsisted down to the Lateran Council held in the year 1215, which, by finally prohibiting the marriage of ecclesiastics, put an end to this order of hereditary succession, and occasioned a resignation of the patronage to the chief lord of the fee, after which the church of Whalley sunk into an ordinary rectory; and this also, after the death of the first incumbent, was further degraded, by two successive appropriations, into an impoverished vicarage.

So singular is the outline of our ancient ecclesiastical story: and, when the reader is further told that this account is merely abstracted from a monkish MS. of the fourteenth century, though purporting to be drawn *ex antiquis et veracibus Chronicis*, he will probably see reason for suspending his assent to so extraordinary a narrative till he finds it corroborated by older and more authentic testimonies.

Now it is surely an inauspicious circumstance that this story commences with a falsehood, for no evidence or probability warrants the supposition that Augustine was ever in Northumbria: and it had been well if his monkish admirers had allowed themselves time to reflect, that, by engaging him in this Northern expedition, they have loaded his memory with a reproach which does not belong to it; I mean that they have exposed him to the charge of having instigated the monks of Bonchor. I do not highly esteem the character of this man: his conduct towards the Christian Britons proves him to have had the narrowest views in religion; and he was besides proud, superstitious, and addicted to an indelicate casuistry, which, devoted to celibacy, argues at least a contaminated imagination. But I am unwilling to condemn him, upon such evidence, of all that complication of fraud and cruelty in which his unthinking panegyrists have involved him; and am happy, at the same time, to reserve the apostleship of Whalley for a better and more evangelical man.[1]

Quamobrem dictus Rogerus continenter vixit et ad sacerdotalem se fecit ordinem promoveri. Consideransque quod beneficia ecclesiastica juxta ordinationem concilii supradicti non debebant ex tunc per concessionem hæreditariam occupari, volensque nobili viro domino Johanni de Lascy, comiti Lincolniæ ac domino de Blagbornshire cognato suo placere, et jus patronatus totius Ecclesiæ suæ de Whalley cum capellis, sibi et hæredibus suis confirmare, ac ipsi transferre, cessit Rectoria et Decanatu ecclesiæ suæ prædictæ, ut sic jus præsentandi ad personatum ejusdem ecclesiæ per dictum comitem et hæredes suos, quantum in ipso fuerat, evidentius affirmaret, solum sibi retinens, per assensum Episcopi, ejusdem Ecclesiæ vicarium, unde Dominus Comes ad personatum dictæ Ecclesiæ de Whalley quendam clericum suum Petrum de Cestria præsentavit. Qui quidem Petrus extitit primus ejusdem Ecclesiæ persona nominatus, atque ad præsentationem ejusdem domini comitis ab episcopo Lichfeldensi Alexandro admissus ad eundem personatum et institutione canonicè ac inductus et eandem Ecclesiam extunc tenuit et possedit per totam vitam suam, videlicet per LIX (quinquaginta novem) annos et amplius. Idem tamen Petrus, pro tempore dicti Rogeri, non habuit de præfata Ecclesia nisi quinquaginta marcas annuæ pensionis nomine rectoriæ suæ, et dictus Rogerus totum residuum Ecclesiæ habuit dum advixit, nomine vicariæ, prout in literis præsentationis et institutionis dicti Petri, et ordinationis Episcopi inde factis, satis liquet. Huic autem Petro successerunt in personatu prædicto, Religiosi viri, abbas et conventus vocati quondam de Stanlaw, nuper de Whalley, et intraverunt in manerium de Whalley, Domino Gregorio de Norbury tunc Abbate, VII id. Ap. anno regni regis Edwardi viginti quatuor, ætatis vero domini Henrici de Lascy comitis Lincolniæ quadragesimo septimo, A.D. M.CC.XCVI. anno bissextili, littera dominicali G. &c.

[1] My sentiments on this subject are precisely the same with those of Dr. Smith, the learned edition of Bede. "Id videtur," says he, speaking of this very story, "erratum esse confundentis Augustinum cum Paullino. Sed tribuunt Augustino scriptores iter boreale consilio multum diverso, hinc ad elevandos (in the English, not the classical sense of

In fact, Augustine seems to have been to the monks what the Theban Hercules was to the Greeks, an object of fond and thoughtless devotion, on whom they were anxious to accumulate the exploits, and to divert the honours, of his brethren. Thus, precisely in another instance nearly akin to the present, they have adorned him with trophies not his own. "In one Christmas Day," says a fragment quoted by Camden,[1] "Austin baptized above ten thousand men, and consecrated the River Swale." Yet the whole story, with concomitant circumstances, is related of Paulinus by Bede, whose authority is incontestible.

But the credibility of ancient facts is sometimes little affected by an error in the names of persons to whom they are ascribed: so that, if the gospel were not preached at Whalley in this century by Augustine, it is far from following that it was not preached there at all in that period; and still further, there is not only evidence to establish the probability of the fact, but to ascribe it to the known apostle of the North of England. This evidence, it must be allowed, is but circumstantial, though surely strong, That Paulinus was diligently employed, under the the auspices of Edwyn, in preaching and baptizing throughout the provinces of *Deira* and *Bernicia*, that vast multitudes flocked to him to receive the ordinance of Baptism, and that he usually chose the banks of rivers as the scene of his ministry, for the convenience of baptizing, is recorded by Bede. His presence at Dewsbury is moreover attested by a cross with an inscription, formerly extant, to that effect; and though the three crosses of Whalley,[2] to which tradition has with one voice assigned the office of commemorating the same event under another name, have no remaining inscriptions, yet their obeliscal form and ornaments of fretwork,[3] used in common by the Norwegians, Saxons, Danes, and other Northern nations, prove their antiquity to be considerable, and probably of no later date than Paulinus. The æra, therefore, of this memorable event, the first preaching of the gospel at Whalley, may, in all probability, be fixed between the years 625, when his ministry commenced, and 631, when he was finally driven out of *Northumbria*[4] by the death of his royal convert.[5]

In one other circumstance my authority must be received with some abatement, as the church of Whalley could not have been exactly contemporary with Paulinus. On this

that word) ejus labores, auctoritatem et miracula; illinc, ad affigendum illi Monachorum Benchoriensium cædem, pari utrinque, ut videtur, veritatis specie."—Note in Bedam, l. 2, c. xiv.

[1] Gibson's Ed. vol. i. p. 88.

[2] "One thing I much notid, was 3 Crossis standing in row at the est ende of the Chapelle Garth. They were thinges *antiquissimi operis*, and monuments of sum notable men buried there: so that, of al the old monasterie of Ripon" (the work of Wilfrid) "and the toun, I saw no likely tokens left, after the depopulation of the Danes in that place, but only the waulles of our Lady Chapelle and the Crosses."—Leland, Itinerary, vol. i. f. 96.

[3] The cross in the churchyard of Bakewell in Derbyshire, and those in the churchyard of Penrith, &c. are in the same taste.

[4] It makes a difference of two miles, only that, according to the hypothesis which I have endeavoured to establish in this edition, Whalley was actually in Mercia. Considerable portions, however, of the parish, even of the present parish, were certainly in Northumbria.

[5] Bede has given an excellent original portrait of our Northern apostle. He described him to have been "vir longæ staturæ, paululum incurvus, nigro capillo, facie macilentâ, naso adunco pertenui, venerabilis simul et terribilis aspectu."—Eccl. Hist. l. ii. c. 16, § 136.

head the testimony of Bede is decisive. "Nondum enim," says the venerable historian, "oratoria vel baptisteria in ipso exordio nascentis ibi ecclesiæ poterant ædificari, attamen in Campodono, ubi tunc villa regia erat, fecit basilicam." This, therefore, and the church of York, were the only places of worship in the Northumbrian kingdom contemporary with the ministry of Paulinus. But the place where he had preached at Whalley would probably be held sacred; crosses[1] would be erected, and divine offices performed there, from the beginning; and the climate would soon admonish the most zealous and hardy congregation, that warmth and shelter are necessary to undisturbed devotion. Such are the trifling abatements with which the testimony of our ancient chronicler is to be received.

The second particular in this account capable of receiving confirmation from external testimony, is the appellation of *White Church under the Leigh*. The probability is, that, after the example of the original church of York, it had first been built of wood, which was afterwards replaced by stone. Hence the name of *Candida Casa*, or Whiteherne, in Galloway, a contemporary or rather prior erection, for which Bede assigns the following reason: "Vulgo vocatur 'ad Candidam Casam,' eo quod ibi ecclesiam de lapide, insolito Brittonibus more, fecerit.[2]" The ancient erections of wood were probably turned black from age, and these rare and recent edifices of stone would, for some time, exhibit a very striking contrast to the eye.[3]

This hypothesis is remarkably confirmed by a passage in Harding's Chronicle:

Kynge Arthure then in Aualon so died,
Wher he was buried in a Chapell fayre,
Whiche nowe is made and fully edified;
[The mynster churche this daye] of great repayre
Of Glastenbury, where nowe he hath his leyre;
But then it was called the blacke Chapell
Of our Lady, as chronycles can tell.

The lxxxiiii chapiter, Ellis Ed. 1812, p. 147.

This black chapel seems to have been made of wood, but in the time of Harding it was certainly "made, and fully edified," of stone.

Kynge Arthure than in Aualon so diede,
Wher he was buried beside a Chapell faire,
Which nowe is made and fully edifiede,
Weste fro the Mynstre Churche of grete repaire,
Of Glastonbury, where nowe he hath his laire,
But than it was called the Blacke Chapell
Of oure Lade, as Chroniclers can tell. Harl. 661, f. 55b.

[1] An ancient form used in the consecration of a churchyard was the erection of a cross in the centre, accompanied with processions, singing, and sprinkling of holy water.—Gough's Sepulchral Monuments, vol. ii. Pref. p. 177.

[2] Eccl. Hist. l. iii. c. 4, § 158.

[3] "Interea sanctum Corpus de illa quam diximus Ecclesiola (de virgis, p. 142) in aliam translatum quæ Alba Ecclesia vocabatur." Sim. Dunelm. p. 145. It is remarkable that a perpendicular rock in Cliviger, the property of the author, blanched by exposure to the weather, has immemorially been called The White Kirk.

But, what adds great weight to the circumstantial evidence adduced in proof of the existence of a church here at a very early period is that the place itself has already been proved to exist in the eighth century, and that it is one of the few towns which, either on their own account or of events connected with them, have obtained a place on the solitary map of the Northumbrian kingdom. Without a previous knowledge of this circumstance, the tradition of a church must have been applied to prove the existence of the place; but now the positive evidence for that fact may be employed to confirm the tradition.

Dismissing, therefore, the name only of Augustine, the particulars of our traditionary account, compared with their respective confirmations from external testimony, will stand thus:

	I.
TRADITION.	CONFIRMATION.
The gospel was preached at Whalley in the beginning of the seventh century, and Whalley stands nearly at the confluence of the Ribble, the Calder, and the Hodder.	At this precise period Paulinus employed six years in preaching and baptizing through Deira, Bernicia, and the northern part of Mercia, and usually frequented the banks of considerable rivers.
	II.
This event was recorded by the erection of three crosses.	His preaching at Dewsbury was recorded by a cross, and the form and decorations of those remaining at Whalley accord with the period assigned to them.
	III.
A church was erected upon the same place, and called the White Church under the Leigh, from some peculiarity about its appearance.	Stone churches of that period were actually denominated White Churches, and they were remarked as an unusual mode of building.

To all these proofs is to be added another confirmation, which contributes greatly to their force, namely, that the compiler of the Monkish record was, probably, ignorant of them all.

Other particulars in this account which require to be established, are, that the incumbents of the ancient church of Whalley were married men; were lords of the town; and were entitled, not parsons or rectors, but Deans.

The first of these, besides that the constitution of the Saxon church is known to have permitted marriage in the secular clergy, will follow from the fact of the benefice having passed in hereditary succession, which remains to be proved in its place.

The second particular, namely, an union of the character of incumbent, and lord of the manor, though unusual, is far from being singular, and it is to be accounted for thus:

At the first distribution of England into dioceses, the endowment was common, and tithes and oblations constituted one general fund which was applied by the Bishop, under certain regulations, 1st, to the support of himself and his own family or college of priests resident at the cathedral church; and, 2ndly, to the maintenance of the country clergy, whether itinerant, as they originally were, or partly itinerant and partly resident, or wholly resident, as they gradually became.[1]

But, in order still further to encourage the erection of churches, which were as yet very inadequate to the general diffusion of religious knowledge, and the general communication of the comforts of religious worship, lords of manors were allured to these acts of munificence within their domains by a concession from the ordinary of the right of patronage, which by the primitive constitution belonged solely to himself, and by the privilege of annexing in perpetuity all tithes and oblations accruing within their own demesne to the service of that particular church. To these was uniformly added a portion of land or glebe, absolutely necessary to the accommodation of an incumbent at a time when almost all the wants of life must be supplied from the immediate produce of the earth.[2]

But though, in general, parishes and manors were for this reason commensurate through the kingdom, and manors and advowsons passed together, yet in these barren Northern tracts the fact was far otherwise. Here no single person in the Saxon times was lord of more than a single vill or township;[3] yet the original parish of Whalley must have consisted of more than 50. This is a strong collateral proof of its high antiquity; for, if we suppose some Saxon lord of Ƕpælleȝ to have erected his White Church under the Leigh before the existence of any other place of worship for many miles around, the people, anxious as they then were for the blessings of religious instruction, would flock thither in multitudes from every quarter, and would be willing to repay the priest for the spiritual benefits they received from him, in tithes and offerings. I mean not here to enter upon a question so much in agitation between Mr. Selden and his antagonists as that of arbitrary consecrations;[4] it is of no importance to the present argument, and the other hypothesis will answer my purpose as well. For the bishop of the diocese, concurring with the devotion of the faithful, and seeing no tendency in the lords of neighbouring manors to erect churches upon their demesnes, might, by his own authority, allot to the incumbent all tithes and oblations accruing from the several manors and townships, however remote, whose inhabitants frequented his church.

Either of these hypotheses will account very satisfactorily for the vast extent of our Northern parishes, Whalley in particular, and for the number of manors and townships which they contain.

[1] See Dr. Newton's Pluralities Indefensible, p. 56. See also Selden's History of Tithes, c. ix. pa. 4.

[2] This hypothesis will bring down the foundation of the church of Whalley about a century lower than the period assigned to it by the author of the Status de Blackburnshire. For I do not recollect an instance of lay foundations of churches till about the year 700, when there are two mentioned by Bede, one erected by Puch, and another by Addi. H. Eccl. l. v. c. 4 and 5. By the year 800 however, they appear to have been common, if we are to credit the charters of confirmation made by Bertulph king of Mercia, and others, to the abbey of Croyland, on the authority of Ingulphus. [These are now generally regarded as fabrications.—J. G. N.]

[3] "Quot fuerunt villæ, tot fuerunt Domini." Status de Blackburnshire.

[4] By this term is meant the right of dedicating tithes accruing from a manor or demesne to any church within the same diocese, at the owner's discretion.

But the extent of the parish of Whalley, and the great value of its tithes and offerings, even in those days of wretched husbandry and slender population, must now be applied to the solution of another difficulty in the constitution of this benefice.

Its incumbents were themselves lords of the town.

We find from Domesday Book that the Church of St. Mary held in Wallei two carucates of land, free from every custom. Now this was not a glebe which could ever have been set apart by the founder for the use of an incumbent, but it was in fact the whole domain of the manor itself.[1] As, therefore, it is scarcely to be conceived that a founder, even in times of the most fervid devotion, would strip himself of his whole estate for the endowment of a parish church, only one other reason of this circumstance remains to be given, namely, that, in consequence of the immense extent of the original parish, what was at first an accessory outgrew its principal; or, in other words, that, the advowson becoming far more valuable than the manor to which it was regardant, the lords, who were also patrons, saw the convenience of qualifying themselves by inferior orders for holding so rich a benefice; and thus the manor itself, having passed for ten descents through a succession of ecclesiastics, ceased to be considered as a lay fee, and grew to be confounded with the glebe of the church.

This hypothesis is countenanced by two singular charters, in one of which, without date, but between the years 1198 and 1208, an incumbent of this church grants to Ughtred the clerk, son of Gospatric de Samlesbury, certain lands to be held *de ecclesia de Whalley, et de me et de successoribus meis in feudo et hæreditate libere solute integre et quiete ab omni sæculari servitio.*[2] And another, somewhat later, grants lands in Dounum, *tenend. et habend. de Deo et omnibus sanctis et de ecclesia de Whalley in feodo et hæreditate libere quiete et pacifice.* I suppress the names and styles of these grantors that I may not forestall evidence which will more properly appear under the next head. But how is it to be accounted for that an incumbent should be permitted to alienate lands in fee to be held of him and of his successors, on any other supposition than that they were originally the demesnes of the manor, and had now acquired a mixed character, being treated partly as glebe and partly as a lay fee?

The account further informs us that these incumbents were styled not rectors or parsons but Deans, and that the reason of this name was, that a certain portion of ecclesiastical jurisdiction was delegated to them by the Bishops of Lichfield, on account of the remote and almost inaccessible situation of the parish.

Here, in the first place, we are not to confound the office of the Deans of Whalley with that of rural deans, a dignity of high antiquity, and once of great importance in the church. For in fact rural deaneries were so far from being hereditary that they were not even offices for life; besides that the jurisdiction of the Deans of Whalley extended merely over their own original parish, whereas that of rural deans originally comprehended ten,

[1] At the time of the Domesday Survey no manor or vill within the parish contained more than two carucates, and not many more than one. *Vide* The History of Property.

[2] Townley MSS. [Coucher Book, tit. 5, No. lv. p. 286; No. lxxxvii. p. 320.]

and afterwards an indefinite number of parishes. Besides it has never been discovered that the Deans of Whalley used an official seal at all, whereas the rural deans had always a seal inscribed with their office, but without a name.

In the same account it is stated that ten persons had held this office in succession, besides an indefinite number of others whose memories are lost in remote antiquity. Those whose names have been here preserved are Spartlingus, Liwlphus Cutwulph, Cudwolphus, Henry the elder, Robert, Henry the younger, William, Geoffry the elder, Geoffry the younger, and Roger.

Should any degree of incredulity remain with respect to the truth of this part of the narrative, it is, like most of the former, capable of confirmation from external evidence. For, though some of the former names in this catalogue rest on the single authority of our monkish record, as we have no remaining charters relating to this parish prior to the reign of Henry I. yet the following personages actually appear either as parties or witnesses to deeds of which the originals or authentic copies are still preserved. Dns. Galfr. Dec. de Þwalley. Joh. frat. Galfr. Dec.; Henr. et Gaufr. fil. Gauf. Dec.; Dns. R. Decanus de Whalley, Ric. frat. ejus; Galfr. fil. Robti. Decani de Whalleia.[1] After these attestations to his veracity, our old chronicler is surely entitled to credit for the earlier part of the line.

But there is a circumstance related of one of these which may be shown at least to be probable, and in character. It is recorded in the same narrative of Liwlphus, second in the catalogue, that he acquired the name of Cutwulph from having cut off the tail of an animal of that species, while hunting in the forest of Rossendale,[2] at a place called Ledmesgreve.[3] On this account I have to observe that the chronology of the line proves this circumstance to have happened about the reign of Canute, and a mere falsary of the reign of Edward III. would almost certainly have acquiesced in the vulgar story of the extinction of wolves by Edgar.[4] But, secondly, the Deans of Whalley, like other ancient and dignified ecclesiastics, were mighty hunters, and enjoyed the right of chace, first to a considerable extent in other manors adjoining to their own domains, and secondly within the forests themselves. The first of these facts is ascertained by the following record in the Coucher Book of Whalley:

> Iste sunt mete infra quas rectores ecclesie de Whalleye ratione ecclesie sue predicte pro libito solebant omni tempore anni venari, videlicet, incipiendo apud le Holpselogh juxta Twisilton usque Downom, et sic per totam terram de magna Merlay et parva usque Hasschaldene supra Penhulton, et sic per altam viam que jacet infra boscum de Penhulton et forestam de Penhull, et sic ultra le Rugg in Kruseteclogh usque aquam de Caldre."[5]

[1] Towneley MSS.

[2] Wolfenden in Rossendale, and Wolfstones in Cliviger, both attest the existence of this animal there, when those names were imposed.

[3] There is a place of the name of Levengreve (Leofwine-greve) not far from Whitforth, but this was never within the forest. I suspect, therefore, that the real scene of this adventure was a place called in the perambulation of Brandwood under Roger de Lacy, about the year 1200, Senesgrene, probably corrupted from Lenesgreve.

[4] I shall hereafter apply the same argument to prove the authenticity of the laws of Canute.

[5] Coucher Book of Whalley, tit. v. p. 334.

But they also claimed and exercised a right of hunting in the forests; for, the abbey and convent having succeeded to all the territorial rights of the deanery, Henry de Lacy exacted an express renunciation of this right from the first abbot on the translation of his house to Whalley.[1]

For the fact of the Dean's exercising spiritual jurisdiction we must (and I think may safely) take the word of our old and well-informed chronicler, for no other evidence can now be adduced on the subject.

On the whole then it appears that the Dean of Whalley was compounded of patron, incumbent, ordinary, and lord of the manor, an assemblage which may possibly have met in later times and in some places of exempt jurisdiction, but at that time probably an unique in the history of the English Church.[2]

Yet a character almost exactly resembling this may actually be traced in the church of Ireland, which, as Mr. Selden[3] observes, bore in many respects a strong resemblance to that of our own country: this was the Corban, Plebanus, or Chorepiscopus, of whom Archbishop Usher communicated a learned and curious account to Sir Henry Spelman;[4] not however distinguishing with his usual accuracy between this ecclesiastic and the archipresbyter or rural dean, an error into which he seems to have been led by Isidore Moscovius. The *Plebanus* of the canon law was, properly speaking, incumbent of a mother church out of which one or more dependent parishes had been taken, and of which he retained the patronage. In an inferior sense it may be yet applied to the parochial incumbents of great benefices, who have the patronage of several dependent chapels.[5] If the *Plebanus* had perpetual chaplains (or a vicar and chaplain) in his own church, he was a dignitary, and always occupied the first stall in his own choir.

Nearly akin to this Plebanus, if not altogether the same, was the Corba, Corban, Comorbanus, all corruptions of the word Chorepiscopus. The office, and the inferior office of Herenach, which much resembled it, was hereditary; was held by persons sometimes only in the inferior orders, and sometimes in none, but always literate persons. The glebe of the Herenach was called *honorem villæ*, or the lordship of the town. Both received institution from the ordinary, and exercised an inferior jurisdiction, one over the tenants of the termonland or ecclesiastical demesnes committed to him, the other over the clergy of his plebania or corbanate. All these are instances of a strong tendency to the seculariza-

[1] Coucher Book of Whalley.

[2] It is not here meant that the mere fact of hereditary succession in benefices was at all unusual in those early times, notwithstanding the general irregularity of the practice, and the particular canons which were directed against it, as that of the synod of Westminster, 3rd Hen. I. "Ut filii presbyterorum non sint hæredes ecclesiarum patrum suorum." But this difficulty was obviated by an *investiture*, which enabled an incumbent, who was also patron, to transfer, during his lifetime, all his rights in a benefice, without the intervention either of bishop or archdeacon. It appears, in particular, that St. Peter's church in Cambridge was thus conveyed. Rot. Plac. 6 Rich. I. rot. 1; and Selden, c. xii. § 4.

[3] History of Tithes, c. ix. par. 4.

[4] Vid. Spelm. Gloss. *in voc.* Corba.

[5] "Plebania est aliud genus beneficii, et majus quam rectoria: habet sub se capellas, et dignitatem esse putant interpretes." Syntagma juris canon. l. xv. c. 24. Weever applies this to our *side-wasted* parishes in Lancashire, and particularly to Whalley. Fun. Mon. p. 180.

tion of ecclesiastical property in very early times, a natural consequence of enormous landed endowments, which always lead either to violent resumptions on the part of the Crown, or, as in the instance before us, to a silent transition from patronage to property, and from the character of incumbent to that of impropriator. It is a fact little known, that fifteen persons held the archbishopric of Armagh itself in hereditary succession, and of these eight were married men without episcopal consecration, but all literate persons.[1]

With what exactness do the several characters of these kindred offices in the Church of Ireland apply to the Dean of Whalley!

For, like the Herenach, he had *honorem villæ*; like the Plebanus (which, however, was not confined to the Irish Church), he had patronage and jurisdiction over several dependent churches, together with a vicar and chaplain in his own; and like the Corban his function was hereditary, tenable also by persons in inferior orders and compatible with the married state.

That he was lord of the town has already been proved; that he was patron of one, at least, of the filial churches, will be proved hereafter; that he exercised jurisdiction over all has been asserted by our author, whose veracity we have been able to confirm in many instances, and to impugn in none; that he had a vicar and chaplain may be proved by the attestations of charters in which "Rog. Rect. *or* Dec., Ughtred Cler., et Gilb. Cap. de Whalley"[2] appear together, and by the stalls, three in number, which yet remain in the choir of the parish church. Lastly, that he was married and had received only the lower orders, is demonstrated by the example of the last Dean, of whom it is affirmed, in contradistinction to his predecessors, "quod continenter vixit et ad sacerdotalem se fecit ordinem promoveri."

Another proof of extreme accuracy in the Status de Blackburnshire is the following. We have before observed, that in this memoir there is an hint of some dependence to which the Deans of Whalley were reduced under the lords of Blackburnshire after the Conquest, which, though it did not break the order of hereditary succession in the benefice, imposed upon them a necessity of obtaining commendatory letters from the lord previous to institution. This was undoubtedly regarded by the latter as a species of patronage: and accordingly, when upon a temporary forfeiture of the Lacies, in the reign of Henry the First, this great fee became vested in Delaval, the latter actually granted to the priory of Kirkby (Pontefract) in Cestriashyre,[3] "Walleyæ ecclesiam et ad eam pertinentia, et

[1] Spelman's Gloss. *in voce* Corba.

[2] Townley MSS.

[3] Cestershyria. The antiquity of this charter will be considered hereafter: but I cannot help remarking here the peculiarity of this description. In Domesday Book we have seen that what is now the part of Lancashire south of Ribble appears to be classed with neither county, but is surveyed by itself under the title of "Terra inter Ripam et Mersam." But in Delaval's charter it is plainly considered as part of Cheshire; and, of the dependent parishes, Slaidburn is afterwards granted by name to the same priory of Kirkby, and the churches of Blackburn and Rochdale are not mentioned at all, because the former had already become private property, and the latter was not yet in existence. It is further remarkable that St. Michael in the Castle is described as a chapel, though endowed with tithes, and St. Magdalen in the Town, together with Colne and Burnley, are called churches, though it does not appear that they ever received tithes at all.

capellam castri de Clyderhow cum decimationibus omnium terrarum dominicalium mei ejusdem castri, et ibi ecclesiam beatæ Mariæ Magdalenæ, et ecclesiam de Calna, et ecclesiam de Brunlaia." A subsequent restoration of the Lacies prevented this alienation from taking effect; but it was contested with the true pertinacity of monks even after the foundation of the abbey, and a lapse of two centuries.

CASE OF THE MONKS OF PONTEFRACT.

[Dugdale, Monasticon Anglicanum, i. p. 658 and p. 898, ed. 1682; edit. of 1825, v. p. 127 and p. 642.]

Quidam antecessorum Comitis Lincolniæ, Hugo de Lavale nomine, dedit jus patronatus Eccl. de Whalley priori et conventui de Pontefracto per cartam suam quem habent, qui præsentaverunt ad eam successive A. B. C. D. qui omnes prædicti admissi et instituti fuerunt; inter quos erat quidam nomine Sparlinge, quo defuncto, successit ei quidam Liwlphus qui cognominabatur Cuttewulfe, eo quod sedens quadam vice in foresta de Rossendale, ad locum qui vocatur Ledmesgreve, respiciendo canes suos currentes, lupum quendam juxta se currentem decaudavit. Defuncto vero prædicto Liwlpho, quidam prædecessor dicti Comitis, vacante dicto prioratu et in sua custodia existente, præsentavit nomine custodis quendam Galfridum ad eandem, qui duxit in uxorem filiam Gospatricii Dni de Samlesbury, de quo genuit filios et filias, de quorum progenie multi adhuc nobiles in illis partibus manent. Defuncto prædicto Galfrido, successit ei Galfridus filius ejus, quasi nomine hæreditario, gratia super hoc prius à curia Romana impetrata; quo defuncto quidam antecessor dicti Comitis præsentavit quendam Rogerum, et post ipsum Petrum de Cestria, prædictis priore et conventu reclamare non audentibus. Vivente autem Petro de Cestria prædictus Comes Lincolniæ Henricus de Lasey nomine dedit patronatum prædictæ Ecclesiæ de Whalley, Coventrensis et Lichefeldensis diocesis, Abbati et Conventui de Stanlawe ordinis Cisterciensis dictæ diocesis, recepta prius ab eis litera obligatoria quod, quotiescumque vacaret, præsentarent ad eam quem ipse aut hæredes sui vellent, et non alium, nisi possent eam in proprios usus impetrare; qua impetrata augmentarent numerum solitum monachorum, ita quod ab illo tempore essent sexaginta ubi prius fuerunt quadraginta, et quod monasterium suum ad territorium dictæ Ecclesiæ transferrent. Postea Nicholaus papa Quartus concessit eis appropriationem ejusdem (cedente vel decedente Rectore), salvis congruis portionibus pro Vicaria. Postea papa Bonifacius revocavit appropriationes concessas per prædictum prædecessorem suum Nicholaum, de quibus non habebatur ipso die jus in re licet ad rem. Postea decessit prædictus Petrus de Cestria octodecimo kalendas Januarii anno Domini Millesimo ducentesimo nonagesimo quarto, quondam ad præsentationem avi dicti Comitis, id est, domini Johannis de Lasey, institutus, qui in vita sua nunquam cedere voluit; quo defuncto prædictus Henricus de Lasey comes, tanquam in jure proprio existens, ingressus est ad dictam ecclesiam, dictos religiosos multis diebus excludendo, qui pro ingressu habendo remiserunt et quietum clamaverunt dicto comiti et hæredibus suis in perpetuum quandam capellam infra limites dictæ Ecclesiæ existentem, valentem annuatim C marcas sterlingorum, et alias multas libertates infra forestas dicti comitis, dictæ ecclesiæ ab antiquo spectantes, ut venandi et feras omni tempore anni ad libitum capiendi; et sic, lectis ante fores dictæ ecclesiæ super hiis instrumentis, die Purificationis sanctæ Mariæ post revocationem prædictam, adepti sunt ingressum, nullum jus ad appropriationem prædictam, ut prædictum est, habentes, præsente populo non parvo et clamante Væ vobis Simoniacis! Postea composuerunt cum domino Rogero de Meauland tunc episcopo contra hujusmodi ingressum provocante, appellante, et sequestrum interponente, de CCCL marcis sterlingorum; de quibus post obitum suum satisfecerunt executoribus dicti episcopi de centum libris sterl. obligantes se et successores suos ad anniversarium dicti episcopi imperpetuum pro residuo faciendum, et sic, pacto et prætio mediantibus, adepti sunt possessiones dictæ Ecclesiæ, nullum jus habentes ad ejusdem appropriationem. Et sic lapsu temporis duodecem annorum devolvitur collatio ejusdem ad Dom^{m} Papam, eo quod de jure vacaret per idem tempus. Ex præmissis patet quod Prior et Conventus prædicti habent cartam et sesynam, quod non est aliud nisi præsentatio cum effectu. Abbas et Conventus prædicti habent cartam solomodo sine sesyna, eo quod nunquam præsentaverunt. Ecclesia vero prædicta valet singulis annis ad minus deductis expensis quinquaginta marcas sterlingorum. Qualiter postea impetraverunt confirmationem prædicti Papæ Bonifacii (nulla facta mentione de conventionibus prædictis), et confirmationem Episcopi qui tunc temporis fuit, pro mille marcis sterlingorum, et confirmationem capitulorum Coventrensis et Lichefeldensis et loci Archidiaconi pro quindecem libris sterlingorum annuæ pensionis, imperpetuum solvendis, non est opus exprimere. Set errores prædictos radicis infectæ. Hec autem sciendum quod omnia præmissa notoria sunt, et quod ab ingressu dictorum religiosorum in dictum beneficium de malo in pejus, usque ad hodiernum diem, ad scandalum cleri et populi dissentio semper pullulavit. Et sciendum quod omnes Rectores dictæ Ecclesiæ usque ad tempus domini Petri de Cestria cognominabantur Decani et non Rectores. Nuper decessit Vicarius dictæ ecclesiæ, cujus portio, secundum ordinationem ordinariorum, valebat centum libras sterlingorum. Et præsentatus est ad vicariam, nuper ordinatam per dominum Papam, nunc quidam capellanus, contra cujus ordinationem appellatum est per Episcopum et Archidiaconum, et causa per impletionem, similiter et collatio eo quod de jure et de facto per annum et dimidium jam vacavit, devolvitur ad Papam.

Such is this singular and important case, very artfully but untruly stated by the prior and convent of Pontefract, or their advocates. In the first place, it was their object to prove the *jus in re*, and therefore, forgetting that Hugh de la Val, from whom they derived their title to the benefice, lived in the time of Stephen, they pretend to prove a presentation, in the person in Liulphus Cudwlph, who lived before the Conquest. In the next place they pretend that an ancestor of the then Earl of Lincoln presented, during a vacancy, as patron of the convent; and that in consequence, on the next avoidance, the representative of the Lacy family presented as in his own right, but of this there is neither proof nor probability. Delaval's charter appears never to have been confirmed; in consequence of which defect his grant to the priory of Pontefract was invalidated, and the advowson returned, with the other estates of the Lacy family, to their former owners.

The later transactions which took place between the Earl of Lincoln, Bishop Meuland, and the monks of Stanlaw were shamefully simoniacal, and the convent of Pontefract expose them *con amore*; but the value of the rectory of Whalley was greatly overrated.

But there is another circumstance in its constitution which may seem almost equally singular with the institution of the Deanery; and that is, the existence of an endowed Vicarage before an appropriation of the Rectory.

This, however, like the other, is a genuine remnant of Saxon antiquity: for, though it has been remarked that vicarages, in the present sense of the word (endowed, that is, in perpetuity with a certain portion of glebe, tithes, and offerings, by an act of the ordinary), rarely occur before the reign of John,[1] yet the institution of vicars in a larger and more general sense is certainly coëval with the first donations of benefices to religious houses, and evidently arose out of the necessity of the case. Neither were these substitutes merely stipendiary curates removable at pleasure, for they appear to have held their offices by institution; but their provision at first was arbitrary, and the subsequent endowment

[1] There is, however, one instance of an endowed vicarage as early as 1129, 29 or 30 Hen. I. Kennet's Par. Ant. p. 90.

of vicarages seems to have arisen from a general abuse of this discretion in the regulars, of which bishops were willing to take advantage, as it contributed at once to an extension of their own authority, and to the independence of a depressed and useful body of men.

But a circumstance which approaches much nearer to the case before us is this: it appears from Domesday, that many benefices were even then, wholly or in part, fallen into the hands of laymen; and the minister actually officiating in such churches, whether he received a portion of the tithes, or by what means soever he were supported, was, both then and later, called "Presbyter qui ecclesiæ servit,[1] sacerdos, clericus ecclesiæ," &c. though a little before that time Thomas, Archbishop of York, 17 William I. in a general confirmation to the priory of Durham, enjoins "ut Vicarios[2] in eis libere ponant." This is the first instance in which the word has occurred to me.

If, therefore, these substitutes were in actual use from the year 800,[3] when appropriations of churches founded by laymen first occur, and were wanted alike in benefices appropriate and those which had been seized by laymen, there can be no doubt that they would be equally employed by the semi-secular Deans of Whalley; and that they were, in fact, so employed, may be proved by the example of the last Dean, who, in conformity to the decree of the Lateran Council, having aspired to the Order of Priesthood, though he resigned the Deanery, retained, or rather presented himself to, the vicarage, with its rights, which were not inconsiderable; for we find that Peter de Cestria, the first and only Rector, who was the presentee of John de Lacy, received from the benefice, during the life of Roger, only a pension of fifty marks, or about a third part of the income.[4] The largeness

[1] Domesday, in Clamoribus Everwykschyre.

[2] Seld. Hist. Tithes, c. 12, part i. and Rog. Hoveden, part i. f. 263. This injunction shows that the ordinary did not yet ordain vicarages, but exhort patrons and lay possessors of benefices to the appointment and liberal payment of vicars.

[3] Seld. Hist. Tithes, c. 9, § 4.

[4] [That portion of the monastic memoir *De Statu Blagborneshire* which has been printed in p. 68 has related how Roger the last Dean, during his lifetime, transferred the church of Whalley to the patronage of John Earl of Lincoln, the Earl presenting thereto his clerk Peter de Chester, but at the same time the Dean retaining to himself, under the name of Vicar, all the emoluments, except a yearly pension of sixty marks. Dr. Whitaker derived the number "fifty" from the memoir *De Statu Blagborneshire*, as printed in the Monasticon, but that "sixty" is correct appears as well from various other MSS. as from the Earl of Lincoln's letter of presentation addressed to Alexander de Stavenby, Bishop of Coventry and Lichfield 1224-1238, which is introduced into the Coucher Book of Whalley, *tit.* 5, No. lxii. p. 293, with these remarks:—

"Quia vero quidam dixerunt, licet male, quod Prior et conventus de Pontefracto præsentaverunt dominum Petrum de Cestria ad Ecclesiam de Whalleye, sequitur hic transcriptum præsentationis pro dicto Petro ad dominum Coventr. et Lich. episcopum facto per dominum Joh. de Lascy, comitem Lincolniæ, quam habemus sigillatam:—

"*Copia presentationis Petri de Cestria ad ecclesiam de Whalley, cedente Rogero ejusdem ecclesiæ Decano.*

"Reverendo Domino et Patri in Christo karissimo domino Alexandro Dei gratia Coventrensi et Lichfeldensi episcopo vel ejus officiali Johannes de Lascy, Comes Lincolniæ, Constabularius Cestriæ, Salutem et debitam cum omni devotione reverentiam. Noverit paternitas vestra me divinæ caritatis intuitu concessisse quantum ad patronum pertinet Petro de Cestria clerico personatum Ecclesiæ de Whalley vacantis percepturo inde annuatim sexaginta marcas annuæ pensionis nomine. Salvo residuo totius Ecclesiæ cum pertinentiis nomine Vicariæ Rogero de Whalley. Quapropter

of the sum reserved to the Vicar will excite the less surprise, when it is understood that the Dean had yet a power, *jure patronatus*, of fixing the endowment for himself, as ordinaries had then scarcely begun to interfere in such concerns, and indeed he could have encumbered his own resignation with such conditions as he thought proper.

This ancient vicarage, however, expired in the same person with the deanery; for, on the death of Roger de Whalley, Peter de Cestria procured from Roger, Bishop of Lichfield, in 1249,[1] a consolidation of both parts of the benefice, after the following form :

REDINTEGRATIO SIVE CONSOLIDATIO VICARIÆ DE WHALLEYE CUM PERSONATU EJUSDEM ECCLESIÆ.

Rogerus Dei gratia Coventrensis et Lichfeldensis Episcopus dilecto filio in Christo Archidiacono Cestriæ vel ejus officiali salutem, gratiam et benedictionem. Noveritis nos secundum Deum et justiciam Vicariam quam Rogerus de Whalleye quondam in vita sua obtinuit in Ecclesia de Whalleye personatui ejusdem ecclesiæ, quam quidam Petrus de Cestria auctoritate nostra obtinet, sibi canonice intitulatum consolidasse. Quare vobis mandamus firmiter injungentes quatenus dictum Petrum vel ejus procuratorem in corporalem possessionem totius Vicariæ et omnium bonorum ad dictam Vicariam spectantium una cum personatu inducatis. Salvis tamen quibusdam possessionibus ab Abbate et Conventu de Stanlawe et domino Rogero de Meuland infra dictam parochiam nomine Ecclesiæ de Blakburn obtentis, et salvis fructibus istius anni usque ad festum Sancti Michaelis, si secundum consuetudinem episcopatus ad opus defuncti debeant reservari. Dat. apud Stanlawe pridie kal. Junii pontificatus nostri anno quarto. (Coucher Book, Tit. 5, No. lxiii. p. 293, compared with Harl. MS. 1830, p. 18, and Lansd. MS. 973, f. 51.)

This resignation of Roger broke the order of hereditary succession, and his surrender of the advowson, together with the act of consolidation, put an end to the peculiar constitution of the benefice itself; but Richard, brother of this incumbent, himself also an ecclesiastic, profiting by the bounty of the Lacies, his kinsmen,[2] settled upon the Villa de Tunlay, and became progenitor of a flourishing family, yet subsisting, after a lapse of six centuries, legitimate descendants and representatives at once of the ancient Deans of Whalley[3] and Lords of Blackburnshire.

Peter de Cestria, the first and last Rector, properly so called, of this church, is supposed, with great probability, by Sir Peter Leycester, to have been a natural son of

eundem clericum ad dictum personatum vobis presento, attentius supplicans quatenus eundem admittere et quod vestrum est eidem facere velitis. Valete."]

[1] [Dr. Whitaker printed this date 1245, but the date of the instrument is evidently the 31st May, 1249, the fourth year of the episcopate of Roger de Weseham. This is confirmed by the following memorandum:—

"Hæc redintegratio facta fuit per dominum Rogerum de Weseham episcopum anno Domini Mcc°xlix. quia ipse consecratus fuit anno Domini Mccxlv." (Marginal note, Coucher Book, Tit. de Whalley, No. lxiii. p. 293.) The "domino Rogero de Meuland" with whom a composition had been made, was then a Canon of Lichfield, and subsequently (in 1257) Weseham's successor as Bishop.

[2] Roger the last Dean of Whalley and Richard de Tounlay or Townley his brother stood in relationship of second-cousins to Henry de Lacy third Earl of Lincoln. Roger had evidently derived his name from his great-grandfather Roger de Lacy constable of Chester, the father of the first Earl, John. The relationship is distinctly stated in the following monastic memorandum: "In 1° et 3° gradu, viz. Johannes in 1° et Rogerus in 3°. Nam soror dicti Johannis comitis Lincolniæ erat avia Rogeri decani, uxor Galfridi senioris, et filia Rogeri Lascy." (Harl. MS. 1830, f. 16 marg. note.)]

Lacy.[1] He was a very long-lived man, having been instituted A.D. MCCXXXV. and dying on the festival of St. Fabian and Sebastian A.D. MCCXCIIII. He was also Rector of Slaidburn, and Provost of Beverley. All that I find concerning him further was, that he vigorously opposed the erection of Altham into a parish church; and that he obtained charter of free warren in his manor of Whalley.[2] His death was the commencement of a new and memorable æra in the history of Whalley.

Before we take leave of this subject, it may throw some light both upon the preceding disquisition, and upon the origin and constitution of the dependent churches which arose out of our ancient parish, to state the respective ranks and rights of these foundations, according to the Saxon laws.

These were of three orders:

1st. The ealdan mýnstre, or mother church.
2nd. The church having a legerstowe, or place of burial.
3rd. The feldcyrce, field kirk, or chapel without a cemetery.

The word ealdan mýnstre appears sometimes to mean the cathedral church; but more generally denotes those churches of ancient erection, to which tithes were due of common right, from the first foundation of parishes in the present sense of the word.[3] Cyrce and mýnstre appear to be synonymous; for not only cathedrals but the larger mother churches had frequently more priests than one, living, probably, in the collegiate manner; and the Saxon monasteries themselves, before the time of Dunstan, usually consisted of secular priests, who lived together without rule and without vows. In this sense Whalley may properly be considered as the ealdan mýnstre, or mother church.

But if a *Thane* had erected on his own *Boeland* (freehold or charter land) a church having a legerstowe, he was allowed to substract one-third part of his tithes from the mother church, and to bestow them upon his own clerk; and so essential was this circumstance of a legerstowe, or cemetery, to the constitution of a church, that even as late as 23 Hen. III.[4] in a case of *quare impedit*, the issue was not whether it were church or chapel, but whether

[1] ["I find mention in the Book of Whalley, fol. 126 b, of one Peter de Lascy, a bastard, called also Peter de Cester, Rector of Whalley." (*Leycester*, p. 513.) To what document Sir Peter Leycester refers is not clear; but in the Coucher Book, Tit. 5, De Whalley, No. xlix. is a charter relating to the sale of certain tenements to Peter de Cestria, Rector of Whalley, to which this memorandum is annexed: Sed quia dominus Petrus de Cestria, cui facta fuit charta proximè precedens, *fuit bastardus*, et non habuit hæredem legitimum, dominus Henricus de Lascy comes Lincolniæ, *&c.* (*see under* SNELLESHOU *hereafter*). Peter de Chester was made Provost of Beverley in 1282, and Prebendary of Bugthorpe in the church of York, 5 Mar. 1287-8. He died in 1294—not 1293, as printed in former editions of this History. "Presentatio hæc dicti Petri facta fuit A° xi. dicti Alexandri episcopi, qui fuit ab incarnatione Domini anno Mccxxxv. Qui quidem Petrus tenuit eandem ecclesiam per annos lix. et moriebatur A° D[i] M°ccexciiij in festo sanctorum Fabiani et Sebastiani,"—Jan. 20. (Harl. MS. 1830, f. 16, marg. note.)]

[2] Tower Record, 12 Edw. Confirmed 20 Ric. II. pars 1, mem. 14.

[3] Leges Eadgari, par. 2. The same distinction is observed in the laws of Canute with respect to the Weregild. Leges Cnuti, par. 3.

[4] Selden, *ubi supra.*

it had rights of baptism and sepulture.[1] But before that time a check appears to have been put to the practice of endowing new parishes, so that foundations claiming rights of sepulture and administration of the sacraments henceforth assumed an intermediate rank between churches of the second order and mere "field kirks," and were called "parochial chapels." To the former class, in this subdivision, belong the filial churches of Rochdale, Blackburn, Slaidburn, &c.; to the second, all the chapels of the old foundation, as Saddleworth, Law, Clitheroe, Colne, Burnley, &c. of which hereafter. This also accounts for the resistance made by Peter de Cestria, in the very period alluded to above, against the erection of Altham into a parish church.[2]

Last in rank was the feldkirk, a mere oratory, or chapel of ease, so called, not from its situation in the country, but from its lying uninclosed and open to the adjoining fields. This had no right or place of sepulture, and no stated endowment; but the founder was required by the same laws of Edgar,[3] without substracting anything from his tithes for the support of his chaplain, to sustain him according to his own discretion out of the remaining nine parts of his income. To this class belonged many chapels of ease within the original parish, since become parochial, some by gradual usurpation, and others by positive concession. Thus the chapel of Samlesbury, originally dependent upon Law, was made parochial by a grant of the rights of sepulture and baptism.[4]

The little chapel of Whitewell, in Bowland, still remaining without cemetery or inclosure, affords a complete example of these humble foundations.

If the subject be not yet sufficiently clear, it may further be illustrated by the several *effects* which these subsequent endowments had upon the rights of their parent churches. For the erection of a church with leȝeɲɼꞇope occasioned a substraction both of tithes and oblations; that of the parochial chapel in later times, of oblations alone; and that of the feldkirk, neither one nor the other.

It may be worth while to observe that the distinction between the second and third of these ranks does not appear to have been understood at the date of Delaval's charter (temp. Hen. I.), in which the now parochial chapels of Clitheroe, Colne, and Burnley are denominated churches, though they never received tithes; and that of St. Michael in Castro is plainly termed a chapel, though its endowment of tithes is expressly mentioned. Hence it may be inferred that in the conception of that age a leȝeɲɼꞇope without tithes constituted a church; and that tithes without a leȝeɲɼꞇope did not.

[1] Selden, *ubi supra*. [2] About the year 1245. [3] Leges Eadgari, *ubi supra*. [4] Towneley MSS.

Drawn by W. Turner A. | Engraved by James Basire

To the Right Honourable SOPHIA CHARLOTTE BARONESS HOWE.

CHAPTER THE SECOND.

LOCUS BENEDICTUS DE WHALLEY.

"Bonum est nos hic esse, quia homo vivit purius, cadit rarius, surgit velocius, incedit cautius, quiescit securius, moritur fælicius, purgatur citius, præmiatur copiosius."—BERNARD.[1]

IN the year 1178,[2] a period when the veneration of mankind for monastic institutions in general was at its height, and when a partial reform of the Benedictine order under St. Bernard had directed for a time the bounty of kings and nobles almost exclusively into that single channel, John, Constable of Chester, founded a monastery of Cistertians at Stanlaw,[3] in Cheshire, not far from his Castle of Halton, endowing it with the villages of Aston, Stanye, and other lands, and appointing that it should be called LOCUS BENEDICTUS:[4] but the situation was low and unpleasant; at spring-tides nearly inaccessible, and sometimes overflowed; besides that the sea made continual encroachments upon the adjoining lands. These inconveniences were patiently endured for about a century; but the vast accession of property which the Barons of Halton received in that interval from the first house of Lacy had enabled them to multiply their benefactions to Stanlaw; and the acquisition of the rectory of Rochdale from Roger de Lacy and of Blackburn and Eccles from John Earl of Lincoln, followed by many private donations in the same quarter, occasioned a vast preponderance in the property of the Monks on the side of Lancashire, and naturally turned their eyes (never wanting in sagacity to discover warm and fertile situations) to a place at once more commodious in itself and better adapted to the inspection of their other estates. Those estates indeed afforded no situation to their taste. The

[1] A sentence usually inscribed on some conspicuous part of the Cistertian houses.

[2] [The monastic chroniclers state that Stanlawe was founded in 1163, the 15th Hen. II. "Iste Johannes post mortem dicti Ricardi patris sui fundavit monasterium de Stanlowe in Wirrall, com. Cestriæ, anno regni regis Henrici secundi, dicti Filii Imperatricis, xv°. Anno gratiæ 1163, post cujus fundationem idem dictus Johannes profectus est in Terram Sanctam," &c. (Harl. MS. 1830, fol. 15 b.) Another passage states that "Anno domini 1172 fundata fuit abbathia de Stanlaw per Johannem Lacy Constabularium Cestriæ et dominum de Halton, qui obiit in Terra Sancta anno sequenti." (Cotton. MS. F. III. fol. 258.) That which is considered the foundation charter, however, and is printed in the Monasticon, and Coucher Book, pp. 1—5, was granted in 1178, the date named by Dr. Whitaker.]

[3] [On a small rock, which rises from a desolate marsh, formerly covered by the tides, at the junction of the river Gowy with the Mersey, is the site of the monastery of Stanlaw. (Lecture delivered by the Rev. R. A. Whitaker, Vicar of Whalley, 2nd Feb. 1869.)]

[4] *Locus*, in monastic Latin, technically expressed a religious house; thus, in missals formerly belonging to monasteries, this suffrage occurs, "ut locum nostrum conservare digneris."

glebe of Blackburn, for instance, was a bed of sand, and that of Rochdale surrounded by morasses; but the parent church of Whalley itself presented, as they truly said, "locum habitationi admodum idoneum;"[1] the glebe was fertile, warm, and spacious; the tithery extensive; the incumbent aged; themselves importunate; and their patron bountiful.

Thus two of the filial churches were reduced once more to their original dependence upon the ealban mẏnꞅꞇꞃe; and Whalley, previously venerable for its ecclesiastical antiquity, became the seat of a flourishing establishment, which continued for two centuries and an half to exercise unbounded hospitality and charity; to adorn the site which had been chosen with a succession of magnificent buildings; to protect the tenants of its ample domains in the enjoyment of independence and plenty; to educate and provide for their children; to employ, clothe, feed, and pay many labourers, herdsmen, and shepherds; to exercise the arts and cultivate the learning of the times; yet, unfortunately, at the expense of the secular incumbents, whose endowments they had swallowed up, and whose functions they had degraded into those of pensionary vicars or mendicant chaplains.[2]

But the secular clergy were not the only persons who felt or fancied themselves to be aggrieved by this translation. The elder convent of Sallay,[3] which was never richly endowed, and whose lands were better adapted to the feeding of cattle than to the growth of grain and other necessaries of life usually raised by the religious houses within their own domains, exhibited a large catalogue of grievances, which, at the distance of more than six miles, they experienced or apprehended from the new foundation. This dispute, however, was compromised by arbitrators of their own order. In fact, the monks knew how to lay their own damages; but the complaint was not altogether groundless, for the introduction of so numerous an establishment into a country scarcely able to support its own inhabitants before, must necessarily be felt in a defect of provisions, or an increase of their price.

Querela.

Hæc sunt gravamina quibus Abbas et Conventus de Salleya se conquiruntur aggravari de translacione abbatiæ de Stanlawe ad ecclesiam de Whalleya.

Primum est quod abbatia de Whalleya nimis prope situata est ad abbatiam de Salleya, contra constitutiones ordinis.

Secundum est quod monachi de Whalleya modo occupant et expendunt decimas ecclesiæ de Whalleya quas monachi de Salleya emere solebant tempore domini Petri de Cestria rectoris dictæ ecclesiæ et tempore

[1] In their petition for the appropriation.

[2] Coucher Book, &c. For proofs of all these particulars, see the Computus of the House for the years 1478 and 1521, which will be given in their place.

[3] [The history of Sallay Abbey is related at full by Dr. Whitaker in his *History of Craven* (2d edit. 1812), pp. 39-58; and at pp. 44, 45 he has given an imperfect copy of the *Querela*, which we have now transferred to the text, as more strictly belonging to Whalley. In his remarks Dr. Whitaker states that "the dispute was finally determined in a chapter of the order held by the abbots of Rievall and Byland." This is not quite accurate. It will be seen that the dispute was referred by a general chapter to the abbots of Rievaulx and Byland as judges, and that, with the assistance and mediation of the abbots of Revesby and Swineshead, the reconciliation took place in the church of the Hospitallers at Boston, in Lincolnshire, on the morrow of St. Peter ad Vincula 1305.]

omnium predecessorum suorum ad sustentationem suam, pro majori parte, sed modo impediuntur per predictos monachos de Whalleya ad dampnum ipsorum de Salleya c. s. per annum.

Item Monachi predicti de Whalleya modo discurrunt per se et per suos servientes et procuratores infra patriam de Craven et in foro dicti Abbatis de Salleya emunt omnimoda blada quæ Monachi de Salleya emere solebant ad sustentacionem suam, et venduntur modo eis blada infra Craven carius causa illorum omni anno ad tertium denarium, ad dampnum ipsorum x. li. per annum, quod oportet ipsos de Salleya emere bladum suum et cariare per xl. sive lx. leugas pessimæ viæ si vivere volunt.

Item quod butirum et caseus ex quo venerunt dicti Monachi apud Whalleyam venduntur carius monachis de Salleya ad tertium denarium, ad dampnum eorum xl. s. per annum.

Item quod maremium, quo monachi de Salleya edificare deberent et edificia sua sustentare, venditur eis carius ad quartum denarium ratione quod monachi de Whalleya modo edificant, et in posterum edificare intendunt, ad dampnum ipsorum de Salleya xxx s. per annum.

Item ferrum et sal venduntur eis carius causa illorum ad tertium denarium, ad dampnum illorum de Salleya xx s. per annum.

Item venditores tanæ in partibus illis, sperantes monachos de Whalleya magnam tanariam habituros, tanam carius vendunt ad tertium denarium, unde tanaria de Salleya fere destructa est, ad dampnum ipsorum c. s. per annum.

Item pisces rarius veniunt apud Salleyam causa illorum, et venduntur carius eis cum veniunt ad tertium denarium, ad dampnum illorum xl. s. per annum.

Item aucæ, gallinæ, ova, et cetera minuta necessaria carius venduntur eis ad tertium denarium quod rarius inveniuntur, ad dampnum illorum xx s. per annum.

Summa omnium dampnorum xxvii li. x s.

Concordia hujus querele.

Cum mota esset contentio per Abbatem et Conventum de Salleya contra Abbatem et Conventum de Whalleya super quibusdam articulis nimia propinquitate et majori caristia venalium, causa propinquitatis Abbatiæ de Whalleya ad Salleyam, datis judicibus a Capitulo generali, dominis videlicet de Ryevalle et de Bella Landa abbatibus, qui dictam causam secundum consuetudinem ordinis pace vel judicio terminarent, tandem vocatis et assistentibus partibus coram dictis judicibus in ecclesia Hospitalorum juxta Sanctum Botulphum in crastino Sancti Petri ad Vincula Anno Domini M° ccc° quinto, mediantibus venerabilibus patribus de Revesby et Swynesheved abbatibus, et annuentibus prefatis judicibus, in hac forma amicabiliter conquievit, videlicet, quod sopitis et extinctis penitus omnibus querelis de temporibus retroactis, deinceps utraque pars bona fide alterius negocium tanquam proprium promovebit commodum et proficuum procurabit. Et si forte monachi vel conversi de Whalleya contra domum de Salleya in aliquo notabiliter excesserint, cum de tali transgressione Abbati et Monachis de Whalleya manifeste constiterit, delinquentes ad abbatiam de Salleya sine mora mittentur puniendi in capitulo monachorum secundum quantitatem delicti et ad arbitrium presidentis. Et si a parte ipsorum de Salleya aliquid tale contigerit, per ipsos de Whalleya similiter punientur. Et si illi de Whalleya decimas venales habuerint quas Abbas et Conventus de Salleya suis usibus viderint competentes, vendentur eis citius et liberius quam aliis, saltem pro pretio quod alii dare volunt. In cujus rei testimonium tam partes quam judices et mediatores huic scripti cyrographico sigilla sua apposuerunt. Datum apud Sanctum Botolphum die et anno suprascriptis. — (*Addit. MS. Brit. Mus.* 10,374, *f.* 136.)

But to return: Stanlaw, notwithstanding the name of *locus benedictus*, appears to have been eminently unblest, for, in addition to the calamities recited above, the tower of the church fell down in the year 1287; and in 1289 great part of the abbey was consumed by fire.[1] These misfortunes would undoubtedly quicken the impatience of the monks for a removal. The advowson of Whalley, together with a licence of translation, had been obtained from Henry de Lacy by charter, dated at Pontefract on the day of the Circumcision A.D. 1283; but Peter de Cestria, the long-lived Rector, survived this transaction ten years, and, after his death, the translation was delayed for three years longer[2] by the want of an appropriation, for which the Bull of Nicholas IV. and the subsequent ratification of the founder were not obtained till 1295; so that it was not before the festival of St. Ambrose, or April 4th, 1296, that Gregory de Northbury, eighth abbot of Stanlaw, and his convent, took possession of the old deanery or parsonage, which was to be their abode during the erection of the new monastery.[3]

The following Inquisition, transcribed from an ancient copy, will prove the value of this donation, and throw considerable light on several particulars in the ancient state of the parish.[4]

INQUISITIO facta de valore et proventibus Ecclesie Matricis de Whalleia, et Capellarum ejusdem, die Veneris proxime ante festum Sancti Georgii, anno Domini MCC nonogesimo sexto, per xxiiij^cr fide dignos juratores et examinatores. Qui dicunt quod—

WHALLEY.]—Decime Garbarum de Whalleia valent viij*l.* Item terra de Dominicis cum firma ville viij marcas. Item parva Mitton cum Henthorn valet v marcas. Item Wyswall valet ix marcas. Item Coldcotes valet xx*s.* Item Magna Penhulton valet viij marcas.[5] Item Reved valet ix marcas. Item Symondston valet vij marcas. Item Padiam cum Whitacre[6] valet xij marcas. Item Hapton et Bryddestwysell valent xij marcas. Item Alteragium Ecclesie ejusdem valet xvj*l.*

CLYDERHOW.]—Item Decime Garbarum de Clyderhow valent xiiij marcas. Item Chatborn valet

[1] ["Anno 1287 corruit magnum campanium de Stanlaw quadam tempestate.

"Anno 1289 combusta est magna pars abbatiæ de Stanlaw." (Cotton. MS. Titus F. III. f. 258.)]

[2] The grant of an advowson to a religious house must be carefully distinguished from an appropriation, or concession *in proprios usus*. The former was merely a transfer of the patronage, and might be transacted without licence by a lay-patron; the latter was an act of the ordinary, or sometimes, as in the instance before us, of the Pope himself, *ex plenitudine potestatis*. During this interval of two years, as the monks never presented a rector, the church must have been considered as litigious, otherwise the Bishop of Lichfield would scarcely have neglected to avail himself of the lapse, and the monks would have lost their turn and their translation together.

[3] ["Tempore dicti Henrici translata fuit Abbatia de Stanlawe apud Whalley propter nimius maris inundaciones. anno Domini 1296 in festo sancti Ambrosii Episcopi." (Harl. 1830, f. 23 b.)

"Anno Domini 1296, Indictione nona, anno bissextili, littera dominicali G. 7 idus Aprilis, anno regni regis Edwardi 24, anno ætatis domini Henrici de Lacy 47, intravit Conventus de Stanlawe in Wirall in manerium de Whalley, presidente Gregorio de Northbury, sub quo isti sunt subscripti monachi—Thorstanus de Cestria," &c. as hereafter in p. 88. (Cotton. MS. Vesp. D. XVII. f. 6.)]

[4] [Another return resembling this, drawn up only two years later, is inserted by Dr. Whitaker among the documents appended hereafter.]

[5] The distinction between Great and Little Pendleton is now unknown, and the Vicar of Whalley receives the altarage of both. Little Pendleton, which is here described as in the chapelry of Clitheroe, appears to be that part of the village in which the Hall is situated. [The name will be found a little south of Pendleton Hall, in a map at the Public Record Office, Duchy of Lancaster, Class XXIX. No. 101.]

[6] Whitaker, from which the author of this work derives his name and descent, is no longer a hamlet in Padiham, but is reduced to a single house—the ancient Hall.

vj marcas. Item Worston valet vj marcas. Item Magna Merley et Parva Merley valent v marcas. Item Parva Penhulton valet xx s. Item Alteragium ejusdem Capelle valet v marcas.[1]

DOWNHAM.]—Item Decime Garbarum de Downham valent x marcas cum Twyselton. Item Alteragium ejusdem Capelle valet iiij marcas. Item Terra de Dominicis de Downham valet j marcam.

COLNE.]—Item Decime Garbarum de Colne cum Alcancotes[2] valent viij marcas. Item Folryges valet vj marcas. Item Ferneside[3] cum Barnesete[3] valet iv marcas. Item Merklesden valet x marcas. Item Parva Merklesden valet xl s. Item Alteragium ejusdem Capelle valet x l. Item Terra de Dominicis de Colne valet vij s.

BRUNLEY.]—Item Decime Garbarum de Brunley valent xv marcas. Item Clyvacher valet x marcas. Item Worstorn valet vj marcas. Item Extwysel valet xl s. Item Brereclyff valet iij marcas et dimidiam. Item Habrincham valet viij marcas. Item Hightenhull[4] valet iiij marcas. Item Alteragium ejusdem Capelle valet xx marcas. Item Terra de Dominicis de Brunley valet j marcam.

CHYRCHE.]—Item Decime Garbarum de Chirche valent iiij marcas. Item Oswaldestwysel valet vj marcas. Item Dukword valet ij marcas. Item Huncotes valet vj marcas. Item Alteragium ejusdem Capelle valet v marcas. Item Terra de Dominicis valet x s.

HASLINGDEN.]—Item Decime Garbarum de Haslingden valent v marcas. Item Alteragium cum Terra de Dominicis valet iiij marcas. Summa ccxj l. vij s.[5]

Ad hec dicit Inquisitio quod octava pars Matris Ecclesie de Whalleia et Capelle ville de Cliderhow et Capelle de Downham de jure et consuetudine pertinet ad Ecclesiam de Blagburn. Item ad alia onera sustinenda et supportanda oportet invenire ibi septem Capellanos, viz. ad Whalley, Clyderhow, Downham, Colne, Brunley, Church, et Haslingden, viz. unicuique Capellano iiij marcas, secundum consuetudinem patrie. Item in procurationibus Domini Archiepiscopi xl s. et in Synodalibus iij s. Item ad inveniendum panem et vinum annuatim xl s. Item ad hec Abbas inveniet ibi xx monachos secundum tenorem Bulle sue cum aliis ministris necessariis in Abbathia de novo constructa cum aliis sumptibus necessariis. Et licet ista Inquisitio capta fuit ex mandato Domini Archiepiscopi Cant' ut postmodum de taxacione vicarie in certis porcionibus ordinaret, tamen hoc per ipsum non fuit factum, sed postea per Dominum Walterum de Langton Coven' et Lich. Episcopum dicta Vicaria fuit ordinata, videliz. Anno Domini Millesimo CC^mo nonagesimo octavo.

Indorsed "Ane old valuation of the Rectorye of Whalley, vndr Mr Roberte Parys hand wrytinge, whome was a monke of the Abbey of Whallye;[6]" and at the foot of the front page is this memorandum "Mr Parysbe his awne hande." *(From the original in Dr. Whitaker's interleaved Edition of* 1811.*)*

[1] The omission of all mention of glebe in Clitheroe proves that the glebe elsewhere mentioned in that place belonged to the chapel of St. Michael in the Castle.

[2] Alcancotes is in the same predicament [as Whitaker]; no hamlet, but a single gentleman's house.

[3] The name of Fernesete is lost. Barnside remains, like Alcancotes, in an ancient manor-house.

[4] This proves that Ightenhill is not extra-parochial, but merely a hamlet within Burnley.

[5] It might be proved, if necessary, that the Rectory was, at this time, nearly equal to the rental of the whole parish: the reason of which is, that the tithes are a tax upon the actual produce, while rents bore a much smaller proportion than at present to the real value: or, in other words, the tenant had a more and the landlord a less lucrative interest in the estate.

It is remarkable that the altarage of Whalley with Padiham exceeded its present amount; one reason of which is, the vast numbers of sheep and lambs, which were not only tithed in kind, but paid a modus to the Easter Roll.

The expression of *Abbatia de novo constructa* can only be understood of some temporary erection for the accommodation of the Monks, as the present Abbey is unquestionably of later date.

[6] [He survived until 1572, as will appear in a subsequent page.]

Before we take leave of the original house, it may be proper to record the names of its abbots, with the date of their respective deaths, which is all the intelligence that can now be retrieved concerning them, excepting that, on the morrow of St. Simon and Jude, A.D. 1259, the Abbot returned from the Council of London with the Bishop of Lichfield's confirmation of the church of Blackburn,[1] and that their foundation consisted of twenty monks, the expenses of each of whom were estimated at v marks, or lxvj *l.* xiij *s.* iv *d.* in the whole.

ABBATES APUD STANLAW.[2]

RADULPHUS, primas Abbas, obiit in festo Sti Bartholomei Aprilis A.D. 1209.

OSBERNUS, secundus, obiit in festo Apostolorum Philippi et Jacobi.

CAROLUS, 3, temp. Joh. Scott, Com. Cest., ob. 3 nonas Jan.

PETRUS, 4, ob. prid. non. Mart.

SIMON, 5, ob. 7 idus Decembris 1268.

RICARDUS THORNTON, 6, ob. 7 idus Decembris 1269.

RICARDUS NORTHBURN, 7, ob. kal. Jan. 1272, nocte Circumcisionis.

ROBERTUS HOWARTH, 8, ob. 10 kal. Maii, 1304, quondam abbas de Stanlaw, having resigned the Abbey, and remained at Stanlaw.[3]

The names of the fraternity, at the time of their translation, were as follow:

1. GREGORIUS DE NORTHBURY, primus Abbas de Whalley, ob. die Sancti Vincentii Martyris, A.D. 1309.

Robertus Hauworth, quondam Abbas de Stanlaw, ob. 10 kal. Maii, 1304.

Fr. Thurstanus de Cestria, Prior, qui in Cristo requievit xiii° kal. Maii 1296, et sepultus in ecclesia parochiali ante altare Marie virginis de Whalley.

2. HELIAS DE WORKSLEIGH, Theologus, Abbas secundus, cess. abbatiam et ob. A.D. 1318, et sepultus est apud Mon. de Baxley.[4]

Fr. Ricardus de Preston.

Fr. Hugo de Heli.

Fr. Symon parvus de Smetlay.

Fr. Johannes de Heli.

Fr. Willielmus de Cestria.

Fr. Rob. de Toftes, ob. 1311.

Fr. Rog. de Melis: in communi negotio domus itinerans usque curiam Romanam, sed in vigiliis Symonis et Jude ibidem obiit.

Fr. Willielmus Workesdelegh.

Fr. Ric. de Rodiherde, postea Abbas de Cumbermare, ob. 1316, sep. in cemiterio ap. Whalley.

Fr. Ric. de Aston.

Fr. Johannes de Buckelegh, al. Bulhaughe.

3. JOHANNES DE BELFELD, Abbas 3tus, ob. 8 kal. Aug. 1323.

Fr. Willielmus de Moston.

[1] [1259 Anno, in crastino apostolorum Simonis et Judæ, rediit Simon quintus abbas de Stanlaw a consilio Londinensi cum confirmatione d'ni Ep'i Cestrensis et Capituli Coventrensis de eccl'ia de Blackburn." Cotton. MS. Tit. F. III. f. 258.]

[2] This catalogue is transcribed from Bib. Cotton. Titus F. III. f. 258. [In a list of the Abbots of Stanlaw and Whalley, Harl. MS. 1830, f. 23, Simon and Petrus the fourth and fifth abbots are transposed.]

[3] This ancient foundation, which, after the translation to Whalley, seems to have subsisted as a small cell down to the general dissolution, is now merely a farm-house, the property of Sir Ferdinando Poole, Bart.; and the demesne belonging to it, a rich grass-farm, appears to be fertilized, rather than injured, by the periodical inundations of sea-water to which it is still exposed. The Abbot of Stanlaw was one of the spiritual Barons who held under the Earls of Chester, and sat in the little parliament of that palatinate, of which there is a pictorial representation in King's Vale Royal.

[4] Boxley, in Kent.

Fr. Willielmus de Segbrokes.
Fr. Robertus de Werington, Prior, ob. 3 non. Sept. 1348.
Fr. Willielmus de Wico.
Fr. Adam de Lostokes.
Fr. Rob. de Midlyton, Prior.
Fr. Rog. de Bromburgh, ob. 9 kal. Sept. 1339.
Fr. Ricardus de Mottrom.
Fr. Ricardus de Wheteley, ob. 13 kal. Maii, 1355.
Fr. Tho. de Upton.
Fr. Rog. de Frodesham.
Fr. Joh. de Walton.
Fr. Warinus de Ines.
Fr. Rob. de Buri, ob. 1311.
Fr. Ricardus Sutton.
Fr. Hen. Storisworthe.
Fr. Hunfredus Niger.
Fr. Tho. de Lene.
Fr. Rog. Pes Leporis.[1]

In all thirty-five.

Of these,[2] however, five were left at Stanlaw, under the government of their old abbot, Robert de Haworth; viz. Upton, Frodsham, Walton, Ines, and Buri; Sutton and Storesworth were appointed to the care of the Grange of Merland;[3] Niger and Lene were left for the same purpose at Staynings; Harefoot, or *Pes Leporis*, at Stanceye; and Worsley was sent to pursue his studies at Oxford,[4] where he afterwards proceeded to the degree of doctor in divinity. Twenty-four, therefore, remain as the original convent of Whalley, a number too considerable to be well accommodated in a single parsonage.

[1] The dates of this obituary are principally from a MS. Cotton. Lib. Titus F. III. f. 258. It is often difficult to trace the parentage of monks; 1st, because they frequently dropped their family name, and assumed a local one; and, 2nd, because they were persons dead in law, and therefore never occur in wills or inquisitions, which might serve to connect them with their father's house. But, in this investigation, one of the best rules is to seek for them, either in the immediate vicinity of the Abbey, if it afforded any family or any place of the same name; or, 2dly, among the tenants and dependants of the house, though more remote. In order to illustrate this latter rule, if we attend to the catalogue above, we shall observe, among thirty-five names, of which the rest belong principally to Cheshire, five who appear to have been natives of the parish of Rochdale. The Abbey of Stanlaw had, at this time, very large possessions in this parish; and appears, from many circumstances, to have been extremely popular among the inhabitants. Again, the higher we ascend towards the origin of local names, the less they are ramified, and the greater is the probability that any person was really born at the place whose name he bears. Laying all these circumstances together, we may, without much hesitation, refer Abbot Haworth to the ancient house of Great Haworth, near Rochdale, which ended about thirty years ago in Radclyffe Haworth, LL.D. Fellow of All Souls College, Oxon. [but see the pedigree of the Haworths hereafter under Great Haworth]; the two Helys to the hamlet of that name; John de Buckelegh to the family of Buckley, which may be traced up to a much higher antiquity; and, lastly, Abbot John de Belfield to the ancient stock of Belfield, in Butterworth, then inhabiting the house so called, and which continued at Cleggswood down to the middle of the last century.

[2] Cotton. Libr. Cleop. C. III. f. 331 b and 332.

[3] Merland, one of the earliest acquisitions of the Abbey of Stanlaw in those parts, is a pleasant village about two miles south-west from Rochdale, with a mere or small lake of about seven Lancashire acres, whence it derives its name. There is a tradition in the neighbourhood of Rochdale that Gooselane was a grange; the only foundation for which seems to have been a resemblance of name to a place also belonging to Stanlaw and Whalley Abbeys, called, in the Coucher Book, [p. 339, Tit. vi. Houses and Rents in Chester, No. I.] Goselone; but the arrangement of that accurate compilation proves the latter place to have been in the vicinity of Chester. It may be worth observing that the morasses about Merland afforded the last retreat in this country to the black game. The mere abounds with trout, perch, and roach; and the village had once a chapel, probably a remnant of the Grange; and is thence denominated, in Speed's maps, A.D. 1610, *Chap. Marland.* It was overlooked by Speed's predecessor Saxton.

[4] [Ad studium Oxon. Helias de Workesdelegh. Cotton. MS. Cleop. C. III.]

It is a matter of some curiosity to determine the site of the ancient Deanery or parsonage of Whalley; for we are not to take it for granted that the abbey was erected on the precise spot where the other had stood, as the monks were empowered by the charter of foundation, "Monasterium in terra Ecclesiæ de Whalley ubicunque sibi viderint expedire de novo construere et edificare." Now there is at the east end of the churchyard a very ancient structure of wood and stone surrounding a small quadrangle, the most ancient form of such buildings, and still denominated the Old Hall.[1] As therefore we have shown the manor and glebe of the deanery to be the same, or rather the one to have been swallowed up in the other, and as the Old Hall of every village uniformly designed the manor or principal mansion-house, it will follow that here was the primitive residence of the Dean, and here the temporary dwellings of the Abbot and his monks. I do not mean to affirm that the individual building now remaining was the house in question, for it scarcely appears, from the style of the timber-work, to be older than Henry VII., but that the real parsonage of Whalley stood upon the same site and bore the same name.

Moreover, this house, though immediately contiguous to the parish-church, had a domestic oratory; for I find that on Wednesday the 28th April, 1306, the altar in the chapel which Peter de Cestria had made in the manor of Whalley, was dedicated by Thomas Bishop of Candida Casa (Whithern or Galloway); and that on the festival of St. Philip and James (being Sunday the 1st May) he celebrated mass, *in pontificalibus*, within the convent of Whalley; that is, I suppose, in the above chapel; [that on the feast of the Invention of the Holy Cross (May 3) he celebrated mass in the parish church; and that on the day of St. John *ante Portam Latinam* (May 6) a great part of the abbey, with the whole precinct, was dedicated by the same Bishop, attended by the Abbat of Combermere and other official personages of importance.[2]]

The foundation-stone [of the conventual church] was laid on the morrow of St. Barnabas, [June 12, 1308,] by Henry de Lacy, [Earl of Lincoln,] in person.[3]

[1] [Taken down in 1866, and further noticed hereafter.]

[2] [Dr. Whitaker was so far misled by inaccurate and imperfect transcripts of the dates regarding the erection of the Abbey, that we are obliged to make important alterations of his text in this page and the next. They are derived, in the first place, from the following more correct copy of what occurred in 1306, subsequently appended by the Author among the documents at p. 131 of his Third edition:—

Anno Domini M ccc sexto, Quarto kal. Maii, feria quinta, consecratum fuit altare in capella quam Petrus de Cestria fecit in Manerio de Whalleye, a domino Thoma Candide Case Episcopo vices Diocesani gerente, in honorem beati Gregorii Pape et aliorum Doctorum. Et kal. Maii, videlicet die sanctorum Philippi et Jacobi quæ dominica habebatur, celebravit idem Episcopus missam in conventu de Whalleye in pontificalibus. Et v non. Maii, videlicet die Inventionis Sanctæ Crucis, quæ fuit feria iii, celebravit in pontificalibus in Ecclesia Parochiali Et pridie non. Maii videlicet die Sancti Johannis ante Portam Latinum, quæ erat feria vi^ta^, dedicata fuit magna pars Abbatiæ cum toto præcinctu ab eodem Episcopo, anno consecrationis ejus xii Pontificatus vero domini Clementis v^ti^ Papæ primo, et regni Regis Edwardi filii Regis Henrici xxxiiii, ætatis vero domini Henrici de Lascy Comitis Lincoln. et Patroni nostri . . Domino Will'o de Lee tunc abbate de Cumbermare et Domino Gregorio de Norbury abbate de Whalleye, Priore Roberto de Werintone, suppriore Roberto de Toppeclive, cellarario Roberto de Middleton, Edmundo Talebot seneschallo de Blakburnshire, Roberto fil' Ad. de Preston constabulario. Litera dominicali B. Epact. xv. Indictionis iiii. Ciclo decennovenali xv Pascha erat iii. non. Apr. Omnia ista medio anno a bisexto.] (Addit. MS. 10374, f 28 b, 24.)

[3] [No fuller account of this ceremony has been preserved than the single line quoted in p. 94 note, and it will there be seen that the work did not actually proceed until 1330.]

This fact will determine a question which has perplexed our writers on monastic antiquities; namely, what parts of religious houses, besides the churches, were actually consecrated; and it seems to have been taken for granted, that the chapter-houses and cloisters only were hallowed, as the former were generally honoured with the interment of some great persons, and the latter were the common cemeteries of the house.[1] But it now appears, that the whole close and precinct received a general benediction from the Bishop; though the other parts of the building, more peculiarly devoted to holy offices, received, no doubt, a more formal and solemn dedication.

But the monks, who must have been much incommoded in their new habitation, would naturally be anxious to provide themselves with better lodgings; and therefore, instead of increasing the number of their religious to sixty, which, according to the second charter of appropriation by Pope Boniface VIII., they were bound to do, we now find them applying all their superfluous income to the erection of a spacious and magnificent abbey, of which their own estimate was 3,000*l.*[2] sterling, an enormous sum in those days.

Abbot Norbury, dying on St. Vincent's day [9th June] 1309, was succeeded by

II. Helias de Workesley, D.D., of whom it may probably be conjectured that he was descended from a celebrated hero in the Crusades, of both his names, commonly called Elias the Giant,[3] who was born at Worsley, and after many triumphs over the Infidels died and was buried at Rhodes.

Of this abbot we know nothing, but that he resigned his charge, and died, according to the MS.[4] A.D. 1318, in the Monastery of *Baxley*, that is, I suppose, Boxley in Kent. Colleges or abbeys, during the time of their erection, require a man of business at their head rather than a scholar. Worsley was probably a scholar, as he was certainly a student, and therefore would naturally prefer a private station in another house, to unquiet pre-eminence amidst the noise of axes and hammers in his own.

On his resignation, of which the precise time is not known, the convent elected

III. John de Belfield, in the beginning of whose government (A.D. 1316, as I presume that Worsley had now resigned) so little progress had yet been made in the building, that we find the monks still unsettled, dissatisfied with their situation, and calling upon their patron for a second translation. The place, which heretofore seemed the great object

[1] *Vide* Fuller's "History of Abbeys."

[2] Petition for the appropriation of the church of Preston. Coucher Book.—The average rent of lands at that time was four pence per Lancashire acre; but, as the intrinsic value of a penny in the reign of Edw. II. was nearly three pence, this is, in reality, about a shilling. Multiply, therefore, by thirty (as thirty shillings are about the average* at present), and this sum amounts to 90,000*l.* But at that time lands were cheaper, in the true sense of the word; that is, the tenant expected a larger profit in his farm, probably by one-half: divide, therefore, by two, and we have 45,000*l.*—No extravagant estimate, if the parts which have perished were equal to those which remain.

[3] Lancashire pedigrees, MS. [For the Workesdelegh pedigree, see pages 55, 888 of the Coucher Book, which preserves several of their charters under Tit. 2, De Eccles, and Tit. 18, De Maunton et Swynton.]

[4] Cotton. MS. Titus F. III. f. 258.

* Much more 1815.

of their wishes, was now become "minus sufficiens, maxime propter defectum bosci, pro meremio ad monasterium suum de novo construendum, et alias domos suas faciendas, ac propter defectum focaliæ et propter districtionem et insufficientiam loci ad blada et alia cariagia Abbatiæ necessaria!" So different is the language of hope and of possession! In consequence, however, of these representations, which surely had no foundation, excepting in that part which related to difficulty of carriage, the monks obtained from Thomas Earl of Lancaster, their patron and the firm friend of their order, a grant of Toxteth and Smethedon, near Liverpool, accompanied with a licence "ut inhabilitatem et insufficientiam loci predicti fugiendo, monasterium suum ab eo loco de Whalley amoveant, et in dicto loco de Tocstath ubicunque sibi viderint expedire ac de novo construant et edificient."—Dat. apud Whalley in fest. Jac. A.D. 1316.[1]

Why this plan never took effect must now be left to conjecture; but as Worsley seems to have resigned the abbey, and to have been succeeded by Belfield a little before this time, the latter might prefer remaining in the neighbourhood of his friends and of the principal estates of his house; and indeed a translation to Toxteth would have brought back many of the inconveniences which attended the situation of Stanlaw.

About this time I am inclined to fix an undated transaction, which is recorded thus:—

> 8 Idus Octobris Gilbertus   episcopus, tunc suffraganeus domini Walteri Coventrensis et Lichfeld. episcopi,[2] dedicavit altare majus in oratorio monasterii de Whalley in honore Sanctæ Mariæ et omnium sanctorum. (MS. Cotton. Titus F. III. f. 258.)

It was one of the offices appertaining to Suffragans to hallow altars. Walter Langton became Bishop of Lichfield in the very year of the translation of this house, and died in 1322; and the most probable account of this dedication seems to be, that, as the work had languished under abbot Worsley, upon his surrender, and upon the resolution having been formed of remaining at Whalley, the fabric was carried on with more spirit. Some of the habitable parts of the house were immediately entered upon. The old manor-house or parsonage of Peter de Cestria was abandoned, and therefore the domestic chapel and altar—consecrated, as we have seen, in 1306—ceasing to be convenient for the devotions of the convent, a temporary oratory was erected upon some site immediately adjoining, for we are not to dream of the high altar in the abbey church, of which the foundations had not yet been laid.[3]

A grant from Adam de Huddleston of his quarry beyond the bridge of Calder in Billington, dated 12 Edw. II. or 1319, proves that the monks were at length setting about their buildings in earnest.[4]

[1] [Coucher Book, pp. 327-530, Tit. 10, No. XLIII.]

[2] [Walter de Langton was Bishop of Coventry and Lichfield from 1296 to 1321. His suffragan here mentioned was Gilbert elected Bishop of Annaghdown (*Enachdunensis*), co. Galway, in 1306; who has been traced as officiating in Dorsetshire and Staffordshire in 1311 and 1312. See Cotton, *Fasti Eccles. Hib.* iii. 53.]

[3] Townley MSS. Ibid.

[4] In the same year, or the next, the abbot and convent obtained Huddleston's moiety of the manor of Billington from Thomas Earl of Lancaster, subject to the life estate of Huddleston, which he had in the said moiety by grant from Henry de Lacy. The licence of mortmain bears date Nov. 10, 12 Edw. II.

The year after, 1320, the convent was visited by Adam abbot of Cumbermere, as visitor of the Cistertian Order, when the stock and finances of the house appeared as follows:

Recepta de Mero a Visitatione ad Visitationem,	ccxcij *l.* x *s.* x *d.*	
Expensa ab ead. usq. ad eand.	ccc xx *l.* xvj *s.* viij *d.*	This excess of the expenses above the receipt seems to imply that considerable sums were now laying out upon the buildings.
Debita Domus in toto	c lxxviij *l.* xj *s.* vij *d.*	
Stauri boves	ccxi	In all, 800 head of horned cattle, and only 837 sheep, a very extraordinary disproportion, and especially at a time when so much more ground lay in common than at present.
Vaccæ	cxcix	
Tauri	vij	
III Annor.	xcvij	
II Ann.	cxxxiij	
Stirci	c xix	The wild cattle in the park, if any such there were, are not distinguished in this account from the common breed.
Affri utriusque sexus	xxxix	
Equi portantes	ix	No draft-horses are mentioned in this account, whence I conclude that the cartage of materials for the building was hired or given; or, what is still more probable, performed by oxen.
III Ann.	xv	
II Ann.	xi	
Pulli	xv	
Porci utriusque sexus	lxxxviij	This was pretty plainly an herd of swine, kept in the woods: they were far too numerous for the farm-yard; and, indeed, though the hog would of course be put up to fatten at that time as at present, he was, in his general habits, more of a wild animal than now, feeding, as his snout imports, on roots, mast, &c., and very far from the filthy impounded glutton to which we have degraded him.
Oves	DCCC xxxvij	

It further appears, from the account of this visitation, that the house were indebted to Gilbert de la Leigh *cl.* sterling, which they had been compelled to borrow, for the accommodation of their patron, Thomas Earl of Lancaster.

This is the last transaction which occurs during the government of John de Belfield, who died July 25, 1323, and was succeeded by

IV. Robert de Topcliffe, who in 1306 had witnessed the general consecration of the precinct, being then a young man, and subprior of the house.

This abbot is memorable for having begun that spacious and magnificent pile the conventual church on the festival of St. Gregory the pope (Feb. 13,) 1330,[1] [after the Earl of Lincoln had laid the foundation stone nearly twenty-two years before. This great work

[1] [The text is here altered from the last edition, p. 70, in which Dr. Whitaker stated that the abbot "laid the first stone on the festival of St. Gregory the abbot, A.D. 1330." Our authority is derived from the following passages of the monastic annals, (confirmed, not contradicted, by the MS. Cotton. Titus F. III. f. 258, cited by Dr. Whitaker):—

"Anno Domini Mcccxxx. die Sancti Gregorii papæ, inceperunt Abbas et Conventus edificare novam ecclesiam conventualem de Whalley, nobili viro Henrico de Lascy, comite Lincoln. ponente primum lapidem in fundamento dictæ ecclesiæ anno Domini Mcccviii. Et prima missa celebrata in ea anno Domini Mccclxxx. fuit, ad quam missam professi fuerunt fratres Johannes de Rutland et Johannes de Dalton." (Marginal note in Harl. 1830, f. 19, 19 b.)

appears to have been slowly but regularly pursued,[1] for, within fifteen years from its foundation, [*i.e.* in 1345,] John de Kuerdale, who had left lands to the abbey of the annual value of five marks, was interred in the new conventual church.[2] The work, however, was not yet carried beyond the nave. The stones of which the church was constructed appear to have been brought from the quarries of Read and Symondstone, for Nic. del Holden and Joh. de Symondstone licence the abbot and convent to dig for stone in Symondstone,[3] *pro fabrica monasterii sui*, A.D. 1336. John del Holt, of Read, granted a similar permission, *in vasto de Read*, 7° Edw. III. or 1333.

This abbot, in the same year in which he laid the foundation of one church, contrived to despoil and ruin another, for, in 1330, by representing the necessities of his house, and the immoderate endowment of the vicarage of Whalley, he prevailed on Roger bishop of Lichfield to annul the former equitable ordination, and to substitute in its place a wretched appointment, which has starved the church from that time to the present.[4]

In the year 1341 we have the following curious account of the provisions of the house from a transcript in Harl. MS. 2064 [p. 322, fol. 31 b]:—

MEM. q^{d} frater Witt de Preston dimisit in officio provisoris conventûs de Whalley feria quarta in capite Jejunii,[5] año dñi 1341, fratri Thome de Routheeliffe succedenti eidem in officio supradĉo, viz.:

cccxxiv de duris Piscibus (that is, stock-fish); et de Salmonibus grossis xxviij; et de Allec' tria milia; et unam copulam de fruct' (probably one basket of dried fruits); et de carcosiis bovinis 8 pretti i marc'; et de baconibus ii; et de caseo xxiv petras; et de butiro i petram et dimidium (this proportion of butter is extremely small); et de riis (racemis) xlii lb. (42*li.*) (the common word *raisin* is a corruption of *racemo*); et de amygdalis lx lb. (60*li.*); et tria millia ceparum; unam lagenam olei Olivæ, et de

"In crastino Sancti Barnabæ apostoli, quæ fuit feria 4, nobilis vir dominus Henricus de Lacy Comes Lincolniæ posuit primum lapidem fundamento ecclesiæ conventualis de Whalley." (Cotton MS. Vesp. D. XVII. f. 14 b.)

From these dates it appears that the church was not actually commenced before 1330, although Henry de Lacy, Earl of Lincoln, (who died in 1312) had laid the foundation stone in 1308,—when the morrow (June 12) of the feast of St. Barnabas fell on a Wednesday (*feria* 4): and that another half-century elapsed before the first mass was celebrated in it, in 1380.]

[1] The importunity of the monks for contributions to carry on their buildings is thus divertingly represented by Chaucer:

"Yeve me then of thy gold to make our cloistre,
Quod he: for many a muskle and many an oystre
Whan other men han ben full wel at ese
Hath ben our food, our cloister for to rese;
And yet, God wot, unneathe the fundament
Performed is, ne of our pavement
N'is a tile yet within our wones,
By God we owen fourty pound for stones." *Sumpner's Tale.*

These good men had not met with a Nicholas del Holden or John de Symondstone.

[2] It is also recorded that the manor-house of Kuerdale was burned down the year following. [See KUERDALE.]

[3] Coucher Book, Tit. 19, No. CXLIV. p. 1061. [See SIMONDSTONE hereafter.]

[4] Vide Chapter III.

[5] [In the MS. miscopied "in capita Gemini." The *feria quarta in capite Jejunii* is Ash Wednesday.]

cymino, 3*li.*; et de Pipere i lb. (1*li.*); de Saffr. i quatron. dimid. [et equos duos, duas sellas cum duobus frenis et capam unam; et de argento in manibus 17*li.* 4*s.* 1*d.*; et item de arrer' de tempore Arnaldi 10*li.* 7*s.* 5*d.*; et item 2 coria bovina et item 6 petras ferri.]

Abbot Topcliffe made considerable acquisitions to the estates of the abbey, was active in recovering the chapel of St. Michael in the castle [of Clitheroe], and seems to have been in all respects a zealous friend to his convent. I have some reason to believe that he was a native of Billington,[1] and that he was the first monk admitted after the translation. He is said to have died 10 kal. March 1350; which date, if it be correct, will prove that he had resigned his charge; a fact not improbable on account of his age, as he had been professed above fifty years.

However this may be, in the year 1342 appears[2]

V. John Lyndelay, D.D.,[3] of whose birth and parentage I regret my inability to give any account, as he was a man who, for many reasons, ought not to be forgotten. For to his care and industry we are indebted for the Coucher Book of Whalley,[4] which is a complete and accurate chartulary or transcript of evidences belonging to that and the parent-house of Stanlaw, digested into twenty titles, every title referring to a distinct parish or township, and to the title page is prefixed the following inscription:

MARIA. IHS. JOHANNES.

Hic liber fuit scriptus tempore bonæ memoriæ Magistri Joh. Lyndelay sacræ paginæ professoris A. MCCCxlvii.

But there is also the strongest internal evidence to prove that he was author of that singular and valuable tract, *de Statu Blackburnshire*, which has preserved so many particulars of our parochial history from the earliest periods, namely, the origin and constitution of the deanery, the state of property before the Conquest, the foundation of the dependent parishes, and a number of circumstances, in attestation of which we have been enabled to adduce such a body of external testimony. For, as this account is carried down to one of the first transactions of Lyndelay, it cannot be prior to his time; and, as it contains not the most obscure reference to any thing of later date, it must, by every rule of criticism, be held contemporary with the last facts which it records. This memoir displays, indeed, a measure of curiosity and intelligence little to be expected in that dark age and

[1] For there was a William de Topcliffe of Billington, who, in one charter, is called his brother; or, what is the same thing, of John de Topcliffe, vicar of Whalley. Townley MSS.

[2] This is proved by the following coincidence of circumstances: John del Clogh grants to Adam de Gristhwaite and John de Topcliffe, in trust for the abbey, 10th part of the manor of Reved, A.D. 1342. And in the *Status de Blackburnshire* we are told: "Tempore Joh. Lyndlay abb. 10ma pars manerii de Revard adquisita fuit."

[3] In the Townley MSS. the name of this abbot is spelt *Livesay;* which, had it been right, would have left no doubt with respect to his family: but, in an original charter now before me, the orthography is as I have given it.

[4] [The Editors reserve what is further to be said both of the *Coucher Book* and the treatise *De Statu* to their Prefatory remarks.]

obscure situation. The latinity of it, though far from classical, is not inferior to the style of the best historians of its time; the technical terms of canon law, in particular, are applied with strict propriety. But as it has been proved to belong to that period, it proves itself to belong to the place; and when these limitations have contracted our inquiries to so narrow a compass, to whom can this germ[1] of the History of Whalley be with any colour of probability assigned, but to the known compiler of the Coucher Book, the contemporary abbot, the accurate and industrious Lyndelay?

The first act which occurs of this abbot is the acquisition of a tenth part of the manor of Read, in 1342; and the next, that of the manor of Choo, and the second moiety of the manor of Billington. The latter of these was an object of great importance, both from its value and its contiguity to the house.

In 1349 he, together with the convent, obtained a license from King Edward III. *ob majorem securitatem suam et domus suæ, quod ipsi Eccl'am et Clausum Abb'iæ suæ muro de petra et calce possint firmare et kernellare.* This was probably the part of the fabric completed under abbot Lyndelay; for thirteen years after, or in 1362, the provincial of the Cistercian order, at his periodical visitation, releases the abbey and convent of Whalley from their rated contribution,[2] *quousque ecclesia conventus sit perfecta et simul dormitorium et refectorium, quæ sunt totaliter construendæ.* The Church,[3] we see, had been advancing very slowly, if at all, during the last twenty years, and the Refectory and Dormitory were not yet begun.

In the same year[4] Henry Duke of Lancaster, patron of the house, granted in trust to the abbot and convent "2 cottages, 7 acres of land,[5] 183 of pasture, 200 of wood, called

[1] It has a right to that appellation; for the first idea of this work was conceived many years ago in the library of St. John's College, Cambridge, after a perusal of the *Status de Blackburnshire*, in the Monasticon Anglicanum.

[2] Towneley MSS.

[3] In the tower of the church there appear to have been five bells, of which I met with the following imperfect memorial, among the papers of my worthy predecessor Mr. Johnson:—"Thomas Talbot of Dinkley, A.D. 1515, gave to the steeple of Whalley one bell, called the morning-bell; the second was consecrated to St. John the Evangelist; the third to St. John Baptist; the fourth in honour of the Assumption of the Blessed Virgin; the fifth to the Holy Trinity, and All Saints, and All Souls going out of this world. This bell was given by Wm. Redcliff of Wimbersley, who gave his body to lie at Whalley, if his dear wife died after him; but, if she died first, she might choose where she would lie, but All Sowls' bell towling for her at her departure, which was A.D. 1505. Roger Fitton of Martholm, in Harwood, gave the third bell; and Matilda, his dear wife, gave an acre of land, and other lands in Harwood and Billington, for good of her poor soul and her consort, to be prayed and sung for in the choir. Also Roger Nowell of Merley gave xix acres of arable land, on condition that every priest of the said house daily, in the canon of the mass, should make special commemoration of the souls of his family, as well the dead as the living. A.D. 1283." ["Four of these remain to this day; three of them are at Downham, and one at Church Kirk, no doubt given by the Asshetons of Whalley Abbey, who were the patrons of those livings. Around the rim of one of the bells is "S'ta Margaretta ora pro nobis," on another "S'ta Katherina ora pro nobis," on another the inscription is unintelligible. (Lecture by the Rev. R. N. Whitaker, Vicar of Whalley, Feb. 2, 1869.)]

[4] Coucher Book; from whence this indenture, in old French, has been transplanted into the *Monasticon.*

[5] Land, in the old law sense, is arable land—*Terra* (says Sir Edward Coke, who always affected quaint etymologies) *à terendo.*

Rommesgreve, in the chase of Blackburn; likewise 2 mess. 126 acres of land, 26 of meadow, 130 of pasture called Standen, Hulcroft, and Grenelache, lying in the towns of Penhulton and Cliderhou, with the fold and foldage of Standen, to support a recluse[1] in a certain place within the churchyard of the parochial church of Whalley; as also two woman servants to attend [her], there to pray for the soul of the said Duke, his ancestors and heirs, and to find them every week 17 loaves of bread, such as is usually made in the convent, each weighing fifty shillings sterling, and seven loaves of an inferior sort and the same weight;[2] also eight gallons of their better beer, and three-pence for their food. Moreover, at the feast of All Saints, yearly, to provide them 10 large stock fishes, one bushel of oatmeal for pottage, one bushel of rye, two gallons of oil for their lamps, one [stone] of tallow for candle,[3] [ten] loads[4] of turf (no coal), and one load of faggots; also to repair their habitations, and to find a [monk, chaplain of the said abbey, of honest conversation, and a clerk to minister to him at mass daily for ever] in the chapel of the said recluse,[5] with vestment [chalice, bread, wine, light, and other ornaments necessary for the said mass]. The successor of the recluse to be nominated by the Duke and his heirs.[6]

This endowment was ample, but turned out, as we shall hereafter see, more to the emolument than either the credit or comfort of the house upon which it was engrafted.

Six years after this time appears another Visitation by the abbot of Rivaulx, as deputy to the provincial of his order; the result of which, I fear, will induce a suspicion that abbot Lyndlay was more of a scholar than either a disciplinarian or economist. For—

[Receptæ an. Mccclxvj . DXXViij*l.* xs.
Expensæ in eod. . DClxxxj*l.* xv*s.* vij*d.*
Recept. an. current. usq. ad diem Visitationis, viz. diem post fest. S. Petri ad Vincula . . ccl*l.* j*s.* v*d.*
Exp. in eod. . ccccxxxviij*l.*
In ultimo computo debetur Duci Lanc. pro Capella Castri Cliderhow, cccl.
Diversis creditoribus, ccxlvij*l.* vj*s.* viij*d.*
Solvend. de pecunia recepta de Abb. de Cumbermere et aliis malefactoribus, clxiij*l.* xij*s.* viij*d.* (At the meaning of this article I can offer no conjecture.)
Debita de claro, DCCxv*l.* iij*s.* iv*d.*
Boves, c.; tauri, ij.; vaccæ, xxx.; bovunculi et juvenc. II ann., xx.; sturci, xx. Summa clxxij.

[1] [*Une recluse* (Coucher Book, p. 1155), not "two recluses," as was printed in former editions.]

[2] [*Paynes conventuales.*] [3] [*Une pier de sur.*]

[4] [*Dys charrez des tourbes*, not "six," as before printed.]

[5] [*Une moigne chappellayn, &c., en la chapelle de la dite recluse*—not recluses, as before printed.]

[6] This is a good specimen of English œconomics 450 years ago: but the provisions vary exceedingly, both in kind and in proportion, from what would be allowed in the foundation of a modern almshouse. Bread and beer seem to have been intended for the principal support of these recluses. Even oatmeal pottage, the wholesome food of our Lancashire peasantry, of which we have here the first mention, must have been a rarity, as one bushel *per annum* would not have supplied a meal per day. Peat was the principal fuel, with a little wood; no fossil-coal; a very small provision of oil for lamps; and of tallow, little better than none. Hence I conclude, that the recluses must have been intended to keep very early hours at night. But, from what follows in their history, it may be feared that some of them *loved darkness rather than light.*

Verveces, cclxxij.; ov. matric., clxxvij.; agni, cvj.; affri ad grang. pro opere, iv.
Monachi, xxix. De quibus III sæculariter evagantes. Conversus I.[1] (Townley MSS.)

From the increase of rents, and great decrease of stock, it appears that the monks had let out a considerable portion of their demesne within the last forty years.

I have met with no other memorials of the house during the life-time of Dr. Lyndelay, who sat at least thirty-five years, as he was alive in 1377, but probably died soon after.

He was succeeded by—

VI. William Selbie, Vicar of Whalley, of whom nothing is remembered but the name. His successor was—

VII. Nicholas de Eboraco, or Yorke, who occurs in 1392; and by inq. appears to have died 5th of Hen. V. or 1417. He was succeeded by—

VIII. William Whalley,[2] undoubtedly a native of this place, in whose time, in the year 1418, Robert abbot of Furness, who had been appointed by the Pope to be the *Reformator* of all monasteries of the Cistercian order, with whom William abbot of Sallay was joined in commission, held a Visitation of the abbey of Whalley, which is recorded in the following terms:

Omnibus et singulis personis nostri Cistertiensis ordinis Robertus abbas monasterii Beatæ Mariæ de Fournisie, Reformator omnium et singulorum monasteriorum predictæ ordinis constitutus auctoritate domini Papæ, et etiam Willielmus abbas monasterii Beatæ Mariæ de Sallay ordinis Cisterciensis. Dum partibus provinciæ Eboracensis pro utilitate ordinis nostræ interessemus advenit persona propria reverendus in Christo pater abbas monasterii Beatæ Mariæ de Whalley et ex parte Dei et ordinis nostri sæpius requisivit de et super reformatione monasterii sui in spiritualibus et temporalibus tam in capite quam in membris; qua requisitione nobis facta accessimus ad præfatum monasterium de Whalley, et lecta coram abbate et conventum diffinitione ordinis generalis cum bulla papali, admissi sumus et eosdem abbatem et conventum unanimi consensu ad reformandum ibidem, in spiritualibus et temporalibus tam in capite quam in membris. Igitur in actu reformationis nostræ noveritis nos ita processisse: Primo, fecimus diligentem et specialem inquisitionem de et super gradu, dignitate, gubernatione, et etiam fideli administratione domini Willielmi de Whalley abbatis monasterii prælibati, in qua quidem inquisitionem fecimus, primo et Fratrem Rogerum de Smethedone et omnes et singulos ejus monasterii monachos tunc præsentes et quemlibet eorum per se et singillatim in verbo sacerdotis ponendo manus ad pectus præstare juramentum quod de infra scriptis articulis purè, nudè et simpliciter dicant veritatem, 1mo vid. utrum dominus Willielmus esset ejus monasterii de Whalley verus Abbas legitime et canonice electus, annon? Item utrum idem dominus Willielmus aliquam notoriam commisit Symoniam, vel etiam incontinentiam, vel si dictus Willielmus fuerit dilapidator, alienator, aut dissipator bonorum monasterii de Whalley, vel si idem Willielmus fuerit fur, homicida, gravis sacrilegus, solempniter perjurus, vel etiam conspirator seu alio aliquo crimine notorie irretitus. Super quibus quidem articulis dominus R. de Smethedon dicti monasterii Prior, juratus et examinatus in verbo sacerdotis, ponendo manum super pectus dicit et affirmat quod idem Willielmus est legitimè et canonicè electus et verus Abbas . . . . . . nec fur nec homicida, &c.—propter quæ seu eorum aliquod a gradu, statu, et dignitate abbatiatus

[1] The *Conversi* were lay brethren. [In prædicti Savignii abbatia non solum Monachi sed etiam Laici quos *Conversos* nuncupant, sub habitu religionis Deo deserviunt. (Acta S. Hamonis monachi Savigneii, apud Ducange, edit. Henschel.)]

[2] In the possession of Mr. Barrett of Manchester is a general pardon granted to William abbot and the convent of Whalley, dated at Westminster a.r. Hen. VI. 3°. Test. Joh. Duc. of Bedford, and countersigned Clitherowe.

merito debet amoveri, sed hoic usque dignè et laudabiliter gubernavit et administravit tam in spiritualibus quam in temporalibus; cui etiam omnes et singuli monachi ejusdem monasterii unaniniter et concorditer in ejus electione spontè et voluntariè eidem suas professiones et obedientiam impenderunt.

Qua quidem inquisitione coram nobis sic ut præmittitur privatim et secreto facta fidelibus et veris testibus domino R. de Smethedon priore et monachis prædictis prout superius recitatur; ex eorum unanimi consensu et voluntate, plenariam et majorem declarationem status, gradus, et dignitatis domini Willielmi abbatis monasterii de Whalley predicti in domo capitulari ibidem coram toto convento ejusdem loci duximus publicandum et de facto fecimus publicari, necnon omnibus et singulis et maximè ejusdem ordinis professoribus innotescimus per presentes. In quorum omnium fidem et testimonium sigilla nostra una cum sigillo conventuali dicti monasterii de Whalley, toto conventu ad hoc consentiente, duximus apponenda. Data sunt hæc et acta in domo capitulari dicti monasterii de Whalley 7mo Apr. A.D. 1418.

The insertion of this instrument may be pardoned, as the form of visiting a monastery has not I think been given by any writer on Monastic Antiquities. (*From the History of Craven*, p. 42, 43.)

After an interval nearly of sixty years, we meet with another notice relating to the progress of the building, for on the eve of Saint Thomas the Apostle, 1425, the convent took possession of a new Dormitory, with a ceremonial thus described:

Memorandum quod anno Domini 1425 in vigilia Sancti Thome apostoli, intravit Conventus de Whalley in novum Dormitorium ad noctem immediate post completorium[1] in ecclesia ab omnibus decantatum. Insuper dominus Willielmus Abbas et totus Conventus processionaliter stantes cantaverunt Hymnum *Te Deum Laudamus*, etc., et cantando Abbas indutus copa cum pastorali virga aspersit aqua benedicta omnia Lecta dormitorii, et post finem Hymni dicta Collecta *Quesumus Domine* ab Abbate et data benediccione exierunt. (Harl. MS. 1830, f. 24.)

This was a striking ceremony, and serves to show with what judgment, and knowledge of the human heart, the gloomy uniformity of monastic life was occasionally varied, by exhibitions calculated to strike the senses and amuse the imagination. It is not impossible that it might have a better effect that, as the hours of severest trial to those who were debarred from the great privilege of their nature were to be passed in that apartment, an awe which, in superstitious minds, would long accompany the remembrance of this outward sprinkling, might be an inducement, where purer ones were wanting, to keep the heart sprinkled from an evil conscience.[2] And, after all the outcry that has been raised against ceremonies, in days of comparative darkness, a real use might thus result from divers washings, and carnal ordinances, imposed on them until the time of reformation.[3]

The Refectory, which, with the kitchens, probably formed the south side of the cloister-court, now destroyed, seems to have been completed in the interval betwixt the year 1362 and 1425. The Dormitory appears to have been the upper story of the western side of the same quadrangle, which is yet remaining, and consisting of one apartment, at least 120 feet in length.

[1] The *Completorium* or *Compline*, in the Romish ritual, is the last part of the evening-service.

[2] Hebr. x. 22.

[3] Hebr. ix. 10.

Abbot Whalley survived the benediction of the Dormitory nine years, and seems to have devoted his latter days to the erection of the Choir of the church, which, however, he did not live to see completed, for he died in 1434,[1] after an active and useful presidency of seventeen years.

Next succeeded

IX. John Eccles, who must have been an aged man at his election, as he was considerably senior in order of admission to his predecessor. There can be little doubt that he was a native of the town whose name he bore, and of which his house had the appropriation. This abbot had the honour of putting the last hand to the fabric of his abbey, at least according to the original plan,[2] after a period of 142 years from the first foundation, for in 1438, [*read* 1435,] "in vigilia Omnium Sanctorum ad vesperas intravit conventus de Whalley in nova stalla, tempore Johannis Eccles Abbatis.[3]"

Notwithstanding this information, which I have no reason to think incorrect,[4] the abbot's stall, which with great part of the rest is still preserved in the parish church, has the cypher W. W. which undoubtedly means William Whalley. But the chronological difficulty may be obviated by supposing that the stalls had been begun in the latter end of abbot Whalley's time, that the abbot's stall had been carved first, and that the choir was not ready for them, or they for the choir, till four years after, as the monks appear to have carried on their works with great deliberation.[5]

Indeed a question naturally arises out of this account, namely, to what concurrence of circumstances it was owing that the completion of an edifice of which every part was wanting either for the accommodation of its inhabitants or for the pomp of worship, had been deferred so long;[6] but the answer is obvious: the Abbey of Whalley, with great revenues, was never rich, and, though the monks had not only neglected to increase their number to 60, as they were bound to do by the Bull of Pope Boniface, but had even reduced their numbers beneath the original establishment of 40, yet, from the two statements of their affairs which have been given, they appear to have been usually in debt. Their founder had indeed bestowed upon them, in addition to their other possessions, a valuable rectory and a rich and extensive glebe, but this was all. He permitted them to take possession of the old parsonage-house, and to provide for themselves better accommodations at their leisure, and, thus circumstanced, they judged wisely to adopt a magnificent plan, and to pursue it, though slowly yet with uniformity, rather than to disgrace themselves and what they conceived to be the cause of God by mean and hasty erections.

But by what mismanagement, it will be asked, were their funds inadequate to the

[1] The Lady Chapel, built by abbot Paslew, seems not to have formed a part of the original plan.

[2] Townley MSS.

[3] Harl. MS. 1830 [f. 24].

[4] [It is incorrect, so far as the date, which (being in Arabic figures in the Harl. MS. 1830, f. 24) was misread 1438, instead of 1435, as we have intimated in the text.]

[5] I now think [adds Dr. Whitaker in 3rd edition, p. 75,] that no more is meant by these words than that the new stalls were substituted for old ones. The choir itself appears to have been finished long before.

[6] It had not been wanting so long.—See the last note [and note [4]].

completing of the present building in a much shorter period? Perhaps by no mismanagement at all.

The claims upon their hospitality were immense, and sometimes drew from them complaints on a subject, which, to do them justice, rarely excited their murmurs without cause. Hospitality was a virtue common to all the religious houses; but the peculiar situation of Whalley, almost at an equal distance between Manchester and Lancaster, in the centre of a barren and inhospitable tract, and in the great route of the pilgrims[1] from north to south, rendered these demands singularly oppressive here. Their liberality in money was also great. The nobility and gentry of the county had corrodies or pensions; the poor friars, the minstrels, the officers of the Ecclesiastical Court in their visitations, and even the servants of ordinary visitants, partook liberally of their bounty. Then again, the most hopeful of their novices were educated at the universities, and encouraged to proceed to the higher degrees, when degrees cost at least half as much in terms of money as at present.[2]

Besides, their demesnes, though rich in pasturage, were not very favourable to the growth of grain. The collection of corn-tithe in kind, throughout the greater part of their parishes, must have been nearly impossible; and the conveyance of the grain they were compelled to purchase, *extra patriam* as they termed it, must have been extremely inconvenient, in consequence of the state of the roads.

On the whole, it will leave no very unfavourable impression of the monks of Whalley to assert, what may be proved from their accounts, that not more than a fourth part of their large income was consumed in their own personal expenses.

But these considerations will be more properly resumed when we enter upon the subject of their receipts and expenditure.

Of the adjoining Hermitage, founded by Henry Duke of Lancaster, nothing has occurred since the foundation; but, in the time of abbot Eccles, an instance of misconduct in a votress of this establishment afforded a pretext, which may seem to have been willingly embraced, for petitioning the King, who was now become patron as Duke of Lancaster, to dissolve an institution which did no credit either to itself or the monastery on which it depended.

It appears, that under the general description of a recluse, votaries of either sex might be included.[3] Accordingly King Henry VI. by [writ of privy seal] dated July 6, a. r. 15°, nominated one "Isola de Hetou de com. Lanc. vidua, quod ipsa pro termino vitæ suæ esse possit anachorita in loco ad hoc ordinato juxta ecclesiam parochialem de Whalley." This

[1] The mention of Pilgrim Cross in Tottington at once marks their route, and the frequency of their journeys. The Shrine of Becket, and of our Lady of Walsingham, probably had many devout and idle visitants from the North; and in the title *De Donis* of the Computus A. 1478, is a sum charged as given "itinerantibus versus Jerusalem."

[2] In the Compotus of 1521 is the following entry: Scolari pro gradu Bac. *9l. 6s. 8d.* which is almost equivalent to *100l.* at present.

[3] [Our author, as before noticed in p. 97, did not correctly understand that the Hermitage at Whalley was founded for one female votary only.]

vow was probably taken in the first fervours of sorrow, which soon wore off, so that the widow grew weary of her confinement, and broke loose from her vows and her cell together. Vowesses like these, who, under pretence of total solitude, were only exempted from the restraints of social retirement, seem to have been in general a disgrace to their profession. Leland mentions an anchoress "in media urbe (of the town of Wakefield) unde aliquando inventa fecunda;" and, among some old charters relating to the parish of Rochdale, I have seen an attestation, *filii monialis* (in the proper sense of anchoress) *de Newbold*. Nay, even among those females who were kept under the stricter discipline of the cloister many it is to be feared were little better than those solitaries who kept their own keys; and friar Wrath, the mischievous spy of Piers Plowman, would remember many instances like that of dame Parnel,[1] though he does indeed hint that her misconduct stood in the way of her advancement.

However, the behaviour of this Isola or Isold de Heton occasioned a representation to the King, which contains the following passage:[2]

TO THE KYNG OWRE SOVEREIGN LORD, &c.

Be hit remembryd that the plase and habitacion of the seid recluse is within place halowed, and nere to the gate of the seyd monastre, and that the weemen that have been attendyng and acquayntyd to the seyd recluse have recorse dailly into the seyd monastre, for the livere of brede, ale, kychin, and other thyngs for the sustentacyon of the seyd recluse accordyng to the compposityon endentyd above rehersyd: the whyche is not accordyng (fitting) to be had withyn such religyous plases. And how that dyvers that been anchores and recluses in the seyd plase aforetyme, contrary to theyre own oth and professyon, have brokyn owte of the seyd plase, wherin they were reclusyd, and departyd therfrom wythout eny reconsilyatyon. And in especyal how that now Isold of Heton that was last recluysd in the seyd plase, at denomynatyon and preferment of owre Sovereign Lord and Kyng that nowe is, is broken owte of the seyd plase, and hath departyd therfrom contrary to her own oth and professyon, not willyng nor entendyng to be restoryd agayn, and so livyng at her own liberte by this two yere and more, like as she had never bin professyd. And that divers of the wymen that have been servants ther and attendyng to the recluses afortym have byn misgovernyd, and gotten with chyld withyn the seyd plase halowyd, to the grete displeasaunce of hurt and disclander of the abbeye aforeseyd, &c.

Please hyt your Highness of our espesyal grase to grant to your orators the abbat, &c.

This petition had the desired effect of delivering the abbey from the shame and vexation occasioned by these disorderly women; for, by letters patent reciting the scandals which had been given by the recluses upon this foundation, Henry VI. dissolved the Hermitage endowed by Henry Duke of Lancaster his ancestor, appointing in its place two chaplains to say mass daily in the parish church of Whalley, for the soul of the said Duke

[1] And Dame Parnel a preests file, priores was she never,
For she had a child in chery time, all our chapter hit wist.

[2] It is now extant at Whalley Abbey in the old book marked A.C., from whence it was transcribed, in the beginning of the seventeenth century, by Weever, and inserted in his "Funerall Monuments," p. 155; but he omitted to mention the reception which it met with, and the effect which it produced. Indeed, it was a representation likely to interest the chastity and zeal of Henry VI. and is far from conveying an unfavourable idea of the state of morals in the house.

Henry, and for his own good estate while living, and on the anniversary of his own death for ever, ordaining an obit to be celebrated by thirty chaplains.[1]

Under the three succeeding princes of the house of York, it is scarcely to be supposed that the latter condition would be performed, unless the monks of Whalley were bold and faithful Lancasterians indeed. It might however be remembered, after the accession of Henry VII., who felt or affected great reverence for the memory of this blameless man, and would in all probability have obtained his beatification, had not the reigning Pontiff (Julius II.), as Lord Bacon[2] observes, "been a man who knew how to distinguish between innocence and sanctity."

Of the house and chapel of these recluses nothing now remains; but they appear to have stood upon the site of those dirty cottages which defile and disgrace the western side of the churchyard.[3]

Nothing further is recorded of the administration of abbot Eccles, who died in the 21st of Henry VI. 1443 or 4.

After his death is a succession of four Abbots, in the space of twenty-nine years, of whom nothing is remembered but their names,[4] viz.

X. Ralph Cliderhow,[5] [or Sclater,] vicar of Whalley.

XI. Nicholas Billington.

XII. Robert Hamond, al. Harwood.[6]

XIII. William Billington.

All probably monk's names, indicating the places of their respective births. Next occurs a man whose name frequently appears in the local transactions of those times.

XIV. Ralph Holden, elected the 11th or 12th Edw. IV. It is in the highest degree probable that this abbot was younger son of Adam Holden of Holden, and Alice his wife, daughter of William Holland of Heaton.

Adam Holden occurs in charters of the year 1411, and is known to have had a son, Christopher, whose eldest son, the first of that name in the direct line, was Ralph, and probably so called after the abbot. There appears also a Ralph Holden, of Aspden, in the

[1] Coucher Book, *ubi supra* [not in the Chetham Society's edition.]

[2] Life of Henry VII. [References to the existing evidences of the proposed canonization of Henry VI. will be found in Trevelyan Papers (Camden Society), vol. iii.]

[3] These nuisances are now removed (1818) at the instance of the Author, by walling-up the doors; which, till within the last five years, opened into the church-yard, on the north and west sides.

[4] [In the list of Abbots, Harl. MS. 1830, f. 23, Nicholas Billington is said to have preceded Cliderhowe, the latter being numbered as eleventh, the former as tenth Abbot.]

[5] The family name of this abbot was Sclater; for there is a receipt, Townley MSS. G. 20, from Joh. Pilkington to Rad. Sclater, Abbot of Whalley, for 6s. 8*d*. 6th Edw. IV.

[6] I have never met with any original charters of this abbot, who must have sat a very short time; but in the Townley MSS. the name is spelt *Harwood;* which I am inclined to think right, as *Hamond* is no common name in the North, and nothing is more probable, than that a native of the neighbouring village of Harwood should have become a monk of Whalley.

year 1454,[1] who seems to have been progenitor of the Holdens of Chargeley,[2] but must have been too young to have been ancestor of the abbot.[3]

In the latter part of this Abbot's time, a great dispute fell out between the abbey of Whalley and sir Christopher Parsons, rector of Slaidburn, on account of the tithes of certain lands called Hall Flatt and Countess Meadows, together with Slaidburn Mill, which, though not included within the forest of Bowland, and actually surrounded, like many other small insulated tracts, by another county, were in fact ancient demesne lands belonging to the castle and castle parish of Clitheroe. Some servants of the abbey, with Christopher Thornbergh, then bursar of the house, at their head, driving away a few tithe calfs from these lands, were set upon by a mob instigated by the rector, who with dreadful outcries of **kyll ye monke, slaye ye monke**, attacking the tithing party, sent them home cruelly beaten, and in a very evil plight. Their next step was to swear the tenants of these bateable lands, upon the crosse of a groat, to pay no tithes but to the rector, whose conduct on the whole appears to have been extremely violent and unwarrantable.

This story, with all its circumstances, is most tragically and lamentably set forth by the sufferers, *recentibus odiis*, in a memorial yet extant in the Coucher Book,[4] and subscribed by the abbots of Salley, Cockersand, &c., for the whole fraternity were up in arms at such an attack upon the property of a monastery and the person of a monk. However, each party appealed to his own ordinary; and, as it did not seem very clear to whom the cognizance of the cause appertained, whether to the Bishop of Lichfield, in whose diocese the abbey stood, or to the Archbishop of York, in whose diocese the tithes accrued,[5] at length,

[1] Townley MSS.

[2] John Holden of Chageley had a second son Ralph, who is referred to in the Townley Pedigree as living 12th Edw. IV.; and, though he is not mentioned as Monk or Abbot of Whalley, I think it most likely (on account of the vicinity of Chageley to Whalley) that he was the person.

[3] At the inthronization of Archbishop Neville, 6th Edw. IV. the great Northern abbots sat at the second table, and were arranged in the following order, in which, it must be understood, they ranked by pairs :—

	I.	
Abbot of St. Maries, York.		Prior of Duresme.
	II.	
Abbot of Fountains.		Abbot of Whalley.
	III.	
Abbot of Salley.		Abbot of Kirkstall.
	IV.	
Abbot of Rivaulx.		Abbot of Bylande.
	V.	
Abbot of Whitby.		Abbot of Selby.
	VI.	
Abbot of Meaux.		Prior of Bridlington.

The rank which these great ecclesiastics bore is strikingly displayed at this feast, in which the temporal barons were placed at an inferior table.

[4] [Not in the Chetham Society's edition.]

[5] Hence it appears that tithe-causes, in the fifteenth century, were cognizable by the ordinary. The Court of Exchequer is never mentioned.

after much wrangling, both parties agreed to refer the dispute to King Edward IV., who, after an hearing before the privy council, determined it very rightly in favour of the house. [1]

This award was further confirmed by letters patent of Richard III., dated Dec. 3rd, an. reg. 2do, from which I transcribe the following passage as a specimen of the language and orthography of that time:

Wee therfore remembring wele that wee be thair founder and protector, by reason wherof wee owe to succor tham in all theyr rights, wole and charge you and every of you, that unto tham in contynnying tham in the same yee be helping aidyng and assistyng to your powers. And in especiall our tenants of Boulond, that yee do pay the said abbot and convent as ye have done aforetyme after the tenor of the said jugement, havyng no consideracyon to noo awarde, bounde, ne dome made contrary to the said jugement withouten assent and wyll of the said abbot and convent, and that yee ne faile to do the premissez as yee will avoyde our great displeasir.

Abbot Holden died in 1480, after having sat about nine years, and was succeeded by

XV. Christopher Thornbergh, junior bursar of the house, whose activity and suffering in the cause which has been related above might possibly recommend him to this dignity; which he enjoyed only six years, and, dying in 1486, [2] was followed by

XVI. William Rede, so called in all probability from the neighbouring township of that name. His government began nearly with that of Henry VII. and ended about four years before it; a period of great tranquillity, such as usually precedes a storm.[3] [He died 13 July, 1507.] [4]

On his decease the convent elected their prior [5]

[1] It is remarkable, that in an inspeximus of 7th Hen. VII. relating to this cause, of which the original is now before me, Edward IV. is styled *Dn. Ed. nuper reg. Angl. quart.* but Richard III. *Dn. R. nuper de facto et non de jure reg. Angl.* Surely personal resentment had its share in this distinction: for Henry VII. no more acknowledged the right of Edward V. on which the usurpation of Richard was grounded, than that of his father. It is curious, that this appellation of Kings *de facto* was applied by the house of York to that of Lancaster, but afterwards retorted.

[2] Comp. A.D. 1487, *ab W. Rede primo.*

[3] The following contract between this Abbot and Sir John Talbot of Salesbury seems to indicate that some considerable buildings or repairs were going on in his time. "This Indenture, &c. bearing date Jan. 28, 6 Hen. VII. witnessyth that William abbot of Whalley hath bought of Sir John Talbot knight a parcel of wood callyd Keyteyhurst, for which ye said Sir John is payd xviij*l.* The Boundes wherof begin at the great Holgh * standing in the southe parte of ye wood without Whitefeld Rawe, so following ye Rawe to Dinkelly Moor, and from, &c. &c. to Ribble Bank—then to Deidweynstobbe, and so following from Deidweynstobbe uppe throgh the Wode, from oke to oke, as they are markyd, and so following y^e skirts of y^e Hurst, fro oke to oke, unto the Holgh Sappeling, standyng in y^e southe parte aforesaid. Y^e seid Abbot to have alle Wode within y^e Boundys aforesaid, except sappeling, holyn, ashe, crabtre, and haythorne, $with^t$ they be deid." Townley MSS.

[4] [1507. 3 idus Julii obiit dominus Willielmus Rede abbas 24 de Whalley. Cotton. MS. Vesp. D. xvii. f. 16.]

[5] [Die Sancti Donati videlicet 7 idus Augusti eodem anno (1507) suscepit in se regimen domus de Whalley dominus Joannes Paslow, et sic regnavit annos 29 et amplius. Cotton. MS. Vesp. D. xvii. f. 16.]

* I have long doubted the meaning of the words Holgh and Holgh Sappeling; but am now inclined to think them synonymous with Hag, in the following passage of Lawson's "New Orchard and Garden, 1597," which I quote from Dr. Hunter's edition of Evelyn's *Sylva*, p. 476:—"I see a number of *Hags;* where, out of one root, you shall see three or four pretty oaks or ashes, streight and tall." I think the meaning is, a large old root, sending up several young stems.

XVII. JOHN PASLEW, B.D., whom his arms, lately remaining in the windows of the abbey, prove to have been of the Paslews of Wiswall.[1] I suppose him to have been son of Francis Paslew, who occurs in charters about the year 1460. To him or to his predecessor, Rede, is to be ascribed that quadrangular building which the Assheton family chose for their habitation, and which appears to have been the abbot's lodgings. I am induced to refer this part of the abbey to so late a period, by some appearances in the wood-work, which I think were peculiar to the reign of Henry VII. and the earlier part of that of his son.

To abbot Paslew[2] also must be ascribed the new chapel of our Ladye of Whalley, referred to in the indentures for erecting the north aisle of Burnley church, A.D. 1533,[3] which appears to have been building A.D. 1521, from a considerable sum charged in the *compotus* of that year *pro fabrica ecclesiæ.* Thus the first twenty years of this abbot passed, like those of his predecessors, in the duties of his choir, in the exercise of hospitality, in attention to the extensive possessions of his house, or in the improvement of its buildings; but a storm was now approaching, before which either conscience or bigotry prevented him from bending, and which brought quick and premature destruction on him and his house.

The religious houses in general were now greatly relaxed in discipline, and many of them dreadfully corrupted in morals. What was the state of Whalley, however, as no report of the visitors is extant, must be left to conjecture; but charity should incline us to think no evil of an institution professedly religious, against which no specific evidence appears.

[1] [The family pedigree occurs hereafter. "The gold finger ring of abbot Paslew was in the possession of Pudsey Dawson, Esq. of Hornby Castle, where I have seen it, and is now in the hands of his nephew, Richard Dawson, Esq."—Lecture by the Rev. R. N. Whitaker, Vicar of Whalley, 12 Feb. 1867.]

[2] To the beginning of Abbot Paslew's time must be referred the following Memorial, written either by himself or one of his monks, in the Leiger Book* of Whalley, out of which it was copied by Weever (Fun. Mon. p. 394):—"A.D. Mvxiii. Hoc anno Jacobus Scotie rex in Borea triumphaliter ab Anglis interemptus est: cujus corpus, quum hæc scripserim (quoniam membrum ab Ecclesia evulsum de hoc mundo abscesserit) huc usque in domo Carthusiensium apud Rychmund mortalibus miserandum spectaculum inhumatum jacet—'Qui videt testimonium perhibuit, et verum est testimonium ejus.'—Lib. Monasterii de Whalley, in com. Lanc."—No very decent application of the words of St. John.

[It might be thought that Richmond in Yorkshire was the place here mentioned, but the house of the Carthusians in question was that at Sheen, near Richmond in Surrey, where the chronicler Stowe himself saw what was said to be the royal deposit, as related in the following passage:—"After that the Earle of Surrey had taken order, and set the North in good quiet, he returned to the Queene, with the dead bodie of the Scottish King, which bodie inclosed in lead (as before is showed), as I have beene informed, was conveyed to Shine, a Monastery in Surrey, founded by King Henry V. where it remained for a time, in what order I am not certaine, but since the dissolution of the house, to wit in the raign of K. Edward the VI. Henry Gray then Duke of Suffolke there keeping house, I have beene showed the same body (as was affirmed) so lapped in lead, thrown into an olde wast roome amongst olde timber, stone, lead, and other rubble." (Annals, 1614, p. 495.) 29 Nov. 1513, Leo X. wrote to Henry VIII. authorising the body of James IV. to be carried to London, and buried in St. Paul's, notwithstanding that he had incurred the sentence of excommunication. Brewer, Letters and Papers of Henry VIII. vol. i. p. 705.]

[3] MS. pen. Auct.

* I have never seen this book.

The Injunctions also of the Visitors, if indeed they gave any particular injunctions, are lost,[1] but the tenor of them may be guessed at from the following articles of relaxation[2] yet extant. (Dodsworth's MSS. at Oxford, vol. lxi. f. 25.)

The relaxacyon of certayne particles of ye Injunctyons given of late in ye monasterie of Whalley, in the conntie of Lancastre, by the Visiters for ye Kynges highness there.

Imprimis, That ye Abbot, havyng one or two discrete brethren of ye said monasterie with hym, may go and ride abrode for ye necessarie business of ye same howse and anie other honest cause, so that they resort not to anie suspecte place or suspecte companie.

Item. That it maie be permitted to two discrete brethren of ye saide howse with lycens of ye abbot to go and ride abrode for ye necessarie business of ye same or for anie other honest cawse, so that they tarie no longer abrode than ye busyness shall necessarilie require, and alsoe ye companie with suspecte and infamed persons be utterlie avoided.

Item. That it maie be permitted to certayne brethren of ye foresaide monasterie with lycense of the abbot to walke for ther bodilie heilth forthe of ye precinct of ye saide monasterie into ye felds adjoyning to ye saide howse thre tymes in a moneth, and ther use honest recreacyon, so that they be at the least foure together, and all suspicious resortes to be avoided, wher . . . . .

Item. That it maie be permitted to certayne discrete seniors, being officers of ye said howse, with lycens of the abbot, to lye in ye chambers heretofore for them assigned, so that all suspicions resortes be avoyded.

Item. That a lecture of divinitie redde in ye saide monasterie thre tymes wycklie may suffice, soe that yt bee done diligentlie, purelie, and sincerelie. (Signed) THOM. CRUMWELL.

How far the following instrument contributed to this relaxation, or whether it does not refer to a subsequent transaction, the reader will judge for himself:

[1] ["General Injunctions to be given on the King's Highness behalf in all Monasteries and other Houses of whatever order or religion they may be," are printed by Burnet, *Hist. of the Reformation*, from Cotton MS. Cleop. E. IV.]

[2] [These articles of relaxation may be illustrated by comparison with the following extracts from similar articles granted by Cromwell to the Monastery of St. Mary of York (*Lansd. MS.* 973, p. 101):

I. Inprimis, that the Abbot may goo foorth of his monastery as well unto his manors and to other places, as also for any other honest cause, and that he beinge foorth may there tarie for like causes, and to take with him three or more of his brethren at his discretion, so that they resort not to any suspecte places or infamyd company.

III. Item, that brethren being offyceers of the said monasterye, with lycense of the Abbot, go abrood for the executyons of their offyces at such times as it shall be thought convenient by the discretion of the Abbott, so that they avoyde the companye of suspecte and infamyd persons.

IV. Item, that the Abbot may lycense certaine brethren of the said house or monasterye to walk furth intoe gardyns or feilds adjoyninge to the said monasterie, and ther to use honest recreation at such times as it shall be thought convenient by the discretion of the Abbot. So that they be at least foure all times in company, and returne to their monasterye againe in due hours, avoydinge also the conversation wth all suspecte and infamyd persons.

VII. Item, that a lecture in Scripture, syncerelye and diligently read three tymes weekeley, may suffice, and that the brethren beinge of the graduats and learned in Scripture, and approved by the Bysshop of the Diocese, may, with license of the Abbot, goe abroad and preache ye worde of God, so that they doo the same purely and syncerely. And also that it may be permitted to such brethren to lye in chambers, to be assigned by the discretion of the Abbot, for their more quiet studie. And also for as much some of the brethren of the said monasterye be well instructed in the Latine, so they may preach the word, so that it be diligently and syncerely taught and expounded.

The General Injunctions mentioned in the preceding note had provided that every day by the space of one hour a lesson of Holy Scripture should be kept, to which all in the convent should resort.]

To all estates due honour and reverence, and to all other commendacioun in our Lord everlastyng. Know ye that we John, abbot of ye monasterie of our blessed Ladie of Whalley, in com. Lanc. by ye assente and consente of ye convente have freely granted untoe ye right honourable Mr. Tho. Crumwell, secretarie-general, visitor and principal official to oure most sovereign Lord Kyng Henry VIII. an annual rent or fee of vi^{li}. xiii^{s}. iv^{d}. yerelie, to be paide at ye Nativitie of St. John Baptist unto ye saide Maister Tho. Crumwell. Wee ye saide abbot and convent have put to ye same our handes and common seale. Yeven at Whalley 1st Jan. 28 Hen. VIII. [1537]. (Townley MSS. G. 16.)

I was once inclined to think that the above relaxation of the visitors' injunctions was purchased by this poor bribe of ten marks per ann.; but an unwillingness to load the memory of Cromwell, who was an open and generous man, with the imputation of accepting money from those whom he had previously determined to ruin, led me to a more exact investigation of the case, which terminated in a different conclusion.[1]

General injunctions to the religious houses, which, by restoring at once the rigour of ancient discipline, at a time when the virtues of monks were probably less acceptable to Government than their vices, seemed rather calculated to irritate than to reform, were issued in the year 1535, and a relaxation would naturally be applied for as early as possible. But the date of this grant to Cromwell is Jan. 1st, 1537, at a time when the monks of Whalley had little leisure to attend to their own accommodations. For the rashness and intemperate zeal of Paslew had now pushed him into the foremost ranks of rebellion; and, as the Pilgrimage of Grace had ended in the confusion of its authors, every art of submission and of corruption was to be employed in order to ward off the impending blow. That the grant before us was intended for that purpose there can be little doubt; yet there is no evidence to prove that Cromwell had any knowledge of the transaction, and *nolenti non fit beneficium*: nay, it is more than probable that, though sealed, it was never tendered; and it is almost certain that, if tendered, he durst not have accepted it. But I suppose that at this time the house was in great consternation: they had committed many overt acts of rebellion, and the abbot was just returned from his unblest pilgrimage, at full leisure to reflect on the consequences of his own conduct. What other expedients were suggested in this hour of distress, to avert the impending blow, we know not; but the charter before us was almost certainly one.

The chronology of the Pilgrimage of Grace[2] will confirm this hypothesis:—

[On Oct. 12, Robert Aske returned from Lincoln into Yorkshire and found the whole North rising from the Humber to the Cheviot Hills. Oct. 16, York received the rebels, and Oct. 20 Pomfret castle and Hull surrendered to them.] On that day Aske and his associates received the King's herald in Pontefract castle. [Oct. 25, the Duke of Norfolk, sent by the King, joined the Earl of Shrewsbury at Doncaster.] Oct. 26, they summoned the Earl of Cumberland to surrender his castle of Skipton. On the same day another

[1] I have since, however, discovered (West's *History of Furness*, App. No. x.) that Cromwell was actually in the receipt of a pension from the abbey of Furness, and was promised an increase of stipend on condition of his standing their good friend against the Earl of Cumberland, who was desirous to lay his hands upon their manor of Winterburn in Craven. (Note by Dr. Whitaker in *Corrigenda* to Third Edition, p. 552.)

[2] [The Editors correct and somewhat amplify this chronology on the authority of the historian Froude.]

party appeared before Doncaster, and began to treat with the Duke. Nov. 14, the King sent a safe-conduct for 300 persons to come to Doncaster. Nov. 26, they were still together; and, though they had laid down their arms, agreed to resume them upon firing of the beacons. [Dec. 2, an agreement was made at Doncaster, whereupon Aske pulled off his badge of the Five Wounds of Christ.[1] A pardon and Northern parliament was promised.] Dec. 9, a general pardon was issued, on condition of future obedience; "notwithstanding which, the clergy of the North still kept the rebellion on foot."[2] [Feb. 3, the Duke of Norfolk arrived at Pontefract with an army composed of men who would do his bidding and ask few questions. Feb. 12. The rebels from Kendal, Richmond, Hexham, Appleby, and Penrith, under one of the Musgraves, attacked Carlisle, but were repulsed and put to flight. On inquiry, this last explosion, like the rest, was traced to the monks; those of Salley, Hexham, Lanercost, Newminster, and St. Agatha being the most guilty.]

Nothing more is known of this melancholy interval till the time of the spring assizes at Lancaster; when John, Abbot of Whalley,[3] was arraigned and convicted of high treason, and sent to his own town for execution, which was performed March 10, 1536-7, upon a gallows erected on a gentle elevation in the field called the Holehouses, and immediately facing the house of his birth.[4] The ignominious part of his sentence seems

[1] [See an article by W. H. D. Longstaffe on the Heraldry of Durham in *The Herald and Genealogist*, vol. vii. 1871.]

[2] Lord Herbert's Life of Henry VIII. p. 480, &c.

[3] It is highly probable that the judge who tried him was the famous Sir Anthony Fitzherbert, as I find him at Furness Abbey within a few days after this event, along with the Earl of Sussex. I had been assured that the indictment of Abbot Paslew was among the records at Lancaster; but, upon a very diligent search, I have not been able to meet with it. There are multitudes of others, for riots, &c. at the same assizes, which prove the disturbances in Lancashire, at that time, to have been very general.

[4] According to the constant tradition of the place. (*Third edit.* p. 140.) An oaken post, which was part of the fatal apparatus, is said to have remained within the memory of aged persons.

[Dr. Whitaker (*Third edit.* pp. 82, 140, apparently on the authority of a Latin memorandum quoted *ibid.* p. 87 *note*, but without reference to its original.) gave the date of Paslew's execution as March 12. We now follow the following memoranda in Cotton. MS. Vespasian D. XVII. f. 16.

1536. 6 idus Martii obiit dominus Johannes Paslew in theologia baccalaureus, 25 abbas et ultimus domûs de Whalley.

4 idus Martii eodem anno suspensus fuit Willielmus Haydocke monachus abbatiæ de Whalley. (*Marginal note,*) In campo vocato *parvo Imps.*

Ricardus Eastgate monachus de Sauley suspensus fuit apud (*the rest wanting*).

Stowe says that Paslew was executed at Lancaster on the 10th, "and the same day with him was hanged, drawn, and quartered John Eastgate, a monk of the same house, whose quarters were set up at divers townes in that shire." Dr. Whitaker (p. 140) understands the latter clause as applying to Eastgate only, and that "Paslew was not dismembered." I think it most probable that it applies to both Paslew and Eastgate. Stowe continues, "And on the 13th (which should be 12th) of March William Haydocke, a monk of Whalley, was hanged at Whalley in a field called *Pediam Guies*, and there hanged long time after." Haydocke's body (that is to say) was allowed to continue suspended for some time entire, whilst those of Paslew and Eastgate were quartered and distributed to other towns. As to the scene of Haydocke's execution, Dr. Whitaker (p. 140) interpreted it to mean "Padiham Green or Padiham Eases, either of which is five miles from Whalley:" but *Le Impe-yard* adjoining the abbey, *i.e.* a nursery for young

to have been remitted out of respect to his order; and he is supposed to have been interred in the north aile of the parish church, under a stone yet remaining. John Eastgate, one of his monks, appears to have suffered with him,[1] and another, named William Haydocke, two days after.

[Robert Radcliffe, Earl of Sussex, then Lord-Lieutenant of Lancashire, was the principal person entrusted with the pacification of the country at this period, and on the 17th of March the royal satisfaction in his proceedings was expressed to him and his fellow-counsellors in the following terms:—

From a paper written by Wriothesley, in a Miscellaneous Bundle in the Chapter-House, indorsed "The mynute of the l'res to my Lord of Sussex, 17 Marcij." (State Papers, 4to. 1830, i. 540.)

Right trusty and welbiloved cousins, and trusty and welbiloved, we grete you well. And have received your letters the 11th daye of this monethe, by the contynue wherof we doo right well perceyve the great dexteritie, circumspection, and diligence which youe have used, as wel in the receyving of the submission of our good subgettes of those parties, as in the punishment of suche personnes as, being themselfes inwardly corrupted, labored and travailed sundry wayes, most traitorously, howe to infecte others; bothe by the sowing of sedition and devisyon amonges our people, and by the mayntenance and receipting of suche traitours as contynuelly devised uppon the same; for the whiche we give unto you our right harty thankes, assuring you that you have therin proceded moche to our contentation.

And wheras upon th'execution of th'Abbot of Whalley, ye have taken ordre for the good direction of the house, and the sauf keping of the goodes, without embesselement, til further knowleadge of our pleasure, approving moche your good forsight therof, we have thought it convenient to signifie unto you that, for as moche as it apperethe that the house of Whalley hathe been so sore corrupt, amonges other, that it shuld seme there remaynethe very fewe therin that were mete to remayn and contynue in suche an incorporation, we thinke it shalbe mete that some ordre be taken for the remotion of the monkes nowe being in the same, and that we shuld take the hole house in to our oune handes, as by our lawes we be justely, by th'attaindour of the said late Abbot, entiteled unto it; and soo devise for such a newe establishement therof as shalbe thought mete for th'onnour of God, our suretye, and the benefite of the cuntrey. Wherfor our pleasure is, that you shall, with good dexteritie, laye unto the charges of all the monkes there their grevous offences towardes us, and our commune wealthe, and therwith assaye their myndes, whither they will conforme themselfes gladly, for the redubbing of their former trespaces, to goo to other houses of their cote, where they shalbe wel entreated or elles wither they woll rather take capacities,[2] and soo receyve seculer habite. Albeit

trees, was probably the spot, coinciding with "the field called *the little Imps*," above named. It is mentioned in the *Coucher Book*, pp. 1176 and 1210.]

[1] [As stated by Stowe (see the previous note). There were two Eastgates, brothers, who both suffered capitally: Richard being a monk of Salley, who had fled to Whalley for refuge and was harboured there, as thus stated by Sanders: "Et quia horum Monachorum unus, qui fratrem Whaliensi in Monasterio habebat, eò confugerat, ingressusque fuerat inscio Abbate qui cœnobio præerat, ille etiam Abbas laqueo sublatus est, variaque strages in alios edita."—*De Schismate Anglicano*, lib. i. p. 121. Richard Trafford the abbot of Salley, together with his prior, suffered at Lancaster, apparently on the 10th March, the same day as Paslew: see Dr. Whitaker's *History of Craven*, p. 83. The same fate attended four other abbats, those of Fountains, Jervaulx, Rievaulx, and Barlings, the Prior of Bridlington, many monks, and five priests of the diocese of Lincoln, besides the better known names of the lay leaders of the Rebellion.—J. G. N.]

[2] [A *capacity* must have been a licence to relinquish their religious vows.]

we require you soo to move them to entre into other houses, that they may chuse the same; for we thinke it cannot be holsom for our comen wealthe to permyt them to wander abrode; and therfore we require you to frame them to that pointe, that they maye entre in to other places, as is aforesaid; wherin you shall do unto us good service; desireng you to advertise us of this matier with all diligence.

As touching th'ordre of the house, in the meane tyme, we desire and pray you to have special regarde that no thing be embeseled, and to lye in a good awayte of the monkes, that they conspire not to the brewing of any inconvenience.

Concernyng th'old man whom you wrote you have respited, uppon the lamentation he made at the barre, and th'allegation of his service thries hertofor against the Scottes and otherwise doon unto us; albeit we cannot but take your steye of him in good parte, yet, considering he hathe soo often receyved our wages, and wold, nevertheles, at the last be thus corrupted against us, we thinke him for an example more worthye to suffer thenne the rest, that before had non experience of our princely puissance, ne had receyved any benefite of us; and soo remytt him unto you to be executed, according to his judgement geven for his offences commytted agains us.

The Earl of Sussex was possibly already occupying the mansion of the late abbot when this letter arrived, and an inventory of the goods belonging to the monastery, taken by his order, is dated on the 24th of March (as will be seen in a subsequent page).

It was here that, on Thursday the 5th of April, 1537, the Earl of Sussex and others of the King's Commissioners received the surrender [1] of Roger Pyle, the abbot of Furness, he "knowing (as he was constrained to admit) the mysorder and evyll liff both unto God and our Prince of the bredren of the said monasterie." This "byll" was signed *Per me Rogerum abbatem Furnesii*, in the presence of the Earl of Sussex, "and also in the presence of Sir Thomas Butler, Sir William Leyland, Johan Cladon clerk, Sir Johan Beron, and Sir Anthony FitzHerbert one of the Kynges justices, beying of the Kynges counsell within the said countie;" who, on the day following, addressed a remarkable letter [2] to the King detailing their mode of procedure with the trembling abbot, and stating that they had committed to ward in Lancaster Castle "twoo of the same monks, which was all we could fynde faultye." Then (referring to a former letter not now extant) they proceed thus in regard to Whalley:—

And wher in our said lettres we wrote unto your Majestye touching the Pryour here,[3] whiche is impotent and aged, his peticion nowe is, that, where the house is boundene to kepe twoo prestes within the parishe churche of Whalley, the parishioners wherof is aboue M^{li} M^{li} M^{li} people, it may pleas your Highnes that hee may bee oone of those twoo prestes, and to haue 6*l.* or 7*l.* a yere for his stipend; whiche if it may so like your Highnes to graunt unto hym, we think it shuld be a good and charitable dede, seeing that he hath beene a monk in this house above fyfty yeres, and is almost $iiij^{xx}$ yeres of age, not like long to contynue.

The letter is signed by Robert Sussex, Anthony Fitzherbert, William Leyland, Henry Farryngton K., John Claydon prest; and there is a subsequent letter of the Earl to the Lord Privy Seal, dated "At Whalley, the xth day of Aprill."]

The attainder of an abbot was understood, how rightly soever, by the Crown lawyers

[1] Printed in Letters relating to the Suppression of the Monasteries, (Camden Society 1843,) p. 153.

[2] [Printed in *Annales Furnesienses.* History of the Abbey of Furness. By Thomas Alcock Beck, esq. 1844.]

[3] Christopher Smith: see p. 134.

of that time, to infer a forfeiture of the house; and accordingly, without the form of a surrender, and without any provision, so far as can be discovered, for the remaining monks, many of whom were probably innocent, the abbey of Whalley, with all its appurtenances, was instantly seized into the King's hands; and thus fell this ancient and opulent foundation.

More caution and less zeal might have prolonged its existence about three years, might have secured a splendid establishment for the abbot, and competent stipends for his subordinate brethren; but the fate of Paslew was not unmerited: it was his duty to suffer for conscience' sake, but nothing can justify his rebellion.

Having thus closed the annals of the monastery, nothing remains but that we record the names of the monks, the extent and value of their possessions, the particulars of their expenditure, their successors in the site and demesnes, and the present state of their mansion.

The following catalogue, beginning with Abbot Topcliffe, whom I suppose to have been the first monk admitted at Whalley, is taken from an imperfect transcript out of one of the abbey registers, which appears to terminate before the year 1500, for it exhibits only four admissions after Paslew, who became abbot in 1506, when it is scarcely to be supposed that he was of less than ten years' standing; and the register itself will shew that nearly one admission took place every year.

Robertus Topcliffe, Abbas 4tus, ob. 10 kal. Mar. 1350.[1]
Fr. Willielmus Morley, Prior.
Fr. Walterus de Cornubia.
Fr. Walterus de Sledmer, hospes monach.
Fr. Robertus Driffield, ob. 12 cal. Mar. 1342.
Fr. Adam Gerston, ob. 1343.
Fr. Willielmus Eccleston, 3 id. Aug. 1346.
Fr. Willielmus Preston, cellerarius, ob. 1343.
Fr. Johannes de Glover, al. Glauster,[2] 3 kal. Ap. 1328.
Fr. Galfrid de Brockhall, al. Burchell,[3] ob. pr. non. Nov. 1339.
Fr. Gilbert de Leigh, ob. 18 kal. Ap. 1336.
Fr. Robertus de Mancestria, pr. id. Sept. 1354.
Fr. Willielmus Boulton, ob. kal. Nov. 1342.
Fr. Johannes Greenacres, ob. 6 kal. Nov. 1353.
Fr. Robertus Stanfield, ob. pr. non. Nov. 1339.
Fr. Robertus Donnington, ob. 1338.
Fr. Robertus Boulton, ob. 12 kal. Ma. 1322.
Fr. Johannes Barton, convers. ob. 1338.
Johannes Lyndelay, S. T. P. abbas 5tus.
Fr. Willielmus Banester.
Fr. Radulphus Pontefr.
Willielmus Selbie, vicar. et postea abbas 6tus.
Fr. Willielmus Singleton, doct. et prior.
Fr. Geoffry de Worston, convers. 16 Ed. III. [1341-2].
Fr. Willielmus Biland.
Fr. Robertus Newton.
Fr. Adam Castleforth.
Fr. Roger Lyndlay, Abbas de Cumbr.
Fr. Henricus Duffield.
Fr. Willielmus Whitmore, interfectus fuit sagitta 5 kal. Nov. 1351.
Fr. Hugo de Bradeley, ob. 6 id. Nov. 1352.
Fr. Johannes Stabulton.
Fr. Richardus Dower.
Fr. Robertus de Selby.
Fr. Johannes de Bedingley.
Fr. Arnald de Embsay, prior.

[1] [1350 10 kal. Martii obiit piæ memoriæ dominus Robertus de Topcliffe quondam abbas 12 de Whalley. Cotton. MS. Vesp. D. xvii.]

[2] [Glaucestr' (de Glovernia). Cotton. MS. Tit. F. xi. and 258 b.]

[3] Birsgill. *Ibid.*

Fr. Alanus de Salley.
Fr. Edmundus de Bromehurst.
Fr. Willielmus de Topcliffe.
Fr. Robertus Pollard.
Fr. Johannes Bolling.
Fr. Johannes Baghill.
Fr. Johannes Halghton.
Fr. Robertus Normanvile, prior et vicar.
Fr. Lucas de Sevell.
Fr. Richardus Hertforth.
Fr. Johannes Burton.
Fr. Thomas de Halton.
Fr. Johannes de Ese.
Nicol de Eboraco, Abbas 7tus, ob. 3 Hen. V. [1414-15].
Fr. Rogerus de Anworth.
Fr. Johannes de Pontefracte.
Fr. Johannes Tollerton, Vicar.
Fr. Thomas Blackburne.
Fr. Johannes Woodhouse.
Fr. Henricus Deyne.
Fr. Johannes Brotherton.
Fr. Thomas Ledes.
Fr. Willielmus Otlay.
Fr. Dionysius Carleton, Abbas de Halton.
Fr. Richardus Cliderhow.
Fr. Robertus Ottrington.
Fr. Johannes Burne.
Fr. Johannes Haiton.
Fr. Johannes Salley, Prior, postea Vicar.
Fr. Willielmus Hert.
Fr. Stephanus Brimstone.
Fr. Johannes Saintpole.
Fr. Thomas Shupton.
Fr. Willielmus Eastbie.
Fr. Johannes Butterie.
Fr. Johannes Dalton, al. Calton.[1]
Fr. Willielmus Darwyn.
Fr. Willielmus Knottingley.
Fr. Robertus Foole.
Fr. Willielmus Hyde.
Fr. Johannes Hesketh.
Fr. Johannes Dorein.
Fr. Johannes Bradforth, Prior.
Fr. Johannes Selbie.
Fr. Rogerus Symthay. [Prior 1418.]
Fr. Johannes Thornere.
Fr. Henricus Bradforth.
Johannes Eccles, Abbas 9, ob. 21 Hen. VI. [1442].
Fr. Johannes Keleby.
Fr. Johannes Wederbie, Prior.
Fr. Thomas Rigley, Abbas de Cumbr.
Fr. Edwardus Steelton.
Willielmus Whalley, Abbas 8, ob. 12 Hen. VI. [1433].
Fr. Willielmus Ashton.
Fr. Laurence Rede.
Fr. Willielmus Morwyke.
Fr. Johannes Preston.
Fr. Ricardus Burghett.
Fr. Robertus Parish.
Fr. Johannes Moore.
Fr. Johannes Downam.
Radulphus Cliderhowe, Vicar. postea Abbas 10.
Fr. Rogerus Norwyke, Prior.
Fr. Thomas Harden.
Fr. Ricardus Neston.
Fr. Nicol. Chatburne.
Nicolaus Billington, Abbas 11mus.
Fr. Ricardus Masham.
Fr. Willielmus Holden.
Fr. Thomas Wood, Prior.
Fr. Robertus Salley, Vicar. de Blackburn.
Fr. Willielmus Ledes.
Fr. Johannes Whitaker.
Fr. Johannes Steresacre.
Fr. Willielmus Dinkley, Vicar. de Whalley.
Fr. Willielmus Thornehill.
Fr. Rogerus Whitaker.
Fr. Thomas Brotherton.
Fr. Johannes Wakefield.
Fr. Robertus Burneley.
Fr. Willielmus Forster.
Fr. Robertus Lyndsay.
Fr. Johannes Harden.
Fr. Rogerus D'Arcy.
Robertus Hamond, al. Harwood, Abbas 12mus.
Fr. Johannes Croston.
Fr. Johannes Bolland.
Willielmus Billington, Abbas 13us.

[1] [Fr. Johannes de Rutland et Johannes de Dalton professi fuerunt, 1380. (Harl. MS. 1850, f. 19b.)]

Fr. Richardus Sealez, Prior et Bursar. 1484.
Fr. Edmund Whalley.
Fr. Milo Bradforth.
Radulphus Holden, Abbas 14 us, ob. 1480.
Fr. Johannes Walton.
Fr. Jacobus Lawe.
Fr. Lauren. Grinlton
Fr. Henric. Hamond.
Fr. Willielmus Wood.
Fr. Johannes Keppes, Prior 16 Edw. IV. [1475-6].
Christopherus Thornbarr, Abbas 15, ob. 1485.
Fr. Johannes Smershall.
Willielmus Rede, Abbas 16, ob. 1505 vel 6.
Fr. Johannes Cliderhowe, Abbas de Hayles.
Fr. Johannes Standen.
Fr. Nicol. Forrest.
Fr. Otwell Whitehead.
Fr. Willielmus Henthorne.
Fr. Radulphus Murton.
Fr. Nicol. Downeham.
Fr. Reginaldus Wood.
Fr. Edmundus Choe.
Fr. Johannes Otes, Prior.
Fr. Johannes Chatburne.
Fr. Jacobus Dugdale.
Fr. Willielmus Forrest.
Fr. Henric. Sallay, vicar. de Blackburn.
Fr. Johannes Seller, vicar. de Whalley, 9 Hen. VIII. [1517].
Fr. Johannes Grinlton.
Fr. Johannes Forrest.
Fr. Robertus Eddleston, bursar. 1521.
Fr. Jacobus Fontaine.
Fr. Thomas Chatburne.
Fr. Thomas Becrofte, oc. 1517.
Fr. Johannes Dewhurst.
Fr. Willielmus Bancrofte.
Fr. Robertus Sudell.
Fr. Radulphus Walmsley.
Fr. Willielmus Preston.
Fr. Henric. Cowper.
Johannes Paslew, prior, postea Abbas 17, elect. 1506.
Fr. Christopher Smith, Prior ultimus.[1]
Fr. Rogerus Cloghe.
Fr. Johannes Rede.
Fr. Milo Whitaker.

This register not having been continued to the dissolution, I can only gather a few scattered names of those who were admitted at a later period. Of those who occur in the foregoing catalogue, Smith the prior, Sudell, and Chadburn survived the dissolution.

The following are from later authorities :

Fr. Nicholas Downeham, bursar with James Fountain, 1509.
Fr. Richard Hill, bursar with Robert Edleston, 1521.
Fr. William Chatburne and John Chester, last bursars, 1537.
Fr. Lawrence Forest, procurator domus 1536.
Fr. Richard Mersden, 1536.
Fr. Robert Parish, 1537.[2]

[*Addition from p.* 516 *of the Third Edition :* From a subsequent examination of all the remaining evidences of the Abbey, I am enabled to add the following names to the former catalogue of monks:—Fr. Rob. Brunley, *granator*, 1509; Fr. William Bancroft, sub-cellarer; Fr. William Whalley, *sacrista*, 1510; Fr. Edmond Haworth,[3] sub-cellarer,

[1] [He survived until 1539, under which year he will be further noticed.]

[2] [See the list of Vicars of Whalley.]

[3] [This sub-cellarer, after his death 7 May 1520, appeared one night to Abbot Paslew, and foretold his death: "Anno Domini 1520 nonas Maii obiit Edmundus Howard monachus de Whalley, Iste post mortem apparuit quadam nocte domino Joanni Paslaw ejusdem Monasterii Abbati et illi predixit, se 16 annos et non amplius vivere." (Cotton. MS. Vesp. D xvii. f. 17b.)]

1529; Fr. Rad. Linney; Fr. Jac. Moore, *portar.*;[1] Fr. Edm. Dinkley, sacrist. 1529. To these may be added, from other evidences in the same collection, Fr. Thomas Law, Fr. Rad. Catteral, Fr. —— Billington, Fr. John Chester, Fr. Ric. Wood, Fr. Tho. Harwood. There was another Fr. Thomas Law, a Carthusian monk of Syon, who also resided at Whalley; but the former Law and Harwood outlived their brethren, and continued, by indulgence, to say mass in one or other of the side chapels of the parish-church till their deaths, the latter of which happened about 1560: a remarkable instance either of toleration or of attachment to the old religion in those who might easily have deprived these poor men of their last remaining comfort.]

To these must be added John Eastgate and William Haydocke, remembered only by their tragical end; and, lastly,

Fr. Thomas Holden, younger son of Gilbert Holden, of Holden, gent. who appears to have been the surviving monk; for I find, from his own papers,[2] that in 1534, being then an acolyth, he received under the convent seal in the chapter house of Whalley a title for the order of subdeacon, addressed to Roland (Lee) bishop of Lichfield. In 1535 he received letters dimissory, and was ordained subdeacon "titulo monachatûs Beatæ Mariæ de Whalley," by John, bishop of Sodor and Man. On the dissolution he appears to have retired to his native place. In 1550 I meet with him once more under the title of Sir Thomas Holden, curate of Haslingden; and in 1574 he was licensed to the same cure at the metropolitical visitation of Archbishop Grindall, held at Preston, by the style of Thomas Holden, clerk, of sober life and competent learning. How long he survived this last transaction I cannot ascertain, for the register of that place does not commence till the year 1607, and the records of the ecclesiastical court at Chester have been searched in vain.

But it is satisfactory to have pursued this ancient stem to its last ramifications, and to have found the surviving monk of Whalley a Protestant minister, thirty-seven years after the dissolution. Had he been aware, in his latter days, how interesting many facts which he alone remembered would one day become, and had he, instead of a few meagre facts and dates relating to himself, recorded the order and economy of the house, the state of its buildings when entire, the tone of morals, piety, and discipline, the intrigues which were carried on, the personal characters of his brethren, the scandal conceived at the King's measures, the particulars of the Pilgrimage of Grace, the distress occasioned by the Abbot's execution, the despair of age and helplessness when driven to penury in a world which had forgotten them, the exultation of youth when restored to liberty and domestic comforts, yet the melancholy with which all must have beheld their noble retreat in solitude and ruin; what a treasure would such a collection of anecdotes and reflections have been at present! But it would probably have required a mind more curious and comprehensive than that of Fr. Thos. Holden.

[1] The Porter was always a monk. But there is a regular charge "pro famulo Portarii," so that the Master Porter, probably, did little more than keep an eye on his deputy.

[2] Townley MSS. G. 16.

The state of their receipts and expenditure will best appear by placing the annual computus of two different periods in opposite columns, so that a comparison of each may be formed by carrying the eye from line to line.

Compotus fratrum Johannis Kypas et Christopher Thornbergh burs. de Whalley, A.D. MCCCCLXXVIII. nec non anno Radulphi Holden abb. vii°.	Compotus fratrum Rob. Edelston et Ric'i Hill, burs. de Whalley, A.D. MDXXI. et anno Dni. Johis Paclewe abbatis quinto decimo.

IN SPIRITUALIBUS.

REC. ECCLESIARUM.[1]		RECEPT. ECCLESIARUM.	£	s.	d.
P. ecclesia de Whalley cum capellis[2]	cxxix*l*. iiij*s*. iiij*d*.	Pro ecclia de Whalley cum capellis .	228	11	8
P. ecclesia de Blacburne .	lxxxix*l*. xvj*s*. ix*d*.	Pro ecclia de Blakeburne cum capellis	133	1	0
P. ecclesia de Rachdall . . .	lxiv*l*.	Pro ecclia de Eccles et de Deyn .	119	10	4½[3]
P. ecclesia de Eccles . } P. capella de Deyn . }	lxxiij*l*. xvijs. v*d*. ob.	De Rachedall cum capellis . .	111	0	1[4]
Sum. . .	cccclvi*l*. xvij*s*. v*d*. ob.	Sume totall . .	592	3	1½

REC. FIRMAR.		RECEPT' FIRMARUM.	£	s.	d.
Pro Cestria . . .	xvij*s*. iv*d*.	Pro Cestria	1	10	8
P. Staney	xx*l*.	P. Stanney	20	0	0[5]

[1] The former of these accounts is transcribed from an original roll, written upon a very large sheet of parchment, with the title and initials beautifully tricked by a pen. The latter is from a copy in the Harl. MS. 2064, ff. 339 b to 341.

[2] In this interval of 42 or 43 years we find the income of the house arising from spiritualities nearly doubled. The proportions paid by the several chapelries within Whalley in 1536 were these:

		£	s.	d.
Whalley, including Padiham, cum stip. sanc. ap. Whalley et stip. S. Leonard de Padiham		39	8	5
Clyderhow cum stip. sancti Martini de Chadburn		13	0	4
Downham cum stip. sancti Leonard et al.		9	18	0
Colne		31	17	3
Brunley cum stip. sanctorum		50	0	0
Church et Altham cum stip. sanct.		22	8	0
Haslingden		7	12	9
Cap. Cast. de Clyderhow	Bowland	12	5	9
	Penhull	24	4	10
	Trawden	8	6	4
	Rossendale stip. sanctorum.			
	Ightenhill Park de perq. capelli.			

From a MS. remaining in the Augmentation Office 1635, but transcribed into the Townley MSS.

[3] Deane anciently, at the appropriation styled capella de St. Maryden, seems to have become in this interval a parish church, as it is at present.

[4] Rochdale, besides the ancient chapel of Saddleworth, seems to have had now Todmorden, Littleborough, which was licensed for mass in 1476, and Milnrow, all erected since the year 1400, as none of them are mentioned in the confirmation of Archbishop Arundel.

[5] These farms appear to have been let out upon a long lease, which accounts for the identity of the rents in the two columns. They were the original endowment of Stanlaw Abbey.

			£	s.	d.
P. Willaton	liijs. ivd.	P. Willaton	2	13	4
P. Aston	viijl. xvs. ivd.	P. Aston	8	15	4
De Acton	xivl. vijs. ivd.	P. Yltley inclus. in parco de Dutton	0	1	0
De mol. ibm.	xxvjs. viijd.	P. Acton	1	8	2
De decimis ibm.	xs.	P. molendino ibidem	1	6	8
De turbaria ibm.	xxs.	P. decimis ibidem	0	10	0
De piscaria ibm.	xxxs.	P. turbaria ibidem	1	0	0
De Weryngton	ijs.	P. piscaria ibidem	1	10	0
De Denton	xijd.	P. Croenton	18	4	0
De Garston	liijs. ivd.	P. molendino ibm	0	18	0
De Akebergh	xxvjs. viijd.	P. Denton	0	1	0
De Croenton	xviijl.	P. Garstan	2	13	4
De Alt	ls.	P. Akebergh	1	6	8
De Chyldwall		P. Warington	0	8	0
De Wygan	iijs. ivd.	P. Wygan	0	3	4
De Stanynges	vl.	P. Alt	2	13	4
De orreo ibm.	xijd.	P. Chyldwall			
De mol. ibm.	xxs.	P. Stanyngs	5	0	0
De Merton	xs.	P. orr. ibidem	0	1	0
De Carleton	xviijd.	P. molendino ibidem	1	0	0
De Banckhouse	ivd.	P. Merton	0	10	0
De Edylswyke	iijs. ivd.	P. Carleton	0	1	6
De Preston	ijs.	P. Ethilliswyke	0	3	4
De Dutton	ivs.	P. Banckhouse	0	0	4
De Ribyleester	ijs. jd.	P. Mawnton	16	18	0
De Edysford	xls.	P. Federforthe	0	13	4
De Wadyngton	ijs.	P. Placea Alic' Morcell[1]	0	3	4
De Clyderhowe	viijl. xijs.	P. Swynton	4	7	0
De Standen	ivl. xiijs. ivd.	P. Gadiswallhede	6	16	8
De Hulcroft	xxjs. viijd.	P. Wolden	9	3	4
De Coldcoates	ivl. viijd.	P. Haghton	2	14	0
De Wyscwall	vjl.	P. Molendino de Hulcroft	0	3	4
De Revede	xijs.	P. Rypull et Westwode	1	5	0
De Cowhope et Brendwood	vl.	P. Westslakks	1	0	0
De Roclyffe	liijs. ivd.	P. Norwico[2]	2	13	4
De Whitworth	vijl. xs.	P. Rachedall[3]	24	18	4½
De Rachdale	xxijl. xs. jd. ob.	P. Whitworth[3]	14	19	2
De Mawnton	xjl. xiijs. viijd.	P. Cowōp[3] et Brendwode	6	0	0

[1] ["A peace of grownd called ye place of Allis Morfield otherwise called Huntingdow."—Survey of Swinton (July 1537); Coucher Book, p. 1239.]

[2] That is Northwich. Here ends the rental of the Cheshire estates originally belonging to Stanlaw.

[3] The rental therefore of these large estates, which included Castleton and Merland, amounted to 45*l.* 17*s.* 6*d.* which, if multiplied by 100, would probably not exceed the present value,—a decisive proof of a fact generally taken for granted that the monks were good landlords, as the rack-rent of lands in Henry VIIIth's time may be averaged at a thirtieth of their present value. Much, however, is to be allowed for subsequent inclosures and improvements.

De Federforth	xiijs. ivd.
De Swynton	ivs. vijd.
De Gadwalshede	ivl. xvjs. viijd.
De Wolden	vl. iijs. ivd.
De Halghton	livs.
De Molend. de Huleroft	iijs. ivd.
Lyrepul et Westwode	xxvs.
De Brendscoles	xxxiijs. ivd.
De Weleton et Withinhall	viijs.
De Stanworth	iijl. vjs. viijd.
De Whyton	xlvjs. viijd.
De Romesgreve	ivl.
De Byllyngton	xxxvijl. xviijs. xd.
De Yitley in parc. de Dutton inclus.	xijd.
De Westslakes	xxs.
De Baldwynshill	xxijs. iijd.
De Norwyco	xxs.
De Brownlay	xxxivs.
De Placea Aliso Morell	iijs. ivd.
De Placea Johannis Clyderhowe	ivl.
De Servitio de Beyllington	xxvjs. viijd.
De Servitio de Coldcoates, Wyswale, et Asterlee	vs.
Sum. tot.	ccxll. xijs. ixd. ob.

	£	s.	d.
P. Molendino ibm	1	0	0
P. Roclyff	2	13	4
P. Stanworth	3	6	8
P. Brendscolles	2	0	0
P. Whelton et Withynhill	0	8	0
P. Witton	2	13	4
P. Romesgreve	4	0	0
P. Brunley	1	14	0
P. Rybchester	0	2	1
P. Dutton	0	4	0
P. Edisforth	2	0	0
P. Wadyngton	0	2	0
P. Placea quondam Johannis Cliderhow	4	0	0
P. Preston	0	2	0
P. Cliderhow	8	12	0
P. Baldwynhill	1	6	8
P. Standen	4	13	4
P. Huleroft	1	1	8
P. Coldcotts	4	1	6
P. Wyswall	6	0	8
P. Rede	0	12	0
P. Byllyngton	35	17	6
P. Servit. ejusdem	1	6	8
P. Parva Harrowode	4	13	4
P. Newfeld et Grenefeld	2	0	0
P. Harrowsbanks in Dutton	3	0	0
P. Calfhagh in Chatterton	0	0	6
P. Smarshall place in Rede	1	0	0
P. terris Jacobi Garthsyde	0	3	4
P. Halstydds in Rachedall	0	1	0
P. Clayton super Moras	0	10	0
P. Penhulton	0	13	4
P. Bagsladhey in Rachedall	0	3	4
P. Molendino de Rossendall	1	5	0
P. Grenewarth apud Stanlow [2]	2	6	8
P. Roelyfswode in Rossendall	0	10	0
P. Molendino de Coptwode	0	3	4
Sum̃. total	281	7	10½

[1] See the preceding page.

[2] Probably a new improvement, and therefore not included in the old rental.

DE PERQUISITIS.

De Stipite Sc̃e Marie[1]	ijs. vijd.
De Sigisterio[2]	xxxiijs. ivd.
De Agistamento Æstiv.	xls.
De Agist. Yemali	ls.
De Superexcresc. in offic. Cellar.	xxjs. vijd.
De Superexcr. in off. Subcellor	ivl. viijs. jd.
De mensa Vicarii[3]	ivl.
De eodem pro pane et vino	xxs.
De eodem pro ort. et vacca	xs.
De mensa Ric. Trygge capelli	xls.
De mensa Wil. Thornb. capell.	xls.

DE PERQUISITIS.

	£	s.	d.
P. Stipite beate Marie[1] et Sc̃i Henr'. apud Capellam	0	1	6
P. Sigistio[2]	1	13	4
P. agistiamento estimale	1	4	0
P. agistiamento yemali	2	14	0
P. supexcr' offic' Subceller'	7	2	7
P. supexcr'. offic' Cellar'	2	15	2
P. mensa Vicarii[3]	2	13	4
P. eodem pro pane et vino	1	6	8
P. eodem pro ortis et vacc'	1	10	0

[1] Here is a very curious fact; to account for which let it be observed that, in the *Compotus* of 1478, this article stands *pro Stip. Sce. Marie*, and in that of 1521, *p. Stip. Sc. Mar. et Sci. Hen. ap. Capellam.* How is this difference to be accounted for? 1st. These were offerings, in the former account at the high altar, which was then the altar of the Virgin Mary; but we have already seen that in Abbot Paslew's time a *Lady Chapel* was erected contiguous to the Abbey Church, so that our Lady in this interval had changed her lodgings, and was become *St. Maria apud Capellam.* So far all is clear; but who is St. Henry, who had the high honour of being associated with the Virgin in her own chapel? The name, as far as I know, is not to be found in the Romish calendar. On this subject, therefore, I can only hazard a conjecture, of which those who are better skilled in the rituals of that Church than myself will judge for themselves. King Henry VI. as we have before observed, at the dissolution of the adjoining hermitage, converted that foundation into a chantry of two priests to sing for his good estate while living and for the soul of Henry Duke of Lancaster, the founder, and to celebrate his own obit yearly with 30 chaplains. I have also conjectured that this appointment, though it would be overlooked in the reigns of the line of York, would probably be remembered and put in execution after the accession of Henry VII. Accordingly we find no mention of it in 1478, which is the 18th of Edw. IV.: but, at a period subsequent to the restoration of the Lancastrian house, here is actually a *Stipes S'cti Henrici*, whatever may be the meaning of the words. The only conjecture, therefore, which I can offer is this, that, though Henry VI. was never regularly canonized, yet the monks of Whalley, who were zealous partizans of his house, and probably also great admirers of his virtues, disappointed by the reserve or by the rapacity of Julius II. ventured upon an act of private and voluntary beatification, and erected a St. Henry for themselves. Were the name of Henry to be found in the canon, my conjecture of course would fall to the ground; but, as that is not the case, the pious and royal patron of Whalley has the fairest claim upon this hitherto unappropriated honour. Since the foregoing remarks were written I have the satisfaction of finding my conjecture established by the following proofs: Henry VI. was actually adored at Windsor by the name of Holy King Henry. (Stowe's Ann. p. 424.) There is also a prayer addressed to Henry VI. in the "Horæ B. V. M. in usum Sarum," printed by Wynkyn de Worde, A.D. 1502. See Gough's *Sepulchral Monuments*, vol. ii. p. 235, [and the Trevelyan Papers (Camden Society), Part. I. p. 53, Part III. p. 2.] And this is now reduced to a certainty, for, in the *Compotus* of 1510, the article stands thus, *Pro Stip. Regis Henr.* [as added by Dr. Whitaker in Third Edition, p. 552. The subject has been before introduced in p. 103].

[2] *Sigisterio, Sigistio.* I once conjectured that the first word, of which the reading is very clear in the original roll, was a contraction of *Sigillisterio*, as the sealings in colleges at present afford a considerable emolument to the senior fellows. But, as these must necessarily vary, according to the number of leases sealed, and the sum charged in these two distant years is exactly the same, I must leave the word to future inquiry and better information.

[3] In the charge for the vicar's table, who appears to have lived a sort of fellow-commoner in the house, it is remarkable that the sum is diminished in the latter account. He probably sat at the monks' table, and the two chaplains, who possibly served the north and south altars in the parish-church, were in lower commons with the novices.

De Tannaria[1]	iij*l*. vj*s*. viij*d*.
De Pellibus boum et vaccarum .	. iv*l*. xiij*s*.
De Corticibus arborum . .	. vj*s*. viij*d*.
De Amerciam. curie . .	. xiij*s*. iv*d*.
De terris R. Cundelyffe, vidz. Brodmede et Grenehey	xl*s*.
De Duscroftes ?[2]	xij*s*.
De servitio ux. Rob. Wode .	. vj*s*. viij*d*.
De ter. nob. dimiss. per Jac. Marshall	. iij*l*. vij*s*.
De mensa Ric. Caterall . . .	l*s*.
De off. Bail. Wapent.[3] . . .	xl*s*.
Sum. . . .	xxxix*l*. xix*s*. ij*d*.
S. tot. Rec. .	DCXXXVij*l*. xj*s*. j*d*.

	£	*s*.	*d*.
P. Tannaria[1]	3	6	8
P. pellibus bovum et vaccũ . .	4	10	0
P. Corticibus arborum . .	0	5	0
P. Amerciamentis curie . .	0	13	4
P. Orto Stabuli . . .	0	5	0
P. Ryddis vendit' apud Wyllaton[4] .	1	6	8
P. Nova Clausura apud Romesgreave .	4	0	0
P. Terris Robti Cundelyf per forisface'	0	4	8
Sum̃.[5] totaƚƚ . .	34	11	9
Sum̃. totaƚƚ recept' .	908	2	9

[This title, consisting principally of prescriptive payments, is very nearly the same in both accounts, excepting a few verbal differences.]

S. tot. . . .	viij*l*. xv*s*. *ob*.

EXPEN' DE FIRMIS EXTERIORIBUS.

	£	*s*.	*d*.
Dño Regi pro Edisforth . .	0	3	0
Eidem pro Snodworth . .	0	0	3
Eidem pro Standen . . .	3	6	8
Eidem pro Baldwynhyll . .	1	0	3
Eidem pro Whitworth . .	0	12	8
Eidem pro Mawnton . . .	0	6	0
Eidem pro Brunley . . .	0	0	2½
Dño de Eland	0	14	1
Dño de Barton . . .	0	0	11
Dño de Worsley . . .	0	7	11
Heredibus Christopher' Holt . .	0	3	0
Monialibus de Hampull . .	0	12	0
Monialibus Cestrie . . .	0	10	0
Abbati de Cestrie . . .	0	9	0
Castello de Liverpull pro Sectis et Wardis	0	11	0
Sum̃ .	8	7	11½

[1] *De Tannaria.* The later of these accounts, it must be recollected, was before the statute 21 Henry VIII. [1529] which forbad priests, whether secular or regular, to engage in such base employments. Of these monkish tanneries it is observed by the witty Dr. Fuller that, "though the monks themselves were too fine-nosed to dabble in tan-fatts, yet they kept others (bred in that trade) to follow their work. These covents having barke of their own woods, hides of the cattle of their own breeding and killing, and, which was the main, a large stock of money to buy at the best hand, and to allow such chapmen they sold to a long day of payment, easily eat out such who were bred up in that vocation." Church History: *History of Abbeys*, p. 282.

[2] What place is meant by Duscroftes I know not, but it is pretty evidently the reading in the original roll.

[3] This was their share of the profit arising from the bailiwick of Blackburnshire, of which they held one fourth part; the Towneleys of Towneley two,—one for Towneley and another for De la Leigh; and the Banastres of Altham the fourth.

[4] *Rydds.* The word may possibly mean riddings or refuse wood grubbed up in ridding or clearing an estate.

[5] On the whole it appears from the former account that the expenses of the house considerably exceeded their

IN DONIS.[1]		IN DONIS.[1]	£	s.	d.
Quat. ord. fratrum	ivs.	Quatuor ordinibus frm	0	4	0
Ministrallis	xxxvjs. vijd.	Ministrallis[1]	2	4	0
Thomæ Dño Stanley[1]	vjl. xiijs. ivd.	Dño de Mowntegylle[1]	2	0	0
Jacobo Harynton Mil.	xls.	Mro Merney	2	13	4
Joh. Savage Mil.	xiijs. ivd.	Hugoni Shereburne armig'	1	0	0
Tho. Pylkynton Mil.	xlvs.	Johanni Talbott armig'	1	0	0
Robt. Sherborne, jun.	xxs.	Mro Snede	1	0	0
Robt. Sherborne, sen.	vjs. viijd.	Mro Rokesbe	0	13	4
John Talbot	xxs.	Thome Strawe	0	6	8
Hug. Radcliffe	xiijs. ivd.	Mro Feirfax	1	0	0
Robt. Ambrose	xiijs. ivd.	Willielmo Brether	0	4	0
Wm. Ambrose	xiijs. ivd.	Math. Standysh	0	13	4
Tristram Legh	xiijs. ivd.	Thome Grymysdych	0	6	8
Henrico Worsley	xiijs.	Laur' Starke	0	10	0
Duobus Generosis	ijs.	Alexandro Ryshton	0	3	4
Petro Smyth	xijd.	Ursariis[1]	0	10	0
Scholari vers. Cockersand	viijd.	Famulo Epi Sodor'	0	2	0
Filiæ W. Heton	ijs. ivd.	Famulo Dñi Regis	0	6	8
Filiæ R. Holand	ijd.	Quibusdam fribus cum aliis	0	3	4
Thomæ Leds	vjd.	Wiltmo Shyreburn cum aliis	0	4	4

income, in the latter the reverse; and the reason is obvious, that, with an increase, chiefly in the spiritualities, to the amount of nearly one third of their annual receipts, the price of the necessaries of life, in some instances at least, appears to have diminished. But of this more hereafter.

[1] Of the three articles which stand at the head of this title, *De Donis*, it would, perhaps, be harsh to observe, that the smallest is for charity, the next for pleasure, and the largest for ambition. The four orders of begging friars have a small and stated contribution of 4*s.*; the minstrels from 1*l.* 16*s.* 7*d.* to 2*l.* 4*s.*; and the Lord Stanley 6*l.* 13*s.* 4*d.* From the amount of the sum paid to the minstrels, more considerable than to the organist of the church, and larger, by nearly one half, than the Earl of Northumberland paid to his "minstraills that be daily in his household" (Northumberland Household Book), it should seem that they were a part of the regular establishment of the Abbey; that these fathers could relish the heroic romance or the pastoral ballad, and that the refectory of Whalley often resounded with the rude but affecting minstrelsy of the times. Yet these men were bitterly inveighed against by the severer orders; and it was even an established rule in some monasteries, that no minstrel should ever enter their gates.—Dr. Percy's Essay on the Minstrels, Notes, xliii.

With respect to the pensions paid to the Lords Stanley and Monteagle, it might be prudent, in times of difficulty and danger, to secure the interest of a great man at Court, even at a high rate; but these were days of perfect tranquillity; and for what service performed, or expected, or from what consideration but mere complaisance, the inferior gentry of the country were thus pensioned, it is not easy to conceive. On the whole, there appears some ground for Piers Plowman's complaint against the religious houses:—

> And of them yt haveth not they take, and geveth hem yt haveth,
> And clerkes and knyghtes and communers that be ryche.
>
> Fol. lxxxii.
>
> Right so ye ryche, ye robe (*not* robbe) that ben ryche,
> And helpyth them yt helpeth youe, and geveth ther no nede is.

[1] Ursariis 10*s*. Another symptom of the progressive decay of discipline is the article before us, which proves that an amusement more boisterous and less elegant than the former was encouraged by the monks in the later period.

Famulis Abbat. de Cumbermere [1]	xx*d*.
Rob. Bolling	xij*d*.
Rad. Walmsley	xx*d*.
Here the parchment is decayed.	
Ric. Herys medico equorum	viij*d*.
Famulo Rectoris de Halsall [1]	viij*d*.
Famulo abb. de Kirkstall [1]	x*d*.
R Bolling Legisperito	xx*d*.
Ballivo Dñi Regis	ij*s*.
Famulo Dñi de Balderston	iv*d*.
Jac. Lawe	xiv*d*.
. . . . .	.
. . . . .	.
Peregrinantibus Jerlam [3]	xvj*d*.
Officiali Dñi Arch. Cest.	vj*s*. viij*d*.
Registro ejusdem	iij*s*. iv*d*.
Summonitori ejusdem	xij*d*.
Doctori Dublinie	vj*s*. viij*d*.
Monacho de Waverley	ij*s*.
Suffraganeo Cestriæ	vj*s*. viij*d*.
Radulpho Coke Heremitæ	xvj*d*.
Duob. fratrib. de Preston	viij*d*.
Joh. Lawe Legisperit.	ij*s*.
Heliæ Worsley [5]	xx*d*.
Cuidam Capellano pretend. jus ad domum nostram gra. titl. [7]	xx*d*.
Coco Tho. Dñi Stanley	xvj*d*.
Famulo ejusdem	ij*s*. viij*d*.
N. Skythorne Cap. gr. tituli	xx*d*.
Jas. Cowpe Cap.	xij*d*.
Sm.	xxv*l*. iij*s*.

	£	*s*.	*d*.
Famulo Regis per vices	0	7	0
Doctori de Lancastr' [2]	0	3	4
Robto Swannesey	0	6	8
Monacho de Tinterne cum aliis	0	4	0
Hug. Chernok	0	2	0
Hen. Felden	0	1	8
Chancellar' Lancastr'	0	3	4
Chancellar Ep'i	0	10	0
Mro Martyn	0	6	8
Mro Clyff	0	3	4
Famulo eorundem	0	6	8
Monachis de Wallia	0	2	0
Monachis de Fontibus	0	2	0
Cuidam presbytero cum cetero	0	1	8
Will'mo Waller, cum aliis	0	2	0
Questoribus	0	3	4
Pauperibus per annum	2	0	0
Forestariis [4]	1	10	0
Baillivo de Wirall	0	1	0
Will'mo Whythove	0	1	8
Offic' Cestrie	0	10	0
Registro ejusdem	0	3	4
Summonitori ejusdem	0	0	4
Ric'o Banke	0	6	8
Capellano apud Wytwell [6]	0	10	0
Sum	£23	19	4

[1] A constant intercourse appears to have been kept up between the two houses of Cumbermere and Whalley, the latter of which had sent three abbots to the former. The abbot of Cumbermere, it seems, travelled with two servants, and his brother of Kirkstall with one only. The vails paid to the servants of an abbot were ten pence, to those of a secular clergyman eight pence, and to those of a lay gentleman four pence: a true scale of the estimation in which they were severally held.

[2] A physician's fee from Lancaster, at least 27 miles, was three shillings and four pence.

[3] Peregrinantibus Jerusalem, *vide supra*.

[4] Perhaps the abbot had a general warrant for venison out of the forests from the Crown. It is not said Forestario de Bowland, but Forestariis, which amounts nearly to a proof that the deer of the other chases were not destroyed in 1521.

[5] The name of the second abbot. This shows how long a Christian name which has once been borne by a distinguished personage is generally kept in families.

[6] Capellano apud Whytewell. As this article is not found in the former computus it amounts nearly to a proof that this chapel was founded in the interval between the dates of the two.

[7] It appears that the monks were accustomed to grant titles for holy orders to young men not professed, but who,

Thus the bounty of the house diminished as its resources increased: a very natural and frequent process.

IN ITERANTIBUS.

Robto Shotylworth et al. usque Horneby	vijs. ixd.
Jake Forster usque Horneby	ijs.
Wm. Cowpere usque Halsall et alibi	xxijd.
Wm. Henthorne usque Cestr.	vjs. viijd.
Wm. Henthorne usque Lanc. et alibi	xxxivs. vd.
Abbat. usque Coldcotes et Wiswall	xxd.
Cuidam de firis usque Preston	ijs. viijd.
Nich. Dewhurst usque Cumbermere	iijs. ivd.
Rob. Full usque London	xxxvjs.
Abbat. in obit. R. Sherburne[1]	ijs. xjd.
Wm. Cowpere usque Heton et Rachdall	xd.
Famulis firis laborantibus in officio ballivi	ivs. vjd.
Miloni Cokkesbut usque Staynings per vices	xvjd.
Famul. nost. usque Lanc. cum Georgio Stanley[2]	xviijd.
Geo. Forster usque Ebor.	viijs. ivd.
M'och. usque Ord.[3]	vjs. viijd.
Milo Bradford usque Wyche	xijd.
Jacobo Dugdale usque Lychfield pro R. Townley[4]	xvjd.
Nic. Forest usque Stanlaw	xijd.
Abbati usque Blackborne	ijs.
Eidem usque Forestam	ijs.
Nico Chatburne usque Preston	ivd.
Rico Clyfton usque Staynings	viijd.
Rob. Hyndley usque Holowaye	xd.
Nic. Chatburne usque Ebor. bis	vijs.
It. eidem usque Tutbury	xxs.

IN ITINERANTIBUS.

	£	s.	d.
Domino Abbi versus Borongh	1	15	0
Eidem versus Bolton	0	10	0
Eidem versus Dorham	1	10	0
Eidem versus Cumbermer' et Stanlawe	5	10	0
Eidem versus Rypon	1	0	0
Christophero Smyth versus Acton	0	13	4
Eidem versus Chester	0	12	0
Laurentio Forest versus Lancastr' bis	1	6	0
Eidem per vices	0	12	0
Lionell Full vers. London ter	4	7	8
Eidem per vices	0	10	0
Rico Crombok versus Hull	1	0	0
Eidem versus Oxforth per vices	1	0	0
Eidem per vices	0	13	0
Petro Deyn versus Manchester'	0	2	0

receiving trifling pensions, were considered as dependents and beneficiaries of the house. In a very exact account of the Chadwicks of Heley drawn up by the late John Chadwick, Esq. I find an example of this practice, for by letters testimonial bearing date Nov. 20th, 1523, the abbot and convent of Whalley commended their beloved in Christ, James Chadwick (who does not seem to have been a monk) to Geoffry Bishop of Lichfield to be received into the order of priesthood. MS. penes Joh. Chadwick, Arm.

[1] I suppose the abbot to have attended the obit of one of the Sherburnes at Mitton, or more probably at the Grey Friars in Preston, for "there lay," saith Leland, "divers of the Shirburns gentilmen." Lel. Itinerary, iv. 21, f. 38.

[2] They had been entrusted with the care of George Stanley [eldest] son of the [second] Lord Stanley, then a boy, [he was summoned to Parliament 15th Nov. 1482, *jure uxoris*. Nicolas, *Syn. of the Peerage*.] and had sent a servant with him to Lancaster. Qu. Whether this young nobleman received a part of his education at Whalley?

[3] Two monks were ordained this year. The difference of the sums may be accounted for from the different distances they might have to travel.

[4] Richard Townley of Townley, Esq. Probably to procure a dispensation or on some business with the ecclesiastical court.

Rob. Hyndley usque Holeway	vj*d.*		
M'ocho ñro usque Ord	xxviij*s.* viij*d.*		
Dno. Abbati usque Stanlaw	iv*l.* x*s.* ij*d.*		
Eid. per vices usque Wiswall	iij*s.* iv*d.*		
Christopher Cowpere per vic. usque Preston	xvj*d.*		
Laur. Radeliffe usque Clyderhow	viij*d.*		
Nic. Thorniber usque Fylde	xij*d.*		
Wm. Strynger usque Bradford	xij*d.*		
Nic. Forest de Stanl. usque Whall.	iij*s.* ij*d.*		
Joh. Kypas et Wm. Henthorne usque Latham	iij*s.* ij*d.*		
Rob. Hyndlay usque Brunley	iij*d.*		
Thomæ	xij*d.*		
S.	xxv*l.* vij*s.* vj*d.*	Suñ	£21 1 4

From this table we shall be enabled to draw some conclusions with respect to the comparative habits of the two abbots Holden and Paslew, by no means to the advantage of the latter. In the year before us Holden made only one journey, and that on the necessary business of the house, to Stanlaw; for the short excursions to Bowland, Blackburn, Wiswall, &c. were only morning rides. But Paslew was perpetually abroad, at Borough (qu. Brough, in Westmerland ?), at Bolton, at Durham (spelt Dorham, the genuine dialect of Whalley), at Cumbermere, Stanlaw, and Ripon. His bounty was considerably less, but his personal expenses were double those of his predecessor. His monks also were more confined. Travelling was, to these prisoners for life, the greatest of all indulgences; yet only five monks were permitted to make any excursions in 1521: in 1478 there were 31; whether it were that at the former period there was more business or greater lenity.

The sums allowed for travelling would amount to about 1*s.* per day. The abbot may be conjectured to have travelled, on an average, with four servants. The prior, Christopher Smith, appears to have been attended by one, and the ordinary monks to have journeyed alone, but all on horseback.

IN VARIIS EXPEN.		IN VARIIS EXPEN.	£	*s.*	*d.*
Dño abbati pro habitu [1]	v*l.*	Dño Abbi pro habitu [1]	5	0	0
Conventui pro habitu [2]	xxxix*l.*	Conventui pro habitu [2]	47	0	0
Provisori Conventus [3]	xliv*l.* xij*s.* iij*d.*	Provisori Conventus [3]	71	16	0

[1] The ordinary habit of a Cistertian abbot was the canonical gown and scapulary of white cloth, but probably of much finer materials than that of the monks.

[2] If we allow forty shillings for the habit of each monk, the number will in one instance a little exceed, and in the other fall short, of twenty.

[3] Every necessary of housekeeping seems to be included in other articles. I do not, therefore, understand what was the nature of this heavy charge.

			£	s.	d.
Pro vino rubr.[1]	xxix*l*. ivs. iij*d*.	Pro vino[1]	33	15	8
Pro vino dulci	lxiijs. iv*d*.	Pro vino dulci	9	0	0
Pro vino per vices	xxxviijs. vij*d*.	Pro Butiro et caseo	25	9	0
Pro cera	xxxvijs. iv*d*.	Pro robis serviene'[2]	17	12	0
Pro filo albo	viijs. iv*d*.	Pro plumbo viz ii. p̃	6	13	4
Pro filo nigro	ivs. xj*d*.	Pro Bobus empt' ad Grang'	3	10	0
Pro pan. lin. et canna	iij*l*. xviij*d*.	Pro aĩalibus empt' ad Staurũ	6	13	4
Pro panno lanæ	xls. ij*d*.	Famulis Abbis[3]	12	0	0
Clericis in Cœna Domini	vs.	Pro cera rubea	0	1	0
Pauperibus in Cœna Domini	vjs.	Pro cera Sacriste	3	0	0
Pro sclatston		Pro Empc̃oe et mutac' vas.	1	15	0
Pro clavis equorum		Pro Filo albo	0	6	8
Pro resina		Pro Filo nigro	0	3	0
Pro ferro Hispanico		Pro Panno lin'	1	6	8
Pro ferro Anglicano		Pro Panno lan'	5	0	0
Pro stanno	ixs.	Pro Oleo ad eccliam	1	1	0
Pro terebris	xs. xv*d*.	Pro Curac̃oe equorum	0	5	0
Pro Sharj.	iijs. vj*d*.	Pro Capistris frenum et fuñ	0	2	6
Pro secur. et astris	xxj*d*.	Pro Clavis equorum	0	15	0
Pro panno profess.[4]	lviijs.	Pro Ferro Hispanico	6	6	8
Pro panno nup. profess.[4]	xlixs. x*d*.	Pro Clavis duplicibus	1	0	0
Eisdem pro scapular. et tunicis	ls.	Pro Clavis singulis	0	10	0
Pro sect. in cur. Christian.	xv*d*.	Pro Stonebrode[5]	0	9	0
Pro sect. apud Lane.	xiijs. ix*d*.	Pro Strebrode[5]	0	2	0
Pro merc. curiæ de Gysborne	x*d*.	Pro Pice	0	1	8
Pro porc. empt. ad Staurum	ijs. ij*d*.	Pro Sclaytstonys	0	10	0
Pro sport.	ivs. j*d*.	Pro Smigmate[6]	0	6	0
Pro equo empt.	xxxiijs. iv*d*.	Pro Cera Abbi	0	7	0
Pro equo empt.	xxs.	Pro Sectis captis apud Lane'	1	2	0
Pro equo empt. scholari	xxs.	Pro vomeribus	0	3	0
Pro equo empt.	vjs.	Pro singulis equorum	0	1	8

[1] In 1504, a mean term between these two periods, red wine was sold at the rate of 4*l*. per dol. or pipe of 126 gallons ; so that the mean consumption of the abbey was about eight pipes *per annum*, besides white wine.—See Fleetwood's Chron. Pret. p. 92.

[2] Suppose five shillings *per ann.* to clothe a servant, and this charge will infer 70 persons of that order about the abbey.—*Vide* Fleetwood, p. 130.

[3] In 1514, the ordinary wages of a common servant of husbandry were 16*s*. 8*d*., and of a maid servant, 10*s*.—Fleetwood, *ubi supra*. Suppose an equal number of each sex, and the abbot had about twenty upon his own private establishment.

[4] The monks, besides novices, seem to have been divided into two classes, the *professi* and *nuper professi*. Their clothing was before accounted for; so that this extra charge for cloth, besides scapularies and waistcoats, is not very intelligible.

[5] I can offer no conjecture as to the meaning of these words.

[6] *Smigma* appears to have been a kind of soap used in washing floors.—Bp. Kennet, Gloss. Par. Ant. *in voce.* ["Smigma est quoddam unguentum vel confectio unguenti; vel saporis, vel aliquarum aliarum rerum boni odoris." Joh. de Jonna, quoted by Du Cange.]

			£	s.	d.
Pro equo empt.	xvjs.	Pro Sellis et hm'	0	16	4
Pro equo empt.	xiijs. ivd.	Pro Calebe	0	3	0
Cuidam medico	iijs. ivd.	Pro pergameno	0	6	8
Itm. pro medico circa	xxixs. vjd.	Pro papiro	0	1	0
Medico equor.	viijd.	Pro Bitumine	0	1	8
Pro Osmundes	xjd.	Pro Calce	1	2	0
Pro Repar. ap. Downham	xxixs. ivd.	Pro Resina	0	4	0
Pro Repar. Mol. de Acton	ijs. ivd.	Pro Canabo	0	12	0
Pro Rep. ap. Holoway	vs. ijd.	Pro Sectis captis apd London	3	3	4
Pro Rep. Ponend[1] de Terfyn	iijs. ivd.	Pro Capellano Castri	4	0	0
Pro Rep. ap. Staynings	xxd.	Pro Contribucōibus studii	2	0	0
Pro Rep. Cancelli de Rachdall	xxs. ivd.	Pro Colleccōne earundem	0	3	0
Pro Rep. ap. Brunley	ijs. ivd.	Pro Cariccōe focalium	0	10	0
Pro repar. librorum	viijs.	Pro cariacōe lapidum	4	10	10
Pro ferram equor.	viijs.	Pro Messione	2	10	0
Pro Grata ferri[2]	ijs.	Pro Cariacōe focalium Conventui	0	10	4
Pro papyro, viz. Reme	ijs.	Clericis in Cena domini	0	5	0
Pro sotular. pauperum[3]	vjs.	Pauperibus in Cena dñi	0	7	0
Pro cella empta	vs.	Pro Sotularibus corundm[3]	0	8	0
Pro Repar. Cellar.	xjs. vjd.	Pro Ciphis lign'	0	0	7
Pro concordia facta, &c.	iijs. ivd.	Collectori dñi Pape	0	7	0
Sedar. pro rata[4]	vd.	Sutrici	0	2	0
Eid. ad acc. Grad. baccal[4]	xxs.	Magistro Operum	0	3	4
Arch. Ebor. in part. subsid.	xxiijs. ivd.	Custodi Orologij[5]	0	3	4
Procurat. Cler.	xiijs. ijd.	Custodi de Chymys[5]	0	3	4
Pro Wayneloth	iijs. ivd.	Monacho Cellar' pro Caddet	0	2	0
Pro Smygmate	ijs. ixd.	Pro collecōe Firme de Clyderhow	0	6	8
Pro oleo ad ecclam	xxixs. ijd.	Pro collecōe Firme de Rachedall	0	6	8
Tho. Sellar pro Deb. Otwel Whithede	iijs. ivd.	Pro collecōe Firme de Eccles	0	3	4
Ric. Newton p. eod.	xijd.	Pro collecōe Firme de Byllyngton	0	3	4

[1] *Ponendum* I take take to be a pound.

[2] Grates and chimneys were beginning to be introduced about a century before this time.

> Nowe hath eche ryche a rule to eaten by himselfe,
> In a privie parler for poore men sake,
> Or in chambre with a chimney, and leve ye chief halle.
>
> Piers Plowman, fol. xliii.

[3] The shoemaker of the poor. It is pleasing to find that the monks employed a person specifically for this benevolent purpose. The word was formed from *subtalaris*, and yet exists in the Scottish Sowter. It must be observed that there is no charge for leather, because their own tanneries supplied it.

[4] A scholar was constantly maintained at the expense of the house in one of the universities, whose annual exhibition we see was 5*l.*; twenty shillings ad acc. grad. bacc. can only have been in part; the real charge, I believe, appears in the next column, viz. 9*l.* 6*s.* 8*d.* Bishop Fleetwood was not accurate in saying that degrees might be taken 260 years ago at five times less charge than in his own time. Chron. Pret. p. 10.

[5] An abbey orologe was proverbial in the time of Chaucer; but we have here also an instance of the antiquity of chimes.

Pro Moss	vijs. ixd.
Pro sotular.	vjs. vd.
. . . .	
. . . .	
Pro iv^or. supellec. ad Hospitium	xs.
Pro Rep. Organor. viz. pro Tynne[2]	xxxl. xs.
Pro Wyre, viz.	ijl. ivd.
Pro Marcour	ixd.
Pro Tinglas	ivd.
Pro Glutino	ixd.
Pro Wainscot	ivs. vjd.
Joh. Organistæ pro labor. suo	xxxvjs. viijd.
Pro focal. empt.	ijs.
Pro eod. ad R. Sherburne	xvs.
Pro Terricid.[3]	xjs. viijd.
Pro Cepo et flot[3]	xijd.
Pro Materia encausti	xijd.
Pro Politridiis[4]	ixd.
Pro butyro et cas.	xxivl. xiijs. vijd. ob.
Pro Messione	xls.
Pro Introduc. garb. dec^m.	xliijs.
Pro caric. focal. et oner.	xxxxvs. ivd.
Pro car. pis. ac vol. ad Stagna[5]	xxxvs.
Pro rob. servient.	xvl.
Famul. abbatis	xl. xjs. ivd.
In Decimas Wapontag.	xls.
Pro concord. fact. cum. J. Haydock	xvjs.
Pro Cilicio ad vestim.[7]	xvjs.
Capellano Castri	ivl.

	£	s.	d.
Pro introduc̃c̃o Garbarum	2	0	0
Pro materiis incausti[1]	0	1	4
In decasis firme de Clyderhow	0	8	0
In decasis de Harrowode buks pro conventu	2	6	8
In Decas. de Newfeld et Grenefeld in propriis manibus	2	0	0
Scholari pro Rat'	5	0	0
Pro Reparac̃oe Terebrorum	0	1	8
Conventui pro termino Sci. Jo. Bapt'	11	6	8
Rad. Wolton pro custodio Westwode et Weteley	0	6	8
Pro tertio monacho apud Stanlaw	1	0	0
Carbonibus marinis Pro sportis et h'	0	9	0
Pro Carbonibus marinis	0	0	0
Reparac̃oe pont' apud Stanlaw	0	6	0
Pro Apro	0	6	8
Pro Empc̃oe vas' conventui	0	19	0
Pro Organis et Reparac'	6	13	4
Pro Bremys vivis pro paludibus[5]	0	10	0
Scholari pro gradu Bacalat'	9	6	8
Pro Cortinis tapetis et sm'	0	16	0
Pro Reparc̃oe apud Wolden	1	10	0
Pro duobus Nowchis et vitro pro Altar'[6]	1	3	0
Henr' Cokshoth pro fact' Domus ap. Padyham	2	2	0
Pro coloribus pictori[8]	0	12	0
Pro vitrac̃oe	0	10	0
Pro monacho Furnesis[9]	4	13	4

[1] These appear to have been colours used in staining glass; if so, this operation was carried on within the abbey: but qu.?

[2] In Abbot Holden's time here was an organ and regular organist, of the latter of which we find no mention in the latter computus. The organ-pipes seem to have been of tin.

[3] Terricidium is turf, and flot the superficial flah. Cepum, I believe to be chips. No mention of pit-coal, which appears in the latter account, though without a charge. *Vide* Padiham.

[4] Politridiis, probably something used in polishing, as emery, &c.

[5] Piscium ac volatilium ad stagnum. Bremys ad paludes. These were store fish and water-fowl for the ponds, of which there are considerable remains about the abbey.

[6] Nowches, I believe, are cruets; but qu.? [A jewel; a necklace: oftener spelt *ouche*.—Halliwell.]

[7] Hair cloth, to be worn next to the skin, for mortification. There is no charge for this article in the latter account. Sixteen shillings were equivalent at least to 8*l*. at present.

[8] These were colours for the limner or illuminator of missals; an art in which, so far as related to colouring, the monks had certainly attained to great excellence. But the drawing, indeed all the drawing of the times, was hard and unnatural.

[9] What was the occasion of so large a payment to a monk of Furness, I do not understand.

			£	s.	d.
Ballivo de Byllington . . .	xxd.				
Jac. Garsyde pro coll. de Rach. .	xiijs. ivd.				
Alex. Holt pro cust. Silvæ ibm. . .	xxd.				
Cust. orolog.	iijs. ivd.				
Mag. oper.	iijs. ivd.				
Monach. cellar. pro cand. . . .	ijs.				
Pro bob. empt. ad Grang. . . .	vijl. ijs.				
. . . .					
Pro duobus pannis de Draper . .	xiijs. ivd.				
. . . .					
. . . .					
. . . .					
Pro tert monach. ap. Stanlaw[1] . .	xvjs. ivd.				
S.	cclxvijl.	Sum̃ . . .	341	8	3

IN DIVER. CAR.		IN DIVERSIS CARIAG^{s}.	£	s.	d.
Pro vino	vl.	Pro Fru^{to}. extra patriam . .	15	0	0
Pro car. sal. . . .	xxvjs. ijd.	Pro ordeo bras. extra patriam . .	8	6	8
Pro car. frut. extr. patr. . .	xvijl. ijd.	Pro providenc' domus . .	4	0	8
Pro car. bras. ord. ext. pat. .	xijl. xixs. ijd.	Pro vino	5	10	0
Pro car. de Craven . . .	xjs. xjd.	Pro sale, viz. xxvj Karrok[2] . .	2	1	6
Item de Fylde	iijs. ivd.				
Item	viijs. ivd.				
Pro car. providen. domus . .	vl. xijs. ixd.				
S. . . .	xlijl. xvijs. ixd. ob.	Sum̃ . . .	34	18	10

IN EMPT. GRANI.		IN EMPCÕE GRANI.	£	s.	d.
Pro frum. empt. extr. patriam, viz. clxxxiv^{q}. j^{b}. ij^{p}. . .	lxxxvl. viijs. xd.	Pro fru^{to}. extra patriam, viz. viij^{xx}. xiiij qrt. iij li. . . .	77	15	3
Pro bras. ord. empt. extr. patriam, viz. clxxiv^{q}. iij^{b}. . . .	lixl. xvjs.	Pro fru^{to}. infra patriam, iiij qrt. vj li. .	7	6	8
Pro ord. empt. de B. R. et H. .	iijl. ivs. iijd.	Pro ord' Bras. extra patriam, viz. v^{xx}. vij qrt. di. . . .	54	18	10
It.	xxxvijs. viijd.	Pro ordeo braseato infra patriam, viz. xxix qt. di. iij li . . .	24	12	4
Pro avenis empt. de B. R. et H. . .	vjl. ijs.	Pro Aven' Bras. infra patriam, iv qrt. ij li. . . .	1	2	4
It. præd.	iijl. ijs. ixd.				
Pisc. empt.	xijs.				
Famulis grang. . . .	xivl. xxd.	Pro Pisc. cum cariacõe . .	0	18	0

[1] A monk still continued to reside at Stanlaw; but why he is called the third monk I have yet to learn.

[2] Karrok, a cart or wain.—*Vide* Spelmanni Gloss. *in voc.* Carrocium.

			£	s.	d.
Pro frum. empt. infra Craven, xvij q. di. j lb.	vj*l*. xviij. iv*d*. *ob*.	Granatori super.	0	4	0
		Famulis grang'	14	1	8
		In cervisiis pro Abbate	5	0	0
		Pro pane empt' apud Wakefeld cum carne	0	7	0
		Pro sectis in curia Christianitatis	0	3	4
		Pro ordio infra patriam vij qrt' dim. vj li	4	4	3
S.	clxxxvij*l*. vij*s*. j*d*. *ob*.	Sumñ	190	13	8

Under this head, in which by-the-bye are several articles strangely misplaced, it may be observed, that the quantity and the price of wheat consumed were very nearly the same in both years; viz. 184 quarters in the first and 187 in the second; the price per quarter nine shillings, more or less. This statement contradicts Stowe's account, who asserts that, in this very year 1521, the price of wheat was 20*s*. per quarter, and it was always dearer in Lancashire than in the London market.

In the article of malt a considerable reduction appears to have been made, as in 1478 the consumption was 174 quarters, and in 1521 only 147; but in the latter is an item of five pounds "in cervisiis pro abbate." But a great advance had been made in the price, the former averaging somewhat more than six shillings per quarter, the latter nearly ten. It was probably this dearth which put them upon the awkward expedient of malting oats.

It is remarkable that the wages paid to the servants of the grange, at an interval of forty-two years, are the same to a farthing.

IN COQUINA ABB.		IN COQUINA ABB'IS.	£	s.	d.
In carne bov. et vac.	l*l*. iv*s*. vj*d*.	In carnibus bovum et vaccarum	72	19	0
In car. ovum	ix*l*. xs.	In carnibus ovum	15	8	0
In car. vit.	vj*l*. ix*s*. ij*d*.	In carnibus vitulorum	8	0	5
In car. porc.	xlviij*s*. vij*d*.	In carnibus porcorum	1	10	0
In car. porcel.	xx*s*. x*d*.	In carnibus porcellorum	0	16	0
In car. edul. agr. et vol.[1]	xxxv*s*. viij*d*.	In carnibus agnorum	0	17	0
In pisc. rec.[2]	xxiij*l*. xvij*s*. iij*d*.	In carnibus edum et volat'	1	10	6
Wil^mo^. Andrew et Jake[2]	xxxiij*s*. iv*d*.	In piscibus Recent'[2]	39	17	3
		Piscatoribus pro Mercede[2]	3	0	0
S.	lxxxxvij*l*. iij*s*. ix*d*.	Sum̃	143	18	11

[1] That is, game and water-fowl.

[2] The corresponding article, in the latter Compotus, proves these to have been the fishermen of the abbey. Modern Catholics acknowledge that the long season of Lent requires all attainable varieties of this innutricious and quickly disgusting species of food; and the monks were fully aware of this inconvenience, and amply provided to alleviate it; for they had (*vide infra*) stock-fish, herrings red and white, salmon, and salted eels in store. The sea afforded various species of fresh fish in vast quantities; their ponds supplied them with bream; the Ribble with excellent salmon and trout; and the Hodder with its own delicious umber. What baskets of the three last must Will. Andrew and Jake

These accounts, and especially the latter, imply an enormous establishment; for, in the year 1533, we are told by Stowe, the faithful chronologist of English economy, that a fat ox sold for xxvj *s.* viij *d.*, a fat wether for iij *s.* iv *d.*, a fat calf for the same, and a fat lamb for xij *d.* But if we multiply the sum total of the latter Compotus by 10, which is less than Stowe's account would allow, here is an annual sum equivalent to 1,400*l.* of modern money expended upon animal food alone in the abbot's private household. Now, in a well-ordered family, when shambles meat sells for 4*d.* in the pound, 20*s.* per week will supply ten persons. But, in the sixteenth century, animal food formed a much larger proportion of the necessaries of life than at present. We will therefore suppose six persons to have been sustained upon this proportion of meat; but 1400 divided by 52 leaves 27 and a fraction: 27 times 6, or 162 persons therefore must have been constantly fed at the abbot's table.

Every conclusion that can be drawn from these comparative statements is unfavourable to the character of Paslew. He was an economist indeed, but not at the expense of his own comforts; for, though the income of his house was much improved, the expenses of the church-service were abridged, the stated allowances of charity were not increased, the general consumption of the house retrenched, the instruments of luxury more amply rewarded, and the cost of his own private establishment greatly augmented. See also the title *De Hiner.*

IN PROVIDEN. DMS.		IN PROVIDENCIA DOMUS.	£	s.	d.
In alec. rub. mel. secte[1] } In alec. rub. vil. secte }	ivl. xvijs. ivd.	In Allec' Rub melior' sect' } In Allec' Rub vilior' sect' }	5	15	0
In alec. alb.	xviijs. viijd.	In Allec' Albis	5	2	0
Pro pisc. dur.	vl.	In piscibus duris	3	12	0
Pro pisc. salsis	vjl. ijs. ivd.	In pisc. salsis	11	10	0
Pro anguillis sals. viz. barclt.	xivs.	In Salmonibus salsis	1	16	0
Pro ol. oliv.	vijs. vjd.	In anguillis salsis	0	11	4
Pro Rac de Coran.	ixs.	Pro Sale, viz. xxvi karrokes	5	3	8
Pro Amygdal.	vijs.	Pro Ficubus et Racemis	0	8	0
Pro Ficubus et racemis	vijs.	Pro Amigdalis	0	6	8
Pro Pipere[2]	xvs. vijd.	Pro Racemis de Coran'	0	5	4

have brought in! Will. Andrew is, I believe, the Christian and surname of the same person; for I find that, in the beginning of Abbot Paslew's time, there was a dispute between him and John Tallbot, of Salesbury, for the latter assaulting Will. Andrew and Rob. Dobson on High Pikestone Edge, in the way from Whalley Abbey to Preston, and taking from them a parcel of fish. This was principally intended to decide the right of a road over that ground, which was determined by award in favour of the Abbey.—*Townl. MSS.*

[1] In the year 1495 white herrings were sold for 3*s.* 4*d.* per barrel.—Fleetw. *Chron. Pret.* But, if we average the red and white at 5*s.* per barrel, here was, in the former year, a consumption of 23 barrels, and in the latter of 45. The use of stock-fish appears to have diminished greatly at the latter period, and to have been replaced partly by salt-fish not dried and partly by herrings. Eels salted and barrelled must have been a rancid and abominable food. Surely the stomachs of many monks must have been affected by the very smell of fish, like that of Erasmus.

[2] This increase in the consumption of pepper proves that the use of pastry and other seasoned cookery prevailed much more in 1521 than forty years before.

Pro Croco	vj*s.* vj*d.*
Pro Zinziber	vj*s.* viij*d.*
Pro Zinziber vir.	ij*s.* vij*d.*
Pro Sawnders [1]	xviij*d.*
Pro avellan. et licor.	xiv*d.*
Pro libis et rice	xxij*d.*
Pro Turnsole alkanet et pynde	viij*d.*
Pro Sucaro inrolat. et al. sp̃ebus [2]	xiv*d.*
Pro Sale, viz. xxi karroks et dim.	xliv*s.* ix*d.*
S.	xxiij*l.* ij*s.* iij*d.*
In Fabrica eccl.	x*s.* xiv*d.*
S. tot. exp.	dclxxxv*l.* iv*s.* vi*d.* *ob.*
Superexer. exp.	xlviii*l.* xiij*s.* v*d.* *ob.*
Sum. rest. de anno p̃terit.	ccccIxviij*l.* xvij*s.* ij*d.*

	£	*s.*	*d.*
Pro pipere	4	2	0
Pro Croco	1	16	0
Pro Zinzibero	0	2	6
Pro Avellanis	0	1	0
Pro libis et thiriaca	0	6	8
Pro Nutmukis	0	1	0
Pro diversis Sp̃ebus	0	0	6
Pro Succareande	0	1	0
Pro sucar.	0	9	0
Pro Turnsoll Alkanet tinsot et at	0	1	0
Pro gariofolis et Maces	1	0	0
Pro licores et Sinamomo	0	4	0
Pro Rices	0	1	0
Pro Oleo Olivo	0	18	5
Pro Zinzibero virido	0	4	0
Pro Sawnders	0	5	0
Pro Dactilis	0	1	0
Pro granis paradisi	0	10	0
Pro Sturg'	0	10	8
Sum̃	44	15	7
In Mercedibus Curie	7	8	4
In Fabrica ecclesie	23	0	0
Sum̃a total' expenc̃	839	11	5½
Sum̃ Recept' super expeñ	68	11	3½

We have now traced from authentic documents the internal arrangements and economy of this establishment, which appears to have consisted of the lord abbot, the prior, about 20 monks, divided into the *professi* and *nuper professi*, besides an uncertain number of novices, 20 servants belonging to the abbot, and 70[3] in the general service of the house: in all probably 120 persons. But besides these the demesnes and revenues of the abbey had to sustain a daily though uncertain and irresistible influx of guests in every rank, from the sovereign to the beggar, whose stay, if it exceeded not three days, was never considered as oppressive. This boundless hospitality however, though eminently useful in some

[1] Sawnders or Sanders is the Indian spicewood; it has a bitter taste and aromatic smell, and was probably used in cookery.

[2] This is a curious fact, as it proves that sugar was in use amongst us before the discovery of America; but the history of this great ingredient in modern luxury is far from being well ascertained. The sugar-cane, however, appears from "Pancirollus de Rebus inventis," tit. 5, to have been grown in Sicily, and sugar to have been manufactured at Venice, though probably in small quantities, some centuries before his time. But it was rather considered as a balsamic or pectoral medicine than an article of food.—Not. ib.

[3] To persons unacquainted with the economy of these houses, the number of servants which I have assigned must appear very great; but this is far beneath the establishment of many of the greater houses. The abbey of Tewkesbury, at the Dissolution, had 144 servants.—Burnet's *Hist. Reform.* vol. i. App.

respects, was equally pernicious in others. If, for instance, in an age of poverty, and when no legal provision for the poor existed, these foundations liberally supplied the wants of age and sickness, they dealt out with undistinguishing hands an equal measure of bounty to "valiant and idle beggars, drove beasts, and michers."[1] If again they afforded a gratuitous and comfortable resting-place to the traveller of every description, the power of exercising this liberality was extorted from the laborious parish priest, who had an antecedent right to those tithes, which the monks with unfeeling rapacity appropriated to themselves. The same cause, together with the magnificence of their buildings, rendered them importunate and never-satisfied beggars, who found an easy access to the beds of the great at seasons when guilt and fear precluded a refusal; and the necessary magnitude of their general expenses made them jealous of the most trivial rights, querulous, irritable, and contentious.[2]

But to return from this digression:—The average consumption of the house may be stated in round numbers, on the authority of the two preceding accounts, at wheat 200 quarters, malt 150 quarters, wine 8 pipes.

For the Abbot's table.		And for the Refectory and inferior tables within the house.	
Oxen and cows	75	Oxen and cows	57
Sheep	80	Sheep	40
Calves	40	Calves	20
Lambs	20	Lambs	10
Porkers	4		

From this statement may be inferred a great disproportion in the quantity of animal food, when compared with the other necessaries of life, to modern habits; for in this table of expenses it may be made clearly to appear, that the value of shambles-meat consumed was, to that of wheat and of malt, in a much higher ratio than at present.[3] The latter circumstance leaves a very favourable impression with respect to the sobriety of a religious house. The quantity of wine accounted for would indeed have allowed a bottle of wine per day to every monk; but it is to be suspected that great part of this luxury was intercepted

[1] General injunctions to the monasteries.—Burnet's *Hist. Reform.* vol. i. App.

[2] See the "Annales Prioratus de Dunstable," published by Hearne; which is little better than an history of petty squabbles.

[3] This computation supposes that the first article, *provisori conventus*, was a charge for shambles-meat on the general account of the house, which is no where else provided for; and the two sums charged under this head are nearly one-half of that which is placed to the account of the abbot's table.

[The large stone troughs still remain, composed of Pendle grit, at the Abbey, at the farm of Easterley, and at the Old Vicarage house at Wiswell, on which the monks salted down half-carcases, or flitches, of beef, in autumn: when beasts were driven down to the Abbey from the Grange above Slaidburn in Bowland, from Merland near Rochdale, from the forest of Rossendale, and other places. Not having sufficient buildings to house the stock in, they drove them down to be slaughtered before they lost their condition, and before the snow and storms commenced in the upper valleys.—R. N. W.]

by the abbot and his guests before it reached the refectory; and who can forbear lamenting that these poor men had scarcely a vegetable to eat [1] or a garden to cultivate!

On the whole, to men who fed so grossly and had so little exercise or labour to correct the effects of repletion, how wise and salutary, even in a medical view, was the institution of fasting! Yet, after all the benefits resulting from temporary inanition, how peculiar must then have been the state of the human body, and consequently the practice of medicine, in monasteries! When men, born in times, and bred in habits, which almost exempted them from the evil, shall I say, or the privilege, of weak constitutions, were often swept away in the midst of their days by inflammatory disorders, or, if they survived to a later period, were knocked down at a stroke by apoplexies, the superadded laziness and plenty of a convent, without such systematic checks, must have been doubly pernicious.

But another circumstance in the habits of monks must have exposed them to putrid and cutaneous disorders;[2] I mean a total inattention to cleanliness, which is to be imputed to the absurdity of their rule: for they had no sheets to their beds, or shirts to their backs: they slept in their ordinary dresses of woollen, and never availed themselves of a practice from which they do not appear to have been prohibited, and which alone rendered the same habits tolerable in the ancients, namely, a constant use of warm baths, which would have removed all impurities from the skin. In us it would produce a strange mixture of feelings, to be repelled from the person of a man of learning or elegant manners by stench and vermin.

Such, then, was the monastery of Whalley, with its several advantages and defects; and in this state it subsisted till the attainder of Abbot Paslew.[3] After that melancholy event, nothing more is recorded of it during a period of two years; after which, on

[1] [The present Vicar of Whalley has found reason to report differently. "Attached to the abbey was a garden abounding with fruit-trees and herbs proper for making salves. Apples, pears, beans, and pot-herbs grew in them, and the sick walked in them that they might enjoy the pure smell of the flowers of the herbs. In the old hedges great numbers of barberry trees were grown which were used for confections."—(Lecture by the Rev. R. N. Whitaker, 2nd Feb. 1869.) It also appears from the Coucher Book that there were several gardens and orchards about the abbey.]

[2] The jaw-bone of one of the abbots, turned up in digging within the choir, had been honeycomed by a scrofulous complaint. [Chap. xxv. of Distinctio quarta of the *Exordium magnum Ordinis Cist.* is entitled De monacho qui sine caligis dormire præsumpsit et propterea per divinam revelationem vetitus est abbas fieri. Chapter xxiv. is Qualiter conversus, qui sine licentia caligas suas lavit, divinitus punitus est.]

[3] It was committed to Braddyll from the day of the Dissolution. I have since met with his first half-year's account, ending at Michaelmas 1537. [In the Public Record Office, Exchequer, Augmentation, Ministers' Accounts 28 and 29 Hen. VIII. No. 89, is the Computus Joh'is Bradyll, Ballivi dn'i Regis pro Whalley nuper Monaster', a large roll, and several other rolls for succeeding years.]

I find that Pedley was Vicar of Whalley at this time; so that he could not have been presented by Archbishop Cranmer. It does not appear that he was a monk: it is therefore not improbable that he was presented by the Crown immediately after the Dissolution. There is no account of the precise time when Vicar Seller died.

It appears, from the account above mentioned, that, immediately upon the forfeiture of the house, Richard Pollard, esq. one of the King's Surveyors General, came down and let the desmesnes from that time to Michaelmas.

April 12th, 1539, the bailiwick of the demesnes was committed, by letters patent of Henry VIII. to John Braddyll, gent. of the neighbouring house of Braddyll and Brockhole, the said demesnes being then seized into the King's hands "ratione attincturæ Johannis nuper abb. ibm." In the beginning of July, this year,[1] died Christopher Smith, who had been 30 years Prior, before the forfeiture of the house. He was interred near the font of the parish church, where the initials X S, and the paten and chalice, expressive of his order, still remain upon a large gravestone, adorned with a cross fleury. (Engraved in the same plate with the crosses in the churchyard.)

In this state everything remained during an interval of somewhat more than 14 years, in which time Braddyll had so profited of the rich deposit committed to his hands, as to be able to convert a trust into property; and accordingly, at a most dangerous period for such an adventure, that is, exactly 20 days before the death of Edward VI., he, in conjunction with Richard Assheton, a younger son of the house of Lever, purchased from the Crown, for the sum of 2132*l.* 3*s.* 9*d.* the whole manor of Whalley and site of the dissolved or attainted monastery thereof, which are particularised in terms extremely interesting, as they perpetuate several names allusive to its former state, which they who love the place and the subject would not wish to be forgotten.[2]

Within four days after this transaction followed a partition of the premises betwixt the two grantees, in which Assheton obtained exclusive possession of the house; but

Hence it appears, that all the live stock must have been disposed of immediately. Under this letting, the land, upon an average, produced about 2*s.* per acre, and cottage-houses from 1*s.* to 6*d.* and even 4*d.* The tenants at will, who appear to have been all the inhabitants of the town of Whalley, occupying, for the most part, five, six, or eight acres each, paid in all 18*l.* 2*s.* 9*d.*; works silver, 12*s.* 11*d.*; demesne lands, 62*l.* 11*s.* 2*d.* Of these, one close, called Portfield, containing 18 acres, was let for 31*s.* The herbage of the park and wood, two miles in circuit, was demised to Alexander Osbaldeston for 12*l.*; and the folds, containing 60 acres, and Standen Hey, containing 120 acres, to ——, for 19*l.*—The Court Grange is mentioned, as is Le Castell. The dove-house was let for 1*s.* 8*d.*; the tan-house to Simon Haydock and John Woodroof (both I suppose of Burnley), for 4*l.*; an enormous rent, when the skins of the cattle slaughtered at the abbey were gone. Abbey Mill, 1*l.*

[1] "1539, July 5th, Seps. Dns. Christopherus Smyth, quondam prior de Whalley."—Reg. Ecc. Par. [The last prior maintained, after the Dissolution, a considerable interest in the possessions of the abbey, of which he was then called the Proctor, as appears by the following (among other) entries in the *Coucher Book*:—

A medow called Heulker, about vii acres, let to Xp'ofer Smith and John Wilkinson, 1*l.* (p. 1181.)

Le Prioris orchard, di. acr. in tenura Xp'oferi Smith, 1*s.* (p. 1210.)

Christ. Smith clearke, late of Whalley, and . . . . . and George Greinfild clerke, houldeth a parcell of grounde called *the leasing steads*, without gate to the water, and payeth yearly for the same (*blank*). (p. 1189.)

Memorandum, that Mr. Bazon, porter of the parsonage of Whalley, shall paie yearley at the towe feastes of the yeare, that is to say, at Michaelmas and Easter, 6*l.* 14*s.* 4*d.* to Chris. Smith clearke, procter of the late monestery of Whaley, now chantery priest in the parish church of Whaley, for his stipend by the yeare, so appointed by the Earle of Sussex. (p. 1190.)

Christ. Smith, 2 acres arable land and 2 roods meadow, 5*s.* (p. 1195.)

" " a messuage, a garden, 3 acres arable land, 7 acres of pasture, and one acre and a half of meadow, 15*s.* (p. 1201.)

[2] [This important document will be found in a subsequent page.]

Drawn by W^m. Turner A. — Engraved by James Basire

To the Right Honourable ASHETON LORD CURZON,

Braddyll retained so much larger a portion of the demesnes, that he paid a compensation to his partner of 467*l.* 16*s.* 8*d.*

Henceforward the site and demesnes of Whalley are to be considered merely as a lay-fee, and will be noticed once more, in their proper place, under the families of Assheton and Braddyll.

Before we proceed to a survey of the existing remains of Whalley, it may not be improper to premise a few observations on the peculiar construction of monasteries in general, and of the Cistercian houses in particular. These may be considered as a short rationale of monastic architecture; and, besides their general use, may assist the reader in understanding the grounds upon which the different apartments in the annexed ichnography have been assigned to their respective uses.

First, then, the quadrangular mode of building, with apartments opening inward, was, of all others, best adapted both to security and to sequestration; and, for one or other of these reasons, it was common to the villas of the Greeks and Romans;[1] perhaps to temples, with their appendages,[2] to the Oriental kanes,[3] to the castles and greater manor-houses of our English ancestors, to colleges,[4] hospitals, and monasteries.

But, as monastic institutions had their origin in the East, it may be presumed that the first hint, not indeed of the general form, but of that peculiar disposition of apartments which prevails so generally in this species of building among ourselves, was ultimately brought from thence, yet varied in such particulars as difference of climate, and the consequent necessity of a change of habits, seemed to indicate.

But, besides, this disposition of apartments, in religious houses, arose partly from the nature of monastic rules, and partly from attention to general convenience. For the very nature of their rule required, in monks, seclusion from the world; yet a necessary regard to health and cheerfulness, even in those who professed to pay little attention to the one,

1 These were certainly quadrangular; and, besides an impluvium, or, as it is called by Suetonius, Aug. c. 92, a compluvium, in the centre, had frequently noble colonnades, resembling cloisters, which surrounded them within. Such appears to have been the house of Byrrhæna, described in Apuleius, Metamorph. l. 2, c. 22. "Atria longè pulcherrima columnis quadrifariam per singulos angulos stantibus."—See also Vitruvius, l. 6. c. 4.

2 A temple discovered at Pompeii, with its dependent offices and apartments, is said to bear a striking resemblance to an ancient convent.

3 The kanes are built in fashion of a cloister, encompassing a court of 30 or 40 yards square, more or less, according to the measure of the founder's ability or charity.—Maundrell's *Journey from Aleppo to Jerusalem*, p. 4.

4 It may be amusing to trace the features which colleges and monasteries had in common, and those which each possessed apart. Both, then, were quadrangular; both had cloisters, refectories, common rooms, libraries, and a distinct lodging for the head of the house; both, too, had magnificent gateways, but the gateway of a monastery entered a close, and that of a college the quadrangle. The college had no common dormitory, no chapter-house, and no church but a chapel: this is remarkably true, even in the most splendid collegiate foundations; for that of King's College itself, though equalling many cathedrals in extent, and perhaps surpassing them all in magnificence, in order to preserve the collegiate character as distinct from the monastic, was constructed without tower, columns, side aisles, or transept. We are to remember that Jesus' College, in the same university, which has a regular church, is an entire nunnery. It may perhaps be said that Merton College at Oxford, which never was a monastery, is an exception to this rule; and Magdalen College, with respect to its tower; but I recollect no other.

and affected to mortify the other, imperiously demanded that the votaries of religion should sometimes behold a more expanded horizon, and sometimes breathe a freer air, than that of the cloister.

The first feature, therefore, of a religious house was the *clausum*, or close, consisting often of 50, or even 90,[1] acres, surrounded by an high and sometimes embattled[2] wall, and entered by one or two magnificent gateways. Beyond this inclosure the religious were not regularly permitted to walk or ride, but on the necessary business of the house.

Within the close were included all the appendages of a large domain, occupied by the owners; as, a grange[3] or farm-house, barns, stables, mill, &c. The reason of this arrangement, at least in the northern parts of England, was obvious, as the live-stock and outbuildings of the monastery were thus completely protected, not only against ordinary depredations, but against the more formidable and periodical plunder and conflagrations of the Scots.

Next was the house itself, situated in the lowest and warmest part of the inclosure; consisting usually of one large quadrangular court, into which the various offices and apartments opened;[4] and to all these a warm and sheltered access in every season was provided, by means of a penthouse cloister, surrounding the whole.

The northern side of this quadrangle was formed by the nave of the conventual church, so placed with great judgment, on account of its height and bulk, as in that position it afforded the best shelter against northern blasts, and in any other would have excluded more or less of sunshine from the cloister, where the aged monks, who could no longer wander far beyond their cells, would naturally wish, with the poet,

"Nostra bibat vernum contracta cuticula solem."—*Juv.* [Sat. ix. 203.]

Attached to the end of the south transept, and with it constituting, in part, the east side of the quadrangle, was the Sacristy, and next the Chapter-house, of which the doors and windows are generally observed to be adorned with peculiar care.[5]

[1] Fifty acres is about the average, but that of Fountains exceeded ninety.

[2] We have already seen a licence granted by Edward III. to kernel and embattle the close wall of Whalley.

[3] The grange of Whalley seems to have been originally without the close, which now makes a very awkward angle, on purpose to comprehend it.

[4] [The conventual buildings arranged round this cloister court or quadrangle were placed in a variety of positions by different orders of monks; but it has been shown by Edmund Sharpe, M.A., F.S.A., a distinguished architect and archæologist, that the Cistercians not only had fixed rules concerning the nature of sites for their buildings, and the style and amount of ornament to be employed in their construction, but that they followed, with very slight variations, one uniform plan. These laws, it is also proved, were most strictly observed for two centuries at least, not only in this country, but on the continent of Europe. The first house of the Cistercians in this country was founded A.D. 1128, at Waverley, in Surrey. (*Communicated by Mr. W. A. Waddington.*)]

[5] In the churches of the Benedictines especially these apartments were very highly adorned; witness the chapter-houses of York, Worcester, Wells, Lincoln, &c. They were, however, generally small in houses of the Cistercian order on account of their position, but sometimes underwent a subsequent enlargement, as at Kirkstall. [This note, and others of Dr. Whitaker in this place, together with portions of the text, are also corrected by Mr. Waddington, assisted by the great experience of Mr. Sharpe.]

The chapter-house was always considered as a part of the church, received the same peculiar consecration, and was honoured with the interment of patrons and other great persons. Here, too, all elections were made; hence, all processions commenced after elections; and here, lastly, all acts of discipline[1] were performed. All these, but the last, were reasons for its contiguity to the former edifice.

[Next in order on the east walk of the cloister is an apartment used probably as a penitentiary where offending monks were incarcerated after sentence passed on them. A slype, or passage, generally divided this room from a long apartment used as the common refectory and day-room of the monks, stretching in a southerly direction far beyond the line of cloister court.

Over the chapter-house was the library or scriptorium; and to the south, over the common refectory, was the dormitory. A flight of steps is generally found in the south transept of the church, communicating with these apartments for the use of the monks during nocturnal services.

Again, opposite to the church, and forming the south side of the quadrangle, were situated the kitchens, principal refectory, butteries, sculleries, &c., a range of apartments necessarily connected with each other, and in the Cistercian houses usually placed on the north bank of a stream, so that all the offal and filth from the offices passed immediately into the current without annoying any other part of the house.

On the western side was the Hospitium, or guest-house, its dormitory occupying the higher story.[2]]

In all this arrangement there appears a great deal of good sense and rational contrivance.

A very dignified part of the monastery is yet unnoticed, namely, the Abbot's Lodging, which was usually attached to or a little removed from the south-east corner of the quadrangle, and so placed as to afford an easy communication with the cloister, chapter-house, and church. This was a distinct residence, pretty much in the style of a large manor-house, and calculated for a splendid establishment, having a hall, kitchen, and sometimes a chapel within itself. The remains of this building are very conspicuous at Kirkstall,

[1] For there ben manye felle frekes . my feeris to aspie,
Bothe priour and suppriour . and oure pater Abbas:
And if I telle any tales . thei taken hem togideres,
And doon me fast frydayes . to breed and to watre,
And am chalanged in the chapitre hous . as I a child were
And baleised on the bare ers . and no breech bitwene.

Such is the complaint of the merry and mischievous Friar Wrath in *Piers Plowman*. [Wright's edit. 1856, vol. ii. p. 87.]

[2] [The lower story at Fountains Abbey is a magnificent apartment groined in stone; the vaulting ribs springing from a long range of columns continued down its centre. This portion is still in a good state of preservation; indeed, the ruin of Fountains is the most perfect of all the Cistercian establishments in the kingdom. Its plan is so clearly traceable, and its buildings are in such condition, that it forms an excellent field for the study of the economy of monastic architecture.—W. A. W.]

though in ruins: at Whalley it was, till within the last thirty years [before 1800], entire. In those cathedrals, particularly Durham, which have preserved their monastic form, the Protestant deans having occupied the apartments of their excluded predecessors the priors, the deanery is yet found precisely in this relative situation.[1] For this position also of the abbot's or prior's apartments a good reason may be assigned; for, in the quadrangle there was evidently no room for them; placed to the north of the church they would have been cold and dark; to the west, too remote from the choir and chapter-house; and to the south, immediately in the way of kitchens and offices. No situation remained, therefore, but to the south-east, or immediately opposite to the choir, where they united the advantages of shelter, sunshine, and contiguity to those parts of the house where the abbot's presence was most frequently required.

With respect to that peculiar instinct, if it may be so called, which seems to have dictated to the Cistercians in the choice of situations, at least for their Northern houses, it may be observed that, though they affected to plant themselves in the solitude of woods, which were to be gradually essarted by the labour of their own hands, and though they obtained an exemption from the payment of tithes on that specific plea, yet they were excellent judges of the quality of land, however concealed, and never set about their laborious task without the assurance of an ample recompence.

But, if any conclusion can be formed from the scenery which they affected, they must have been men of taste as well as judgment, who had better eyes for landscape than their abstracted patron, St. Bernard.[2]

[1] To illustrate these remarks, compare the annexed ground-plan with those of Kirkstall and Fountains in Burton's Monasticon Eboracense, and with Browne Willis's Ichnography of the Cathedral of Durham, vol. i. p. 223. On the progress of Norman and Gothic architecture as displayed in these buildings, I forbear to make any remarks, for the subject has often been treated of late, and is now pretty generally understood; but, if the reader wishes to see it discussed in a masterly manner, he is referred to Mr. Bentham's Remarks, *History of Ely*, sect. 5 and 6, where he will find the genuine science of James Essex united with the fine taste and critical discernment of Mr. Gray, or to *Observations on the Faery Queene*, vol. ii. from p. 184 to 198, by Mr. Thomas Warton, who has treated Norman and Gothic architecture, not indeed with professional exactness, but with that felicity of real genius which illustrates and adorns every subject that it touches. To all these may now be added the more elaborate and critical elucidations of Dr. Milner.

[2] St. Bernard, in a fit of devout abstraction, is said to have walked a whole day along the Lake of Lausanne without perceiving it. (*Vita Bernardi*, l. 3, c. 1, p. 2014, edit. Par. 1632.) For this absence of mind, or want of taste, he is sneered at by Mr. Gibbon (*Decline and Fall of the Roman Empire*, c. 59), who certainly beheld the same scene from the windows of his library at Lausanne with no mixture of those affections which engaged the Abbot of Clareval. I cannot often accord either in my feelings or conclusions with this great but disingenuous historian; yet in the present instance I can no more conceive than himself how piety is promoted by insensibility, or how the sanctity of Bernard would have been endangered by a moderate use of his eyes in contemplating some of the most beautiful works of the Creator. I have what was meant for a portrait of Bernard in painted glass, preserved out of the wreck of the long gallery at Whalley, but it is only appropriated by the crozier, the glory, and the white Cistercian gown; for the man who sat for this picture must have been a plump and jovial monk of later days, not the pale and meagre *saint*, much attenuated by the discipline, and more by the disease, of fasting, for Bernard was long afflicted by a constriction of the œsophagus. How happy for himself that he thought abstinence a duty! [This head is now, 1871, at The Holme.]

Drawn by Wm Turner J. — Engraved by James Basire

To Richard Henry Beaumont Esqr F.S.A. of Whitley Beaumont in Yorkshire, and of Little Mitton near Whalley this Plate is inscribed, as a small acknowledgment of the many valuable communications received from him in the Progress of this present Work by his obliged and humble Servant the Author.

A copious stream to the south, a moderate expanse of rich meadow and pasture around, and an amphitheatre of sheltering hills, clad in the verdant covering of their native woods beyond,—these were features in the face of Nature which the earlier Cistercians courted with instinctive fondness; where these combined it does not appear that they ever abandoned a situation which they had once chosen; and where these were wanting, it is certain that they never long or willingly remained.

Thus Tulket, which was abandoned for Furness, Stanlaw for Whalley, and Barnoldswick for Kirkstall, though not deficient in general fertility, wanted all these peculiarities of situation and beauties of landscape.

We now proceed to a particular survey of the remains of Whalley Abbey as they exist at present.[1] First, then, the whole area of the close, containing 36 acres 3 roods 14 poles, is still defined by the remains of a broad and deep trench which surrounded it; over this were two approaches to the house through two strong and stately gateways yet remaining. They are constructed in that plain and substantial style which characterised the Cistercian houses, a style which approximates to that of fortification, and shows that the monks did not obtain a licence to kernel and embattel without an end in view. [The central portion of the north-west gateway is almost entire, and is a fine specimen of Late-Decorated architecture, probably of the middle of the fourteenth century. It is of two stories, the higher being supported on stone groining springing from wall corbels. To this upper room, however, there is now no staircase; access must have been gained from apartments north and south of the existing portion. But though there are three side doors of communication, nothing is now to be seen even of the foundations of these buildings.[2] The north-east gateway[3] is of much later date and more complete, with its angle buttresses and battlemented parapet. It possesses a spiral staircase in an angle turret which leads to the second story and the roof.] Within this area, and on the verge of Calder, which formed the south-west boundary of the close, was the house itself, consisting of three quadrangles, besides stables and offices. Of these the first and most westerly was the cloister court, of which the nave of the conventual church formed the north side; [the south transept, sacristy, chapter-house, penitentiary, and portion of common refectory the east; the kitchens, principal refectory, &c. the south; and the guest-house the west. The roof of the cloister was supported on wooden posts, the corbels for bearing the rafters being still visible in the walls. The area within was the monks' cemetery, and some ancient gravestones are still remembered within it. In the south wall of this quadrangle is to be seen

[1] [For the careful Plan, which has been substituted in the present edition for that which previously appeared, the reader is much indebted to William Angelo Waddington, Esq., architect, of Burnley, author of *Architectural Sketches on the Calder and Ribble*, 1869.]

[2] [The north-west gateway is about 130 yards further to the west than is shown on the plan. This is drawn in Mr. Waddington's work above named, together with a view of the Cloister Court, showing the entrance to the Chapter House, and another of one of the south-west angles of the monastery, showing the Monks' Day-Room.]

[3] [The remarks inserted by Dr. Whitaker in his *Corrigenda*, third edit. p. 552, have not been overlooked; but it is evident that the architectural friend whose opinion he quotes placed the erection of the north-west gateway about 150 years too late.]

a wide arched recess which has evidently contained the lavatory.[1] The groove of the lead pipe is still conspicuous, as is also another for the reception of a wooden rail on which the towels hung.

Standing in this court we observe that only a few fragments of the mighty fabric of the conventual church now remain;[2] of these more will be said hereafter.

The library and monks' dormitory were also destroyed by Sir Ralph Assheton. Of the buildings to the south nothing is now to be seen but a portion of the north wall of the refectory, &c. pierced by two or three moulded doorways; but the eye rests with satisfaction on the beautiful doorway of the chapter-house, with its numerous pateras, and the richly moulded and traceried windows on either side, with many shafts, and an amount of carving which serves to illustrate the peculiar care which was bestowed on the decoration of this building. The other doorways are devoid of carved ornaments, but have moulded arches and jambs. The windows of the day-room have mullions with simple tracery heads. The south-west angle is generally admired, being more ornate and decidedly picturesque. There are many insertions of windows and other departures from the original design in this range, but the predominating style is that of the transition from the Decorated to the Perpendicular. The guest-house to the west is almost entire, but its buttresses have been much broken and some of its windows destroyed. It is now used as a barn and cow-house.]

Beyond this court to the east is another quadrangular area, formed by the choir of the church on one side, the opposite side of the chapter-house, &c. on another, a line of ruinous buildings on the third, and a large distinct building, itself surrounding a small quadrangle, on the fourth. This appears evidently to have been the abbot's lodgings; for which reason, as being best adapted to the habits of an ordinary family, it immediately became

[1] ["Adjacent to the refectory was the lavatorium, or place for washing for the monks, and, although we know that they were anything but cleanly in their persons, it is curious to trace how careful the abbots were to have a good supply of pure water for the establishment. * * * There are two beautiful wells in Wiswell and Whalley,—one in the field above Mr. Cottam's cottage, the other near Ingham's Wood, both circular, with hewn ashlar steps, which were the reservoirs from which they drew their supplies, and which attest the value that they put upon a good water supply. From these heads an inch leaden pipe, of which there used to be specimens in the cottage until the late sale, conducted the water; and if any one will search in the bottom of the field called Sheep Hey, he will find remains of the pipes still existing. The monks were fond of wells, and on Ascension Day the rustics in some places used to assemble around them, dance, chant psalms, and encircle them with emblematical flowers, which was called Well-flowering. In June 1847, when driving the piles for the piers of brickwork of the railway viaduct opposite to the lower corner of Titus Edwards's cottage, the workmen came upon the wooden framework composing the cloughs or outlets of the ponds or canals constructed by the monks. The framework was very strong—so strong that the contractor would not allow it to be disturbed; and in front of it there extended a thick board, pierced with small holes, less than half an inch, which would appear to have been placed there to keep the fish in."—Lecture by Rev. R. N. Whitaker, Vicar of Whalley, 2 Feb. 1869.]

[2] [Mr. Waddington has remarked that, though we still have in England many perfect monastic churches of other orders, there is not one of the Cistercians that is not roofless and in ruins. This has probably arisen from their secluded sites, away from large populations that might have adopted them for parochial use.]

PLAN OF WHALLEY · ABBEY.

1870.

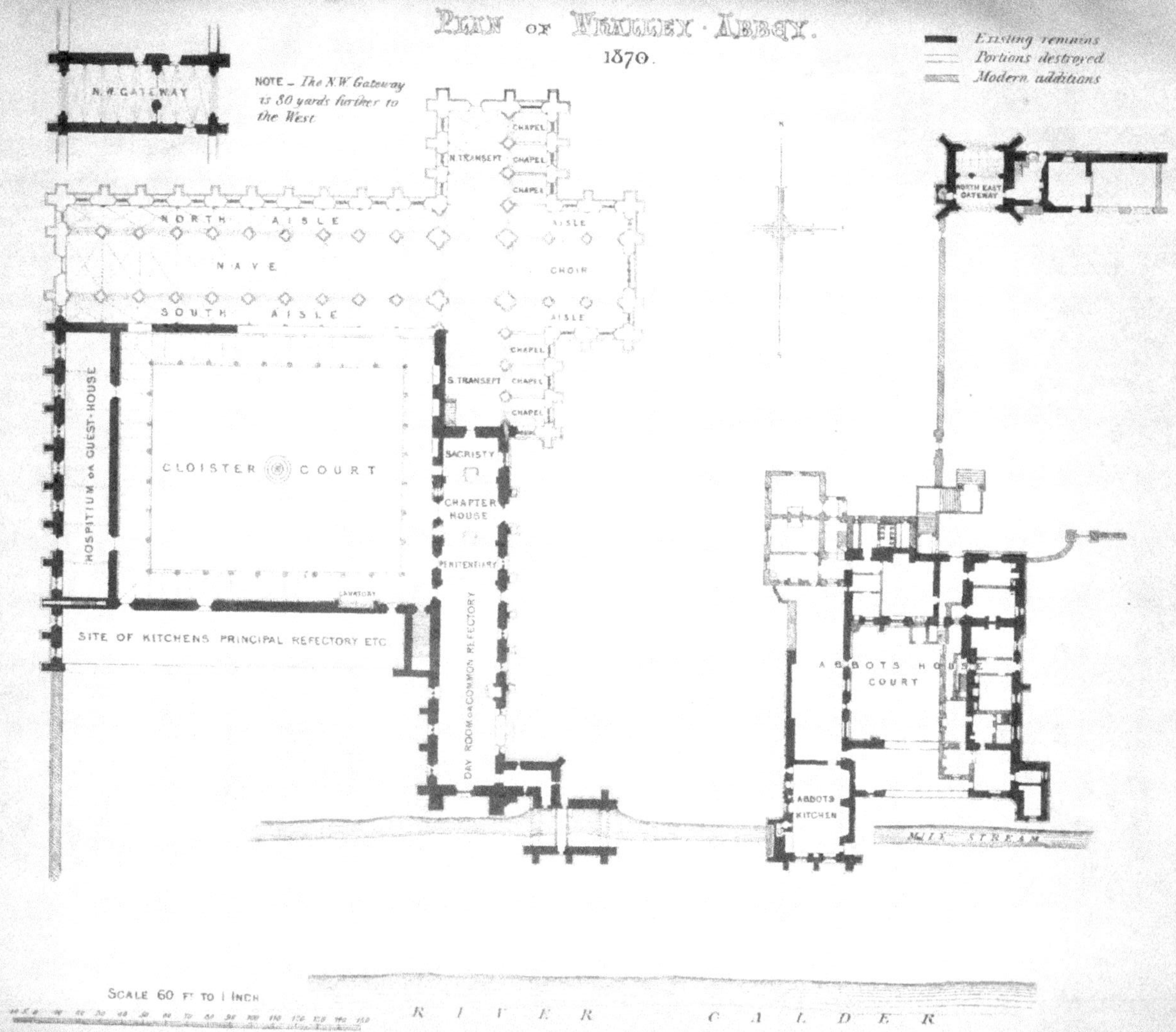

the residence of the Asshetons, [who in their additions piled up the beautiful fragments of the abbey in many grotesque forms. Very little of the original building is now left. Its best apartments, amongst them a gallery nearly 150 feet in length, have been demolished. It was enlarged in 1862 (as shown on the Plan) without regard to the style of the original structure, and is now formed into two distinct residences.] The ancient Kitchen, the *Coquina Abb'.* of the Compotus, whence such hecatombs were served up, remains, though roofless, with two huge fireplaces. On the southern side of this building is a small but very picturesque and beautiful ruin mantled with ivy [presenting a very elegant window of Transitional character]. It appears to have been a chapel, and was probably the abbot's private oratory.

But to return to the conventual church itself, which [would rank amongst the finest of the Cistercian order in Europe, and] exceeded many cathedrals in extent. As before stated, it has been levelled nearly to the foundation. This work of havoc was probably an effect of that general panic which seized the lay-owners of abbeys, on the attempt made by Queen Mary to restore the monks to their cloisters. "For now (says Fuller) the edifices of abbeys, which were still entire, looked lovingly again on their ancient owners; in prevention whereof, such as possessed them for the present, plucked out their eyes by levelling them to the ground, and shaving from them, as much as they could, all abbey characters."[1]

[1] From the following particulars, which I have since met with in the Account Books of Sir Ralphe Assheton, it appears that a considerable part of the church, together with much of the cloister court, remained above 120 years after the Dissolution, when they were demolished at a considerable expense, and for no assignable cause:—

"1661, P^{d} for pulling down the old walls over the inner close, 1*l.* 10*s.* 6*d.*

"1662, Pulling downe the old abbey walls this winter:

"P^{d} Henry Clayton and Ja^{s} Rushton in p^{t} for pulling down the old part of the steeple and those side walls adjoining to it, at 3*d.* per yard, 26*s.* 8*d.* More to them, being the whole, for pulling down 223 y^{ds}, as per note 29*s.* 2½*d.*

"More to d°, for pulling down the end of the close wall next to Gilly's house, and a peice adjoining to the barn side, at 6*d.* per yard, 25*s.* 6*d.*

"More to them for pulling down 136¾ y^{ds} of the old steeple, at 4*d.* per yard, 2*l.* 5*s.* 7*d.*

"P^{d} in part for pulling down 14 y^{ds} of the highe cloister walls next the dove coat, at 6*d.*, 7*s.* More, in full, for the same side, 9*d.*

"In part for the other, &c. &c. In all, for this work, 1*l.* 15*s.* 8*d.*

"P^{d} John Gilbert for taking down the great window or door at the head of stairs in the cloisters."

To compensate, however, for this havoc, Sir Ralphe Assheton, in the years 1664 and 1665, fitted up the Long Gallery, which, in little more than a century, followed the fate of its predecessors, and is itself become a ruin, without the charm of antiquity.

This work of destruction left a very curious remain for future speculation. In the south wall of the building which I have called the dormitory is a hollow space, almost from top to bottom, which has apparently had no opening but by a breach in the wall. It contains a narrow staircase, at the bottom of which is a small arched space on the level ground, just capable of containing a narrow bed, and at the top is a narrow opening through one of the external buttresses of the building for air and light. It could not, therefore, be intended for the tremendous Vade in Pacem, but it was, probably, the "teter et fortis carcer" for refractory monks, into which the Liber Loci Benedicti informs us that one of the fraternity was thrust for attempting to stab the Abbot of Kirkstall in the chapter-house. The breach through the wall by which this singular excavation is entered, is now wide enough to admit a man's body with some

However, in the month of August 1798, permission having been obtained from the guardian of the present owner to investigate the foundation by digging, a very successful attempt was made to retrieve the whole ichnography of the church,[1] of which there were no remains above the surface to assist conjecture, or to guide research, but one jamb of the west window against the wall of the dormitory, a small portion of the south wall of the nave, a fragment of the south transept, and another jamb of one of the side chapels eastward from the last. An inequality in the ground eastward from the transept in an adjoining orchard showed the half-pace into the choir, of which the outline to the north and east was also defined in the same manner. Upon these slender data we proceeded first to investigate the foundations of the columns towards the west end, and having ascertained the distance of one from the south wall, the width of the south aisle, and consequently of the north, followed of course; another digging, immediately to the north, ascertained the width of the middle aisle, and a third from east to west gave one intercolumniation; the length of the nave being already given by the remains of the transept, the number of columns was now proved. A right line drawn along the remnant of the south wall, and continued to the intersection of the nave and transept, proved the length of the latter on the south side, and consequently also on the north. The choir evidently appeared to have had two side aisles, [and each transept the three eastern chapels, so common in churches of this order].

The site of the choir being determined, it remained to investigate its contents beneath the surface. Accordingly, under the high altar nothing appeared but a bed of undisturbed and native sand; but beneath the second half-pace, immediately leading up to it, were turned up many broken remains of a painted pavement, consisting of small glazed floor-tiles,[2] adorned with various devices, and of different forms and dimensions. At the foot

difficulty; but as there is no appearance of a doorway, the probability is, that the prisoner was walled up, and that a small aperture only was left to admit his provisions. Had he been left to expire in his dungeon, it is evident that no aperture would have been left for light or air.

[1] [Mr. Gregson, in his *Fragments of Lancashire*, published a restoration of the Abbey Church of Whalley drawn by Mr. Palmer, who was an architect in Manchester, and who was employed in 1816-17 in the restoration of the Collegiate Church, of which he wrote the description appended to Dr. Hibbert's *History of the Foundations of Manchester*. He died in 1846, at the age of 64. Gregson's plate of Whalley Abbey Church is incorrectly entitled a view from the South-East instead of the South-West. But it has besides many architectural faults. The style displayed is totally at variance with the date ascribed to it (1409), as the existing portions exhibit the characteristics of a date at least forty and the church at least sixty years earlier. The transept is a departure from all rules of proportion. The Cistercian cloister-walk was covered with a simple roof, supported on wooden posts, and not an elaborate stone erection as shown, which certainly exists in the Benedictine churches at Wells, Worcester, Canterbury, Gloucester, &c., and also in those of the secular canons at Lincoln, Salisbury, &c. The existing portions of the structure are very badly drawn, and the whole is disproportionate and in exaggerated perspective. The small elevation of the dormitory and west end of the church is open to the latter objections; the porch is unusual, and the buttress pinnacles could never have existed as they are represented.—W. A. Waddington.]

[2] ["Close to the foundation of the only remaining columns of the south transept in the abbey is still remaining part of the original floor of the conventual church. It is composed of encaustic tiles, many of which are still found. All those in the nave were turned up and dispersed at the time when orders were given to dismantle the building.

of the stalls a narrow rectilinear filleting of the same material had bounded the whole. On some was inscribed the word MARIE in Longobardic characters.

This pavement had been deeply bedded in mortar, but was altogether displaced, and turned down from one to three feet beneath the surface, where several skeletons were found very entire and in their original position, but without any remains of coffins, vestments, or other ornaments, as appeared upon a most minute investigation. These, however, were beyond a doubt the abbots of Whalley. From the confused state of the original pavement the whole floor of the presbytery, from the foot of the stalls, appeared to have been successively covered with gravestones, all of which, however, had been removed, excepting fragments of two; one of these had a groove, once inlaid with a filleting of brass, and the other, beneath which lay the skeleton of a tall and robust man, had deeply cut upon it the stump of a tree raguled. This I conjecture to have been a thorn, intended as a rebus upon the name of Christopher Thornber, the fifteenth abbot, who died in 1486. In this search we narrowly missed the fragments of the gravestone of Abbot Lindley, which were casually turned up on this very spot A.D. 1813. On one, in the Longobardic character of Edward the Third's time, were the letters IOH, and on the other . . . . . AJ HVIV . . .

From these data, slender as they may seem, I arrive at my conclusion thus: 1st. None but abbots were interred in the high choir; 2nd. The characters cannot be later than the latter end of Edward the Third, when the old English black-letter was substituted in its place. From the foundation to this time three Johns had been abbots of Whalley, Belfield, Topcliffe, and Lindley. The termination of the surname must have immediately preceded the word *hujus*, but the letters AJ can only have formed the termination of Lindelai, the old orthography of the word.

There is no doubt but that if permission could be procured from the present liberal owner to clear away the earth from the foundations, and open out the ruins—as the Marquess of Aylesbury explored Jervaux Abbey, in Yorkshire, not long ago—many valuable discoveries would be made, and disputed questions set at rest; for instance, the truth or incorrectness of the report handed down to us that 'the terrace,' which extends from the abbot's gateway to the present farm-house, is composed of the beautiful carved stone fragments of the doors, windows, and arches of the mutilated buildings, thrown into this rampart to disguise observation. The tombs of the abbots, under the high altar, would then with other curious subjects be explored, and it would be known whether the abbots who are buried there were men of large stature and noble deportment, as has been currently believed."—(Lecture by Rev. R. N. Whitaker, Vicar of Whalley, 2 Feb. 1869.)

"Old Richard Eatough (of a family which had been woodmen to the abbey and to Lord Howe for many generations,) was fond of detailing to me forty years ago stories of the abbey and of its later owners, and he informed me that after the destruction of the Conventual Church and the Abbot's Lodge such was the quantity of beautiful carved angels, flowers, and other ornamental work, that they filled all the rooms on the south and east side of the Abbot's Gateway until there came a very productive year of corn, when the tenants, instead of stacking it, turned out the carved work into the open air and substituted the corn. Nor was such destruction confined to the woodwork, but the stained glass which had gloriously adorned the great window of the Conventual Church was wheeled away by barrowloads, and cast into the river Calder, from whence Dr. Whitaker (after a high flood) recovered some fine specimens, which he put up in the staircase of his own house at the Holme, where they remain at this day." (Lecture by the Rev. R. N. Whitaker, 19 Feb. 1867.) Some other fragments were placed in the windows of the church at Langho.]

The remains of the Lacies, wherever deposited after their removal from Stanlaw, had undoubtedly been preserved with religious reverence, and inclosed in magnificent tombs. But in these researches there were no appearances which justified even a conjecture that we had discovered them. Where they were placed after their translation is perhaps of little importance; but the following Indulgence, granted with a view to facilitate that work, will gratify the curious reader :—

Sancte matris ecclesie filiis universis ad quos presens Scriptum pervenerit. Nos Anianus miseracione divina Bangorensis ecclesie Episcopus notum fieri volumus per presentes, quod, de Dei omnipotentis misericordia et gloriose Virginis Marie omniumque Sanctorum meritis confisi, omnibus nobis jure diocesano subjectis et aliis quorum Diocesani hanc nostram indulgenciam ratam habuerint, vere penitentibus, qui ad monasterium Loci Benedicti de Stanlaw, ordinis Cisterciensis, Coventrensis et Lichfeldensis dioc. accesserint et ibidem pro animabus Constabulariorum Cestrie et Comitum Lincolnie fundatorum dicte domus, et quorum corpora ibidem sepulture traduntur, omniumque fidelium defunctorum devotas preces fuderint Altissimo, vel qui ad emendationem periculosi accessus ad dictum monasterium de bonis sibi a Deo collatis aliquam elemosynam fecerint, vel si contingat propter periculum maris fugiendum dictum monasterium ab eo loco amoveri, et fratres in loco tutiori sibi habitaculum querere, et ossa patronorum suorum predictorum et aliorum nobilium ibidem humatorum inde ad locum quieti religiosorum competentiorem transferre, qui ad ista procuranda dictis fratribus condigna caritatis subsidia fecerint, Triginta dies de injungenda eis secundum antiquos canones pœnitentia misericorditer relaxamus. In cujus rei testimonium presenti scripto sigillum nostrum apposuimus. Dat. apud Aberconewy in Snaudon, Incipiente Anno Domini M°. CC°. octogesimo tertio. Et anno regni Regis Edwardi filii regis Henrici undecimo.[1]

The conquest of Wales was now completed; and, accordingly, Bishop Anian speaks of the Conqueror as his sovereign. No reasonable account can be given of this indulgence from so remote a prelate, but that Henry de Lacy was attending upon Edward the First at Conway Castle, then either building or recently built, where he met the Bishop ot Bangor coming to pay his court also.[2]

The mention of "Aberconway in Snowdon" is, perhaps, an older authority[3] than Mr. Pennant was acquainted with, for styling the environs of that mountain Snowdonia.

[Other documents to the same purpose, obtained during the course of the six next ensuing years, run as follows :—

Indulgence. 1287.

Universis Christi fidelibus, etc. Petrus permissione divina Archiepiscopus Montis Regalis salutem in Domino. Quoniam ad hoc ecclesie suffragia pro mortuis sunt inventa ut peccata viventium que non fuerint per satisfaccionem debitam expiata post mortem eorum qui caritatis in statu decesserint per premissa

[1] From the original at Whalley Abbey. [Now bound up in Dr. Whitaker's own copy of the *History of Whalley.* The seal gone. Indersement: xxx[ta] dies indulgencie bn'factorib; n'ris et ꝑ aïab; fūdator' orātib;.]

[2] [On comparing the other Indulgences which ensue, it will be doubted that this was solicited by Henry de Lacy in person. Anian archdeacon of Anglesey was elected Bishop of Bangor in 1267, and was still living in 1305.]

[3] ["Aberconweye in Snaudon" occurs also in the same year, 1283, in the Fœdera of Rymer, vol. ii. p. 240; also three times in the *Statuta de Rothelan*, 12 Edw. I. 1284, *e.g.* "in Snaudon et terris nostris Walliæ adjacentibus." See the *Record of Carnarvon*, p. 119.]

suffragia expientur, ad quorum gratiosam prestationem Salomonis auctoritate nos invitans mortuo prohibet gratia prohibenda eorum precibus qui gratiam hujusmodi pro fidelibus defunctis implorant non debemus eandem inhumaniter denegare, ut cum pro nobis per aliquos similis forte gratia postulabitur in futurum ipsum denegare petitoribus ex nostris demeritis non contingat, cum grate ex parte magnifici viri domini Henrici Comitis Lincolnie super concessionem hujusmodi gratia pro animabus quorundam antecessorum suorum fuerimus cum instantia requisiti, de omnipotentis Dei ac virginis matris ejus, cujus ministerio deputati sumus licet indigniter, ac Apostolorum Petri et Pauli auctoritate confisi, omnibus vero penitentibus et confessis, quorum Diocesani hanc nostram Indulgentiam ratam habuerint, qui monasterium de Loco Benedicto Coventrensis et Leichfeldensis diocesis adierint vel alias honoraverint, et pro bone memorie domini Edmundi de Lacy et antecessorum suorum omniumque defunctorum fidelium animabus atque nostrum *orationem dominicam* cum *salutatione beate virginis* dixerint mente fida, quadraginta dies de injuncta sibi penitentia misericorditer relaxamus. In cujus rei testimonium, *etc.* Dat. Burdegal. 13 kalendarum Maii, anno Domini 1287. (Harl. MS. 2064, f. 69.)

(Peter Gerra of Campania was in 1266 chosen Bishop of Sora in the Terra di Lavoro, in 1278 Bishop of Reati, and in 1286 Archbishop of Monte Reale in the Val di Mazara, near Palermo in Sicily. He served several times as papal legate, especially in 1281 to Alphonso X. of Castile, then in 1288 to Philip IV. of France and Edward I. of England. In 1296 he became Archbishop of Capua, and in 1299 Patriarch of Aquileia. He died 12 Feb. 1301.—Pirri, *Sicilia Sacra*, i. 463; Ughelli, *Italia Sacra*, i. 1205, v. 96, vi. 342.)

Presentibus ac posteris presens scriptum inspecturis vel auditurıs patefaciat quod nos Arnaldus permissione divina Dertusensis epūs de omnipotentis Dei miti misericordia, gloriose virginis Marie matris ejus, beatorum Petri et Pauli Apostolorum, omniumque sanctorum Dei meritis et precibus confidentes, omnibus parochianis nostris et aliis quorum Diocesani hanc nostram ratam habuerint Indulgentiam, de precibus suis vere penitentibus, qui ad ecclesiam conventualem Loci Benedicti de Stanlaw Coventrensis diocesis ubi conventus adhuc moratur, vel ubi nobilis vir dominus comes Lincolnie ipsos transferre et de novo fundare proponit, causa devotionis accesserint, et ibidem pro animabus d'ni Rogeri de Lacy quondam Constabularii Cestrie, domine Mathilde de Clare uxoris ejus, et successorum eorundem ibidem humatorum omniumque fidelium defunctorum orationem dominicam cum salutatione gloriose virginis dixerint fidemente, vel ibidem pia intentione audiverint verbum Dei, vel fratribus dicti loci aliqua subsidia fecerint caritatis, quibus adjuti pondus diei et estus facilius queant portare, quadraginta dies de injuncta eis penitentia Deo propitio misericorditer in Domino relaxamus, testimonio presentium quas ad instanciam prefati Comitis sigilli nostri munimine roboravimus. Dat. apud Sanctam Mariam Clovensem festivitate Omnium Sanctorum anno gratie 1288. (Fol. 70.)

(Don Arnal de Jardino was elected in 1272 or 1273 Bishop of Tortosa in the province of Tarragona in Spain. He died 20 July 1306.—Villanueva, *Viage Literario à las Iglesias de España*, v. 91.)

Universis Christi fidelibus, *etc.* Aimo permissione divina Vercellensis Episcopus salutem in Domino. Obsequium beneplacitum totiens opinamur impendere Altissimo quotiens mentes Christi fidelium ad caritatis et misericordie opera exitamus; de Dei igitur omnipotentis, ministrorum Petri et Pauli Apostolorum ejus, necnon beati Eusebii Episcopi et martyris patroni nostri omniumque sanctorum meritis confidentes, omnibus parochianis nostris et aliis quorum Diocesani hanc nostram habuerint Indulgentiam ratam, de peccatis suis vere contritis et confessis, peccataque sua dimittentibus, qui ad ecclesiam conventualem Loci Benedicti de Stanlaw Coventrensis et Leichfeldensis diocesis causa devotionis accesserint et ibidem pro anima nobilis viri domini Edmundi de Lacy quondam Comitis Lincolnie et antecessorum suorum ibidem humatorum, necnon pro anima domini Henrici de Lee quondam vicecomitis Lancastr' omniumque fidelium requie defunctorum devotas preces fuderint Altissimo, vel ibidem fideli devotione audierint verbum Dei, seu fratribus dicti loci aliqua subsidia fecerint caritatis, Quadraginta dies de injuncta eis penitentia misericorditer relaxamus. In cujus rei testimonium presentibus sigillum nostrum fecimus apponi. Dat. Vercell' 15 kalend' Julii anno gratie 1289. (Ibid. fol. 69.)

(Aymo Avogadrus was elected 71st Bishop of Vercelli in Piedmont in 1272, and died 1303.—Ughelli, *Ital. Sacra*, iv. 798.)

Sancte matris ecclesie filiis universis ad quos presentes littere prevenerint, nos miseratione divina Bonefacius Parentinus, Parronus Larrinensis, et Leotherius Verulanus episcopi, eternam in Domino salutem vestram. Cum Altissimo totiens nos obsequium opinamur impendere quotiens Christi fidelium animos ad caritatis et misericordie opera excitamus, de omnipotentis Dei miti misericordia, gloriose virginis Marie genetricis ejus, Beatorum Petri et Pauli Apostolorum, omniumque Sanctorum Dei meritis et precibus confidentes, omnibus nobis jure diocesano subjectis et aliis Christi fidelibus quorum Diocesani presentis Indulgentie assensum et ratificationem prebuerint, de peccatis suis vere penitentibus et confessis, qui ecclesiam conventualem Loci Benedicti de Stanlaw Coventrensis diocesis, Cisterciensis ordinis, devotionis causa adierint et ibidem pro statu Universalis Ecclesie et pro statu nobilium virorum dominorum Henrici de Lacy comitis Lincolnie dicte domus patroni et domini Othonis de Grandisono dum vixerint et pro animabus eorundem cum viam universe carnis fuerint ingressi, et progenitorum predicti Comitis ibidem humatorum omniumque fidelium requie defunctorum devotas preces fudarint Altissimo, seu fratribus dicti loci grata aliqua subsidia fecerint caritatis in loco ubi adhuc sunt vel ubi predictus Comes ipsos transferre proponit, quibus adjuti pondus diei et estus facilius valeant portare, singuli nostrum singulas dierum quadragenas de injunctis secundum antiquas canones penitenciis misericorditer in Domino relaxamus, testimonio presentium quas ad instanciam predicti domini Othonis de Grandisono et fratris A. de Leyke predicti Comitis procuratoris sigillorum nostrorum munimine roboravimus. Dat. Beat. (*sic*) kalend. Augusti anno gracie 1289, Pontificatus domini Nicholai pape quarte anno secundo. (Ibid. fol. 69 b.)

(The three seals attached are engraved in the Plate of Episcopal Seals. They are those of—

Bonifacius, 38th Bishop of Parenzo in Istria, who granted, in 1299, Indulgences to those who visited the relics in the church of St. Anthony in Padua. Ughelli, *Italia Sacra*, v. 408.

Petronus or Patronus, 6th Bishop of Larina in the province of Benevento, who subscribed in 1288 an Indulgence to the church of the Carmelites of Siena. He was removed from the administration of his church before 1291, "suis exigentibus culpis," and died under Boniface VIII. still suspended. Ughelli, viii. 304.

Lotherius II. who succeeded in 1285 as 30th Bishop of Veroli in the Campagna of Rome. In 1287 he was one of eleven Bishops who granted an Indulgence of forty days to the cathedral church of St. Andrew in Carinthia. In 1289 he subscribed an Indulgence granted to the Carmelite Friars of Siena. He died in 1314. Ughelli, i. 1399.)

Sancte matris ecclesie filiis, *etc.* fratribus Loci Benedicti de Stanlowe etc. ad reparacionem periculose . . . ad monasterium suum quod inundaciones maris jam in magnam partem consumpsisse dinoscantur manus prorexerint adjutores, vel grata subsidia ejusdem fecerunt caritatis quibus adjutis facilius se ad habitacionem securiorem queant transferre, seu pro benefactoribus et fundatore dicti loci [et] animabus antecessorum videlicet magnifici viri domini comitis Lincoln. idem humatorum, *etc.:* 40 dies misericorditer in Domino relaxamus, *etc.* sigillum nostrum apposuimus. Dat . . . . cate kal. Augus. anno gracie 1289. (The place and bishop's name omitted.) (Ibid. fol. 66 b.)]

The following epitaphs, absurd as they are, having been really hung over the tombs of the Lacies at Whalley, I deem it not improper to afford them a place :

Epitaphium Comendacionis Rogeri Lacy.

Hic sepelitur herus generosus in orbe Rogerus
Conjuge cum cara quam mors prostravit amara.
Forti Sampsoni similis fuit atque leoni,
Tauro cornuto pungendi semper acuto.
Tectum torace nullus superare valebat,
Regnum cum pace miles sub rege regebat.
Nullus Trojanus sibi par fuit in probitate,
Victor in etate fuit, alter Waspasianus.
Gentes linguarum male credente *(sic)* variarum,
Sectas Persarum, Medorum, Spartiatarum,
Grecos, Creteuses, Romanos bella moventes,
Francos, Flandrenses, nautas portis rapientes,
Hic dum pugnavit, pugnans pugnando domavit.
Vivus ut optavit, defuncto tumba paratur :
Pictor adornavit petram sub qua tumulatur.
Inferni claustro careat perflatus ab austro
Sit prece conventus fulgoris in arce retentus.
Inclita matrona dicto digna Matilda corona
Sit cum matre pia Christi conjuncta Maria.
Qui legis, absque mora, pro fundatoribus ora.

Epitaphium Commendacionis Johannis Lacy.

Egregii comitis en hec est tumba Johannis,
Hostibus immitis cunctis dum vixerat annis.
Jure suum Comitem luget Lincolnia mitem,
Quem plangunt unum Cestrensia castra tribunum.
Anglia flet rite tali caruisse quirite,
Et Stanlowe bonum dolet amisisse patronum.
Christo devotus miles fuit undique notus,
Wallia, quem Scotus, timuit mundus quoque totus,
Gallus et Hispanus, Normannus, Britoque, Danus,
Almannus gnarus bello, Lumbardus avarus,
Indus, et obscenus Gentilus, atrox Saracenus,
Æthiopes fuscy, Greci, Babilonia, Tuscy,
Rex et Soldanus, omnis populusque prophanus,
Hunc cum cernebant armatum, corde tremebant.
Vicit eum vermis qui victor erat in armis,
Sic et vincemur pro quo dicendo precemur.
Ultima censura cum venerit illa futura
J. comes a dira servetur Judicis ira.

Epitaphium Commendacionis Johannis de Lacy, comitis Lincolniæ, et Fundatoris iij. Loci Benedicti de Whalleya.

Ut in hoc loco legitur, sub hac structura tegitur cor comitis Johannis,
In carne non plus clauditur set a carne divi[di]tur in universis annis.

Cordis et carnis unitas efficitur dualitas et paritas partita :
O misera conditio, tam flebilis divisio nunquam fuit audita.
Tristantur cives Cestrie, plangunt primates patrie, nec volunt consolari,
Flet Pontefracti populus, vir, uxor, senex, parvulus, non cessant lachrimari.
A solis ortus cardine cuncti debent ex ordine rurales et burgenses
Magni, minores, pariter, pro cunctis singulariter lugent Lincolnienses.
Nec mirum, flos militie jam marcuit, letitie spes est exinanita,
Quia post hunc in seculo carnali visus oculo nòn erit vigens ita.
Heu ! planctus fit perpetuus cum pugil tam precipuus privatus sit hac vita ;
Planctus, ploratus, gemitus nunquam cessabunt amplius secula per infinita.
Ut Job simplex, ut Salomon doctus, et sicut Absolon pulcher, et Sampson fortis,
Ut Joseh fuit providus, ut Mars in bello validus, totius dux cohortis.
Hic erat mundi lilium, solempnitas nobilium, se tamen equans imis.
Ut Moyses mitissimus, ut Josue justissimus, plus audax Gedione,
Vellem fari quis fuerit, sed nulla dici poterit humana ratione.
Non fuit inter millia tam promptus quis ad prelia, sub armis tam discretus,
Nullus ad arma promptior, in armis nec ferocior, post arma tam quietus.
Lorica corpus, galia frons, ense femur, lancea manus ecce munitur,
Scuto latus protegitur, morte tamen subigitur, per hoc non impeditur.
Castra, domus, familia, et opes, et has similia non poterunt prodesse :
Lira, plausus, et predia, jam nulla dant remedia quin mori sit necesse.
Et jam consumptis carnibus nunc esca datur vermibus qui fuit tam probatus ;
Nunc ejus aula tumulus, et vermis suus famulus, et lira fit ploratus.
Sit transit mundi gloria, sic vita transitoria disperdetur et deletur,
Sic desinit dies hominis, sic et ominis laus nunquam finietur.
Johannes Dei gratia, fertur sine fallacia nomen interpretetur,
Precemur ergo singuli ut iste prece populi cum sanctis glorietur :
Et Christus vera veritas det ut sua posteritas sit heres ejus morum,
Et hanc in cunctis prosperet, et hunc a penis liberet eternis infernorum.

Epitaphium Commendacionis Edmundi Lacy.

Mors probat Edmundi, brevis est quod gloria mundi,
Mendax et mundus, quamvis quandoque secundus.
Scandere qui primo cum ceperit lapsus in ymo
Monstrat quod mundus est labilis atque rotundus :
Nichilque fit in mundo quod non pertransit eundo,
Protinus a mundo cum sit quasi vas sine fundo.
Ergo det Edmundo Deus a contamine mundo
Uti jocundo vultu Christi rediundo.
Respice qui transis, in me circumspice quid sis,
  Exemploque mei sis memor ipse tui.
Sum quod eris, quod es ipse fui, mundoque superstes
  Flórueram mundo, terra cinisque modo.
Quid probitas, quid opes, quid honor, quid gloria mundi,
  Omnia quid fuerint, cum cecidere docent ?
Hic jacet et funus Cestrensis jure tribunus.
Me pro posse bonum sensit domus ista patronum.

Since the first edition of this work was printed, several original documents relating to Whalley Abbey have come to light. The first of these is a thick octavo volume,[1] entitled *Liber Loci Benedicti de Whalley;* the contents of which are very miscellaneous. It seems to have been a kind of original register or day-book, beginning with the translation of the convent from Stanlaw, and ending about the year 1346. The whole is extremely abbreviated and difficult to be read. The contents are minutes of leases and other contracts, letters, tables of weights and measures, sermons, and poetry. Of these the most curious specimens are given below. The two first are letters from Gregory de Norbury, the first abbot, to Elias de Workesley, afterwards his successor, and to William de Brooke, who was probably professor of divinity at Oxford when the former took his doctor's degree in that faculty.[2] The academical reader will observe that the language of the schools was the same five centuries ago as at present. To incept and to respond, at least, have the same meaning now.

Scolari ad congratulandum cum Inceperit.

Carissimo suo si placeet mag^{ro} et amico Nonno W. de B. suus totus et semper Fr. G. vocatus abbas de W. id modicum quod est et quod potest. Ad congratulandum vobis et sancte societati scholarium in inceptionis vestre solempnitate affectuosissimè venire vellemus et merito teneremur si corporis imbecillitas permisisset, sed absentes corpore, spiritu vobiscum erimus, orantes Deum, ut hic possitis incipere cum honore et in gloria consummare. Ceterum pro beneficiis que dilecto filio et commonacho nostro Fr. H. facitis et fecistis, vestre dilectioni ad quantas et quales possumus gratiarum assurgimus actiones, salutantes vos per eundem, et sicut ad presens potuimus respicientes, non tamen sicut voluimus, Deus novit, si facultas voluntati copiosius respondisset. Valete semper in D^{no} IHU Xro, salutantes ex parte nostra si placeet magistrum cum scholaribus et omnibus aliis quos vestra discrecio fore decreverit salutandos. *Cauda.*[3] Nonno W. de B. per suum [G.] Abbtem de Wh. (Fol. 86 b.)

Monacho cum Responderit.

Salutem quam sibi in Christo. Scripsit nobis Nonnus[4] W. de B. quod in scolis nostris nuper publicè et honorificè respondisti, de quo novit Deus gavisi sumus admodum, utpote profectum tuum totis visceribus affectantes. Quod autem mutacio monete te gravavit ex nobis ipsis conjicimus, quia similia passi sumus, nec tamen defectum tuum ad plenum relevare possumus istâ vice; facimus tamen interim quod possumus, mittentes tibi per latorem presentium xs. sterl. et alios xs. pollard:[5] et per vicarium de W. xxs. pollard:[5] alii qui promiserint

[1] [Now in the British Museum, Addit. MS. 10,374, having been purchased in 1836. A distinct account of this and of the other original archives of the abbey quoted in the History will be found in the Introduction to this Edition.]

[2] William de Brooke, a Benedictine, had taken his doctor's degree, with great magnificence, in 1298, a little before this time. Wood, Hist. et Antiq. Univ. Oxon. lib. i. p. 24. With whatever credit to himself Worsley had performed his exercises, the abbot's slender remittances would be very inadequate to the expensive feastings formerly used on those occasions. For which see Wood, *ibid.*

[3] Cauda, *i. e.* the address.

[4] Nonnus was a title of reverence whose origin and etymology are very uncertain. Juniores, autem Priores suos Nonnos vocant quod intelligitur paterna reverentia. Reg. Sc'i Benedicti, cap. 62, ap. Du Cange, *in voce.* From the feminine Nonna, which is used by St. Jerome in Ep. ad Eustochium, is undoubtedly derived the word nun.

[5] Pollards and Crokards were a base coinage cried down in 1299, about the date of this letter. See Matthew of Westminster in that year, and Spelman's Gloss. *voce* Pollard.

domi non erant; de iis tamen in posterum sis securus, nec te moveat quod plures sterl. non mittimus ut rogasti, q̃uia re vera à tempore recessus tui non increverunt thesaurariam nostram de nostris receptis v solid. stl. Mittimus nichilominus per eundem latorem ad opus nonni W. de B. xx s. quorum medictas est de sterl. et alia de pollard. Ceterum si possitis agere cum magro H. prece vel precio quod ipse impetraret nobis licentiam remanendi à Capitulo per literam dni Cistertiensis quia graviter infirmati fuimus anno isto necdum plene convaluimus, multum ei teneremur, et tue utilitati possemus commodius providere. Vale semper in Xp̃o, fratre et fili karissime, qui te incolumem custodiat, et spiritu proficere faciat in sanctitatem et virtutem.

The next epistle relates to the oppression which the abbot and his house experienced from Bishop Langton, who, in addition to his jurisdiction over them as his diocesan, was now Treasurer of England.

Archidiacono pro consilio requirendo.

Venerando discrecionis viro et domino in Christi visceribus amplectando Magistro R. de R. Archidiacono C[estrensi] suus tocius et semper frater G[regorius] vocatus Abbas de W[halley] id modicum quod est et quod potest. Quam verum sit illud verbum veritatis in evangelio, *In mundo pressuram habebitis*, cotidianis nostris angustiis experimur. In hujus enim mundi mari magno flebiliter fluctuantes dum ad portum putamus potissime pervenire, negato respiracionis solacio, proch dolor, ab hiis qui passis compati de jure debuerant repellimur in profundum. Ecce enim venerabilem patrem Dei permissione C. et L. Episcopum quem secundo ab urbe redeuntem dum duplicem nobis gratiam et benedictionem speravimus reportâsse, vice versâ duplici nos afflictione fatigat, quia solutis jam eidem per nos C Marcis de illis Mille in quibus ei tenebamur, quas per ministros regios immisericorditer de bonis nostris temporalibus fecit fieri cujuscunque, cum putaremus ipsum de residuo micius acturum imposterum, alteram aciem gladii bisacuti ad ecclesiam jam convertens, omnia bona nostra ecclesiastica exposuit venditioni præconizari faciens solempniter in ecclesiis, comitatu et mercatis, ut ad certos diem et locum mercatores conveniant empturi de dictis bonis nostris quod sibi viderint plus valere. Unde cum tam spiritualia quam temporalia pro prece maxima sint exhausta qualiter nostra simul stabit congregacio penitus non videmus et ab invicem discedere seu dispertionem facere et maxime in absencia patroni nostri amarissimum arbitramur. Et ob hoc, venerande dne et amice, si placet rescribere dignemini per latorem presencium secundum quod vobis videbitur quid nobis in hoc casu consulcius sit agendum. Et si aliquam vel aliquas de ecclesiis nostris in S. pro liberand. nobis de manu homicidis ad firmam recipere volueritis vel aliquem amicorum vestrorum noveritis recepturum, adquiescimus libentissime quantum sive evidentissimo dampno poterimus vestris beneplacitis et mandatis. Venissemus vel misissemus ad vos aliquem de nostris super hiis specialiter locuturum si licuisset pre valitudine nisi timuissemus homicidianos ne forte in proprio eorum staret suspicio vel tumultus. Valeat vestra reverenda dilectio. Salutem in domino Jesu Christo. (Fol. 87.)

The same circumstances drew from the abbot this eloquent and affecting complaint, addressed to Thomas of Lancaster:

Une Playnte.

A tresbonorable home e sun tres cher seingnur en Deu sire Thomas de Lancastre, Frere Gregor' Abbe de Whall. Salutz, ove touz honurs e reverentes. Pur ceo qe tout nostre refuit e esperaunce de socour en terre principalment pent en vous sire apres nostre avowe e seingnur le Counte de Nichole, a vous come a sovereyn ayde terrien mustroms noz grevaunces. Sachez, honure sire, qe nostre Evesque de Cestr' par sun poer e male volente qil ad eu, ia lungement devers nos a tort, en taunt ad noz grevaunces e ennuys com-passe countre la priere du Rey, de nostre seingnur le Counte, de vo^s^ sire, voz mercy,[1] e des autres plusours noz amys, e outre mesure tendue e fet no^s^ ad escumeger depecea, e les pluis avaunt de nostre mesun, qe la deneyent guyer, e apres la sentence, la capcioun sur no^s^ p̃chase, par vint no^s^ ne usoms en les ammones nostre avowe demorer, ne ne pooms ordre ou religioun garder, ne servise Deu, ou nostre dette a noz beinfetours mortz ou vifs rendre, ne autre estat de religioun meyntenir, mes come forbaniz de Countee en Countee fuyr. Dount no^s^ vo^s^ reqeroms cher seingnur pur Deu et pur voz grauntz bounteez qe pite vo^s^ emprenge de no^s^, et voillez sire quant verrez oure convenable prier nostre seingnur le Rey pur no^s^, qe il, si li plest, pur lamour le Counte et vostre priere sire, comaunde estat de Religioun a no^s^ estre grauntee, et alegge noz ennuys auaunt nomeez jusqe la venue nostre avowe en terre; kar mout harrioms voider ses ammones pur rien, qe puist auenir saunz sun comaundement, qe si fraunchement les ad graunte a no^s^. E sachez sire qe ne mye par nostre defaute no^s^ fet nostre Euesque ces tortz et duresces, countre le graunt de la Court de Rome, et countre les apeaus qe fet avouns a mesmes la Court: mes pur sa dure volunte demaunde a queus no^s^ ne pooms atteyndre. Dount, cher sire, pite vo^s^ emprenge. Salutz en Ihesu Crist. qe vo^s^ garde cors et alme e la dame vostre compayngne, et bone engendrure vos doynt en haste." (Fol. 96.)

Next follows[2] an apology from Abbot Gregory, on the plea of bad health, for not obeying a summons to parliament;[3] and an appointment of a proxy:

Excusatio et procuratio ad Parliamentum.

Universis sancte matris ecclesie filiis ad quos presentes littere pervenerint Frater G. Abbas loci Benedicti de Wh. salutem in omnium Salvatore. Quia adversâ corporis valetudine ad presens prepediti, cum prelatis, magnatibus et patribus regni coram domino Rege in parliamento suo London, secundâ die dominicâ quadragesime proximo futuro ad colloquendum et tractandum super negociis dictum dominum Regem et regnum contingentibus personaliter interesse nequimus: dilectum commonachum nostrum fratrem E. de R. procuratorem seu excusatorem nostrum ordinamus facimus et constituimus per presentes. Dantes eidem potestatem plenariam tractandi et faciendi in dicto negotio omnia que facere possemus si nos contingeret personaliter interesse. Ratum habituri et gratum quicquid per eundem nomine nostro, et communitatem cleri, ac ordinis nostri ibidem coram dicto domino Rege seu quovis locum ipsius tenentem fuerit ordinatum. In cujus rei, etc. Dat. apud locum benedictum de W. in festo beati Petri in Cathedra, Anno, etc. (Fol. 119 b.)

The next is a commendatory epistle to the Abbot of Kirkstall, sent with a delinquent monk. It is accompanied with a kind of pass.

Venerabili in X^to^ Patri et cum omni reverencia nominando domino Abbati de K(irk-tall) suus tocius et semper frater G. dictus Abbas Loci Benedicti de Wh. salutem cum omni reverentia et honore: Quia ex decreto visitatorum nostrorum lator presentium fr. nomine monachus noster et sacerdos pene conspiratorum est addictus, et eandem penitentiam humiliter et devotè per annum et amplius jam peregit, quem salvâ pace fratrum et ordinis disciplinâ ad presens in domo nostrâ retinere non possumus, dilectam paternitatem vestram attencius exoramus, ut eundem cum debitâ vestium quantitate ad vos missum inter vestros ad tempus retinere velitis, ordinate tractantes et ab aliis tractari facientes, quousque licentiam habuerimus revocandi eundem a Capitulo generali. Ita quod sit ultimus sacerdotum in ecclesia, nec celebret; omni sexta

[1] [Probably a clerical error for "marie"—your wife.]

[2] [Not so in the MS. volume, for there is an interval of 24 folios.]

[3] [This was the Parliament held at London on 6th March, 1300. Seventy-nine abbots, priors, &c. received summonses: among them the forty-ninth was addressed "Abbati de Stanlow." The writ to the Abbot of St. Augustine Canterbury is dated "apud Berewycum super Twedam, xxix. die Decembr." *Parliamentary Writs*, vol. i. p. 84, No. 4.]

feria in adventu et quadragesima in pane et aquâ pœnitens in capitulo accipiat disciplinam, nisi grandis solempnitas, vel evidens infirmitas aliquam exegerit dispensationem. Promittentes nos vobis vicem similem rependere, si quod absit casus talem emiserit vel majorem. Valeat vr̃a reverenda paternitas, s. i. d. I. X. Dat. *ut in patentibus.*

Emissio.

Reverendo patri in Christo domino venerabili Abbati de Wh. *et cetera.* Latorem presentium fratrem R. nomine rotarium strenuum et subtilem conversum domus nostre quem ad presens culpis suis exigentibus ad pacem quorundem in domo propria retinere non valemus dilecte paternitati vestre cum plenitudine vestium duximus transmittendum: rogantes attencius quatenus eundem in congregatione vestra ad tempus suscipere et secundum ordinis disciplinam tractare dignemini. Ita quod omni vi[ta] feria sit in pane et aqua et omni capitulo quo interfuerit vapulet usque ad proximam Pascham, et esu carnium careat per annum, nisi grandis *et cetera usque* Promittentes—quousque mutuo fruamur colloquio vel aliud de eo vobis direxerimus in mandatis. Valeat *et cetera.* Dat. *ut in patentibus.* (Fol. 130 b.)

These are very curious particulars in the monastic discipline.

Littere Viatice et patentes.[1]

Universis ad quos presentes littere pervenerint Fr. G. dictus abbas Loci Benedicti de Whalley et ejusdem loci Conventus, salutem in Domino: Latorem præsentium fratrem nomine monachum nostrum, quem ad abbatiam de K(irkstall) transmittimus, universitati vestre recommendamus, attencius supplicantes quatenus eidem per vos transeunti, nullam molestiam, dampnum, seu gravamen inferri permittatis, sed in vie et vite necessariis quibus indiguerit misericorditer assistatis, eterna pro temporalibus recepturi. Veruntamen pedes eat. Dat. etc. Anno, etc. Valeant eidem per dies proximo subsequentes.[2] (Fol. 131.)

Several inferences may be drawn from the singular document before us. First, Kirkstall, which, being of the same order and of the foundation of the same family, is undoubtedly expressed by the initial K, was little more than forty miles from Whalley. Yet a poor monk could not travel on foot from one to the other, without some risk of being robbed, or otherwise injured. Secondly, there were no inns by the way. Thirdly, his pass, though addressed to all men, was in Latin; consequently, all but the clergy, and some perhaps of them, must have taken the bearer's word for the meaning of it. I strongly suspect, therefore, that the English language, at this time, was scarcely written at all. French was the court language, and in French the monks wrote to their patrons. There is not a vestige of their native tongue in this volume, though filled with minutes of the most familiar transactions.

Reverendo in Christo patri domino Abbati de B. Frater Gregorius vocatus Abbas de Whalley salutem cum omni reverentia et honore. Fratrem I. monachum vestrum Dominica Septuagesima cum plenitudine vestium recepimus, minori tamen quam eidem in hâc regione *que frigidissima est, precipue hyemis tempore,* perspeximus oportere. Unde pro certo noveritis quod ipsius indigenciam libentissimè sup-

[1] [This title is plural, and refers to the whole series of five letters, of which the first only is here given; at the end of the fifth is a marginal note, *Patentes usque huc.*]

[2] [The next "littere viatice" end "valeant eidem quantum necesse fuerit," the next "valeant eidem per x dies."]

pleremus, sed tantis debitis et multis etiam incommodis aliis sumus ad presens onerati quod nostris propriis prout deceret vel oporteret indumenta non possumus providere; quapropter vestram rogamus paternitatem quatenus eidem subvenire dignemini in hac parte. Ceterum, cum calamus quassatus non sit omnino conterendus, iterum vobis preces affectuosas pro ipso et cum ipso porrigimus, quatenus ab hâc ignominiosissimâ qua detinetur penâ in hoc instanti generali capitulo vestrâ ope absolvatur, et ad proprie matris gremium misericorditer revocetur: scientes certissimè, si id feceritis, quod de ejus anima quam regendam suscepistis securè respondebitis, et pariter laudem cum honore ab omnibus qui hoc factum audierint adquiretis. Speramus enim per Dei graciam et per vexacionem que sibi jam tribuit intellectum, quod omnibus diebus quibus vixerit ipsum inveneretis promptiorem ad omnia que vestre sederint voluntati. Valt. (Fol. 132.)

This epistle is probably addressed to the Abbot of Byland. It affords another proof that the climate of the hilly part of Lancashire was much colder formerly than at present. No one would now feel it necessary to make a change in his clothing after he had removed from any of the adjoining counties to Whalley.

Hitherto we have seen the monastic discipline as exercised upon humbled and penitent offenders: the next memorandum lays open a scene of desperate and incorrigible depravity.

Pateat universis per presentes quod cum nos W. dictus Abbas de C(umbermere) concomitantibus nobiscum venerabili Abbate de V(alle) R(egali) et domino R. coabbate nostro de D(eulacres) die, etc. Anno, etc. ad filialem domum nostram de W(halley) accessimus ad litere domini Abbatis Cistertii nobis directe executionem faciendam super inquisitione emissionis Fratris R. de A. Monachi de W(halley), qui dicto domino Abbati Cistertii retulit se per venerabiles Abbates de F(ontibus) et de K(irkstall) minus justè a domo propriâ fuisse eliminatum, quibus data fuit plenaria commissio per patrem Abbatem dictam domum de W(halley) visitandi, et correctiones faciendi secundum demerita tam in capite quam in membris. Invenimus dicte domus venerabilem Abbatem ab omnibus criminibus per predictum Fratrem R. de A. et complices suos sibi maliciosè impositis legitimâ purgatione tocius conventûs unanime[1] et dictum Fratrem R. ritè et justè emissum. Insuper non solum diligenti inquisitione mediante, verumetiam publicâ famâ omnium conventualium conclamante, indisciplinatum nimis et exordinatum, necnon, et quod dolentes referimus, à longo retroacto tempore gravibus viciis et sordibus diffamatum, utpote conspirationis, furti, ac incontinentie criminibus miserabiliter inquinatum, et quod magis dolendum in venerabilem Abbatem de K(irkstall) coram nobis in pleno capitulo cum cultello acuminato extracto manus injecit violentas. Pro quibus excessibus intolerabilibus qui toti ordini maximum scandalum gravarint ipsum carceri perpetuo decrevimus mancipandum. In cujus rei testimonium sigillum nostrum presentibus est appensum, et sigilla venerabilium de Valle Regali et de D. Abbatum apponi procuravimus. Dat. loco die et anno supradictis. (Fol. 132 b.)

I have ventured to fill up the initials of these abbots, Valeroyal, Deulacres, and Cumbermere: the last of whom was Richard de Rodierd, formerly a monk of Whalley, where he was interred, A.D. 1316. The criminal appears to have been Fr' Ric. de Aston.

Pro negociis in Capitulo.

Reverendo patri in X^{to} domino venerabili Abbati S(avigniensi), suorum minimus fr. G(reg.) vocatus Abbas de W(halley) tam devotam quam debitam reverentiam cum salute. Licet tanquam filius non degener vobis esse debemus, honoris causâ, non oneris, multum tamen donec fortuna blandior arriserit, onus nostrum

[1] Some word or words apparently omitted.]

supplicantes vobis imponimus, honorem quem Dominus voluerit libencius impensuri. Cum igitur jam diu et gravi infirmitate detenti anno isto ad capitulum generale propter imbecilitatem corporis accedere non possumus, et ob hoc litteratorie nostram illic absenciam excusemus, vobis, sancte pater, ea que ibidem haberemus facere suggerimus, ut vestro si placet consilio et auxilio fulciantur. In primis petimus et rogamus, ut si contributio Angligenis per capitulum imposita, quam propter inhibitionem regiam sub pœnâ gravi in Angliâ solvere vel trans mare mittere non audemus, solvi debeat omni modo; vos si placet pro ratâ nostrâ cavere velitis vel à mercatoribus mutuando vel alias prout potueritis faciendo, et nos mandato vestro super hiis indilatè respondebimus et contante.[1] Est autem porcio nos contingens xxxii li. et di. marc. sterling. Item ut emissi nostri pro conspiratione jam per triennium[2] possint licitè, si se humiliaverint et conventus consenserit revocari, vel saltem ubi moram traxerint de licentiâ capituli celebrare, et Monachi novicii aput nos recipi non vetentur. Item quia vicinus Abbas noster de domo S(allay), que per quinque leugas à nobis distat, et sita est in provinciâ separatâ, in quâ nec passum pedis habemus de terrâ, nec domus nostra in aliquo communicat cum eadem, sepius comminatus est de nimiâ propinquitate et vicinitate nostrâ se in capitulo conquesturum, si de hoc fieri mentionem audieritis, pro nobis interponere dignemini preces vestras. Audacius scripsimus vobis, non quasi in aliquo horum minimo meruerimus exaudiri, sed inde trahentes fiduciam quia super et in omnibus agendis nostris vestram inoletam bonitatem nobis sensimus adjutricem. Valeat vestra rev. paternitas semper in domino Jesu Christo, nec valeant in eternum qui vos nuper turbaverint in Angliâ, nisi resipuerint et dignè correxerint culpam suam. (Fol. 135.)

Abbot Norbury is always pleading indisposition. The tremendous curse, in the end of this letter, must have been meant either for Edward the First or Bishop Langton his treasurer—the sovereign or the diocesan of the writer![3] As Norbury died in 1309, all the foregoing papers are to be dated between the year 1296 and that time.

During the reign of Edward the Second I meet with few memorials in the Liber Loci Benedicti. The latter part of the volume affords two curious poetical compositions of the earlier part of Edward the Third's time. The first is a sarcastic effusion of triumphant loyalty after the battle of Neville's Cross,[4] in the form of an epistle from David Bruce to his friend Philip de Valoys, whom the writer was too good a courtier to style respectively Kings of France or Scotland.

[1] [*i. e.* in ready money.]

[2] [As the Concordia with Salley, before related in p. 85, was made in 1305, this conspiracy among some of the monks of Whalley cannot be placed later than 1302.]

[3] [Our author's inference is mistaken, because the last sentence of the preceding letter was thus incorrectly printed in previous editions, "Valeat vestra rev. paternitas in D^{no} J. X^{o}. Nec valeat in eternum qui nos nuper turbavit in Anglia, nisi resipuerit et digne correxerit culpam suam." The word "vos" is obviously employed because Savigny, to which the letter is addressed, was in France.]

[4] [The battle of Neville's Cross, near Durham, was fought 17 Oct. 1346, while Edward III. was besieging Calais after the victory of Crécy. It is fully described in a paper by Robert White, esq. in the *Archæologia Æliana*, New Series, vol. i. pp. 271—303. The present poem is not included among the curious compositions of the like nature edited by Thomas Wright, M.A., F.S.A., in his *Political Songs*, printed for the Camden Society in 1839, and in his *Political Poems and Songs relating to English History*, from the Accession of Edward III. to the reign of Henry VIII. in two volumes, 1859, 1861, in the Chronicles and Memorials of Great Britain and Ireland in the Middle Ages, published under the direction of the Master of the Rolls. But various other poems, both in Latin and English, made on the same battle, will be found in Mr. Wright's series, but he has overlooked a remarkable one, formerly published in Hutchinson's History of Durham, vol. ii.]

Ceste est la copie de letre que David le Bruys maunda a Philippe de Valoys Roy de Fraunce.

Ore escoutez de Davyd le Bruys
Come a Philippe de Valoys maund Saluz.
Per ceo qe avoms entenduz
Qe moult de gentz avoms perduz,
Vous face a savoir qe bien tard
Si avoms fait notre part.
Taunt avoms tenuz voz maundementz
Qe nous sumes perduz et noz gentz.
La terre d'Escoce ay refuse,
Et en Engleterre su demore
Tout soul saunz nul amy,
Et en garde d'autruy.
Jeo me confesse a toutes gentz,
Qe trop avoms fate malement
Quant nous entrams en Engleterre,
En absence le roy de lever guerre.
Qare nous n'avoioms rien a faire
Mes grant meschance pur nous aquere.
Nous entendismes bien passere
Parmy la terre saunz destourbere
Meis L'ercevesqve[1] ove poeir grauntz
Nous vynt toust encountraunt.
Le Percy et le Moubray
Se perdent bien al journay.
Nous n'avoyoms grace ne poeir
Encountre lour bataille estere
A la novelle[2] Croyce du Dureme.
La perdymes nostre Realme.
La fumes pris en fuaunt;
Philippe, gardez vous de taunt,
Qe nous fumes pris en nostre trespas,
Dount sumes venuz de hautz en bas,
Come la Fortune est ordyne,
Primes mountams de gre en gre
Quant estoy venus al pluys haute,
Si perdy moun regne qe ore me faute.
Vous me maundastes par verite
Qe en Engleterre ne seroit trouve
Fors chappellayns, dames et moignes
Et autres femmes et berchers:
Meys trovames illoeques graunte gentz,
E ceo nous vynt en confusement.
Dount nous avoms bien apareeu
Qe le Roy du ciel est toust somelu
En qil soit ove son poeir,
Le Roy du ciel luy voet aidere
Pur ceo sumes de sa partie—
Escoutez, Philippe, qe jeo en die,
Tout soit il nostre frere en ley
Moult avoms trespasse vers luy,
Et tu, Philippe, en graunt outrage
Retenez son heritage:
Estoit a grant sire avaunt,
Heritage est descendaunt,
Qe nul homme ne poet juger
Qe heritage doit remounter,
Meis descendre de gre en gre,
Cest est ley par verite.
Moun piere Robert, quant il vesquist
Roy d'Escoce, a tort luy fist,
Et nous regnames apres sa mort
Si avoms trove nostre tort.
Qui en fausyne se regna,
Le tierce gre ne avera ia.
Nos avoms regne a taunt en cea,
Regne ore qi qe pourra.
Meis ore, Philippe, avysez vous,
Si prenez ensaumple de nous,
Sicome avoms fait et les noz,
Si ferreiez vous et les voz.
Vous me maundastes vostre messagere
Qe a Loundres dussoms encountrere
Voz gentz sount venuz devaunt,
Philippe, ore vos ajourne taunt.
Vostre Seneschal fait purveance
Meis vous demorez trope en Fraunce.
Pur ceo, Philippe, hastez a nous
Qi la sumes trovez trestoutz. (Fol. 110.)

The whimsical copy of macaronic verses which follows, a mixture of loyalty and discontent, proves the English character to have been much the same in the fourteenth and nineteenth centuries. An allusion to the youth of Edward the Third shows that they

[1] Archbishop Zouch.
[2] So in the MS. but probably by mistake of the writer for "Neville."

ought to have preceded the former. The stanza is a quintain, consisting of four motley lines, French and Latin, closed by a Leonine hexameter, or pentameter, in the latter language.[1]

Dieu roi de mageste per personas trinas
Notre Roi et sa meisne ne perire sinas,
Grantz maux li fist avoir ac maximas ruinas.
Celui qi lui fist passer partes transmarinas :
  Rex ut salvetur : falsis maledictio detur.

Roi ne deit afier de guerre extra regnum ire,
Si noun la comune de sa terre velint consentire,
Par treson veit home sovent quam plures perire,
A qi dener assurement nemo potest scire.
  Non eat ex regno Rex sine concilio.

Ore court en Engleterre de anno in annum
Le xvme dener, pur mal faire est certe dampnum,
Il fait avaler qe solerent sedere super scamnum,
Et fait a vendre a comune gent, vaccas, vas, et pannum.
  Non placet ad summum quindenum sic dare nummum.

Une chose est encountre fei unde gens gravatur,
A peyne vient la moyte al roy in regno quod levatur,
Pour ceo qil nad le tout entier prout sibi datur,
Le poeple doit le pluys doner et sic cincopatur.
  Nam que taxantur regi non omnia dantur.

Uncore pluys grieve as simples collectio lanarum
Qe les fait vendre comunement divicias earum
Ne poet estre qe tiel counsail assit Deo carum,
Ensi destrure le poverail est opus avarum.
  Non leges sanas teneo regi dare lanas.

Uncore est pluys encountre la pees, ut testantur gentes,
Dun sak deux pieres ou treys nimium librantes,
Questio qi avera cele layne quidam respondentes
Ceo ne averoi Roi ne Royne, set tantum colligentes.
  Pondus lanarum tam falsum constat amarum.

Et puis qe le Roi vodra tam multum cepisse,
Entre les Riches si purra satis invenisse,
Et pluys auxi come mest avis et melius fecisse
Des grauntz partie avoir pris et parvis pepercisse.
  Qui capit argentum sine causa peccat egentum.

[1] [This remarkable poem was printed by Dr. Whitaker without the 4th, 7th, 9th, 10th, and 16th stanzas, which are now supplied. It was edited (with an English translation) by Mr. Wright in his *Political Songs*, (Camden Society 1839), p. 182, from Harl. MS. 2253, as a *Song against the King's taxes*. There are many various readings, but little affecting the meaning. The terminating French words of each line are intended to rhyme as well as the Latin.]

Mes home ne deit al Roi retter talem pravitatem,
Mes tout al faux counsailer per ferocitatem.
Le Roi est joesne bacheler, non habet etatem
Nulle malice compasser, set omnem probitatem.
  Consilium tale dampnum confert generale.

Poi grieve as grauntz granter regi sic tributum ;
Les simples qi deveient doner contra Dei nutum
Tiel counsail par qi il vient est vitiis pollutum ;
Ceaux qi grantent ne paient nyent est male constitutum.
  Nam concedentes nil dant regi sed egentes.

Coment freit home bon espleit ex pauperum sudore
Que les Riches esparnier deit, dono vel favore?
Ses grantz vodrei lever Dei pre timore ;
Le poeple pluys esparnier qui vivit in dolore.
  Qui satis es dives non sic ex paupere vives.

Jeo vei al seicle qu'ore court gentes superbire,
Daltruy biens tenir grant court, que cito vult transire.
Quant vendra al haut judgment, magna dies ire,
S'il ne facent amendement tunc debent perire.
  Rex dicet reprobis Ite, Venite probis.

Dieux qi fustes coroune cum acuta spina,
De vostre poeple eiez pite gratia divina
Qe le seicle soit allege de tali ruina.
A dire un grosse verite est quasi rapina.
  Res inopum capta non gratis fit quasi rapta.

Tiel tribut a nulle foer diu nequit durare ;
De voide bourse qi poet deners manibus tractare?
Les gentz sount a tiel meschief quod nequeunt plus dare.
Jeo me doute s'il eussent chief quod vellent levare.
  Sepe facit stultas gentes vacuata facultas.

Il y ad grant escharste monete inter gentes,
Qe homme poet venir en marchee, quam pauci sunt ementes ;
Tout eyt homme bestes moebles, equos vel bidentes,
A peyne prendra nul dener, tam multi sunt egentes.
  Gens non est leta cum sit tam parca moneta.

Si le Roi freit moun counsail tunc vellem laudare,
D'argent prendre le vessel Monetam parare,
Kare mielz vaudreit de fust manger pro victu nummos dare
Ke dargent le corps servir et lignum pacare.
  Est vicii signum pro victu solvere lignum.

Lour commissions sont trop cheres qui sunt ultra mare,
Qe lour terre ne soit de poer eosdem sustentare,
Jeo nei sei coment purront animas salvare
Qe d'altruy biens voilent vivre et propria salvare.
  Non dubitant penas rapientes res alienas.

Dieux par son sayntisme noun confundat errores
Et touz qi pensent faire treson ac pacis turbatores,
Ke voides soient par temps tales vexatores,
Et conferme si lui pleise inter reges amores.
  Perdat solamen qui pacem destruit. Amen. (Fol. 146.)

Internal evidence fixes this odd composition to the year 1337, when Edward the Third obtained 20,000 sacks of wool from Parliament, in order to bribe the Flemings, before his first expedition to France. With respect to the advice offered in the fifteenth stanza, it may be supposed that the author did not mean the plate of his own house. Edward, however, seems to have taken the hint, for he plundered the Lombard merchants, on this occasion, of all their gold, silver, and jewels. Considering the age in which they were uttered, the sentiments contained in these verses are unusually bold; but the monks were great complainers; and the reputed sanctity of their character, their seclusion, and mutual confidence, enabled them to speak, and even to write, with impunity, what would have been highly penal to other men.

The Liber Loci Benedicti contains many sermons, which appear to have been preached in the Abbey Church. I have selected the following, not because it is either better or worse than its companions, but as being less abbreviated, and therefore more legible. It is marked by the initials I. de Gl. which must refer to Fr. John de Glovernia, who died in 1328.

Fac tibi duas tubas argenteas ductiles, quibus convocare possis multitudinem.

Fratres mei dilecti, cum isti Imperatores, Reges, et alii plerique inferiores prandere volunt, tubis convocant comessuros. Congregati ergo et discumbentes, quidam cum architriclino, quidam cum medioeribus de populo, quidam verò cum garcionibus in aule medio, vel exteriùs in atrio, priusquam comedant, orationem faciunt, sicq' cum gratiarum actione leti suscipiunt degustanda. Nos etiam, karissimi, ad prandium Dei id est audiendum verbum Dei tubâ id est campanâ hac convocati habemus inter nos plerosque cum architriclino, id est cum Deo vel cum ipso predicatore discumbentes, hoc est, subtilia et sublimia sencientes; quosdam autem cum medioeribus de populo sedentes, id est ipsâ veritatis planicie contentos, non sensum profundiorem vel exponere obscuriorem expetentes; alios verò cum garcionibus, id est, simplicioribus residentes, narrationes et si que sunt que risum excutiant auscultantes. Igitur antiquum propositum aggrediamur: oret unusquisque quatenus Deus nobis aperiat hostium sermonis, ut digna ad ipsius honorem et istorum omniumque sanctorum promere valeamus, et in confusionem sint Sathane et omnium satellitum ejus, et ad nostrarum salutem proficiant animarum.

Fac tibi duas tubas, &c.—Quadripartitum officium habebant tube in veteri lege; sicut dicitur in histor. Numb. 11; videlicet, in multitudine convocandâ, ad castra movenda, ad bella committenda, et ad festa celebranda—et hec tanguntur in textu in capitulo suprascripto. Sic et Xpc in hunc mundum veniens ad expugnandos hostes fidei, ad convocandos proprios ad cultum Dei, ad movenda castra per viam caritatis, ad predicanda festa perpetuo jocunditatis: merito voluit uti tubis, id est, istis Apostolis inter alios precipuis, de quibus ait

Pater filio incarnato, *Fac tibi duas tubas, &c.*, in quibus verbis tria veritates potuerunt annotari, videlicet vasorum precipuorum evidens expressio ibi *Fac tibi duas tubas*, metalli perlucidi excellens conditio ibi *argenteas ductiles*, et multitudinis divise conjungens vocatio ibi *quibus convocare possis multitudinem.* Sed hec pocius de proprietate dictionum quam de edificatione morum dicta sunt, unde in verbis premissis de istis sanctis mystice intellectis 3ª veritates inveniuntur, primo prolacionis auctoritas ibi *Fac tibi duas tubas;* secundo predicacionis claritas, ibi *argenteas ductiles;* 3º utilitas, ibi *quibus convocare posses multitudinem.* Primum commendat patris preceptum in eo quod officium predicacionis temere non usurpant, et quod proprium erat sacerdotum tubis clangere, unde Numeri 10 *Filii Aaron sacerdotis clangent tubis.* Secundum commendat eloquencia propter documentum, quod argentum inter omnia metalla est clarissimum, et sonum habet dulcissimum, unde Proverbiar. 10 *Argentum electum lingua justi.* Tertium commendat utilitas propter meritum et premium et consequentem effectum, unde Act. iv. *Multitudinis credentium erat cor unum et anima una.* Circa primum notandum quod apte per tubas apostoli designantur. Tuba enim per flatum oris sonat, magnum sonum reddit, aggregat, excitat, terret. Primo inquam tuba per flatum oris sonat, et apostoli non solum per epistolas suas, sed et ore suo sonando et vivá voce predicando Christum predicabant. Et hoc faciebant cum labore, quod notatur in flatu continuantes aliquo diem cum nocte, sicut legitur Ac. 20: *Protraxit sermonem usque in mediam noctem. Protraxit*—ecce flatus laboriosus: *sermonem*—ecce sonus oris: *usque in mediam noctem*—ecce labor continuatius. Faciebant ergo quod precipitur in Psº. *Buccinate in neomenia tuba. Buccinate*—hoc est, annunciate: *tuba*, i.e. predicatione aperta: *in neomenia*, i.e. in novilunio: hoc est, in tempore gracie sive glorie. Sed quid dicitur *buccinate*? Quia preceptum in Israel est et judicium Deo Jacob.[1] Preceptum ergo Dei est quod habetur in Joh. *Hoc est preceptum meum ut diligatis unice.* Judicium vero Dei est quod ultioni extreme districtionis servatur. Qui itaque renuit audire et facere preceptum timeat quia ipsum percipiet judicium. De hâc tubâ tipice legitur Jos. 6, ubi dicitur quod Josue precepit sacerdotibus ut tollerent tubas et incederent ante archam Dñi, et populus armatus precederet, et vulgus reliquum sequeretur sacerdotibus tubis concrepantibus et populo tacente, sicque facerent circuientes Jericho VII diebus, die autem septimo circuirent septies, et in septimo circuitu, sacerdotibus tubis clangentibus, dixit Josue ad populum, Vociferamini. Igitur clamante populo et tubis sonantibus, postquam in aures multitudinis vox sonitus increpuit, ilico Jherico corruit. Josue ergo, id est X̄p̄e, precepit sacerdotibus, id est Apostolis, ut tollerent tubas, id est magnificam celestemque doctrinam, et precederent archam, id est ecclesiam. Quia autem populus armatus precederet, et vulgus reliquum sequeretur, Judeorum et gentilium tipum gerit. Quia vero septem diebus cecinerunt, et in septimo septies, significatur quod usque ad finem seculi quid septem dierum vicissitudine volvitur non desinunt predicari. Sed muri Jherico tubis sacerdotalibus corruerunt? hoc est, quod cultus ydolorum et fallacia divinacionum monstrata arte demonum, commenta augurum et magorum et dogmata philosophorum, sua superstitione elata, funditus sunt subacta. Et vos, fratres dilectissimi, tubá estote buccinantes et concrepando narrantes invicem et absentibus verba Dei que ex ore predicatoris auditis, ut tuba veritatis dici possitis, et si non per omnimodam similitudinem, saltem per aliqualem imitacionem. Sed forte dicet aliquis: Ergone magnum est homini esse tubam? Nunquid aurum vel argentum nos esse velis? Nunquid non melior est homo quam metallum? Cui ego, Respondeo sicut quod dicit beatus Augustinus super Johannem Omelia 47,[2] Esse aliquid predicitur dupliciter per proprietatem rei aut similitudinem. Per proprietatem? nolo vos esse tubam vel aliquod metallum, sic nec ipsi Apostoli fuerunt; Per similitudinem verò volo vos esse tubam et hoc argenteam; Tubam, ut que bona esse discitis unice doceatis; Argenteam autem, ut pretiosa

[1] [Psalm lxxx. 5.]

[2] [The passage here referred to is probably that beginning "Per similitudinem Christus multa est quæ per proprietatem non est." Aug. in Joannis Evan. Tract. 47, sec. 6. Translated in Dr. Pusey, Lib. of the Fathers. "By way of similitude Christ is many things which he is not in the nature of the things themselves. By similitude both is Christ a rock, and Christ a door, and Christ a corner-stone, &c. &c." Aug. on St. John, p. 626.]

sint id est celestia, et non plumbeam ut sint vilia vel terrena. Item magnum sonum reddit tuba, et sancti isti apostoli non minima, non abjecta, non parva, sed de magnis magna predicabant; et ideo per magnum sonum eorum revocati sunt homines à cultu Diaboli ad cultum unius veri Dei, eosque qui in tenebris ignorancie jacebant et peccatis et viciis et carnis voluptatibus serviebant, ad intuitum luminis evangelice veritatis excitabant, et ea quo eis antea dulcia esse videbantur horrere fecerunt. Impleverunt ergo utrique quod precipitur Ys 58, *Clama, ne cesses quasi tuba*, &c. Hec autem agentes multitudinem demonum ab hoc mundo exterruerunt, et populum Dei in fide Trinitatis informantes ab eorum cultura servicio et subjectione liberaverunt. De hoc habetur Judicum 7 ubi dicitur quod Gedeon et trecenti viri ingressi partem castrorum media nocte ceperunt tubis canere, et tenuerunt sinistris manibus lampades et dextris tubas, et omnia castra turbata sunt et fugerunt vociferantes ululantesque. Sed trecenti viri insistebant tubis nichilominus personantes. Gedeon ergo, id est Xpe, et trecenti viri, id est Petrus et Paulus apostoli in fide Trinitatis armati, ingressi partem castrorum, quia inceperunt ab Jherosolomis predicare, mediâ nocte, quia ante apostolorum predicationem mundus totus in tenebris ignorancie dormitavit, et verum lumen omnino nescicus pictatis peccatis et viciis extitit deformiter obfuscatus, ceperunt tubis canere, id est magnâ et altà voce Xpm predicare, et tenuerunt sinistris manibus lampades et dextris tubas, quia salutem corporum temporalem dispiciebant que per sinistram accipitur, predicacioni totâ devocione insistebant quod per dextram designatur, et sic castra mundi turbata sunt, id est templorum pontifices seipsos turbaverunt, et seditionem in populo commoverunt, vociferantes contra apostolos pro eo quod contra ritum ydolorum docuerunt, et ululantes fugerunt id est finem suum similem lupis fetidis ostenderunt.

Item tuba aggregat, excitat, et terret, unde Esdr. 4, *In quocunque loco audieritis clangorem tube, illuc concurrite ad nos*, &c. Et Act. 2. *Multitudo convenit*, pro primo, et infra, *Stans Petrus levavit vocem suam*, pro 2°; et infra, *Compuncti sunt corde;* pro tertio; et 13, *Pene universa civitas convenit audire verbum Domini.* Ecce primum. Sed blasphamantes in deos terrens et gentes ad devotionem excitans subdit, *Vobis oportebat primum loqui verbum Dei, sed quoniam repellitis illud*, &c. ecce tertium, *Ecce convertimur ad gentes;* ecce secundum. *Audientes autem gentes gavise sunt et crediderunt*, excitati videlicet benignitate Xpi et tantorum doctorum, de quibus potest dici illud, Mac. 3, *Tuba cecinerunt hii qui erant cum Juda, et congressi sunt et contrite sunt gentes.* Hii, id est Apostoli Petrus et Paulus qui erant cum Judâ, id est cum Christo, tubâ cecinerunt ut populum excitarent, et congressi sunt ut plures aggregarent, et contrite sunt gentes cum ritus gentiles vel potius ipsos demones exterminarent. Et in hiis omnibus predicacionis auctoritas commendatur. (F. 52—f. 54.)

If such were the taste and style of all discourses preached in the religious houses, those who occupied the place of the unlearned would have little reason to complain that they were written in an unknown tongue. But this was properly a *Concio ad clerum*. The duty and excellence of preaching, however, might have been enforced by arguments more cogent, and drawn from topics more evangelical, than these jejune and fanciful allegories. Their own Bernard would have afforded many better models.

The following important Documents relating to the Appropriation of the Rectory and the Endowment of the Vicarage of Whalley, I have judged proper to be inserted in this place, from the "Liber Loci Benedicti," into which they were transcribed at the time.

Littera Regis de Appropriacione Ecclesie de Whall. Ad Papam.

Sanctissimo in Xpo patri Dno B(onifacio) providencia divina sacrosancte Romane et universalis Ecclesie summo Pontifici, E. Dei gratia Rex Angl. Dus Hybn. et Dux Aquitann' cum omni reverencia et honore devota pedum oscula bor'.[1] Divine provisionis acies, que in sua disposicione non fallitur neque fallit, ad hoc vos in terris suum vicarium ordinavit, ut supplicancium votis, que comitatur honestas, ac profectus sequitur animarum, et annuatis benignius et de specula preeminencie vestre gregem respicientes dominicam, prout unicuique opus fuerit, rorem ei vestre paterne dulcedinis infundatis. Hec profecto spem nobis uberrimam suggerunt, hec firmam fiduciam subministrant, quod nostre supplicacionis devocionem, que de cordis intimo prodit affectu, ad exaudicionis benigne graciam admittetis. Cum igitur, septennio jam elapso, ad nostram instanciam et vestram, sancte pater, si recolitis, pro nobis intercessionem, felicis recordacionis D^ns N[icholaus] Papa IIII., concesserit viris religiosis Abbati et Conventui Loci Benedicti de Stanl., Ord'is Cisterc', Coventr' et Lych. Dioc', quòd dictam Abbatiam suam, quam progenitores dilecti et fidelis nostri H[enrici] Com' Lync' fundaverunt, et amplis, prout potuerunt, dotaverunt possessionum largicionibus, et que nunc ad eum statum noscitur devenisse, cùm fundata fuerit supra quendam fluvium, per quem fluxus et refluxus maris habetur, quòd propter superexcrescentes inundaciones et impetus maris ejusdem, quod diebus ac noctibus a fluxu et refluxu non cessat, extra consuetos alveos debachando, terminosque suos transgrediendo antiquos, et locum suis alluvionibus[2] destruendo et adnichilando predictum, Abbas et Conventus Abbatie predicte ibidem absque corporum et animarum rerumque suarum periculo et dampnis nequeant commorari, cum totalem destructionem et exterminium finale murorum et domorum Abbatie prefate marinus impetus infra tempus modicum comminetur, ita quòd non adiciet[3] ut resurgat, transferre possent ad ecclesiam de Whall[eye] predicte Dioc', et in ejusdem ecclesie solo, cedente vel decedente rectore, officinas sibi et mansiones necessarias construere, eandem ecclesiam in usus proprios eisdem abbati et Conventui de munificencia sedis apostolice concedendo, maxime cum dictus Comes, zelo caritatis et virtute compassionis inductus, Jus patronatus quod in eadem habebat ecclesia, dictis Religiosis sub spe translacionis hiis optinende, de consensu nostro speciali jam diu et concessisset, ac ibidem cultum divini nominis augmentandum decrevisset, juxta augmentum facultatum ecclesie supradicte, prout de hiis omnibus per factum supradicti predecessoris vestri vestre sancte paternitati liquere poterit evidenter, nuper circa festum Purificacionis Anno Dñi M^occo n^o quarto, rectore supradicte ecclesie de Whall[eye] ab hac luce subtracto, iidem religiosi, necessitate querende habitacionis compulsi, et auctoritate ut predictum est sedis apostolice communiti, de consensu eciam diocesani et archidiaconi dicti loci, sue indempnitati sufficienter assecuracionum satisfactum, dictam ecclesiam sunt ingressi, ipsam cum juribus et pertinenciis suis sibi in usus proprios applicando, et habitacula que defuerant ad opus Conventus sui magis necessaria in solo ejusdem infatigabiliter construendo. Quia ergo necesse est vestre sanctitatis inchoata feliciter caritatis opera auctoritatis et confirmacionis vestre cumulo consummare, sancte paternitati vestre ex intimo cordis affectu et omni affectione qua possumus supplicamus, quatenus, caritatis intuitu, et nostre si placet supplicacionis interventu, statum dictorum Religiosorum, qui ad appropriacionem prefate ecclesie cum juribus et pertinenciis suis, et translacionem eorundem à loco periculoso in quo nunc sunt ad alium competenciorem in solo dicte ecclesie faciendam, concessionesque felicissime recordacionis prefati predecessoris vestri super premissis prehabitam auctoritatis vestre munimine dignemini confirmare, seu vestre sancte paternitatis benevolencia premissa de novo concedere. Attendimus enim et habemus pro constanti quòd anime vestre et animabus predecessorum et successorum vestrorum non modicum proficiet factum istud, cum pro eisdem viginti monachi in collegio novi monasterii assumendi ultra numerum in priori monasterio solitum observari, devotas oraciones Altissimo effundere teneantur. Conservet D^ns vitam vestram feliciter incolumem ecclesie sue sancte per tempora longiora.—Dat. &c.

[1] *i.e. beatorum.* The contraction occurs a second time [in p. 162.]

[2] The sense of this word is inverted. *Alluvions*, in the language of the Civil Law, are increments made to estate, by aggestions of soil from floods, or by the receding of rivers.

[3] Such appears to be the reading, from whatsoever word it is corrupted. [*Adicere* pro *adjicere*, ap. Rymer, ii. 99, et alibi passim, nec raro apud antiquos. Glossarium Manuale ad Scrip. Med. et Infimæ Latinitatis.]

Item eidem Comes Lync' de hoc ipso.

Sanctissimo in Christo patri B(onifacio) divina providencia sacrosancte Romane et universalis Ecclesie summo Pontifici, suus filius devotus H. Com' Lync' devota pedum oscula ẗor'. Considerantes quantâ devocione et fidei puritate olim progenitores nostri preclarum Cist' ordinem confovere sollicite studuerunt, quodque iidem, ordinem ipsum favore benevolo prosequentes, Monasterium Loci Benedicti de Stanl., Coventr' et Lych' dioc., quo adhuc ejusdem ordinis Monachi pro animarum eorundem progenitorum nostrorum et nostra salute virtutum Domino jugiter famulantur, fundaverunt, intuitu caritatis idem dotando monasterium quibus potuerunt possessionibus, ac optantes effici laudabilis imitator eorundem, religiosis viris Abbati et Conventui dicti loci Jus patronatus ecclesie de Whall' ejusdem dioc. ad nos spectans, caritatis contemplacione duximus conferendum, piam paternitatem felicis recordacionis D^{ni} N. pp^{e} IIII predecessoris vestri requirentes humiliter ac devote, ut cum predicti situs monasterii maris turbini fuerit tam vicinus, quòd adversus fluctuum ejus tempestuosos impetus ullo remedio muniri non possit, quin inundacionum intemperie terra circumquaque latenciis consumatur, religiosis ipsis dignaretur misericorditer indulgere, quòd ad Ecclesiam de Whall. supradictam, cujus jus, ut premittitur, sibi concessimus, patronatus, de ipsius possent licentia se transferre, eandemque ecclesiam, cum suis juribus et pertinenciis habere valerent et retinere perpetuo propriis suis usibus applicatam, et ipsius possessionem ingredi, alterius cujuslibet irrequisito consensu, ipsius ecclesie cedente vel decedente rectore. Hoc proviso quod per aliquos fratres ipsorum apud dictum locum de Stanl., quamdiu dictus locus possit inhabitari, Altissimo quam honestius poterit serviatur. Idem vero pater sanctissimus pauperum desolationi compatiens visceribus pietatis, ac super hiis sui gratia favorabiliter annuens votis nostris, dictam ecclesiam de Whall. cum omnibus juribus et pertinenciis suis, dictis Religiosis concessit in forma qua petivimus possidendam, sicut per transcriptum littere sanctissimi patris vestre sanctitati luculentius poterit apparere. Post lapsum vero temporis Rectore prefate Ecclesie de Whall. ab hac vita migrante circa festum videlicet Pur' beate virginis Anno Domini M°cc° nonogesimo quarto, statim dicti Religiosi juxta tenorem literarum papalium dictam Ecclesiam de Whalleye sunt ingressi, subsecutis nichilominus approbacionibus tam diocesani quam archidiaconi dicti loci sue indempnitati sufficienter asserencium satisfactum, sicut per eorum instrumenta super hiis confecta plenius est videre, et mundi malicia vacantes Deo, ac simplices, importunis et cautelosis argueiis indies inquietat, volentesque, si Deus permiserit, quòd dicti religiosi karissimi nostri, quos maris violencia à primis sedibus suis in proximo ejiciet et expellet, in loco quem eis providimus ubi etiam ad opus ipsorum ex magna parte habitacula sunt constructa, diebus nostris inconcusse et stabiliter radicentur, vestram sanctam paternitatem flexis cordis nostri genibus humiliter exoramus, ut pro Dei misericordia, et precum nostrarum intuitu, facto felicissime recordacionis dicti D^{ni}, vestrum prebere velitis assensum, et illud auctoritatis vestre munimine confirmare, seu vestre sancte paternitatis benevolentia premissa de novo concedere. Attendimus siquid et pro constanti tenemus, quod si sancte paternitati vestre placuerit in premissis votis nostris annuere que ut credimus a rationis tramite non discordant, non solum acceptum erit Deo, et ipsius ecclesie exinde proveneret laus et honor, sed vestre vestrorumque predecessorum et successorum animabus augebitur suffragium salutare, maxime cum viginti monachi ultra monachorum numerum in priori monasterio solitum observare ratione appropriacionis sepedicte ecclesie in collegio novi monasterii assumendi pro vestrum et predecessorum ac successorum vestrorum animabus devotas oraciones Altissimo effundere teneantur. Valeat excellens et sancta paternitas vestra semper in d^{no} Ihu Xp̃o. (Fols. 92-93.)

The monk who was deputed to negociate this important transaction at the Court of Rome appears to have been Richard de Rodierd, afterwards Abbot of Cumbermere. Of his appointment, the *Liber Loci Benedicti* supplies the following notices :

A noble bier e lur cher soingnur sire Henry de Lasey, Counte de Nichole, les soens si li plest Abbe e le Couent de Wh. saluz, reverence, e honur. Cher sire, nous vous prioms especialment que Richard de R. nostre clerk, portour de ceste lettre, voillez si vous plest ayder e counsailler entour nos beseingues purchacer en la Court de Rome, que nous ne auioms pas le leisir ore aparmes mes de purveer autre clerk. E, sire, les coustages et les mises que vous freez en leide e le counsail entour nous besoingues a vous voloms pleinement restorer, sicome est countenu en une lettre obligatoire la qele nous vous aveoms. E sachez, sire, que nous avoms done poer a mesmes celi Richard a obliger nostre mesoun a certeine soume de aver per vostre counsail. E donez fey, Sire, si vos plest, a ceo que le vauntdist Richard vos dirra de bouche de part nous. A Deu, Sire, qe vos gard a touz jours. (Fol. 97.)

Obligocio.

Pateat universis per presentes, quòd nos Abbas et Conventus de Wh. tenemur, et per hoc scriptum fatemur nos obligari nobili viro Domino Henr' de Lasey Com. Lync'. in omnibus sumptibus et expensis quos vel quas fecerit pro negociis nostris in Cur' Romana expediendis, eidem vel suo dicto attornato hanc literam deferenti, cum ad partes Anglicanas redierit, fideliter persolvendę. In cujus, &c. Dat. &c. Anno, &c.

Potestas Obligandi.

Universis pateat per presentes, quod nos Fr. Gregor' Abbas Loci Benedicti de Whall. et ejusdem domus Conventus Cist' ordinis Coventr' et Lych' dyoc' constituimus, facimus, et ordinamus dilectum nobis in Xpo Ricard. de R. clericum, procuratorem et attornatum nostrum, ad negocia nostra in Sancta Romana Curia expedienda, ac etiam ad mutuum nomine nostro contrahendum usque ad sexaginta marcas sterlingorum, vel ad valorem eorundem, aut ultra aut citra, prout indiguerit, à quocunque poterit Christiano, cum consilio tamen et assensu nobilis viri Dni Com. Lync. Dantes eidem potestatem obligandi nos et domum nostram predictam, ac litteras obligatorias et convencionales nomine nostro conficiendi, et omnia alia faciendi que facere possemus si nos contingeret personaliter interesse. Ratum habiturum et gratum omnem contractum per eundem nomine nostro cum quibuscunque initum, et omnem scriptum super hoc sub quacunque forma verborum conceptum, et quicquid in premissis vice nostra duxerit faciendum cum consilio tamen et assensu domini Comitis supradicti. In cujus, &c. Dat. apud Wha. in pleno loci capitulo, &c. Anno, &c. (Fol. 97 b.)

Procuratorium.

Universis pateat per presentes quod nos F'r Gr' Abbas loci benedicti de Wh. et ejusdem domus conventus Cist' ordinis Coventr' et Lych. dyoc' dilectum nobis in Xpo Ricard de R. clericum procuratorem nostrum legittimum constituimus facimus et ordinamus per presentes in omnibus causis et negociis nos et domum nostram predictam qualitercunque contingentibus, coram quibuscunque judicibus quibuscunque diebus et locis contra quoscunque adversarios nostros. Et ad impetrandum in Sancta Romana Curia privilegia et indulgencias et quascunque alias litteras tam simplices quam legendas favorem nostram seu justiciam continentes. Et ad contradicendum litteris quibuscunque in Curia contra nos impetrandis et ad procedendum ibidem si necesse fuerit in omnibus causis nos et ecclesias nostras qualitercunque tangentibus. In judices et loca consentiendum conveniendum et recusandum prout justicia et status noster in curia suadebit. Et ad appellandum et prosequendum ibidem si necesse fuerit, et ad omnia alia et singula faciendum que in predictis vel circa predicta fuerint necessaria ac etiam opportuna. Ratum et gratum habiturum quicquid dictus procurator noster nomine nostro fecerit in premissis. In cujus, &c. videlicet sicut proximo anno, &c.

Viatica.

Universis ad quos presentes littere pervenerint Fr. G. vocatus Abbas loci benedicti de W. et ejusdem domus conventus salutem in Domino. Noverit universitas vestra quòd lator presentium, Ricard. de R(odierd) nomine, clericus noster est, et a nobis versus Curiam Romanam pro negociis nostris ibidem expediendis directus. Pro quo universitatem vestram specialiter exoramus quatenus eidem per vos transeunti nullam molestiam inferatis, vel inferri, quantum in vobis est, permittatis; sed in hiis quibus indiguerit, caritatis intuitu et ordinis reverencia, misericorditer dignemini subvenire, ut omnium bonorum que fuerint in ordine participes effici merito valeatis. Dat. &c. anno, &c. (Fol. 98.)

The next is a letter, apparently written by one of the Earl's officers, in order to remove some dissatisfaction which the abbot and convent had conceived against Rodierd, for delay.

Commendacio exsecutoris negociorum istorum.

Eximie religionis et venerande discrecionis viro domino Abbati de W(halleye), suus B. de R. affectum servicii et honoris. Si in agendis vos et ecclesiam vestram contingentibus, propter que Ricardum clericum vestrum ad Romanam Curiam misistis, non est ut expediret et credebatis processum; dicto Ricardo non imputetis, quoniam ipse, ut prudens et solicitus procurator, in hiis fecit quod potuit, dominum meum Comitem et alios sollicitandos vigilanter et diligenter excitando, ex quo est de diligencia merito commendandus. (Fol. 98.)

The effect of these petitions and exertions appears in the Papal Bull which follows:

Bulla Secunda de Ecclesia de Wh.

Bonifacius Episcopus,[1] servus servorum Dei, dilectis filiis Abbati et Conventui Monasterii Loci Benedicti de Whall. Stanl.[2] Cisterciensis ordinis, Coventr. et Lych. dyoc', salutem et apostolicam benedictionem. Sub sacre religionis habitu, mundi spretis illecebris, que cum blandiuntur illudunt, virtutum Domino[3] militantes, per laudabilium actuum studia meruisse noscimini, ut apostolice sedis consueta benignitas, favorabiliter annuens votis vestris, illius vos et monasterium vestrum gracie munere prosequatur que vobis et ei fore dinoscitur opportuna. Exposita nobis siquid petitio vestra continebat, quod cum olim in monasterio quod tunc in loco qui Locus Benedictus de Stanl. Cisterc' ordinis, Conventr' et Lych. dyoc. vulgariter dicitur habebatis (habitabatis) propter inundaciones equoreas cum mare dicto monasterio sit vicinum, ac alias etiam incommoditates multiplices, absque gravi manere periculo non possetis. Venerabilis frater noster Coventr' et Lych. episcopus benigne intendens super hoc divine vobis pietatis intuitu salubriter providere, transferendi monasterium ipsum ad locum illum, quem vobis dilectus filius nobilis vir Henricus de Lasey, Comes Lync. monasterii memorati patronus, duceret deputandum, vobis concessit auctoritate ordinaria facultatem. Ac idem Comes gerens in votis ad locum in quo ecclesia de Whall. ejusdem dyoc. sita est, in qua ipse nullusque alius jus patronatus habebat, Monasterium transferri prefatum, tam patronatus, quam omne jus aliud, quod in eadem sibi competebat ecclesia, pio ductus affectu ea vobis intentione concessit ut ad locum eundem dictum monasterium transferretur, et de proventibus ejusdem ecclesie viginti monachi ultra monachorum numerum in prefato monasterio solitum observari in eorum assumendi collegio congrue substentacionis stipendia optinerent, qui pro Romanorum pontificum dictique Comitis animarum salute devotas preces Altissimo fundere tenerentur: Felicis quoque recordacionis Nicholaus papa quartus, predecessor noster, volens vos ubere favoris et gracie prosequi specialis, sepefatam Ecclesiam cum omnibus capellis, juribus et pertinenciis suis, vobis vestrisque successoribus in usus proprios concessit et auctoritate apostolica imperpetuum deputavit, eadem vobis auctoritate nichilominus concedendo ut cedente vel decedente ipsius ecclesie rectore, possetis illius possessionem auctoritate apprehendere propria, cujusvis assensu minime requisito, vobisque licentiam tribuit predictum monasterium ad locum prefatum, ubi jam dicta consistit

[1] [Benedict VIII. was elected Pope 24 Dec. 1294, and died 11 Oct. 1303.]

[2] [Whall. is scored out, and Stanl. written after it in the line.]

[3] [*Sic orig.* perhaps for virtute Domini.]

ecclesia, sine juris alieni prejudicio transferendi. Reservatâ de proventibus ejusdem ecclesie Vicario perpetuo inibi servituro, ad vestre presentacionis instanciam per diocesanum instituendo predictum, congrua porcione de quâ commode substentari valeat, jura episcopalia solvere ac alia eidem ecclesie incumbencia onera supportare, prout in literis predecessoris ejusdem super hoc confectis plenius dicitur contineri. Sicque vacante postmodum ecclesia supradicta per obitum quondam Petri de Cestria[1] rectoris ejusdem, vos possessionem ipsius ecclesie fuistis pacificam assecuti, ac demum ad locum eundem prenominatum transferre monasterium curavistis. Verum quia universas provisiones, reservaciones, concessiones quibuscunque personis à predecessore factas eodem de quibusvis ecclesiis et ecclesiasticis beneficiis vacaturis per constitutionem à nobis ante vacationem illius ecclesie editam cassavimus, irritavimus, et vacuavimus, cassas, irritas, et vacuas nunciavimus, vos mutuentes vobis ex cassacione, irritacione, ac vacuacione hujus pro eo quòd post constitucionem ipsam, licet antequam de ea ad vestram perveniret noticiam ecclesie predicte fuistis possessionem adepti, circa eandem ecclesiam prejudicium imminere nobis humiliter supplicastis, ut providere super hoc vobis paterne solicitudinis studio dignaremur. Nos itaque, volentes vos, divine pietatis intuitu, et consideracione dilecti filii nostri R. tituli sancte Potentiane presbyteri Cardinalis[2] nobis super hoc cum instancia supplicantis, prosequi dono gracie specialis, translacionem hujus monasterii supradicti ad locum eundem, et concessionem ipsius ecclesie de Whall. sicut premittitur, vobis factam, auctoritate apostolica ex certa scientia approbavimus, vobis auctoritate predicta nichilominus indulgentes ut vos in prefato loco sub vestri ordinis observancia perpetuo remanentes omnibus privilegiis, indulgenciis, concessionibus, libertatibus et immunitatibus que ante translacionem monasterii memorati noscebamini optinere, possetis uti libere sicut prius, et predictam ecclesiam cum omnibus capellis, bonis, juribus, et pertinenciis suis, juxta tenorem concessionis predecessoris ejusdem, in usus proprios sive, obsistat hiis nostra cassacio seu constitucionis edicio sive non, perpetuo retinere. Confirmavimus insuper auctoritate predicta porciones terrarum, redditnum, et proventuum vicarie loci predicti de Whall. per nos, sicut asseritis, Perpetuo Vicario ibidem sicut predicitur Domino servituro ad sustentacionem ipsius, et jura episcopalia aliaque onera subportanda que prefate incumbunt ecclesie, secundum quod idem predecessor voluit assignatas. Nulli ergo omnino hominum liceat hanc paginam nostre approbacionis, concessionis, confirmationis infringere, vel ei ausu temerario contraire. Si quis autem hoc attemptare presumpserit, indignacionem omnipotentis Dei et beatorum Petri et Pauli Apostolorum ejus se noverit incursurum. Datum apud Urbem Veterem XII kal. Julii Pontificatus nostri anno tercio.[3] (Fol. 98—99 b.)

In Dei nomine Amen. Facta diligenti inquisitione super valore fructuum et proventuum Ecclesie de Whall. et Capellarum eidem adjacencium, necnon oneribus eisdem incumbentibus, eaque inquisicione in omni sui parte expressius per Religiosos viros Abbatem et Conventum de Whall. et Dominum Johannem ad vicariam in eadem ecclesia ordinandam presentatum acceptata et approbata, coram nobis Archidiacono Cestrensi et Officiali Domini Coventr. et Lych. Episcopi ac Officiali dicti Archidiaconi, dicti patris quorum tenores, videlicet tam commissionis quàm inquisitionis, sequuntur: W(alterus) permissione divina Coventr' et Lych. Episcopus, dilectis in Xro. filiis Archidiacono Cestrie, Magistro Waltero de Thorp Officiali nostro, Canonicis in ecclesia nostra Lych. ac etiam Officiali dicti Archidiaconi, salutem gratiam et benedictionem. Ad inquirendum super vero valore fructuum, proventuum, et obvencionum quorumcunque ad ecclesiam de

[1] [Obiit A.D. M°. cc°. xc°. III°. Marginal Note in a later hand.]

[2] [Robert, French by birth, *doctor egregius*, occurs, 1285, as 19th abbot of the famous abbey of Pontigny, in the diocese of Auxerre, one of the four houses called the daughters of Citeaux; chosen in 1293 twenty-eighth abbot of Citaux; promoted by Cælestine V. in 1294 to be a priest-cardinal under the title of St. Pudentiana. He was commonly known as the White Cardinal, from never laying aside the robes of his order. He died at Parma, in Italy, in Aug. 1305. Gallia Christiana, vol. xii. col. 447, vol. iv. 997. Migne, Dictionnaire des Cardinaux.]

[3] The former Bull of Nicholas IV. to the same effect, has been printed by Dugdale and Dodsworth. Mon. Ang. vol. i. This, and all the instruments contained in the present account, have not been published before.

Whall(eye), nostre dioc. et ad capellas ejusdem qualitercunque pertinencium, pariter et de oneribus eidem ecclesie et capellis ejusdem ex quacunque causa incumbentibus, ac eciam ad ordinandam et faciendam ibidem vicariam competentem prout mandatum apostolicum id requirit, et ad facienda omnia et singula in hac parte que nos facere debemus, si presentes essemus, vobis vices nostras committimus cum canonice cohercionis potestate. Quod si non omnes hiis exequendis interfuerint, duo vestrum, presentia tercii minime expectata premissa, nichilominus exequentur. Dat. London. III. kal. Julii consecracionis nostre anno secundo.

Inquisicio[1] facta de valore et proventibus ecclesie matricis de Whall. et capellarum ejusdem, et de oneribus predicte ecclesie incumbentibus, die Mercurii proximo post festum Assumptionis beate Marie Virginis, Anno Domini M°cc° nonagessimo octavo. Decime garbarum ville de Whalleye valent iiij li. Decime garbarum de Wysewalle valent vj li.: et distat de Whalleye per dimidiam leucam. Decime garbarum de Coldecotes valent xx s. et distat per unam leucam. Decime garbarum de Hennethorñ et Mittoñ valent lxvj s. viij d. et distat ab ecclesia matrici per unam leucam. Decime garbarum de Peniltoñ valent vj li. et distat per duas leucas. Decime garbarum de Reved valent iiij li. et distat per duas leucas.[2] Decime garbarum de Symondestan valent xl s. et distat per tres leucas. Decime garbarum de Padiam valent viij Marc'. et distat per tres leucas. Decime garbarum de Haptoñ et Briddestwysel valent viij Marc'. et distat per quatuor leucas. Alteragium matricis ecclesie predicte valet x li. et terra de Dominicis valet c s. Decime garbarum capelle de Cliderhou valent xvij li. Alteragium ejusdem valet iiij li. et distat per tres leucas. Decime garbarum de Dounam valent c s. Alteragium ejusdem cum terra de dominicis valet iiij Marc. et distat per v leucas, et ecclesia de Blakeburn est dotata ab antiquo in octava parte predicte ecclesie de Whalley cum capellis predictis. Decime garbarum capelle de Caune valent xiij li. Alteragium valet vj li. et distat per viij leucas de Whalleye. Decime garbarum de Brunleye valent xv li. Alteragium cum terra de dominicis valet x li. et distat per viij leucas. Decime garbarum capelle de Alvetham cum alteragio valent ix li. et distat per ij leucas. Decime garbarum capelle de Chirche valent x Marc. Alteragium cum terra de dominicis valet iiij marc. et distat per iiij leucas. Decime garbarum capelle de Haselingdene valent xl s. Alteragium valet xl s. et distat per viij leucas.[3]

[1] This differs very materially from the Inquisition already given, of which the total amount was no less than ccxl. viis. The monks, in a short interval, had evidently contrived to procure a much lower valuation. It may be amusing to the reader to compare the respective values of the great tithes in several of these townships at two very distant periods.

	1298			1810		
	£	s.	d.	£	s.	d.
Read	4	0	0	38	0	0
Pendleton	6	0	0	49	14	0
Wiswall	6	0	0	62	11	0
Downham	5	0	0	50	0	0
Altham, deducting Alterage	7	0	0	65	0	0
Simonstone	2	0	0	20	0	0

On the whole, about a tenth of the present rate: yet, in 1289, the nearest point at which I can approach the year 1298, wheat sold for 6s. per quarter, and oats for 2s. Each of these sums might, in 1810, nearly be multiplied by 20. It follows that twice as much grain was grown in the parish of Whalley 600 years ago as at present. But at this time the rent of land was little more than 4*d*. per Lancashire acre. In 1812, upon an average, from 40*s*. to 50*s*. Such was the ancient advantage in favour of the tenant; and, for the same reason, little land in comparison was demised to tenants, and large demesnes were occupied by the owners.

[2] These distances prove the leuca to have been the old computed mile.

[3] To this is subjoined in a later hand—"S'mª estimaco'is veri valoris eccl'ie de Whall' c.xxxvii li." [Note on top margin of f. 100ᵇ.]

Hec sunt onera contingencia Abbatem et Conventum de Whalleye, nomine ecclesie de Whalleye. In sustentacione xx monachorum ultra solitum numerum. Item in x libris annuatim Capitulis ecclesiar. de Coventr. et Lych. Item ecclesie de Whalley in xls. pro procuracionibus. Item in iijs. pro Synod. In sustentacione vij capellanorum. Item in xxs. pro pane et vino. Nos Commissarii supradicti, considerata estimacione fructuum ecclesie et oneribus eidem incumbentibus, ac eciam ipsius ecclesie onera lata, diffusa, periculosa, de consilio domini Decani et Capitulorum [Coventr. et] Lych. ad ordinacionem vicarie in ecclesia de Whalleye predicta processimus in hunc modum:—

In Dei nomine amen. Ordinamus vicariam ecclesie de Whall(eye) debere consistere in manso competenti et xxx acris terre et prati adjacentibus, una cum housbote et haybote in bosco abbatis et conventus et communa sufficienti pro animalibus suis infra predictam parochiam et cum animalibus Abbatis et Conventus. Item in alteragio matricis ecclesie de Whall. et capellarum omnium eidem adjacentium, capella seu ecclesia de Alvetham duntaxat excepta, de qua ad presens propter litem super ea motam nichil duximus ordinandum. Item in terris de Brunleye, de Dounum et de Chirche. Item ordinamus dictos Abbatem et Conventum onus refectionis tocius cancelli et sustentacionis ejusdem, necnon duas partes omnium extraordinariorum onerum, Vicarium terciam partem et omnia onera ordinaria debere agnoscere. Hanc autem ordinacionem nostram perpetuo fore decrevimus valituram. Salva tamen patri predicto et successoribus suis potestate eam augendi, minuendi, et corrigendi, prout Deo acceptabile, et sibi processu temporis videbitur oportunum. Actis et datis Lych. die Veneris proximo ante Nativitatem b'e Marie Virginis Anno Domini supradicto. (Fol. 99 b—101.)

[The claims of the Archdeacon of Chester on the impropriation of the church of Whalley were satisfied by a pension of 100s., as related in the following documents:

Memorandum quod die Veneris in crastino Invencionis Sancte Crucis, Anno Domini M°CC° Nonog. sexto, apud Cliderowe in presencia discretorum virorum subscriptorum, inter Magistrum R. Archidiaconum Cestriensem et fratrem Gregorium Abbatem de Qualleg' et ejusdem loci Conventum expresse taliter fuit actum, videlicet cum idem Archidiaconus ab ipsis religiosis secundum formam obligacionis sue centum libras sterlingorum ratione indempnitatis Archidiaconatus sui pro appropriacione ecclesie de Qualleg' efficaciter petivisset, post altercationem super hoc habitam aliqualem remisit idem Archidiaconus exactionem totaliter hujusmodi pecunie que sibi virtute obligacionis eadem aliqualiter competebat, sub hac tamen condicione et forma quod iidem religiosi Archidiacono prefato et suis successoribus imperpetuum darent Centum Solidos annui redditus de proventibus ecclesie de Qualleg' predicte in festo sancti Egidii Abbatis, et hoc fideliter promiserunt se facturos cum omni securitate que per Archidiaconum vel suum consilium poterit provideri, hoc expresse adjecto quod cartam super hoc duplicatam sigillabunt, et nihilominus veniet Abbas in curiam domini Regis in cancellaria vel scaccario et factum istud pro se et suis successoribus personaliter recognoscet. Et hoc faciet cum super hoc per eundem Archidiaconum fuerit congrue requisitus. Et nihilominus coram loci diocesano hoc idem facient dicti religiosi per procuratorem sufficientem qui ad hoc potestatem habeat specialem. Convenit etiam quod facta securitate plena prout superius est notatum fiet eis restitucio litere obligatorie centum librarum. Et ad hoc fideliter observanda que dicti religiosi promiserunt prestiterunt juramentum corporalem Abbas predictus, fratres Umfredus et Ricardus de Rodiard commonachi dicte domus, fratre Johanne de Bellefeld dicte domus commonacho assistente et ibidem presente. Et hec acta fuerunt in presencia dominorum Will'i de Nunny, Thome de Fisschebourñ, J. de Hanleg', Henr' de Cumpton, et Will'i vicarii de Blakebourn, magistrorum Henrici de Clyton et Henrici de Dounum, Roberti de Hepehales, Thome le Surreys, Will'i de Alvetham, Ade Russel et multorum aliorum. In anno etc. sigilla partium presenti memorando alternatim sunt appensa. (Harl. MS. 3868, fol. 30 b, being part of the Register of the Abbey church of Lichfield.)

Obligacio pensionis C. Solidorum Archidiacono Cestrie de bonis Whalleye.

Universis sancte matris ecclesie filiis presentes litteras inspecturis vel eciam audituris Frater Gregorius Abbas loci Benedicti de Whallay et ejusdem loci conventus ordinis Cisterciensis salutem in Domino sempiternam. Attendentes dampna et incommoda varia que ex appropriacione ecclesie parochialis de Whallay auctoritate sedis Apostolice nobis facta poterunt processu temporis jurisdictioni archidiaconali et archidiaconis qui pro tempore fuerint imposterum pervenire, volentesque eorum indempnitati sicut convenerit prospicere plenius in hac parte, damus et concedimus pro nobis et successoribus nostris tenore presencium, Magistro Roberto de Radeswell nunc Archidiacono Cestrie et suis successoribus Archidiaconis ejusdem loci in perpetuum Centum solidos annui redditus bone et legalis monete solvendos eisdem vel eorum attornatis de proventibus et obvencionibus ecclesie de Whallay memorate in ecclesia sancti Johannis Cestrie die Egidii Abbatis [Sept. 1.] Ad quam solucionem ut premittitur futuris temporibus fideliter faciendam obligamus specialiter fructus proventus et obvenciones quascunque ecclesie predicte ita quod liceat loci archidiacono qui pro tempore fuerit vel ejus officiali ad solucionem dicte pecunie si in eadem vel ipsius parte defecerimus ecclesiam predictam supponere ecclesiastico interdicto et proventus ac obvenciones ipsius eo pretextu libere sequestrare, ac de eisdem sine quolibet obstaculo levare integraliter pecuniam memoratam. Et hujusmodi quidem donacionem et concessionem ac solucionem dicte pecunie suo termino ut premittitur absque omni dolo, cavilla commune et omni fraude bona fide promittemus pro nobis et successoribus nostris fideliter futuris temporibus in perpetuum servaturos, ac etiam nos facturos. In cujus rei testimonium sigillum nostrum unanimi consensu nostro presentibus est appensum. Hiis testibus: domino Witto de Nunny, Tħma de Fisseburn, Rob'to de Hepeshal, Will'o de Alvetham, dño Johe de Hanles, Tħma Surreys, magr̃o Henr. de Clayton et multis aliis. Dat. apud Whallay die dominica proxima post festum Invencionis Sancte Crucis. Anno Domini Millesimo ducentesimo nonogesimo sexto. [(6 May, 1296.) (Ibid. fol. 36.)]

[The petition of the Abbey of Whalley to the Archbishop of York for the appropriation of the church of Preston has been cited by Dr. Whitaker, in p. 91, as containing an estimate that the cost of their new buildings would exceed 3,000*l*. A copy of it now follows: it is undated, but must necessarily be earlier than 1356, when the church of Preston and five others were granted by Henry Duke of Lancaster to his college in the Newark at Leicester.[1]

Supplicatio.

Significant vestre paternitati reverende seduli oratores vestri C. Abbas et Conventus Monasterii Loci Benedicti de Whall. in com Lanc., Cisterciensis ordinis, Coventr. et Lich. dioc., quod terre possessiones et tenementa in Grangiis de Stanl. et Staneye in com. Cestr. prope maris fluxum situate et situata, ad prefatum Monasterium, Abbatem et Conventum ejusdem pertinentes et pertinentia pleno jure, per ejusdem maris impetun, cui non possunt resistere quovis modo, fuerunt et sunt Monasterio Abbati et Conventui supradictis irrecuperabiliter amisse et ablate, amissa etiam et ablata, ad valorem et dampnum cc marc. annui

[1] [See the charter in Nichols's *History of Leicestershire*, vol. i. Appx. p. 109. Dr. Whitaker, again referring to the present petition in his *History of Richmondshire*, ii. 425, remarks:—"Not long before that event (the grant to the college of Leicester) the abbot and convent of Whalley cast a longing eye upon this wealthy benefice, and presented a petition to the Duke of Lancaster for a donation of it; but, great as their interest then was with the descendant of their founder, the application did not succeed. A copy, however, of the supplication was carefully entered in the Coucher." But the petition is evidently addressed to the Archbishop of York. The petitioners state that the patronage and advowson of Preston already (*dudum*) belonged to them by the presentation and collation of Henry Earl of Lancaster. This *might* be the first Earl Henry, who died 1345; Henry his son was created Duke in 1351.]

redditus et profectus. Nonnulle insuper terre possessiones et tenementa eorundem infra com. Cestr. predictum in locis de Acton, de Aston, de Bacford', de Winlnton, de Cestr' et de Norwico tamen propter locorum et personarum distanciam, tum propter alias locorum eorundem temporumque importunitates maximas et inevitabiles, tot et tantis dispendiis jugiter exponuntur, quod Monasterio Abbati et conventui supradictis omnino fere sunt steriles et inutiles: nec eisdem profectui solito cedunt, set potius cotidianis oneribus atque dampnis. Nonnulli etiam redditus et proventus eorundem Monasterii, Abbatisque et Conventus per assiduas quorundam malefactorum infestationes infra Com. predictum, quibus nullo modo poterunt obviare, eisdem Abbati et Monachis nunc ad tempus, nunc imperpetuum ad dampnum cc libr. annis singulis detinentur. Monasterium etiam de Whalleye supradictum tam in fabrica ipsius ecclesie, quam in dormitorio, refectorio, claustro capitulari et quibuscunque aliis domibus et officinis tanto et tali Monasterio necessariis competentibus semper fuit et adhuc est de toto noviter construendum, et quacunque competenti structura miserabiliter destitutum. Ad cujusmodi edificiorum necessarios et rationabiles sumptus tria Millia librarum sufficere non valebunt: necnon in hospitalitate et aliis diversis oneribus, eo quod in solo sterili et vasto situatum est, a diu fuit et adhuc est ultra vires ejusdem tam importabiliter oneratum, quod ad sustentacionem LX Monachorum, qui in dicto Monasterio secundum primariam fundacionem ejusdem Deo et beate Marie die et nocte jugiter famulantur, et debent annuente Domino imperpetuum famulari, et ad fabricam ipsius ecclesie, dormitorii, refectorii, claustrique capitularis et aliarum domorum prefato Monasterio et personis ejusdem competenter necessarie facienda, hospitalitatemque et alia onera eidem Monasterio et personis ejusdem incumbentia supportanda, Monasterio Abbati et Conventui supradictis, absque magno subsidio extrinsecus adhibendo, proprie non suppetunt facultates, set prefatum Monasterium et fabrica ecclesie ipsius et aliarum domorum absque competentibus reparacione et structura, prefatique Abbas et Monachi absque victualibus et aliis necessariis competentibus in scandalum totius ordinis verisimiliter imperpetuum remanebunt: nisi de magno et competenti suffragio eisdem celerius succuratur. Quare supplicant eidem paternitati vestre humiliter et devote, quatinus parochialem ecclesiam de Preston in Amoundernesse vestre Ebor' diocesis in Archidiaconatu Richemundie, dudum ad presentacionem et collacionem nobilis viri domini Henrici Comitis Lancastrie spectantem, cujus patronatum et advocacionem iidem Religiosi viri eis et eorum Monasterio jure perpetuo auctoritate sufficiente in hac parte canonice possidendam ex collacione dicti domini Comitis, quantum pertinet ad laicalem donacionem, legitime sunt adepti, cujus etiam fructus, redditus et proventus annui, secundum taxacionem decime . . . li. valorem annuum non excedunt, eis et eorum Monasterio de Whall. supradicto unire canonice et in usus proprios imperpetuo assignare dignemini intuitu caritatis. Salvo tamen pro perpetuo vicario in eadem ecclesia ad eorundem presentacionem per vos instituendo et etiam servituro congrua porcione quam ad XX li. sterlingorum de eisdem Religiosis viris per eundem vicarium annuatim percipiendo, taxare dignemini in pecunia numerata, non obstante quod vos ipsi venerabilis pater, seu Capitulum vestrum Ebor., aut loci Archidiaconus, dictos fructus, redditus vel proventus in eadem ecclesia tempore vacacionis ejusdem percipere consuevistis, et cum aliis non obstantiis et clausulis oportunis.] (Fol. 17.)

The following is a grant of a corrody to the De la Leghs of Hapton.

Copia scripti G. de Legh et Joh. fil. sui.

Noverint universi per presentes quod Nos Frat. G. Abbas Loci Benedicti de Stanlawe et ejusdem domus Conventus tenemur et hoc scripto nostro obligamur ad inveniend. Gilberto de la Legh et Johanni filio et heredi suo, vel alteri eorum diucius superstiti, qualibet septimana octo panes conventuales et totidem lagenas cervicie conventualis vel xij denar. et pro garc. suo xiiij panes de Cret. per septim. vel duos denarios. Item ad festum Sancti Martini in hyeme duo corpora boum vel dimidiam marcam, duos porcos vel xl denar. et quatuor corpora arietum vel duos solidos et octo denar. Recipient autem annuatim dicti Gilbertus et Johannes filius ejus, vel alter eorum diucius superstes seu eorum nuncius, hec omnia apud Whall. vel Blak. si maluerint, a nobis vel successoribus nostris, vel a monachis nostris locum nostrum ibidem tenentibus, in prescriptis porcionibus vel pecunia si maluerint pretaxata[1] ad festa Sancti Michaelis et Pasche pro equalibus porcionibus persolvenda. Ad que omnia fideliter observanda obligamus nos et successores nostros et omnia bona nostra in Blakeburnshir' districtioni Ballivoř domini Com̃ vel cujuscunque domini feodi ejusdem ut liceat eisdem nos distringere per dicta bona nostra ad observacionem omnium premissorum. Pro hac autem liberacione habenda nominatus Gilbertus pro se et filio suo dedit nobis quandam summam pecunie in usos nostros et domus nostre commissam pre manibus. In cujus rei testimonium presentibus literis sigillum nostrum commune est appensum. Hiis testibus: Symone Noel, Rogero fratre suo, Willmo. de Heskayth, Olivero de Stansfeld, Magistro[2] Henr' de Clayton, Magistro Henr' de Dounom, Ricardo de Ruysheton, Roberto de eadem, Ada de Aspeden, Johanne filio Symonis de Reued. Dat. apud Locum Benedictum de Stanlawe die dominica proximo post festum Sancti Barnabe Ap̃li, Anno Domini M°cc° Nonagesimo Quinto. (Fol. 6.)

Istud prenotatum scriptum Dominus Helias Abbas, successor predicti Domini Gregorii Abbatis, confirmavit per quoddam novum scriptum cum sigillo communi domus. De quibus quidem scriptis Gilbertus de Legh fecit nobis quietamclamacionem. Post mortem vero dicti G. Johannes filius ejus portavit brevem domini Regis ad placitandum nos de predicta liberacione coram Justiciariis assignatis ad sedendum de diversis querelis et placitis apud Laucastriam. Set quia dicti Justiciarii non venerunt, idem Johannes placitavit nos de eadem liberacione in Curia de Cliderhou per quandam cedulam in hec verba: Johannes de la Legh querit de . . Abbate et Conventu de Whalleye de placito injuste detencionis panis, cervisie, carcosium boum, porcorum, et arietum. Plegium de presente, Gilbertus de Legh. Quod quidem placitum in eadem Curia per dilaciones secundum consuetudinem patrie usitatas per aliquod spatium temporis remansit. Tandem capto die amoris inter nos et eundum Johannem sub hac forma amicabiliter conquievit, videlicet quod predictus Johannes remisit liberacionem pro garcione suo, duo corpora boum duos porcos et quatuor corpora arietum que in festo Sancti Martini debuit percepisse vel pecuniam pro eisdem rebus, videlicet xxi s. et iiii°r denar. et retraxit placitum de Curia supradicta, reddiditque nobis vetera scripta de liberacione sua quorum primum scribitur supra ex altera parte folii de verbo ad verbum. Et nos eidem Johanni fecimus quoddam novum scriptum de liberacione panis et cervisie in hec verba:

Pateat universis per presentes quod nos frater Robertus Abbas Monasterii Loci Benedicti de Whalleye et ejusdem loci Conventus concessimus Johanni filio Gilberti de la Legh unum corrodium videlicet octo panes conventuales et octo lagenas cervisie conventualis de Cellario dicti Mon. nostri de W. qualibet septimana ad totam vitam ipsius Johannis per visum nuncii sui percipiendas. Et concedimus quod predictus Johannes dictum corrodium capiat pro quindena simul quando voluerit. Ad hoc ut predictum est fideliter faciendum obligavimus nos et successores nostros et Manerium nostrum de Bilyngton in Blakeburnshire, ad quorumcunque manus devenerit. Ita videlicet quod quandocunque predictum corrodium a retro fuerit in parte vel in toto, tunc bene liceat dicto Johanni per totam vitam suam in predicto Manerio de Bilyngton distringere et districcionem quam ea occasione fecerit retinere quousque de predicto corrodio plenarius sibi fuerit satisfactum. In cujus rei testimonium sigillum nostrum commune presentibus apposuimus. Datum in supradicto Monasterio nostro de Whalleye die Veneris proximo post festum sancti Gregorii Pape anno regni Regis Edwardi tertii post conquestum xiiii^{mo}. (Friday, 17th March, 1340.)

Et sic retrahuntur de antiqua liberacione xxj s. et iiij d. annuatim ut superius est expressum. (Fol. 6b.)

Memo^{m} quòd Gilbertus de Legh senior dixit Priori et Cell. de Whalleye et prelibatis monachis dc̃e domus, parum ante Natł̃e Anno Domini M°ccc°xxxvi, apud Whalleye, tunc existens in camera Domini Elie quondam Abbatis dc̃e domus, quòd dimisit in festo Inventionis Sc̃e Crucis ultimo preterito Gilberto fil. Joh' de Legh filii sui, tot equas gravidas cum fetibus, ut duo pulli ad minus dari deberent ad decimam. Et tot vaccas cum vitulis, ut quinque vituli ad minus dari deberent ad decimam. Dimisit etiam eidem oves matrices

[1] [*Prætaxare, i.e.* prius numerare, assignare.]

[2] What were these *Magistri?* Clearly not Knights, as they follow persons without title.

cum aliis bidentibus ccxl. Agnos lx. Inde decima: sex. Quatuor sues porcantes. Ideo petantur de eodem Gilberto Juniore pro decimâ duo pulli, quinque stirci, et vellera lane xxviij. et agni sex, et tres porci, et decima[1] albi pro vaccis et ovibus matribus. (Fol. 1 b.)

[The terms of some other corrodies are not less curious.

Pateat universis, etc. nos frater Gregorius Abbas Loci Benedicti de Stanlaw et ejusdem loci Conventus etc. dedimus domino Wil. de Burton capellano caritatis intuitu et pro consilio fideli ipsius in omnibus habendo fraternitatem ordinis nostri et a tempore confeccionis presentium quoad vixerit in domo nostra honestum hospitium cum sufficienti focali et qualibet hebdomada ad opus suum decem panes conventuales et septem lagenas cervisie conventualis: Inde adventu vero et quadragesima et tribus diebus in septimana reliquis temporibus piscem sicut uni monacho de conventu, et per annum quemlibet unum carcosium bovis et dimidium ad precium sex solidorum, bacones duos vel quatuor solidos, duo carcosia ovium vel duos solidos, duas petras de casco et duas de buttiri et garcioni suo per quamlibet septimanam panes de cret' viginti unum et de cervisia secunda tres lagenas et dimidiam, et diebus piscium piscem sicut uni de garcionibus Abbatis. Preterea dedimus domino Will'o foragium et pasturam pro hyeme et estate ad 24 oves cum ovibus nostris, et ad quatuor averia cum averiis nostris in pastura meliori ubi oves nostre pasturant et averia. Hec omnia nos inventuros dicto d'no Will' pro toto tempore vite sue bona fide compromisimus et obligamus dum sibi in domo nostra placuerit habitare, quamdiu vero alibi manserit panem et cervisiam tantam ut prescriptum est percipiat vel de aliis exigend'. In cujus rei testimonium, &c. (Harl. MS. 2064, f. 77*b*.)

Omnibus ad quos presens scriptum etc. frater Gregorius dictus Abbas Loci Benedicti de Stanlaw et ejusdem Loci Conventus salutem etc. Nos concessisse Gilberto de Rushton et Eve uxori sue seu alteri eorum diutius superstiti septem panes et septem lagenas cervisie conventualis in qualibet septimana recipiendas apud Whalley solend' eisdem vel eorum certo nuncio vel eorum alteri diutius superstiti et duo carcosia bovina pretium amborum dimid' marc' et duo carcosia porcina pretium amborum 40[d] et quatuor carcosia ovina pretium omnium 32[d] recipiend' quolibet anno apud Whalley in festo sancti Martini in hyeme. Item duas petras casei et duas petras butiri recipiendas ad eundem locum in festo sancti Egidii. Ad istam autem convencionem bene et fideliter faciendam obligamus nos et successores nostros et omnia bona nostra in Blakeburnshire existentia discretioni et potestati Ballivorum domini ejusdem feodi et liceat eisdem nos distringere per omnia bona nostra tam ad observacionem convencionis principalis quam refusionem dampnorum et expensarum si que vel quas incurrerint ratione desertus nostri vel occasione convencionis non servate. In cujus rei, etc. (Harl. MS. 2064, fol. 77 b.)

The next was granted in return for 40 marks to William Le Mercer de Stanlaw, who was to live in the abbey or in the town of Whalley as he pleased.

Pateat universis etc. frater Gregorius abbas Loci Benedicti de Whalley et ejusdem loci Conventus concessimus, etc. Willo le Mercer dicto de Stanlaw per totum terminum vite sue novem panes conventuales et quatuordecim panes de creit, novem lagenas melioris cervisie conventualis, et quatuor lagenas secunde cervisie percipiendas singulis septimanis in cellario conventuali per se vel per suum attornatum de nobis et successoribus nostris in domo de Whalley predicta vel Stanlaw in quocunque conventus extiterit. Item duo corpora bovina precii octo solid' et quatuor porcos ejusdem precii, tres petras buttiri et tres petras casei ac dimid' mibar allectis conventualis percipiendos per singulos annos in festo sancti Martini in hyeme toto termino vite sue et loco superius memorato; licebit etiam eidem Willo prescriptam annonam cariare vel asportare ac suam per omnia voluntatem facere de eadem absque contradiccione vel retinemento. Et si predictus Will extra Abbatiam in villa de Whalley habitare voluerit providebimus eidem competentem mansionem

[1] That is, the Easter dues: a proof of the antiquity of the Easter Roll.

cum communibus aysiamentis liberam ab omni servitio nos contingente vel ad nos pertinente dabimusque sibi vel suo attornato cum annona superius distincta tres bigatas feni per singulos annos et in tempore herbagii herbagium uni equo sufficiens; si vero intra Abbatiam maluerit habitare providebimus eidem locum competentem et focale sufficiens cum herbagio et feno quantum sufficit ad sustentacionem unius equi; predictis bigatis feni nobis interim reservatis. Pro hac autem concessione dedit nobis prefatus Witt pre manibus quadraginta marcas bonorum et legalium sterlingorum, de quibus nos profitemur bene fore pacatos. In cujus rei, etc. (Harl. MS. 2064, fol. 81 b.)

Obligation of 1,000 marks to the Bishop of Lichfield, to be paid by half-yearly instalments of 100 marks; and his release.

Universis sancte matris ecclesie filiis ad quos presentes littere pervenerint Fr. G[regorius] Abbas monasterii de W. et ejusdem loci Conventus salutem in Domino. Noveritis nos teneri venerabili patri domino W[altero] de L[angton] Dei gratia C[ovent.] et L[ichf.] episcopo in M. marc' argentis, solvendis eidem Domino vel suo certo attornato terminis subscriptis, in crastino clausi Pasche proximo sequente c. marc' et in festo sancti M. proximo sequente c. marc' et sic eisdem terminis de anno in annum cc. marc' dicto domino [W.] Episcopo solvend' donec eidem domino Episcopo de predictis M. marc' plenarie fuerit satisfactum. Et ad predictam solucionem predictis terminis de anno in annum ut premittitur dicto domino [W.] Episcopo fideliter faciendam obligamus nos et successores nostros et omnia bona nostra mobilia et immobilia dicto domino Episcopo, subicientes nos et successores nostros jurisdictioni et cohercioni cujuscunque judicis ecclesiastici aut secularis quem idem dominus Episcopus duxerit eligendum, ad compellendum et cohercendum tam nos quam successores nostros ad observacionem omnium premissorum absque omni placito et juris solempnitate nullo excepcionis beneficio nobis quo ad id aut nostris successoribus valituro, quotienscunque et quandocunque idem judex ex parte dicti domini Episcopi fuerit requisitus. Renunciantes quoque omni beneficio et remedio tam facti quam juris per quod predicta solucio impediri valeat quomodolibet seu differri. In cujus rei testimonio, etc. Dat. etc. (Addit. MS. 10,374, fol. 66 b.)

Omnibus has litteras visuris vel audituris W[alterus] Dei gracia C. et L. Episcopus salutem in Domino. Cum G. Abbas de W. et ejusdem loci Conventus nobis teneretur in M. marcis per scriptum suum obligatorium: Noveritis nos recepisse et habuisse de eodem [G.] Abbate predictas M. marcas. Et volumus quod dictum scriptum obligatorium vacuum sit et irritum in cujuscunque manus fuerit inventum. In cujus. Dat. anno. (Ibid. fol. 73.)

Grant of a life annuity of 5*l*.

Pateat universis per presentes quod nos , . Abbas et Conventus Loci Benedicti de W. tenemur dilecto nobis in Christo R. de H. in *cs.* sterlingorum pro fideli servicio et auxilio suo nobis et nostris impenso et imposterum impendendo cum de eo necesse habuerimus Solvendos eidem R. de camera nostra annuatim apud W. toto tempore vite sue, videlicet ad Nativitatem Sancti Johannis Baptiste et ad Nativitatem Domini per equas porciones. In cujus rei, &c. Dat. etc. (Ibid. fol. 66.)

Roger de Meuland, the bishop of Lichfield and Coventry (who has been already named in p. 80), died in 1295 a creditor of the abbey to the amount of 200 marks. This sum was remitted by his executors, on condition of the monks undertaking to observe a commemoration of his death on the 16th December for ever:

Pateat universis ad quos pervenerit hec scriptura quod nos frater Gregorius Abbas de Whalleya et ejusdem loci Conventus, ordinis Cisterciensis, Coventrensis diocesis, ad beneficia que venerabilis pater Rogerus de Meuland quondam Coventrensis et Lichfeldensis episcopus nobis et monasterio nostro multipliciter contulit dum vivebat nostre consideracionis aciem convertentes, illud etiam sincere mentis affectu pensantes quod executores ejusdem patris post mortem ipsius nobis de quodam debito in quo eidem tenebamur dum vixerat, Ducentas marcas liberaliter remisissent. Volentesque eidem patri per orationem necnon suffragia et alia caritatis opera cum ad presens aliis non indigeat vices rependere debitas ut tenemur, Volumus et fideliter concedimus ac pro nobis et successoribus nostris imperpetuum bona fide promittimus per presentes quod annis singulis videlicet septimo decimo kal. Januarii anniversarium obitus sui diem tempore perpetuo observari in nostro monasterio et celebrari faciemus sicut unquam ibidem pro aliquo episcopo fieri consuevit. Ita quod omnes et singuli monachi nostri monasterii in sacerdocio constituti missam pro anima ejusdem patris et animabus omnium fide Domini defunctorum eodem die specialiter celebrabunt. Et si aliqui ex causis legitimis prepediti celebrare nequeant eo die tunc teneantur infra octo dies ante diem illum vel infra octo continue post ea illud fideliter adimplere. Et ad perpetuam hujus nostre gratuite permissionis et oblacionis memoriam et ut id nostrorum successorum auribus imperpetuum inculcetur hanc nostram promissionis litteram de verbo ad verbum in nostro Martirologio inseri fecimus que similiter penes executores dicti patris residet nostri sigilli munimine roborata. Dat. et Act. in capitulo nostro apud Whall Idus Junii anno Domini M° cc° Nonog° Nono (13 June 1299.) (Harl. MS. 3868, fol. 36 b. being f. 310 b. of the Register of Lichfield.)]

The following is a statement of a case for the consideration of lawyers. The intermixture of lands in the Forest of Bowland, between the parishes of Whalley and Slaydburne, is extremely difficult to be accounted for, and is scarcely understood to the present day.

Capella Sancti Michaelis in Castro de Cliderhou, infra fines et limites parochie ecclesie de Whall. Coventr. et Lich. dioc. notorie situata à centum annis elapsis et amplius, at ante omne tempus humane memorie vel prescripcionis, dotata fuit per assignacionem dominorum de Blakeburnschire et Bouland de decimacionibus et aliis proventibus ecclesiasticis omnium dominicarum terrarum suarum infra dicta loca de Blakeburnschire, qui est in dicta dioc. Coventr' et Lich., et Bouland, qui est in dioc. et provincia Ebor. Juxta quam assignacionem clerici et capellani eidem capelle per collacionem sive assignacionem decanorum de Whall. dictorum dominorum incumbentes decimaciones et proventus predictos tam in Blak. quam in Bouland ut premissum est per tempus eandem pacifice possidebant. Infra dictum autem Dominium de Bouland dicte Ebor. dioc. est quedam ecclesia parochialis videlicet ecclesia de Slayteburn ejusdem Ebor. dioc. juxta et infra cujus fines sunt quedam terre dominice dicti dominii de Bouland, de quarum decimacionibus et proventibus dicta capella dotata fuerat ut premittitur, et ejusdem capelle ac matricis ecclesie de Whalleye Rectores easdem decimaciones virtute dotationis, assignacionis et possessionis ejusmodi pacifice per omnia possidebant usque ad tempus cujusdam Rectoris dicte ecclesie de Slayteburn jam incumbentis, qui xx et v annis duntaxat jam elapsis quasdam terras dominicales infra fines parochie sue predicte ad firmam cepit, et in persona propria occupavit, ut decimaciones dictarum terrarum ecclesie sue predicte de Slayteburne appropriaret, et à dictis capella de Clid. et ecclesia de Whalleya ac earundem Rectoribus per cautelam hujusmodi detinerit. Decimaciones tum quorundam aliorum dictorum dominicalium infra fines et limites dicta pochie de Slayteburn consimiliter existentes dimittit idem Rector dicte ecclesie de Whall. et capelle de Cliderhou liberas, prout antea fuerant, et quietas ab omnimoda impetitione sui et suorum.

Abbas igitur et Conventus de Whall. dictam ecclesiam parochialem de Whall. cum prefata capella beati Michaelis in Castro de Cliderhou, et cum omnibus aliis juribus et pertinenticiis eorundem in usus proprios optinentes, decimaciones dictarum terrarum dominicalium in Bouland quas dictus Rector occupavit per antea ut est dictum, tanquam jus dictarum suarum ecclesie de Whall. et capelle de Clid. dudum repetentes, tandem de expresso consensu dicti Rectoris fecerunt dictas decimas extra custodiam et possessionem utriusque partis penes Sen. de Bouland reponi duobus annis jam elapsis, neutri parti liberandas donec per viam et processum juris vel amicabilis compositionis fuerit definitum cujus parti de communi consensu debeant finaliter liberari.

Et quum Dominus Archiepiscopus Ebor. dictas partes Boulandie ut dicitur in proximo visitabit, et verisimiliter estimatur quod dictus Rector de Slayteburn coram dicto Archiepiscopo in suâ visitacione contra prefatos Abbatem et Conventum super jure suo de predictis decimacionibus infra limites sue parochie ut premittitur provenientibus movebit litem, specialiterque quod Ar[l]ep̃s eidem Rectori pro amplianda jurisdictione sua plus justo favebit: Ideirco dicti Abbas et Conventus circa omnia per suum procuratorem provocationem quandam et appellationem ad Cur. Romanam directa et ad Cur. Cantuar. tuitor' fecerunt, ut moris est, interponi.

1°. Queratur igitur à jurisperitis an, cum dc̃o ecclesia de Whall. et capella de Clid. notorie situate sint infra Dioc. Coventr. et Lich. et sint de jurisdictione ordinaria Archidiaconi Cestr. et Episcopi Coventr. et Lich., teneatur Abbas de Whalleye, racione decimacionum quas percipit infra limites provincie Ebor. nomine dictarum suarum ecclesie et capelle, coram dicto Domino Archiepiscopo comparere, exhibiturum vel allegaturum titulum percepcionis dictarum decimacionum, cum dictus Abbas jurisdictioni dicti Archiepiscopi aliunde nullatenus sit subjectus.

Q°. 2. Item queratur, quid et qualiter allegari debeat coram illo, cum dictus Abbas nihil habeat exhibend. nisi possessionem prescript. ab antiquo.

Q°. 3. Item queratur, si dictus Archiep̃us sequestrum interponat in dictis decimacionibus, vel eas adjudicet ecclesie de Slayteburn, dicto Abbate non vocato vel non obtemperante suis mandatis, quid vel qualiter sit agendum.

Q°. 4. Item queratur, an dicta causa per appellacion' tuitor' possit in eventum ad Curiam Cantuar' devolvi et ibidem ulterius agitari.

De capella Castri de Cliderhow queratur plus in secundo folio proximo ubi scribitur, Petrus de Cestr' quondam Rector ecclesie parochialis de Whalleye, *etc.* (Addit. MS. 10,374, fol. 6 b—7 b.)

Memorandum de munimentis Abbatis et Conventus de Whalleye, que Magister Rogerus de Motelowe habuit secum versus Curiam Romanam: videlicet quatuor Bullas, unam scilicet generalem Alexandri pape de omnibus rebus et tenementis pro tempore suo spectantibus ad Mon. de Whalleye, confirmatam. Item aliam Bullam Bonifacii octavi de appropriatione Ecclesie de Whalleye, et de translatione Couventus. Item terciam Bullam de ordinacione vicariarum de Blakeburn, Rachedal, et Eccles. Item quartam bullam de confirmacione ordinationis vicariarum. Item ordinacionem Domini Rogeri Conventr. et Lich. Episcopi, super Vicaria de Whalleye. Item habuit copias relaxationum de pensionibus Capitulorum Coventr. et Lich. et Archidiac. Cestr. sub signo Notarii puppliei. (Fol. 27 b.)

This appears to have been when the abbot and convent were soliciting a confirmation of the second endowment of the vicarage at the Court of Rome.

Next in the MS., though out of chronological order, is the curious renunciation of the right of hunting within the forests, by Gregory the first Abbot.

Copia quiete clamacionis venacionis Ecclesie de Whalley.

Omnibus ad quos presens scriptum pervenerit, frater Gregorius Abbas Loci Benedicti de Stanlowe et ejusdem loci Convent. salt̃ in Domino. Quum nobilis vir Dominus Henr. de Lacy Com. Linc. dederit et concesserit nobis et successoribus nostris Ecclesiam de Whalleye in proprios usus in perpetuum tenendam, licet quidam Rectores quondam ecclesie predicte jus fugandi et feras capiendi infra forestas predicti Comitis se vendicaverint habere, ut de jure ecclesie predicte de Whalleye: Nos pro nobis et successoribus nostris remisimus et in perpetuum quieteclamavimus totum jus et clameum quod habuimus seu aliquo modo habere poterimus fugandi seu feras capiendi infra forestas predicti Comitis, vel heredum suorum, seu infra aliquem locum qui ad forestam vel ad chaceam pertineat; Ita quod nec nos nec successores nostri de cetero aliquod jus vel clameum fugandi vel aliquod aliud capiendi infra forestas vel chaceas predicti Comitis, vel heredum suorum, seu infra aliquem locum qui ad forestam vel chaceam pertineat ratione predicte ecclesie de Whalleye, exigere vel vendicare poterimus. In cujus rei testimonium huic scripto sigillum nostrum commune apposuimus. Hiis testibus: domino Roberto filio Rogeri, Willielmo le Vavasour, Johanne de Hodel, Roberto de Herteford, Jac. de Neville, Roberto de Schirburn, Johanne Spring, &c. Dat. ap. Stanlawe, Anno Domini Mcclxxxxiiii. (Fol. 27 b.)

The following instrument is a deed of sale of a slave and his family.

Omnibus, &c. Gregorius Abbas et Conventus loci bn. de W. sal'm. Noveritis nos, pro nobis et singulis successoribus nostris, dedisse, concessisse, et tradidisse dilecto nobis in Christo I. G. et assignatis suis R. fil. I. fil. A. de W. nativum nostrum cum tota sequela sua, et omnibus rebus suis habitis et habendis, pro centum solidis sterlingorum nobis a predicto Johanne traditis et solutis; Ita quod predictus R. cum tota sequela sua et omnibus rebus suis ut prediet. est, liberi sint, soluti et quieti ab omni calumpnia, seu qualibet vexatione n'ri vel successor' n'ror' d'etor' imppetuum. Ita quod nec nos nec successores nostri aliquid juris vel clamei in predictis ratione nativitatis de cetero quomodo poterimus vendicare. Salvo tamen jure nostro et calumpnia nostra versus quoscunque alios nativos nostros. In cujus rei testimonium huic carte nostre, quam ad majorem securitatem fecimus indentari, tam nos quam predictus I sigilla nostra mutuo apposuimus. (Fol. 62 b.)

[Among the *Littere multiplices et private* the following occur:]

Universis ad quos presentes littere pervenerint Fr.   dictus Abbas de S. salutem in Domino. Licet nuper ad instanciam domini Abbatis de C. in visitatione sua apud W. ad quandam cedulam articulos quosdam contra Abbatem dicti Loci editos continentem sigillum nostrum apposuerimus, non tam eo animo hec fecimus ut testaremur ipsos articulos omnino veros esse, aut per hoc factum nostrum dĉo Abbati respondendi pro statu suo via precluderetur, quin potius testificavimus per presentes quòd cum sepedicto Abbati de W. a dicto patre . . . Abbate suo si gratis cedet curialitas camere, et alia humanitatis solacia coram nobis liberaliter offerentur, et ipse de hiis non curaret, asseruit nichilominus plena voce libentissime se cessurum, nihil de hiis curialitatibus affectando, si ammotis quatuor aut quinque accusatoribus suis, quorum quidam infames erant et notorie defamati, tota reliqua communitas conventus sui seu pars sanior coram domino . . . . Abbate de H. qui tunc aderat et nobis singillatim seu in communi, privatim vel publice, modo debito requisita mallet vel dignius esse diceret ipsum cedere quam dicimus inter ipsos auctoritate regiminis presidere, ad quod prefatus pater Abbas penitus non consensit. In cujus etc. Dat. etc. (Fol. 129.)

Venerabili Patri suo in Christo et cum omni reverentia nominando domino A. Abbati de C.[1] suorum minimus Fr. G. vocatus Abbas de W. cum debita subjectione salutem. Equum qualem petitis libentissime misissemus, si facultas respondisset voluntati. Super hoc sufficienter excusare nos poterit lator presentium, si hiis que vidit velit veraciter testimonium perhibere. Ceterum mala nobis facta causa vestri non meminimus, aut debere fieri scienter meruimus, nec ad nos spectat bonor' vestrorum taxacio que Deus multiplicet et augmentet, angustiati tum fuimus graviter nos et omnes nostri pro ratâ contribucionis nobis impositâ anno preterito et gravius anno isto, quia, si illi benevoli estimatores bonorum nostrorum ecclesiasticorum debita que incurrimus et sumptus quos fecimus pro eisdem appenderent equâ lance, non preponderaret pars nostra tam largiter quam loquuntur. Quia revera Ecclesia de W. quam forsitan exaggerant in immensum subductis expensis quas causâ ejusdem fecimus, et Vicarii porcione non multum de claro huc usque rece-

[1] Cumbermere. It was very ungracious in the Abbot of this house to beg a horse from his brother of Whalley whom he appears to have been at that very time oppressing by an unjust taxation.

pimus, nec forte recipiemus per quinquennium proxime secuturum. Si igitur justum sit coram Deo et ordine tam pro non habitis, quâm habitis, nos taxari, vos videritis. Valeat vestra sancta Paternitas semper in Dno. (Fol. 129.)

Venerabili patri et cum omni reverentia nominando domino . . Abbati Savign'. sui semper humiles et devoti in Christo filii Fr. G. vocatus Abbas de W. et ejusdem loci conventus cum debita subjectione salutem. Quum ratione appropriationis Ecclesie de W. nobis nuper facte videtur nonnullis onera circumstancia non pensantibus nostra possessio non minimum excreuisse, et ideo in contributionibus ordinis summam nobis impositam ultra solitum augeri multum de jure debere. Ideo verum valorem dicte ecclesie prout ex singulis particulis que nos contingunt elici potuit bona fide et sana conscientia vobis in scriptis transmittimus, notantes nichilominus aliqua de oneribus e diverso, ut pensatis que rite pensanda sunt, quodlibet de claro nobis accrescat ratione cujus rata nostra super antiquam consuetudinem debeat augmentari advertere possit vestra discretio, et secundum hec venerabili patri nostro de C. mandare dignemini ut manum suam temperet in taxando. Valeat vestra Reverenda Paternitas semper in Dno IHU XRO. *Cauda,* Dno Venerabili Abbati de Savign', per suum de Whalley.

[Sic fuit valor ecclesie de Wh. estimatus et Abbati Savign' destinatus quantum pertinet ad abb. et con.

Vendicio garbarum vel valor. De villa de Whall. v*li.* xiii*s.* iiii*d.* De Hennethorne et Mitton lxvi*s.* viii*d.* De Wysewalle, vi*li.* xiii*s.* iiii*d.* De Penilton parva et magna, v*li.* De Merleye parva et magna, lxvi*s.* viii*d.* De Cliderhowe, xiii*li.* vi*s.* viii*d.* De Worcheston, l*s.* De Chatteburn, xl*s.* De Dounum viii*li.* De Twiselton, xxx*s.* De Reued, iii*li.* De Simundeston, iiii*li.* De Whitacre, xxx*s.* De Padiam, v*li.* De Hapton, vi*li.* De Briddestwisel, xxvi*s.* viii*d.* De Aluetham, vi*li.* De Clayton, xl*s.* De Acrington, xl*s.* De Chirche, xl*s.* De Oswaldestwisel, lxvi*s.* viii*d.* De Duceworth, xx*s.* De Honecote, iiii*li.* De Haselingden, lx*s.* De garbis capelle de Brunleya, xxiiii*li.* De garbis capelle de Caune, xv*li.*

Summa omnium garbarum—c.xxxvi*li.* x*s.*

Rec. Firmarum De Whall. x*li.* De Caune, ix*s.* De Haselingden, iii*s.* iiii*d.* De Cliderhowe, iiii*s.* iiii*d.* De Aluetham, xiii*s.* iiii*d.* De Reued, xviii*d.* De Briddestwisel, vi*d.* De Molend. lxvi*s.* viii*d.* De Dominicis, liii*s.* iiii*d.*

Summa omnium Firmarum—xvii*li.* xii*s.*
Summa tocius red'.—c.liiii*li.* ii*s.*]

Sic eidem Abbati de S. onera incumbentia monstrabantur.

Ad sustentacionem xx Monachorum lxvi*li.* xiiii*s.* iiii*d.* videlicet cujuslibet v marc'. per annum.

Capitulis Coventrens' et Lich. et Archidiacono xv*l.* annuatim.[1]

Ecclie de Blak. xlv*s.* v*d.* annuatim.

Pro decimis congregandis, cariandis et domibus conducendis, x*l.* annuatim.

In extraordinariis, utpote regiis exactionibus, cardinalium, nunciorum domini pape procuracionibus, denar' Mercedalibus vel libralibus, et hiis: secundum casum.

Itm edificatio sive constructio nove Abbie.

Indebitatur Domus ratione dicte ecclie, utpote Episcopo jam defuncto in c*li.* solutum.

Episcopo succedenti et Domini Regis Thesaurario in M. marcis solutum.

Simoni de Alvetham pro resignatione juris sui, si quod habuit, in capella de Alvetham, in xx*li.* solutum.

Pro expensis factis circa dictam ecclesiam in Curia Romanâ, regiâ, Cantuar' et Consistor' Lich. ccc*li* solutum.

Sma omnium onerum preter ea secundum casum, iiiixxxiii*li.* xix*s.* ix*d.* annuatim.

[1] *Annuatim* and *solutum* are written throughout in a smaller hand.

Universis pateat per presentes quod cum nobis fratri N dicto abbati de T. per venerabilem in Christo patrem dominum [J.] Abbatem Savign' facta fuerit commissio que sequitur in hec verba: UNIVERSIS presentes litteras inspecturis frater Johannes dictus Abbas Savign' salutem in Domino. Notum facimus quod anno Domini M°CCC° octavodecimo tempore generalis capituli facta fuit diffinitio que sequitur in hec verba: QUERIMONIA abbatis de Whall. qui conqueritur de patre abbate suo de Cumbermar' eo quod nimis taxavit eum de contributione committit generale capitulum priori . . . Abbati de Savign' per se vel alium ut inquirat super hoc diligencius veritatem, et inde faciat quod justicia suadebit. Et quia pluribus aliis negociis prepediti ad dictam terram personaliter non possumus accedere, dilecto et fideli coabbati nostro de T. committimus vices nostras, quod super hoc secundum tenorem dicte diffinicionis veritatem inquirat, et inde faciat quod sibi justicia suadebit. In cujus rei testimonium sigillum nostrum unicum quo utimur litteris presentibus duximus apponendum. Dat. Anno Domini M°CCC° vicesimo die Jovis post Resurrectionem Domini. [23 Apr. 1320.] Nos Abbas de T. predictus, hujus commissionis auctoritate, associato nobis ven. Abbate de Furnes, unà cum discretis viris dominis Gulielmo Bursario et Ricardo le Soterel Suppriore Savign. accedentes personaliter ad domum de Whalley predictam, ubi comparentibus coram nobis partibus predictis, ac earum rationibus et allegationibus quas in scriptis dare vel oretenus[1] dicere voluerint hinc inde auditis plenius et intellectis, consideratisque taxationibus,[2] tam super decima ad verum valorem, quàm super contributionibus aliis factis, quas dicte partes ad earum intentionem fundandam coram nobis exhibuerint et approbarint, ac super hiis omnibus habita deliberacione matura, de assensu partis utriusque diffinimus et diffiniendo senteneiamus et pronunciamus quòd cum dictus Abbas de Cumbermar' dicto filio suo de Whall. imposuerat Centum et sex libras bonorum parvorum turonum de ducentis et duodecim libris ejusdem monete sibi et generacioni sue pro contribucione de anno Dni M°ccc° octavodecimo impositis: dicta summa Centum et sex librarum restringatur ad quater viginti libras monete predicte; residuum vero ejusdem contribucionis dictus Abbas de Cumbermar' sibi et ceteris filiis suis distribuat prout viderit faciendum: Ita tamen quod ex hac nostra restitutione, moderacione, vel decisione nullam pro futuris temporibus prejudicium generetur. Expensas quoque quas dc̃s Abbas de Whall. se asseruit fecisse occasione querele memorate de utriusque partis assensu taxavimus ad centum solid. sterlingoram, quos dictum Abbatem de Cumbermar' dicto filio suo de W. hinc ad proxime sequens festum Natal. Domini solvere debere adjudicavimus in hiis scriptis. In quor' omnium premissorum testimonium sigillum nostrum una cum sigill. dicti domini Abbatis de Furnes et parcium predictar' presentibus est appensum. Dat. apud dictam domum de W. primo die Mensis Junii, anno Dni M°ccc° vicesimo.

1 [Johannes de Lustriaco, 16th Abbot of Savigny, succ. 1319.]

2 [Cumbermar' solvit pro spiritualibus suis pro decima secundum taxacionem veri valoris . xxjli. vijs. xjd. ob.

Deulacress solvit pro eadem causa	xviijli. ijs. ijd.
Whalley solvit	xxjli. ijs. xd. ob.
Hulton solvit	xls. vd. ob.

Taxacio locorum subscriptorum secundum quod inveniebatur apud Lich. in rotul. collectorum.

Temporalia Abbatis de Cumber. in Archid. Staff.	xjli. iis. iiijd.
Item in Archid. Cestr.	xxijli.
Item in Archid. Salop	xxixli. xs.
Item in Archid. Derbeye	xxxjli. xixs. vijd.
Taxacio ecclesie de Sondon	xij marc.
Taxacio ecclesie de Alstansfeld	xx marc.
Taxacio ecclesie de Acton cum capellis	xxij marc.
Norton quum percipit in ecclesia de Drayton	iijs.
Temporalia abbatis de Deulacr' in Archid' Cestr'	xxixli. xvs.
Item Archid. Staff.	xxxvijli. xiijs. viijd. (Marg. note lixs. vjd.)
Taxacio ecclesie de Lek.	xlij marc. (Marg. note iijl. xvs. iiijd qr di.)
Taxacio ecclesia de Sondbach	xxxiiij marc.

From these instruments alone we learn that Whalley, and consequently Stanlaw, were filial houses, dependent upon Cumbermere, in Cheshire. The whole family of children was styled *Generatio*. In the taxation referred to in this transaction, the Abbot appears to have acted oppressively and injuriously to his daughter of Whalley. The other dependent houses were Deulacres and Hulton, both in Staffordshire. I meet with no other trace of dependence in the later transactions of Whalley; and perhaps this oppressive taxation may have induced the monks of our house to assert their own independence the sooner. The contest, however, was settled for the present, by the following agreement:—

Venerabilibus in X^{to} Patribus D^{nis} de B(iland) et de C Abbatibus, Fratres W(ilhelmus) et G(regorius) de C(umbermere) et de W(halley) dicti Abbates salutem cum omni reverentia et honore. Quum super querela dudum in capitulo generali proponitam, ad quam terminandam judices dati estis, ex mutua caritate patris ad filium, et filii ad patrem, concordavimus in hunc modum; videlicet quod nos Abbas de Cumbermar' et successores nostri, quoties collecte seu contributiones de cetero fient in ordine, summam nobis et generationi nostre impositam, convocatis filiis abbatibus nostris, fideliter et expresse notificabimus, et in ipsius summe distributione seu divisione per omnia secundum formam distinccione 7°, capitulo primo, traditam procedimus. Nos vero Abbas de W(halley) et successores nostri sic et ceteri coabbates filii de C. summam nobis taliter impositam acceptabimus indilate: vestram sanctam paternitatem devote et humiliter exoramus, quatenus formam istam si placet acceptantes, eam in scriptis dentatis utriusque parti tradendis redigere dignemini, reservata vobis et successoribus vestris auctoritate compulsionis parti parere nolenti imposterum faciende. In cujus rei, etc. Dat. apud W(halley) tali die et apud C(umbermar') tali die. Anno. 302. (fol. 138).

Chapel of Clitheroe.

Venerabili in Xpo p̃ri et dnõ dnõ Rogero dei grã Coventr. et Lichf. Ep̃o, suus si placet filius humilis et devotus Vicarius ecclesie de Whalleye omnimodam reverentiam, obedientiam et honorem, &c. per Mandatum ṽrum reverendum nuper recepi, scilicet eo qui sequitur tenore. ROGERUS permissione divina Coventr' et Lichf. Ep̃us dilecto in Xp̃o filio vicario ecclesie de Whalleye ñre Dioc. graciam et benediccionem. Querelam Religiosorum virorum Abbatis et Conventus de Whalleye, ecclesiam ipsam de Whalleye cum suis capellis in usus proprios optinent' noviter recepimus, continentem quod, licet cura poch' totius pochie predicte ecclesie de Whalleye, omniumque et singulor' pochianorum ejusdem, ad vos racione vicarie ṽre pertineat et pertinere debeat, ac Vicarius qui pro tempore fuerit curam hiis per se et suos capellanos exercere teneatur, vos tamen curam poch' Capelle infra Castrum de Clyderhou scituate, prefate ecclesie de Whalleye annexe, et dependentis ab eadem, subire et agnoscere sicut in ceteris capellis dependentibus, absque causa rationabili temere recusatis, in ipsorum religiosorum prejudicium non modicum et grave periculum animarum. Quocirca vobis quantum de jure possumus firmiter injungendo mandamus quatenus, si sit ita, curam parochialem capelle supradicte prout justum fuerit, et ad vos pertinere dinoscitur, subire ac solerter et diligenter exercere nullatenus omittatis. Alioquin tenore presentium peremptorie vos citamus quod tercio die juridico post dominicam quâ cantatur *Misericordia Domini*,[1] coram Comissario ñro in Ecclesia ñra Cath. Lichf. comparere curetis canonicum si quod habeat, quare ad agnoscend' et exercend' curam parochiale' capelle supradicte compelli minime debeatis, in forma juris propositur' et receptur' ulterius in hac parte quod justicia suadebit. Quid autem in premissis feceritis et duxeritis faciend' prefatum Commissar. dictis die et loco certificetis per literas vestras patentes. Dat. London. XVII kalen. Aprilis Año dñi M°CCC° tricessimo quinto. Scire velit vestra Dñacio Reverenda quod adversâ valetudine gravissimâ prepeditus personaliter non potui comparere, set procuratorem meum in premissis sufficienter instructum vobis destinavi: et sic mandatum vestrum quatenus potui reverenter sum executus. Dat. apud Whalleye Idus April. Anno dñi M°CCC° Tricesimo sexto

[1] Introit from Ps. xxxiii., sung on the Second Sunday after Easter.

To the sale of a slave and his family may be added the hiring of a servant for life:—

Universis, &c. Noveritis nos unanimi consensu et pari voluntate concessisse Galfrido dicto K. pro servicio quod nobis hucusque servivit et serviet in futuro, victum et vestitum in domo nostra de W(halley) pro toto tempore vite sue, dum tamen fideliter se habuerit et honeste; Ita quod, dum in stabulo ex more servierit, vel in alio servicio sibi per nos assignando, locum unius servientis competenter et sufficienter tenere potuerit, dabimus ei in victualibus et vestitu, sicut unus garcionum de stabulo . . Abbatis pro illo tempore recipere consuevit. Si autem infirmitate vel senio prepeditus ad talem locum tenendum sufficere non valuerit, inveniemus eidem sustentationem suam inter familiares in infirmitorio secularium, sicut uni talium solitum est ministrari, etc. (fol. 75.)

Some conclusion, with respect to the general knowledge of the Monks of Whalley, may be formed from the following entries in different parts of the *Liber Loci Benedicti*.[1]

Memor. quod in Anglia sunt Ecclesie parochiales	lx^{ml}.vi.
Ville	lij.M^{l}.$^{\text{xx}}_{\text{iiij}}$
Feoda Militum	xl.M^{l}.cc.xv.
De quibus Religiosi occupant	xxviii.M^{l}.xv.
Comitatus	xxxvi di. (Fol. 104.)

The following table will show that they had some principles of husbandry:—

Terra	Alba	Argillosa—Frumentum, fab. aven.
		Marlosa—Frumentum.
	Nigra.	Petrosa—Frumentum, fab. aven.
		Siliciosa—Uniuscujusque seminis grano apta, maxime vescis; et ista terra nutrit cuniculos.
		Temperata, apta uniuscujusque seminis grano.
		Sabulosa—Siligini.
	Rubea	Argillosa—Frumentum, fab. aven'.
		Marlosa—Frumentum, aven'.
		Sabulosa—Siligo, Ordeum.
		Temperata, Mixta, Petrosa, Siliciosa — Apta uniuscujusque seminis grano. (Fol. 23 b.)

Ad restinguend. sanguinem de naribus vel vulneribus medicina probata.

Deus propicius esto huic famulo tuo N. ne de suo corpore amplius gutta sanguinis exeat. Sic placet filio Dei, sic Sue genetrici Marie. In nomine Patris cessa, sanguis. In nomine Filii cessa, sanguis. In nomine Spiritus Sancti cessa sanguis ab hoc famulo Dei. In nomine Sc̄e Trinitatis. (Fol. 79 b.)

[1] [Similar tables are not uncommon in old writers. Thus, Higden:—"Tunc sunt in Anglia, præter Cornubiam et insulas, triginta sex shiræ, provinciæ, sive comitatus. Quas omnes fecit Willelmus Conqæstor describi, et per hydas seu carucatas dimetiri, et inventi sunt comitatus triginta sex et dimidium; villæ vero quinquaginta duo millia et octoginta (another reading, 62,080), ecclesiæ parochiales quadraginta quinque millia duo, feoda militum 60,015, de quibus religiosi habent 28,015 (19,015) feoda: sed hodie nemoribus succisis novalibusque procisis, multo plures sunt hidæ et villæ quam tunc erant." (*Polychronicon*, lib. i. ch. xlix. vol. ii. pp. 89, 90. Master of the Rolls' Edition.) Higden was a monk of St. Werburgh's, Chester, who seems to have taken his vows in 1299, and who wrote his chronicle to 1352. He was therefore a contemporary of the writer of the above.]

Pur estauncher Saunk.

Longevus miles lancea latus Salvatoris aperuit: et continuo exivit sanguis et aqua,[1] sanguis redempĉois et aqua baptismatis. In noĩe p̃ris ✠ cesset sanguis ✠. In noĩe filii ✠ restet sanguis ✠. In noie sp̃us sc̃i ✠ non exeat sanguis amplius de ore vel de vena vel de naso. (Fol. 79 b.)

They had an opportunity of trying the efficacy of this charm, within a short time after it was written, upon one of their brethren, who was shot with an arrow. As he died of the wound I am compelled to suppose that the charm was forgotten.

Nota:

- De Lino
  - quod 24or Cuscute lini faciunt quod Anglice dic^r Cherf.
  - quod 24or Garbe faciunt unum Thrave.
- De Corio
  - quod 10 Cor. faciunt unum Dik.
  - quod 10 Dik. faciunt unum Last.
- De Ferro
  - quod 6 Petr. faciunt unam Duodenam.
  - quod 13 Duodene faciunt unum Seem *(inserted in later hand and ink.)*
  - quod 25 Petr. faciunt unum Band.
- De Cera
  - quod Libra cere ponderat 25 Solid.
  - quod 8 Lib. cere faciunt Petram.
- De Sepo et de Canabo 16 Libr. faciunt Petram.
- De Lana
  - quod 12 Libr. faciunt Petram.
  - quod 30 Petr. faciunt unum Saccum.
- De Speciebus
  - quod Dragma ponderat 2 d. ob.
  - quod Uncia ponderat 20 Dragm.
  - quod Libra ponderat 20 Solid.

Nota:
- quod 26 Pedes faciunt unam Rodam vel Perticatam terre.
- 10 Rode in longi^ne et 4 in lati^ne, vel 20 in longi^ne et 8 in lati^ne, faciunt unam Acram.

Distempera[2] ad scribendum:
- Azorium cum albo vino et gummy, vel cum glarea ovi.
- Vermiculum cum glarea ovi et modico salis et aque.
- Viride Græcum cum albo vino et croco et modico mellis.
- Crocum cum glarea ovi.
- Sinopide cum glarea ovi.
- Brasill'. Id'm. (Fol. 23.)

[1] This legend is alluded to by Peirs Ploughman, who has converted the epithet *Longævus* into a proper name, *Longeus.* [In Legenda Aurea, cap. xlvii is *De sancto Longino* (edit. Graesse, p. 202-3). He was a centurion of Isauria, and suffered martyrdom at Cæsarea in Cappadocia, and his feast is on 15th March. Peter de Natal. lib. iii. c. 201. According to Bollandus, Actæ Sanctorum, Martii, tom. 22, p. 375, the Latin writers have probably derived the name from the apocryphal gospel of Nicodemus. The following form of this charm, in mingled English and French, occurs, among others, in the MS. Harl. 273, fol. 112 b:—*Pour sang estauncher.* In nomine patris, etc. Longes the knyht him understod, to cristes syde his spere he sete. þer com out water and blod. In the nome of þe holy gost asta blod, at cristes wille ne drople þe namore. Beau sire dieu ihesu crist auxi veroiment come Longes le chevaler vous fery de une launce ale coste destre, taunge al cuer, de quei il ne saneit, dont il issist sang e eawe, de queis il recouvrist la vewe, vous pri auxi veroiement que cest sang estancher e vous commaund en soun seint noun: vous sang qe vous estaunchez pater noster ter ave, etc. Longes is said to have become blind, and to have recovered his sight on touching his eyes with the blood of Christ.]

[2] [*Distempera* comes before *Nota* in the MS.]

But the most singular circumstance in this volume is, that it contains the Runic Alphabet, together with some other contractions, of which it does not appear how they came to the knowledge of the monks, or what use they made of them.[1]

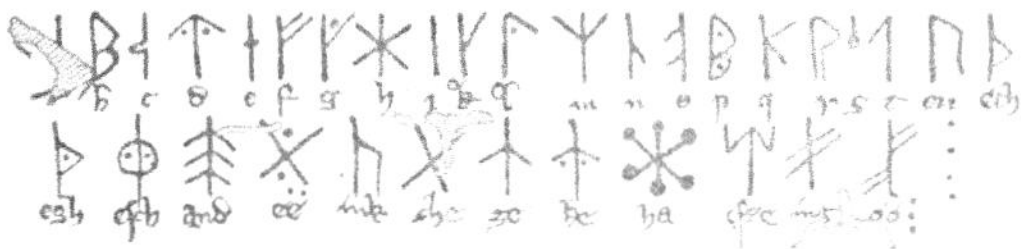

The attestation of the following instrument is sufficiently curious to procure the insertion of the whole :

Memorandum quod Anno gratie etc. ad festum tale ita convenit inter viros religiosos Abbatem et Conventum Loci B(enedicti) de W(halley) et Dm A. de H.[2] Militem : videlicet quod dicti . . Abbas et Con. unanimi consensu capituli sui concesserunt dicto domino A. ad totam vitam suam xls. sterlingorum percipiend. apud W. in festo Sci Mich. major. annuatim. Dictus vero dominus A. e contra versus dictos Religiosos, ea securitate qua fidelem militem obligari convenit, se astrinxit quod eisdem in omnibus negociis et necessitatibus suis fidele consilium et auxilium impendet toto tempore vite sue sine fraude, calumpnia, seu qualibet fictione. Et quod decimas garbarum de dominicis carucis suis in terra quam tempore confectionis presentium coluerit per easdem annis singulis libenter recipiet ad voluntatem dictorum Religiosorum pro pecunia memorata. Ita quod eisdem decimis perceptis literas acquietantie faciet dictis Religiosis de xls annuis antedictis. Ad majorem vero hujus rei securitatem huic scripto cyrographato utraque pars sigillum suum mutuo apposuit. Testibus Deo, Beata Maria, et Omnibus Sanctis patronis ecclesie de W. (Addit. M.S. 10,374, f. 66 b.)

I shall next insert one of their Contracts for the Sale and Delivery of Wool :—

Hoc anno solvit mercator pro manibus liiij li.[3]

Universis presentes litteras inspecturis Fr. R. de W. (Rob. de Warrington) Prior domus de W(halley) et Fr. R. de M. (Moston) dicte domus Cellararius Procuratores . . . . Abbatis et Conventus domus predict. salutem in Domino. Noveritis nos, nomine procuratorio dictor. Abb. et Conv., teneri et obligari A. B. Burgensi et Mercatori de L. per bonum compotum inter nos nomine quo supra ex parte una et dictum A. ex

[1] [A more careful fac-simile of these Runes is now presented than was given in the former edition, where the second line was entirely omitted. The shaded spots denote worm-holes in the page. The Editors are favoured by Mr. Eiríkr Magnússon with the following remarks: "The first line represents the Scandinavian Runic alphabet, not the Anglo-Saxon. The writer differs from other authorities in representing *c* by the third character in the first line, which is a corrupt representation of the common rune for *s*, occurring even more frequently than the drop-like character here afterwards shown for that letter. It is clear that the writer knew not the phonetic value of the rune for þ *th* the aspirate, or that for ð *th* soft. He has also mistaken for *esch* the character used for *x*. Out of the compound runes following the last-mentioned character little is to be made. But it is almost certain that the whole must have been copied from an Icelandic MS., which is attested by the graphic correctness of the strokes. It seems likely that the scribe was a Frenchman, as he gives the sound of the rune for *u* as *ou*. EIRÍKR MAGNÚSSON."]

[2] [Incorrectly read "A. de B." by Dr. Whitaker, and explained by (a mistaken) conjecture to mean Adam de Blackburn.]

[3] [Written in small characters over the middle of the first line.]

altera factum de omnibus factis habitis inter dictas partes pro toto tempore preterito, in viii saccis bone lane[1] diete domus et iv. saccis medie lane et loccarum electar' domus ejusdem. Que quidem tota lana antedicta debet per preparatorem dicti A. parari, brusari, et in sarpellario ejusdem A. insaccari, et per pondus dĉe domus debitum et consuetum ponderari. Et illos xii. saccos lane predicte promittimus et tenemur reddere et deliberare predicto A. vel suo attornato apud villam Sĉi B(otulphi)[2] sumptibus dĉe domus et expensis die Sĉi Petri ad Vincula in forma subscript', scilicet anno D'ni, &c. tres saccos bone lane et unum saccum medie lane et loccarum electarum. Et anno D'ni, &c. quinto [*i.e.* 1305], duos saccos et dimid' bone lane et i. sacc. medie lane et loccarum electarum. Et anno Domini, &c. vi^{to} duos saccos et dimid' bone lane et unum saccum et dimid. medie lane et loccar' electar' sine ulteriori dilatione. Et pro quolibet sacco bone lane modo predicto non soluto promittimus et tenemur reddere et pacare dicto A. vel suo attornato x li. et pro sacco medie lane et loccarum electarum x. Marcas sterlingas infra octo dies post quemlibet terminum supradictum non observatum. Et si contingat dictos . . . Abbatem et Conventum in secundo vel tertio anno plus habere de lana quam superius dictum est concedimus dicto A. in recompensacionem curialitatum dicte domus ab eo impensarum quod habeat illud plus in hac forma scilicet quemlibet saccum bone lane dicte domus pro x. marcis et quemlibet saccum medie lane et loccarum electarum pro vi. marcis sterlingis. Et illud plus dicto A. vel suo attornato dictis loco et termino in forma predicta deliberare promittimus et tenemur. Pro quibus omnibus antedictis fideliter adimplendis obligamus dictos Abbatem et Conventum et eorum successores et omnia bona dicte domus mobilia et inmobilia presencia et futura capiend. distringend. detinend. per quoscumque vicecomites et ballivos sub quorum districtione tam ultra quam citra mare inveniantur. In cujus rei testimonium sigilla nostra presentibus sunt appensa. Dat. etc.

Prec. Sac. { bone lane x. mrc / medie lane vi. mrc } in vendicione.[3]

In 1304 the abbey owed to Henry de Lacy, Earl of Lincoln, seventeen sacks of good wool for 85*l.* sterling, received from Simon N. constable of Clithero.

Omnibus sancte matris ecclesie filiis presentes litteras inspecturis frater G[alfridus] dictus Abbas loci Benedicti de Whalley et ejusdem domus conventus salutem in Domino sempiternam. Noveritis nos teneri ac etiam presenti scripto nostro obligari domino H[enrico] de L[aci] Comiti L[incolnie] in xvii. saccis bone lane de proprio instauro domus nostre pro quater viginti et quinque libris sterlingorum quas a Simone N. constabulario de C[lithero] in magna necessitate nostra aput W. pre manibus nomine dicti domini Comitis recipimus, solvendos eidem domino Henrico Comiti vel suo certo attornato apud sanctum B[otulphum] die sancti Petri ad vincula in forma subscripta videlicet, Anno *etc.* quarto [A.D. 1304] octo saccos et dimidium. Et Anno Domini etc. quinto [1305] octo saccos et dimidium sine ulteriori dilacione. Que quidem tota lana antedicta debet per preparatorem dicti domini Abbatis et Conventus parari, brusari, ac in sarpellario eorum insaccari, et per pondus diete domus debitum et consuetum ponderari. Pro quibus omnibus et singulis antedictis fideliter adimplendum obligamus nos et successores nostros ac domum nostram predictam et omnia bona nostra mobilia et immobilia presencia et futura capienda, distringenda, et detinenda per quoscunque vicecomites et ballivos sub quorum districcione inveniantur. In cujus rei testimonio sigillum nostrum commune presentibus est appensum. Dat aput W. in festo Annunciacionis etc. Anno Domini M.°CCC° quarto incipiente. [25 Mar. 1304.] (Fol. 73.)

[1] [*Bone lane.* In a previous contract they promise to sell A. B. "sexdecem saccos lane de suo proprio instauro sine Coth', gard, ing^{a}, grisa, scabie, putredine, pellicea refutabili, unctura, Elact', Bard', sine sorele et omni vili vellere." (Fol. 64.)]

[2] [The port of Boston in Lincolnshire.]

[3] Note on the bottom margin of fol. 65.

AGREEMENT WITH J. B., MERCHANT OF FLORENCE, MUTUALLY ANNULLING ALL CLAIMS ON EITHER SIDE.

Notum sit omnibus hoc scriptum cyrographatum visuris vel audituris quod ita convenit inter Fratrem G[alfridum] Abbatem de W. ordinis Cisterciensis Coventr' et Lich' dyocesis et ejusdem loci Conventus ex parte una, et J. D. Mercatorem de Societate Mercatorum de Florenc' ex altera, videlicet, quod dictus [Galfridus] Abbas et Conventus domus predicte, pro se et successoribus suis, omnes acciones, peticiones, querelas, demandas ac debita que inter eos fuerint a mundi initio usque ad diem confectionis hujus instrumenti causa alicujus lane ab eis empte seu alicujus alterius contractus inter eos prehabiti dicto Mercatori ac sociis suis omnino remisit et relaxavit. Dictus autem J. pro se et sociis suis hoc idem erga predictum Abbatem et Conventum domus predicte facere concessit, ita quod si aliquod instrumentum penes alteram partem per quod aliquid exegi poterit inveniatur, pro nullo penitus habeatur, sed omnino careat suo robore et virtute. In cujus rei testimonium partes alternati huic scripto bipartito sigilla sua apposuerunt. Dat. etc.

[The following is the Abbot of Whalley's acceptance of the new Cistercian constitutions[1] made by Pope Benedict the Twelfth:

In Dei nomine Amen. Ego Frater R(obertus) de T(opcliffe), Abbas de W(halley), protestor in hiis scriptis me fore paratum ad recipiendas Constitutiones sanctissimi in Christo patris nostri Domini Benedicti Pape XII^{mi}. personis nostri ordinis ut dicitur indictas et in ultimo nostro generali capitulo promulgatas, cum reverentia qua teneor et devocione; necnon easdem velle observare, eisque quatenus de jure teneor libenter obedire, nedum secundum quod nuda verba modo videntur sonare, set magis ad mentem condentis, seu secundum quod nostri dicti ordinis capitulum generale ipsas judicaverit observandas juxta modificaciones, interpretaciones, declaraciones, vel exposiciones earundem, si que super hiis in posterum fuerint subsecute. (Fol. 139.)

Sale of the Abbey and its Demesnes.

The letters patent of King Edward VI. by which the manor of Whalley with its appurtenances was sold by the Crown to Richard Assheton and John Braddyll, both of Whalley, gentlemen, (as already stated in p. 134,) is printed at length in the Chetham Society's edition of the *Coucher Book of Whalley*, pp. 1175-1183, and it does not appear necessary to repeat it entire: but its descriptive portions are here appended, more fully and correctly than they were given by Dr. Whitaker, in fulfilment of his remark that they are "particularised in terms extremely interesting, as they perpetuate several names allusive to its former state, which they who love the place and the subject would not wish to be forgotten":—

Totum illud Dominium et Manerium nostrum de Whalley in com. nostro Lancastrie, ac totum parcum nostrum ac omnia terras et ten. nostra vocat. *Whalley Parke*[2] in dicto com. nostro Lancastrie cum suis

[1] [Benedict XII. who had been a Cistercian (Abbot of Font Froide), after several conferences with the Abbot of Citeaux and the four principal Abbots of the order at Pont de Forgue (in the diocese of Avignon), made a constitution in the year 1334, containing many regulations of this order. Arbois de Jubainville, Abbayes Cisterciennes, p. ix.]

[2] [" There is a parke called Whalley Parke which lieth on the north-east side of the towne of Whalley, and is in the distance from the late monestere one bow-shot, well replenished with timber and underwood, for three parts of the same parke is covered with wood. There is very little plean ground or land within the same parke; but for that

juribus membris et pertinentiis universis nuper Monasterio de Whalley in eodem com. Lancastr. modo dissolut. quondam spectant. et pertinentibus ac parcell. possessionum inde existent. Ac totam capitalem Domum et scitum dicti nuper monasterii de Whalley in Whalley in dicto comit. Lancastrie, ac omnia domos, edificia, horrea, stabula, columbaria, ortos, pomeria, gardina, stagna, vivaria, terram, fundum et solum et hereditamenta nostra queeunque infra scitum, septem, ambitum, circuitum, et procinctum dicti nuper monasterii existen. ac omnia illa domos, edificia, terras, prata, pasturas, ortos, pomeria, gardina, horrea, stabula, et hereditamenta nostra quecunque vocata seu cognita per nomen vel per nomina de Rogerashes, Gresyardes, Sykesdongarth, le Common Stable, le Gousehouse, le Newehouse, Brodryddynge, le Geez alias Gez,[2] Helker,[3] Morehey, Catterall wypes, Wheatley, Newfelde, Westwoode, Ellker, Tunneworth hays, hyghe Tunneworthe, Tunneworthe Ryddynge, Claycroft, Brighehay, Oxheye Wood, Portefeyld, Longley, le Intake, Roughhey, Graves, Crowparke, le Asshes, le Fermery Garthes, le Kytchyn Garthes, le Prior's Orchard, Parry's Orchard, Marston Orchard, Wordell Orchardes, le Abbotes Orchard, Hyll Orchard, Harwood Orchard, Danby Orchard, Haydock et Woodes Orchard, le Prior's Orchard, More's Orchard, le Proctor's Orchard, Southeseller Yard, le Impeyarde, Abbotes Kychyn Garth, le Proctor's stable de Blakborne, le Haggehouse, le Hay Barne apud Grange, Cleyfelde, Smythes Howse, le Henne howse, le Oxe howse, le Mason's lodge, Barne crofte, le Old stable, le Howker stable, le Bourde house juxta le Smythes forge, Lawsyng stedes, Barrowclough, le Foure Acre Heye et Kylne, Pyg hyll, Crabtres Oxhay, le Six landes, Clafe Hay, le Plot of Medowe, Robert Feyldes, Crose Feylde, Buckflatte alias Buckfoote, Castell, Hiyhe Lynge, Kirkyng Henhurst, Hallyclyf, Breeley Close, Shepe hey, le Tiethe barne, Whitacre Orchard, Dynkley Orchard, le Procter Stable, Standenfoldes et Standenhey. Necnon omnia alia mesuagia, molendina, cotagia, tofta, crofta, terras, tenementa, domos, edificia, horrea, stabula, columbaria, stagna, vivaria, ortos, pomeria, gardina, prata, pasturas, pascuas, lesuras et hereditamenta nostra quecunque cum omnibus et singulis eorum pertinentiis universis modo vel nuper in separalibus tenuris sine occupationibus Will. Shotylworth, Georgii Shotylworthe [and fifty-eight others[4]] in villis, campis, et parochiis de Whalleye et Blackburne &c. Ac omnia terras et hereditamenta nostra vocata *Whalley Parke*, necnon omnes boscos et subboscos infra eundem parcum, ac omnia terras et tenementa, prata, pasturas, et hereditamenta nostra vocata seu cognita per nomina de Whetley (and other places already named). Tenend. de nobis, heredibus et successoribus nostris in capite per servicium quadragesime partis unius feodi militis. Ac reddendo annuatim nobis heredibus et successoribus nostris ut ad Ducatum nostrum Lancastrie ad manus ballivi wapentagii de Blackborneshyre &c. et pro terra et pastura vocat. Standen hey 6*s*. 8*d*. ac de et pro septem acris jacentibus inter terras dominicales dicti nuper monasterii 2*s*. Test. 16 Junii anno regni septimo.

[*i.e.* notwithstanding,] there is very good pasture, and for need would be meddow; and thorrow the same parke runeth a fair river called the water of Calder, wheirin is taken salmon, trout, with other good fish; and the harbage of the same parke is leten for twelve pound by the year—the said parke contayning about by estimation two miles—and there is in the same parke upon this vision xxx deare." Survey taken 29th June, 29 Hen. VIII.—Coucher Book, (edit. 1849) pp. 1201, 1202.]

[1] [See among "the demesne lands" in the Survey or Rent-roll of the same period "a close of pasture" called Brode[ryddynge] of six acres, and another "called the Jes" of seventeen acres, both let to Robert Low. *Coucher Book*, p. 1184.]

[2] ["A medow called Houlker," containing seven acres, and several of the others that follow, will be found in the same document.]

[3] [From these Dr. Whitaker (Third Edition, p. 106) selected the names of Christopher Thornebarre, Thomas Chatborne, Robert Sudyll, and James Lawe, remarking that "these were poor monks who had clung to the old house like a few surviving bees about a suffocated hive:" but though the names are the same as some of the former monks (see p. 114), they were assuredly not the same persons, nor of the number of the monks at the forfeiture. Christopher Thornbarre was the abbot who died in 1485 (see p. 113).]

[A Survey or Rent-roll of the possessions of the late Abbey compiled about the same time is printed in the Coucher Book, pp. 1183—1254.

THE INVENTORYE[1] of all the gooddes belonging to the Monasterie of Whalley, taken by the Erle of Sussex and others of the King's Counsell, the xxiv[th] day of Marche in the xxviij yere of the Reigne of our Sovereigne Lorde Kyng Henry th'eighte.

Plate remaining in the Bowser's[2] Howse.

Fyrst ij large stondinge cuppes with covers of silver and gilte.[3]
Item another cuppe gilte with a cover stondinge vppon three lyons.
Item ij stondinge cuppes with a cover parcel gilte.
Item one salt with a cover gilte.
Item a basyn parcell gilte with a ewer of playen silver.
Item ij stondinge pottes of silver.
Item iij plain bowels of silver.
Item a basyn parcell gilte.
Item ij sallts with one cover gilte.
Item ij nuttes harneste with silver gilt with ij covers, thone without a knoppe.[4]
Item a dosen spones.
Item another dosen spones with ragged knoppes.
Item iij drinking ale cuppes parcell gilte.
Item ij small cuppes with one cover.
Item a little stondinge cuppe with a cover plain gilt.
Item a goblet with a cover parcell gilte.
Item ij plain bowlles.
Item a little piece of silver.
Item iij spones broken and one hole.
Item a litle masar.
Item a minstrel's scochyn and a litle scochen with a black lyon.[5]
It. a stondinge cuppe with a cover and an egle on the toppe gilte.
It. another stondinge cuppe parcill gilte with a cover and a pellican on the toppe.
It. ij white goblets.
It. one white bowl of silver.
It. ij small drinking cuppes, one gilte, thother parcill gilte.
It. one large stonding powncéd[6] bowlle with a cover parcill gilte of my Lord Mount Egle's gifte.

Plate remayning at Cockersand.

It. there iij silver bowlls.
It. ij wyne pottes waying iiij[xx]vj vnces as apperith by an Indenture made betweene the abbots of Whalley and Cockersand.

The Hostery.

It. in the chefe chamber there iij fether beddes, j materes, iiij boulsters, ij coverings, iiij[or] blankettes of fustian, iiij[or] blankettes of cloths, and vj coverlettes.
It. in the parlor benethe, ij fether beddes, ij boulsters, j pillowe of downe, j coveringe, iij coverlettes, ij per fustians.
It. in the galary chamber, ij fether beddes, ij boulsters, ij coverings, ij coverlettes, ij par of blankettes.
It. in the other galary chamber, ij materes, ij boulsters, iiij coverlettes.
It. in the over bishoppis chambre, iij fether beddes, iij boulsters, iij p[er] blankettes, the one of fustian

[1] The more complete Inventory which now follows was not seen by Dr. Whitaker. It has been edited twice since his time, by Mr. Hulton at the close of the *Coucher Book of Whalley*, pp. 1255—1265, and again (without reference to the Coucher Book) by the Rev. Mackenzie E. C. Walcott, B.D., F.S.A., in the *Transactions of the Historic Society of Lancashire and Cheshire*, 1867. In the latter place, by some accident, it wants at the commencement the first thirteen items. Some inaccuracies in both copies are now amended.

[2] *i.e.* the Bursar.

[3] The same four standing cups will be found in the subsequent Inventory, p. 189, with their weights.

[4] Mentioned in the subsequent Inventory, p. 189, as Nutts for Ale.

[5] The badge of a travelling minstrel, and another of some nobleman. Mr. Hulton suggests possibly the *purple* lion of Lacy.

[6] *i.e.* punched, or decorated by stamping little holes.

and the other ij of clothe, iij coverings, and iij coverlettes.

It. in the middel bishoppis chamber, j fether bedd, j boulster, j payer of blankettes, j coverlett, and a covering of say.

It. in the lower bishoppis chamber, ij fether beddes, ij boulster, iij blankettes, j covering, and iij coverlettes.

It. in the ladis chambers, vj materes, ix coverlettes, iij coverings, and pillowes vj.

It. in the Kinges receyvour's chamber, j fether bedd, j boulster, j materes, another bolster, iiijor coverlettes, and ij paier of blankettes.

It. xx payer of lynnen shetes.

It. x payer of canvas.

It. iij old coverings unservisable.

It. iij pillowes of downe.

It. ij carpets.

It. v hanginges unto beddes.

It. iiijor borde clothez and iij coppeborde clothez.[1]

It. xxvi. quysshions.

It. x candlestikks.

The Abbott's Chamber.

It. there his owne bedd, j materesse with blankettes and a litle covering.

It. in the utter chamber, j fether bedd, iij coverlettes, ij blankettes, and a bedd for his chamberlayen.

The Abbotes Dynynge Chamber.

It. there j cuppeborde.

It. a long settel.

It. ij chayers.

It. iij carpettes.

It. j dosen of old quishions of verdors.

It. a hanging candlestick in the middeste of the chamber.

The Buttery.

It. there ij bordeclothes of diaper.

It. another bordeclothe and ij wasshing towells of diaper.

It. xvij napkins of diaper.

It. xiij bordeclothes for the hall.

It. viij towelles for the hall.

It. xx napkins.

It. xij candelstikks.

The Brewe Howse.

It. there ij leades.

It. a meshe fatte.

It. j keling lead.

It. j. killer (*i.e.* a cooler).

Bake Howse.

It. there j leade.

The Abbott's Kychen.

It. there iiij garnishe[2] of pewter vessell.

It. there more ij dosen of vessell.

It. xj brasse pottes.

It. x pannys.

It. ij frying pannes.

It. ivor paier of pothokes.

It. ix rosting spittes.

It. ij brasse mortars wth a pestell.

It. ij brassen ladels.

It. j scommer of brasse.[3]

It. j scommer of iron.

It. j grydeyron.

It. iiij drientubbes.

It. other tubbes and hogsheddes xiij.

It. ij dressying knyves.

The Graunge.

It. there l. draft oxon.

It. vj stires of iiij yeres.

It. vij steres of iij yeres.

It. xij steres of ij yeres.

It. stere of j yere.

It. cowes iiijxx.

It. hoggeshepe[4] iiijxx.

It. x swyne.

It. xij horses for the ploughe and carte.

The Convent Kitchen.

It. there vj pottes.

It. iiij pannys.

It. ij spyttes.

It. j brassen morter.

It. j pestell to the same.

[1] Cloths for the dining-tables and for the cupboards, *i.e.* sideboards.

[2] A set or service.

[3] A skimming ladle.

[4] Sheep two years old.

It. xxxij dishes.

It. xxij doblers.[1]

It. xxxiij sawsers.

A litle Chamber in Dortour.[2]

It. there xv chalises with their patens all gilte.

The litle Revestury next unto the Lybrary.

It. there a large crosse of silver and gilte wth ij imagies of Mary and John.[3]

It. another crosse with the iiij Evangelistes gilte.

It. a large holy-water fatt with a sprinkelle of silver parcell gilte.

It. ij small sensairs of silver and gilte.[4]

It. one crowche[5] of silver and gilte with a staffe of silver.

It. another crowche of silver and gilte sett with saphours, without a staff.

It. ij candelstikkes of silver parcell gilte.

It. a litle shippe for frauncensence with a spone parcell gilte.

It. a bell of silver without a clapper.

It. a paier of crewettes of silver and gilte.

It. another paier of crewettes of silver.

It. a miter of silver and gilte, sett with safours, emerodes, balas, and turkesses, as evill as can be.[6]

It. another miter made all of nedelwork.

It. a payer of knett gloves with a roose of gold imbroydered sett with perle and ij small safours in eyther of them.[7]

The foresaid Revestury next unto the Galary.

It. there one cope [of] Venise gold with Lord Mount Egle's armes.

It. another of clothe of gold with the seid Lord Mount Egle's armes.

It. another of clothe of bawdeken with an image of Jhesus on the breste.

It. another of white damaske bawdekin with an image of Seinte Martine on the breste.

It. ij. other of red velvett imbroidred with flowers.

It. another of white coursse satten imbroidred with roses of gold.

It. ij other grene velvett braunched.

It. ij other of satten of bridges[8] imbroydred with doble vervour and ploughes.

It. ij other of redd doble sarsenett with flowers and nedelwerke.

It. another of black velvett imbroidred with a posie of gold letters.

It. another of velvett uppon velvett white.

It. ij other copes old of grene bawdekyne with m of gold imbroydred on the breste of eyther of them.

It. another cope geven unto the sequestern[9] that had the keepinge of all the seid copes.

It. there one vestment of red clothe of gold with an image on a crosse on the bak with tynnacles for a deacon and sub-deacon belonging to the same.

It. another of blewe baudekin wth a crucifix on the bak wth all thinges thereunto belonging for deacon and subdeacon.

It. another of blewe baudekyn in like maner with all things thereunto belonging for deacon and subdeacon.

It. ij baners of sarsnett, wherof one redd and thother grene.

The Standeries[10] *in the Churche.*

It. there a vestment of blak velvett wth a posie of letteres of gold imbroidered, with things thereunto belonging for deacon and subdeacon.

It. another vestment of redd velvett with a crucifix imbroidered, with all things thereunto belonging for deacon and subdeacon.

It. another vestment of grene velvett with an image of Seinte Michell imbroidred on the bak, with all things thereunto belonging for deacon and subdeacon.

[1] Dishes of larger size.

[2] In the Dortour or Dormitory.

[3] Compare the description of these crosses in the Inventory of 1536, p. 189.

[4] The *Thuribula* there mentioned.

[5] There described as *Baculus pastoralis*.

[6] Pope Clement IV. had ordered that the mitre of an Abbot should be embroidered with gold only, to distinguish it from the Bishop's. Fosbroke's *Monachism*. But this mitre was set with precious stones as evil (heavy) as could be. (Note by Mr. Hulton.)

[7] *i.e.* each glove was embroidered on the back with a jewelled rose.

[8] Bruges.

[9] Sacristan.

[10] Chests or wardrobes.

It. another vestment of white coursse satten imbroidred with an image of the Trynitie on the bak, with all things thereunto belonging for deacon and subdeacon.

It. another of redd bawdekyn with a blew crosse, with all thinges thereunto belonging for deacon and subdeacon.

It. another old vestment of coursse redd bawdekyn, with all things thereunto belonging for deacon and subdeacon.

It. another old vestment of blak velvett imbroidred, wth all things thereunto belonging for deacon and subdeacon.

It. another old vestment of blewe coper tynsell, with all things there unto belonging for deacon and subdeacon.

It. there be xiij other vestments of Dornyx[1] and fustian that ar dayly occupied in the churche.

The Store House.

It. there in iron by estimacion x c. and in leade lx ston.

Rob'te Sussex.
Wyll'm Leylond.
Antony Fitzherberte.
Henry Farryngton.
John Claydon, p̃st.

The Abbey Kitchener's last Account.[2]

Dyverse somes of money leid oute by me Jamys More, monke and kechyner to the late Abbot of Whalley, for and concernynge dyverse caitls bought by the seid Jamys of dyverse persons, as hereinafter dothe particulerly appire by parcells whiche came to thuse of the seid house from the last daye of December until the daye of Marche then next folowynge yn the xxviijth yere of the reign of Kynge Henry the viijth, for whiche somes of money the said Jamys asketh allowance:—

First payde to Edmunde Taillor, Fisher, for ——— salt salmons, spent in the seyd late abbot's kechyn syns the tyme of his accompt	xxv^{s}
Itm. Payde to the seid Edmunde for xj freshe salmons, bought of the said Edmunde to thuse, &c. of the seid house, there spent by the seid tyme .	xxv^{s}
Itm. Payde to Will'm Newbbet for fresh fishe	iij^{s} iiij^{d}
Itm. Payde for vj capons, bought at Fastynge even of dyverse psons . .	ij^{s}
Itm. Payde for xxxv hennes, bought of dyverse psons	v^{s} x^{d}
Itm. paid for eggs, butter, chese, bought of dyverse persons betwixt Cristmas and Fastyngs evyn, spent yn the seid house	xxiiij^{s}
Itm. Payde for mustersede	v^{s}
Itm. Bought of William Fische viij potts hony, pric'	x^{s}
Itm. Bought of Anthony Watson vij gallons hony	ix^{s} iiij^{d}
Itm. Bought of John Colthirst ij gallons hony	ij^{s} iiij^{d}
Itm. Payde to Richard Jackson for xvij^{c} sperelyngs	ix^{s} viij^{d}
Sum of the payments	vj^{li} xviij^{d}
Itm. The same Jamys askyth allowance of xiiij^{s}, whiche the seid late abbot dyd owe hym at the tyme of his last accompt, whiche endyd at Cristmas last past, as yt dothe appire by the accompt of the seid Jamys More . .	
Itm. The late abbot of Whalley dyd owe unto the seid Jamys More, for a grey stagg that the seid late abbot dyd by of the same Jamys by the space of a yere syns	x^{s}

By me James Mor.

[1] Dornix,—stuff made at Doornix or Tournay.

[2] Communicated to this Edition by the Rev. R. N. Whitaker, Vicar.

Status Mon. beate Marie Virginis de Whalley, 1536.[1]

INVENTARIUM OMNIUM ET SINGULORUM BONORUM MOBILIUM.[2]

Vasa sacrata pro vestibulo deputata.	UNC.
In primis xvi Calices de arg. deaurat. et ponderant	ccclxxix.
Duo paria Thuribul' de arg. deaurat. .	lxiv.
Una navis de argento pro Chrismat.' .	ix.
Unum par Phialar' de arg. deaur. .	viij.
Unum par Candelabr. de arg. . .	l.
Baculus pastoralis de arg. capite deaur. .	cvi.
Caput alterius Baculi de arg. deaur. .	xxxii.
Una Crux de auro	xxx.
Alia Crux de arg. deaur. . . .	lxii.
Alia Crux de arg. deaur. . . .	viii.
Alia Crux ex ligno cum argento cooperta.	
Una Pax de argento	xii.
Una Mitra ornat. cum lapid' viz. Perls, super argent.	

Vasa argentea in Cellario et in Camera Abbatis.	
In primis tres Salsar' de arg. deaurat. cum II^bus coopertoriis	lvi.
i Bassyn et i Ewer de arg. . . .	lxix.
iiii Bolls de arg.	lviii.
ii Bolls de arg. parcel gylde . . .	xxxvi.
iii Standyng Cups wth Covers deaur. .	lxxxx.
i Standyng Cupp parcel gylde . .	xxiv.
A Nest of Gobletts wth a Cover . .	lx.
A Goblet with a Cover all gylde . .	xxvi.
i other Goblet wth a Cover parcel gylde .	xxvi.
ii Wyne Potts de arg.	xlii.
iii Ale Cupps parcel gylde . . .	li.
iii letyll Ale Cups wth ii covers parcel gylde	xxxviii.
i Doss. Spones all gylde . . .	xxiv.
ii Doss. Spones wth gylde heds . .	xxxii.
i Doss. Spones	xii.
ii Nutts[3] for Ale, harnyshed wth Sylver.	
ii Massers[4] for the Convent halle harnyshed wth Sylver.	

From a paper in the Augmentation Office, I am now enabled to add several particulars to my account of this house after the attainder.

The Abbey and demesnes were immediately committed to the custody of Braddyll. In the course of two or three weeks Richard Pollard, esq. one of the King's surveyors, came down and let the demesnes in parcels for the first half year, or from Lady's Day to Michaelmas. Hence it appears that all the live stock must have been already disposed of. But, besides the demesnes, the tenants at will, who were all the inhabitants of the town, occupying with their houses small tenements of five, six, or eight acres each, were compelled to enter into new contracts, probably at advanced rents. Yet the whole sum paid by them was only 18*l*. 2*s*. 9*d*. per annum : the price of houses from 1*s*. to 6*d*. and even 4*d*. each. The demesne lands averaged about 2*s*. per acre, Lancashire measure, and at this low rate produced 62*l*. 11*s*. 2*d*. The herbage of the park and wood (the Lord's Park), two miles in circuit, was demised to Sir Alexander Osbaldeston for 12*l*. This, I suppose, was pretty near the current price of land at the time. Every acre of land, then let for 2*s*., is now worth thirty times the sum ; and yet the price of the necessaries of life is not advanced

[1] I find, by a comparison of hands, that this was written by Rob. Paris, al. Parishe, one of the last monks.

[2] [This must be a fragment, for a status of the monastery and an inventory of all the moveable goods would include much more than the plate.]

[3] A very early instance of the use of cocoa-nuts as cups.

[4] Massers, *i.e.* mazer or maple bowls, called by Ralph de Diceto, ad ann. 1182, Cuppæ Mazerinæ.—Vide Junium in voce. Ex aceris nodis sive tuberculis crispo macularum discursu conspicuis fiunt scyphi insignes.—Ib.

in the same interval more than ten or twelve fold. The reason of this disproportion is, that, in times when there is no trade, farmers must live wholly from the produce of their farms, and therefore require a much larger profit in them. This was also a reason why landowners retained so large a portion of their estates in their own occupation.[1]

The following reflections may not improperly close this part of the subject:

Had the Dissolution of Monasteries been conducted on other principles than sacrilege and rapine, had the application of their revenues been directed by those high ideas of the inalienable nature of tithes and offerings which prevailed a century later, and, in consequence, their spiritualities completely restored to officiating incumbents, while the temporalities, instead of being squandered with thoughtless prodigality, had been disposed of at an extended value, the necessities, even of Henry VIII. might have been abundantly supplied, and a wealthy yet not overgrown establishment have been formed as the basis of Reformation. But as it was in fact conducted, nothing but the overruling Providence of God could have procured even a decent reception for the reforming clergy. For, on the sites of these great foundations, and among people, above all others, bound to the old religion by interest, by imagination, by gratitude, and by regret, *they* were turned out, armed indeed with the word of God, but destitute of all external means to conciliate or to reward. On the very sites where whole districts had so lately been feasted and pensioned, *they* had neither kitchens for hospitality, nor purses for alms. Dejected and dissatisfied, and many of them, it is probable, deeply tinctured with old prejudices, they performed their stated offices without spirit, and without effect, and they transmitted to their successors a people only Christian inasmuch as they had received the rite of baptism, and only not Catholics because the mass had been abolished among them.

[AGREEMENT ON THE TITHE OF HAY MADE IN 1333.

INDENTURA testatur quod cum controversia mota fuisset inter religiosos viros fratrem Robertum Abbatem de Whalley et ejusdem loci conventu [*sic*] ordinis Cesterciensis ex parte una et parochianos capellarum Ecclesiæ Whalley, viz. de Burneley, Colne, Alvetham, Church, Haslingeden, parochianosque villarum de Symondeston, Padiham, Twiselton, Hapton, Rochedham, Downam, Pendleton et Chatburne ex parte altera pro decima feni, dicta controversia sub hac forma tandem amicabiliter quievit, viz. quod omnes et singuli dicti parochiani et eorum heredes tam presentes quam futuri imperpetuum solvent de cetero singulis annis fide media dictis abbati et conventui et eorum successoribus pro decima cujuslibet plaustrate feni unum quadrantem argenti bone etc. tempore quadragesimali quando computant procuratoribus dictorum abbatis et conventus de aliis minutis decimis in Ecclesia de Whalley et in Capellis ejusdem supra dictis, &c. Dat. apud Whalley in festo Sancti Hillarij Anno Domini 1333. (Harl. MS. 2077, f. 128.)]

[1] At the death of Sir John Townley, of Townley, A.D. 1541, the whole estate was valued at 100*l*. per annum. The same, when stripped of all additions by purchase or inclosures, is now worth 3,000*l*. Nor was the price of land in this district greatly advanced in the reign of James the First. In the year 1612 the demesnes of Townley were surveyed, and valued at 2*s*. per acre. In the Parliamentary Survey, about 40 years after, the same lands averaged between 4*s*. and 5*s*. Eight shillings per acre was about the average rent of farms here in the reign of Queen Anne. In half a century more it had increased in a ratio of two and a half to one. In the same interval, from that time to the present, it may generally be considered as trebled again.

[(Augmentation Office, Miscellaneous Book, vol. vii. fol. 19.)

SEQUITUR brevis quedam Declaratio totius valoris omnium terrarum et possessionum Attinctorum in partibus Borealibus et existentium infra circuitum Philippi Lentall judicis domini Regis earundem terrarum in Comitatibus predictis.[1] Anno regni ejusdem domini nostri nunc Henrici VIII^{vi}. Dei gratia Anglie Francie et Hibernie Regis, Fidei Defensoris, in terris Anglicane et Hibernice Ecclesie supremi Capitis, xxxvi anno.

(*Extract.*)

Whalley nuper Monasterium in com. Lancastr' et Cestr' infra recepta Johannis Keehyn Receptoris generalis ibidem.

	Summa Annui Valoris. Prima facie.	Repensuris.	Remanet.
Dominium sive manerium de Whalley	iiij^{xx}x li. xiiij s. iiij d.	iiij li. xij s. vj d.	iiij^{xx}vj li. xxij d.
Dominium sive manerium de Byllyngton	xlv li. vj s. iiij d.	,, li.	xlv li. vj s. iiij d.
Wysewolde et Wytton	xvij s. vj d.	,, li.	xvij s. vj d.
Padyham	vj d.	,, li.	vj d.
Chatborne	xiij s. iiij d.	,, li.	xiij s. iiij d.
Clayton	x d. cancellatos.	,, li.	x d. cancellatos.[2]
Penhulton	lvjs. ij d.	,, li.	lxvj s. ij d.
Cliderowe	xiij li. xviij s. x d.	viij s. iiij d.	xiij li. x s. vj d.
Croenton et grang' de Staynynges	c s. xd. ob.	,, li.	c s. xj d. ob.
Colcotes	viij s. viij d.	,, li.	viijs. viij d.
Acryngton	xiij s. iiij d.	,, li.	xiij s. iiij d.
Cadeleswalhed, Walden Magna, Walden Parva et Willaton Manerium	xli s. iij d.	,, li.	xlj i. iij d.
Harrowes bankes	lxv s.	,, li.	lxv s.
Rosendale	lxv s.	,, li.	lxv s.
Burneley	xxxiiij s. viij d.	,, li.	xxxiiij s. viij d.
Standen juxta Clyderowe	ix s. iiij d.	,, li.	ix s. iiij d.
Romesgreve et Maunton	lv s. viij d.	,, li.	lv s. viij d.
xvijs viijd xxxijs			
Downham et Rede infra parochiam de Whalley	xlix s. viij d. cancell.	,, li.	xlix s. viij d. cancell.[2]
Maner' de Spotland, Chatterton, Whyteworthe, Tonge, Roclyff, et Brandwood	lxxi s. iiij d.	,, li.	lxxj s. iiij d.
Harwood Parva	ix s. iiij d. cancell.	,, li.	ix s. iiij d. cancell.[3]

[1] Viz., Lancaster, Chester, York, Lincoln, Rutland, and Suffolk.

[2] Quia conceditur inter alia Johanni Braddell' et heredibus imperpetuum per literas patentes domini Regis xxiij^{tio} die Martii anno xxxvi^{to} Regis.

[3] Quia responsum est domino Regi de eadem in Curia Augmentationis revencium Corone.

	Summa Annui Valoris. Prima facie.	Repensuris.	Remanet.
Castleton et Hundersfeilde . .	xxij s. iiij d. ob. q^{a}.	,, li.	xxij s. iiij d. ob. q^{a}.
Maneria de Wheleton et Wythinhill	xviij s. vij d.	,, li.	xviij s. vij d.
Preston in Aunderness . . .	ij s.	,, li.	ij s.
Bankehouse in Wharton . .	iiij d.	,, li.	iiij d.
Barston et Sikebarthe . . .	iiij li.	,, li.	iiij li.
Denton	xij d.	,, li.	xij d.
Rybchester	ij s. j d.	,, li.	ij s. j d.
Swynton, Haugton, Westslacks, Kepull, Westwood et Merland .	xxiv s. ij d.	,, li.	xxiv s. ij d.
Marton	x s.	,, li.	x s.
Elleswycke	iij s. iv d.	,, li.	iij s. iv d.
Carleton	xviij d.	,, li.	xviij d.
Wygan	vj s.	,, li.	vj s.
Warrington	viij s.	,, li.	viij s.

Com. Cestr'.

Graung' de Acton et Aston . .	xxxvij li. xj s. ij d.	,, li.	xxxvij li. xj s. ij d.
Graunge de Stanlowe . . .	xiij li. vj s. viij d.	xx s.	xij li. vj s. viij d.
Graunge de Stanye . . .	xlij s.	,, li.	xlij s.
Bakeforthe	xx s.	,, li.	xx s.
Northwyche	v s. iiij d. cancell'.	,, li.	v s. iiij d. cancell'.[1]
Nantwyche	v s.	,, li.	v s.
Civitas Cestr.	iiij li. vij s.	xxviij s.	lx s.
Waddington in Com Ebor. . .	ij s.	,, li.	ij s.
Rector' de Whalley	ccxxxvij li. xiij s. iiij d.	l li.	ciiij^{xx}vij li. xiij s. iiij d.
Rector' de Blackeburne . .	cxxxix li. ij s. ij d.	xxvj li. xiij s. iiij d.	cxij li. viij s. x d.
Rector' de Rachedale . . .	cij li. vij d.	xxij li.	iiij^{xx} li. vij d.
Rector' de Eccles	cxiiij li. xviij s. viij d.	x li. xiij s. iiij d.	ciiij li. v s. iiij d.

Summa totius valoris terrarum et possessionum pertinencium Monasterio de Whalley predicto.	VIII^{c}xxix li. xviij s. ob. q^{a}. viz. in Com.	Lancastr'	VII^{c}iiii^{xx}j li. iij s. ij d. ob. q^{a}.
		Cestrie	xlviij li. xij s. x d.
		Ebor'	ij s.
Repensuris diversis modis.	cxvj li. xv s. vj d. viz. in Com.	Lancastr'	cxiiij li. vij s. vj d.
		Cestrie	xlviij s.
		Ebor'	,, li.
Et sic remanet ultra omnia Repensura in computis ministerii.	VII^{c}xiij li. ij s. v d. ob. q^{a}. viz. in Com.	Lancastr'	VI^{c}lxxj li. xv s. viij d. ob. q^{a}.
		Cestrie	xlvj li. iiij s. x d.
		Ebor'	ij s.

Repensuris in Computo Recepto hoc Anno . . . lxxvj li. ij s. iiij d. q^{a}.

[1] Quia responsum est domino Regi de eadem in Curia Augmentationis revencionum Corone.

The very curious paper which now follows was unknown to Dr. Whitaker. It contains minute directions for the lections, or lessons, to be read throughout the year in the Refectory or Infirmary at Whalley, "according to the use and laudable custom of this *Locus Benedictus.*" No such document has occurred for any other English monastery :[1]

Quicunque scire desiderat quomodo libri Veteris ac Novi Testamenti necnon Sermones sanctorum patrum secundum usum et laudabilem consuetudinem hujus Loci Benedicti legi debeant in Refectorio vel Infirmatorio, legat hanc sequentem scripturam et inveniet.

Advent, First Sunday. Dominica prima Adventus Domini legantur in refectorio Sermones beati Bernardi Abbatis.[2] In Adventu Domini legatur Isaias propheta in refectorio, et incipiatur ibi ubi lecciones finales terminantur.[3] Post Ysaiam prophetam legantur Sermones beati Bernardi, incipiat lector ubi finerit dominico die.[4] Post Sermones sancti Bernardi legatur Alredus de undecim oneribus. Advent, Third week. Septimana tertia legantur quatuor Omelie beati Bernardi super Evangelium, *Missus est*,[5] et incipiatur feria quarta, post quas omelias legatur Alredus usque ad vigiliam Nativitatis Domini. Dec. 6. St. Nicholas, Bp. of Myra. Die Sancti Nicholai Episcopi legatur legenda sanctorum.[6] Dec. 21. St. Thomas, Ap. and M. Die Sancti Thome apostoli legatur legenda sanctorum.[7]

Christmas. In Nativitate Domini legantur Sermones beati Bernardi. In die Nativitatis Domini

[1] Illustrations from the *Usus Ordinis Cisterciensis*, the Cistercian Breviary, and other authentic sources, are appended in the footnotes, which will materially assist the reader in his perusal, and will afford him some idea of the great pains bestowed by my coadjutor the Rev. Ponsonby A. Lyons, as well upon this as upon the other documents now for the first time accurately edited in these pages.—(J. G. N.)

[2] S. Bernardi Abbatis Claræ Vallensis Sermones de Tempore. In Adventu Domini (seven sermons). Migne, Patrologiæ Cursus Completus, clxxxiii. col. 35—56.

[3] That is, where the lessons in the Breviary, which had been read in the church, end. In Adventu Domini; Dominica prima Esayas incipiatur ad Vigilias: et deinceps totus legatur per Adventum, non solum ad Vigilias, sed et in refectorio prout tempus expetierit. Usus Ordinis Cisterciensis, Paris 1643; cap. l.

[4] Sermones xxxii. in Adventu Domini de oneribus in capp' xiii. et seq. Isaiæ prophetæ. Migne, cxcv. 361—502. Alredus is one of the many synonyms of Aelred third abbot of Rivaulx in Yorkshire. He died 12 Jan. 1166, aged between 57 and 67. (Acta Sanctorum, Bollandus, Januarius, tom. i. p. 749.) These sermons are usually quoted as Aelredus De oneribus Isaiæ. He thus enumerates the eleven burdens in his first sermon (omitted by Migne).—Sanctus Isaias undecim nobis onera prophetica describit: Onus Babylonis, Onus Philistiim, Onus Moab, Onus Damasci, Onus Ægypti, Onus deserti Maris, Onus Duma, Onus in Arabia, Onus Vallis Visionis, Onus Tyri, Onus jumentorum Austri. La Bigne, Maxima Bibliotheca Veterum Patrum, tom. 23, p. 5 G. In the MS. the transcriber has written *omnibus* in mistake for *oneribus*.

[5] De laudibus Virginis Mariæ. Super verba Evangelii, *Missus est angelus Gabriel*, etc., Luke i. 26, 27. Four homilies and preface. Migne, clxxxv. 55—87.

[6] Leg. sanct. cap. iii. De Sancto Nicolao, p. 22—29. "Legenda Sanctorum que alio nomine Lombardiæ vocitatur Historia." Title of the Nurenberg edition of 1492. It is best known as Legenda Aurea, and was written by Jacobus de Voragine, born about 1230, Archbishop of Genoa 1292, died 1298. It was a most popular book. Echard says that the manuscript copies are nearly innumerable, and he mentions thirty-eight Latin editions. (Scriptores Ordinis Prædicatorum, i. 435.) There are twenty-three Latin editions in the British Museum. That here referred to is by Dr. Th. Graesse: Lipsiæ, 1846, 8vo.: 214 chapters and 957 pages, of which 101 are additions to the original work. The monks of Whalley read more than one-fifth of the whole.

[7] Cap. v. De Sancto Thoma Apostolo, p. 32—39.

legantur Sermones beati Bernardi.[1] De Sancto Stephano, Johanne, et Innocenciis Sermones beati Bernardi. Septimana Nativitatis Domini legantur fines leccionum que lecte erant ad vigilias in die Nativitatis Domini,[2] preter omeliam super evangelium *liber* generacionum,[3] post fines omnium leccionum legantur Sermones Bernardi de Nativitate Domini,[4] postea si necesse fuerit legantur Sermones beati Bernardi de nativitate Domini[5] usque ad finem Sancti Silvestri. St. Silvester, Pope, Dec. 31. In die Sancti Silvestri legatur De vita ejusdem in parvo passionario.

Circumcision, Jan. 1. In die Circumcisionis Domini legantur Sermones beati Bernardi.[6] Post Circumcisionem Domini legantur epistole beati Pauli.[7] Post epistolas legatur vita Sancti Silvestri. Post vitam Sancti Silvestri legatur sanctus Augustinus de verbis apostoli[8] usque ad lxx^{am}. Epiphany, Jan. 6. In die Epiphanie legantur Sermones beati Bernardi.[9] Dominica prima post octavam Epiphanie legantur Sermones beati Bernardi de nuptiis in Cana Galilee.[10] St. Vincent, Jan. 22. Die Sancti Vincencii legantur legenda sanctorum.[11] Conversion of St. Paul, Jan. 25. In conversione Sancti Pauli legantur Sermones beati Bernardi.[12]

Purification of B. M. Feb. 2. In purificacione beate Marie legantur Sermones beati Bernardi.[13] Septuagesima. Dominica in lxx^{a} egantur Sermones beati Bernardi.[14] Deinde super Abvil'.[15] In lxx^{a} legantur quinque

[1] In Nativitate SS. Innocentium. Sermo unicus. Migne, clxxxiii. 129—132.

[2] The Lessons for Christmas are taken, in the Cistercian Breviary, from Isaiah, chapters ix., xl., and lii.; from St. Leo Magnus, Sermo xxi., In Nativitate Domini nostri Jesus Christi, i. cap. i. (He wrote ten sermons on the Nativity.) Migne, liv. 190—193; from S. Jerome on Matthew; from St. Gregory the Great, xl., Homiliarum in Evangelia Libri duo. Lib. i. Hom. viii. § 1. Migne, lxxvi. 1103—1105: from Bede, Homilia vi. In aurora Nativitatis, Migne, xciv. 34—38: and from Bede, Homilia vii, In die Natali Domini. Ibid. 38—44.

[3] S. Eusebii Hieronymi Commentariorum in Evan. Matthei Libri Quatuor, lib. i. caput i.; of which the first few sentences were read as a lesson. Migne, xxvi. 21—26.

[4] In Nativitate Domini, (five sermons). Migne, clxxxiii. 115—139.

[5] In vigilia Nativitatis Domini, (six sermons). Migne, clxxxiii. 87—116.

[6] In Circumcisione Domini, (three sermons). Migne, clxxxiii. 132—142.

[7] Si tempus a circumcisione usque ad lxx. breve fuerit non solum in Ecclesia: sed etiam in refectorio legantur Epistolæ Pauli, quod fiet secundum quod cantor ordinaverit. Usus Ord. Cist. cap. viii. p. 17.

[8] Two classes of St. Augustine's Sermons, De Verbis Domini and De Verbis Apostoli, are found thus named in MSS. of the ninth century. When both classes are found in the same MS. the first of the Sermones de verbis Apostoli is numbered 65; but the order of those De Verbis Domini varies in different MSS., of which an instance occurs in this paper.

[9] In Epiphania Domini, (three sermons). Migne, clxxxiii. 141—152.

[10] Dominica Prima post Octavam Epiphaniæ, (two sermons). I. De Miraculo facto in Nuptiis (Jo. ii. 1—11), &c. II. De Spiritualibus Nuptiis. Migne, clxxxiii. 115—130.

[11] Cap. xxv. De Sancto Vincentio, pp. 117—120.

[12] In Conversione S. Pauli, (two sermons). Migne, clxxxiii. 359—365.

[13] In Purificacione beatæ Mariæ, (three sermons). Migne, clxxxiii. 364—372.

[14] In Septuagesima, (two sermons). Migne, clxxxiii. 161—168.

[15] Johannes Alegrin of Abbeville. Sermones de Tempore, id est in Epistolas et Evangelia totius anni. Marrier, Bibliotheca Cluniacensis; Preface, p. 6. None of the sermons of this author ever seem to have been printed, but MSS. of the various series are not uncommon. His Summa Festivalis is in MS. Reg. 3 A. ix.; his Dominicales Sermones in Harl. 4951, and Reg. 2 E. ix. All are folio volumes. He was born at Abbeville of the noble family of Alegrin. Doctor of Theology at Paris 1220. He was Master of the Schools of Paris, and taught Theology there for several years. He was canon of St. Vulfran in Abbeville. Occurs as Dean of Amiens 1218. Consecrated Archbishop

[St. Matthias, Feb. 24.] [Ash-Wednesday.] [First Friday in Lent.] [First Saturday in Lent.] libri Moysi deinde Josue Judicum et Ruth' usque ad dominicam Passionis Domini.[1] In die Sancti Mathie apostoli legitur legenda sanctorum.[2] Feria quarta in capite Jejunii legantur Sermones beati Bernardi.[3] Dominica prima xl° leguntur sermones beati Bernardi. Feria sexta ejusdem septimane legitur sermo beati Bernardi, De languido jacente juxta piscinam.[4] In die sabbati legitur sermo beati Bernardi de transfiguracione Domini.[5] Post historiam Ruthe leguntur sermones beati Bernardi super Psalmum, *Qui habitat.*[6] Postea si necesse fuerit legitur Sanctus Augustinus super Johannem. [Tuesday after 3rd Sunday in Lent.] Feria iij^a post tertiam dominicam Quadragesime legitur sermo Sancti Augustini de verbis Domini, *Si peccaverit in te frater tuus.*[7] [St. Gregory, Pope, Mar. 12.] In die Sancti Gregorii legitur legenda sanctorum.[8] [St. Benedict, Abbot, Mar. 21.] In die Sancti Benedicti Abbatis leguntur sermones beati Bernardi.[9] [Annunciation B.M. Mar. 25.] In Annunciacione beate Marie leguntur sermones beati Bernardi.[10] [The week before Palm Sunday, or the two weeks before Easter.] In Passione Domini legitur Jeremias propheta,[11] post Jeremiam prophetam legitur Sanctus Augustinus super Johannem. [Palm Sunday.] Dominica in Palmis leguntur sermones beati Bernardi.[12] [Holy Thursday.] In Cena Domini sermo beati Bernardi.[13] [Good Friday.] In Parasceve Augustinus super Johannem.

[Easter Eve.] In vigilio Pasche legitur sermo beati Bernardi: *vicit leo de tribu Juda.*[14] Postea Augustinus super Johannem. [Easter day and week.] In die Pasche et septimana leguntur sermones beati Bernardi.[15] Deinde sermo beati Leonis pape, De passione Domini.[16] [Friday in Easter week.] Feria vi^ta ejusdem septimane legitur omelia Origenis leccione evangelica,[17] *Maria Stabat.* Deinde si necesse

of Besançon 1225. Cardinal Bishop of Sabino Sept. 1227. He had been appointed Patriarch of Constantinople by Honorius III. but was kept in Rome by Gregory IX. He died in 1237.

[1] Reliqua pars vero (Genesis) si quid ab his vigiliis residuum est, aliique libri qui sequuntur usque ad libros Regum in refectorio legantur. Ubi hoc sollicite provideatur ut ante Dominicam qua canitur officium *Judica me Deus,* perfecti sint (that is, before the 5th Sunday in Lent). Usus Ord. Cist. cap. xi. p. 21.

[2] Cap. xlv. De Sancto Matthia apostolo, pp. 183—188.

[3] In capite jejunii et in quadragesima. (Seven sermons.) Migne, clxxxiii. 167—186.

[4] Not in his printed works.

[5] Nor this.

[6] In Psalmum xc., *Qui habitat,* Sermones septem decim. Migne, clxxxiii. 185—234.

[7] S. Aug. Episcopi, Sermo lxxxiii. (alias De verbis Domini 16). De verbis Evan. Mat. xviii. 15—18. Et de verbis Solomonis, Prov. x. 10 (12 chapters). Migne, xxxviii. 506—514. Sermo lxxxiii. (alias De verbis Domini 15). In verbis Evan. Mat. xviii. 21, 22 (7 chapters). Migne, 514—519.

[8] Cap. xlv. De Sancto Gregorio, p. 188—202.

[9] In Natali S. Benedicti Abbatis, Sermo. Migne, clxxxiii. 375—382.

[10] In festo Annuntiationis Beatæ Mariæ Virginis. (Three sermons.) Migne, clxxxiii. 383—393.

[11] Librum Hieremiæ Prophetæ his diebus tam in Ecclesia quam in refectorio legendum. Usus Ord. Cist. cap. xvi. De duabus hebdomadis ante Pascha, p. 31.

[12] In Dominica Palmarum. (Three sermons.) Migne, clxxxiii. 253—262.

[13] In Cæna Domini. De Baptismo, Sacramento altaris et Ablutione Pedum. Migne, clxxxiii. 271—274. Also another sermon considered spurious, Item in Cœna Domini Sermo, clxxxiv. 949—954.

[14] Sermones de Diversis, lvii. De septem signaculis per Christum solutis. *Ecce vicit leo,* etc. Apoc. v. 5. Migne, clxxxiii. 680, 681. See the next note.

[15] In die Sanctæ Paschæ et tempore Resurrectionis. Sermo I. De septem signaculis que solvit Agnus. II. Ad Abbates. De lectione evangelica *Maria Magdalena.* III. De mersione Naaman septies in Jordano. Migne, clxxxiii. 273—284.

[16] S. Leo Magnus, Sermones v., vi. De passione Domini. Migne, liv. 491—495. Sermones inediti, ii.; lvi. 1135.

[17] The seventh of nine Homilies ascribed to Origen, printed at Cologne 1475 with S. Gregoriæ Omeliæ (44). It has been printed alone by William Faques in Abchurch Lane before 1510; an English translation was printed by

First Sunday after Easter.
Easter week.
St. Ambrose, Bp. of Milan, Ap. 4.
First week after Easter.
St. Mark. Evan. Ap. 25.
SS. Philip and James, May 1.
Rogation days.

fuerit legitur Augustinus super Johannem, die sabbati. Dominica in Albis leguntur sermones beati Bernardi. In ebdomada post pascham leguntur Actus Apostolorum. In festo Sancti Ambrosii legitur legenda sanctorum.[1] Septimana prima post octavam pasche dum canitur historia *Si oblitus fuero*[2] leguntur epistole canonice, deinde Beringer'.[3] In die Sancti Marci evangeliste legitur legenda sanctorum.[4] In die sanctorum Apostolorum Philippi et Jacobi legitur legenda sanctorum.[5] Feria ii. iii. iiii. in rogacionibus in primis legitur sermo beati Bernardi, deinde legenda sanctorum de letania majore et minore,[6] deinde *Quis vestrum habebit amicum* super Abvil', postea Beringer'.

Vigil of Ascension.
Ascension Day.
St. Barnabas, June 11.
Trinity Sunday.
Corpus Christi Day, Thursday after Trinity Sunday.
Monday.
7th Sunday after Trinity.

In vigilia Ascensionis incipiatur Secunda pars super Abvil', *Elevata est nubes.* In die Ascensionis legitur sermo beati Bernardi.[7] Feria vi^{ta} die sabbato sermones beati Bernardi, postea Berenger' usque ad Pentecostam. In die sancti Barnabi apostoli legatur legenda sanctorum.[8] In die Pentacoste, feria ii. iii. et iiii. leguntur sermones sancti Bernardi,[9] deinde Augustinus super Johannem usque ad dominicam sequentem. In festo sancte Trinitatis legitur Augustinus de verbis Domini, sermo lxiiii^{us} de una Trinitate trinaque Unitate.[10] In festo Corporis Christi legitur tractatus de corpore Christi in libro qui vocatur *Examеron Basilii.*[11] Feria ii^{a} post festum sancte Trinitatis incipiatur liber Regum cum prologo in Refectorio, et deinde leguntur iiii^{or} libri Regum,[12] postea ii^{o} libri Paralipomenōn. Dominica vii^{a} post festum Sancte Trinitatis leguntur Beati Ber-

Reginald Wolfe in 1565, A Homilie of Mary Magdalene, &c. An old Italian translation was published by Rossi, in his Quatuordici seriture Italiane, i. 197—250.

[1] Cap. lvii, De Sancto Ambrosio, pp. 251—259.

[2] The beginning of the Responsorium after the First Lesson sung on the 4th and 5th Sundays after Easter. A Responsorium is sung after each lesson. Cum autem Responsorium *Si oblitus fuero tui* incipitur, Epistolæ Canonicæ leguntur. Usus Ord. Cist. p. 57.

[3] Expositio in Apocalypsin, frequently attributed in MSS., and by many writers, to Berengarius of Tours, a disciple of Abelard, and a renowned writer in his day. He died Jan. 1088, æt. 90. This book is printed by Migne, xvii. 765—970, with the title Expositio super septem visiones libri Apocalypsis, and is attributed to Berengauches, a Dominican monk of Ferrieres. It has also been attributed to St. Ambrose.

[4] Cap. lix. De Sancto Marco Evangelista, p. 265—271.

[5] Cap. lxv. De Sancto Philippo Apostolo, p. 292, 293; cap. lxvii. De Sancto Jacobo Apostolo, p. 295—303.

[6] Cap. lii. De letania majore et minore, p. 312—316.

[7] In Ascensione Domini (five sermons). Migne, clxxxiii, 299—324.

[8] Cap. lxxxi. De Sancto Barnaba Apostolo, p. 346—352.

[9] In Festo Pentecostes (three sermons). Migne, clxxxiii. 323—334.

[10] Sermo LII. (alias 63 de Verbis Domini), de Trinitate. Migne, xxxviii. 354—364. In the very fine MS. Burney 37 it is numbered xxv. "Citatur a Floro ad Galat. titulo sermonis in Trinitate. Plerisque autem MSS. inscribetur, De Una Trinitate Unaque Trinitate." Migne, Ib.

[11] The Hexameron of Basil consists of nine homilies on the creation, to which are often added in Latin copies (as in MS. Reg. 5 F. xvi) two supposititious homilies, De Hominis Structura. The Tractatus de Corpore Christi was perhaps chapters v. to viii. of Basil's book, De Spiritu Sancto, or else some treatise on the Incarnation (of which Migne, ccxix. 448, enumerates nineteen,) written in the same MS. volume which contained the Hexameron, or one on the body of Christ, of which Migne gives ten. See ccxviii. 680—81, or perhaps Thomas Aquinas, Opusculum 58, De venerabili sacramento altaris. The Officium de Corpore Christi in the Cistercian (as in the Roman) Breviary is by Thomas Aquinas, Opusculum 57. Opusculum 58 occupies sixty columns of the folio edition of the Opusculæ, Venice, 1498.

[12] Tempore illo quo canitur, *Deus omnium exauditor est* (responsorium after second lesson sung from the third to the eleventh Sunday after Pentecost) usque ad Kalendas Augusti leguntur quatuor libri Regum, et postea duo libri

Nat. of St. John Baptist. June 24. SS. Peter and Paul. June 29. Trans. of St. Thomas the Martyr, July 7.

nardi de septem panibus et fragmentis misericordiarum.[1] In Nativitate sancti Johannis Baptiste sermo sancti Bernardi.[2] In vigilia et in festo apostolorum Petri et Pauli et in octavo leguntur sermones beati Bernardi.[3] In translatione Sancte Thome martyris legitur vita ejusdem. Post duos libros Paralipomenōn legitur vita Sancte Thome, postea leguntur sermones beati Bernardi de obedientia et de humilitate et de labore,[4] postea Augustinus de verbis Domini usque dum incipiatur historia, *In principio*.[5] In festo sancte Marie Magdalene legitur legenda sanctorum. In festo Sancti Jacobi Apostoli legitur legenda sanctorum.[6]

St. Mary Magdalene, July 22. St. James the Apostle, July 25. Lammas, Aug. 1. St. Peter ad vincula.

Ad vincula Sancti Petri legitur legenda sanctorum.[7] In kalendis Augusti dum cantamus *In principio*, leguntur libri Salomoni, id est, Parabolæ, Ecclesiastes, Cantica Canticorum,[8] deinde Sapientia et Ecclesiasticus; post librum Ecclesiasticum legitur Augustinus de verbis Domini usque ad festum Sancti Bernardi,[9] tamen infra octavas Assumpcionis beate Marie legitur sermo beati Bernardi. De Assumpcione ejusdem Attu'[10] post finem librorum Salomonis. In die Sancti Laurentii legitur legenda sanctorum.[11] In Assumpcione beate Marie leguntur sermones beati Bernardi.[12] In festo Sancti Bernardi Abbatis legitur vita ejusdem in magno passionario. In festo Sancti Bartholomei legitur

St. Laurence, Aug. 10. Assumption V. M. Aug. 15. St. Bernard the Abbot, Aug. 20. St. Bartholomew, Aug. 24.

Paralipomenōn. Usus Ord. Cist. cap. xli. *Quomodo legantur libri in refectorio à Pentecoste usque ad Kalendas Novembris*, p. 73.

[1] Dominica VI. post Pentecosten. Sermo I. De evangelica lectione, ubi turba triduo sustinens Dominum septem panibus reficitur. Sermo II. De septem misericordiis. Sermo III. De fragmentis septem misericordiarum. Migne, clxxxiii. 337-344.

[2] In Nativitate S. Joannis Baptistæ. Sermo, de lucerna ardente tripliciter et tripliciter lucente. Migne, clxxxiii. 397-404.

[3] In vigilia SS. Petri et Pauli Apostolorum. Sermo, De triplici auxilio quod a sanctis accipimus. Migne, clxxxiii. 403-406. In festo SS. Petri et Pauli (three sermons) ib. 404-416.

[4] De diversis Sermo II. De obedientia, patientia, et sapientia, etc. clxxxiii. 542—546. De Diversis Sermo XLI. De virtute, obedientia, et septem ejus gradibus, clxxxiii. 653, 661. De diversis Sermo XX. De verbis Domini, Omnis qui se exaltat humiliabitur, etc. Luc. xviii. 14. clxxxiii. 292—294. De diversis Sermo XXXVI. De altitudine et bassitudine cordis. Ibid. 637—639. De div. Sermo XXXVII.-XXXIX. (three sermons), In labore messis. Ibid. 639—647.

[5] *In principio Deus antequam terram faceret*, etc. Responsorium after the first lesson for the first Sunday in August sung during August. Cap. xcvi. De sancta Maria Magdalena, p. 407—417.

[6] Cap. xcix. De Sancto Jacobo majore, p. 421—430.

[7] Cap. cx. De Sancto Petro ad vincula, p. 455—461.

[8] Si kalendæ evenerint die Dominica, eadem die inchoetur historia. Si vero Kalendæ in secunda vel tertia aut quarta feria evenerint, in Dominica quæ easdem kalendas præcedit, assumatur historia. Quod si kalendæ in quinta vel sexta feria aut Sabbato apparuerint, Dominica sequenti imponatur historia. Usus Ord. Cist. cap. xxxix. *De quatuor historiis quæ cantantur à Kalendis Augusti usque in Adventum Domini*, p. 71.

[9] A kalendis vero Augusti usque ad kalendas Septembris interim dum canitur *In principio Deus*, legimus Proverbia Salomonis, et postea Ecclesiasticus, et deinde Cantica Canticorum, et librum Sapientiæ, id est, *Diligite justitiam*, et postea librum Jesu fili Sirach, id est, *Omnis sapientia*. Usus Ord. Cist. cap. xli. p. 73.

[10] Perhaps the book ascribed to Melito Bishop of Sardis, De transitu Virginis Mariæ which was condemned by Pope Gelasius and rejected by Bede. It is printed in Migne's Patrologiæ Cursus Completus, Series Græca, v. 1231-1240. Tischendorf in his Apocalypsis Apocryphæ, p. 124-136, has printed it from several MSS. (without the first chapter, which begins with the name of Melito) under the title of Transitus Mariæ. B.

[11] Cap. CXVII. De Sancto Laurentio Martire, p. 488—501.

[12] In Assumptione B. V. Mariæ (four sermons). Migne, clxxxiii. 415—430. In Dominica infra Octavam Assumptionis Sermo, In duodecem prerogativis B. V. M. 429—438.

Beheading of St. John the Baptist, Aug. 29.

legenda sanctorum.[1] In Decollacione Sancti Johannis Baptiste legitur legenda sanctorum.[2]

Translation of St. Augustine, Sept. 6.
First Sunday in September.

In festo Sancti Augustini legitur legenda sanctorum,[3] deinde de vita Sancti Bernardi usque dum incipiatur historia, *Si bona*,[4] que dum incepta fuerit leguntur libri Jacobi, post librum (*sic*) Jacoby leguntur libri moralium beati Gregorii usque dum incipiatur *Peto Domine*,[5] que dum incepta fuerit legitur Thobias, deinde Judyth et Hester, postremum Esdras et Neemias. In Nativitate beate Marie sermo Sancti Bernardi.[6] In Exaltacione Sancte Crucis legitur legenda sanctorum.[7] In festo Sancti Mathei legitur legenda sanctorum.[8] In festo Sancti Michaelis Archangeli Sermones beati Bernardi.[9] In festo Sancti Iheronimi legitur legenda sanctorum.[10]

Nativity B. M. Sept. 8.
Holy Cross Day, Sept. 14.
St. Mathew the Apostle, Sept. 21.
St. Michael the Archangel, Sept. 29.
St. Jerome, Sept. 30.

October.

In kalendis Octobris dum cantatur historia *Adaperiat*[11] (*worn*) duo libri Machabeorum,[12] et incipiat lector ibi in refectorio ubi iiii^ta leccio finem fecerit,[13] post librum Neemie leguntur libri moralium Sancti Gregorii, post libros Machabeorum leguntur iiii^or libri evangeliorum[14] usque dum incipiatur historia, *Vidi Dominum*.[15] In festo Sancti Dionysii legitur legenda sanctorum.[16] In festo Undecim Millium Virginum legitur legenda sanctorum.[17]

St. Denis the Areopagite, Oct. 9.
Eleven thousand virgins, Oct. 21.

November.

In kalendis Novembris dum cantatur historia [*Vidi*] *Dominum*, legatur Ezechea

[1] Cap. cxxiii. De Sancto Bartholomeo, p. 540—548.

[2] Cap. cxxv. De decollatione Sancti Johannis Baptistæ, p. 566—575.

[3] Cap. cxxiv. De Sancto Augustino, p. 548—566.

[4] Si bona suscepimus de manu Dei, etc. The responsorium after the first lesson for the first Sunday in September. In kalendis Septembris quando canitur, Si bona suscepimus, Job. Usus Ord. Cit. cap. xli. p. 72.

[5] S. Gregorii Magni Moralium Libri, sive Expositio in Librem B. Job, Libri 35. Migne, lxxv. 509—1162, lxxvi. 1—782, 1,335 columns. *Peto, Domine, ut de vincula hujus improperii absolvat me*, etc. Responsorium after the first lesson for the third Sunday of September. In eadem mense mutatur historia alia, id est *Peto Domine*, et tunc legitur prius liber Thobiæ, deinde Judith, postea Hester. Ac postremo Esdras. Hanc autem historiam: i. *Peto Domine* nec ante pridie idus Septembris, nec post xiiij Kalendas Octobris, sed in his septem diebus ubicunque dies Dominica evenerit incipimus, excepto quod quando solemnitas Sanctæ Crucis die Dominica evenerit Dominica precedente festum dicatur, *Peto Domine*. Usus Ord. Cist. cap. xli. p. 74.

[6] In Nativitate Beatæ Mariæ, sermo, De Aquæductu. Migne, clxxxiii. 437—448.

[7] Cap. cxxxvii. De exaltatione Sanctæ Crucis, p. 605—611.

[8] Cap. cxl. De Sancto Matheo Apostolo, p. 622—628.

[9] In festo S. Michaelis (two sermons) Migne, clxxxiii. 447—454.

[10] Cap. cxlvi. De Sancto Hieronymo, p. 653—658.

[11] *Adaperiat Dominus cor vestrum in lege sua*, &c. Responsorium after the first lesson for the first Sunday in October, and sung during the month.

[12] In kalendis Octobris leguntur duo libri Machabeorum dum canitur, *Adaperiat Dominus*. Usus Ord. Cist. cap. xli. p. 74.

[13] That is, the reader was to begin at 1 Mac. i. 17. In libro tamen Machabeorum primum, ibi lector in refectorio incipiat ubi quarta leccio fecit finem. Usus Ord. Cist. cap. xli p. 74.

[14] Et cum perlecti fuerint (Macchabees) legimus quatuor libros Evangeliorum in refectorio tantum usque ad passiones, et dimissis passionibus quod reliquum est legatur. Usus Ord. Cist. cap. xli. p. 74.

[15] *Vidi Dominum sedentem super solium excelsum*, etc. Responsorium after the first lesson on the first Sunday of November and throughout the month.

[16] Cap. cliii. De Sanctis Dionysio, Rustico, et Eleutherio, p. 680—686.

[17] Cap. clviii. De undecim millibus virginum, p. 701—705.

propheta, et incipiat lector post lecciones feriales trium Ebdomadum, postea legitur Daniel et incipiat lector post lecciones feriales unius septimane vel duorum. Deinde leguntur xii Prophete, post xii Prophetas legitur Gregorius super Ezechielem usque adventum Domini.[1] In festo Simonis et Jude legitur legenda sanctorum.[2]

SS. Simon and Jude, Apostles, Oct. 28.

All Saints, Nov. 1.

St. Martin of Tours, Nov. 11.

St. Clement, Pope and Martyr, Nov. 23.

St. Katherine, V. and M. Nov. 25.

St. Andrew the Apostle, Nov. 30.

In festo Omnium Sanctorum leguntur sermones beati Bernardi in parvo passionario.[3] In festo Sancti Martini leguntur sermones beati Bernardi in parvo passionario.[4] In festo Sancti Clementis leguntur sermones beati Bernardi.[5] In festo Sancte Katherine legitur legenda sanctorum.[6] In vigilia et in die Sancti Andree apostoli leguntur sermones beati Bernardi.[7]

In omnibus ceteris dominicis diebus leguntur expositiones morales super evangel' in libro quem vocamus Abvil'. In (*torn away*) collacionem semper leguntur hi quinque libri, videlicet Vitas patrum,[8] Quid noceat claustralibus,[9] Dialogi Sancti Gregorii,[10] Diadema[11] monachorum, et Expositio[12] Hugonis super Regulam Canouicorum.

FINIS.

[1] S. Gregorii Magni Romani Pontificis Homiliarum in Ezechielem Libri duo. (Twenty-two homilies.) Migne, lxxvi. 785—1072.

[2] Cap. clix. De sanctis Symone et Juda Apostolis, p. 705—711.

[3] In festo Omnium Sanctorum. Sermones V. Migne, clxxxiii. 447—482.

[4] In festo S. Martini Episcopi. Sermo. De exemplis obedientiæ. Migne, clxxxiii. 489—500.

[5] De S. Clemente Papa et Martyre. Sermo. De tribus aquis—on Ps. cxv. 15. Migne, clxxxii. 499—502.

[6] Cap. clxxxii. De Sancta Catherina, p. 789—797.

[7] In festo S. Andreæ Apostoli. I. De tribus generibus piscium. II. De quatuor cornibus crucis. Migne, clxxxiii. 291—293.

[8] Vitæ Patrum, sive Historiæ Eremeticæ Libri decem, a work ascribed to St. Jerome, many editions of which were issued by the early printers. There are eleven Latin editions previous to 1520 in the British Museum. The best is that of Heribert Rosweyd, a Jesuit; Antwerp, 1615, folio, pp. 1011, reprinted in Migne's Patrologia, lxxiii. and iv. Vitas Patrum is frequently used as the title of the book not only in printed editions but in MSS. as old as the ninth century.

[9] In the Catalogue of the MSS. of the Episcopal Library at Durham, MS. V. I. 12, Art. 6, is De duodecim Abusionibus Claustri, etc. Sic incipit "Duodecim sunt abusiones Claustri." In fine: "Explicit, tractatus Hugonis de Sancto Victore de 12 Abusionibus Claustri." Catalogues of the Library of Durham Cathedral (Surtees Society), p. 141. This MS. evidently consists of chapters xi.—xxiii. of the Second Book, De Claustro Animæ, Libri iv. of Hugo de Folieto, Prior of St. Laurence of Amiens 1153 to 1174.

[10] Sancti Gregorii Papæ Dialogorum Libri iv., de vita et miraculis Patrum Italicarum, et de eternitate animarum. Migne, lxxvii. 149—430. (Greek and Latin in opposite columns.) The Benedictine editors say that the MSS. of this work are almost infinite, and that there was scarcely any ancient monastery in which two or three copies were not found.

[11] Smaragdi Abbatis Diadema Monachorum (100 chapters). Migne, cii. 593—690. Smaragdus became known about the middle of the eighth century. He dedicated a book to Charlemagne before he became emperor, which was in 800. He was Abbot of St. Mihiel, in the diocese of Verdun, about 806; at Rome in 810. He died 25 Oct. soon after the translation of his Abbey in 819. Hilduinus his successor occurs 825.—Gallia Christiana, xiii. 1272. Zedler, Universal Lexikon. Migne, Dict. de Patrologie.

[12] Hugo de S. Victore (died 11 Feb. 1140, æt. 44), Expositio in Regulam Beati Augustini. Migne, clxxvi. 881—924. It has been frequently printed.

SEALS ATTACHED TO WHALLEY CHARTERS.

The Plate of Ecclesiastical Seals which faces this page was inserted in this History by Dr. Whitaker without further explanation than that given in the Latin line at its head, that it represents the seals of ancient Bishops and Chapters which were appended to the charters of the monasteries of Stanlaw and Whalley, and to the confirmations of the churches of Whalley, Blackburn, and Rochdale. They were unfortunately derived from no better originals than very rude pen-and-ink drawings in the Harleian MS. 2064, one of the MSS. of Randle Holme, who copied them, together with the charters to which they were attached, from the originals then at Whalley. They are considerably "improved" in drawing by the engraver Basire, and consequently can only be regarded as affording a general idea of the devices of the seals, and imperfect copies of their legends. With this explanation, the present Editor will do what he can towards describing them.

1. Seal of the Priory of St. Mary of Coventry. The Virgin and Child.

SIGILLVM SANCTE MARIE DE COVENTRE.

This seal is engraved in the Monasticon Anglicanum, edit. 1826, Plate VIII. fig. 6, but from so imperfect an impression that the Holy Child is omitted and the legend varied.

Counterseal of a Prior named Henry. The device of this I cannot undertake to specify: nor do I find it in the Harl. MS. 2064.

2. Alexander de Stavenby, Bishop of Coventry 1224.

Counterseal: the device is evidently an antique gem, apparently of Hercules. The legend is too blundered in copying to be interpreted.

This seal was attached to a charter relating to the chapel of Walton, which is printed in the Coucher Book, edit. Chetham Soc. p. 84.

3. William de Cornhill, Bishop of Coventry 1214–1223.

The counterseal represents the bishop praying to the Son of God, held in the arms of the Virgin, in the terms of this hexameter:

SIS ROGO FILI DEI GULIELMO DUX VIA VITE.

This seal was affixed to a charter relating to the church of Rochdale, printed in the Coucher Book, edit. Chetham Soc., p. 139.

4. Perron, Bishop of Larina 1289. The Virgin and Child between the moon and sun; below, the bishop between two stars.

Counterseal, the Holy Lamb.

5. Boniface, Bishop of Parenzo 1289.

6. Leother, Bishop of Veroli 1289.

Counterseal, apparently an owl.

These are the three seals attached to the Indulgence printed in p. 146.

7. Roger de Meuland, Bishop of Coventry and Lichfield 1257.

He was the third Roger who had occupied the see, and in order to identify his seal this is inscribed across the seal, ROG' III., under heads probably intended for Saint Alban and Saint Chad. Below are his two cathedral churches. Beneath his feet merely an architectural bracket, ill copied.

8. Seal of the Abbat of Stanlaw—

SIGILLVM ABBATIS DE LOCO [BENEDICTO].

This seal is attached to a charter relating to the churches of Rochdale and Blackburn in 1277. (Harl. MS. 2064, fol. 307.)

…scoporum et Capitulorum Veterum ad Chartas Cœnobiorum de Stanlaw et Whalley et ad Confirmationes Ecclesiarum de Whalley Blackburn et Rochdale olim appensa

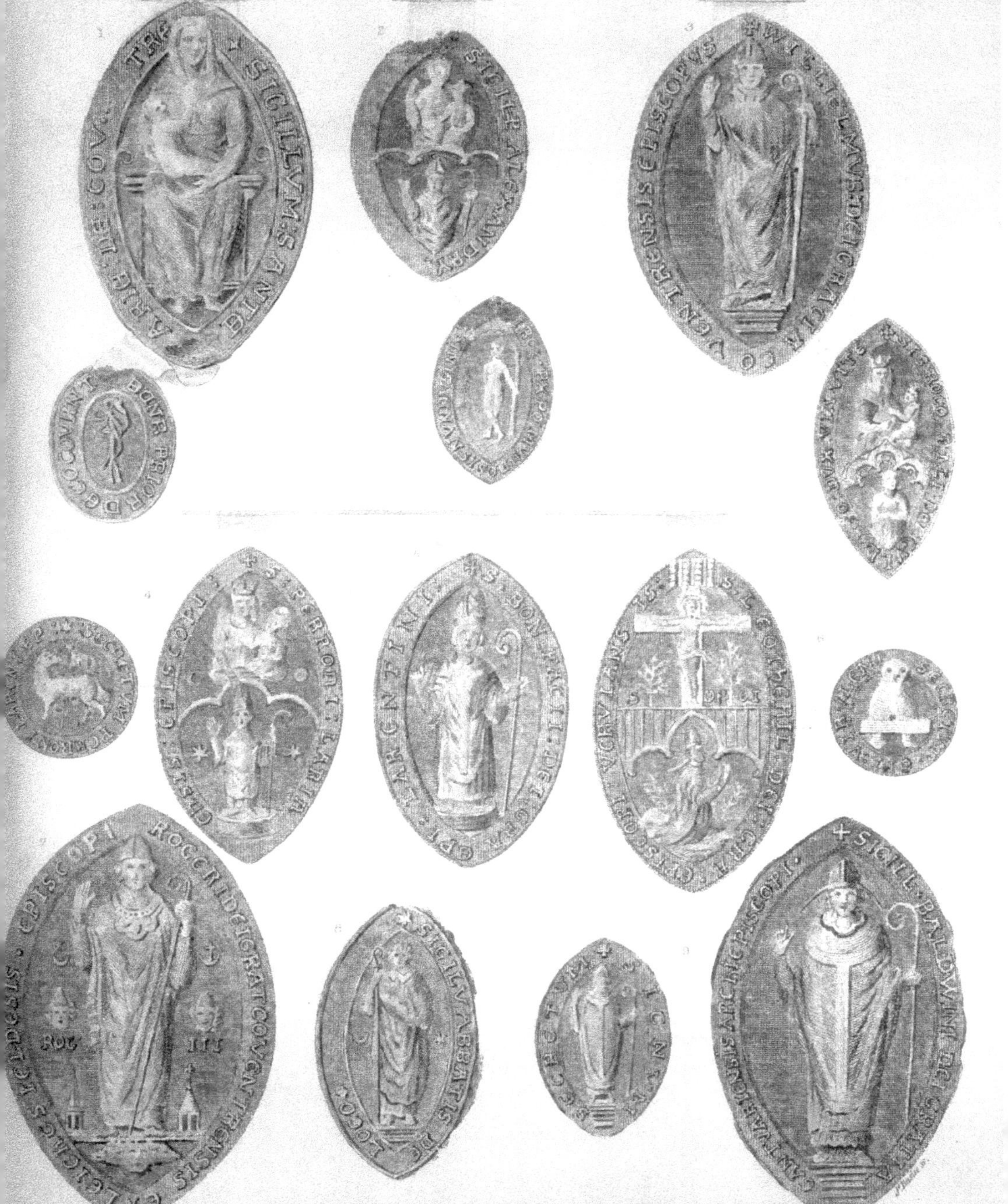

Erudito et amicissimo viro Thomæ Starkie A.M. Vicario de Blackburn de se pariter et opere suo multis omnibus optime merito hanc tabulam D.D.D. T.D. Whitaker.

9. Baldwin, Archbishop of Canterbury 1184. Counterseal, his figure repeated: SIGNVM SECRETVM. (The inverted crescent behind his head is a mistaken alteration of the dependent infulæ of his mitre.)

This seal was attached to the archbishop's confirmation of the charter of Richard Bishop of Coventry, of Staney and Eston to Stanlaw. Harl. MS. 2064, fol. 307. Coucher Book, edit. Chetham Soc. p. 15.

The Seal of Whalley Abbey, which was unknown to Dr. Whitaker, is now engraved for the first time. It is from an impression in green wax attached to a charter in the office of the Duchy of Lancaster, Class X. Box A. No. 124, being Henry Duke of Lancaster's foundation of the Hermitage of Whalley (see pp. 96, 97,) dated (at the beginning) Whalley, 10 Dec. 34 Edw. III. and at the end, 2 Jan. 10th year of the duchy of the said Duke. The shields on this seal are those of the founder or patron, as Constable of Chester and Earl of Lincoln. The legend, S' COMVNE ABB'IS ET CONVENTUS LOCI B'N'DICTI DE WHALLEY.

From the Visitation of the North, by Thomas Tonge, Norroy, in 1530. (Harl. MS. 1499, f. 45, fol. lxviii.)

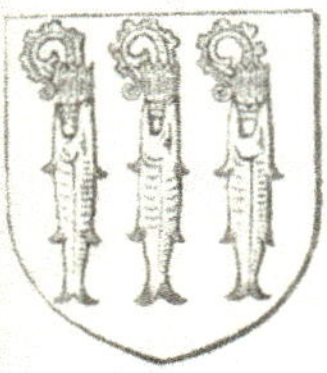

These be the armys of the monastery of Whalley of White Monkes, which armes belongeth to the said monastery.

Be yt noted, John Lacy, Constable of Chester, and hys heyres after, Erles of Lincoln, founded the monastery of Whalley of White Monkes, in the Countye of Lancaster, of whom descended Alice, wife to Thomas Erle of Lancastre, whiche Alice, daughter and heyre to Henry Lacy, Erle of Lyncoln, by whom our souverayne lord the Kyng restyth Founder of the said Monastery.

The following MS. note by Dr. Whitaker was written on p. 110 of the third edition of this work :—

"Mr. Johnson, Vicar of Whalley, has recorded in his papers that he had seen a charter of Henry de Lacy granting a right of fishery in Ribble and Hodder on all days excepting Sundays, 'ministris et fratribus domus de Whalley.' The fishery of Calder they must have had already, and I consider their armorial bearings, viz., three salmons in pale, pierced by as many croziers or, as an allusion to the right so conferred or before enjoyed in these three rivers and to the noble fish with which they then abounded."

Notwithstanding the three fish may be thus pleasantly regarded, I must add that I am still inclined to adhere to the earlier description which I find of them, as being more consistent with the ordinary significance of ancient armory. They are termed *whales* in Edmondson's "Complete Body of Heraldry," I have no doubt upon competent official authority: and so again by Moule in his "Heraldry of Fish," and by Mr. Dyer Longstaffe, the Editor of Tonge's Visitation for the Surtees Society: and this customary echo to the sound of the name receives confirmation from several families of Whalley bearing whale's heads. J. G. N.

CHAPTER THE THIRD.

PARISH CHURCH AND VICARAGE OF WHALLEY.

HAVING now traced, to the several periods of their duration, the ancient Deanery, the short-lived Rectory which followed, and the magnificent Abbey which rose upon the ruins of both, we are next to consider the Vicarage, which has survived them all, and will probably continue as long as an ecclesiastical establishment remains in England.

The regular ordination of a Vicarage in this church did not take place immediately upon the appropriation, nor even till five years after the death of Peter de Cestria, the last incumbent. In the mean time, it may be presumed that the monks of Stanlaw, while they were preparing for their own translation, were careful to have the cure supplied by chaplains; and, for two years afterwards, by some of their own body. But, in the year 1298, Walter Langton, Bishop of Lichfield, endowed[1] the second Vicarage of Whalley in a spirit more favourable to the wants and merits of a respectable incumbent than to the rapacity of craving monks. For he ordained the vicar's portion to consist in a manse and thirty acres of meadow and (*terra*) corn land adjoining, with housebote and haybote in

[1] Copies of most of these endowments, &c. remain in the Coucher Book, and among the Towneley MSS. but they have been already given from an authentic and original source, the *Liber Loci Benedicti* (see pp. 160 *et seq.*)

The ancient glebe of the Rectory or Deanery, as we have already seen, was the entire demesne of the manor of Whalley; but it is remarkable that all vestiges of the glebe, granted to the vicar under the first endowment, have not yet disappeared, though it was so quickly merged in the Abbey demesne again. In the Inquisition of Survey, taken before Roger Nowell, Esq. &c. A.D. 1616, the glebe was described as lying in divers parcels about the Nether Town, together with two tenements near Clerk Hill, one occupied by Mr. Crombock, and the other by Henry Hammond, gent. (a near relative of the famous Dr. Henry Hammond). The cottages to the east, with their gardens (though the site of the ancient hermitage) are described as parcel of this glebe, and those on the north, *but without any gardens.*—The lands near Clerk Hill are still distinguished by the name of Glebe [and some near Nethertown also. R. N. W.]

But saith this survey, "By the terrier there should be 41a. 2r. 20 falls of glebe, yet it appears that by two recoveries, one bearing date 26 Edw. I. of 15 acres, and the other 12th Edw. III. of 60 acres, that in Whalley were 75 acres of glebe. (I am unable to account for this last fact, as the second endowment, which stripped the vicarage of the best part of the glebe, had taken place long before the 12th of Edw. III.) Moreover, to this glebe belonged common on Whalley Moor, and also common of pasture in the moors of Billington, and the vill of Harwood, between Rotilegh Clough and the Divises of Billington, excepting 60 a. of moor and pasture within the same Divises, reserved when this common was granted, viz. A.D. 1314." So far the Inquisition, which records a very singular fact, namely, that right of common appertained to the glebe of Whalley in another parish.

the abbey woods, and common of pasture for his cattle in the park,[1] along with those of the convent, in the altarage of the mother church and chapels, that of Alvetham excepted, which was then litigious. Likewise in the glebe lands of Brunley and the other chapels,

This may partly be explained by the following record in the *Liber Loci Benedicti* [now printed in full]:

De divisis factis inter Magnam Harwod, medietatem ville Billyngton quam d'ns Adam de Hudleston miles quondam habuit, et aliam medietatem ejusdem ville quam nobilis vir d'ns Henricus de Lasey comes Lincoln' habuit.

Die veneris proximo ante festum Sancti Johannis Baptiste Anno regni Regis Edwardi xxx°iiii. (17 June 1306), de assensu et voluntate nobilis viri domini Henrici de Lascy, comitis Lincoln, facta fuit hec concordia apud Altosfes inter Willielmum, de Heskayth, Joh'em filium ejusdem Will'i, Rogerum Noel, Adam filium ejusdem Rogeri, Alexandrum Hurel et Margaretam uxorem ejus, querentes, ipsos Will'm, Rogerum, et Alexandrum et Margaretam uxorem ejus esse disseysitos de libero tenemento ipsorum Will'mi, Rogeri, Alexandri, et Margarete uxoris sue in Magna Harrewod in Com. Lanc. ex una parte, et dominum Ad. de Hudleston militem, tenentem predictum liberum tenementum asserentem idem tenementum esse in Bilyngton, de quo libero tenemento predicti Willielmus, Rogerus, Alexander et Margareta uxor sua quesiti fuerunt ipsos esse disseysitos ex altera. Que quidem concordia talis est: scilicet incipiendo ad quandam sepem antiquam super ripam aque de Kaldir subtus le Fallyngtreker, descendendo per illam sepem usque ad quendam rivulum propinquiorem terre, quam terram Robertus Spekes tenuit die confectionis presentis scripti in Bilyngton, et sic ascendendo per dictum rivulum versus summitatem cujusdam montis qui dicitur Bellesetenabbe linealiter usque ad quoddam fossatum ibi de novo constructum. Et sic de illo fossato per foveas ibidem factas et lapides ibi per loca positos directe usque ad le Horelowe, et del Horelowe per foveas ibi de novo factas et lapides ibidem positos usque Snoddeworth qui locus de Snoddeworth est in occidentem. Et sic erunt de cetero divise inter Magnam Harrewod et Bilyngton predictas imperpetuum. Ita scilicet, quod terre, bosci, vasta et tenementa omnia de quibus contencio inter eos fuerat, et que sunt ex parte dictarum divisarum, ubique versus Magnam Harrewod, remanebunt in separali predictis Willielmo, Johanni filio ejusdem Willielmi, Ade filio Rogeri Noel, Alexandro Hurel et Margarete uxori ejus ut liberum tenementum suum in Harwod. Et post decessum ipsorum Alexandri et Margarete uxoris sue qui tenent dicta tenementa versus Harrewod nomine dotis dicte Margarete, simul cum dictis Willielmo, et Ad. pro indiviso tenementa illa in Harrewod remanebunt predictis Willielmo, Johanni filio suo et Ad. fil. Rogeri et heredibus ipsius Johannis et ipsius Ade quieta de predicto domino Ad. de Hudleston et heredibus suis imperpetuum, tenendum de capitalibus dominis feodi per servicia inde debita et consueta. Et terre, bosci, vasta et tenementa omnia unde contentio fuit inter eos que sunt ex altera parte dictarum divisarum versus Bilyngton remanebunt in separali dicto domino Ade in forma subscripta videlicet quod tota medietas terre, bosci, vasti et tenement. omnium remanebit dicto domino Ade et heredibus suis imperpetuum. Et tota altera medietas terre, bosci, vasti et tenementorum omnium ultra divisas predictas versus Bilyngton remanebit dicto domino Comiti et heredibus suis post decessum dicti domini Ade imperpetuum quieta de heredibus dicti Ade. Et hec concordia facta fuit in presentia dicti domini Henrici de Lascy Comitis Lincoln. ad predictam concordiam pro se et heredibus suis imperpetuum tenendum consentientis et illam ratificantis. Et in omnium suprascriptorum testimonium parti istorum scriptorum cyrographatorum tripartitorum penes dictum dominum Comitem remanenti: predicti Will'm's, Joh., Ad. de Hudleston, Rogerus et Adam fil. dicti Rogeri, Alex. et Margareta uxor ejus sigilla sua apposuerunt. Et alteri parti penes dictum dominum Ad. de Hudleston remanenti sigilla dictorum domini Comitis, Will'i de Heskayth, Joh. fil. ejus, Rogeri, Ad. filii sui, Alex. et Margarete uxoris sue sunt apposita. Et tertie parti penes dictos Will'm, Joh'em fil. ejusdem Will'i, Rogeri, Ad. filium ejus, Alex. et Margaretam uxorem suam remanenti sigilla dictorum domini Comitis et domini Ade sunt apposita. Hiis testibus, dominis Will'o le Vavasour, Will'o de Stopham, Ad. de Waleton, Will'o Banastre, militibus, Thom' de Fisheburn, Henr' Lescrop, Edmundo Talbot, Thom' le Sureys, Simone de Alvetham, Ric'o de Ruyshton, Rob'to de eadem, Ad. del Clogh, et aliis. Dat' apud Altoftes die et anno supradictis. (Add. MSS. 10,374, fol. 77 b-78.)

[1] From this early mention of a park, it appears to have been inclosed before the foundation of the abbey, and probably under the deans. It was afterwards called the Lord's Park, and extended from near the town to Parkhead in length, and from Calder to the turnpike-road in breadth, a fertile and beautiful piece of ground. [See before, p. 183].

&c. This was a fair and liberal distribution of the benefice, which, though it allowed to the monks the rich and spacious glebe, excepting thirty acres, and all the tithes of the parish, great and small, still left the incumbent in a respectable and independent situation.

These conditions were endured for a season, because they were the best that could be obtained from a prelate of good sense, spirit, and humanity; but, after the death of Langton, who survived this transaction twenty-four years, a bishop succeeded, of whom it is observed by Godwyn, that, after having sat thirty-eight years, he had done nothing worthy of commendation, *nisi forte hoc ab illo recte factum dicamus, quod mortuus est.* This was Roger de Northborough, a man much more acccommodating to the views of monks, and accordingly, by a second ordination, dated at Manchester, 12 kal. Apr. in the year 1330, after reciting the immoderate endowment of the present Vicarage, the barrenness of the place, the great resort of strangers, the increased number of monks, the expenses incurred in building, &c. this bishop having examined the abbot and vicar in person, and the convent by their proctor, and exacted an oath from all parties to abide his ordination, decrees that the Vicarage in future shall consist in a competent manse, with a yard within the abbey close, to be erected at the expence of the house, in hay sufficient for one horse, with four quarters of oats, and in sixty-six marks, payable in money; in consideration of which, the vicar should undergo all ordinary burdens of the said church, the chapel of Alvetham, concerning which the suit was now determined, and all the other chapels; that he should also find a priest for each chapel, with bread and wine for the communion, &c.; and moreover, that he should distribute the sum of 13*s.* 4*d.* on the morrow of St. Michael, yearly, to the convent, as a pittance.

Henceforward the vicar became little better than a mere stipendiary, burdened, moreover, with the expences of the sacramental elements, and with the support of seven priests, to officiate in the dependent chapels.

These are the seven chapels of the old foundation, all of which not only existed, but were endowed with competent glebes before Henry de Lacy's grant of the advowson, A.D. 1284. And all these glebes, though merged from the time of this ordination in the glebe of the rectory, remained till the late sale of one moiety of the rectory, distinct from all other property, and generally contiguous to the churches to which they originally belonged.

The following table will necessarily suggest two observations: 1st. that these glebes have uniformly been allotted with a reference to the ancient oxgang; and 2dly, how little that admeasurement varied from itself in seven distinct instances.

COMPARATIVE TABLE OF THE CHAPELS OF THE OLD FOUNDATION IN THE PARISH OF WHALLEY, WITH THE MEASURE OF THEIR RESPECTIVE GLEBES IN OXGANGS AND ACRES.

Name.	Æra.	Oxgangs.		A.	R.	P.
CLIDERHOW	all mentioned in Delaval's charter, and therefore existing temp. Henrici 1mi.	2		43	3	0[1]
St. Magdalen, in villa CALNE		2		35	2	0
BRUNLEY		2		35	0	0[2]
ELVETHAM	founded by H. fil. Loswine, circ. R. Ric. 1mi. [1189]	4	originally endowed as a parish church; but, upon being reduced to a state of dependence, the glebe appears to have been restored to the manor.			
DOWNUM	uncertain, but all founded before the year 1284.	2		36	0	20
CHURCH		2		32	0	10
HASLINGDEN		1		15	0	0

I have lately met with the original, from which the following instrument is transcribed, among the charters at Towneley. [It is dated in 1393, and exonerates the parishioners resident in the chapelries of Colne, Burnley, Church, and Haslingden, from contributing to the repairs of the church of Whalley, charging those living in Whalley, Clitheroe, and Downham :]

Pateat universis per præsentes, quod cum in visitatione Domini Archidiaconi Cestriensis quam in Decanatu de Blackburn ultimo exercuit, compertum fuit quod ecclesia parochialis de Whalley in coopertura, parietibus et fenestris, et cemiterium ejusdem in clausura multiformes patiebatur defectus, in defectu parochianorum dictæ ecclesiæ et capellarum de Colne, Brunley, Church, et Haselyngden, ab eadem ecclesia dependentium ; super quibus dictus Dominus Archidiaconus parochianos capellarum prædictarum ad certos diem et locum super dicto comperto fecit coram eo officiali suo ut ejus commissario evocari. Qui quidem parochiani capellarum dictarum eisdem die et loco sibi assignatis coram nobis commissario dicti Domini comparuerint, et quandam relaxacionem sive renunciacionem in scripto redacto diversis sigillis cum sigillo officialis Cestriensis signato per parochianos de Whalley, Cliderowe, et Downum factam, dictos parochianos de Colne, Brunley, Churche, et Haselynden, ut videbatur, omni onere dictæ ecclesiæ parochiali de Whalley faciendo exonerantem, et ipsos parochianos de Whalley, Cliderowe, et Downum in omnibus onerantem, judicialiter exhibuerint et ostenderint : unde nos commissarius dicti domini officialis die et loco dictis parochianis capellarum prædictarum assignatis in hac parte legitime prætendentes, habita publica proclamatione in judicio . . . . nemine se opponente, dictos parochianos capellarum prædictarum de Colne, Brunley, Chirche, et Haselyngden, consentientibus omnibus in hac parte requisitis, quatenus officium nostrum præmisso concernit, ab officio nostro dimisimus per decretum. In cujus rei testimonium sigillum officii dicti domini officialis præsentibus est appensum. Datum apud Werington iiij kal. Aug. anno Domini Mccc° nonagesimo tercio. (29 July 1393.) (*From Addenda to the Third Edition.*)

[1] It now appears to me more probable that this was the half-carucate belonging to the chapel of St. Michael in Castro. The measure is too large for two oxgangs of rich land, and not too small for half a carucate of the same quality. Still I hesitate. After all, is it probable that the chapel of St. Magdalen would be unendowed with any glebe? And may not the basis of the estate of the Asshetons in Clitheroe, with the exception of the fourteen burgage houses, have been the half-carucate in question? [I have since discovered that this was the glebe of St. Michael in Castro. *Corrigenda*, in Third Edition, p. 552.]

[2] As per survey, anno Eliz. 36, though now increased by the inclosure of the commons of Ightenhill, temp. Jac. I. to 48 a. 2 r. 4 p.

In the endowment of these ancient chapels a very laudable attention, we see, was paid to the independence and comfort of the incumbent; and two oxgangs, or somewhat more than thirty Lancashire acres, appear in general to have been thought adequate to his support. Whether, before the first appropriation, these chaplains were entitled respectively to the whole of their own altarage, or to what part of it, or to none at all, does not appear.

But it is difficult to stop the progress of injuries when once begun; for, even in Langton's ordination, liberal as it was in some respects, the vicar was first robbed by the monks, and then sent to seek his remedy by seizing the glebes and manses of the dependent clergy. From this sentence, however, the terms of which were, perhaps, as easy as Langton could impose, no appeal lay but to the Court of Rome, where every ear was closed to a representation of the secular clergy against the monks; so that from this time forward the poor chaplains were compelled to hire a residence where it could be found, and to purchase the necessaries of life where they could be obtained, when there was scarcely any exchange or commerce, and that out of a poor pittance of about five marks per annum.

But the influence of superstition gradually improved the condition of these incumbents again: chantries began to be founded and endowed with competent revenues; the lands were often within a convenient distance of the church, and furnished with decent houses; Burnley alone, though but a chapel, resembled a little college of priests, and had no less than four altars well endowed.

This order of things, like all the former, had its day. But another revolution was now at hand, which swept away, with undistinguishing rapacity, the rewards of piety and wages of superstition. At the dissolution of chantries, 1 Edw. VI. no distinction whatever was made in these foundations between the incumbent and the chantry priest; and though the former was sometimes, not always, permitted to remain in possession of his own church,[1] he was turned out once more upon the world, without manse or glebe, and compelled to subsist upon a miserable and ill-paid stipend, allotted him by the Commissioners of pious uses; and in this abject and impoverished state did these foundations continue till the gradual operation of Queen Anne's Bounty restored their ministers to much of the comforts of independence, though seldom to a convenient and appropriate residence.

Of all the measures by which unprincipled men disgraced the Reformation, none contributed more, by the manner in which it was conducted, to injure that excellent cause, than the dissolution of chantries, a measure in which, after the rich harvest of Henry's plunder was exhausted, it seemed to be the sole object of a profligate court to gather the miserable gleanings of sacrilege without regard to the service of God or to the cause of religion; in which, by diminishing the numbers of the clergy, they destroyed much of that

[1] Some chapels were demolished, as Chatburn (but see that township in the parochial survey); others dissolved and sold again to the inhabitants for divine service, as Littleborough and Milnrow (Towneley MSS.); others again left standing, but without endowment or minister, as Holme; even the great parochial cures of Burnley, Colne, &c. were stripped of everything, and their incumbents paid by trifling pensions.

influence which near inspection and personal intercourse with the people always produces, and, by impoverishing the foundations which remained, they effectually prevented the introduction of learned and able preachers. For the effect was what might be expected—the inferior clergy of that and the succeeding times have been too often contemptible for their poverty among the rich, their ignorance among the refined, and their bad morals among the devout; so that, from the want of a well-informed, respectable, and respected ministry, a country antecedently superstitious and stupid has never been thoroughly evangelized to the present day. Religion, indeed, in the reign of Edward VI. exhibits a spectacle at once pleasing and melancholy. The King, a boy, a scholar, and a saint; the bishops learned, sincere, and zealous; the courtiers selfish and corrupt; the inferior clergy, with a few shining exceptions, illiterate and useless; and the common people, after being deprived of their old forms, standing at gaze with an excellent liturgy in their hands, which, from the want of a preaching ministry in the country, they had neither been taught to esteem nor to understand.

After this account of the Chapels within the parish on the old foundation, it may not be improper to give a short view of those which have arisen since. Both these, indeed, and the former, will be treated more distinctly in their several places; but it may assist the recollection to bring them under the eye at once.

In the general confirmation of archbishop Arundel, A.D. 1400, the Chapels of the old foundation are recognized, and no more; so that it is certain that no new religious erections had taken place during a period of 116 years.

After this, the next foundation was,

Padiham, for which the licence of mortmain bears date 30th Hen. VI. Then,

Whitewell, Holme, Marsden,—all, erected, as appears from their architecture and some other evidence, between the reign of Henry VI. and Henry VII. Then,

Newchurch in Rossendale, 3rd Hen. VIII. which, by an instance of good fortune peculiar to itself, was permitted, I suppose in consideration of its poverty, to retain the original manse and glebe. Then,

Goodshaw, 32nd Hen. VIII. Then,

Newchurch in Pendle, 35th Hen. VIII. These three last in consequence of the planting of the forests. Afterwards, at an uncertain period,

Accrington, taken out of Alvetham; concerning the foundation of which the episcopal registry at Chester affords no information; but it is mentioned in Harrison's Description of Britain, p. 66, as extant in 1577. And, lastly,

Bacop, in Rossendale, consecrated A.D. 1788.

But it is high time to resume the immediate subject of this chapter.

Three vicars of Whalley (John, who appears to have been the first; Rich. de Chadsden, who, in 1310, resigned, at the request of Thomas Earl of Lancaster[1]; and Richard de Swinfleet,) enjoyed this benefice under the endowment of Walter Langton. The last was succeeded by one William le Wolf de Kirklauton, a native probably of Church Lawton, in

[1] A copy of the Earl's letter to this effect remains in the Coucher Book.

Cheshire, who not only submitted to what he was unable to prevent, namely, the last wretched appropriation, but was reduced, by a most arbitrary practice, exercised in other instances upon the poor vicars, to bind himself by oath never to procure an augmentation.[1] He was followed by John de Topcliffe, brother of the abbot,[2] whose name perpetually appears with that of Gristhwaite, vicar of Blackburn, in the charters of this period, as trustees, to take lands for the benefit of the house; and after his death, which happened about 30th Edw. III. the abbot and convent presented no more secular priests, but retained the benefice in their own hands till the dissolution. No usurpation of the monks gave greater offence, or was more injurious to the interests of religion than this, when, not content with the original appropriations, they had begun in some instances to devour the endowed vicarages, by appointing only chaplains to serve them; and in others, as in that before us, to nominate one of their own body, who, instead of keeping hospitality upon his benefice, was merely a boarder in the convent. The real advantage which they derived from these scandalous presentations was, that a regular, being under the obligation of the vow of poverty, could not touch the fruits of his own benefice, which of course accrued to the common stock of the house. This practice, after many remonstrances and complaints of the commons in parliament, produced a well-meant statute, 4 Hen. IV. [c. 12] providing, *inter cætera*, "that from henceforth in every church appropried a secular person be ordained vicar perpetual, and that no religions be any wise made vicar in any church so appropried, or to be appropried by any means in time to come." But this was unfortunately a law without a sanction; no penalty having been annexed to the breach of it: the abuse, therefore, continued till the 10th of Henry VI. "when a bill was brought into parliament requiring that in every church appropriated, or to be appropriated, a secular person be ordained perpetual vicar, to do divine service and keep hospitality; and that if any religious, or men of holy church, which have or hold any churches in proper use, from henceforward suffer such vicarages to be inofficiate, without a vicar resident there for six months, that the same churches be disappropried and disamortized for ever, saving only to the said religious their patronage in the same." This was vigorous and decisive; but the poor King was instructed to reply, "Le Roy s'avisera," and this inveterate evil continued in unabated malignity till the dissolution, to which it had its full share in contributing.[3]

The monks might have taken warning from the invective, shall I call it, or the prophecy of Piers Plowman, who, long before these statutes, boldly taxed them with want of charity and hospitality upon their appropriated benefices, and warned them of the consequences in a strain exceeding, as we should suppose, the powers of natural sagacity and foresight.

[1] [See this curious document hereafter, p. 225. Dr. Whitaker's statements in this place must be compared with the corrected institutions of the Vicars, hereafter, p. 211. John de Topcliffe preceded William le Wolf, but he also followed him, being admitted Vicar a second time; and there were two other Vicars, of whom Whitaker was unaware, before Selby.]

[2] There was a third brother resident in Billington, which I suppose to have been the native place of the family.

[3] See Bishop Kennet's Case of Impropriations *passim*.

Little had lordes to dow to geve londes from her heyres
To religious that have no ruthe if it raine on her autres;
In manye places ther the persons (appropriators) be hemself at ease
Of ye pore have they no pitye and that is ther charite.
And ther shall come a king and confesse you religious,
And amende monials, monkes and chanons,
And then shall the abbot of Abbingdon and al his issue for ever
Have a knocke of a kynge and incurable the wounde.

After the dissolution of the monastery, by deed of exchange between King Edward VI. and Archbishop Cranmer, dated June 12th, anno regni primo, the appropriate rectories of Whalley, Blackburn, and Rochdale, with the advowson of their several vicarages, are granted to the see of Canterbury, under the following very inaccurate description: "omnes illas rectorias nostras et ecclesias de Whalley, Blackburn, et Rachdale, nuper monasterio sive abbatiæ de Whalley nuper dissolutæ dudum spectantibus, ac etiam omnes illas capellas nostras de Padiham, Clyderhow, Coln, Brunley, Churche, Altham, Haslingden, Bowland, Penhull, Trawden,[1] et Rossendale, et capellam nostram de Clyderhowe, necnon omnes illas capellas nostras de Leeke (mis-written for Law), Samlesbury, Saddleworth, Butterworth, &c. et advocationem et jus patron. vicariarum eccl. p'dict. de Whalley, Blackburn, et Rachdale, dictæ nuper mon. dudum spect."[2]

In consequence of this acquisition, Archbishop Cranmer appears to have collated soon after, but certainly before the 7th of the same reign, Edward Pedley,[3] S. T. B. to the vicarage of Whalley. He was the first Protestant vicar, and was interred Dec. 5, 1558, with this eulogy in the register, "egregius Concionator," a proof of care and fidelity on the part of this apostolical bishop, in providing a faithful preacher for so large a parish, not always imitated by his successors.[4] He received 46*l*. from the great tithes.

After this, I find, by a receipt of Archbishop Whitgift's, A.D. 1588, of which a copy is inserted in the old book marked A. C., that the vicar received out of the great tithes the sum of 30*l*. per annum.

During the Usurpation, and for some time afterwards, the stipend was 38*l*., of which I am unable to say why it varied from the original endowment of 66 marks.[5]

[1] Qu. Was Trawden a mistake for Marsden?

[2] Lambeth MSS. Misc. vol. xiii. No. 21.

[3] From the first half-year's account made by Braddyll, at Michaelmas 1537, it appears that Pedley was then vicar. [Payment of his pension as Vicar occurs in the Ministers' Accounts 28 and 29 Hen. VIII. No. 29. (Augment. Off.) He was, therefore, Vicar before the dissolution, and probably originally appointed by the Abbot and convent.]

[4] This is an early and happy exception to my former strictures; but it is not long before we meet with this expression in a letter to a succeeding archbishop, "Whalley hath as ill a vicar as the rest." [See note in p. 213.]

[5] Immediately after the Restoration the ten curates subscribed 40*s*. each, and deputed Mr. Moore to wait on Archbishop Juxon with a petition for the Easter-roll, when a promise was obtained at the next renewal, which happened a little while before Juxon's death. Sir Ralph Assheton valued the Easter-roll at 120*l*. but it was found to fall considerably short of that sum. Afterwards, as the trust was not very clearly expressed, Mr. Gey made an attempt to appropriate the whole to himself: this occasioned an Exchequer suit, which ended in a decree to this effect: "That a trust did exist, and that the vicar should assign over to such persons as the major part of the curates should appoint."

But upon the accession of Archbishop Juxon, this benefice, and the parochial chapelries dependent upon it, received a noble and most judicious augmentation by a grant of the whole Easter roll and surplice fees, which he reserved out of the rectory and tithery of Whalley upon the renewal of a lease, on condition that the several curates should receive the same within their respective cures, and should pay to the vicar for the time being, in different proportions, the sum of 42*l.*, which, with 38*l.* heretofore paid, would augment the stated income of the vicarage to 80*l.*

By this benefaction, however, in consequence of the depreciation of money, and the great increase of population, the curates have greatly the advantage, as they now receive (in consideration of certain fixed annual payments, making up, in the whole, the above sum of 42*l.*), besides their own surplice fees, formerly paid to the farmers of the rectory, all the customary payments due at Easter; that is to say, for communicants, for house debts, for kine, for calves, for hay, for plow, for lambs, for sheep sold, for swarms of bees, and for foals, throughout the whole rectory of Whalley, the tithery of Bowland excepted.[1]

On a subsequent renewal, Archbishop Sancroft also, in the year 1685, gave a great fine, received by him from the lessees of Whalley, Blackburn, and Rachdale, in Lancashire, to purchase lands, and settle annual pensions, for the stipends of the curates of the chapels of ease before unprovided for.[2]

The first transaction which occurs after the Dissolution is a lease of twenty-one years, from the Crown, of the Rectory of Whalley, bearing date July 8th, 30th Hen. VIII. to Sir William Pickering, knt. for the rent of £237 13*s.* 4*d.*

Next is a lease from Pickering to Richard Assheton, as under-tenant, dated Sept. 12th, 32 Hen. VIII. This was the first footing which the Asshetons obtained at Whalley.

Thirdly, another from Henry VIII. a. r. 35, to Sir John Dauntzey, knt. who, in 37 Hen. VIII. gave it to his natural son, who soon after assigned it to Richard Assheton in

[1] Trust Deed of 1688, pen. auct.—The most exact account of the Easter-roll is contained in an Inquisition of Survey for the Rectory of Whalley, taken by Roger Nowell, of Read, esq. and others, A.D. 1616, in which it is thus stated: "Also for lambs and calves of all numbers under seven, for every lamb an halfpenny, and for every calf an halfpenny, at Easter. If there be odds of calves or lambs under or above seven, there must be paid one halfpenny for each below seven and ten, and so from ten to seventeen. And for swarms and foals, one of ten or seven, *ut supra.* Also where any person sells any sheep after Candlemas, and before the same be clipped, then the seller is to pay for each an halfpenny at Easter. Also for every cow a penny at Easter. For himself or herself, and every other communicant resident in his house, a penny at Easter. Also an ancient duty called house-duty and offering-days. If there be man and wife fourpence-halfpenny, except in some places of the chapelries of Burnley and Colne, where they pay threepence-halfpenny. And in both cases, where there be more married persons in the house than the housekeeper and his wife, for every such, over the said fourpence-halfpenny, threepence-halfpenny. Also for every foal a penny, every swarm a penny, under ten or seven *ut supra*; but where ten or seven they pay *ut supra.* For every plow or draft a penny, and every half plow or draft an halfpenny. For every garden within the chace of Trawden a penny." What follows, as it has become quite obsolete, is very curious: "Also the parishioners, except in the chace above mentioned, are accustomed to pay an ancient duty called 'Holy-loaf money.' Thus every year fifty-two houses in every ancient chapelry in the said parish do pay a penny-halfpenny a piece; and next year fifty-two other houses do the like: and the next year after, fifty-two other houses; and so from fifty-two to fifty-two, till all the chapelry be gone over, then beginning again with the first, and so for ever."

[2] Bishop Kennet's Case of Appropriations, p. 308. Ex Reg. Lichf.

consideration of the manor of Downham, &c. (*vide* Downham). Pickering's lease was to expire in 1558, and Dauntzey's term was forty years from that time.

Fourthly, the remainder of this term was surrendered to Abp. Whitgift, 26th Eliz. who granted the first lease from the see of Canterbury to Ralph Assheton, esq. the elder and Ralph Assheton the younger, for the lives of the last Ralph and of Ratcliff Assheton, sons of Ralph the elder and of Richard son of Richard Assheton of Downham, brother of Ralph.

Lastly, the rectory of Whalley itself, after having been held under renewed leases from the time of Edward VI. by the Asshetons, and, after the marriage of the co-heiresses of the last Sir Ralph Assheton, by the families of Curzon and Lister, was, in the year 1799, alienated in perpetuity to the lessees under the sanction of an Act of Parliament by the present Archbishop of Canterbury; and thus, after having hitherto preserved at least a shadow of its original destination to ecclesiastical uses, the whole is finally desecrated and become a lay-fee.

[The Vicarage of Whalley continued in the patronage of the Archbishop of Canterbury, until it was alienated to the feoffees of the late William Hulme in the year 1846; since which time the stipends of the different incumbencies in their gift have been very largely augmented.]

Temp. in quibus occ.	Vicarii de Whalley.	Patroni.	Vacat.
1298	Johannes, vic. de Whalley	Abb. et conv. de Whalley	Incert.
1309	Ric. [or Radulph.] de Chadsden [1]	Ep. Langton, jure devoluto	Incert.
1311	Ric. de Swinflet [2]	Abb. et conv. de Whalley	Per resig. Chadsden.
1330	Johannes Topeliffe [3]	Iidem	Per resig.
1336	Wm. le Wolf de Kirklauton	Iidem	Per mort.
1342	Johannes de Topeliffe, 2° admissus	Iidem	Per mort.
1348	Johannes de Walton	Iidem	
1349	Robertus de Neuton	Iidem	Per mort.
	Fr. Will. Selby, postea abbas	Iidem	Incert.
July 12 1379	Fr. Rob. Normanvile, prior [4]	Iidem	Per resign.
June 7 1381	Fr. Johannes de Tollerton [5]	Iidem	Incert.

[1] Inst. Vic. Wh. ap. Lond. non. Maii 1309. Ibid.

[2] Non. Jun. 1311. Licentia concessa R. de Swinflet adeundi Romam in negotio vicariæ de Whalley. Ibid.

[3] Joh. de Topcliffe inst. Vic. Whall. non. Oct. 1330. Ibid.

[4] iiii Id. Julii 1379, apud Heywood, Rob. de Normanton, Pr. et Mon. de Whalley, inst. ad Vic. de Whalley vac. per res. Ibid. This nearly fixes the period of Selby's election to the abbacy. [The registers of Lichfield, prior to the foundation of the See of Chester, are bound in 14 folio volumes, and the records of the Archdeaconry of Chester are found under a separate title in each, and are pretty entire from the time of Walter de Langton (whose register is the oldest now remaining) to the year 1513, when they cease. In these records are contained many institutions or admissions of the Priors of Burscough and Holland, but none of the Abbots of Whalley, who were probably exempt from episcopal jurisdiction. Of the chantries within the compass of this work [few] are noticed but that of St. Katharine of Eccles and St. Leonard of Padiham. The rest were either not founded, or their officiating priests were stipendiaries only. The regular chantry priests received canonical institution. (Dr. Whitaker, in his Addenda et Corrigenda to the First Edition.)]

[5] Fr. Joh. de Tollyton inst. Vic. Whall. 7 Id. Jun. 1381. Ibid.

Temp. in quibus occ.	Vicarii de Whalley.	Patroni.	Vacat.
1411	Fr. Johannes de Salley, prior[1]	Iidem	Per resig. Tollerton.
1426	Fr. Rad. de Cliderhow,[2] postea abbas	Iidem	Incert.
1453	Fr. Will. Dynkley,[3] S.T.B.	Iidem	Per res. ut videtur
1488	Fr. Johannes Seller[4]	Iidem	Per mortem.
[1534	Fr. Robert Paryshe[5]	Iidem	
1536	Mr. Edward Manchester, B.D.		
1537	Edwardus Pedley, S.T.B.		Per resig.
April 8, 1558	Georgius Dobson, dec. rur. de Blackburn; sep. Maii 23, 1583	Queen Elizabeth	Per resig.
Oct. 9, 1581	Robertus Osbaldeston, M.A.	Arch. Cant.	Per mort.
Aug. 11, 1605	Petrus Ormerod; sep. Feb. 11, 1631	Richard Chadderton	Incert.
Feb. 21, 1631-2	William Bourn	Arch. Cant.	Incert.
1651	William Walker		
1656	William Moore		
1663	Stephen Gey; sep. Oct. 12, 1693	Arch. Cant.	Per mort.
1693	Richard White, A.M.; sep. Nov. 19, 1703	Arch. Cant.	Per mort.
Dec. 8, 1703	James Matthews; sep. July 19, 1738	Arch. Cant.	Per mort.
Sept. 25, 1738	William Johnson, A.M.	Archbishop Potter	Per resig.
July 2, 1776	Thomas Baldwin, LL.B. died at Leyland, Jan. 11, 1809	Arch. Cant.	Per mort.
1809	Thomas Dunham Whitaker, LL.D.	Arch. Cant.	Per mort.
[March 11, 1822	Richard Noble; died at Whalley, Nov. 29, 1839, aged 62	Arch. Cant.	Per mort.
Jan. 1, 1840	Robert Nowell Whitaker, M.A.	Arch. Cant.	Per mort.]

Of my predecessors, from the Reformation to the present day, the following are the only notices which I have been able to collect :—

Pedley received at his death an eulogium which has certainly not been applicable to some of his predecessors, *egregius Concionator*.[6]

[1] Joh. Salley, mon. Whall. inst. Vic. Whall. Nov. 7, 1411, post res. Tollerton. Ibid.

[2] Apud Haywood penult. Oct. 1426, Rad. de Cherehow (*sic*) inst. ad Vic. de Whalley. Ibid.

[3] Sept. 11th, 1453, Wm. Dynkley inst. p. res. R. de Clid.—This fixes the date of R. de Cliderhow's election. Ibid.

[4] Nov. 24, 1488, Joh. Seller mon. inst. Vic. Whalley post mort. Wm. Dinkley. Ibid.

[5] [This Vicar is now inserted in the list for the first time. His name occurs in the Valor as at once Vicar of Whalley and receiver of the rectory of Eccles. The Commission for taking the Valor is dated 25 Jan. 26 Hen. VIII. 1535, and the returns were to be made before the Octaves of Holy Trinity in the same year, 31 May 1535.

Pensio annuatim soluta Roberto Parrysshe vicario de Whalley xij li. Feodum Roberti Parryshe receptoris rectoriæ de Eccles per annum iiij li. (Valor Eccles. v. 229.)

Vicaria de Whalley. In manibus Roberti Parryshe monachi valet in pensione annuatim recepta de abbate de Whalley per compositionem xij li. Inde in pensione annuatim soluta episcopo Cestriensi xl s. Denariis solutis archidiacono Cestriæ pro sinodalibus et procurationibus per annum xliij s. Elemosina annuatim distributa in die obitus Rogeri nuper episcopi Cestriensis xiij s. iiij d. In annuali redditu resoluto gardianis ecclesiæ de Whalley per annum xx s. Et remanet clare vj li. iij s. iiij d. Inde Decima xij s. iiij d. ob. (Ibid. p. 230.)

His interment is thus entered in the Parish Register:

1572. Robertus Paris, alias Birche, capellanus vet. de Winsum.

Some of the abbey documents transcribed by Paris have appeared in p. 87.]

[6] See the previous notice of him in p. 209.

Dobson, whom Bishop Pilkington characterised as being an "ill Vicar," appears to have been eminently illiterate.[1]

Of Osbaldeston, I know not how nearly or how remotely he was allied to the ancient house of that name, nor what became of him. He was not interred at Whalley.

I strongly suspect Ormerod to have been a son of the parent house of Ormerod in Cliviger.[2] He constantly resided, and appears to have done his own duty. Every entry in the Register from 1605 to 1631 is in his own hand; and it is remarkable that a baptism and burial are entered by him on the fifth day before his own interment.

Of his successor, Burn, nothing is known.

Walker was never properly Vicar, having probably been intruded by the governing powers during the Usurpation.

Moore was a judicious and able divine, whose ministry must have been a blessing to the parish. By the kindness of the late Mr. Brand, Secretary to the Society of Antiquaries, I am possessed of a very scarce little volume written by him, and dedicated to Sir Raphe Assheton, entitled "The grand Enquiry, who is the righteous man, or the Character of a true Believer in his Approaches towards Heaven, by William Moore, Rector [?] at Whalley, in Lancashire. London, 1657." The orthodoxy, piety, and good sense of this little work lead me to suspect that Whalley had the best minister under the worst government. From the parish accounts, it appears that he resigned his vicarage A.D. 1663. He removed to Rothwell, in Yorkshire, where he died A.D 1664; and being styled, in his epitaph, Minister of that parish, I suspect that he only resigned Whalley for a better benefice, though I once supposed him to have gone out upon the Bartholomew Act.

Stephen Gey was incumbent and resident upon this benefice thirty years: he appears to have been a discreet and prudent man. (His Epitaph will be found in a subsequent page.)

Richard White, A.M. of Emanuel College, Cambridge, for now we arrive on the confines of recollection, was vicar ten years. I find in the parish accounts that on coming

[1] [Dr. Whitaker here alludes to a letter addressed by Dr. Pilkington, Bishop of Durham, to Archbishop Parker, and written probably in 1564; it relates chiefly to a vacancy in the Vicarage of Rochdale, and will be found in *Parker Correspondence*, p. 221. The zealous Pilkington freely tells the archbishop, "Your cures, all except Rachdale, be as far out of order as the worst in all the country The old Vicar of Blackburn resigned for a pension, and now liveth with Sir John Biron. Whalley hath as ill a Vicar as the worst. And there is one come thither that hath been deprived or changed his name, and now teacheth school there; of evil to make them worse. If your Grace's officers lust, they might amend many things. I speak this for the amendment of the country, and that your Grace's parishes might be better spoken of and ordered. If your Grace would, either yourself or by my lord of York, amend these things, it were very easy. One little examination or commandment to the contrary would take away all these and more."

[On the 27th May 1575 the parishioners of Whalley alleged an Information against Sir George Dobson, Vicar, to the Bishop of Chester. He was charged with teaching "in ye Churche ye Seven Sacraments, and he persuadeth his parishioners that they shall come and receive but in one kynd, and in any case to take it not as common bread and wyne as they may take it at home or elsewhere. That he gives at Easter to certein of his Parishioners consecrated Oasts, saying that in them is Salvation. In his reply he said that for thirty or forty years past he had behaved himself as a man of hys callyng ought to do.]

[2] [He was not very nearly related, as he was of the Gambleside family of Ormerod: see hereafter, under Whalley Grammar School.]

to take possession of the benefice he was met with great ceremony by the principal inhabitants, and that the penthouse window behind the pulpit was made for his accommodation.

He was succeeded by James Matthews, whom I may be allowed to call, as Bishop Godwin called his own predecessor Kitchin, the great dilapidator of the see of Llandaff, *fundi nostri calamitatem.* He was a needy man, of whom I have but too convincing proofs that he took money for presentations to the curacies, and that he set the lowest offices, such as those of parish clerk and sexton, to sale. By his means too, and not without a valuable consideration, the patronage of six, if not seven, of the curacies was alienated from the vicarage under the 1st George I. His example, however, appears to have operated as a warning to the dignified patrons of the living of Whalley, never more to intrust so poor a benefice with so rich a patronage annexed to it, in the hands of any but a man of property.

On the decease of Matthews, Archbishop Potter presented William Johnson, M.A. of Magdalen College, Cambridge, a native of Wakefield, and related to himself. He was of the Johnsons of Rushton Grange, in Bowland.

William Johnson, of Walsh Whittle, co. Lanc. gent. Pensioner of King James I. J. P. co. Lanc. = Eulalia, dau. of Mr. Wood, of Wood, co. Oxon.

Ferdinando Johnson, ob. s.p. — William Johnson, of Rushton Grange, in Bowland. = Mary, dau. of Dr. John Chambers, Dean of Carlisle and Vice-Master of Trin. Coll. Cambridge. — Richard Johnson, B.D. Fell. King's Coll. Cambridge. Fell. Coll. Ch. Manchester. Reader of the Temple, London, &c. *See Lancashire MSS. vol. xli. p.* 193.

Alexander Johnson, of Rushton Grange, aged 10 years 1665. *Dugdale's Visitation.* = Mary, daughter of James Bellingham, of Levens, in Westmerland, esq.

Alex. Johnston, of Rushton Grange and Wakefield. = Elizabeth, daughter of William Lawson, of Wakefield, merchant. — Alan Johnson, of Wakefield, attorney at law, afterwards of Temple Belwood in 1784. = ...dau and heir of..... Popplewell, of Temple Belwood, co. Lincoln.

William Johnson, A.M. Vicar of Whalley. = Elizabeth, daughter and co-heiress of Richard Tatlock, of Prescot, Esq. attorney at law. — Alan Johnson, of Temple Belwood, Esq. living 1783. — Richard Popplewell Johnson, of St. John's Coll. Camb. B.A. 1772, M.A. Rector of Ashton upon Mersey 1783. = ... — Alexander, 3d son, living 1783. — Mary. — Elizabeth.

[The additions made to this pedigree have been supplied by Mr. Canon Raines.]

On his accession to the benefice he found the ancient vicarage house, by the supineness of his predecessor, ready to fall to the ground; he therefore applied to his patron Archbishop Potter, who generously bestowed a quantity of excellent oak from the rectorial glebe sufficient to rebuilt it. With this material help he began the work, and has left it on record that he expended three years' income of his benefice on the structure, which is so durably and excellently finished, that more than thirty years of utter neglect, which would have reduced a flimsy fabric of the present day to rubbish, had little perceptible effect upon it. Mr. Johnson was a man of strong understanding, a keen and caustic wit, and an unconquerable spirit, which last quality he displayed in many disputes with his parishioners, who were always worsted, and above all in a contest with Archbishop Secker and his diocesan Bishop Keene for the patronage of the valuable curacy of Newchurch in Rossendale.

On this occasion that great and excellent metropolitan was so ill-advised as to lay claim to the presentation of all the unalienated curacies in the parish as appropriator. In order to establish his claim, a search was instituted at his request by Bishop Keene in the Registry at Chester, which, instead of producing any precedents of nominations by the appropriator, led to the discovery of an unattested copy of a decree of the Commissioners of Pious Uses in the reign of Edward VI. vesting the patronage of the Chapel of Rossendale in the Bishop of the Diocese. This brought forward a second competitor in the Diocesan himself; but, to the infinite advantage of his successors, Johnson maintained so firm and even menacing an attitude, that, after three years of legal skirmishing, during which the question was never brought to an issue, both the prelates fairly gave up the point, and Bishop Keene was contented to licence his antagonist's presentee. The question should never have been moved at all, but this event has set it at rest for ever.

Mr. Johnson resigned the living of Whalley, May 1, 1776, and survived to the year 1792. He was interred in the church of Prescot, where he had spent the last years of his life. He left a multitude of papers relating to his transactions as Vicar of Whalley, which, having been carefully arranged and bound up by the present Incumbent,[1] form a folio volume. Among these are many original Letters from Archbishop Secker, Bishop Keene, &c. a few of which, relating to his spirited contest for the rights of patronage belonging to his church, are here subjoined.

To the Bishop of Chester.

My Lord, Oct. 20, 1762.

I was this morning surprized with an account of Mr. S. being refused a licence to the Curacy of Rossendale upon my nomination; for what reason I cannot conceive, since I apprehend there can be no doubt of my right. It is very extraordinary that there should be no claims of this kind before my time, and so many since. I cannot recollect that anything has been done since I became Vicar to prejudice the rights and privileges of the Rectory[2] of Whalley, but much in support of them; so that, if ever the right of nomination to Rossendale Chapel belonged to the Vicars of Whalley, it still remains so, and whoever the person is who pretends to a right of nomination may with equal justice dispute his Grace of Canterbury's right of presentation to the Vicarage of Whalley, and is as well entitled to the one as the other. Not to trouble your Lordship any longer on this subject, I should be glad your Lordship would do me the honour to enquire into the reasons why my clerk has been rejected, and why my antagonist is concealed from me, seeing I cannot well proceed before I know my adversary, and am desirous of putting an end to this dispute with all expedition, as it is a populous chapelry, and the parishioners may suffer inconveniences for want of a minister, &c. W. J.

Sir,

I have received your letter, expressing your surprize that your nomination to Rossendale Chapel is not accepted, because there can be no doubt of your right. In your mind there is none; but in others there is, or you would not have met with obstruction. You say the person who litigates this point with you might as well litigate the Archbishop's right to the presentation of the Vicarage of Whalley; but that is not

[1] [It bears the following inscription: "Hunc Librum, ex schedis disjectis concinnatum et compactum, Successoribus commendat T. D. Whitaker; unâque memoriam haud jure interituram Wilhelmi Johnson, quondam Vicarii de Whalley, A.D. 1809." Other volumes have since been added, and the series now forms a record as well of facts, as of the letters and documents which relate to the history, both of the Mother Church, and of the offset Incumbencies, now some forty-six in number. See *Notitia Cestriensis*, ii. 303.]

[2] A slip of the pen for Vicarage. [No: the writer refers to the Rectory, appropriate to the Archbishop.]

likely to be; for it is the Archbishop himself, who, on having been applied to by various persons for the Curacy, has looked into his papers, and thinks he has a right, and means to prosecute it; and why they who refused Mr. S. his licence should have concealed it I cannot tell, for it was not intended to be a secret by any one. I must acquaint you farther, that since the Archbishop has entered his caveat, I have reason to think that I have some right to this chapel; and if the arguments should prove as solid as they appear specious, I shall prosecute my right against his Grace and you too.

Notwithstanding what I have said, unless I am well satisfied in my own mind that my claim is well grounded, I will not create you vexation and expence; and I am sure I can venture to affirm the same of my friend the Archbishop, &c. E. C.

May it please your Grace,

I am concerned to hear, by a letter from my good Lord of Chester, that your Grace is the person who has entered a caveat against my nomination to Rossendale Chapel—an adversary I did not suspect: and moreover, should I get clear of your Grace, his Lordship is so generous as to declare that I am in some danger from *him*. It would have pleased me better to have had less powerful opponents; but, since it happens so, neither your Grace nor his Lordship will, I hope, be offended at my doing my utmost in defence of what I think my right: and if your Grace would honour me with your reasons for opposing me, it would add to the favours received by W. J.

SIR, Lambeth, Nov. 11, 1762.

My reason for desiring that the Bishop of Chester would not immediately licence any person to serve the Cure of Rossendale was, that applications were made to me as Patron of it, the Impropriator being thought to be such of common right, and the nomination to the chapels being expressly reserved to the Archbishop, in the lease of the Rectory.

I have not, hitherto, been able to inform myself sufficiently concerning the strength of this argument: but I am very willing to hear anything which you have to alledge on the other side, and hope a contest by law may thus be prevented: but, if it cannot, your endeavours to defend your claim will give no offence to, &c. T. CANT.

May it please your Grace,

It appears that the Vicar of Whalley for the time being has always nominated to the chapels within the Rectory of Whalley; nor have any of your Grace's predecessors, of whom I have seen several (and most of the chapels have been vacant in my time), ever made any claim.

The nomination to the Chapels being expressly reserved to the Archbishop, in the lease of the Rectory, can only be intended as a bar to the Lessee, who, without such an exception, might possibly be entitled to the patronage both of the Vicarage and Chapels; but, by such a reservation, the Archbishop's right is secured, which right, by his Grace's presentation, devolves upon the Vicar, he being instituted and inducted to all and singular the rights, privileges, &c. thereunto belonging. This I apprehend to be the situation of all livings impropriate. I know no instance of an incumbent not nominating to the chapels under him, except where his right has been legally alienated. I would not presume to make the least encroachment on your Grace's rights; and it gives me great uneasiness that there should be any doubt, at this day, to whom the nomination belongs, &c. W. J.

To the Bishop of CHESTER.

MY LORD,

As, probably, there may never again be a Vicar of Whalley in circumstances to assert his rights, I would willingly fix them on such a footing as to put them out of the power of dispute.

If your Lordship's pretensions have no other foundation than the Decree supposed to be passed in the Duchy Court, I am persuaded that the rights and privileges of the Rectory of Whalley are in no danger, as that decree contains nothing that can affect them; and for this plain reason, because neither Patron nor Incumbent are parties; and therefore nothing foisted into the Decree, by artifice or iniquity, can operate so as to vest a right in your Lordship against the Vicar.

In these Letters there was more of law and reason than either the Patron or Diocesan knew how to answer; and, accordingly, the first was silent; and the second, after some skirmishing, fairly gave up the cause, in the following elegant Letter:—

REV. SIR,—The contest between you and me, concerning the patronage of the Church in Rossendale, took its rise accidentally, from some papers being found while my officers were searching into the claim of the Archbishop.

When the different foundations of my right were drawn together, they did appear to me, and others whom I consulted, to be of validity enough to form a pretension to the nomination of that Chapel, and I then acquainted you with such my intention.

After I despaired of finding the original decree, I stated my case, and laid my materials before Mr. Wilbraham, with a resolution either of proceeding at law or desisting from my claim, as his opinion should direct me; and as it is his opinion that the materials I produced would not support a trial at bar, I did immediately determine to give up my pretensions.

I should at that time have written to you, and declared my readiness to licence your clerk, if I had not thought it incumbent upon me to inquire whether the Archbishop had still any objections to your nomination. His Grace did not with his usual exactness answer my letter. On my return to town last week I waited upon him; and he then apologised for not writing, from his having been making some farther researches into this affair, and desired I would give him a little more time.

On these facts, which I affirm to be true, I think I can vindicate myself from the charge of unnecessary delay.

Whatever others may say or think on this subject, I please myself with reflecting that I neither wantonly formed my pretensions nor prosecuted them peevishly. I can easily conceive that a clamour may have been made, not only among the Laity, but some of the Clergy too, against a Bishop endeavouring, as it may be called, to deprive one of his Clergy of his right; but as I have suffered, in different parts of my life, from my conduct having been misrepresented or misapprehended, I have long learnt to be content with the approbation of my own mind, not indifferent, yet not over-solicitous, about the precarious judgment of other men.

ED. CHESTER.

The next Incumbency affords no materials for narrative or remark.

May the present Incumbent be permitted, for the sake of truth and accuracy, on a subject however unimportant, to subjoin the following facts and dates. [These autobiographical passages are transferred to the Introduction to this Edition.]

I must now turn back to a temporary and curious state of ecclesiastical affairs, within this and the neighbouring parishes, which was happily terminated in the restoration of the old episcopal government in the year 1660. Few ecclesiastical documents of this period remain.

In the archiepiscopal library at Lambeth is a MS. marked 912, which throws considerable light on the state of our church establishment in this parish during the usurpation of the last century. It is an inquisition taken at Blackburn, June 25th, 1650, before Richard Shuttleworth, esq. and others, by commission under the Commonwealth seal for inquiring and certifying the number and value of all parochial vocations, &c. within the parishes of Whalley, Blackburn, and Rochdale. After the Restoration this document was found among the records of the House of Commons, and, by an order of that House, delivered into the hands of Archbishop Juxon, the proper depositary.

By this inquisition it is found, 1st, that the parish of WHALLEY consists of thirty-five townships; that Mr. William Walker, an able and orthodox divine, is now minister, and receives from Mr. Thomas Assheton, farmer of the rectory, a stipend of 38*l.*

2nd. That the chapelry of PADIHAM is parochial, consisting of the townships of Padiham, Hapton, Simonstone, and Higham Booth, containing 232 families and 1,106 souls: the minister, John Breares, A.M. who receives a stipend of 6*l.* 19*s.* 2*d.* from the receiver of the county, and 33*l.* from the county commissioners; and that the inhabitants desire to be made a parish.

3rd. That the chapelry of COLNE consists of that township, Foulrig, Marsden, and Trawden, containing in the whole 400 families:—That the minister, John Horrocks, A.M. an able divine, receives 11*l.* 10*s.* from the farmer of the rectory, by order of the county commissioners; and that the inhabitants desire to be made a parish.

4th. That the chapelry of CLITHEROE consists of that township, Chatburn, Worston, Mereley, and Heyhouses; in all about 400 families:—That the minister, Mr. Robert Marsden, an able divine, receives 11*l.* 10*s.* out of the duchy rents, and 25*l.* from the commissioners of the county; and that the inhabitants desire to be made a parish.

5th. That the chapelry of DOWNHAM, containing in that township 300 families, and in Twiston 40, is parochial:—That the minister, George Whitaker, A.M. receives 10*l.* from the farmer of the rectory and 30*l.* from the county commissioners; and that the inhabitants desire to be a parish.

6th. That ACCRINGTON is not parochial; that it consists of the township of Accrington vetus et nova, &c. containing 200 families:—The minister, Mr. Roger Kenyon, an able and orthodox divine; and that the inhabitants desire to be made a parish.

7th. That ALTHAM is parochial, consisting of Altham and part of Clayton, which contain 150 families:—Minister, Mr. Thomas Jolly, an able divine, who receives 10*l.* from the rectory and 30*l.* from the commissioners: the inhabitants desire to be made a parish. That,

8th. Brerecleve and Extwistle, being distant from Whalley five miles, and from any other chapel almost six,[1] and consisting of 100 families, desire to erect a chapel for themselves.

9th. That the inhabitants of Newlaund, Reedley Hallows, Filly Close, and Ightenhill Park, distant one and a half mile from Burnley, desire to be united to that church, and to be made a parish.

10th. That the chapelry of BURNLEY consists of that township, Haberghameaves, and

[1] These distances are not accurate, but the request was reasonable. Indeed, a place of worship is exceedingly wanted in this remote and uncivilized tract.

Worsthorn, and contains upwards of 300 families:—The minister, Mr. Henry Morris, an able and orthodox divine, receives from the duchy 11*l*. 10*s*. from the inhabitants 4*l*. 8*s*. 2*d*. and from the commissioners 24*l*. 1*s*. 10*d*.

11th. That the chapel of Holme has no minister or maintenance, but that the inhabitants desire that it may be made a parish church, and that the parish consist of Cliviger, Worsthorn, and Hurstwood; in all, 100 families.

12th. That the chapelry of Church consists of Church, Oswaldtwisle, Huncote, and part of Clayton, containing 200 families; and that the minister, James Rigby, A.M. receives 10*l*. from the rectory, and 30*l*. from the county commissioners. The inhabitants desire to be made a parish.

13th. That Henthorn, Coldcoats, and Wiswall, desire to be continued to the parish church.

14th. That the chapelry of Haslingden consists of that township and part of Rossendale; viz. Newhallhey, part of Rawtonstall Booth, Oakenhead Booth, Constable Lee Booth, and part of Crawshaw Booth; in all, 300 families:—Minister, Mr. Robert Gilbert, suspended by the divines.[1] The inhabitants desire to be made a parish. Number of families, 300.

15th. That Newchurch in Pendle is parochial, the chapelry consisting of most part of Pendle Forest, and containing 150 families:—That the minister, Mr. Edward Lapage, an able divine, receives 39*l*. from the commissioners of the county:—That Weetlee and Roughlee desire to be annexed and made a parish.

16th. That Goodshaw, not parochial, has a chapelry consisting of 70 families; but no minister or maintenance, saving a messuage and backside, value 10*s*.; but that the inhabitants desire to be made a parish.

17th. That Whytewell, not parochial, has a chapelry of 116 families, but no minister or maintenance. The inhabitants desire to be made a parish.

18th. That Newchurch in Rossendale is parochial, and consists of Dedwen Clough, Tunsted, Wolfenden Booth, and part of Wolfenden and Bakeop; in all, 300 families:—Minister, Mr. Robert Dewhurst, an able divine, who receives no allowance but what the inhabitants give, who desire to be made a parish.[2]

Thus we see that out of one overgrown parish it was proposed to the commissioners to carve no less than seventeen; a change of little importance in itself, and probably intended to answer no other purpose than that of placing the Clergy on a footing of entire equality, better suited to the genius of a republic than subordination. Let not these men, however, be defrauded of the praise which they really deserve; for, if they made their ministers equal, they paid them almost equally well; and, if none of their preferments were adequate

[1] That is, I suppose, by the Classis. We are not informed what was the offence.

[2] What was now become of the valuable estate belonging to this church, which escaped the Commissioners of Pious Uses under Edward VI. and still belongs to it?

to the rewards of superior merit, all afforded enough to raise them above sordid poverty, and to secure them from utter contempt.

And, for the incumbents themselves, though bigoted beyond measure to an ecclesiastical government in which every one was flattered by bearing a part, though narrow in their tempers and detestable in their politics, yet, by zeal and diligence in their ministry, by sobriety, and even severity in their conversation, they had acquired an influence over the minds of their hearers, which too many who followed them, under a better establishment, have forfeited and lost. Hence the formidable separation which took place on the subsequent exclusion of these men from their pulpits; and hence, in part, the origin of modern sects, almost without number and without name, which threaten, but too obviously, the downfall of our civil and ecclesiastical establishments. Dislike, indeed, will always be conceived, with or without cause, against every thing which bears the stamp of legal authority; but this is a reason for more, and not less, circumspection in the clergy. "Offences will come; but woe unto that man," and above all, to that minister, "by whom the offence cometh." Under the present state of ecclesiastical discipline, too little can be done by the most conscientious diocesan. Of fornication, adultery, incest, though notorious enough to scandalise a whole neighbourhood, it is not easy to procure legal evidence. But a process like the *Fama clamosa* in the Church of Scotland (which condemns, with great reason, him who, above all others, ought to abstain from the "appearance of evil," and will not,) would remove the bold offender, who now defies authority, and disgraces his function with impunity. Let not this short digression be thought unseasonable: it is, unhappily, very far from being unconnected with the present subject.

Yet, the ample testimonies here given to the ability of these men are to be received with some degree of caution. Several of them, however, were graduates: and Jolly, who distinguished himself long afterwards, in a scene which will be noticed below, though credulous, and perhaps enthusiastic, was not devoid of literature. How they became possessed of their benefices, and with what circumstances of justice or cruelty their predecessors were excluded, we are nowhere told.[1] The Presbyterian discipline was set up in this county as early as 1645 or 1646, and is known to have continued till the year 1650, in which this inquisition was taken.[2] The whole county was divided into nine classes; but in which of these the parish of Whalley was included I have not been able to learn, as none of their proceedings are extant but those of the second class, consisting of Bury, Bolton, Middleton, Rochdale, Radcliffe, and Dean; and these exhibit a medley of carelessness, injustice, and disorder, which prove that men not altogether unqualified to teach may yet be very unfit to govern.[3]

[1] Walker's *Sufferings of the Clergy*, p. i. p. 40.—One of their proceedings was, to deny baptism to base children: another was, to thrust unordained persons (unordained even by their own forms) into churches and chapels, from whence, after proof of ignorance or misconduct, they removed them with equal facility, annulling all the baptisms they had administered.

[2] It seems then to have been superseded by the Independent or Congregational plan.

[3] Since this was first printed, I have been favoured, by the late L. N. Starkie, esq. of Huntroyd, with an original

At the close of the last century, Whalley became the scene of a long and desperate conflict, which was carried on by prayers, arguments, and mutual defiances, between nine Puritan ministers, at the head of whom was the above-mentioned Thomas Jolly, and a supposed demoniac of Surey (now Surey Barn) named Richard Dugdale. After all, it is

MS. formerly belonging to Mr. Alexander Norris, of Hall in the Wood, near Bolton, entitled "Ministers' Orders." From this book it appears that every hundred in the county had its Classis, under the Presbyterian Government. It is dated 1649. I transcribe the following particulars relating to the hundred of Blackburne:—

Mr. John Bell, Minister at Accrington Chappel.

By an Order of this Comm. 5th Dec. 1645, there is 40*l.* p. an. allowed to an able Divine at Accrington Chap.

Mr. Bell is approved by the Classis att Whalley, 9th Nov. 1647.

Mr. John Briars, Min[r] at Padiam.

By an Order of the Com. of this County, 13 Jul. 1648, there is 33*l.* 10*s* per an. allowed to Mr. John Bryars Min[r] of Padiham, and 25*l.* 2*s.* 6*d.* due in arrears att Midsomer before.

Mr. Bryars is nominated in the Ordinance for the Classis.

Mr. Henry Morres, Min[r] at Burnley.

By an Order from the Com. of this County, Jul. 13, 1648, there is 24*l.* 6*s.* per an. allowed to Mr. Hen. Morres, and 18*l.* 4*s.* due in arrears at Midsomer before.

Mr. Morres is nominated in the Ordinance for the Classis.

Mr. Rich. Redman, Min[r] of Lowchurch, in Walton.

By Order of the Committee, there is 40*l.* per an. allowed to Mr. Redman, Min[r] of Low Ch.

Mr. Redman is nominated in the printed Ordinance for the Classis. Hee is p[d] till the 14 Aug. 1647.

Mr. Rob. Marsden, Min[r] att Clytherow.

Itt appeares, by the certificate of John Howorthe, that ther is payd from Mr. Ashton, of Whaley, to the Min[r] of Clitherow, 11*l.* 10*s.* and from the King 3*l.* 10*s.* And by Order of the Com. of this County, of the 20th Nov. 1645, there is allowed to Mr. Rob. Marsden 25*l.* augmentation, to make upp the rest 40*l.* per an.

Mr. Marsden is approved by the Com. of Divines at Preston, Aug. 12, 1645.

Mr. James Shaw, Min[r] at Balderston Chappel.

By Order of the Com. of this County, 25th Sept. 1646, ther is 40*l.* per ann. allowed for a Min[r] at Balderston.

Hee was approved on, as Min[r] at Balderston, by the Com. of Divines att Bolton, July 7th, 1646. He is paid upp till the 8th of Oct. 1647, by Charles Gregory.

Mr. Jonas Browne, Min[r] at New Church in Pendle.

By Order of the Com. of Lanc. 2nd Feb. 1647, ther is allowed him and his successors 40*l.* per an. and 20*l.* then in arreare.

Hee is approved on, by the Comm. of Ministers at Whalley, March 11th, 1646.

Mr. John Worthington, Min[r] of Tockholes Chappell.

By an Order of this Comm. of the 25th Dec[r] 1646, there is 40*l.* per an. allowed to an orthodox Divine, to officiate the Cure at Tockholes Chappel.

Mr. Worthington was ordained at Manchester, for Ouldham, 15th April, 1647.

Mr. George Whittaker, Min[r] att Downham.

By Order of the Com. of this County, 13 Jul. 1648, there is 30*l.* per an. allowed to Mr. Geo. Whittaker, Min[r] of Downham, and 15*l.* then in arreare ordered to be payd him.

Mr. Whittaker is approved by the Com. of Min[r] April 1st, 1645.

Mr. John Horrox, Min[r] att Colne.

By an Order from the Dep. Lieutenants, of the 26th June, 1645, there is 13*l.* 10*s.* augmentation allowed to Mr. John Horrox, Min[r] at Colne.

Mr. Horrox is approved, by the Comm. of Divines, the first of April, 1645.

more than probable that the man was either a lunatic or impostor: the latter, undoubtedly, if we are to believe the tradition of the place, which reports that he was effectually exorcised by a threatened commitment from a neighbouring magistrate.

Of this transaction, however, the triumphant party, for so they deemed themselves, thought fit to publish a most injudicious and ill-written narrative, which has been employed by an acute, though concealed, enemy of Christianity, to discredit the miracles of the primitive Church; and through them, it is to be feared, those of the Gospel itself.[1] They

Mr. James Rigby, Min^{r} at Church Kirke.

By an Order from the Com. of this Countie, of the 3d Aug. 1648, there is 30*l.* per an. allowed to Mr. James Rigby, Min^{r} at Church Kirk, and his successors there.

Mr. Rigby was ordained, by the Presbytery of Blackborne, at Church Kirke, 1st of Aug. 1648.

Mr. Rich. Redman, Min^{r} at Law Church.

By an Order from the Com. for plund^{d} Min^{rs}, of April 21, 1647, there is 40*l.* per an. out of the Rectory of Exton, sequestered from James Anderton, Pap. allowed to a Min^{r} at Low Church.

Mr. Redman is nominated, in the Ordinance, for the Classis.

Mr. Alex. Gilbert, Min^{r} at Tockholes Chap.

By an Order of the Com. of this Countie, of the 25th of Dec^{r}, 1646, there is 40*l.* per an. allowed to an orthodox Divine, to officiate at Tockholes Chap.

Mr. Gilbert was ordained Min^{r} here Apr. 10th, 1649.

Mr. Edward Lapage, Min^{r} at New Church, in Pendle Forrest.

By an Order, formerly entered for Mr. Browne, there is 40*l.* per an. allowed.

Mr. Lapage is approved by the Classis, at Whaley, 8th of May, 1648.

Mr. Joshua Bernard, Min^{r} at Over Darwin Chap.

By an Order of the Com. at Manchester, of the   of Jan. 1648, there is 40*l.* per an. allowed to Mr. Bernard, Min^{r} at Over Darwin, together with the arrears due unto him.

By a Certificate of the Inhabitants of the Chappelrie of Over Darwin, it appears that Mr. Bernard was in arreare for twoe yeares and a q^{r}, ending the 3rd of Dec^{r}, 1649.

Mr. Bernard was ordained the 4th of Dec^{r}, 1649, at the Chappel of Over Darwin, by the Classis of Blackborne Hundred.

Mr. Richard Smethurst, Min^{r} at Samsbury Chappel.

By an Order of 13 Dec. 1649, there is 40*l.* per an. allowed to Mr. Rich. Smethurst, Min^{r} at Samsbury Chappel, and the arreares due unto him.

Mr. Smethurst was ord^{d} by the Minst. of Blackborne Classis, and sent to Samlisbury Chappell by them the 4th of Dec. 1649.

By a Certificate the 10th Dec^{r}, under the handes of the Chappelrie, it appeares that he hath served here 20 weekes.

(On a loose piece of paper.)

By Order of the Comm. of this Countie, of 18th Oct. 1649, there is 40*l.* per an. allowed to Mr. James Critchly, Min^{r} at Langoe Chappel, and 20*l.* for his arrear.

Mr. Critchley was approved for that place by the Classis, at Whally, 10th Jul. 1649.

(Under Loynsdale Hundred.)

In another hand: This should be in Blackborne Hund.

Mr. John King, Min^{r} at Chipping.

By Order from the Committee of plundered Min^{rs}, 17th June 1647, allowed 27th Aug. following, there is 50*l.* per an. allowed out of the Tythes of Chipping, sequestered from Christopher Harris, delinquent, to John King, Min^{r} of the Par. Church of Chipping.

[1] See Dr. Middleton's Inquiries into the Miraculous Powers, p. 232.

thought themselves happy, no doubt, in their exemption from the restraint which a canon of the Church[1] imposes upon such adventures; but the event has abundantly proved the wisdom of a constitution, which vests in the ordinary a right to prohibit the intermeddling of hot-headed and credulous men in circumstances so delicate and suspicious. It is to be observed that Mr. Gey, the Vicar of Whalley, though applied to, prudently forbore to interfere.

The remote situation of Whalley, and the adjoining benefices, was probably the occasion of some neglect on the part of Archbishop Parker, of which he was admonished by Bishop Pilkington, a native of Lancashire.[2] This state of things produced the following spirited memorial, in which the unknown writer, with great appearance both of law and reason, strikes at the root of the grievance, and boldly maintains that the benefices in question were actually disappropriated, and became presentative again. I have very lately met with this memoir among the Towneley manuscripts.

Instruction for my L^d^ of Canterburies Benefices in Lancashire.

1st. It appereth by the original donations that there was a simple grant, or guift, of the advowsons and patronages onlie of the parishes and churches of Ratchdale, Blackburn, and Whalley, unto the Abbey of Whalley, as within is mentioned.

2d. The saide churches at the tyme of the saide sev'all donacions thearof were wholly aneyent, presentable benefices; and from tyme to tyme before had been occupyed and possessed by ecclesiastical incumbents, and nev^r^ till afterwards weare thralled and subjected to the state of Romish impositions.

3d. Aft^r^ that the saide Abbye was possessed and invested in the patronage of the saide sev'all churches and parishes, the abbot and convent there did then make suite to the b'p of Roome for the perpetual appropriations of the saide churches and parishes to the saide Abbey; and that a vicar perpetual might be ordayned in every of the saide sev'all churches and parishes, to have cure of sowles, and to be endowed with a certain pensi'on of monye, and glebe lands for their mayntenance; which was grawnted accordingly, as may and doth appear.

4th. It^m^. By this kind of Romish dispensacyon and popish apostolical ordinac'on (as they tearme it) the saide churches of free presentable benefices were made poore appropriated vicarages; and soe ever since have contynued and remayned, as to my lord of Canterburies grace himselfe is not unknowen.

5th. It^m^. The late King Henry VIII. of famous memorie, depely considering the heavie yokes and intolerable bondage wherwith all his lovyng subjects were greavously opressed, thro the tyrannie of the Bishop of Roome, in these and other his dispensations and Romish impositions, did therefore enact and ordayne, in his High Courte of Parlement, y^t^ all faculties, dispensations, and appropriations whatsoever, heretofore procured from ye see of Roome, should bee utterly voyded and of none effect.

6th. It^m^. Forasmuch as ye saide impropriations did procede and take their authority from that dispensing power and seat of iniquity, and therefore were most justlye abolished and annihilated in law, by this meanes it came to passe that all benefices by authoritie from the see of Rome were disappropriated, and brought again to the ancient state of presentative benefices.

7. It^m^. For the better explayning of ye desolution of the appropriations papistical above meneioned, for so much as ye same were not onlie derogatorie to ye true religion and service of Almightie God, but alsoe were verie prejudicial to the aneyent prerogative and royal dignities of the Imperial Crowne of this realme, it was and is further enacted, in statute above mentioned, that whosoever shal plead in anie court any

[1] *Vide* 72nd canon.

[2] [See the extract already given in page 213, note.]

dispensacyon or appropriacion proceeding from ye Courte of Roome shal therby incur ye penalty of premunire made 16 Ri. IId.

8. Itm. Although the statute aforesaide touching the exonerating of ye people of this realme from popish oppression and foreign impositions was repeled A. 1 Mar.; yet ye same among others is effectuallye revived A 1 of oure sov'reign ladie Qu. Eliz. as to those who are learned in ye laws is well knowen.

9th. Itm. Forsomuch as after dissolution of ye saide impropriations, by force of ye statutes above mentioned, the sd abbot and co'vent did nevr seeke for nor obtayne at ye Kinges Majs hands, nor at ye ordinarie of ye diocese, anie new impropriacion in law, but only continued the former usurpation and wrongful intrusion into ye state of ye saide churches, and soe contynued ye same until the dissolution of the then sd abbey and monasterie. By this it is apparent that ye sd abbot and convente, at ye verie instant tyme of ye dissolution of ther saide monasterie, had noe other state in ye churches and benefices of R. B. and W. but only *jus presentandi.*

10. Itm. Where by the Act of Dissolution of Monasteries ye Kinges Majestie had noe other state geven to him than onely such interest and state as was invested and remayned in ye saide abbot and covente, which was onely *jus presentandi*, it behoved Mr. Cranemerr, then archbushop of Canterburie, to have sought a further right and interest in ye saide benefices then eyther remayned in ye sd abbot and co'vente or in ye Kinges Majestie at that tyme, which because he did not, it doth consequentlie follow that ther was no state of impropriation in him at all.

11. Itm. If the King's Maj.'s letters patent be allowed as of force to make ye saide benefices impropriations, to this it may be answered, that ye law of ye land requires consente of ye bushop diocesan, together with ye incumbent, and a sufficient reservation and endowment of ye fruites, both for reliefe of ye poore and maintenance of ye vicars: all which rights and circumstances ought to be expressed in a solemn authentical instrument of real composition; but in these p'tended impropriations of R. B. and W. there is not observed anie such course of law at all (other than from ye Pope).

12. Itm. Forsomuch as no lawful state of impropriation in ye saide church remained or was invested in Mr. Cranemerr, then a'b'p, it must needes follow yt ye said a'b'p had no right nor authoritie in law to demyse and sett to ferme ye saide benefices.

13. Itm. If either the Kinges Majs prerogative royal, or anie other objection, be laide forth to weaken ye truth of ye p'misses, yet ye strength of ye commune law of the lande, together wth ye statutes of H. IV. Ri. II. and H. VIII. doe apparently carrie such force in right, equitie, and conscience, agst these and such like impropriations, as before anie indifferent judge will make the truth hereof manifest.

14. Itm. The p'misses considered, it behoveth my Ld of Canterburie his Grace, not onlie to have a care of his owne due right in ye p'misses, but alsoe to provide better maintenance for the ministers sevving in ye severall cures of these benefices; which being grete p'shes, and contayning among them well nigh 4,000 households in all, it is good reason that ye state of their churches, ye government of ye people, ye right of their tithes, &c. be gravely and depely considered.

And this the rather for that the inhabitants of these three parishes (under colour of pretended leases from Mr. Cranemerr,) have bene oppressed wth exactions and fines to ye sum of 6,000 marks and above. Yet ye poore people are forced, at their owne proper costs and charges, to allow and paye manie of their ministers wages serving at ye chapells in ye saide p'ishes.

With respect to the operation of the statute 1st George I. on the rights of Mother Churches over the augmented Chapels which are declared benefices, and those of which the patronage is alienated, the following clause will prove that they remain what they were:—"That no Rector or Vicar of the Mother Church, having cure of souls within the parish or place where such augmented Church or Chapel shall be situate, shall thereby be divested or discharged from the same: but the cure of souls, with all other parochial rights and duties, shall hereafter remain in the same state, plight, and manner as before the making of this Act, and as if this Act had not been made."—1 Geo. I. c. x. § 4.

So groundless is the doubt of Dr. Burn, whether, in such augmented cures, the duty of canonical obedience, heretofore owing by the Curate to the Rector or Vicar, does not cease.

[*Undertaking of William le Wolf of Kirklawton, Vicar of Whalley, not to seek any increase of the new foundation of Whalley Vicarage*, 1336.

Universis sancte matris Ecclesie filiis presentes litteras inspecturis: Wiltms dictus le Wolf de Kyrkelautoñ perpetuus vicarius ecclesie de Whalleye Coventr' et Lich dioc' salutem in Domino sempiternam. Habita consideracione ad inmensa et innumera beneficia per religiosos viros dominos meos . . . . Abbatem et Conventum Moñ Loci Benedicti de Whalleye, ordinis Cisterc', dicte dioc', michi . . . . [*erased*] . . . . et impensa, volen . . . . [*erased*] eisdem obsequium gratitudinis impendere ac quantum in me est omnimodam litem pro temporibus futuris inter dictos Religiosos et me super augmentacionem dicte vicarie de Whalleye precavere: Sacrosanctis inspectis evangeliis et in verbo sacerdocii non ad hoc coactus, set mea mera et spontanea voluntate ductus, hoc unum eisdem promitto et fide media veraciter assero, quod ex nunc pro meo perpetuo dictos Religiosos super Augmentacionem dicte vicarie de Whalleye per me dictum Wiftm non inquietabo nec per alios quoscunque inquietare procurabo, aliquid ab eisdem aliqualiter exegendo, contra formam ordinacionis ven' in Christo patris domini Rogeri de Northburgh Dei gratia Coventr' et Lich' Episcopi de eadem vicaria anno Domini M°ccc° Tricesimo cum cause cognicione factam, una cum confirmacionibus Capitulorum suorum, Coventr' et Lich' super eadem ordinacione postmodum subsecutis. Et ad majorem hujus rei evidenciam presentibus sigillum meum apposui in testimonio premissorum. Dat apud Whalleye die Lune px̃ post festum sancti Luce Evangeliste, anno Domini M°.ccc°.xxx. sexto, 20 Oct. 1336. (Addit. MS. 10,374, f. 24 b.)

W. de L. perpetuus vicarius ecclesie de N. gave a similar engagement to the Abbot and Convent of Stanlawe on the feast of Trinity 1289. (Addit. MS. 10,374, f. 25.)]

BOOK III.

CHAPTER THE FIRST.

ORIGIN, PROGRESS, AND RAMIFICATIONS OF PROPERTY.

IN that obscure period which intervened between the final retreat of the Romans and the origin of the Northumbrian kingdom this wild and remote tract appears to have been once more reduced almost to a state of nature; for, though not absolutely depopulated, it must have been thinly sprinkled and feebly occupied by the poor depressed remnant of its aboriginal inhabitants. Accordingly, no vestiges of their language can be traced but in the names of great natural objects, which belong to a much earlier period, no remains of their works,[1] and no memorials of their habitations.

The Saxons, therefore, are to be considered with respect to this portion of Britain almost in the light of prime occupants: they seem to have had nearly an universal blank before them, without fortresses to subdue, or towns to seize, or names of artificial objects to continue. Unlike the Norman Conquest, which, five centuries after, transmitted into the hands of new masters a country already built and planted, a system of society already formed, a local nomenclature already established, this revolution gave birth to a new era of manners, language, and religion. Hence it appears, not only that our *villare* is almost entirely Saxon, but that our local names are generally formed from those of the first Saxon possessors, combined with some attribute of place, as the cot of *Hun*, the home of *Elvet*, the boundary of *Oswald*.[2]

Or, if intended to express some peculiar circumstance in the situation of a village, still the name is significant in the Saxon language, as *Clayton*, *Brunley*, *Merelay*, *Downum*, and many more.[3]

But after the Norman Conquest this process was reversed: local denominations were

[1] That is, of this later period.

[2] Huncot, Elvetham, Oswaldtwisle.

[3] The few exceptions to this rule have already been considered in Book I.

now fixed; but something was wanted to remove the confusion incident to single names of persons, especially in a language of so little copiousness as the Saxon; and hence owners of lands, laying aside the inconvenient mode of calling them by their own names, began to borrow distinctive personal appellations from *them*. Yet these appear to have been changeable at first, and to have been descriptive merely of present habitation; so that, if a son, for example, quitted the place of his paternal residence, he would assume a new denomination from the estate to which he had removed. Thus, even brethren of the same house frequently adopted different surnames, which were continued by their descendants. This remark is grounded on the authority of our oldest charters, in which the first subscribing witnesses (men of landed property) are denoted by local surnames; while their inferiors, who follow, if not designated by their occupation,[1] have nothing more than the rude Saxon Christian name,[2] though sometimes distinguished by a patronymical addition.[3]

But, to return from this digression.

The original distribution of property into manors or townships, within this parish, whenever it took place, appears to have been very regularly conducted; and the general principle upon which it proceeded was evidently this:—that under a system of military colonization every subordinate chief should receive a proportion of land adequate to the support of himself, his family, and immediate dependants. And this proportion in the parish of Whalley never exceeded two carucates of land, and never fell short of one.

Seated upon this domain, the Saxon leader, softened into a peaceful *lageman*, was occupied in husbandry and pasturage: here he erected his rude but independent mansion, surrounded by the huts of his shepherds and husbandmen, over whom he exercised the primitive rights of *sac, soc*, &c. &c.; and such appears to have been the origin of our manors, vills, or townships (for the terms were at first convertible), which, having commenced in the earliest period of the Northumbrian kingdom, still subsist, with little alteration but in the orthography of the names, the increase of their population, and the extent of their cultivated lands.

In all the succeeding tract of time few townships appear to have originated, and none have been depopulated and lost.[4]

The carucate, as a measure and principle of distribution to families, is mentioned as early as the laws of Ina;[5] and the twelve followers of Joseph of Arimathea are said each to have received his hyde or carucate of land.[6] In the days of Saxon freedom and inde-

[1] As John Pincerna, Lucas Citharædus, &c.

[2] As Swaine, Hosebert, &c.

[3] As Hen. fil. Leofwine, &c.

[4] The township of Merclesden, now Marsden, is the only one which can be proved to have originated since the Domesday Survey. I am not speaking at present of villages within the forests, for they are all of much later date. "Ad forestas dixi villas non competere." Spelman.

[5] Leges Inæ XXXII, &c. Hence it is, that by conversion the word *familiæ* is rendered, by the Royal Interpreter of Bede, Ƿyðelanðeṛ.

[6] I mention this fact merely to show the antiquity of this principle of distribution; for, if we reject the whole story

pendence amongst us, these lands were held in socage; that is, for a certain render or service, immediately, and *in capite*, of the crown.—"Vulgaris opinio (says the author of the *Status de Blackburnshire*), tenet et asserit, quod, quot fuerunt villæ, vel mansæ seu maneria hominum, tot fuerunt domini, nedum in Blackburnshire, verum etiam in Rachdale, Tottington, et Bowland, quorum nullus de alio tenebat, sed omnes in capite, de ipso domino Rege."

This representation is confirmed by Domesday Book, which, though it passes over the hundred of Blackburn with an indistinctness strongly implying the obscurity of the place, and perhaps the difficulty of access to it, has ascertained, with sufficient exactness, the number and independence of the manors contained within it, and the proportion of each to the original carucate.

We will once more, therefore, lay before the reader a copy of that record so far as it relates to the hundred of Blackburn; and, after a few remarks, will compare it with known and positive facts, from later authorities, respecting the extent of freehold (that is, the only original) property within every manor.

In Blacheburne Hundret.

Rex Edwardus tenuit Blacheburne, ibi II. hidæ et II. carucatæ terræ. Ecclesia habebat II. bovatas de hac terra, et ecclesia Sc̄tæ Mariæ habebat in Wallei II. carucatas terræ quietas ab omni consuetudine.

In eodem Manerio[1] silva I. leuva longa et tantundem lata, et ibi aira accipitris.

of St. Joseph and St. Patrick, these lands must at latest have been bestowed by Ina. A.D. 704. *Vid.* "Mon. Angl." tom. i. pp. 10, 11.

[1] Familiar as the term manor is now become to us, I know not whether it has ever been defined with precision.—The word itself, though found (I believe for the first time) in the charters of Edward the Confessor, is unquestionably Norman: but the peculiar species of private and local jurisdiction which we now express by the term was unquestionably known to our Saxon ancestors; and the *lageman habens socam et sacam super homines suos* was indisputably the same character which was afterwards termed lord of a manor. Coke Litt. c. 9, s. 73.

But the idea of jurisdiction is in many of our manors forgotten; and the popular sense in which the word is now understood implies little more than a peculiar right to kill game within certain limits, although such a privilege depends upon a distinct grant of free chace, which many manors never possessed at all, or upon prescription.

It may assist the reader, however, in perusing the following parts of this work, to be informed that the word *manerium*, as referring to the subject of this work, in the ancient evidences from which it has been taken, bears four senses:—

1st. The whole hundred (*manerium sive hundredum*), in which it is synonymous with Honor. *Vide* Domesday, in the passage quoted above.

2nd. A single vill. township, or sometimes hamlet, under the jurisdiction of a lord holding, before the Conquest, of the Crown *in capite*, and afterwards of the chief lord of the fee. This is the sense of the word where it first occurs, in the passage of Domesday before us, referring to the town of Whalley alone; and such are all our real mesne manors at present,—commensurate, that is, with townships or hamlets.

3rd. An arbitrary collection of mesne manors never granted out by the chief lord of the fee, but in later times grouped together under the name of one manor for the convenience of holding courts. For ordinarily the Court Baron, as well as Customary or Copyhold Court, must be held within its own manor; but if a lord be seized of two or three manors, then, by custom, courts may be held upon one for all. Coke, Litt. *ubi supra*. And thus Colne, Ightenhill, Accrington, and Tottington have obtained the appellation of manors.

Ad hoc Manerium vel Hundretum adjacebant XXVIII. liberi homines, tenentes V. hidas et dimidium et XL. carucatas terræ pro XXVIII. Maneriis. Silva ibi VI. leuvis longa et IIII. leuvis lata, et erat in supradictis consuetudinibus.

In eodem hundreto habebat rex Edwardus Hunnicot de II. car. terræ, et Waletune de II. car. terræ, et Peniltune de dim. hyda.

Totum Manerium cum hundreto reddebat Regi de firma XXXII l. et XI. solidos. Hanc terram totam dedit Rogerius Pictaviensis Rogerio de Busli et Alberto Greslet, et ibi sunt tot homines, qui habent undecim carucatas et dim. quas ipsi concesserunt esse quietas usque ad tres annos, et ideo non appreciantur modo.

This is sufficiently perplexed: a little attention, however, will enable us to remove every difficulty, and to extract from it a pretty accurate representation of the state of property at that early period.

1. It must be remembered that the hundred of Blackburn consisted, at this time, of the parishes of Whalley and Blackburn alone: those of Ribchester and Chipping, now annexed to it, being surveyed in Amunderness.

2. Here were, in the time of Edward the Confessor, 40 carucates and 5½ hides, held by 28 freemen for 28 manors, of which the whole rental was xxxij*l*. ij*s*.

3. Deduct one-third for the number of manors and carucates in the parish of Blackburn, which is nearly the proportion, and there will remain for the parish of Whalley, in integral numbers, about 19 manors, consisting of 30 hides or carucates, and paying a rent of xxj*l*.

4. Our original manors, therefore, some consisting of one carucate and others of two, may be estimated, one with another, at 1½ carucate each.

5. Every hide or carucate paid about xiij*s*. Consisting, therefore, as they did, of 8 oxgangs each, and the oxgang, on an average, of 16 acres, the mean rent per acre would be one penny and a fraction. The carucate, by the same rule, would measure 128 acres; and the whole amount of ancient freehold lands surveyed by Domesday in the parish of Whalley would not exceed 3,840 acres, Lancashire measure.[1]

4th. In the last sense this word is used with great laxity in ancient inquisitions, &c. to denote little more, if anything, than a capital messuage or mansion-house. In this sense, Hesandforth, Catlow, Blakay, Greenfield, and others, none of which were ever vills or hamlets, or ever enjoyed manerial jurisdiction, are sometimes styled manors. *Vide* Townel. MSS. This last use of the word is also common in the monkish historians, *maneriorum edificator extitit.*—Matt. Paris, *sub an.* 1251. *Stanmure abbas Joh. manerium construxit.*—Lib. St. Albani, as cited by Spelman *in voce.* [*Manerium de Kyverdale fuit integraliter combustum.* Add. 10374, fol. 142.]

[1] It may assist the reader, in understanding this survey, to be informed that the bovate or oxgang, here averaged at 16 acres, fluctuated between the two extremes of 11 and 18 acres in different places, and sometimes even in the same township (*vide* Padiham), according to the quality of the land: but in the parish of Whalley, in general, lands were anciently divided, according to the mode in which they were estimated or measured, into the *terra bovata, i.e.* oxgang land, and the *terra rodata, i.e.* rode land. The first of these was ancient inclosure, which, having been time immemorial under the plough, was measured by the quantity which one ox (of which it appears from hence that there were eight in a caruca) could plough in one season. The second was land lately reclaimed and thrown into cultivation; and it may be proved, by the following authorities, to have been synonymous with essart:—"One essart, called Swainey rode—Martin's essart, or Martin rode—One essart called Malyn rode." Burton's Mon. Ebor. under Kirkstall. This word rode, which in the dialect of the parish of Halifax becomes royde, is plainly a participial substantive, formed

6. But further, we have here the first hint of tenure in villenage, which appears to have commenced in this parish after the Norman Conquest, since no notice is taken of it as having existed in the Confessor's time; but it is merely affirmed by Domesday, that there *are* homines or homagers, besides the 28 free tenants, who hold XI et dim. carucates, and that they are free from the geld for three years, and therefore not rated now, evidently, I think, because these lands were but in the infancy of cultivation. After the confused and careless survey of the parish in Domesday is thus reduced to order, little would be wanting to put this account on a footing with the more accurate parts of Domesday but the names of the several manors, vills, and hamlets, and the particular admeasurement of each.

And, happily for our purpose, this defect will be supplied by that most exact record, the Inquisition[1] after the death of Henry de Lacy, the last Earl of Lincoln, taken A.D. 1311, from which I have extracted the following table of manors and freehold lands. It must be premised that I have discarded all those which are held in thanage (a tenure the nature of which will be ascertained hereafter), namely, Oswaldtwisle, Read, Henthorn, Twisleton, Simonstone, and Padiham, because there is the strongest reason to conclude that they were parts of the $11\frac{1}{2}$ carucates held in villenage[2] at the time of the Domesday survey, and have never been regularly granted as manors, but have acquired the right by gradual usurpation and connivance.[3]

Manor.	Measure.	Ancient Tenure.
Whalley	2 carucates . .	Frank almoigne
Huncot	2 carucates . .	Never granted out

from the provincial verb *rid*, to clear or grub up. Again, ridding, or riding also, which yet remains in the names of many fields, may be proved to be synonymous with essart, and therefore confirms the former etymology. Thus: "One essart called Todhill riding—An essart called Tullin riding." Burton's Mon. Ebor. from Charters circ. 1258.—Lastly, the word essart itself is supposed by Spelman (*voce* Foresta) to be corrupted from *exserere*, and to be the opposite of *deserere*. But surely the meaning of the term might have led him to the *sarrio* of the *Rei Rusticæ scriptores*; which, in barbarous Latin, became *exsarrio*, and the participle passive *exsartus*, *i.e. essarted*.—I have been the more diffuse in explaining this word, because Thoresby, and after him Mr. Watson, without any account of its origin or etymology, have contented themselves with defining royd land, *terra debilis et inculta*.

[1] It may be proper to observe, once for all, that inquisitions *post mortem* are of little value but for the purpose of finding an heir. Their descriptions are almost always in round numbers, which must generally be false, *e. gr.* 100 *acras terræ*, 50 *prati*, 200 *jampnorum et bruceræ*; and it is not uncommon, in two successive generations, to find the same premises estimated at twice the quantity, or perhaps one half. But after the death of the last Earl of Lincoln, leaving a single daughter, on whose decease, without male issue, the vast estates of the family were settled upon the Crown, it was thought necessary to make a strict and accurate survey, and for the jurors to find with equal exactness according to the result. To this circumstance we are indebted for one of the most valuable documents from which the History of Whalley has been compiled. There is extant, indeed, another general inquisition of the Honour of Clitheroe, after the death of Henry Duke of Lancaster, but it is comparatively slight and inaccurate. [See the prefatory account of Record authorities prefixed to this volume.]

[2] The rest of these lands I suppose to have lain in the parish of Blackburn, as there is no room for them in that of Whalley.

[3] See Read and Oswaldtwisle, where the steps of this usurpation may be traced.

Manor.	Measure.	Ancient Tenure.
Peniltone and Coldcoats	1½ an hide	Peneltone in mil. serv. Coldcoats in frank almoigne
Little Mitton	1 carucate	Mil. serv.
Wiswall	2 carucates	Mil. serv.
Clitheroe	1 carucate	In demesne
Merlay mag.	2 carucates	Mil. serv.
Merlay parv.	1 carucate	Mil. serv.
Worston cum Chatburne	7 oxgangs or 7-8ths of a carucate	Never granted out
Downham	1½ carucate 1½ oxg.	Mil. serv.
Alvetham with Clayton	1 carucate	Mil. serv.
Accrington vetus, originally an hamlet under Alvetham	½ a carucate	Frank almoigne
Haslingden	1 carucate	Never granted out
Brunley, 1 car. cum Habergham eaves ½ car. and Townley cum Brunshaw ½ car.	2 carucates	The two first constituting one manor, never granted out. The latter in mil. serv.
Colne	1 carucate	Never granted out
Folrig	2 carucates	Mil. serv.
Cliviger, 2 car. and also the grange of Kirkstall Abbey, which appears originally to have belonged to the parish of Rochdale, 1 car.	3 carucates	Two manors, one in mil. serv. the other consisting of Holme, Dineley, and Cliviger Dean, in frank almoigne
Briercliffe, 1 car. with the hamlets of Worsthorn and Extwisle, ½ a car. each	2 carucates	Three manors, the first never granted out, the second held in mil. serv., the third in frank almoigne
Hapton, 1 car. with Bridtwisle, ½ a car.[1]	1½ a carucate	Two manors in mil. serv.

Before I dismiss this subject, it may be proper to subjoin a few observations on the Manors held in Thanage, which have been excepted out of the former catalogue, and must now be assigned to a baser origin than their neighbours.

These are

Manors.	Measure.
Read	7 oxgangs
Simonstone[2]	7 oxgangs
Padiham[2]	4 oxgangs
Twisleton	1 carucate
Oswaldtwisle	2 carucates
Henthorn	½ a carucate

In all 5 carucates, 3 oxgangs.

[1] The accuracy of these measurements will be proved from the Inquisition of 1311, under the survey of the several townships.

[2] I conceive these to have been originally one township, forming a carucate. The latter was never granted out.

Now, whoever attends to the earlier passages of lands in Read and Oswaldtwisle will find no vestige of a formal grant of those manors from the chief lord; but the mention of services, and the word manor, appears to have been introduced by stealth, and the right established by subsequent usurpation on one part and inattention on the other.

The above-mentioned facts, together with the peculiarity of the tenure, first induced a suspicion, in which I am now confirmed, that these townships never formed any part of the ancient free lands of the parish in the Saxon times, but were in fact a portion of the 11½ carucates held at the time of the Domesday survey by homines or homagers, that is, in villenage.

This supposition is countenanced by the nature of the tenure in question.

For Thanage was originally a service to a thane, or to the lord of a manor. These services were generally commuted for by rents; and theinage may be proved to have existed in Lancashire at an early period; for in the 11th year of Henry III. or 1227, when a tallage was made in this county, the tenants in theinage paid ten marks to have respite that they might not be tallaged.—Mag. Rot. Pip. 11 Hen. III. 3 Rot. 1 Lanc.

Strictly speaking, the thanage rents paid in the Saxon times to the great thanes or earls of counties were free rents, *but they were also paid by copyholders to lords of manors.*[1]

On the whole, there appears a strong presumption that this was in fact the earliest species of tenure in villenage amongst us.

It will now be satisfactory to remark the coincidence between these two ancient records, though at the distance of more than two centuries from each other. For, if we dismiss the manors held in thanage on the presumption that they are parts of those lands which are mentioned in Domesday as held in villenage, and if we also consider the hamlets as separated, after the time of the Conqueror, from the vills to which each belonged, we have here again 19 manors, precisely the number collected from Domesday; but instead of 30 carucates, the result of our former computation, we have, in the inquisition of 1311, only 27½ carucates, and half an oxgang; which, however, at the same average rate per oxgang, will prove the former conjecture to have approached very nearly to the truth; as, instead of 3,840, it will leave 3,520 acres for the real extent of our ancient freehold lands within the parish during the Saxon and early Norman times, a coincidence, notwithstanding the actual difference of numbers, scarcely to be expected in two records so independent and so remote from each other.

What a picture does this statement hold up of population and culture amongst us, in those ages; for if, excluding the forest of Bowland, we take the present parish of Whalley as a square of 161 miles, from this sum at least 70 miles, or 27,657 acres, must be deducted for the four forests or chaces of Blackburnshire, which belonged to no township or manor, but were at that time mere derelicts, and therefore claimed, as heretofore unappropriate, by the first Norman lords. There will therefore remain, for the different manors and

[1] For this information I am indebted to Thomas Astle, Esq.

townships, 36,000 acres, or thereabouts, of which 3,520, or not quite a tenth part, was in a state of cultivation, while the vast residuum stretched far and wide, like an ocean of waste interspersed with a few inhabited islands. But these latter wastes differed essentially from the forests, in having been defined and appropriated to their several townships from the very origin of property, by permanent natural boundaries;[1] such as the brook in the valley, the *sike*[1] or *clough*[1] on the mountain-side, or the *deal* of *heaven water*[1] upon the summit. Such were our primitive vills and townships; that is, little more than points of property and culture, about which successive inclosures have been extended in concentric circles, till their circumferences nearly touch each other; and the country has so totally lost its ancient character and aspect that it is not easy for a mind familiarised to its present state to conceive of the other, even in imagination.

But, could a curious observer of the present day carry himself nine or ten centuries back, and, ranging the summit of Pendle, survey the forked vale of Calder on one side, and the bolder margins of Ribble and Hodder on the other, instead of populous towns and villages, the castle, the old tower-built house, the elegant modern mansion, the artificial plantation, the park and pleasure-ground, or instead of uninterrupted inclosures, which have driven sterility almost to the summit of the fells, how great must then have been the contrast when, ranging either at a distance or immediately beneath, his eye must have caught vast tracts of forest ground stagnating with bog or darkened by native woods, where the wild ox, the roe, the stag, and the wolf had scarcely learned the supremacy of man; when, directing his view to the intermediate spaces, to the windings of the valleys, or the expanse of plain beneath, he could only have distinguished a few insulated patches of culture, each encircling a village of wretched cabins, among which would still be remarked one rude mansion of wood, scarcely equal in comfort to a modern cottage, yet then rising proudly eminent above the rest, where the Saxon lord, surrounded by his faithful cotarii, enjoyed a rude and solitary independence, owning no superior but his sovereign.

This was undoubtedly a state of great simplicity and freedom, such as the admirers of uncultivated nature may affect to applaud. But, though revolutions in civil society seldom produce anything better than a change of vices, yet surely no wise or good man can lament the subversion of Saxon polity for that which followed. Their laws were contemptible for imbecility,[2] their habits odious for intemperance. And, if we can for a moment persuade

[1] These are the peculiar phrases of our ancient perambulations.

[2] The Saxon laws, by substituting pecuniary mulcts for corporal punishments, confounded two species of obligation. Hence, the very idea of guilt would gradually be lost, and the laws would be understood not so much to punish crimes as to advertise licences for the perpetration of them upon certain terms. Strictly speaking, bodily sufferings, judicially inflicted, alone are punishments: of these, the exact proportion will be adjusted by every legislator according to his views of justice or mercy. But there is one offence commuted in this code for money, which no Christian lawgiver can, consistently with the obedience he owes to an higher law, avoid punishing with death. See Gen. ix. 6, which is a Noachian precept, and therefore of universal obligation. Thus much, however, must be allowed, that, while systems of legislation excessively severe defeat their own end, because human nature revolts at the execution of them, the Saxon, like all other mercenary laws, were for an obvious reason pretty sure of being enforced.

ourselves that their language has any charms, it is less perhaps from anything harmonious and expressive in itself, or anything valuable in the information which it conveys, than that it is of rare and not very easy attainment;[1] that it forms the rugged basis of our own tongue; and, above all, that we hear it loudly echoed in the dialect of our own vulgar. Indeed, the manners as well as the language of a Lancashire clown[2] often suggest the idea of a Saxon peasant; and prove, with respect to remote tracts like these, little affected by foreign admixtures, how strong is the power of traduction, how faithfully character and propensities may be transmitted through more than twenty generations.

From a people occupied, like the Saxons, in rearing and devouring the produce of their own lands, posterity had little to expect; and, accordingly, the subject of this history cannot boast one Saxon charter, one remnant of Saxon architecture,[3] properly so called; and, independently of general history, we have no remaining evidence, but that of language, that such a race of men ever existed amongst us. I do not even recollect that a Saxon penny or a Northumbrian styca has ever been turned up within the parish.[4]

The Normans were a more abstemious and polished people: their lawyers, with more chicane, had infinitely more knowledge of the principles of jurisprudence: their ecclesiastics, though more devoted to the Court of Rome, had a greater share both of piety and learning; their princes alone, haughty, unjust, and cruel, gave a conquered people reason to look back with regret on the mild, though unskilful, sway of their native monarchs.[5]

As scribes and architects, in particular, they were men to whom this district was greatly indebted; for our only castle, our oldest remaining churches, our most curious and valuable records, are all early Norman.

Such was the state of property and manners when the house of Lacy, which will be the subject of the next chapter, became possessed of Blackburnshire. But, before we go on to that part of the subject, it may be proper to consider the effects which this great revolution produced upon the state of property in this extensive district. The simplicity, there-

[1] I do not mean to say that a little knowledge of the Saxon language is not of easy attainment, but that any further progress in it is to an Englishman attended with that peculiar difficulty, whatever it may be, which is always experienced in making ourselves masters of a dialect akin to our vernacular language, yet abounding in other idioms.

[2] See that truly original work, the "Lancashire Dialect," in which the author, my old acquaintance, besides the praise of having drawn a most faithful and diverting picture of rustic manners, while he supposed himself to be doing little more than transcribing the modern jargon of his own parish, was in reality perpetuating words and forms of speech which had subsisted before the Conquest. His glossary proves that he had sometimes a glimpse of this fact: but his knowledge of the Saxon language was too confined to show him, in its full extent, what would have delighted him beyond measure, the merit and importance of his own achievement. *O si sic omnia!*

[3] I should ascribe the remains of very early architecture in the churches of Clitheroe and Colne, by far the oldest in the parish, to an æra somewhat but not much posterior to the Conquest. There is no evidence that either of those churches was founded before that event: we know that they existed soon after.

[[4] See, however, in p. 37, the notice of the styca of Keanred, found at Anchor Hill, Ribchester, in 1829.]

[5] I am not displeased to find that Mr. Gibbon is of the same opinion. "England," says he, "was assuredly a gainer by the Conquest." Chap. lvi. note 28. He refers also to William of Malmesbury, De Gestis Anglorum, l. 3, p. 101—102.

fore, and independence of Saxon tenures, was completely destroyed; a tract of country which had been parcelled out among twenty-eight lords now became subject to one, and all the intricacies of feodal dependence, and all the rigours of feodal exaction, wardships, reliefs, escheats, &c., were introduced at once.—Yet, perhaps, the rights thus acquired were seldom exercised in their utmost extent. The Saxon lords, though reduced to a state of galling dependence, do not appear, in general, to have been actually stripped of their fees; and we have one instance in which the old possessor of a manor before the Conquest alienates, after that event, in his own name. What a man, in such circumstances, is permitted to transfer, he has been previously allowed to retain.[1]

But these remaining rights, for the destruction of which many trains were laid, gradually merged in the superior fee,[2] where, perhaps, the greater part of them still remain; but others were successively re-granted in military service or frank almoigne: subordinate freehold properties were also cantoned out in socage; tenures in villenage, which had commenced, as we have seen,[3] immediately after the Conquest, were extended and encouraged; and thus, by successive steps, the origin of all landed property within the hundred, some later copyholds alone excepted, is to be traced to voluntary concessions of the Lacies, or their successors of the house of Lancaster.

Yet we are not to consider these grants as acts of pure beneficence; for, beside the personal service which they required, they were frequently charged with pecuniary payments nearly equivalent, at first, to rack-rents; but their real value, which is great indeed at present, grew out of the operation of causes little understood at the time, either by lord or vassal, namely, the certainty of the render, the diminishing value of money, and the perpetuity of the title.

[1] *Vide* Downham.

[2] The existence of a race of mesne lords, and their gradual extinction long after the Conquest, is no chimerical hypothesis. An instance will occur under the manor of Worsthorn, in which one of these (about the time of Henry II. as appears from the attestations,) granted lands to be held of himself and his heirs. Yet, in the reign of Edward I. the manor had reverted to the chief lord of the fee, and was by him granted out again.

[3] The progress of these, during a period of more than two centuries, will be accurately traced under every township, by lights borrowed from the great Inquisition of 1311.

CHAPTER THE SECOND.

LORDS OF THE HONOR OF CLITHEROE.

RESPECT only to general opinion, and to the authority of Dugdale, which has been held decisive, induces me to place at the head of this catalogue

ILBERT DE LACI,[1] a Norman adventurer, on whom the Conqueror undoubtedly conferred the great fee of Pontefract; but, as he is unnoticed under the survey of Blackburnshire by the authentic record of Domesday, which was completed in the last years of the first William, and died early in the reign of Rufus, there is no evidence to prove that he was ever connected with the subject of this history. Ilbert, however, left a son,

ROBERT DE LACI, who was certainly lord of Blackburnshire, though it is now impossible to discover by what means he became possessed of it.[2] As, however, the Hundred of Blackburn at the time of Domesday constituted a part of those vast possessions which the Conqueror granted to Roger de Busli and Albert de Greslet, the probability is that Lacy acquired this fee from them, and held it under them. This opinion is strengthened by a charter of Henry I.[3] granting Boeland to this Robert, son of Ilbert, to be held of the Crown *in capite*, as it had heretofore been of Roger de Poitou.

[1] This name is spelt with all the laxity of ancient orthography, *Laci*, *Lacy*, and *Lascy*. The earlier part of Dugdale's account of this family, Baronage, vol. i. p. 98, *et seqq.* is singularly inaccurate. He seems to have been principally misled by a Ms. in Bibl. Bod. (G. 9, Cant.) f. 77 b. which is little better than a collection of traditionary tales. Where I shall have occasion to differ from him, I shall do it on the authority of original charters, and assign my reasons. [The name is probably derived from a place now called Lassi, in the department of Calvados in Normandy. "Among the families who became seated in England at the time of the Conquest, none obtained more extensive possessions or attained to higher dignities than the Lacis. The first settler was an Ilbert de Laci. The account of his lands in Yorkshire fills seven pages of Domesday Book, and he had other lands in other counties. His Yorkshire lands form what in later times has been called the Honor of Pontefract. . . . . . I am unwilling to dwell upon what has already been often and well told; and I would refer those who wish for further information upon this subject to the *Lacies Nobilitie* of Sir John Ferne, to the Baronage of Sir William Dugdale, to the Antiquities of Cheshire by Sir Peter Leycester, who has corrected many errors committed by the author of the Baronage, and, last of all, to the beautiful history of this house incorporated by Dr. Whitaker in his History of Whalley." Joseph Hunter, *South Yorkshire*, vol. ii. pp. 200, 201.]

[2] [In the "Account of Clithero Burgage," printed in Gregson's Fragments, p. 288, from Kenion's MSS. is an assertion that the Conqueror gave the whole Wapentake, with all its franchises, to Ilbert Lascy.]

[3] Dugdale, *ubi supra*.

That he was possessed, however, of this fee, by whatever means he acquired it, there can be no doubt, as he confirmed the original charter of Merlay, granted by Ilbert his son to Jordan le Rous.[1]

Robert, however, did not long enjoy his inheritance in peace, for, an. 1mo. Henry I. having espoused the better cause of Robert Curthose, he was dispossessed of all his lands by that monarch, and is stated by Dugdale to have gone twice into banishment, from which he did not return a second time.

After the second banishment of Robert we are told by the same writer that the fee of Pontefract (including that of Clitheroe) was granted first to [William] Travers,[2] and secondly to Hugh de la Val. The latter fact is certain; but it appears equally certain that Robert actually returned, and was restored, for we find him confirming several grants of churches made by Delaval during his temporary possession to the priory of Nostel, which was of his or perhaps his father's foundation.[3]

With equal certainty and on similar authority it may be proved against Dugdale that this Robert the First[4] founded the castle of Clitheroe, for it did not exist at the time of

[1] *Vide* Merlay.

[2] [Dr. Whitaker (following Dugdale in this error) gave this name as Henry Travers; but the words of Dugdale's authority are: "Ea tempestate (A.D. 1135) Willielmus cognomento Transversus, qui honorem Fracti pontis (sic enim quoddam oppidum nominatur) ex dono Henrici regis habuerat, a quodam milite homine suo Pagano nomine apud ipsum oppidum letali vulnere percussus, post triduum in habitu monachali mortuus est. Et quem patri suo Roberto de Lesci rex Henricus abstulerat, Ilbertus de Lesceio filius ejus mox eundem honorem recuperavit." Richard of Hexham (edit. Twysden) 310; not Simeon of Durham, as Hunter, ii. 201. And see also John of Hexham, ibid. col. 262.]

[3] The following are instances extracted from Burton's Mon. Ebor. of several alternate grants and confirmations between these parties:—

CHURCHES.	GRANTORS.	CONFIRMATIONS.
Batley	Robert de Lacy	Hugh De la Val, Henry I. Alexander III.
South Kirkby	Guy (*sic*) de la Val	Robert de Lacy.
Featherstone	Hugh de la Val	Robert de Lacy, King Stephen, Alexander III.
Huthersfield	Hugh de la Val	Robert de Lacy, Alexander III.
Rothwell	Hugh de la Val	Robert de Lacy, Alexander III.
Warmfield	Hugh de la Val	Robert de Lacy, Alexander III.

We now see the reason why the monks of Pontefract failed in their claim upon the Church of Whalley, under Delaval's grant (see before, p. 77): it was never confirmed, and all alienations made under an attainder, unless confirmed by the party attainted after his restoration, are held *pro infectis*.

[4] I now find that I had overlooked another hypothesis with respect to the foundation of this castle, which will assign to it a still higher antiquity, namely, that it was the work of Roger of Poictou himself. For it appears from Domesday, under Bernulfswic, that Berenger de Todeni had held XII car. of land in that place, *sed modo est in Castellatu* Rog. Pictaviensis. We know that it was a disputable point much later whether Bernoldswic was or was not in Blackburnshire; and what can be meant by *Castellatus* if there was now no castle at Clitheroe? It may be answered that the word refers to Roger's great fee of Lancaster; but this is impossible, for, at the time of the Domesday Survey, *Longcaster* and *Chercalongcastre* were surveyed *inter terras regis* in Amunderness not yet granted out, and were so far from having a castle or being yet at the head of an Honor, much less a County, that they are taken as vills or berewicks appertaining to the manor of Halton. All is darkness and confusion with respect to the foundation of the Castle and Honor of Lancaster, and particularly with respect to Roger of Poictou, of which name there must have been two persons, for how could it be supposed that a follower of the Conqueror should forfeit under Stephen?

the Domesday Survey; and in the interval of Delaval's possession, during the banishment of Lacy, we find the former expressly granting, under the dependencies of the church of Whalley, *capellam Sci. Michaelis in Castro de Clyderhow.*

It was indeed antecedently to be expected that the 28 manors within the hundred, now united into one Honor, should not have remained two generations longer without a common centre: a temporary residence at least was required for the lord, a court-house for the transaction of his business, and a fortress for the defence of his lands. In a country not abounding with strong positions an insulated conical rock of limestone rising out of the fertile plain between Penhull and Ribble would naturally attract his attention, and here, therefore, the first Lacy of Blackburnshire and second of Pontefract fixed the castle of Clitheroe, the seat of his barony, to which a numerous train of dependents during a period of seven succeeding centuries have owed homage and service. Robert de Lacy also founded the Cluniac priory of St. John in Pontefract, to which, however, he refused a confirmation of the church of Whalley, granted by his disturber Delaval, and, dying, left two sons, Ilbert and Henry.[1]

ILBERT DE LACY, the oldest son of Robert and the companion of his exile, was distinguished by his fidelity to King Stephen, and by his valour in the Battle of the Standard, fought near Northallerton; and, having married Alice, daughter of Gilbert de Gaunt [afterwards remarried to Robert de Mowbray[2]], died without issue. He was therefore succeeded by his brother

HENRY DE LACY the first, who, rivalling his ancestors in the devout liberality of the times, A.D. 1147, founded a Cistertian abbey at Barnoldswick, and afterwards translated it to the more genial climate of Kirkstall. He is remembered as lord of Blackburnshire by having granted out the manor of Alvetham, with Clayton and Accrington, to H. son of Leofwine, which was the second alienation of that kind after the accession of his family to the Honor of Clitheroe. Of the successive restitutions of these brothers by Stephen and Henry II. to the estates of their family, related by Dugdale in a narrative inextricably confused, after the decisive evidence before adduced that the restoration really took place under Robert their father, it is now become superfluous to speak; suffice it therefore to say, that Henry, of whose marriage however nothing is recorded,[3] left a son

ROBERT DE LACY the second, of whom it is very confidently told by Dugdale, on the authority of his MS.[4], that he founded the castle of Clitheroe and the chapel of St. Michael, with the consent of Geoffry dean of Whalley. The falsehood, however, of this story has

[1] Rob. de Lacy confirms to the abbey of Selby the manor of Hamelden, given by his father for the soul of Hugh his brother. Lands quitcl. here by John son of Hugh de Lacy, of Gateford. Burton's Mon. Ebor. p. 395.

[2] [Addit. MS. 26,741, f. 262.]

[3] [His wife is omitted by Dugdale; but elsewhere she is thus mentioned: "Iste Henricus duxit in uxorem sororem Willielmi Vesci rectoris de Berwic, et genuit ex ea Robertum. Nescitur ubi sepultus fuit; creditur quod ipse in Terra Sancta obiit vij kalendas Octobris." *Historia Laciorum*, in the Monasticon, under Kirkstall. Further, her name was Albreda, as appears by a charter of her son Robert de Lacy to the Abbey of Kirkstall quoted in Brooke's *Discovery of Errours*, 1594, p. 63, also in Addit. MS. 26,741, f. 262b.]

[4] MS. in Bibl. Bodl. G. 9, Cant. f. 98b.

already been proved. He married Isabella, daughter of . . . ., and, dying without issue, [August 21,] 1193,[1] was interred in the abbey of Kirkstall. With him ended the male line of this great family,[2] and in fact the blood of the Lacies itself, so that he had no other resource than to devise his vast estates, consisting of sixty knight's fees, to his uterine sister [3] Awbrey, daughter of Robert de Lizours, who married

Richard FitzEustace,[4] lord of Halton, and constable of Chester, who died sometime before 1178, 24 Hen. II. leaving

[1] [" Inventum est in chronicis abbatiæ de Kyrkestall pro anno regis Henrici quarto et Anno Domini mcxciii. mensis Augusti die xxj., viz. xij. kal. Februarii (*sic*) obiit bonæ memoriæ dominus Robertus de Lasey, secundus fundator monasterii de Kyrkestall, et ibi sepelitur." *Monasticon Anglicanum*, 1682, p. 857. " Iste Robertus obiit anno Regis Ricardi primi et anno quarto Anno Domini 1193, et duodecimo kalendas Septembris." Duchy of Lancaster, Class xxv. Bundle AA. No. 8 (7). Dr. Whitaker had here adopted the erroneous date " 12 kal. Feb." following the Monasticon and the Cotton MS. Tib. A. xix. f. 60 b.]

[2] With him too terminates my unpleasing task of detecting the perpetual errors of Dugdale and his authorities. Sir Peter Leycester will henceforward be my guide, in whose account of the Constables of Chester I have not been able to detect a single mistake; but Sir Peter Leycester wrote, as every historian if possible ought to do, from original evidences. [Whatever the merits of Leycester, I cannot allow the expression " the perpetual errors of Dugdale " to pass without a protest. Dugdale, no doubt, fell into some errors, like every mortal genealogist; but they are not those of a blunderer, and his great merit is that, like Sir Peter Leycester, he always cites his authorities. J. G. N.]

[3] [" Et iste Ricardus duxit sororem Roberti de Lascy quæ vocabatur Awbray Lisours, de qua genuit duos filios, scilicet Johannem constabularium, fundatorem domus de Stanlowe, et fratrem Robertum hospitolarem, et duas filias, scilicet Saram et Abreiam. Sara fuit data Roberto de Aldeforde. Altera vero scilicet Abreia data fuit Henrico Beset. Et notandum quod Abreia ista fuit soror Roberti Lascy ex parte matris et non ex parte patris, quia pater Aubreiæ fuit Robertus de Lysours. Successit tamen dicto Roberto de Lascy in heredem quia nullum heredem habuit de se genitum nec alium tam propinquum." Harl. MS. 1830, f. 4, 4b. But these statements of the monastic historian are now shown to be unfounded, as will appear in the following notes.]

[4] [The family of Albreda de Lizours had been seated at Sprotborough in Yorkshire from the time of the Conqueror, when Roger de Busli included that manor in his great fee. The following account of the family is abstracted from that given by the historian of South Yorkshire: " Among the principal of the persons who attached themselves to Roger de Busli was Fulk de Lizours. He is supposed to have been a relation of Roger. His name, and that of Albreda his wife, are joined with those of Roger de Busli and Muriel his wife in the foundation deed of the priory of Blythe. In the time of the sons of the Conqueror appear two brothers, Fulk and Torard, both known by the addition de Lusoriis or de Lizours. Whether they were sons of the former Fulk, or that this Fulk is the same person, does not appear on the face of any record. Torard was the ancestor of the Lizours of Nottinghamshire, where they continued for some centuries; while Fulk had the lands of Sprotborough, with a portion of the Nottinghamshire lands. The charters in the coucher of Blythe relating to lands at Billingley show that Fulk had a son named Robert de Lizours. He made an illustrious marriage with the widow [*l.* cousin] of Henry de Lacy."

Subsequently to his writing the foregoing, Mr. Hunter arrived at a different conclusion in regard to the manner in which the family of Lizours was substituted for the first race of Lacy. It was founded on the following passage of the Pipe Roll of 1131: " Robertus de Lusoriis reddit compotum de viij li. vj s. viij d. ut ducat in uxorem sororem Ilberti de Laci. In thesauro iiij li. Et debet iiij li. vj s. viij d." (Magnus Rotulus Pipæ 31 Hen. I. edit. 1833, p. 8.) Upon which, as editor, he made the following remarks in his Preface: " A new view is opened of a very important fact in the history of one of the great feudal tenancies of England, which became at length, as it still continues, a fief of the Crown, the Honor of Pontefract. The original grantee was an Ilbert de Lacy, whose great possessions are described in Domesday Book. From him descended other Lacies, who held this fee till the reign of Richard I. when Robert, the last of them, deceased without issue. On his death the fee descended to Albreda de Lizours, of whom there exists a fine of the fifth year of King Richard, showing her in possession, and to whom she disposed of it. The question is how Albreda stood related to the last Laci last seized; and Dugdale, together with the whole body of later genealogists,

John, constable of Chester,[1] and lord of Halton, who, A.D. 1178, founded the Cistercian abbey of Stanlaw, the parent of Whalley. He died at Tyre, on a crusade, A.D. 1190, 2nd Richard I., leaving issue by Alice, sister of William de Mandeville, Roger, who

has followed the *Historia Laceiorum*, an historical fragment written not earlier than the time of Henry VI. printed in the *Monasticon* from a chartulary. The writer of this little piece of history declares Albreda to have been half-sister, *ex parte materna*, to the last of the Lacies. But as it would show a rule of descent of which it is presumed no similar instance can be produced from those times, and might, if admitted, lead to general conclusions that were erroneous in respect of the inheritance of feudal tenures under the early monarchy, it is of importance to observe that in this Roll there is an entry in the accounts for Nottinghamshire and Derbyshire that Robert de Lizours paid 8*l.* 6*s.* 8*d.* that he might take to wife the sister and heir of Ilbert de Lasci, a second of that name, and there can scarcely be a doubt that Albreda, the issue of that marriage, was cousin and heir, and not half-sister, of the last Lasci, and therefore a partaker of the blood of the Ilbert de Lasci who was the original grantee from the Conqueror.

The two lines of descent will be made apparent at one view by the following table:

Lords of Pontefract.	*Lords of Sprotborough.*	*Barons of Halton and Constables of Chester.*	*Lords of Knaresborough.*	*Barons of Malton and Alnwick.*
Ilbert de Laci, died 1090.	Fulk de Lizours.	Nigel constable of Chester.		William Tyson.
Robert de Laci.	Fulk de Lizours.	William fitz Nigel, d. 1133 constable of Chester.	John de Burgo, *monoculus.*	Alda, mar. Yvo de Vesci.
Ilbert II. Henry, d. ... Albreda, m. 1131. = Robert de Lizours.		Agnes, 2 wife. = Eustace fitz John, slain 1157. = Beatrix.		
Robert last of the elder line of Laci, died 1193.	Albreda de Lizours, lady of Sprotborough. = Richard fitz Eustace, d. bef. 1178. = 2 husband, William fitz Godric (or de Clairfait).			William de Vesci, ob. 1184.
John fitz Richard, constable of Chester, d. 1190.	Roger fitz Richard, ancestor of the family of Clavering.	William fitz William, ancestor of Earl FitzWilliam, and of Sir Joseph Copley, Bart. now of Sprotborough (1871).		William de Vesci, ob. 1253.
Roger constable of Chester, made heir by his grandmother Albreda in 1194, and assumed the name of Lacy; died 1211.				John de Vesci, ob. 1289. William, ob. 1295, s.p.l.
John de Lacy, constable of Chester, became Earl of Lincoln in 1232.				

I cannot close this note without mentioning with regret that, notwithstanding that the passage of Mr. Hunter's preface above recited was extracted at full in the Appendix to the First Edition of Baines's History of Lancashire, vol. iv. p. 765, in order to point out this very important amendment in the Lacy genealogy, yet it has been overlooked in the new edition of that work, 1870, where at vol. ii. p. 14, the old statement is repeated, that on the death of Robert de Lacy, "his possessions were inherited by his maternal sister Aubrey." Nor has the discovery been duly introduced into Courthope's *Historic Peerage*, 1857, or Burke's *Dormant and Extinct Peerages*, 1866, for in both these works Albreda Lisours is still designated as "his half-sister." Mr. Hulton again, in the *Whalley Coucher Book*, 1847, pp. 2, 76, scarcely ventured to deviate from Dugdale's account, although he had an intimation of the passage in the pipe-roll of 31 Hen. I., derived from Dodsworth,—still unaware of Hunter. So venerable and pertinacious is error, and so difficult is it to substitute truth in its place. J. G. N.]

[1] That the name of Lacy, to which he had not the slightest pretension, should be popularly given to the founder of Stanlaw is no more extraordinary than any other vulgar error: but it is singular, indeed, that this mistake should have been committed in a charter of Whalley Abbey itself, where Henry de Lacy expressly styles [its first founder "quidam antecessorum nostrorum, Johannes de Lasey nomine, constab. Cestrie." Coucher Book, p. 190.]

succeeded him,[1] Eustace surnamed of Chester, Richard a leper, Peter, whom I conjecture to have been Peter de Cestria the long-lived Rector of Whalley,[2] and Alice. This

ROGER DE LACY,[3] the terror and scourge of the Welsh, for his severe executions upon whom, together with the general ferocity of his temper, he was denominated *Hell*,[4] succeeded to the fees of Pontefract and Clyderhow, in consequence of a fine, levied between himself and Aubrey his grandmother, devisee under the will of Robert de Lacy, in 1195, or little more than a year after the death of the latter; Richard FitzEustace and John his son not having lived to enjoy this great inheritance.

He was now lately returned from the Holy Land, whither he accompanied Richard I. in the third crusade, having assisted at the memorable siege of Acre,[5] where so many of his countrymen and equals perished.

There is something evidently allusive to the temper and achievements of Roger de Lacy in his great seal, of which some drawings have been preserved. On the obverse side, instead of the equestrian figure usual in that situation, is the spirited figure of a griffon rending the body of some other animal;[6] and on the indorsement, an armed man

[1] So Sir Peter Leycester, and this is confirmed by a fine levied at Clyderhow, 7 Ric. I. before Roger de Lacy in person, where we meet with some other persons of the Halton family, of whom I do not know that they are mentioned anywhere else. Coram Rog. de Lacy, Const. Cest., et fratre Roberto, filio Ricardi avunculi Rogeri, Eustatio fratre suo, &c. [Elsewhere the wife of John de Lacy is thus described: "habuit in uxorem Aliciam Vere uxorem (*sic*) Willielmi Mandeville Comit. Essex. Vid. 5 Ric I. habuit exitum Rogerum, Eustachium, Richardum cui pater dedit villam de Moore, Galfridus testis cum Rogero fratre suo in anno 5to Joh'is, Alicia. Addit. MS. Brit. Mus. 26,741, f. 262 b.]

[2] See in the Coucher Book, (Chetham Soc.) p. 94, a charter in which he styles himself "Petrus de Lasey rector ecclesie de Whalleye. As before noticed in p. 80, he is stated to have been a bastard son. (Ibid. p. 280.)

[3] ["This Roger was living at the time of the death of his relative Robert de Laci, and there was a fine levied in the King's court at Winchester on April 21, 5 of Richard I. that is, about a year after the death of Robert de Laci, by which Albreda passed to her grandson all the Laci lands, he quit-claiming at the same time to her the lands which had been Robert de Lizours her father's. (This most important document was first made public by Sir Peter Leycester. It is printed also in Ormerod's *History of Cheshire*, i. 510.) This Roger was the founder of a second family of Laci, for he assumed that surname, and seated himself at Pontefract, abandoning his hereditary house of Halton. His usual style was Roger de Laci, constable of Chester, by which description I have seen his name in an original charter of Albrey de Vere, Earl of Oxford, which, if, as I believe, of the first Earl, shows that the name of Laci was used by him immediately on his entering on the Laci fee." Hunter, *South Yorkshire*, ii. 202.]

[4] ["Rogerum de Hell, a Vallensibus ita cognominatum eo quod eosdem Wallicos, Regi Angliæ rebelles, tanquam inferni (*sic*), undique devastavit." *Historia Laceiorum.* Such is the authority for this oft-repeated soubriquet; which, notwithstanding, seems an exceedingly unlikely one. Among the witnesses to a charter of John de Scotia, Earl of Chester, which is printed by Ormerod, iii. 308, occurs the name of *Rog' Hell senescallo Cestr'*, the original, it may be suspected, of this imaginary nickname of the Constable.]

[5] It is curious and edifying to contrast the scenes which took place respectively before this obscure and remote place (St. John de Acre) at the close of the 12th and 18th centuries. In the former, the armies of France and England are seen fighting together against the Moslem infidels, under the common banner of the Cross; in the latter, appears a Christian knight leading a Mohammedan army against a host of apostate Frenchmen, crusading in the cause of atheism.

[6] [In perfect impressions of this device it will be seen that it is the serpent which is really stinging the neck of the griffin; the latter being, no doubt, intended to typify Wales, in allusion to the name of Griffith (Griffinus) borne by

trampling on the body of an enemy, whose head he holds up triumphantly with the right hand, while the left sustains an antique heater shield.

In this crusade he was accompanied by William de Bellomonte, ancestor of the Beaumonts of Whitley Beaumont, in Yorkshire, who received from his patron the grant of ten oxgangs of land in Huddersfield, and who, from the frequency with which he attests the charters of Roger, appears to have been almost his inseparable companion for the remainder of their lives. It was the practice of those days for dependents to adopt, with some distinction, the armorial bearings of their patrons; it has always been usual to add to them some charge in memory of signal achievements, and thus a lion rampant in the shield of the Beaumonts attests their ancient connexion with the house of Lacy,

the Welsh princes. As for the reverse, it appears to be one of those antique cameos which were continually adopted into the English seals of the period: but, unfortunately, this is only preserved (so far as has hitherto been found) in the rude tricking by Randle Holmes (Harl. MS. 2064, f. 307,) from which the engraving in the Plate is derived.

In another seal attributed to Roger de Lacy, being a signet of small dimensions, there is an antique gem of a human head, which is circumscribed VIRGO EST ELECTVS A DOMINO. But qu. did not this really appertain to the Prior of Pontefract? It is engraved in *Vetusta Monumenta*, vol. i. pl. liv.

The Constables of Chester, who were engaged in constant warfare with the Welsh, appear to have adopted the device of the serpent stinging the griffin as early as the reign of Henry I., when it first appears in the seal of William FitzNigel, four generations before Roger de Lacy. The engraving here given is from the Tabley MSS. Lib. C. 139 b. where it is attached to the charter printed in Ormerod's *History of Cheshire*, i. 507, note. It will also be found (less perfectly drawn) in Sir P. Leycester's *Antiquities of Cheshire*, edit. 1673, p. 261. William his son had a similar seal. (Ormerod, i. 508.)

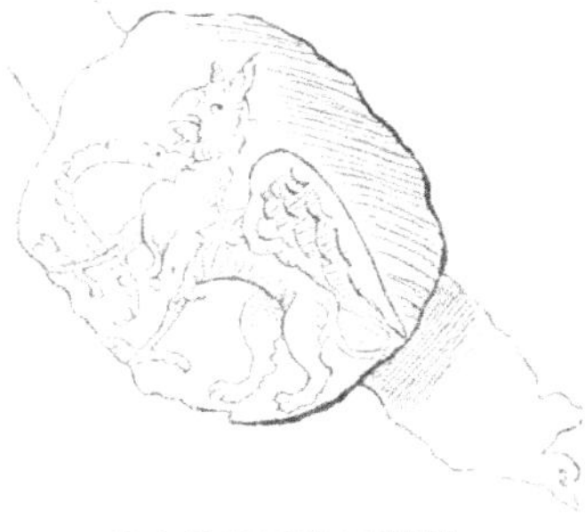

SEAL OF WILLIAM FITZNIGEL.

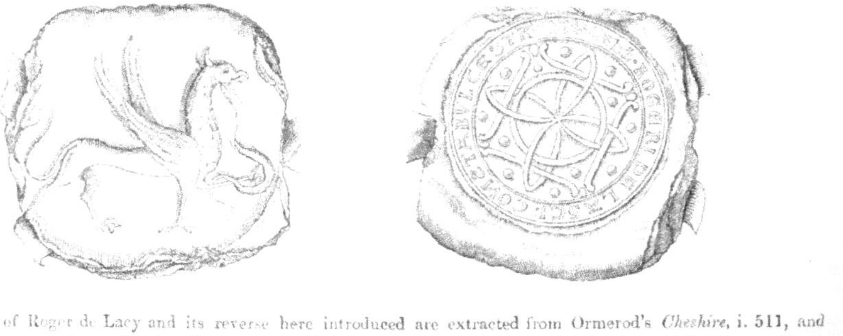

The seal of Roger de Lacy and its reverse here introduced are extracted from Ormerod's *Cheshire*, i. 511, and were engraved from an impression in white wax, appendant to a charter in the possession (1816) of Mr. Thomas Sharp of Coventry.

The interlaced device which Ormerod (ibid.) calls "the fret," occurring on the reverse of the seal of Roger, is certainly meant to echo to the surname of Lacy. Heralds have given it the name of the Lacy fret.]

and an orle of crescents alludes (not obscurely) to some triumph over the standard of Mohammed.[1]

In his connexion with the Honor of Clitheroe, Roger de Lacy gave to the abbey of Stanlaw the lordship of Merland, the advowson of the church of Rochdale, with four oxgangs of land in Castleton (the valuable glebe of the present vicarage), and Brandwood, an uncultivated tract, then considered as part of Rossendale. The Coucher Book of Whalley proves with what enthusiastic ardour this example was followed by the inferior proprietors of lands in that district, who seem for a time to have been even ambitious of stripping themselves and their families to enrich this popular foundation. Roger de Lacy also granted the villa de Tunlay, and manor of Coldcoats, with Snodworth, to Geoffry son of Robert dean of Whalley. He served the office of sheriff for the county of Lancaster in the 7th, 8th, and 9th of Richard I., and is found occasionally presiding in his own courts at Clitheroe. He died Oct. 1, 1211, and was interred in the abbey of Stanlaw,[2] leaving, by Maud de Clare his wife, a daughter married to Geoffry dean of Whalley; and

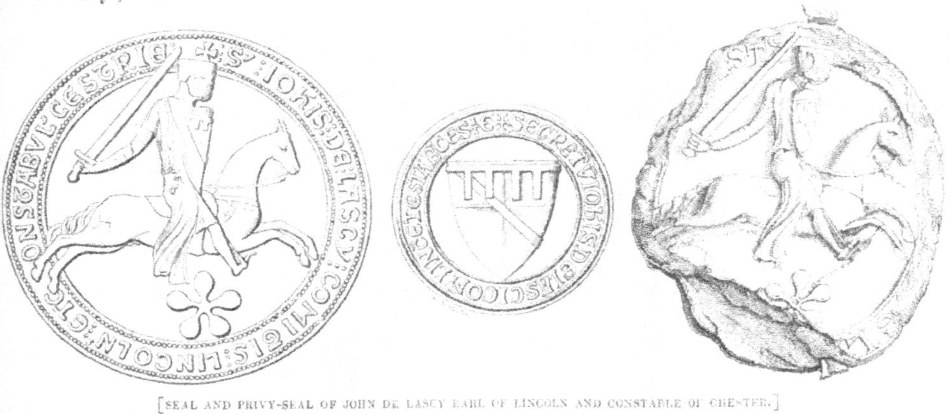

[SEAL AND PRIVY-SEAL OF JOHN DE LASCY EARL OF LINCOLN AND CONSTABLE OF CHESTER.]

[1] The above affords a similar instance in the family of Neville, and probably of the same date.

[I do not know to what coat of Neville our author here alludes: but in regard to the coat of Beaumont his heraldry must certainly be dismissed as imaginary. The lion of Beaumont is of gold, borne on an azure field, which is gerated or *semée* either with fleurs de lis, with billets, or crescents, in the several branches. The family was French, claiming descent from the royal house of France; and a branch which remained in that country, seated at Brienne-sur-Aube in Champagne, retained the same coat, but geraty with billets. As for crescents, they are a common kind of gerating, and the fancy that they, in any family, allude to the Crusades is entirely unproved. J. G. N.]

[2] [" Anno Domini 1211 obiit Rogerus de Lacy, secundus fundator et novicius loci Benedicti de Stanlaw, in festo Sancti Remigii. Cui successit Johannes filius ejus." (Cotton MS. Titus F. III. f. 258.) The designation "novicius" implies that he had been invested with the monastic habit in his fatal illness, as was then a frequent custom. "Habuit exitum Johannem, Rogerum, Robertum qui assumit cognomen de Constable." (Add. MSS. 26,741, f. 263.) From Robert the family of Constable, of Flamborough in Yorkshire, is said to be descended. Peacham, *Compleat Gentleman*, 1622, p. 171.]

JOHN DE LACY, who, after the death of Alice de Aquila, his first wife,[1] without issue, married Margaret, daughter and coheiress of Robert de Quincy, son of Saher, Earl of Winchester. This Robert had married Hawys, fourth sister and coheiress of Ranulph Blondeville, Earl of Chester and Lincoln, who gave to her, in the distribution of his lands and honours, the latter earldom,[2] *scilicet quantum ad me pertinuit, ut inde Comitissa existat.* From her it descended to Margaret her daughter, who, marrying John de Lacy as above, Henry III. by patent[3] dated 23 Nov. 1232, reg. 17, re-granted it to the said John, and the heirs of his body begotten upon Margaret his then wife.[4] John de Lacy granted the two medieties of the rectory of Blackburn to the monks of Stanlaw, and the manor of

[1] ["Alice, daughter to Peter de Aquila: she was buried at Norton abbey." Sir Peter Leycester.]

[2] [Shortly before his death, which occurred at the castle of Wallingford in Berkshire, on the 28th Oct. 1232. The charter by which he transferred the Earldom of Lincoln is still extant in the British Museum, and is printed in the *Topographer and Genealogist*, vol. i. p. 313. See "The Descent of the Earldom of Lincoln," a paper by John Gough Nichols, in the Lincoln volume of the Archæological Institute, 1848, p. 271. Immediately after the Earl of Chester's death the Countess Hawise transferred the Earldom of Lincoln to her son-in-law John de Lacy, an arrangement no doubt contemplated by his uncle the late Earl, and completed and confirmed by royal charter on the 23rd November, 1232. Ibid. p. 272.]

[3] [The date of this patent was within one month of the death of the Earl of Chester. "In terms equally simple with those employed in the first transfer of the Earldom, the King declared that, at the request of Hawise de Quency, he had granted to John de Lacy, Constable of Chester, those twenty pounds which Ranulph late Earl of Chester and Lincoln had received as the third penny of the county of Lincoln, *by the name of Earl of Lincoln*, and which the said Earl had in his life given to the said Hawise his sister; and which twenty pounds John de Lacy was to have and hold *by the name of Earl of Lincoln*, to him and his heirs issuing of Margaret his wife, the daughter of the said Hawise, for ever." (Memoir on the Earldom of Lincoln, p. 272.) Four years later, at the marriage and coronation of Queen Alianor in 1236, John de Lacy is mentioned by Matthew Paris simply as "Constable of Chester," and the passage is very interesting, as showing the feudal relationship of the Constable to the Earl. "The Earl of Chester [then John le Scot,] carried the Sword of Saint Edward which was called *curtana*, before the King, as a sign that he was Earl of the Palace, and had by right the power of restraining the King if he should commit an error. The Earl was attended by the Constable of Chester, who kept the people away with his staff when they pressed forward in a disorderly manner." John de Lacy in his seal as Earl of Lincoln (of which the engravings given on p. 243 are lent by the Archæological Institute,) adheres to the old coat of his family, but possibly the cinquefoil under his feet may have some allusion to Lincoln, though it is generally considered to be the special badge of the county of Leicester. The second engraving of the great seal is from Ormerod, i. 513, and apparently, judging by the remaining letters, from a different matrix, though the same design.]

[4] [The Countess Margaret was remarried to Walter Marshal, the fourth of five brothers who successively inherited the Earldom of Pembroke, and who also died without issue 24 Nov. 1246. There is in the British Museum a charter (Harl. 52 H. 44) in which she styles herself Countess of Lincoln and Pembroke; and in a charter of Maurice abbot of Kirkstall cited hereafter she is so designated. The annexed seal of Margaret de Lacy offers a very remarkable assemblage of early heraldic devices. In the centre is the old coat of Lacy surmounted by a flaming star or sun, with or without any special meaning. The margin, in place of a legend, is occupied alternately with the mascle of Quincy, and a double-tailed lion, possibly to typify that she was twice a Countess, for the lion was borne by both her husbands. The original is in the treasury of St. John's college, Cambridge.]

Little Merlay to William de Nowell; and, dying July 22, 1240, was interred with his ancestors at Stanlaw. He obtained from Henry III. a grant of divers privileges within the Honor of Clitheroe, and particularly the Furca or Gallows at Clitheroe and in Tottington.[1] His son and successor was

Edmund de Lacy [born 1230], who,[2] dying in the lifetime of his mother, never assumed the title of Earl of Lincoln.[3] He was educated at court under the immediate eye

[1] Towneley MSS.

[2] ["Anno Domini M°cc°xxx° natus est Eadmundus de Lascy filius Johannis com. Lincoln. et constabularii Cestriæ." (Cotton MS. Cleopatra C. III. f. 328.) As he did not survive his mother, the heiress of the Earldom, he never actually succeeded to that dignity, though there are some documents in which he is styled Earl of Lincoln by courtesy, as mentioned in the memoir on the Earldom before quoted, p. 273. "Post mortem autem dicti Johannis de Lacy, filius ejus Edmundus de Lacy constabularius et non comes vixit xiij annos et moriebatur Anno Domini Mcclviij nonas Junii et sepultus jacet apud Locum Benedictum juxta patrem suum." (Harl. MS. 1830, f. 6.) "Anno D'ni M°cc°lviij° obijt Eadmundus Lascy ix kal. Junii." (Cotton MS. Cleop. C. III. f. 328 b.) "Anno 1258 obiit Eadmundus de Lacy filius Johannis, quartus fundator, non. Junii, cui successit Henricus filius ejus. Horum ossa sunt modo apud Whalley." (Cotton MS. Titus, F. III. f. 258.)]

[3] [The great seal of Edmund de Lacy is roughly represented in the Plate, fig. 6. It has been lately better engraved, but from a fractured impression, in The Yorkshire Archæological and Topographical Journal, vol. i. p. 169, as here repeated. The legend appears to have been SIGILL' EADMVNDI DE LASCY CONSTABVLARII CESTRIE.

His signet is also engraved in the Plate, fig. 7; but the original is really smaller, as in the woodcut. It has a shield of the three garbs of Chester, and the legend: SECRETV. EADMVNDI DE LASCI.

The engravings here inserted are contributed by the *Yorkshire Archæological and Topographical Association*, from their Journal, vol. i. p. 169; having been copied from a charter now in the possession of Charles Jackson, Esq. of Doncaster. The same seal was used by Edmund de Lacy at Easter 1258 (shortly before his death) to a confirmation charter to Roche Abbey (ibid. p. 173).

of King Henry III. and probably by his procurement married, to the great indignation of the good people of England, Alice de Saluces, a foreign lady, related to the Queen, and daughter of a nobleman of Provence.[1] He died June 5, 1258,[2] and was buried at Stanlaw; leaving

Henry de Lacy [born 1251 [3]], the last and greatest man of his line, who, from his peculiar connexion with the subject of this work, as well as his own personal qualifications, is entitled to a larger and more distinct commemoration than his ancestors.[4]

[1] [This statement is derived from the historian Matthew Paris. There are two curious passages in his chronicle relating to this marriage: the first stating that Peter of Savoy, Earl of Richmond, (the Queen's maternal uncle and brother to Boniface archbishop of Canterbury,) "brought from his distant province some unknown ladies, in order to marry them to the nobles of England whom the King was educating as his wards;" and the second relating that the King stayed at Woodstock from the feast of St. Vitalis (April 28) until the morrow (May 2) of the apostles Philip and James, in 1247, in order to be present at the marriages of Edward (titular) Earl of Lincoln and Richard de Burgh, upon whom the young Provençal ladies were then bestowed. Richard de Burgh died before the end of the same year (as mentioned by Matthew Paris), and of his bride no other notice occurs; but the wife of Edmund de Lacy is identified as Alice daughter of Manfred marquis of Saluzzo, by Beatrix of Savoy, which Beatrix, after the death of her husband in 1244, was remarried to Manfred, a natural son of the Emperor Frederick, and afterwards King of Naples and Sicily. The Marquis of Saluzzo was fourth in descent from the marriage of Boniface marquis of Saluzzo with a former Alice of Savoy in the twelfth century. And it is a fact hitherto unnoticed by our own peerage-writers that Alice Countess of Arundel (ob. 1292), the wife of Richard Earl of Arundel (1272-1302), was niece to the wife of Edmund de Lacy, being a daughter of her brother Thomas Marquis of Saluzzo, who lived until 1299. See Guichenon, Histoire Généalogique de la Royale Maison de Savoie, 1778, vol. i. p. 273, vol. iii. pp. 290, 318.]

[2] This favour he had granted to the monks seven years before, when he gave them the advowson of one moiety of the church of Blackburn, "cum corpore meo apud Standlawe sepeliendo, si contingat me in Anglia in fata decedere." Coucher Book of Whalley, (Chetham Soc.) p. 77.]

[3] ["1251. Natus est Henricus de Lacy 3 idus Januarii." MSS. Cott. Vesp. D. xviii. f. 17b. and Cleop. C. iii. f. 328.]

[4] [For a full biography of the Earl of Lincoln the reader may be referred to "The Siege of Carlaverock, by Sir Harris Nicolas," 4to 1828, introduced by the remark that his name occupies a prominent place in the records of almost every public event of his time. In the expedition to Scotland 1300, which the old poem of *Le Siege de Karlaverok* commemorates, the Earl of Lincoln led the van of the invading army.

Henry li bons Quens de Nicole	Leading the foremost squadron on
Ki provesté embrasce e acole,	Comes Henry the good Earl of Lincoln,
E en son cuer le a severaine,	Whose prowess hugs with close embrace,
Menans le eschele promeraine	In his brave heart its sovereign place;
Baner out de un cendal safrin	On his silk banner saffron-died
O un lioun rampant purprin.	A purple lion ramps in pride.

Dying at his house near London, which had previously been the town residence of the bishops of Chichester, but which ever since his time has retained the name of Lincoln's Inn, Henry Earl of Lincoln was buried in St. Paul's cathedral, and an engraving of his monument may be seen in Dugdale's History of that church. "Anno 1310 obiit dominus Henricus Lacy Comes Lincolniæ et Constabularius Cestriæ in die Sanctæ Agathæ virginis anno ætatis suæ 60, et sepultus fuit in ecclesia Sancti Pauli Londini ad australem partem altaris Sanctæ Mariæ virginis. Cujus animæ pro sua magna misericordia propitietur Deus. Amen." (MS. Cotton. Titus F. iii. f. 258.)

There is a good impression of the first great seal of Henry Earl of Lincoln attached to the Addit. Charter 1438 in the British Museum (and a cast may be obtained from Mr. Robert Ready of that establishment). It is of the usual round

[On attaining his majority he was admitted to the degree of knighthood together with the King's nephew Edmund of Almaine,[1] and fifty-four other gallant bachelors, upon the feast of St. Edward held at Westminster in the year 1272; and on the same occasion prince Edmund and he were respectively girt by the aged King Henry III. (in the last year of his reign) with the swords of the Earldoms of Cornwall and Lincoln. It was, however, five years after before he obtained livery of the fee which his ancestors had usually received *nomine Comitis Lincolnie*, with all the arrears from the time of his investiture.]

He was the confidential servant and friend of Edward the First, whom he seems not a little to have resembled in courage, activity, prudence, and every other quality which can adorn a soldier[2] or a statesman. In 1290 he was appointed first commissioner for rectify-

form, but only 2½ inc. in diameter, and bears his equestrian figure in chain mail and surcoat, a large sword brandished in his right hand, and a crest in the form of an inverted crescent above his round-topped helmet, the visor of which is formed of crossed bars. On his shield, and on the housings of his horse, repeated in front and rear, are the arms of Lacy, Quarterly, a bend and file. Legend, S. HENRICI DE LACI COMIT' LINCOLNIE ET CONSTABVLAR' CESTR'. This is engraved in the Miscellaneous Plate of Seals, &c. in Dr. Whitaker's History of Craven.

The counter-seal of this is a small signet, of the size of our present sixpence. It bears the same shield of arms, with a file of five points, and on either side of the shield a garb. Legend: SECRETVM HENRICI DE LACI. This is the same which is represented in the accompanying Plate, fig. 8, but magnified beyond its real size. The bird in the first quarter is a misapprehension of part of the file or label. This signet occurs attached to a charter dated 1274 in the Duchy of Lancaster office.

At a subsequent date, the Earl relinquished his family coat for the rampant lion then generally affected by Earls, and which in his case was of the unusual tincture *purpure*, on a golden field. The great seal and accompanying counterseal, shown in these engravings,

are from a charter dated 1303. A variation of the counterseal (of the same size) has occurred in the Duchy of Lancaster office: having the same shield flanked not by dragons, but by lions, their backs towards the shield, and their heads hidden behind it. With the same inscription, SIGILLVM SECRETI.

[1] [Son of Richard Earl of Cornwall, King of the Romans, who had died in 1271.]

[2] Though he were not a long-lived man, his services began with the reign of Edward, and continued beyond it, for in the 1st year of Edward he besieged and took the castle of Chartley in Staffordshire, which Robert de Ferrars

ing the abuses which had crept into the administration of justice, especially in the Court of Common Pleas—an office in which he behaved with exemplary fidelity and strictness. In 1293 he was sent ambassador to the French king to demand satisfaction for the plunders committed by the subjects of France upon the goods of the English merchants. After the death of Edmund, Earl of Lancaster, he was appointed commander-in-chief of the army in Gascony, and viceroy of Aquitaine. In 1298 he raised the siege of the castle of St. Katharine near Toulouse, and expelled the French from the confines of that country. In 1299 he led the vanguard at the memorable battle of Falkirk. In the parliament of Carlisle, in the last year of Edward I. he had precedence of all the peers of England after the Prince of Wales; and, by a rare fortune, after the death of his old master, he seems to have retained the confidence of his son. This Earl died at his house of Lincoln's Inn, Feb. 5th, 1310, aged 60 years, and was interred in St. Paul's cathedral, where were erected, over his remains, a magnificent tomb and cross-legged statue in linked mail, which perished with many others in the great fire of London, but happily not until they had been perpetuated by the hand of Hollar.

Henry de Lacy received from his sovereign, in recompence of his services, the Honor of Denbigh in Wales, and additionally to his other titles styled himself, in consequence, Dominus de Roos and Rowennock. Over the gate of Denbigh castle his statue in robes is still preserved, and there, or at Pontefract, for traditions vary, his eldest son, the last heir male of the family, perished by a fall.

As lord of the Honor of Clitheroe, the many remaining evidences of this Earl's transactions prove him to have been active and munificent. For, besides many grants of inferior consequence, he rewarded his seneschal Oliver de Stansfeud with the manor of Worsthorn, and the Delaleghs and Middlemores with the manor of the grange of Clivacher; he confirmed and extended the privileges of his borough of Clitheroe; and, above all, he gave to the monks of Stanlaw the advowson of Whalley with its dependencies, procured the removal of their abbey to that fertile and beautiful site, attended, as it appears, the translation in person, and laid the first stone of their conventual church.[1]

He married Margaret daughter of Sir William Longespée,[2] by whom he enjoyed all the lands, though not the title, of Earl of Salisbury; they had two sons, Edmund and John, and two daughters, Alice and Margaret. Of the two sons, both of whom died young, various accounts are given. One tradition is, that Edmund the eldest [born in 1271] was drowned in the draw-well of Denbigh castle;[3] but it appears from another account,

had entered and detained by force from Hamo l'Estrange, to whom it had been granted by Henry III. upon the attainder of Ferrars.

[1] [See before, p. 90.]

[2] [This marriage had been arranged in his boyhood, when his father fined in ten marks to the King for leave to contract it, Feb. 9, 41 Hen. III. (1257). MS. Dodsworth, lvi.]

[3] [Leland says of the gate-house of Denbigh castle, "On the front is set the image of Henry de Lacy Erle of Lincoln in his stately long robes .... Sum say that the Erle of Lincoln's sunne felle into the castelle well, and there dyed: wherupon he never passid to finische the castelle." Itinerary, vol. vi. fol. 61.]

that in 1282, the year in which Edward I. granted to Henry de Lacy the two cantreds of Roos and Rowennock, he gave to Edmund de Lacy his son Maud de Chaworth, then only five years old, in marriage,[1] but that Edmund died young, and that John his brother, running upon a turret of Pontefract castle, fell down and was killed. It is not probable that both these children perished by violent deaths, but rather that one tradition has been propagated out of the other. Of the two daughters, Margaret also died before her father,[2] who left of consequence his sole heir

ALICE DE LACY, who married at the age of 9, in her father's life-time, Thomas Plantagenet, Earl of Lancaster, and carried along with her an inheritance even then estimated at 10,000 marks *per annum*.

THOMAS EARL OF LANCASTER, though idolized by the monks, was both a weak man and a bad subject, bustling without vigour, and intriguing without abilities, so that, after having long disquieted the kingdom, by an influence which his vast possessions alone created, he at length suffered himself to be overpowered by Edward II. a man as weak as himself, and was beheaded at his own manor at Pontefract, March 22, 1321, leaving no issue.[3]

Of his transactions in the Honor of Clitheroe I recollect no memorial, excepting that, by charter dated at Whalley on the feast of St. James, A.D. 1316, he gave to the abbot and convent of that place Toxteth and Smethedon, as a more convenient site for their abbey. The monks, as we have seen, complained of their present situation: they wanted fuel, building timber, and even an extent of domain at Whalley; but when the charter of Toxteth was obtained these inconveniences were instantly removed, and they thought it prudent to retain their new grant and their old situation.[4]

[1] [" Cui rex Edwardus isto anno [1282] dedit maritagium Matilde puelle quinquennys filie et heredis Patricii de Chauworth, quam genuit de filia Will'mi de Bellocampo Comitis de Warwyke, quam postea duxit uxorem Hugo Despenser. Iste itaque Edmundus dominus et filius Henrici de Lacy statim juvenis est defunctus, nullo post se relicto herede de corpore suo procreato." (Cotton. MS. Cleop. C. III. f. 335 b.) At the marriage, when the bride was five years old, the bridegroom was eleven, having been born in 1271 : "Anno Domini Mcc°lxxi natus est Eadmundus filius Henrici de Lasey x. kl. Sept." (Ibid. f. 328 b, and Vesp. D. XVII. f. 17 b.)

[2] [" Dictus igitur Henricus Com. Lincoln. de prefata Margareta uxore sua genuit aliam filium nomine Johannem et filiam unam nomine Alesyam. Sed Johannes iste priusquam annos nubiles attigisset super turrem quoddam in Castro de Pontefracto incaute discurrens lapsus est ultra muros et in terram collisus et constructus protinus expiravit, nullum post se sui corporis relinquens heredem." (Ibid.)

The Earl of Lincoln married for his second wife Joan, younger daughter and coheir of William Martin lord of Kemoys in Pembrokeshire, a baron of Parliament. He had no issue by her : and on her surviving him, her marriage was granted to Ralph de Monthermer; but she chose to marry, without his or the King's licence, Nicholas Lord Audley, and from that marriage all the subsequent Lords Audley have descended. See Dugdale, Baronage, i. 106; Courthope, Historic Peerage, pp. 35, 317.]

[3] [An impartial biography of Thomas Earl of Lancaster, by Sir Harris Nicolas, will be found in *The Siege of Carlaverock*, 1828. 4to. pp. 265-269.]

[4] [See the particulars before stated in p. 92.]

Of Alice de Lacy there is a very disgraceful story[1] told by Walsingham; and, were it

[1] I will only mention, on the authority of a memorandum in Dodsworth's MSS. which I have mislaid, that the fact which gave rise to the tragedy of Sir John Eiland, of Elland, was a fray between the retainers of Earl Warren and the husband of this lady, on her account. This nearly fixes the era of that transaction, but not of the old song upon the same subject; concerning which Mr. Watson, History, p. 176, critically observes, "that it was penned some time after the facts," that is, a ballad, precisely in the style of Sternhold and Hopkins, was penned sometime after the earlier days of Langland and Chaucer. Doubtless.

[Dr. Whitaker seems to cite Walsingham either from memory, or at second hand: but that historian assigns a precise date to the abduction of the Countess of Lancaster, namely, the Monday before Ascension day in 1317: "Anno gratiæ Millesimo trecentesimo decimo septimo, qui est annus regni regis Edwardi a Conquestu secundi decimus, tenuit rex Natalem, &c. . . . . . Eodem anno, die Lunæ Ascensionem Dominicam precedente, rapta est Comitissa Lancastriæ nobilis viri domini Thomæ comitis Lancastriæ uxor legitima, apud Caneforde in Dorsetia, per quendam militem de domo et familia Johannis comitis Warrenniæ, convocatis ad illud factum detestabile fautoribus (ut dicebatur) assensu regio plurimis Anglicorum; ducta est autem pompose nimis in despectum comitis dicti Lancastriæ ad dictum Warennæ comitem, ad castellum suum de Rigate. Dumque sic fœmina duceretur, ecce in itinerando, inter sepes et nemora inter Haulton [Alton, in Hampshire] et Farnaham existentia, ductores vident eminus vela et vexilla. Aderant enim sacerdotes cum populo facientes processionem more solito circa campos. Ductores igitur dictæ comitissæ timore subito et horrore percussi, putantes comitem Lancastriæ vel aliquos per ipsum missos ad auferendum dictam dominam et tantam injuriam in ipsos vindicandam, cum omni celeritate fugerunt, domina pene sola relicta, sed rei tandem veritate comperta, reversi sunt cum minis et pompa. Cum quibus quidam miseræ staturæ, claudus et gibbosus, suisque perpetuo intendens maliciis (Richardus dictus de Sancto Martino) dominam (proh dolor!) supradictam delusam miserabiliter (magno suffultus adjutorio) in suam exegit uxorem, firmiter protestatus quod ipsam fide media cognovit carnaliter antequam fuerat desponsata comiti supradicto, quod etiam plane prædicta domina palam ubique recognovit, ac etiam verum esse fatebatur, nullo ducta timore. Ac sic quæ toto tempore vitæ suæ nobilissima fuerat reputata domina, subito vergente rota fortunæ, quod dictu turpe est, per totum orbem spurcissima meretrix acclamatur. Igitur dictus Richardus se supra se extollens, nomine uxoris suæ præsumit in curia regia vindicare comitatus Lincolniæ et Sarum, sed incassum, prout rei gestæ sequentia plenius explanabunt. Fama facti hujus ad Summi Pontificis aures allata, misit idem Pontifex duos Cardinales, ut pacem facerent inter regem et barones et præcipue Thomam comitem, ut patebit inferius loco suo." Watson, in his Memoirs of the Earls of Warren and Surrey, vol. ii. p. 19, adds that "This affair occasioned a divorce between the Earl of Lancaster and his Countess, and the Earl, in a spirit of revenge, demolished the castle of Sandal near Wakefield, belonging to the Earl of Warren, wasting his manors on the north side of Trent."

After his death the Earldom of Lincoln was restored to her 20 Dec. 1322 (as shown by various documents cited in the memoir on the earldom before quoted, p. 276); she shortly afterwards married Ebulo le Strange, (younger son of the Lord Strange of Knockyn,) who having no issue by her was summoned to parliament as a Baron only until his death in 1335. Before the 5th of July in the following year the Countess had taken as a third husband Hugh de Freyne, a knight of Artois, who also was in consequence summoned to parliament, but not by the title of Earl. He died before the end of the same year (1336); and the Countess, dying on the 2d Oct. 1348, was buried by the side of her second husband Ebulo le Strange, in the conventual church of Barlings in Lincolnshire.

There are several seals of Alice Lacy, varying in design and remarkable for their heraldry, which is not entirely obvious to interpretation.

In one, the round seal engraved in this work, Fig. 10 of the Plate, the coats of the Earldoms of Lincoln and Salisbury are impaled together, representing her claim as heiress to both those dignities—an early and very remarkable example of impalement. Dr. Whitaker has mentioned (Third Edit. p. 181 note) that the impression from which this was engraved was found "wrapped up in a note written by Bishop Tanner." It has also been engraved in the History of Lacock Abbey by Bowles and Nichols, 1835, p. 148.

In an oval seal used by her 55 Hen. III. the only device is a shield of Chester (three garbs) suspended to a three-headed tree. Legend, SIGILLVM A . . . DE LASCI. (Harleian Charter, 52 H. 43.)

either pleasant or edifying to rake into the dust of libraries for ancient scandal, I could relate more to the same purpose than has ever yet appeared; suffice it, however, to say that after having married two other husbands, Eubulo l'Estrange and Hugh de Frenes, she died A.D. 1348, [at her castle of Bolingbroke, co. Lincoln,] and was interred in the [neighbouring] abbey of Barlings, next her second husband. With her expired the name of Lacy, which, even if she had left issue, would scarcely have been continued at the expense of Plantagenet.

But to return: in the year 1294, Henry de Lacy, despairing of male issue, surrendered all his lands to the King, who regranted them to the said Earl for the term of his life, and after his decease, to Thomas Earl of Lancaster, and Alice his wife, and the heirs of their bodies; failing of which they were to remain over to Edmund the King's brother (a remarkable proof of the Earl's attachment to the royal family,) and to his heirs for ever.[1] By this act the Honor of Clitheroe became united to the Earldom of Lancaster. Thus much is generally known: but the following particulars, which ascertain some important steps about this time in the descent of the Honor of Clitheroe, have been retrieved from an original decree of Edward III. relating to the advowson of St. Michael in the Castle.[2] On the attainder of Thomas Earl of Lancaster, the Honor of Clitheroe and hundred of Blackburn were instantly seized into the King's hands, and remained in the Crown till the beginning of Edward III.'s reign, when, with the exception of Ightenhill Park, they were granted for a term of life to

QUEEN ISABELLA, of whom we have several transactions in this capacity upon record.[3]

In another oval seal (4 Edw. II.) she is represented at full length, standing on an architectural bracket, attired in a flat headdress and flowing robes, her right hand held open by her side, and her left raised to her breast. On either side, suspended on trees, are two shields, one of the three garbs of Chester, and the other pretty clearly only a plain chief, and, if so, not easily explained. The legend SIGILLV' ALESYE DE LASCY. (In the collection at the British Museum, from that of George Baker, F.S.A. the historian of Northamptonshire.)

A third oval seal, resembling the last in design, appeared as a tail-piece in the former editions of this work; but in this she holds up a shield in either hand; one is that of the lion of Lincoln, and the other quarterly,—the bend which would have completed the arms of Lacy being omitted, perhaps by error of the draughtsman. Legend: SIGILLV' ALESIE . DE . LASCI.

[1] [Dr. Whitaker here wrote evidently under a little mental confusion. Edmund the King's brother was not a different party, but the actual Earl of Lancaster; whilst his son Thomas the espoused husband of the heiress was not as yet Earl, but merely heir apparent to that dignity. The provision of remainder to the father would be in order that the heiress might be transferred to another son, had Thomas died before the consummation of the marriage. Thomas Earl of Lancaster is said to have been of full age at the death of his father in 1296, but he could scarcely have then been quite twenty, as his father's marriage was in 1276. Alice de Lacy was not unsuited to him in respect of years, for it appears that she was born on Christmas Day 1281. The inquisitions on her father's death vary, as such documents usually do, in regard to her age, but that for the county of Denbigh—in which she was very probably born, is more precise and reliable:—"fuit etatis xxix annorum die Natali Domini ultimo preterito." (Inq. dated at Dynebagh, on Sunday before the feast of St. Peter in Cathedra, 21 Feb. 4 Edw. II. 1311.) At her espousals she was in her 9th year. (Cotton. MSS. Cleop. C. III. f. 336.) This would thus be in 1290.]

[2] Pen. auct.

[3] No. 2 in the Plate is the seal of this Queen, appended to her charters as lady of the Honor of Clitheroe. [It is

Previously however to her death the attainder of Thomas Earl of Lancaster had been reversed, on the plea that he had not been tried by his peers; so that immediately upon that event Henry Duke of Lancaster succeeded to this Honor and Hundred, by virtue of the above-mentioned entail upon Edmund the King's brother and his heirs.

Of Henry Duke of Lancaster, as lord of the Honor of Clitheroe, the recorded transactions are the following: he founded an hermitage for [a female] recluse in the churchyard of Whalley;[1] granted the bailiwick of Blackburnshire to the abbey and convent of Whalley, together with the Townleys, Delaleighs, and Alvethams; and the manor of Downham to John de Dyneley.[2] This was the last alienation of a manor by the lord paramount within this Honor, as Great Merlay was the first. He died March 24th, 1360, leaving by his wife Isabel, daughter of Henry Lord Beaumont, two daughters and coheirs: Maud married to William Count of Hainault, and Blanch to John of Ghent, fourth son of King Edward the Third, Earl of Richmond, and afterwards in her right Duke of Lancaster.

John of Ghent, Duke of Lancaster, received by this marriage, as the purparty of Blanch his wife, besides the fees of Pontefract and Lancaster, properly so called, the hundred of Blackburn or Honor of Clitheroe, with its appurtenances, thus described: "The wapontake of Clyderhow, with the demesne lands there, the royal bailiwick of Blackburnshire, the manors of Tottington and Rachdale, the lordship of Bowland, the vaccary of Bouland and Blackburnshire, the forest of Blackburnshire, and park of Ightenhill, with the appurtenances in Blackburnshire." A few inquisitions and other acts of little importance are all the evidences which remain of his having exercised these extensive rights.[3] He died February 3, 1398, leaving a son,

Henry of Bolingbroke, Duke of Lancaster, then in banishment, who returning the year following deposed his unfortunate master Richard the Second; after which the Honor of Clitheroe, as a member of the Duchy of Lancaster, merged in the Crown.[4] But Henry the Fourth, conscious of the weakness of his title to the latter, and foreseeing that upon a restoration of the right heirs the Duchy, which was his own undisputed inheritance, would now, of course, as an accessory, follow the fortunes of its principal, "quia magis dignum trahit ad se minus dignum," with the consent of Parliament, anno regni 1mo, made a charter entitled "carta regis Henrici 4^{ti} de separatione Ducat. Lanc. a Coronâ;"

copied from the drawing in Harl. MS. 2064, f. 322, and was attached to a charter dated at Stratford le Bow, 26 June, 6 Edw. III. On the counter-seal is a shield quarterly of 1. England; 2. France; 3. Navarre; 4. Champagne.]

[1] [See before, in p. 97.]

[2] No. 1 in the Plate is the great seal of this Duke, appended to the grant of the manor of Downham, of which the original in green wax is in the possession of William Assheton, esq.

[3] I have an impression of the seal of John of Ghent, but in too mutilated a state to be engraved. It has, as usual, an equestrian figure on one side, and on the other quarterly France and England, with the label of three points. [Such a seal of John of Ghent is described in Sandford's Genealogical History, second edit. p. 249, but I am not aware that it has been engraved. It is his privy seal as King of Castile and Leon which is engraved in Sandford (both editions) and copied in Nichols's *History of Leicestershire*. J. G. N.]

[4] Fleetwood's Antiquity and History of the Duchy of Lancaster, MS. p. 36.

Sigilla Dominorum Veterum de Blackburnshire.

and in this charter it is declared that the Duchy of Lancaster "remaneat, deducetur, gubernetur, &c. sicut remanere, deduci, gubernari deberet, si ad culmen dignitatis regiæ assumpti minimè fuissemus." Notwithstanding this, all grants of lands, &c. passed under the great seal of England alone, through the remainder of this reign, and till the third of Henry V. when it was ordered that no transactions relating to the Duchy should be deemed valid "sub aliquo alio sigillo præterquam sub sigillo nostro pro Ducatu prædicto."[1] And thus the matter rested till the deposition of Henry the Sixth, when Edward the Fourth, whose respective titles to the Crown and to the Duchy were precisely those of the House of Lancaster inverted, reasoning on the same principles with Henry IV. passed an act entitled "actus incorporationis necnon confirmationis inter alia ad Coronam Angliæ in perpetuum de Ducat. Lanc." providing, however, that the said dukedom should be and remain a corporate inheritance, and should be guided and governed by such officers as in the times of Henry IV. V. VI.

After all, Henry the Seventh,—who, independently of these acts of mere power, had the only legal title to this great inheritance, as heir in tail after the death of Edward son of Henry VI. under the deed of settlement upon the heirs male of John Duke of Lancaster and Blanch his wife,—in the first year of his reign repealed the former Act of Edward IV. and entailed, along with the Crown, the Duchy of Lancaster, with its appurtenances, upon himself and the heirs of his body lawfully begotten.

These were the fortunes of the Honor of Clitheroe while it continued a member of the Duchy of Lancaster; that is, to the Restoration of Charles II. when that prince, in consideration of the eminent services of General Monck, bestowed it upon him and his heirs, from which time to the present it has passed in the following channel:

George Monck, Duke of Albemarle, 1st grantee, ob. 1669, æt. 70. = Anne Clarges, ob. 1676.

Christopher, Duke of Albemarle, died in Jamaica, A.D. 1687 or 1688, ob. s.p. = Lady Elizabeth Cavendish, dau and coh. of Henry, Duke of Newcastle, died æt. 95, without issue by either husband. = Ralph, Duke of Montagu, died Mar. 9, 1708-9. = First wife, Lady Elizabeth Wriothesley.

John, Duke of Montagu. = Lady Mary Churchill, dau. of John Duke of Marlborough.

Isabella. = Edward Hussey, Earl Beaulieu.

Mary. = George Brudenell, Earl of Cardigan, afterwards Duke of Montagu.

Elizabeth. = Henry, Duke of Buccleuch.

Henry-James, 2nd son, Baron Montagu of Boughton.

---

[1] Fleetwood's Antiquity and History of the Duchy of Lancaster, MS. p. 36. Qu. whether by Act of Parliament? but so Fleetwood.

Christopher Duke of Albemarle, leaving no issue by his wife, who was daughter and coheiress of Henry Cavendish, Duke of Newcastle, gave her his estates; of which she died possessed 28 Aug. 1734, æt. 95, having, secondly, married Ralph Duke of Montagu, whose son and heir by a former wife, John Duke of Montagu, succeeded to his property, leaving two daughters: Isabella, married first to the Duke of Manchester, and secondly to Edward Earl Beaulieu; and Mary, married to George Brudenell Earl of Cardigan, afterwards Duke of Montagu. Ralph Duke of Montagu died March 9th, 1708-9. Elizabeth, daughter and heiress of George Duke of Montagu, married, in 1767, Henry Duke of Buccleuch, and had issue a second son, Henry James Baron Montagu of Boughton, on whom the Honor of Clitheroe was settled, after the decease of the Duchess, his mother. [On his death in 1845, without male issue, it became the property of his cousin the present Duke of Buccleuch and Queensberry.]

Drawn by W^m. Turner A. — Engraved by James Basire

To the Right Honourable THOMAS LORD RIBBLESDALE,

This Engraving is respectfully inscribed by — The Author.

CHAPTER THE THIRD.

CASTLE OF CLITHEROE AND CHAPEL OF ST. MICHAEL IN CASTRO.

HAVING now traced the several grants, descents, and limitations of this Honor, from its first foundation to the present time, we will return to the Castle of Clitheroe, its seat.

As the *Castellatus Rogeri* is expressly mentioned in Domesday, and the Castle of Lancaster was not then in existence, there can be little doubt that Roger of Poictou was the real founder of the Castle of Clitheroe. The summit of the rock on which it stands was not sufficiently extensive to admit of a very spacious building, and nothing more appears to be intended by the founder than to provide a temporary retreat for his dependants from the predatory incursions of the Scots, or a temporary residence for himself when business called him to this part of his domains. Of the original Castle of Clitheroe nothing is now left but the keep, a square tower of small dimensions, which, though much undermined, remains firm as the rock upon which it was erected; but, from an engraving of the building when entire, taken from a drawing made immediately before it was slighted by order of Parliament, it appears to have had a gateway-tower on the site of the present modern gates, with a round Norman arch, and a lofty flanking-wall running along the brink of the rock, and turning first on the back of the present steward's house, and secondly behind the present court-house, towards the keep. Within this bailey is no appearance in the engraving either of the Chapel of St. Michael, or of any other buildings.

Coeval with the foundation of the castle, and a part of it, was the Chapel of St. Michael in Castro,[1] erected and amply endowed by the founder, with licence of the Dean of Whalley, for the purpose of having Divine service performed, and the sacraments administered to his household servants, shepherds, and foresters. This is proved by the important charter of Guy de la Val, the immediate grantee after the attainder of Robert de Lacy, which conveys to the priory of St. John of Kirkby (Pontefract), amongst other things—"Capellam castri mei de Clyderhow, cum decimationibus omnium terrarum dominicarum mearum," &c.

This grant was long contested, but the advowson of the Castle chapel appears, under every change, to have followed the fortunes of the mother church, nor did the founder, or his immediate successors, ever claim the right of presentation.[2] At length Henry de Lacy granted the second mediety of the church of Whalley to the monks of Stanlaw, without any reservation of the Castle chapel; yet, upon the death of Peter de Cestria the last rector, he seems to have repented in part of his own liberality, and thought proper to keep forcible possession of the church till the monks compounded for admission by a constrained surrender of this indisputable right; the people, we are told,[3] crying out in indignation at so foul a compromise, *Væ vobis Simoniacis!*

Having obtained possession, however, they renewed the claim, and, under two spirited abbots, Topcliffe and Lindlay, carried on a long and obstinate suit against their successive patrons. Lindlay in particular presented a petition in full parliament, stating the wrongful detention of this chapel, with its appurtenances, till at length the cause seems to have been finally determined in favour of the Abbey, 39 Edw. III. Yet, after all,

[1] Our ancestors were extremely attentive to secure to themselves the comforts of religious offices, in situations where they might occasionally, and for a long time, be shut out, as in case of a siege, from their parish churches. And the splendour of the religious foundations within their castles kept pace with that of the fortresses to which they were attached. Thus the greater castle had a college, as St. George at Windsor, St. Clement at Pontefract; the smaller a chantry, as at Clitherhoe; and the peel, or fortified manor, an oratory, by license of the ordinary. In the greater castles are sometimes found specimens of the round churches, as at Ludlow.

[2] [A more complete view of the various transactions regarding the chapel of Clitheroe will be found in the appendix of documents now placed at the end of this chapter. The surrender of the chapel to the Earl (No. 1) was passed in full chapter at Stanlaw at the beginning of 1294. The statement (No. 13) however dates the "usurpation" of the Earl from 1296: and the recovery of their "right" by the monks in 1334. There are various documents regarding this In 1349, Henry Earl of Lancaster regranted (No. 14) the Castle chapel to Whalley Abbey, and the King confirmed that grant shortly after (No. 15). In 1363 the Duke and Duchess of Lancaster were again endeavouring to reassume the nomination of their own domestic chaplains: but after the contest had been pursued for a short time the monks were finally triumphant.]

[3] See p. 77.

though the transaction was closed in the form of a regular decree of the court, a compromise seems to have taken place; for, in a compotus of the abbey, 1368, I find the following entry: In ult. comp. debetur Duci Lanc. pro Capella Castri de Clyderhow cccl.

This was at least equivalent to a purchase of the advowson, as the whole income was estimated, in the Inquisition of 1311, at 13*l.* per annum.[1]

The several particulars of this endowment may best be learned from the confirmation of Urban IV., which states them to consist in half a carucate of land in Cliderhow, together with the tithes of all the demesne lands in Calderbotham, Blackburnshire, and Bowland, particularly specifying the tithe of venison,[2] at that time, perhaps, the best part of the endowment, excepting the glebe, even to a chaplain who was no epicure. The records of this long suit, of which the originals, with their beautiful seals appendant, are now before me,[3] furnish a complete catalogue of the chaplains of St. Michael, while it was pending. Of their predecessors we know nothing, save that one was Richard the first of Townley, who held this chapel by the gift of his brother Roger, about the time of the second Lateran Council, or 1215.

CAPELLANI.	VAC.	PATRONI.
William de Nunny	per mort.	Hen. de Lacy, Com. Linc.
Richard Camell	per mort.	Edwardus II. ratione attinc. Tho. Com. Lanc.
Roger de Lacy	per mort.	Idem.
Richard de Towneley [4]	per resig.	Regin. Isabella.
John de Wodehouse	per resig.	Eadem.
Henry de Walton	per mort.	Henricus Dux Lanc.

[1] [Rather more: "Idem Com. Lincoln. habuit ibi advocacionem Capelle in Castro, que Capella valet per annum xiiij li. vj s. viij d." Inq. 2 Edw. II. Duchy of Lanc. copy.]

[2] Tithe of venison, however, or indeed any other tithe of the forests, was not due of common right, but by special grant, for this reason, saith Spelman (Glossarium, art. Forestæ): "Quod episcopis et parochiarum rectoribus ovium cura, non ferarum demandata erat." But by this rule, in order to claim tithe of wool, the clergy ought to have charge, not of the flock of Christ, but of the sheep of the field. His next reason is not so childish; "Exhorruit nempe Deus cruentam venationem." This is true; for every pang that man wantonly, and for his own gratification, adds to the sufferings of a creature agonising under the prospect of immediate death, is a sin of no common magnitude. But the text, which the learned Etymologist has adduced to establish the truth, proves rather "exhorruisse Deum venationem incruentam;" that, as animals pursued by hunters might be caught in toils, or chased to death without a wound, they were in the situation of things strangled, and could not lawfully be eaten without a previous effusion of blood. Lev. xvii. 13. "Every moving thing that liveth is given to man for meat." Gen. ix. 3. And where animals can only be caught by hunting, and our object is not gratification from the chase, it is undoubtedly lawful. But the invention of fire-arms has made a great revolution in the morality of field sports. Unexpected and instantaneous death may now be inflicted, almost to a certainty, upon the poor object of our pursuit; and, therefore, what was lawful to our forefathers is become criminal in us.

[3] On the division of the demesnes of Whalley Abbey they fell into the hands of the Braddylls; and on the purchase of their moiety of the manor by the late Sir James Whalley Gardiner, Bart. were transferred among the title-deeds to him.

[4] There is no account of this man in the pedigree or charters of the family.

CAPELLANI.	VAC.	PATRONI.
John de Stafford . . .	per resig. . . .	Edwardus III. jure regis.[1]
Richard de Moseley[2]; resigns to the		

Abbot and Convent A.D. 1334. In consequence of this resignation, they seized the whole endowment into their own hands, reducing the chaplain from an independent and opulent beneficed man to a mere stipendiary; besides which they, together with the Ordinary, appear[3] to have compelled the Vicar to take upon himself the cure and charge of souls within the Castle chapelry; in consequence of which the chapel of St. Michael in Castro is yet assigned in the King's books to the patronage of the Vicar of Whalley. In this state, or nearly so, the chapel of St. Michael continued till the 1st Edw. VI. when it fell with the other chantries, and has since been so totally demolished that its particular situation within the area of the castle is no longer remembered. Some small benefactions, however, it appears to have received in this interval, which were very properly allotted by the Commissioners of Chantry Lands at the Dissolution to the unendowed chapel of Whitewell, in Bowland.

In the year 1521 it appears, from the Computus of the Abbey, that the chaplain of St. Michael in Castro received a stipend of 1*l*.

The castle of Clitheroe, with the demesnes and forests, is, strictly speaking, extra-parochial; and, in consequence of this foundation, the latter are denominated the Castle Parish to the present day.[4]

But as the Forest of Accrington is now included within that chapelry, and Trawden within Colne, the whole of the graveships of Rossendale within Newchurch, Haslingden, or Bury, and all the booths of Pendle, except Reedly Hallows, Filly Close, New Laund, and Wheatley Carr, within Colne; Padiham, or New Church in Pendle: these exceptions alone, together with Ightenhill Park, are now termed extra-parochial, and their inhabitants marry at Clitheroe.

Ightenhill Park, however, was not originally extra-parochial, but parcel of the Chapelry of Burnley. This is proved beyond a doubt, by the Inquisition of the Rectory, A.D. 1298.

Documents relating to the Chapel of St. Michael within the Castle of Clitheroe.

1. The Abbot and Convent of Stanlowe in 1294 grant the Chapel within the Castle of Clitheroe to Henry Earl of Lincoln and his heirs for ever. Great Cowcher of the Duchy of Lancaster (or Carta Regum), vol. i. fol. 60.

Omnibus ad quos presens scriptum pervenerit: frater Gregorius Abbas loci Benedicti de Stanlowe et ejusdem loci Conventus: salutem in Domino. Cum nobilis vir dominus Henricus de Lacy comes Lincoln. dederit et concesserit

[1] On the plea that the Duke had alienated the advowson to the Abbey and Convent without the royal licence.

[2] [Richard de Moseley was appointed to Clitheroe by Queen Isabella, 6 March, 1338, in exchange for the rectory of Dewsbury, and resigned the chapel to the abbot and convent of Whalley in the following year (see p. 259). He was then rector of Earl's Barton, in Northamptonshire.]

[3] See the Letter of William le Wolf, vicar of Whalley, to the Bishop of Lichfield, his ordinary, already printed, p. 225.

ecclesiam de Quallay in proprios usus nobis et successoribus nostris in perpetuum tenendam, licet Capella infra Castrum de Cliderhou sita sit infra limites parochiales ecclesie predicte de Quallay; volumus et concedimus pro nobis et successoribus nostris quod idem comes et heredes sui vel assignati eandem Capellam in perpetuum habeant et teneant cum omnibus juribus rebus et possessionibus que ad predictam Capellam pertinent. Ita scilicet quod nec nos nec successores nostri, nec aliquis per nos, aliquod jus vel clamium in predicta Capella, seu juribus, rebus, et possessionibus que ad eandem Capellam pertinent seu pertinere solebant, decetero aliquo modo exigere vel vendicare poterimus. In cujus rei testimonium huic scripto sigillum nostrum commune apposuimus. Hiis testibus, dominis Roberto filio Rogeri, Will'o le Vavasour, Johanne de Hodleston, Roberto de Hertford, Jacobo de Neville, Roberto de Schirburn, Johanne de Spring militibus, et multis aliis. Dat. apud Stanlowe in pleno capitulo nostro die Lune proximo ante festum Purificacionis beate Marie virginis, anno Domini Millesimo cc^{mo} nonagesimo quarto (Monday, Feb. 1294).

This charter is followed in the Great Cowcher by the Abbot of Stanlaw's renunciation of the right of hunting in the forests, which is of the same date, and was witnessed by the same persons, and has been printed at p. 174.

2. Letters patent of Queen Isabella declaring that on the resignation by her clerk John de Wodehouse of her free chapel within the castle of Cliderhou she had granted the same to Sir Richard de Moseley by way of exchange for the said Richard's church of Dewsbury. Dated at Woodstock, 6 March, 8 Edw. III. (1334). Printed in the Coucher Book of Whalley (Chetham Soc.) p. 234.

3. Letters patent of King Edward III. surrendering to the abbot and convent of Whalley the chapel of Cliderhou, lately granted to John de Wodehouse. Dated at Northampton, 18 March, a. r. 8 (1334). Printed ibid. p. 228.

4. Letters patent of King Edward III. acknowledging the receipt into his chamber from the abbey of Whalley of 300 marks in which the abbot had been bound by recognisance made in the King's Chancery, "pro capella castri de Cliderhou." Dated at Folkingham, 27 April, a. r. 8 (1334). Printed ibid. p. 235.

5. Letters patent of Queen Isabella, tenant for life of the castle of Clitheroe, reciting the King's letters of the 18th March, made with the assent of his great council, and ratifying the same, notwithstanding she had recently presented Richard de Moseley to the said chapel. Dated at Coventry, 13 May, 8 Edw. III. (1334). Printed ibid. p. 229.

6. Answer of Roger bishop of Coventry and Lichfield to a petition from the abbot and convent of Whalley, conveying his license and authority to their acquiring the chapel. Dated at Sallowe prid. id. Maii (May 14) 1334. Printed ibid. p. 230.

A memorandum follows, in the Coucher Book, p. 231, stating that after the preceding measures had been taken, Richard de Moselay, then in occupation of the chapel, very urgently impleaded the convent by a writ of *scire facias* in Chancery, until they compounded for his interest by an annual pension of 40*l.* which they granted by the charter next described:

7. Grant to Richard de Moselay, clerk, of an annual rent of 40*l.* for life, to be paid at Merland, co. Lanc. from the manors of Steyninges, Cho, Merland, and Blackburn. Dated at Whalley on Tuesday next after the feast of the Exaltation of the Holy Cross (Sept. 14.) 8 Edw. III. (1334). Printed ibid. p. 233.

8. Quitclaim of Richard de Moselay, rector of Earl's Barton, in the county of Northampton, of all his right and claim in the chapel of St. Michael in the castle of Cliderhou. Dated at Whalley on Friday next after the feast of St. Edward the King and Confessor (14 Oct.) 1334. Printed ibid. p. 234.

9. Mandate of Roger bishop of Coventry and Lichfield directing the Vicar of Whalley (probably William le Wolf) to answer the complaint of the Abbot and convent of Whalley that he refused to undertake the parochial care of the chapel within the Castle of Clitherhow, although it was annexed to the church of Whalley. Dated at London 17 kal. April, 1335 (March 16, 1335-6). Printed at length in the present volume, at p. 178.

10. Answer of the Vicar, acknowledging the receipt of the mandate, which he recites word for word, as was customary. Dated Idus April, 1336 (April 17.) Printed ibid.

11. Mandate of the Official of the Bishop of Lichfield to William le Wolf, vicar of Whalley, that the Bishop in his Visitation had decided that he was responsible for the cure of souls of the parishioners of the chapel of the castle of Clitheroe, and ordering his obedience under pain of the greater excommunication: otherwise he is to appear at Lichfield on the 13th April, 1339, to answer to this summons:

Officialis venerabilis patris Rogeri Dei gratiâ Coventrensis et Lichfeldensis Episcopi et ipsius in quibuscunque correcionum negociis Commissarius: vicario ecclesie de Whalley salutem in Auctore salutis. Nuper contra vos auctoritate dicti patris occasione quorundam compertorum in visitacione quam idem pater in Archidiaconatu Cest' tunc exercuerat legitime procedentes, curam animarum parochianorum in Capella Castri de Cliderhou consistencium, ad vos et successores vestros pertinere debere pronunciavimus, necnon Religiosos viros dominos Abbatem et Conventum Monasterii de Whalleye, ecclesiam de Whalleye cum Capella Castri de Cliderhou et aliis suis pertinenciis in proprios usus optinentes, ad inveniendum Capellanum ydoneum in Capella Castri de Cliderhou supradicta singulis diebus divina celebrantem, ac etiam clericum eidem Capellano monstrantem condempnavimus sentencialiter et definitive justicia suadente, vos tamen curam de qua premittitur agnoscere subire et exercere, juxta vim, formam et effectum pronunciacionis nostre supradicte recusastis et adhuc recusastis minus juste, prout ex querela dictorum Abbatis et Conventus accepimus nobis facta. Quocirca vobis sub pena excommunicacionis majoris firmiter injungendo mandamus, quatenus hujusmodi nostre pronunciacioni parere quatenus ad vos pertinet nullatenus omittatis. Alioquin tenore presentium peremptorie vos citamus, quod compareratis coram nobis vel nostro Commissario in ecclesia Cathed' Lichefeld' secundo die Juridico post dominica qua cantatur Officium *Misericordia Domini*,[1] canonicum si quod vobis competat in hac parte propposituri et prosecuturi cum effectu, facturi ulterius et recepturi juxta negocii qualitatem et naturam quod justicia suadebit. Quid autem in premissis duxeritis faciendum, nos vel nostrum Commissarium dictis die et loco certificetis per literas vestras patentes harum seriem continentes. Dat. Lich. xv kalen' Aprilis, anno Domini M°ccc°. xxxviii° (18 Mar. 1339). Add. 10374, f. 86, b.

Istud Mandatum prescriptum missum fuit per Officialem domini Coventr' et Lich. Episcopi domino Will'mo dicto le Wolf tunc vicario ecclesie de Whalleye ad subeundam et agnoscendam curam parochianorum Capelle Castri de Cliderhou pertinencium sub pena excommunicacionis majoris juxta pronunciacionem sentencie super hoc facte per eundem Officialem.

12. Sentence of the Commissary of the Bishop of Coventry and Lichfield that the vicar of Whalley shall have the cure of the parishioners of the castle chapel. Dated at Lichfield, ii. id. Maii, 1339. (Printed in the Coucher Book, p. 235.)

13. Statement made by the Abbot and Convent of Whalley in 1345 regarding their recovery of the Chapel:—

Petrus de Cestria quondam Rector ecclesie parochialis de Whalley, Coventr' et Lich. dioc', in personatu dicte ecclesie predecessor Abbatis et Conventus Monasterii de Whalley, ordinis Cisterciensis, ejusdem dioc', qui prefatam ecclesiam in suos usus jam optinent appropriatam, ac alii ejusdem ecclesie Rectores dicti Petri predecessores a tempore cujus contrarii memoria hominum non existat, capellam beati Michaelis in Castro de Cliderhou infra fines et limites parochie dicte ecclesie de Whall. notorie situatam, tanquam capellam eidem ecclesie annexam et ab eadem dependentem tenuerunt, occupaverunt et pacifice possederunt, decimacionesque dominicalium terrarum de Blakeburnschire et de Bouland, eidem capelle deputatas, per dominos prefati Castri de Cliderhou dicte ecclesie patronos antiquitus assignatas, ut de jure ejusdem sue ecclesie perceperunt, et de decimacionibus illis taliter perceptis, una cum aliis ejusdem capelle proventibus, libere per omnia disposuerunt absque contradiccione vel resistencia cujuscunque. Post decessum autem ejusdem Petri: cum dicti Abbas et Conventus Monasterii de Whall. possessionem dicte Matricis ecclesie de Whall. cum suis capellis et juribus universis canonice apprehendissent et in usus proprios assumpsissent perpetuo possidendam, precedentibus ad hoc et concurrentibus omnibus et singulis que de jure requirebantur quomodolibet in hac parte, Nobilis vir dominus Henricus de Lascy Comes Lincoln. et dominus Castri de Cliderhou et de Blakeburnschire, dicte ecclesie patronus ac fundator Monasterii antedicti, dictos Abbatem et Conventum possessione dicte capelle, vi et potentia dominacionis, absque auctoritate vel consensu eorum aut ordinarii cujuslibet spoliavit, eandem capellam cum decimacionibus et proventibus predictis, tanquam capellam liberam, de facto duntaxet, cum de jure non potuit, sibi nequiter usurpavit, et ipsius capelle patronatum ad totam vitam sibi retinuit minus juste, necnon clericis suis eandem capellam contulit, et per seneschallos suos de Blakeburnschire dictos clericos in eandem capellam instituit, ac in ejus corporalem possessionem induci mandavit et fecit, concessu dictorum Abbatis et Conventus vel Diocesani aut alterius Ordinarii cujuscunque minime requisito. Quam quidem possessionem Patronatus dicte capelle taliter usurpatam domini Castri de Cliderhou et de Blakeburnschire post mortem prefati domini Comitis Henrici, videlicet dominus Thomas quondam Comes Lan-

[1] Introit from Ps. 33 (*Misericordia Domini plena est terra*) and name of the second Sunday after Easter. The summons was for the 13 April, 1339.

castrie successor suus immediatus, dominus etiam Rex Anglie Edwardus tercius, et domina Regina Mater ejus, continuarunt et absque alio justicie titulo per multa tempora occuparunt, dictamque capellam suis clericis quam pluribus vicissim et successive contulerunt, ipsos in eadem capella propria presumptione instituendo et corporaliter inducendo, irrequisitis consensu et auctoritate Diocesani seu alterius Ordinarii cujuscunque.[1] Dicti etiam clerici taliter instituti, vel potius intrusi, decimaciones et obvenciones omnimodas eidem capelle ut premittitur deputatas per manutenentiam dominorum suorum libere perceperunt et de eisdem ad libitum disposuerunt, de servientibus insuper dictorum dominorum, necnon de tenentibus dominicalibus eorundem correcciones capitulares et omnimodam jurisdiccionem ordinariam, nullo privilegio sedis apostolice vel aliunde habito in hac parte muniti, sibi temerarie usurpabant et sic usurpatam per non modica tempora exercebant, videlicet per xxx et viii annos videlicet ab anno Domini Millesimo cc° Nonagesimo sexto usque ad annum Domini Millesimum CCC tricentesimum quartum.[2] Quo anno dicti Abbas et Conventus, declarato jure suo quod ad dictam capellam habuerunt coram domino Rege et consilio suo, optinuerunt eandem capellam tanquam annexam ecclesie sue supradicte, et ab eadem dependentem sibi restitui, de expresso consentio ejusdem domini Regis et consilii sui, amoto quodam Ricardo de Moselay clerico suo, ejusdem capelle tunc illicito detentore, sicque dicti Abbas et Conventus anno quo supra in festo Sancte Trinitatis (22 May, 1334) in dictam capellam intraverunt, et eam cum suis pertinenciis predictis, tanquam jus ecclesie sue de Whall. supradicte, sibi canonice assumserunt in usus proprios perpetuo cum dicta ecclesia possidendam, ejusque possessionem hujusmodi usque ad festum Sancti Jacobi Apostoli (25 Julii) anno Domini Millesimo ccc°xl quinto pacifice tenuerunt. Quo elapso, dicti Abbas et Conventus de Whallsye prosequentes jus suum quod ad dictam capellam habuerunt erga dominum Regem, qui dominium de Blakeburnschir' tunc temporis possidebat, propositisque et ostensis hiis que ad declaracionem sui juris sufficere videbantur, coram dicto domino Rege et Consilio suo, tandem idem dominus Rex de expresso consensu consilii sui predicti eisdem Abbati et Conventui eandem capellam tanquam annexam ecclesie sue de Whalleye predicte et ab eadem dependentem reddidit et retribuit, amoto quodam Ricardo de Moselay clerico suo, ejusdem capelle tunc illicito detentore. Sicque dicti Abbas et Conventus hiis premissis Anno videlicet Domini M°ccc°xxxiiii^{to} in festo Sancte Trinitatis in dictam capellam intraverunt et capellam cum suis pertinenciis predictis tanquam jus ecclesie sue de Wh. sibi canonice assumpserunt in usus proprios cum dicta ecclesia perpetuo possidendam ejusque possessionem a die predicto usque in presentem festum Sancti Jacobi Apostoli Anno Domini M°ccc°xlv° videlicet per xi annos et amplius jam pacifice tenuerunt. (*Liber Loci Benedicti*, Add. MS. 10,374, f. 10 b.)

14. Charter of Henry Earl of Lancaster declaring that he surrendered to the abbey and convent of Whalley the advowson of the chapel of Clitheroe, which he had recently granted for life to his clerk Henry de Walton. Dated at his manor of the Savoy, 24 Aug. 1349. Printed in the Couchet Book, p. 1169.

15. Confirmation of the same by royal letters patent, 10 Feb. 1350. Ibid. p. 1171.

16. Letters Patent of Edward III. restoring the advowson of the Castle Chapel to John Duke of Lancaster and Blanche his wife, the Abbot and Convent of Whalley having taken possession of it without the King's licence and thereby forfeited it, after having obtained a grant from Henry Earl of Lancaster by a false suggestion:—

Edwardus Dei gratia Rex Anglie: dominus Hibernie et Aquitanie. Omnibus ad quos presentes littere pervenerint: salutem. Supplicarunt nobis carissimus filius noster Johannes dux Lancastrie, et Blanchia uxor ejus, quod cum Henricus nuper Comes Lancastrie ad prosecucionem Abbatis et Conventus de Whalleye pretendencium se jus habere in Capella Sancti Michaelis infra Castrum de Cliderhowe cum suis juribus et pertinenciis quibuscumque racione paro-

[1] Another statement of this character has been printed in the Coucher Book of Whalley, p. 226. The monks speak in it as freely as here of the conduct of their patrons, stating that Henry Earl of Lincoln had given the chapel "cuidam clerico suo, nomine Will'o de Nuny, et quantum in ipso fuit injuste a Matrice ecclesia de Whalleye et non sine gravi periculo animæ suæ seperavit."

[2] The other statement says, "usque ad annum d'ni Edwardi regis Anglie tertii post conquestum quintum" (*i. e.* 1331), when Robert de Toppecliffe then abbot presented his petition to the King in his full parliament, stating that inter cetera the said chapel was annexed to his church of Whalley, and was not a free chapel as the King supposed, because it had not baptism nor burial, nor any privilege from the apostolic see as other free chapels had in various parts of England, but all the parishioners of the chapel baptize and bury in the church of Whalley.

chialis ecclesie ipsorum Abbatis et Conventus de Whalleye quam ipsi in proprios usus tenent dederit et concesserit prefatis Abbati et Conventui advocacionem Capelle predicte que est parcella dominii de Blakeburnshire, quod est de hereditate prefate Blanchie et quod de nobis tenetur in capite ut dicitur, habendam et tenendam eisdem Abbati et successoribus suis imperpetuum; dictusque Abbas et Conventus virtute donacionis et concessionis predictarum eandem Capellam in proprios usus tenendam ingressi fuerint, licencia nostra super hoc non obtenta, per quod advocacio Capelle predicte ad manus nostras tanquam nobis forisfacta jam devenit: Velimus eisdem Duci et Blanchie advocacionem predictam habendam sibi et heredibus suis concedere graciose. Nos habito respectu ad hoc quod prefatus Comes advocacionem predictam prefatis Abbati et Conventui per suggestionem minus veracem ut dicitur in forma predicta alienavit: Nolentes prefatam Blanchiam occasione suggestionis hujusmodi exheredari: set volentes eosdem Ducem et Blanchiam in ea parte favore prosequi graciose: de gracia nostra speciali dedimus et concessimus pro nobis et heredibus nostris prefatis Duci et Blanchie advocacionem predictam habendam et tenendam sibi et heredibus nostris per servicia inde debita et consueta imperpetuum. Ita quod post mortem eorundem Ducis et Blanchie, si ipsi sine herede de corporibus suis legitime procreato obierint, dicta advocacio eisdem personis et eodem modo et per eadem servicia tenenda remaneat, quibus personis et prout advocacio predicta remansisse et teneri debuisset si ipsa per prefatum Comitem nunquam alienata fuisset, set post decessum ejusdem prefate Blanchie jure hereditario descendisset. In cujus rei testimonium has litteras nostras fieri fecimus patentes. Teste me ipso apud Westm. duodecimo die Decembris, Anno regni nostri tricesimo septimo (1363). (Great Cowcher of the Duchy, vol. i. fol. 60 b.)

17. Bond of the Abbot and Convent of Whalley obliging them to pay to John Duke of Lancaster, in instalments, within three years, 500*l.* according to its title, "pro licentia optinendi ad prosequendum jus suum de capella castri de Cliderhow." Dated at Whalley 23 Aug. 38 Edw. III. (1364). Printed in Coucher Book, p. 1169.

18. Indenture between John Duke of Lancaster and the Abbot and Convent of Whalley, the Duke allowing them to sue him for the Chapel:—

Ceste endenture faite perentre lui nobles homes Johan Duc de Lancastre dune parte et les Abbe et Covent de Whalleye dautre part tesmoigne, que come les dites Abbe et Covent eient souvent suez per peticion au dit noble duc leur patron et avowe en clamantz davoir droit a tenir la Chapelle de Seint Michiel deinz son Chastel de Cliderowe en propres oeps come annexe a leur esglise de Whalleye, et empriantz au dit noble duc de sa bone grace et en oevre de charite faire a eux droit en celle partie, ou les soeffrer presuire leur dit droit a la comune ley saunz estre grevez ou dune damage ou duresce a eux ou a leur conseil ou eidantz per celle cause: le dit duc come celui qest obeissant a la ley de la terre et qui nulluy voet destourber a presuire per la ley, si ad octroiez et grante bonement per cestes lettres leur requeste avantdit, et promys a eux que pur nulle seute qils ferront vers lui et la duchesse sa compaigne per processer de ley per la cause suisdite, il ne nul desoens ferra as ditz Abbe et Covent, ne a leur eidantz ou conseillantz damage, grevance, ne duresce, en destourbance de leur dite perseute encontre la comune ley, mes le soeffra estre terminez a plus tost qil purra bonement sanz offense de la ley. Issint toutes voies que nulle seute serra faite en prejudice nostre tresredoutez Seigneur le Roi: ne au dit duc. En tesmoignance de quelle chose a ceste endenture les parties avant dites entrechaungeablement ont mys leur sealz. Donne a Londres le xvi jour de Feverer, lan du regne nostre Seigneur le Roi Edward tierz puis le conqueste trent noesisme (1365). (Great Cowcher of the Duchy, vol. iv.)

CHAPTER THE FOURTH.

HONOR OF CLITHEROE, WITH THE FORESTS AND OTHER DEMESNES.

THE Honor dependent upon this Castle is commensurate with no other division, civil or ecclesiastic. It extends over the present parishes of Whalley and Blackburn, which constituted the original hundred; over those of Chipping and Ribchester, anciently included in the hundred of Amunderness; over Bowland, in the wapentake of Staincliff; over the manor of Tottington, within the hundred of Salford; and over that of Rochdale, partly within the former wapentake and partly within Agbridge in Yorkshire. But it coincides most nearly with the original parish of Whalley, the whole of which it covers, and no where passes the boundaries of it, but to take in the manor of Tottington. Within this extensive tract all manors and estates, of what tenure soever, are held of the Castle of Clitheroe,[1] the common centre from which all landed property has emanated, and to

[1] Feoda heredum Comitis Lincoln. in Blakeburneschir' (meaning the lands holden by military service).

[Inquisitio Wapentachie de Blakeburnschire: Symon le Herice, Adam de Blakeburn, Adam Noel, Henricus de Clayton, Adam de Bilyngton, Will's de Caldecotes, Johannes de Wynkedlegh, et Ricardus de Caterale.]

Joh. de Pountchardon tenet xii. partem 1 feodi Militis in parva Mitton de feodo com. Lincoln et ipse in capite de de domino Rege et pertinet ad dotem Comitisse Linc'.

Adam de Blakeburñ et Rogerus de Arches tenent quartam partem 1 feodi Militis in Wysewall et Hapton de dicto feodo et pertinet ad dotem.

Henr. Gedelyng tenet decimam partem 1 feodi Militis in Tounneleye, Coldecotes, et Snoddeword de dicto feodo et pertinet ad dotem.

Comes tenet in manu sua in dominico decimam partem 1 feodi Militis in Twysilton et pertinet ad dotem ut supra.

Adam de Preston tenet decimam partem 1 feodi Militis in Extwysil de dicto feodo et pertinet ad dotem ut supra.

Radulfus de Mitton tenet quartam partem 1 feodi militis in Aghton, Merelelay et Lyvesay de dicto feodo et pertinet ad dotem Comitisse.

Robertus de Cest. tenet quartam partem 1 feodi Militis in Dounom de dicto feodo et pertinet ad dotem ut supra.

Johannes de Grigleston tenet octavam partem 1 feodi Militis in Folrik de dicto feodo et pertinet ad dotem Comitisse.

Will's Marescallus tenet decimam partem 1 feodi Militis in Mereleye et pertinet ad dotem Comitisse.

Hugo de Parva Mereley e tenet quinquagesimam sextam partem 1 feodi Militis de dicto feodo et pertinet ut supra.

Gilbertus fil. Henr' tenet decimam partem 1 feodi Militis in Ruyschetoñ de dicto feodo et pertinet ad dotem Comitisse.

Ad. de Bilyngton tenet Medietatem 1 feodi Militis in eadem et pertinet ad dotem ut supra.

Heres Hugonis de Alvetham tenet octavam partem 1 feodi Militis in eadem de dicto feodo et pertinet et cetera.

Hugo Fytton tenet quartam partem 1 feodi Militis in Harwod de dicto feodo.

Henr. de Clayton tenet octavam partem 1 feodi Militis in eadem de dicto feodo.

Liber Loci Benedicti. [Add. MS. 10,374, f. 127 b.]

which, in case of escheat, it must return.[1] It has already been proved that in the Saxon times manors and townships or hamlets were commensurate: it has also been observed, and must now be repeated, that a new and arbitrary distribution of manors has long since taken place, merely for the purpose of accommodating the stewards in holding their courts. Thus, all the original manors within the parishes of Whalley and Bury remaining in the hands of the lords, excepting one or two in the immediate vicinity of Clitheroe,[2] have been grouped together, without regard to their ancient rights and distinctions, and are now combined under Colne, Ightenhill, Accrington, and Tottington;[3] and the reason of this arrangement was, that in each of these places,[4] and in no others within their circuit, was an ancient manor-house, to which the stewards and homagers might conveniently resort. To these inferior courts the copyholders and wapentake tenants alone owe suit and service; the lords of manors and freeholders owing suit of court at the Castle alone.[5]

Let it be remembered, that each township had originally around it a large tract of common marked out by certain boundaries. Now, wherever a township was granted out as a manor, the property of the common followed as an appendage, and belonged to the mesne lord; but where the ancient freehold was merely granted and cantoned out in parcels to free tenants, the herbage alone of the common belonged to the freeholder, and no inclosure could take place without permission from the superior lord. These inclosures, however, began, as we have seen, at a very early period, and such lands were always granted in villenage. Agreeably to this representation, the great Inquisition after the death of Henry de Lacy affords instances, in almost every township, of lands held in bondage: these are of the old copyhold tenure, or copyholds by prescription. But it has been already observed, that, besides the tracts of common originally appertaining to town-

Henry Gedelyng must have been a trustee, and the name an ancient *soubriquet* or nickname; for Gedling, at that time, expressed precisely the same idea with the vulgar Lancashire word "Madlin" at present. It is used by Chaucer for an idle vagabond,

"That seemed like no gadeling." R. R. 938.

[1] Excepting in case of particular grants, which amounts to the same thing.

[2] Ex. gr. Chatburne and Worston, for which the courts were held at Clitheroe before Edward III. [To these is to be added Pendleton, which, though once belonging to the Houghtons, has long since merged into the principal fee. 2nd Edit. Addend. and Corr.]

[3] Thus, to the very destruction of all ancient landmarks, the forests themselves are now included under these factitious manors, viz. Pendle under Ightenhill, Trawden under Colne, and Rossendale and Accrington under Accrington. Further, it is to be observed, that copyhold lands are held by copy of court-roll under some specific manor. Wapentake lands are those which hold in villenage of the Honor of Clitheroe in general. Thus, for example, the manor of Cliviger, as distinct from the grange of ditto, though anciently granted to the Townleys, has been lost; but on this account it has, with other original manors, long since granted out, and still continuing to be held as such, never been included in Ightenhill, or any other of the factitious manors; but, the commons of that township having been claimed by the superior lords on the extinction of the mesne manors, all inclosures from them are granted as wapentake lands.

[4] *Vid. Inquisition. post mort. Henrici de Lacy*, where a manor house is expressly mentioned in each of these places, and nowhere else.

[5] *De tribus septimanis in tres septimanas*, in the language of our ancient charters, inquisitions, &c.

ships, there was an immense extent of forest lands absolutely unappropriated, which belonged to the lords merely as derelicts, and which remained nearly in a state of nature till the 23rd of Henry VII. when they were successively granted out as copyholds; but this tenure being found insecure in the reign of James I. gave rise to a very oppressive attempt at a general resumption of lands so held, and ended in a compromise with the Crown, ratified by an Act of Parliament, confirming and constituting them copyholds of inheritance. This was the origin of the newhold, or of copyholds by statute.[1] I have merely hinted at this transaction here, as it will be detailed hereafter, in order to show that it is with lands of these two species, their grants, surrenders, admissions, &c. that the above-mentioned courts are concerned.

Since this work was first printed the Assheton MSS.[2] have furnished me with the original Custumale, the Magna Charta of Blackburnshire, A. 3 Hen. IV. the usages of which before that time seem to have been preserved only by tradition.

Hec Indentura facta apud Brunlay die Martis proximo ante festum Purificationis B. Marie Virginis anno regni Regis Henrici Quarti post Conquestum Anglie tercio coram Thoma Radclyf de Wimmerlegh tunc Senescallo de Blakburnshire, testatur quod ad requisitionem omnium tenentium .... consuetudin' infra Wapentachium predictum.

Inquisicio de consuetudinibus fuit dicto die Mart' et capta fuit certis de causis inter ipsos tenentes motis per sacramentum Willi Mersden, Gilberti del Legh, Joh'is Parker de Ightynyll, Uchtredi Schotilworth, Robti de Blakey, Willi Foldes sen. Willi de Britwissell, Joh. Tatfsall sen. Ric. Tatfsall sen., Nic. Both..... del Riley de Hawkyshogh, Johis Ellot, et Joh. del Legh, qui dicunt super sacramentum suum quod hec sunt jura et consuetudines sue: Qui tenent aliquas terras et tenementa secundum consuetudinem manerii ut de honore Lincoln, quibus antecessores sui a tempore quo non extat memoria usi fuerint; videlicet: Si aliquis tenens terras seu tenementa secundum consuetudinem manerii inde obierit seizitus, tunc ejus proximus heres in propria persona sua vel per attornatum suum veniet infra tria halmota tunc proxime tenenda post obitum superioris tenentis ad faciendum finem racionabilem cum D^{no} pro eisdem terris et tenementis, si fuerit in Anglia. Et si rectus heres non veniet et fuerit in Anglia in propria persona, nec per attornatum, ad faciendum finem cum D^{no}, et modo debito proclametur 1°, 2do, et 3°, ad tria halmot tunc prox. tenenda, quod tunc licitum erit D^{no} per ejus Senescallum dicta terras et tenementa extraneo dimittere, et sicut dicunt quod rectus heres pro se et heredibus suis clameum suum in perpetuum amittet.

It^{m}, dicunt quod post obitum sive decessum alicujus tenentis seiziti per virgam, cujus terre et tenementa sic tenentur D^{no} secundum consuetudinem predictam, illa terre et tenementa descendent de herede ad heredem prout terre et tenementa liberorum tenentium per communem legem Anglie descendunt.

[1] All the lands held by tenants at will, and not granted out at the death of Henry de Lacy, or afterwards, previous to this act, as having not been held by copy of court-roll, for time whereof the memory of man is not to the contrary, undoubtedly belong to the latter tenure. The titles of all inclosures subsequent to the said act stand upon the same foundation.

[2] "The usages of this wapentake, or hundred, appear to have been merely traditional till the reign of Henry the Fourth, when they were reduced to writing in the following Custumale, which I discovered among the MSS. at Whalley Abbey, the monks having been better depositories of records than careless and illiterate stewards. The roll, however, from which I transcribe is in some places nearly illegible." 2nd Edit. p. 211.

[In the Coucher Book, vol. iv. p. 1163, is an indenture respecting "la comune chartre de Blakeburnschir'" deposited in Whalley Abbey on the feast of Philip and James, 6 Edward III. by Sir Adam de Clyderhow, Henr. de Clayton, and Nich. de Holden per comun assent de toutȝ les bonesgentȝ de Blakeburnshire.]

It^{m}, dicunt quod licitum erit cuilibet tenenti terras et tenementa secundum consuetudinem manerii per suum custodem in curiam et manum D^{ni} sursum reddere ad opus cujuscunque voluerit, ac eciam ea vendere et alienare cuicunque sibi viderit melius expedire, necnon ea recipere et finem pro eisdem cum D^{no} per ejus Senescallum facere, et cum necesse fuerit in eadem curia pro eisdem respondere.

It^{m}, dicunt quod quilibet talis tenens potest in manus D^{ni} sursum reddere terras et tenementa sua que tenet secundum consuetudinem manerii ad opus cujuscunque sibi placuerit in presentia Senescalli D^{ni} ib'm, tam in curia quam extra curiam, ac eciam in absencia Senescalli in manum Prepositi ib'm, vel in manum alicujus vicini sui ad proximum halmotum alterius tenendum.

It^{m}, dicunt quod illi ad quorum opus terra sive tenementa sic tenentur de D^{no} secundum consuetudinem manerii sursum reddere sive per vendicionem sive per descensum, finis inde quem facient cum D^{no} erit—videlicet cum D^{no} duplicabunt (firmam) unius anni ad maximum, nisi graciam meliorem inde habuerit de D^{no} vel Sen^{o} loci.

It^{m}, dicunt quod nulla mulier habebit dotem, nisi solummodo de illis terris et tenementis de quibus erit maritus seizitus per virgam curie.

It^{m}, dicunt quod nullus extraneus per minas veniens inter tenentes D^{ni} secundum consuetudinem manerii vertens in auxilium sibi perquisitum sive conductum de generosis patrie ad implacitandum aliquem vel aliquos tenent' predictorum in halmot D^{ni} de Blakburnshyre ad aliquod implacitum in eisdem intrandum versus tenentes predictos vel aliquem eorum per Senesc. loci vel ejus locum tenentem ullo modo receptus erit.

It^{m}, dicunt quod custos alicujus tenentis terras et ten. de D^{no} secundum consuetudinem, etsi infra etatem existet, ipse idem custos erit computato primo cum venerit ad etatem xv annorum, et in hoc consuetudo manerii sequitur communem legem Anglie.

It^{m}, dicunt quod si quis tenens D^{ni} secundum consuetudinem manerii obierit et seizitus habuerit plures filias, omnia terre et tenementa de quibus pater illarum obierit seizitus erunt equaliter partita cuilibet sororum illarum, sicut filie liberorum tenentum habent secundum communem legem Anglie.

It^{m}, dicunt quod nulla Esson. jacet in Halmot inter ter' et ten' [in it' alias partes] in quovis placito.

It^{m},[1] dicunt quod si contingat quod Rotuli Halmotorum sive Wapentache de Blackburnshyre sint perditi negligencia vel aliquo alio modo per Senescallos vel eorum clericos, in quibus quidem aliquis finis de terris et tenementis de domino secundum consuetudinem manerii . . . . quod si recti heredes talium tenentium qui fines fecerant voluerint petere inquisicionem, XII homines de tenentibus D^{ni} . . . . ad inquirendum utrum fines facti fuerint per antecessores suos, necne; et si inveniatur, quod tunc heredes eorum pro racionabili fine inde cum D^{no} faciendo erunt recepti coram Senescallo loci.

It^{m}, dicunt quod bene liceat cuilibet tenenti secundum consuetudinem predictam omnia terras et tenementa sua que tenet de D^{no} secundum consuetudinem predictam, ad firmam dimittere racionabili tenenti absque fine aliquo modo cum D^{no} faciendo.

It^{m}, dicunt quod licitum est eisdem tenentibus recipere et habere arbores et subboscum crescentes super *le Costom Land* infra tenuram propriam ad reparacionem domorum et sepium suorum edificatorum et edificandorum super tenementis suis de *Costom Land*, quotiens et quum oportuerit.

It^{m}, dicunt quod quilibet talis tenens de jure habere debet infra le Fens de Penhill a festo S'c'i Michis Arch'i usque ad festum Pentecostes tunc proxime sequens unum jumentum pro IIII d. et duo averia pro II d. D^{no} solvend'.

It^{m}, dicunt quod quilibet talis tenens haberet liberacionem per forestarium D^{ni} de Penhill, Rossyndale, et Trowden . . . . Accrington ad domos suas quociens et . . . . de fœno et Risshes solvend' pro plaustrato 1 d.

[1] This may seem to have been dictated by aforesight almost prophetical. See the next paragraph.

In quibus omnium consuetudinum testimonium juratores predicti . . . . . necnon Thomas de Radcliff, Senescallus . . . . . . die anno et loco huic . . . . . . sigilla sua apposuimus.

To the Honor of Clitheroe anciently belonged these officers,[1] whose fees were as follows:

	£	s.	d.	
Receiver of the Honor	15	13	4	
Master Forester of Blackburnshire . .	(No fee mentioned.)			
Master Forester of Bowland . . .	6	13	4	
Steward of Blackburnshire . . .	3	6	8	
Constable of Clitheroe Castle . . .	10	0	0	
Porter of the Castle	3	0	8	
Keeper of Radholme Park . . .	1	10	4	(Harl. MS.
[Keeper of Lathgrim Park . . .	2	0	6]	240, f. 41.)

[Thomas d'ns Stanley, Rec' d'nii de Clyderowe . vj li. xiij s. iiij d.
Joh'es Cays parcarius parci de Musbury p. ann. . (*blank*)
Joh'es Talbot parcarius parci de Ightenhull . xxx s. iiij d.
Joh'es Hunt custos chacee de Trowden . . lx s. viij d.]
(Fees of Officers of the Duchy, 22 Edw. IV. Harl. MS. 433, f. 317 b.)

Lastly, grantees of the bailiwick from Henry, Earl, afterwards Duke, of Lancaster, by charter dated 25th Edward III. These were the Abbot and Convent of Whalley, Gilbert de la Leigh, John de Alvetham, and Richard de Tunlay, whose representatives still continue to exercise this office by deputy;[2] and the Towneley family, so late as the year 1687,[3] and perhaps later, continued to enumerate, in settlements, &c. not a moiety, but two fourth parts, of the bailiwick of Blackburnshire, one for De la Leigh and another for Townley.

Of this curious grant, yet extant in the Coucher Book of Whalley, the following is an extract, as the whole would be too long for transcription:

Coste endenture fait perentre ly noble Seignur Henry Counte de Lancastre, Derby, Leycestr', et seneschall Dangleterre dune parte et Labbe et couent de Whalleye, Gilbert de la Legh, Johan de Aluetham, et Richard de Towneley dautre parte, tesmoigne qe le dit Counte ad done et graunte et per per ceste presente chartre endente conferme as ditz Abbe et couent et lours successours et as ditz Gilbert, Johan, et Richard et a lours heirs, la Baillie del Wapentak de Blakeburneschir, oue toutz les profits, comoditez, et toutz outres appurtenaunces a la dite Baillie regardauntz; cest assauoir qe les ditz Abbe et couent et lours successours, Gilberte, Johan, et Richard, et lours heires troueront un home a chiual et deaux a pie de y estre baillifs a faire loffice qe a la dite baillie appartient, les queux serrount presenter, de an en an par eaux, lours successours et lours heirs deuant le Seneschal de dit Count ou de ses heirs qe pur le temps serra a la proscheyne court tenue a Cliderhou apres le feste de Seint Michel larchaungel, et seruientz de faire toutz choses

[1] Serjeant Fleetwood's MS. account of the Duchy of Lancaster, &c.

[2] [The Towneleys and Waltons of Altham still hold the office, and till lately appointed a bailiff, who attended at the court of the hundred. Coucher Book, p. 1164. Note by the editor, W. A. Hulton, Esq.]

[3] From original papers pen. Auct.

queuz attient a la dite Baillie, et leal accompte rendre de toutz choses queux a la dite Baillie nommement des rentes, ferms, fyns, et des amerciementz puauntz les putures deinz la dite Baillie auxsi entierement come les Bailifs queux furent en temps Monsr. Hen. de Lacy jadys Count de Nichole prisetrent deinz le pureeynte meisme la Baillie, hors prys les tenauntz le dit Counte qi tiegnent de ly a volunte queux auaunt ces hours ne soiyent (grauntez) puture doner, etc.—Coucher Book, p. 58. [p. 1164 Chetham Society's edition.] [1]

Of the Master Foresters of Blackburnshire, though several names will occur in the following narrative, I am not able to give any connected list. The office itself appears to have existed from the origin of the Honor, and to have determined with the commission of approvement in the 23rd Hen. VII. 1507-8.

The necessary intervention of the Senescalls, or Stewards, in all legal transactions between the lords and their tenants, has rendered it no difficult task to exhibit a pretty complete succession of names in their office, which appears for several centuries to have been an object of ambition to the first families of the county; but which, about a century ago, began to be entrusted to common agents resident upon the place, for which reason the series is not continued beyond that period. The following catalogue, from Gilbert de Clifton, has been extracted from a valuable collection of local MSS. at Browsholme, with some additional names inserted in their proper places. The foregoing names I have collected from charters without date, and cannot therefore undertake to settle their relative places with exactness.

Senescalli de Blackburnshire.

Adam de Dutton, temp. Rog. et Joh. de Lacy. [2]
Robertus de Cancia et Alanus Clericus, temp. Joh. de Lacy, qui ob. 1240.
Nicholas de Burton. [Coucher Book, p. 956.]
Williehnus de Burch.
Gilbertus de Hocton.
Henricus de Torboc. [Coucher Book, p. 134.]
[Johannes de Bosco. *Ibid.* p. 1032.
Henry de Clayton. *Ibid.* p. 104.
Galfridus de Dutton. *Ibid.* p. 279, &c.
Symo de Heris. *Ibid.* p. 127.
Henricus de Kyrkeby. *Ibid.* p. 1127.
Petrus de Santon. *Ibid.* pp. 1077, 1112.]
Gilbertus de Clifton, 3 Edw. I. 1274-5.
Adam de Blackburn miles, 12 ejusd. 1283-4.
Henricus de Kighley, 16 ejusd. 1287-8.
[Hugo de Biron.]
Robertus de Hepple, 22 ejusd. 1293-4.
Simon de Balderston, 32 ejusd. 1303-4.
Edmundus Talbot, 32 ejusd. 1303-4.
Robertus Sherburne, 34 ejusd. 1305-6.
Johannes de Midhope, 10 Edw. II. 1316-17.
Willielmus de Tatham, 17 ejusd. 1323-4.
Rich. de Radcliffe, 6 Edw. III. 1331-2.
Willielmus de Tatham, ad 13 ejusd. 1339-40.
Johannes de Radcliffe, ad 22 ejusd. 1348-9.
Willielmus Laurence, ad 27 ejusd. 1352-3.
Ric. de Radcliffe, et Rob. de Singleton cum eo pro eo an.
Idem ad 38 ejusd. 1364-5.

[1] [The grantees were to pay a yearly rent of 5½ marks. Rendaunt per an al dit Counte et a ses heires cynk marcs et demy a la feste de seint Michel. Coucher Book, p. 1165.]

[2] This Adam de Dutton is one of the witnesses to the foundation charter of Stanlaw, A.D. 1178; and a Dominus Adam occurs as steward in charters of John de Lacy, who succeeded A.D. 1211: so that, if both these names design the same person, which I believe, he must have held the office at least 33 years.

Godfr. Foljambe, eod. anno.
Ric. de Towneley, a 39 ad 46 ejusd. 1365-6 to 1372-3.
Gilb. de la Leigh, 49 ejusd. 1375-6.
Tho. Radcliffe, 8 Ric. II. 1384-5.
Joh. de Poole, 9 ejusd. 1385-6.
Tho. Radcliffe, 10 ejusd. 1386-7.
Robertus Urswick, 16 ejusd. 1391-2.
Hen. Hoghton, 12 Hen. IV. 1410-11.
Joh. Stanley mil., 8 Hen. VI. 1429-30.
Ric. Tunstal mil., 38 ejusd. 1459-60.
Tho. Dns. Stanley, a 3 ad 19 Edw. IV. 1463-4 to 1479-80.
Tho. Comes Derbie, ad 19 Hen. VII. 1503-4.
Petrus Legh mil., a 21 ejusd. ad 2 Hen. VIII. 1505-6 to 1510-11.
Ric. Tempest mil., ad 28 ejusd. 1536-7. [Appointed 16 Dec. 1511. Duchy Register.]
Tho. Clifford mil., 30 ejusd. 1538-39. [31 Oct. 1527. *Ibid.*]
Arthur Darcy mil., 36 ejusd. ad 4 Edw. VI. 1544-5 to 1550-1.
Tho. Talbot mil., 1 Phil. et Mar. 1554-5.
Tho. Talbot mil. et Joh. Towneley arm. 4 ejusd. 1557-8.[1]
Joh. Towneley, arm. 1 Eliz. ad ejusd. 1558-9.
Ric. Molineaux, arm. a 24 ejusd. ad 36, 1581-2 to 1593-4.
Willielmus Assheton, arm. 39 ejusd. 1596-7.
Ric. Molineaux, mil. et Ric. Vic. Molineaux, a 42 Eliz. ad 5 Car. I. 1599-1600 to 1629-30.
Jacobus Dns. Strange et Johannes Byron, miles. Baln. ad 16 Car. 1640-1 [appointed 12 Car. I.]
[Ric'us Vicecomes Molyneux, 16 Car. I.]
Nicholas Assheton, arm. 1653.
Andrew Holden, gen. et John Lawe, gen. 1656,[2] 1658.
Caryl vicecom. Molineux, [et Ric'us fil' et heres ejus apparens 6 Aug. 1660,] 14 Car. II. 1662-3.
Joh. Baynes, arm. 26 ejusd. 1674-5, et 27 ejusd. 1675-6.
Tho. Stringer, mil. 33 ejusd. ad 1 Jac. II. 1881-2 to 1684-5.
Anth. Parker, arm. 2 Gul. et Mar. 1690-1.
Tho. Coulthurst, arm. 4 Ann. 1704-5.

[1] [Philip and Mary appointed Tho. Talbot mil. and Joh. Towneley, gen., or the survivor, to the office 13 Nov. (1556), 3 and 4 A. R. Talbot having died, and Towneley having resigned, Queen Elizabeth issued new letters patent 23 Mar. 1581 for Ric. Molyneux.—Duchy of Lancaster, Book of Commissions, &c. No. 5, f. 32.]

[2] During the Usurpation. After the Restoration Holden was continued as Deputy. About the same time I meet with a Thomas Forster, esq. calling himself lord of the manor of Ightenhill, and Edmund Stephenson, gent. his steward.

FORESTS.

And ðeþe ȝepexen	Ibique crescit
Þuða ꝼorteþn mýcel	Sylvarum saltus ingens,
Þuniað on ðam þicum	Sinus possident
Þilða deoþ moniȝe	Terræ quam plurimæ
In deopa dalum	in vallibus profundis
Deoþa unȝeþim	Damarum turba innumera.

Vet. Poem. Sax.[1] ap Hickes Thes. vol. i. p. 193.

Before we enter upon a particular survey of the Forests of Blackburnshire and Bowland, it may not be uninteresting to give a short abstract of the laws and customs of our ancient forests in general.

The word Forest,[2] in its original and most extended sense, implied a tract of land lying out (*foras*), that is rejected, as of no value in the first distribution of property; but though immense quantities of ground falling under this description undoubtedly subsisted in England from the earliest times; though the whole country of Deira, or Deoþalond, may be considered as one immense forest; though from the name of those beautiful animals with which they were filled, and the coverts with which they abounded, our Saxon ancestors had long distinguished these retreats by the names of Bucholt and Deorꝼald,[3] there is no clear evidence to prove that they were reserved for the peculiar recreation of our monarchs, and still less that they were placed under a distinct code of laws before the reign of Canute, who, in A.D. 1016, promulgated the *Constitutiones de Foresta*.[4]

[1] [De Situ Dunelmi et de sacris reliquis qui ibidem habuntur.]

[2] Manwood, who wrote upon this picturesque and curious subject with no taste, and with all the pedantry of his age, gravely proves that there were forests in Judea, from Ps. l. 10—"All the beasts of the forest are mine." When men have long been confined to the professional use of terms, it never seems to occur to them that they have a more popular and extended signification.

[3] These are also proper names of two of our forests, one in Hampshire and Wiltshire, the other in Shropshire. Topographers reckon 69 forests in England, but the enumeration is far from being complete.

[4] Lord Coke, Inst. 4, 320, expresses a doubt with respect to the genuineness of these constitutions, because they are nowhere referred to in the general laws of Canute, and because the 30th constitution of the former is inconsistent with cap. 77 of the latter; as if the virtual alteration, and even repeal, of a former statute by a later, afforded a presumption against the authenticity either of the one or the other. But for what purpose should they be fabricated? I will make the most favourable supposition for Lord Coke's hypothesis—namely, that they were devised for the purpose of confronting an early and merciful code with the sanguinary system of forest laws, which prevailed after the Conquest. But this opinion is encumbered with insuperable difficulties; for, 1st, these constitutions, like the other acknowledged laws of Canute, have been written in Danish: this is proved by the many Danish words, which the translator has actually left interspersed with his own version; and which, though many of them are so corrupted as to be unintelligible in their present form, are yet capable of a good sense by slight literal alterations.

2nd. I recollect no instances of forgeries after the Conquest, but of charters, and those by monks, and for their own advantage: these, moreover, were in Latin; because the Normans either did not understand their Saxon evidences or treated them with contempt.

In these constitutions, therefore, we have the first outline of that singular system which, from the anxiety of the first Norman princes to secure to themselves the envied pleasures of the chace, afterwards became very artificial; which is now very picturesque and amusing indeed to us, who view the apparatus of it at a distance; but was oppressive and cruel in an high degree to those who had the misfortune to live within its grasp.

By these laws, the supreme jurisdiction over the forests of England was committed to four *Thegenes* (thanes or principal barons); an inferior authority delegated to four *Lesthegenes* (homines mediocres, or lesser barons); and the immediate custody of each entrusted to two *Tinemen* (minuti homines); whose office it was to guard by nightly watches against offences of vert and venison.

The sanctions of this code were chiefly pecuniary, saving that in two cases, first of having offered violence to one of the four great thanes, and secondly, of having slain a staggon, or royal beast, the free man forfeited his liberty and the slave his life.

The supreme administration of the forests, however, fell by degrees into the hands of one chief justiciary, till, in the year 1184, Henry II. divided the forests of England into two jurisdictions, north and south of Trent, which gave rise to the two *itinera*, or *eyres*, still nominally subsisting. Over each of these he placed four justices; viz. two clerks and two knights, together with two servants of his own household, as wardens, over all the other foresters.

Each of these *itinera*, however, gradually fell back under the jurisdiction of one.

But after the Conquest a much more material alteration took place in the internal

The barons, and even secular clergy, being more illiterate, were less inventive, and therefore less to be suspected of such fabrications.

Again, during the first reigns after the Conquest, our countrymen groaned, rather than remonstrated, under the tyranny of the Forest Laws: it is not probable, therefore, that such an instrument would be fabricated before it was wanted, and might be pleaded with some effect.

But in the reign of John, though the Saxon characters were generally in use, and though the dialect of the time was a semi-Saxon, it would have been difficult to find even a monk who could have written the language of the laws of Canute. Some of them are occasionally found in MSS. (not in charters) as low as the reign of Edward III. or perhaps lower. The convenient and compendious character þ was, I believe, the last.

Lastly, in these laws the wolf is spoken of as actually existing; which, though we know it was, not only in the time of Canute, but for a considerable time after the Conquest, yet it only subsisted in remote parts of the island: and it is almost certain that a monkish falsary of later days, better acquainted with chronicles than facts in natural history, would have acquiesced in the common opinion of the extinction of wolves by Edgar. Once for all, as we shall have frequent occasion to differ on the subject of legal antiquities with Lord Coke, it may be necessary to say, that though he greatly affected this species of knowledge, he was, in fact, a poor etymologist, and a worse critic, even in his own science. His understanding was clear and acute, rather than comprehensive; and having narrowed the attention of his whole life to a single point, the common law, he became, of course, a consummate master of it. Among those who rise to the highest ranks in his profession, it may be remarked that there are persons of two descriptions; the first consisting of men, who by the compass and universality of their talents attain to great eminence in other sciences, at the same time that they illustrate and adorn their own: such were More, Bacon, Hyde, Hale, Murray, Blackstone. The next is made up of those who, wanting the illumination of native genius and the polish of acquired literature, with great knowledge and much practical usefulness in their own peculiar walk, are only to be considered as a more dignified species of attornies—and such appears to have been Lord Coke.

government of the forests, by which a man, even a free man, trespassing against the King's venison, was condemned to a punishment worse than death, namely, mutilation and loss of eyes; a penalty which, from the assizes of Henry I. and Richard I. appears to have been inflicted with no sparing hand.

To return, the constitution of the forests being thus fixed by Henry II. we find their officers, under the chief justices, to have consisted of the wardens, now first introduced, of foresters, verdurers, regarders, agisters, woodwards, sometimes called woodreeves, and bedels, whose respective offices are ascertained with great exactness in the old writers on this subject.

Forests were generally exempt from the operation of both civil and ecclesiastical law: they belonged, in strictness, to no parish, hundred, county, or diocese; and accordingly they had pleas of their own, greater and less. The former held every third year, by the chief justice or his deputy: the latter, that of *Swainmote,* which carries its inferior rank and rustic character in the name, summoned thrice in every year. Besides these was a court of attachment, subordinate to both the former.

The pervading principle of forest law was essentially different, either from humanity or general policy—*Adeo ut* (says the Black Book of the Exchequer) *quod per leges forestæ factum fuerit, non justum absolute, sed justum secundum leges forestæ dicitur;* and what was worse, the rule and measure even of this factitious justice was the *arbitrium solius regis, vel cujuslibet familiarium ad hoc specialiter deputati.* We may therefore cease to wonder that, under a system like this, it was equally criminal to lop an holly and to fell an oak; or that it was even more penal to kill a stag than to murder a man.

Forests are either natural, such as have been above described, or factitious; for it was held a branch of ancient prerogative in the kings of England to afforest, under certain forms, at pleasure, the lands of the subject, for their own sovereign amusement.

This formidable right, however, appears to have been rarely exercised. Never, perhaps, but in two instances, by William the Conqueror, in afforesting great part of Hampshire; and by Henry VIII. in creating the forest of Hampton Court. The latter, however, seems to have comprehended little but lands previously belonging to the Crown. But the wide and unfeeling devastation committed by the former was followed by an awful lesson to those who pervert the first principles of justice and mercy for their own brutal gratification; since, in a tract where he had made the blood of man to be lightly regarded, in comparison with that of beasts, three of his own immediate descendants actually shed their own blood in the pursuit of these very animals.[1]

[1] These enormities frequently drew heavy complaints from the historians and other writers of those times; out of which, for the reader's amusement, rather than to excite his compassion, I will select one from John of Salisbury in his Polycraticon:—"A novalibus, sui arcentur agricolæ, dum feræ habeant vagandi libertatem: illis, ut augeantur, prædia subtrahuntur agricolis; cum pascua armentariis et gregariis, tum alvearia à floralibus excludunt, ipsis quoque apibus vix naturali libertate uti permissum est."—The first part of this complaint is rational, but the latter puerile and trifling. The writer had probably never asked himself by what mode of inclosure, or by what act of prerogative, hive-bees could be shut out from the flowers of the forest. But truth is an ingredient equally necessary in good rhetoric and in good morals.

But though succeeding Kings, as Henry II. Richard I. and John, never ventured upon acts of similar devastation, that is, never afforested in a manner equally oppressive with that of the Conqueror, yet, without absolutely depopulating villages, destroying inclosures, or extending the utmost rigour of the Forest Laws beyond their former bounds, they enlarged far and wide the limits of the forests themselves; and this, among other grievances, provoked the barons (who, to do justice to their humanity, were not the principal sufferers) to extort from King John the first charter of the forests, in which the deforestation of all those recent additions to the ancient forests was expressly stipulated; but, before the necessary regulation took effect, the King died, and nothing material was done till the 9th Hen. III. when a second charter, to the same effect, having been extorted from his necessities, orders were given that inquisitions should be held, and perambulations made, in order to distinguish the lands afforested by the late kings from old and rightful forests. Little, however, in the remoter parts of the kingdom especially, was done to this effect through the remainder of that long reign.[1]

But, in the beginning of the reign of Edward I. the work was seriously undertaken. A commission was issued, under the great seal, to cause all the true and ancient forests to be mered and bounded by certain land-marks; all newly afforested lands to be severed from the former, and the boundaries of each to be returned into the Court of Chancery.[2]

And these lands, so disforested, were called *Pourallees*, or *Purlieus*, from Fr. *pourallée*, a perambulation; yet, notwithstanding all these steps, as lands of this peculiar description had never been completely afforested, so they were never considered by the lawyers as entirely restored to their original rights, but as partaking of a middle nature and constitution between free and forest land, and were therefore placed under certain laws and regulations peculiar to themselves.

But this wise and excellent prince rendered a much more essential service to English liberty by his general confirmation of the *Carta de Foresta*, in which all the arbitrary and all the sanguinary parts of the old code were abolished at once; and it was expressly declared, "that no English subject shall henceforward lose life or limb for any trespass of vert or venison; but, if any one be convicted of killing the King's deer, he shall be sentenced to pay an heavy mulct; which, if he cannot discharge, he shall lie in prison one year; after which, if he be unable to find pledges, he shall abjure the realm."[3] This surpassed even the Saxon law in clemency[4] and moderation.

Our next inquiry will be into the animals which these laws had for their object to protect.

[1] Carta de Foresta, 9 Hen. III. 1224-5.

[2] Assiz. et Const. Forest. 6 Edw. I. et seq.

[3] Spelman *in voce* Foresta.

[4] Excessive severity always leads to the contrary extreme; and, accordingly, the royal forests have long been undisturbed retreats of poachers and deer-stealers. But, while I am writing this, a bill is brought into Parliament for the better preservation of game in the King's forests, of which the principal enactment is *to punish persons poaching in the forests in the same manner with those who are convicted of that offence on private grounds*. So that it now requires additional rigour to put these parts of the royal domains upon a footing which the Norman princes would have encountered a rebellion rather than have consented that they should be reduced to.

It were a tedious and pedantic task to pursue the old foresters through all the barbarous terms by which they distinguished beasts of venery or chace, their haunts, foot-marks, excrements, and other particulars equally unimportant.[1]

But the two following extracts, one from the Constitutions of Canute, A.D. 1016, and the other from Dame Juliana Berners, authoress of the Book of St. Alban's, who flourished about 1480, will shew in general what was the nature of this distinction, and also how little agreed foresters of different periods were among themselves with respect to the particular objects of it.

By Const. Canute 24, the staggon or stag alone is considered as the true *fera forestæ*, or beast of venery: he is otherwise denominated, by way of eminence, *fera regalis*; and by Const. 27, in the same collection, it is declared, "Quod sunt aliæ bestiæ quæ dum inter septa et sepes forestæ continentur, emendationi subjacent, quales sunt Capreoli, Lepores, Cuniculi: sunt et alia quamplurima animalia, quæ, quanquam intra septa forestæ vivunt et curæ mediocrium subjacent, forestæ tamen nequaquam censeri possunt, qualia sunt, Bubali, Vaccæ, et similia. Vulpes et Lupi nec forestæ nec venationis habentur, et proinde eorum interfectio nulli emendationi subjacet; Aper vero, quanquam forestæ sit, nullatenus tamen animal venationis haberi est assuetum."[2]

We will now hear the Prioress of Sopewell deliver her scientific precepts:

Mi dere sones, where ye fare be frith or by fell
Take gode hede in hys tyme, How Tristrem[3] woll tell:
How many maner bestes of venery there were,
Listenes now to oure dame, and ye shullen here.
Fowr maner bestes of venery there are:
The first of hem is a hert, the second is an hare,
The boor is one of tho,
The wolff, and no mo:

And where so ye comen in play or in place,
Now shal I tell you which ben bestes of chace,
On of tho a bak, another a doo,
The fox and the marteryn, and the wilde roo,
And ye shal, my dere sones, other bestes all,
Where so ye hem finde, rascal hem call,
In frith or in fell,
Or in forest y you tell.

Without attempting to reconcile differences in opinion, or rather in language, which a

[1] The curious reader, however, is referred, for all these particulars, to Manwood, Forest Laws, c. 4.

[2] In this constitution I discover the passage alluded to by the solicitor-general St. John, in his inhuman speech a the trial of the Earl of Strafford. "We give law," said that unfeeling accuser, "to hares and deer, because they are beasts of chace; but we give no law to wolves and foxes, because they are beasts of prey, but knock them on the head wherever we find them."—Clarendon, Hist. Reb. fol. ed. vol. i. p. 183.

[3] "Sir Tristram, an ancient forester, in his worthy Treatise of Hunting."—Manwood.

revolution of five centuries had produced, we will now leave the King and the lady to adjust these points between themselves.

For, indeed, which were beasts of venery and which of chase is to us a matter of small importance; but, as some of these animals in the royal forests have long been extinct, while others, perhaps less likely to sustain themselves against the strength and cunning of man, are yet remaining; as a new and beautiful species appears to have been introduced at an uncertain period; and as it is always a pleasing exercise of the understanding to investigate the causes which produce important changes in animated nature, we will now attempt to assign a few probable reasons for these circumstances.

First, then, in the earlier periods of society,[1] the bulky and timid quadrupeds which minister to the sustenance of man, if not taken under his protection, are the first which fall under his ravages.

To this class belonged a gigantic species of deer,[2] which became extinct in England too early to be noticed even in the laws of Canute: to this also belongs the stag, together with the bubalus, or wild bull, of which the last continues in some ancient parks, while the former, though more numerous, is yet rapidly decreasing. These were the first and easiest prey of savages, because their haunts were easily discovered, their swiftness was greater than their sagacity, their strength easy to be subdued by perseverance, and their powers of resistance almost nothing.

In the same class must be ranked a smaller tribe; the *Capreoli, Lepores, Cuniculi,* of Canute's Constitutions, of the two former of which it may reasonably be asked why, with much greater swiftness though less sagacity, the first is within little more than two centuries become extinct in England, while the second everywhere abounds.

Both, we see, were alike placed under that partial protection of man which was intro-

[1] No fact contributes more, in my mind, to verify the Mosaic history, than the account given in Gen. iv. 2, by which the sheep appears to have been placed under the protection of man from the beginning. Nothing but inspiration, or, what is the same thing, specific instructions from the Almighty, could have directed the attention of a creature so helpless and ignorant as man then was to another creature so totally devoid of strength, swiftness, and sagacity, before the latter had perished from the earth. Beasts of prey were guided by a swifter impulse, and would have discovered its relish long before he had learned its uses. Our old unthinking historians tell us, that Henry I. stocked his park of Woodstock with panthers, ounces, leopards, &c. never considering what was to become of its gentler inhabitants. But immediately after the Creation, or rather the Fall, the world itself, though upon a larger scale, must have been nearly in the same state. I suppose, therefore, that in some instances like the present specific instructions were given to man; and in others, a particular Providence watched, for a season, over the feebler animals.

[2] This animal, of whose existence in England there is no evidence but that of its gigantic horns, of which several pairs have been found in Lancashire (Leigh, p. 184, &c. &c.), is mentioned by Giraldus Cambrensis, as remaining in Ireland in his time. He describes it as of the shape of a stag, and the bulk of an ox. I have not the work of Giraldus at present to refer to; but am certain of the fact, as he reports it; and his account is confirmed by the great number of horns and skeletons belonging to that animal which are found in Ireland. Leigh called the horns which he has engraven, in his History of Lancashire, those of the Canadian stag; by which, I suppose, he meant the elk, whose horns, however, are palmated; and thence too, with his usual sagacity, he inferred the universality of a Deluge. As if an indigenous animal, extinct in his time, could not have died in a Lancashire bog.

duced by the Forest Laws, and is still continued in uninclosed manors or chaces; but the one did not want and the other disdained to accept the closer protection of a park; for it is scarcely possible to impound an animal which can bound almost twenty feet perpendicular.[1]

The roe and hare, therefore, were necessarily left to take their chance for life together in the forest or in the field. But an animal like the former, bringing forth once a year, and at most two at a birth, did little more than provide for a succession of its species against the contingence of natural death, in a secure and protected state. Placed, therefore, out of that protection, it could only have subsisted, at least in populous districts, by means of a quality which it did not possess, namely, sagacity added to swiftness; while the other, by producing three or sometimes four together, perhaps too by the singular property of superfœtation,[2] multiplies much faster; and by the acuteness of its hearing, and the rotundity of its eye, together with its habits of vigilance and universal caution, though otherwise helpless in itself, and very partially protected by man, preserves its species undiminished in the midst of enemies. The bulk of the roe, too, which rendered it a better mark and more difficult to be concealed, was another unfavourable circumstance.

The third and most helpless of these animals, the rabbit, is obviously preserved, partly in consequence of having been made property, and partly by its own instinctive habit of subterraneous concealment.

But, after the time of Canute, another species of deer seems to have been introduced, of which, though it is become the most numerous of the whole genus, the great ornament of our parks and forests, and even yet the second luxury of our tables, the history is very obscure: this is the common fallow deer; with respect to which, it is really extraordinary that so accurate and well-informed a zoologist as Mr. Pennant[3] should acquiesce in the common opinion that the spotted kind were brought from Bengal and the brown from Norway to Scotland by James I. at the time of his marriage. This opinion must of course bring down the introduction of the first variety to a later period than the discovery of the Cape of Good Hope; whereas the species was unquestionably found in England two centuries before. I will now state what has occurred to me upon the subject, not as being at all satisfactory, but in order to invite a more accurate investigation.

In the Squire of Low Degree, which is alluded to by Chaucer, in the Rhyme of Sir Thopas, and is probably not long anterior to his time, we find merely this enumeration of

[1] In Leland's time the roe remained in the marches of Wales; at present it is found in no part of the island, but in the highlands of Scotland; and at Blair, in Athol, where the breed most abounds, it is seen indiscriminately within the park and without, passing and re-passing the pales at pleasure.

[2] This fact is denied by Mons. Buffon, but asserted by our countryman Sir Thomas Browne, a man not inferior to the French naturalist in exactness of observation and philosophical incredulity. Instances of extra-uterine conception, which may possibly have led to the other opinion, are certainly observed in hares. See Plot's *Hist. of Staffordshire*, p. 253.

[3] History of Quadrupeds, vol. i. p. 35, &c.

forest-beasts, *harte and hynde, and other like;* but in the romance of St. Degore, which is supposed by Mr. Warton[1] to be contemporary with the former,

For to hunt for a dere or a do.

This may be referred to the end of Edward II. or beginning of his son's reign. A little after, we find the following passage in the romance of Hippomedon.[2]

Ipomydon with his Houndis thoo,
Drew downe bothe Buk and Doo.

And again,

Alle the Game of the Forest,
Herte and Hynde, Buk and Doo.

WARTON, *Hist. of Eng. Poetry*, i. 199.

While Caxton was printing the Golden Legend he had a present from William Lord Arundel, of a buck in summer and a doe in winter. And about the same time they are mentioned by dame Juliana Berners in the passage quoted above.

But it is not to be dissembled that, though the silence of Canute's Constitutions of the Forest seems to prove them not indigenous in England, yet the Saxon Bucholt occasions a little hesitation; still, the word may either be derived from bucken, beech-trees, or, which is more probable, may denominate the deer genus universally.

If, however, the buck and doe be not indigenous, from what country and at what period between the time of Canute and that of Edward II. or III. they were introduced, I am yet to be informed. Can any evidence be adduced to prove that they were imported by the later crusaders from the East? If our hierozoicon be accurate, the fallow deer was known in Judea as early as the time of Solomon, 1 Kings iv. 23.[3]

The rascal tribe (from which it does not appear why the marten should be excluded) consisted of the otter, the badger, the weasel, and, in Leland's time, of the beaver also. To these ought to be added (if the name were not unworthy of him), another beautiful and harmless forester, the squirrel; and a sixth, well entitled to the appellation, who, if his courage had been in any degree comparable to his strength, activity, and fierceness, would have been a formidable animal indeed: this is that shy and treacherous native of the woods, the wild cat, of which our common household cat is a diminutive and degenerate variety; who, with all the habits of domestication, retains every propensity of savage life: fawning, yet irascible; alternately indolent and indefatigable, vigilant and sluggish;

[1] Hist. of English Poetry, vol. i. p. 180.

[2] It must be observed that, whatever may be the hero's name or age, and wherever the scene is laid in the old romances, the manners are contemporary with the writers, and purely English. Thus, too, Shakespeare's Theseus is a mere English sportsman.—*Midsummer Night's Dream.*

[3] And long before.—See Deuteron. xiv. 5; where the *Dishun*, rather than the *Jackmur*, appears to be our fallow deer; as Jerom, who must have been well acquainted with the animals of the country where he lived, renders the former *Pygargus*.

voracious, though patient of abstinence; fond of warmth, yet capable of enduring all the extremities of cold; cunning, but almost altogether indocile; and thievish, when pampered to the utmost.

The wild boar, which appears to have existed in England during the reign of Canute, is to be referred partly to the present class and partly to the following.

2d. The next tribe, which disappears before the skill or courage of man, are the larger animals of prey, of which the wolf,[1] as it attacks the more valuable domestic animals, and sometimes man himself, will not long be endured after the invention of fire arms, except where his retreats are nearly inaccessible.

His congener the fox now exists in England, either by connivance or contempt: for, were this paltry animal once to be abandoned by sportsmen, or were he, instead of confining himself to petty larcenies in the hen-roost, or on the common, now and then to seize an infant, the species would not be permitted to remain for twelve months.

But, as we descend in the scale of predatory animals, their extinction becomes proportionably difficult: their fecundity and diminutive size, together with the nature of their haunts, near to themselves and inaccessible to man, enabling them to defy the vanquisher of nobler beasts, and to carry on their petty but teazing and innumerable depredations without a possibility of redress.

After the animals, which, in one way or other, were either protected or tolerated in the forests, we are next to consider such as were forbidden. These were four: the goose, the hog, the sheep, and the goat. For the first of these prohibitions, which would probably not be executed with rigour, I know no reason, unless there be something in the scream or dung of that uncleanly and vociferous fowl particularly offensive to deer; of the second, the reason is obvious, as hogs would have made too free with mast and acorns; the third must have resulted from observing a circumstance, which I have often attended to, but never heard remarked, namely, a visible aversion between deer and sheep; deer will attach themselves to cows, and goats to horses; but nature seems to have implanted a mutual antipathy in the two other tribes, for the purpose of preventing unnatural commixtures between animals not sufficiently remote from one another in size, to hinder that evil without a strong repulsive instinct.

[1] Dr. Caius acquiesced in the vulgar opinion of the extinction of wolves in England by Edgar. "Regnavit," says he, "Edgarus circ. A.D. 959, a quo tempore non legimus nativum in Anglia visum lupum." I have already affirmed, that they certainly existed among us to a much lower period, and will now produce the latest positive evidence I have met with upon the subject. The [Cistercian] abbey of Fors, in Wensleydale, was founded A.D. 1145; that is, nearly two centuries after the reign of Edgar; and some time after, Alan, Earl of Bretagne, gave to the monks of that abbey the flesh of wild animals, killed by wolves, in the forest of Wensleydale. These men must have been both stout and vigilant to make the gift of any value; but the grant ascertains a curious and important fact in English zoology. *Vide* Burton's Monast. Ebor. under Fors Abbey [p. 371.] [Si vero fratres ipsi, vel aliqui suorum servientium carnem alicujus feræ in mea foresta invenirent, cum Dei benedictione illam accipiant, feræ dico quæ luporum morsu peremptarentur. Mon. Angl. V. 569. See also in Rymer the later royal commission issued in 1281 to Peter Corbet for taking wolves in the five counties of Gloucester, Worcester, Hereford, Salop, and Stafford.]

The reason why the goat was included in these prohibitions is very obvious, as he must have been a capital offender against vert and grenehew.[1]

Another tribe of animals was partially forbidden within the forests, from a very different motive. In the varieties of the dog, Providence seems to have raised up a faithful and necessary ally to man in his warfare or intercourse with other quadrupeds. In this alliance he was too formidable to be overlooked by the jealousy of a forest legislator. Accordingly we find that,

1st. The greyhound and the spaniel, from their strength and swiftness, were absolutely prohibited within the verge of the forests.

2d. The mastiff,[2] a stout but not an active dog, was allowed to be kept, when incapacitated for mischief by one of the two following operations, either genucission, sometimes termed hoxing, which was the more ancient practice,[3] or expeditation, otherwise called lawing,[4] that is, striking off three toes of the fore feet, which is still in use.[5]

3d. By the Constitutions of Canute, it was lawful to keep the velter or langeran,[6] and the ramhundt,[7] by the former of which I understand the terrier, and by the latter the

[1] Manwood, p. 238.

[2] The etymology of this word has never been made out. Manwood says, (Forest Laws, c. 16,) in the old British speech, meaning, I suppose, old English, they do call him Mase-thefe. This is childish, besides that, in old English, the word would have been not Mase, but Mate, as *ex. gr.* a great wooden tower, which Richard I. raised against the Saracens, was called Mate griffon. Dr. Caius, the learned author of that scarce little work *De Canibus Britannicis*, is not much more happy, as he derives the words a *maste sagino, est enim crassum genus canum et bene saginatum catenarium hoc*; on which I have only to observe, that, if the mastiff had nothing better to feast upon than mast, he would not long be *genus crassum et bene saginatum*. What follows will, I think, lead to the same origin of the word: *scio Augustinum Niphum Mastinum (mastivum nostri vocant) pecuarium existimare et Albertum, Lyciscum, ex cane et lupo genitum.* This leads me to suspect both the name and the breed to be Spanish, for in that language the word Mestino really signifies the lyciscus, or wolf-dog; but the word mestizo, a mongrel, is, I believe, the genuine parent of mastiff. This was Junius's conjecture (*in voce* mastiff), and is strikingly confirmed by the manner in which it is pronounced by the common people in Lancashire, *i. e.* not mastiff but mastiss.

[3] Or hocksinewing. Henry II. introduced the modern practice of lawing. Assiz. Woodstock, art. 6.

[4] Or hambling. Hence the vulgar word hample, to limp.

[5] In Bowland expeditation is not governed by the species, but by the size of the dog—an iron ring being kept as a gauge, through which every foot that will pass escapes the operation.

[6] In these constitutions almost all the Danish words which the translator has retained are corrupted. I would read, therefore, instead of Langeran, which is nonsense, Lanȝȝun or Longsnout, from ȝȝun; in the Lancashire dialect *groon* or *groin*, a sharp snout. I meet with the word also in old Scottish poetry.

Came like a sowe out of a middin,
Full slepy was his Grunye. (*Dunbar.*)

[7] Ramhundt is pretty obviously the common sheep-dog. Hund in Danish, as in modern German, being co-extensive with the generic term dog itself. Of this Dr. Caius admonishes his friend Gesner: "Hounde—a vocabulo vestrati *hunde*, quod canem in universum apud vos significat." I will just beg leave to add, that in the time of Caius, whose book *De Canibus Britannicis* was first published A.D. 1570, three species of hybrid animals were common in England, of which two are now rare, and the last I think unknown. 1st. The *lyciscus* or mungrel between the dog and the wolf. 2d. The *lacena*, bred between the dog and the fox. 3d. The *urcanus*, between the dog and the bear. Of the existence of this last I should have doubted, had not Dr. Caius, a man of integrity and science, declared that it abounded in his time.

sheep dog, as the diminutive size and base propensities of these kinds secured the nobler animals of chace and venery from their attacks.

4th. No prohibition whatever is laid upon the keeping of staghounds, either because it was supposed that no one would dare to attack the King's deer openly, and with whole packs of dogs; or because, certain privileges to kill deer having been granted to peers, bishops, &c. on their way to and from parliament, it would be understood that whatever was not included in these indulgences was prohibited of course.[1]

It only remains that we throw together a few miscellaneous facts relating to the administration of the forests.

In the privileges of a forest were contained all the subordinate rights belonging to chaces, parks, and warrens, as *omne majus continet in se minus.*[2]

In strictness of law none but the King could have a forest, for no subject could grant a commission to hold a court of justice seat; but there are exceptions to this rule, as will appear below.

To a forest, besides the justice seat, appertained the two inferior courts of swainmote and attachment, with foresters, verdurers, regarders, and agisters; a chace was entitled to keepers and woodwards only.

Fifteen days before midsummer, and fifteen after, were called the fence month, in which all hunting was strictly forbidden, the hinds being then either big with young, or having just calved.

The forests were generally driven twice a year, once immediately before the fence month, in order that no disturbance might be given to the hinds, does, or fawns; and, 2dly, about Holyrood day, when the agisters began to take in cattle.[3] At these times all who had common right upon the forest came to the pounds, where a roll of the *gaits* they were entitled to was kept, surchargers fined, and foreigners who had cattle straying within the limits amerced, or sometimes the beasts forfeited.

No forester was permitted to arrest an offender against vert or venison, unless he were taken with the manour, which he might be in the four following situations, viz. Stable-stand, Dogdraw, Back-bear, Bloody-hand.

[1] In the present state of manners it will scarcely be believed with what tribes of dogs our ancient nobility, and even dignified ecclesiastics, were accompanied on their journeys. "Now," says the accurate observer and bitter satirist of his contemporary clergy, Piers Plowman,

> Is Religion a pricker on a palfry, from maner to maner,
> An heape of houndes at his . . . . as he a lorde were.

And we are told that A.D. 1216, an archdeacon of Richmond, on his visitation, came to the priory of Bridlington with ninety-seven horses, twenty-one dogs, and three hawks. (Dugdale's Monasticon, vol. ii. p. 65.)

It is well known that, upon the death of a bishop, his kennel of hounds was due, at common law, as a mortuary to the King. Archbishop Cranmer was an excellent horseman, and fond of hunting. One of his successors, Archbishop Juxon, was probably the last prelate in England who kept a pack of hounds: but there was an Irish prelate of later times, T[wisden] Bishop of R[aphoe, 1747–55] a little man, but mighty hunter, whose example in this respect, as well as others, probably has been monitory to his brethren in that kingdom, and who closed a life of indecorum and irregularity in a manner more horrid than was ever openly told.

[2] Manwood, p. 52.

[3] Ibid. p. 235.

Stable-stand, when a man was found with a long bow, or cross bow bent, or standing with greyhounds in his leash, ready to let them slip.

Dogdraw, when a man had already wounded a deer, and was found drawing after him with an hound or other dog, to recover him in his flight.

Back-bear, when actually carrying off a deer which he had killed. And

Bloody-hand, when a man was found coursing, or returning from coursing, within the forest, in a suspicious manner, with his hands embrewed in blood.

All these were to be arrested and committed to prison, where they were to await the court of justice seat, unless delivered by the King's especial command.

Verdurers were judicial officers sworn to keep the assizes of the forest, and to receive and enrol all presentment of trespasses against vert and venison.[1]

The verdurer was also a kind of coroner, who, with ludicrous solemnity, held an inquisition *super visum corporis*, over the slain deer.

The regarder was to view and inquire of similar trespasses.

Foresters were sworn to preserve the vert and venison, to attend the wild beasts, to attach and present offenders. These were of two kinds, 1st. ordinary foresters, holding their offices during pleasure, though under the great seal; or, 2dly,[2] foresters of fee, who held the office to them and their heirs, paying a fee farm to the King. These were the real efficient guardians of the forests, and they had under them inferior servants, called underkeepers or walkers.

Next to the foresters ranked the bedels of the forest, whose office was merely to execute processes, and to make garnishments of the courts of Swainmote and Attachment.

The lowest officer in this catalogue was the woodward, to whom belonged only the care of wood and vert, an object then deemed of no importance, excepting as it regarded the accommodation of the deer.

The ensign of the woodward's office was a bill, as he was not empowered to bear a bow, which belonged to his superiors.

To enliven this dry detail, we will now conclude with a beautiful portrait, drawn by Chaucer, of an ancient forester, in the person of the Squire's Yeoman, of which the costume is most exact.

> And he was cladde in cote and hode of grene;
> A shefe of peacock arwes bright and kene
> Under his belt he bare ful thriftily,
> Wel coude he dresse his takel yemanly:
> His arwes drouped not with fethres lowe.
> And in his hond he bare a mighty bowe;
> A not-hed hadde he with a boune visage
> Of wood-crafte coude he wel alle the usage.

[1] Manwood, c. 21.

[2] This explains the term in the old ballad of Adam Bell, &c.

> And forty forsters of the fee
> These out-laws had yslaw. Percy's Ancient Songs, vol. i. p. 179.

Upon his arm he bare a gaie bracer,
And by his side a swerd and a bokeler,
And on that other side a gaie daggere,
Harneised wel and sharpe as point of spere:
A Cristofre on his breste of silver shene,
A horne he bare, the baudrik was of grene,
A Forster was he sothely, as I gesse.

Prologue to the Canterbury Tales.

We will now return from this long digression.

To the Honor of Clitheroe appertained a very extensive and wild domain, which was divided into the forests of Blackburnshire and Bowland,[1] as the former was subdivided into those of Pendle, Trawden, Accrington, and Rossendale; and, after the marriage of Alice de Lacy with Thomas Earl of Lancaster, all were included in the common description of foresta de Lancaster.

This, in exception to the general rule, was a forest in the strict sense of the term, before it came united to the crown, "For," saith Manwood, "the Earl of Lancaster, in the time of Edward II. and III. had a forest in the counties of Lancaster and York, in the which he did execute the forest laws as largely as ever King of this realm did; and, even at this day, there are no records so much followed as those that were executed by the said Earl in his forests."—Forest Laws, p. 72.

Those of Blackburnshire and Bowland were high and barren tracts, rejected at the first distribution of property, when townships were planted, and commons mered out in the fertile and sheltered grounds beneath; in this state they remained among the last retreats of the wolf, and the abode of stags, roes,[2] and bubali, or wild cattle, which are mentioned by Leland as remaining not long before his time at Blakeley,[3] and of which tradition records that they were transplanted into the dean's or abbot's park at Whalley, whence they are reported, on the same evidence, to have been removed after the dissolution to Gisburne park, where their descendants still remain.[4]

A domain so stocked would probably be preferred by a Norman hunter to the most

[1] This is the distribution uniformly observed in the Tower records, where, so far as I recollect, the subdivisions of the Forest of Blackburnshire are never mentioned.

[2] The existence of the roe in Bowland is pretty plainly indicated by the word roe-cross in the perambulation. But, independently of particular evidence, there can be little doubt of the fact, for, though now confined to the highlands of Scotland, it was once general in England, was referred to in the forest laws, and was mentioned by Leland as actually remaining in his time in the marches of Wales. *Vide supra.*

[3] ["Wild bores, bulles, and falcons bredde in times paste at Blakele." Itin. vii. 57.]

[4] In Mr. Bewick's History of Animals is a good account, and better engraving (for his wooden cuts have a spirit peculiar to themselves) of this animal. He mentions a tradition that they were drawn to Gisburne by the power of music: whatever truth there may be in this, there is no doubt of the general fact, that wild animals are capable of being affected very strongly by melody; and it requires not always the hand or lyre of Orpheus to work upon their feelings, for, in the year 1782, I saw at Edinburgh a stag who had followed the bagpipes of an highland regiment from his native mountains, *tractus dulcedine cantus.* [In his *History of Craven* Dr. Whitaker subsequently published a plate representing the wild cattle at Gisburne.]

fertile portion of his territories. And our ancient lords appear to have been sufficiently jealous of this part of their territories; for while they grant, with wonderful liberality, free chace and warren to their dependants over more cultivated tracts, it is always, excepting in a single instance, with a reserve of the *feræ bestiæ* within the *haiæ dominicales*,[1] and, in that one instance, the indulgence extended only to *ad unius teli jactum*.[2] The ancient deans of Whalley possessed and certainly exercised the right of hunting within the forests, which had been transmitted to them from the earliest times; but it was regarded with little complacency by the lords; and, before the translation of the abbey of Stanlaw to Whalley, Henry de Lacy extorted from Gregory, the first abbot, an express renunciation of that privilege[3], which, as he was probably no outrider that loved venery,[4] like his secular predecessors the deans, would be obtained from him without reluctance. But, at an

[1] Parks have sometimes been defined to be forests inclosed; and forests, open parks. But it appears that the forests themselves were sometimes bounded by hedges or paling, here called *haiæ dominicales*. This word is of such extent, and appears so frequently in the composition of local names amongst us, under its dialectical varieties of *hey*, *hay*, *hawe*, *hag*, *haigh*, that it may be worth while to investigate its origin, meaning, and different applications. 1st. then, Ƿæȝ the original Saxon word, signified merely a hedge, and this was softened down into the old French word *haie*, or *haye*. All the other varieties of the word are to be traced to these two sources, accordingly as different places happened to be more strongly tinctured with the old language of the country, or with that which had succeeded it. Thus the hawthorn is the hedgethorn, and the hagber (in the dialect of Lancashire), the bird cherry, is the berry of the hedge: in this sense it is used by Chaucer, "There is neither bush nor haye." R. R. But, by an easy metonymy, the word was transferred from the inclosing fence to the area inclosed by it. These were sometimes woods, sometimes pastures, and sometimes parks: of all these, instances will now be adduced. 1st. In the Pipe Rolls 17 Henry III. we have "Haga de Burchenwode." Again, Robert de Lacy grants "boscum qui vocatur la Haia de Akerington," and in Briercliffe is a wood called Haughton Hag. 2nd. The many heys in Lancashire were pastures inclosed with hedges. 3rd. Parks were frequently denominated haigh, hay, or de la haye. Thus the well-known Rothwell Haigh near Leeds (Hopkinson's MSS.) was the park belonging to the manor-house of the Lacies at Rothwell. The out-park of Skipton castle is called the hawe park, and that of Knaresborough the haye park. To these instances may be added the forest of Hay, in the marches of Wales. But this last application of the word will lead to another inquiry nearly akin to our present subject. To the ancient economy of our royal and baronial castles usually belonged two parks, one (a park inclosed with a wall, Chaucer) probably for fallow deer, after the introduction of that species; the other for red deer, fenced with a hedge and paling; or, in the words of Bracton, l. 2, c. 40, No. 3, "vallatum fuit et inclaūsatum fossato, haia, et pallatio." These were contemporary with the forests and forest laws; the park of Woodstock, which, however, is the first on record, being mentioned as early as Henry I.: so that Mr. Pennant was mistaken in supposing that parks had their origin in the destruction of forests. But in ancient times every considerable manor-house had its park, and the old patent rolls abound with *licentiæ imparcandi*.

These greater and more remote inclosures for deer, surrounded by the *fossatum*, *haia*, *et pallatium*, were the hay parks mentioned above; and the words, as well as many remains, in Musbury, Cliviger, &c., prove the manner in which these *haiæ dominicales* were constructed, viz. with a ditch and rampart surmounted by pales. This last word is, in all our ancient charters, expressed by Bracton's word *pallatium*, and the old plural form of the word pale, which was *paliz*, has given origin to Paliz-house, in Habergham-eaves, (very improperly called Palace-house,) and to the word *palliser*, or keeper of the pales, an office, so far as I know, peculiar to the forest of Knaresborough (Ext. For. de Knaresborough, MS. pen. Auct.), since grown, like Parker, Forester, &c. into a proper name, which will call to mind a pious Metropolitan of the last [the 17th] century, and a gallant Admiral of this [the 18th].

[At Shenston in Staffordshire, and at Beverley, Newsham, Sheriff Hutton, Topcliffe, and other places in Yorkshire, the same officer is called the Paler or Payler of the parke, in Harl. MS. 240.]

[2] Vide MERLAY MAGNA. [3] [See before, p. 174.] [4] Chaucer.

uncertain period during the occupancy of the Lacies, the first principle of population commenced;[1] it was found that these wilds, bleak and barren as they were, might be occupied to some advantage in breeding young and depasturing lean cattle, which were afterwards fattened in the lower domains. Vaccaries, or great upland pastures, were laid out for this purpose;[2] booths or mansions erected upon them for the residence of herdsmen; and, at the same time that herds of deer were permitted to range at large as heretofore, lawnds, by which are meant parks within a forest, were inclosed in order to chase them with greater facility, or by confinement to produce fatter venison. Of these lawnds, Bowland had Radholme and Leagram, Pendle had New and Old Lawnd, with the contiguous park of Ightenhill, Rossendale had Musbury, and Accrington Newlaund.

But in process of time, when the lords no longer visited these remote parts of their territories periodically, in order to consume their produce, these vaccaries were demised to tenants, first at will, and afterwards for years; and, in the 22nd of Henry VII. (1506–7) that wary prince first issued a commission for their approvement at advanced rents, directing, what it seems his letters patent alone were unable to perform, that they should be converted into copyholds, and held in perpetuity.

They were under the superintendance of two master foresters, one for Blackburnshire, and one for Bowland, and the former had under him an inferior keeper in each, of which that of Rossendale inhabited the chamber of the forest, and had the direction of other still inferior officers, termed graves (from the Saxon Gerefa, præpositus), or reeves of the forest.

These observations on the history and constitution of the forests are intended as an introductory sketch to render the following details more intelligible; but it may not be improper to add that they still bear the marks of original barrenness and recent cultivation, that they are still distinguished from the ancient freehold tracts around them, by want of old houses, old woods, high fences (for these were forbidden by the forest laws[3]), by peculiarities of dialect and manners in their inhabitants, and lastly, by a general air of poverty, which all the opulence of manufactures cannot remove.

To confirm these remarks, and to prevent the possibility of offence, we will call upon the old inhabitants to describe their soil and climate for themselves, which they are ready to do with great truth and simplicity. "We find," say the jurors (in the time of James I.) "that the quality of the said boothes and vaccaries is cold and barren; yet, by manuring, marling, and tilling, will yield a certain grain called oats; and, after such marling and

[1] It is to the credit of the monks that the first systematic attempt at inclosing and reclaiming any portion of these wastes was made by them. Vide Brandwood, under Rossendale.

[2] "By vaccary," saith Sir Edward Coke, "is signified a dairy house." But the following quotation will prove vaccaries to have been large upland breeding farms.

Henry VI. A.R. 9, grants a vaccary, called Batterax, for 32 *vaccæ*, 1 bull, and their issue (*exitu eorum*), both at summer pasture, and hay in winter. Vide BOWLAND.

[3] If a man have licence to inclose any ground within the forest, he may not inclose the same *cum altâ haiâ et fossato, vel cum alto pallatio.* Assiz. Forest. de Lancaster, 12 Edward III. Manwood, c. 10.

tillage, in a short time it will grow to heath, ling, and rushes." And, in an humble petition to the King, they declare, "that the soil of their country is extremely barren, and, as yet, not capable of any other corn but oats, and that in dry years, and not without continual manuring every third year, and that they have no timber trees within many miles thereof." It is difficult to read this account without shivering.[1]

The last circumstance, however, though indisputably true, is hard to be accounted for. The forests had been originally overspread with native woods of oak, hazle, birch, alder, and pine, and it is easy to conceive how these might have grown up and extended themselves, while graminivorous animals were rare upon the earth; but how, after having covered the face of the country for centuries, and after having produced, by the dropping of their seeds, a perpetual undergrowth of rising plants, they should at length decay and perish without the hand of man, is a difficulty more easy to state than to solve: yet that they did so perish is demonstrable, for the mosses abound not only with trunks, but stools of trees, too large by far to have been destroyed by beasts, yet without a vestige of the stroke of an axe, and in a state which proves them to have sunk within the surface of the earth by gradual decay. As an attempt, however, at a solution of this fact, I will hazard the following conjecture: that, after a long period of time, the rotting of neglected woods may generate too large a proportion of soil, consisting of vegetable particles alone, and that the roots of the surviving trees, unable at length to strike into the original surface of the ground, have to extract their nutriment out of a substance which the whole analogy of nature shows to be either noxious or innutritious at least, namely, the exuviæ of their own species.

Another singular fact is this, that in the peat mosses, which are known to be powerful preservers of animal substances, no horns, or other remains of deer, have ever (so far as I know) been discovered, whereas in the bogs of Ireland the skeletons and antlers of the great segh deer, a much rarer animal everywhere than the stag, are far from being unfrequent.

A third circumstance, which deserves to be attended to in the general history of these forests, as it proves not merely that they were rejected at the first colonization of the country after the Saxon conquest, but that they were antecedently in a state of nature, is, that they must have been utterly unoccupied by the Romans. This fact has been observed by antiquaries concerning our forests in general. Mr. Lambard, in particular, remarks that no monuments of Roman antiquity are to be met with in the Weald of Kent. The same reflection may be made upon the Chiltern Hills, upon Bernwood Forest, and all those parts of England which were of old uncultivated woods and deserts.[2] And

[1] In the year 1698, "a very late harvest, for there was much corne never housed, but som persons cut it and gave it there catall, and at the Newe Church in Pendle there was corne to house in the latter end of December. Mr. White, our vicar, tould me he saw some to house February 12th, which belonged to the clarke of the New Church in Pendle." MS. Journal of Thomas Braddyll, Esq.—This calamity probably has not been paralleled till the disastrous year 1799, from the effects of which the poor of this country are now (May 1800) suffering many of the horrors of famine.

[2] Bishop Kennet's Par. Ant. p. 11.

accordingly, in our Blackburnshire chaces, I know not that a coin, fibula, or other trifling relic has ever been discovered, to prove that they had ever been traversed by that active people. Bowland alone, from its situation, was unavoidably crossed by the great road[1] from Coccium to Bremetonacæ.

We will now go on to a particular survey of the Forest of Blackburnshire, considered, 1st, with respect to its general history; 2nd, with respect to that of its four subordinate divisions. The first important transaction affecting this forest, in general, is explained by the following

Commission for Grauntinge of the Forrests,

In anno vicesimo secundo Henrici septimi.

Henry, by the grace of God, Kinge of Englande and of France, and Lorde of Irelande, to our trustie and well-beloved the Stewarde that nowe is, and that hereafter shall be, of our possessions of Blakburne-shyre, within our countie palatyne of Lancaster, greeting. For so much as heretofore we, by our l'res of commission under the seale of our dutchie of Lancaster, have deputed and appointed Sir John Boothe and others to vewe and survey all our groundes, castles, and lordshyps within our said countie palatyne, and thereupon to improove the same and every parcel of them for our most singuler profitt and advantage, whereupon we understand that our said commissioners have indeavoured themselves, surveying and approving the same accordinge to our saide commission and pleasure, and have made graunte and promisse of lease of certaine of our landes and tenements within our saide county, to the tenor and effect of a schedule to these our l'res annexed, to certaine persons, to have and to hould to them and their heires for terme of lyfe or lyves, or for terme of yeares after the custome of the manor by copie of court roll, for execution and accomplishment whereof we have authorized, and by these presentes authorize and geve you full authoritie and power by these our l'res, callinge unto you the saide Sir John Boothe, and by his advyse to sett and lett all suche of our said landes and tenements as bee or lye within your said office, to the said personns for suche rents yearlie as bee contained in the said schedule, to have and to houlde to them and to their heires or otherwise, for terme of liefe or yeares, at the libertie or choise of our said tenantes, and for the full accomplishment of the said promisse and graunte, taking sufficient security of the said persons for the sure paimente of the same rente, as yee shall see best and most convenient. And also that upon the death or exchaunge of everie tenant, that yee make newe lease or leases to such personne or personnes after the deathe or exchaunge of any such tenant or tenants of the same, as the same land shall happen to be granted by you, takinge of everie suche tenant as shall happen to exchaunge or decease, one whole yeares rent of the said tenemt. and that yee shall take for a fine, accordinge as other our tenentes there, beinge copiehoulders, tyme out of mynd gave and used to paie in suche cases, over and above their ancient and oulde yearelie rent of the same, provyded and alwaie foreseene that yee, by color of your said leases, doe not demyse our said rent, fynes and gersomes, nor other duties, due and demandeable for us in that parte. And these our l'res shal bee unto you at all tymes sufficient warant and discharge in this behalfe; whiche our l'res wee will that yee doe enter into your court rolles, there to remaine of recorde for the more suertie of everie of our said tenants, for their saide

[1] A considerable portion of this road was lately uncovered in the estate of Knolmere, where it appeared to be a pavement of broad and heavy stones, very artificially wedged and compacted together. But the most extraordinary circumstance was, that no wheel-carriage had, as far as could be discovered, ever traversed it. It follows, therefore, that the baggage of the Roman armies, except what was borne by the legionaries themselves, was wholly conveyed along these mountainous districts on horseback. This difficulty of conveyance will partly account for a fact which I have already stated as highly probable; that the line from Ribchester to Overborrow was abandoned, in the reign of Philip, for that which passed by Blackrod and Lancaster.

leases, to bee had and made accordinglie. Geven at our cittie of London, under the seale of our saide duchie, the 19th daie of Maie, in the 17th yeare of our reigne. (1502).

The effects of this commission will be explained hereafter. But it may be necessary to observe here, that it was a commission to approve and not to disforest; as the following example, in which especial provision was made for the preservation of the deer, will abundantly prove:

"Feely Close always hath beene agisted to ye sume of IX*l*. XI*s*. VIII*d*. and noe more, because of ye recourse yt ye deere of Pendle hathe thereunto, and yt was thought by us that they should have the same yt saveinge ye like course of deere as hath been used afore." Comm. Henry VII. *ut supra.*

Other facts to the same purpose will occur under Rossendale.

In consequence of this commission grants of the vaccaries were made, and upon the faith of these titles, houses were built, and improvements, such as the soil was capable of, were made; lands were bought and sold; the first grantees died off, and their heirs or other representatives were regularly admitted in perfect security for more than a century, when the Crown lawyers of James I. discovered, or pretended to discover, that copyholds of inheritance could not be created, that the lands of the newhold tenure were of the nature of essart lands, and the occupants a sort of tenants by sufferance. This was a thunderstroke, as it shook to the foundation the titles to twenty-five thousand Lancashire acres of land, and destroyed the comforts and the hopes of many families who lived in competence and quiet upon these new improvements, without any other resources.

It may not be uninteresting, at least to the descendants of the parties concerned, to give a short abstract of the proceedings in this transaction.

1st. An Information exhibited by Sir John Brograve, Knt. in the Duchy chamber, against Richard Townley of Townley, Richard Shuttleworth of Gawthorp, Nic. Townley of Royle, Nic. Banastre of Altham, Esqrs. &c. who have unlawfully, according to their pretended titles, without any title, right, custom, warrant, or authority, entered and intruded into certain lands, parcels of the honor, castle, manor, or lordship of Clitheroe, in the manors of Colne, Accrington, and Ightenhill, and in the forests or chases of Rossendale, Pendle, Accrington, Trawden, &c.

2d. A letter directed to Mr. Auditor Fanshaw, and Ralph Asheton, of Lever, Esq. deputy steward, signifying that there were within his Majesty's Honor of Clitheroe divers lands which have been only granted by the steward, and by warrant to the steward made, which parcels have been improved out of his Majesty's forests and chases, there commonly called lands of the newhold, which are only, however, of the nature of essart land, and cannot be claimed by custom or prescription to be copyholds,[1] &c. offering, however, in his Majesty's name, to perfect their respective titles to the said essart lands, and requiring them to convene the tenants, in order to receive proposals from them for that purpose.

Dated Ap. 5th, 1607. And signed J. SUFFOLK, H. NORTHAMPTON, SALISBURY.

[1] The lawyers evidently mistook the meaning of this word (*essart*), which they confounded with purpresture or encroachment: whereas essarts were often held by the firmest titles, and nothing was more common than for the ancient lords to grant lands, *essartas et essartandas:* which would be nonsense, if rendered encroached and to be encroached.

3d. Next follow a set of articles to be inquired of and presented by the jurors, concerning the nature, extent, and other particulars of the lands commonly called newhold.

4th. Then a presentment of the booths within Rossendale, and of the rents severally paid by each, with distinct and particular answers to the articles of inquiry.

5th. The humble petition of a multitude of his Majesty's tenants and copyholders, stating their claim under the commissions of Henry VII.; their long undisturbed possession; the regularity of their admissions; the barrenness of the country; the great sums which they and their ancestors had expended upon improvements; the extreme distress to which they were reduced by staying the ordinary course of admittances (which it seems had been resorted to in order to force them to a composition); and praying that the said restraint of accustomed admittances may be repealed, &c.

6th. A tender of a confirmation of the respective titles of the tenants to the newhold lands, by decree and act of parliament, on the payment of twenty years' ancient rent.

Dated May 16th, 1608. Signed Salisbury. Julius Cæsar. Tho. Parrie.

7th. A letter from Rich. Townley, of Townley, Esq. and others, relating to a general contribution towards soliciting and defraying the expences of this business, and stating that, through the fantastical persuasion of the vulgar sorte that handes set to an instrument will bind them to they know not what inconveniences, they are enforced to rest only on promises: now, in respect the vulgar sorte is knowne to be variable and may alter from this 2d resolution, least the peevishness of some few should disadvantage or discredit our undertaking, we are of opinion that this, by Mr. Auditor's and your good meanes made known to the Privy Council, will worke such effect, y^t according to ye proverbe, "The fryers shall not be beaten for the nunnes' fault."

Signed, Ric. Towneley. Edw. Rausthorn. And others.

The superior proprietors were evidently aware of their own danger, and willing to compound for their estates upon any reasonable terms, but had to encounter that levity, selfishness, and obstinacy in the lower orders, which, as long as human nature is the same, will encumber and embitter all public concerns in which they have any part.

8th. A number of letters and instructions from Sir Thomas Walmsley, knt. one of the justices of the Common Pleas, and Ralph Ashton, esq. commissioners concerning the four forests, the last addressed to Robert Cecil, Earl of Salisbury, treasurer, and Sir Thomas Parry, knt. chancellor of the Duchy, reporting the progress they had made, and stating the several difficulties which occurred.

9th. A commission from the Crown stating that a general agreement had taken place for the confirmation of the titles to the newhold, at twelve years' rent (not twenty, which was first demanded), and for assessing the mean rates of payment, directed to Sir Tho. Walmsley, kt. Ralph Ashton, Tho. Walmsley, John Braddyll, Rob. Holden, Ric. Greenacres, Savile Radcliffe, esqs. Lau. Habergham, gent. &c. Dated Nov. 17th, 1608.

10. Then after several intermediate steps of little consequence follows the decree for the assurance of titles within the four forests, February 1608.

11th. And, lastly, an Act of the 7th Jac. 4 Sess. entitled, an Act for the perfect creation and confirmation of certain copyhold lands in the honor, castle, manor, and lordship of Clitheroe, or in the severall Mannors or Lordshippes of Derby, Accarington, Colne, and Ightenhill, in the county of Lancaster. (Private Act No. 3.)

The consideration paid for this assurance was 12 years' ancient rent, or 3,763*l.*; and thus the poverty of James I. and the chicane of the Crown lawyers, by an act of temporary oppression, conferred a most substantial benefit upon the tenants of the Newhold, and opened the way to many subsequent inclosures and improvements. In fact this transaction appears to have been but a part of a general scheme carrying on at the same time for extorting money from the tenants of the Crown whose titles were not perfectly secure. The attempt at a resumption of the Border Lands held in cornage,[1] on pretence that, upon the Union of the Two Crowns, service in cornage had necessarily ceased, was a parallel instance.

Whatever might be the deficiency of the Act of 7th Jac. this composition appears to have been set aside, and much severer terms imposed, as will appear from the following fragment [of a Petition to Parliament], which proves the matter not to have been finally settled before the Restoration :

. . . . of Clitherowe, parcel of the Duchy [of Lancaster] upon the King's behalf by the then Attorney of the Dutchy . . . . . ll in qu . . . . . and the inclosures and improvements of Commons [upon th]em made; upon a Commission for that purpose issued in the . . . . . year of King James his reign, came to composition with his Majesties Commissioners, and agreed to pay for confirmation and settlement thereof forty years' copyhold rent: the one moiety upon passing Decrees for that purpose in the Court of Dutchy Chamber, and the other moiety within one moneth next after the same should be confirmed by Act of Parliament.

Decrees of all the several manors and places so compounded for were passed, and the first moiety of the Composition Money thereupon paid in King James his time: And in the sixteenth year of the late King Charles a Bill for confirmation thereof passed both the Houses of Parliament; but through the distractions then growing was prevented of being perfected by the royal assent.

The said late King Charles in the fifth year of his reign granted by letters patents the second moiety of the said Composition Money remaining in the Copyholders' hands to the Navy and Tower Creditors towards satisfaction of certain debts contracted by Sir Allen Apsley in victualling the Navy and Tower: who in the year 1650 obtained from the pretended Parliament then sitting an Act to confirm to the said Copyholders their customs and improvements according to the said Compositions and Decrees: and to compell them to pay the remaining moiety of Composition Money to the said Creditors, with a *nomine pœnæ* of £5 *per diem* upon default of payment after the 1st of September next following.

Several of the Copyholders failed in providing their money, which caused their deficiency of payment according to the Act. But the *nomine pœnæ* being great and the Creditors severe in levying it according to the power given them, those that were careful of preserving their estates and preventing further damage procured and paid the whole moiety, together with a great overplus, amounting to £5,833 in all, for satisfaction of the said moiety and *nomine pœnæ* forfeited, and so freed themselves and many others who are still behinde with their due proportionable parts, and yet have no security for confirmation of their customs and estates.

All which considered, the said Copyholders, having long since, as aforesaid, paid their whole composition to the King's use, do humbly pray the said Decrees and their Customes may be confirmed according to their contract by the Parliament, and that power may be given to certain Commissioners to leavy the moneys in arrear and reimburse to those that have laid out above their proportions so much as shall reduce the payments and account to an equality and due proportion according to a Bill prepared for that purpose.

[1] *Vide* Burn and Nicolson's History of Cumberland and Westmorland. [4to. 1777, vol. i. pp. 16 et seq. But it has been shown in an essay by Francis Morgan Nichols, esq., F.S.A., printed in the Archæologia, vol. xxxix. pp. 349-356, that Littleton and all legal writers have been mistaken in understanding cornage to have been derived from the winding of a horn at the approach of the Scots or any other enemy. It was really a tax on horned cattle, equivalent to the Saxon *Horngeld*.]

The Forest of Blackburnshire was subdivided into those of Pendle, Trawden, Rossendale, and Accrington. Of these in order.

[*Copia scripti de Blakeburnschire.*

(This is very likely the *comune chartre* deposited at Whalley: see p. 265, note.)

Henry de Lacy counte de Nichole et conestable de Cestre a toutz ceaux qe cest escrit verrount ou orrount Salutz en nostre Seignour. Sachez nous avoir graunte et par cest nostre present escrit conferme a touz nos fraunkes homes de Blakeburnschir qe eaux et lours heirs et toutz lours tenauntz a toutz jours mes soient quites des alures de nostre chastel de Cliderhou a fere et a piture du chival nostre chief forester et de son garceon les queux soloient sojourner a custages du payis. Nous avons ensement graunte pur nous et pur nos heirs qe si nule manere de beste sauvage soit trove morte deynz les devises de Blakeburnschir qe par ceo pas ne soient chalengez grevez ne amerciez tout soit ceo qe ils ne troveisent ne ne presentent par ky cele beste soit morte. Sauve a nous et a nos heirs nostre querel vers les meffesours quant nous troverons queux ils serrount. Ensement nous volouns et grauntons pur nous et pur nos heirs qe la ou nous et nos auncestres solions avoir en Blakeburnschir deux seriaunts a chival et deux au pee qe desormes ne eions nuls ne nos heirs a nul jour en Blakeburnschir forsqe un soul seriaunt a cheval ovesqe un garceon pur son chival garder et un soul seriaunt au pee a custages du payis. Issi ne purquant qe quant mester serra le garceon le seriaunt soit receu et condu pur seriaunt a pee pur office de seriaunt faire. Et qe nul boef de seysine ne soit prys par nous ne par nos heirs ne par nos seneschals de nul de nos fraunkes homes avantditz ne de lour tenauntz fors taunt soulement de ceus qe teynent par service de Chyvaler ou en Thaynage et de ceaux soit nul boef prys tauntqe al heir soit rendu seysine de sa terre. Toutes cestes fraunchises allegeaunces et fraunche custumes volouns et grantouns pur nous et pur nos heirs qe toutz nos fraunks homes de Blakeburnschir et lours heirs et lours tenauntz ayent et tienent a toutz jours Issi qe nous ne nos heirs rien de droit ne de claym ne puissons a nul jour vers eaux demander ne chalenger en les services et les custumes qe par cest escrit sount relessez ou a eaux rechargier de nulle chose encountre les allegeaunces a eaux par cest escrit grauntez. Sauve a nous et a nos heirs toutes autres maneres de services et de custumes a nous dues et acustumes le queux ne sount mye par cest escrit relessez. Et hors prys en tout cest graunt Sire Robert de Holland et Elizabeth sa feme et lours heirs, Sire Johan Devias et Cecile sa feme, et lours heirs et toutz les tenauntz de Samelsbyr les queux nous forepreneuns pur ceo qils ount escrit severamment par eaux. Et qe toutes cestes choses avauntdites soient fermes et establies a toutz jours a ceo nostre present escrit avouns fait mettre nostre seal a ces tesmoignes, Sire Will'm de Botiller, Robert le fitz Roger, Will'm le Vavasseur, Johan de Hodleston, James de Nevile, Wauter Bek, Will'm de Stopham, Wakelyn de Arderne, Adam de Hodleston, Robert de Hertford, chyvalers. (Coucher Book, p. 1161.)

Quitclaim of Maurice Abbot of Kirkstall to Margaret Countess of Lincoln and Pembroke of 20 wagon loads of timber from the Forest of Blackburnshire, for an annuity of 10*s*.

Omnibus Christi fidelibus ad quos littere presentes pervenerint Mauricius Abbas de Kirkestal et ejusdem loci Conventus salutem eternam in Domino. Noverit universitas vestra nos quietum clamasse domine Margarete Comitisse Lincoln et Penbr' meremium viginti plaustrorum quod capere consuevimus in tercia parte foreste de Blakeburnsyre ipsam Margaretam Comitissam contingentem nomine dotis sue quoad vixerit pro decem solidis argenti quibus nobis assignavit idem Comitissa per litteras suas patentes recipiendis apud Pontefractum die Sancti Egidii singulis annis tota vita sua de Ballivo suo de Blakeburnsyr qui pro tempore fuerit. In cujus rei testimonium has litteras nostras dicte Comitisse fieri fecimus patentes. Dat' apud Hauton in crastino sancti Benedicti Abbatis anno regni Regis Henrici tricesimo tercio (22 March, 1249). (Great Coucher of the Duchy, I. 80.)

Charges of Queen Isabella against the Abbot of Whalley and others for Transgressions in the Forest.

Abbas de Whalleye distringitur ad respondendum domine Isabelle Regine Anglie de quibusdam transgressionibus eidem Regine factis. Abbas venit et calumpniatus est, quod fecit servientes suos scindere diversas quercus virides et siccas in bosco de Romesgreve et cum plaustris suis per diversas vices eas cariare apud Whalleye injuste, ad dampnum

Regine xls. Abbas venit et dicit quod emit Buscam[1] in bosco de Romesgreve quam fecit scindere et cariare et nullam aliam per preceptum suum, nec ipso sciente, et super hoc tetendit legem, et habet diem ad faciendam legem suam ad proximum, *etc.*

Idem Abbas calumpniatus est quod ipse et Arnaldus de Emmeseye commonachus suus injuste fugaverunt diversa animalia agistata ad herbagium Regine de Brendewod per Ministros Regine usque faldam Regine de Roclif et ibidem ea imparcaverunt, Ita quod Regina agistamenta eorum amisit, ad dampnum Regine xl s. Abbas dicit quod ipse et dictus Arnaldus animalia inventa in suo separali fugaverunt, et in falda sua propria imparcaverunt et non in falda Regine, et super hoc tetendit legem. Et habet diem *etc.*

Idem Abbas calumpniatus est quod Adam de Bradeschagh commonachus suus cum aliis injuste fugavit C. animalia ad herbagium Regine quod positum fuit in defensa pro salvagio Regine, ita quod per eadem averia dictum herbagium depastum fuit et calcatum ad dampnum Regine lx s. Et quia dictus Adam de Bradeschagh non est presens, dictus Abbas habet diem suum ad proximum, *etc.*

Idem Abbas calumpniatus est, quod J(ohannes) de Rad(eclyve) Custos terre Regine in Blakeburnschire et Bouland per preceptum domine Regine et consilii fecit seisire in manu Regine diversa terras et tenementa que dictus Abbas adquisivit infra dominium de Blakeburnschire. Idem Abbas post seisinam captam nomine Regine, dicta terras et tenementa manu operabatur et proficuum suum inde fecit, et predictam seisinam fregit ad dampnum Regine C. s. Abbas dicit quod habuit licenciam de dicta domina Regina ad adquirendas xxx libratas terre infra dominium suum in Comitatu Lancastrie, qui tantas terras adhuc non adquisivit ibidem, et quod terras et tenementa que sic adquisivit manu operabatur et proficuum suum inde fecit, sicut ei bene licuit, sed nullam injuriam dicte Regine fecit. Dictum est eidem Abbati per Seneschallum quod ulterius responderet ad querelas. Abbas dicit quod satis sufficienter respondit, et petit judicium. Et judicium ponitur in respectu pro defectu judicis.

Idem Abbas calumpniatus est quod fecit purpresturam de vasto Regine apud Blakeburn ad dampnum Regine C. s. Abbas dicit quod nullam purpresturam de vasto Regine fecerat ibidem. Et super hoc tetendit legem. (Addit. MS. 10,374, f. 128.)

Littera domini Regis missa Johanni de Radecliff ad liberand' decimas de agistiamentis, fenis, et omnibus aliis rebus decimabilibus.

E. per la grace de Dieu *etc.* a notre bien ame Johan de Radeclif Seneschal des terres notre treschere dame et myere de Bouland et de Blakeburnschir saluz. Notre cher en Dieu Labbe de Wh(alleye) nous monstra nadgaires coment il avoit demande dismes des Ministres et tenauntz notre dite dame et Miere de sa Seignourie suisdite parochens le dite Abbe de sa eglise de Wh(alley), cestasavoir de feyn, agistemen'ez et autres choses dismables, et sur ceo vous luy respondistes, que par resoun que tieles dismes ne furent mye paiez illoeques devaunt ces houres, et notre dite dame et Miere nad estat en la dite Seignourie forsque a terme de sa vie, la reversion ent a nous regardaunt, vous nosastes tel charge surmettre a la dite Seignourie, ne a les tenauntz dy celle saunz assent et comandemente de nous. Et pour ceo que nous estoioms bien enfourmez, que dismes sont dues a Seynte eglise de tous lieux parsitz surdaunte deyniz les boundes de paroche, et nyent voisauntz que ceo que appartient de droit a Dieu et a Seynte eglise soit southretrete par nous ne par les noz: vous signifiasmes par nous autres lettres que en cas que les dites dismes ne feussent detenuez par autre cause si noun par resoun que eles ne ount mye estie paiez avaunt ceste houre, que adonques feissez ordyner, qe dismes feussent paiez au dit Abbe de foyn agistementz et toutes autres choses dismables deynz les boundes de sa paroche avantdite. Nient countresteaunt qil nen ad estie seisi devaunt ces houres. Et ja auoms entenduz iqe coment qe par vertue de notre dit comandement vous avez fait liverere audit Abbe certeynes parcells de dismes susdites, niyentmeyns vous luy avez detenuz et detenez uncore les dismes des agistementz et de southboys deynz la dite Seignourie en prejudice de luy et de sa eglise avant dite, per qi vous mandoms, qe si ensi soit adonqes luy facez deliverere et soeffrez avoir et enjoyere entierement meismes les dismes, cestasavoir si bien des agistementz et de southboys come dautres choses solome leffect de notre primer mandement avauntdite. Et ceo ne lessez. Done souz notre prive seal a Westm' le xvi jour de Juyl. Lan de notre regne Dangleterre vyntisme second et de France noefisme. (16 July 1348.) (Addit. MS. 10,374, f. 7.)

[1] Ligni seu arboris stipes, caudex focarius, Gall. *Busche.* Du Cange.

CUSTOMS OF THE HONOR OF CLITHEROE.

The Customs of the several Manors and Copyhold Lands within the Honor of Clithero in the County of Lancaster are as followeth, Per Jer. Ainsworth 1670.

The said Honor of Clithero doth consist of these several manors, viz.: 1. Chadburn, 2. Worston, 3. Pendleton, 4. Colne, 5. Ightenhill or *Heigham*, 6. Ackrington, 7. Tottington and 8. the wapentake copyhold lands of Blackburn parish; and their several courts are and, time out of mind, have been holden and kept as followeth:[1]

Chatburn.—Chatburn, Worston, and Pendleton be three little manors, having only one court kept for them altogether at Clithero Castle, which is called an Halmot Court, and is both a court leet and copyhold court.

The greaves[2] of the manors do make return of jurors at the court in manner (to wit), for Worston one, for Pendleton two, and for Chatburn three, and so after this rule and proportion until a full jury be returned.

Colne.—The manor of Colne consisteth of ancient copyhold land and the Forest of Trawden, and these have the like court, which is kept at Colne, and either of them a greave, and these greaves do make return either of them a jury.

Ightenhill.—The manor of Ightenhill likewise consisteth of copyhold lands, whose halmot court is kept at Burnley, and of the Forest of Pendle, which hath a halmot court within itself at Heigham.

Ackrington.—The manor of Ackrington Old, Huncote, and Haslingden, which are ancient copyhold lands, and of Ackrington New and Rossendale, which are forest lands, and all these have one halmot court kept together at Ackrington, and two grand juries, the one returned by the greaves of Ackrington Old and Haslingden and the rest by Ackrington New and Rossendale.

Tottington.—The manor of Tottington hath one halmot court, which is kept at Halcome within the said manor, wherein is no forest lands, and therefore hath but one grand jury for the said manor; there is likewise a court leet there kept for that which was called the fee of Tottington, which consisted of these several townships (to wit), Bury, Middleton, Chatterton and Foxdenton, and Ackrington, at which said court leet these several townships have time out of mind appeared as at their proper leet, and the constables of these towns make return of juries to inquire and present as followeth (to wit), Bury 4 men, Middleton 4, Chatterton and Foxdenton 4, and Ackrington 2.

The bailiff is Thomas Greenhalgh, Esq. who hath the same of inheritance, and to him all precepts concerning this court leet are directed. The suitors which are called and appear at this court leet are Charles Earl of Derby for Bury; Sir Ralph Ashton, Knt. and Bart. for Middleton; Edward Ashton, Esq. for Chatterton and Foxdenton; Robert Lever, Esq. for Ackrington.

[1] The General Courts of the Duke of Buccleuch and Queensberry, for the several manors and forests within the Honor of Clitheroe, are now usually holden as follows:—

The Halmot Court and Court Baron for the Manor of Chatburn, Worston, and Pendleton, at Clitheroe Castle.

The Halmot Courts and Courts Baron for the several Manors of Accrington Old-hold and Accrington New-hold, at the Court House in Haslingden.

The Halmot Court and Court Baron for the Manor of Tottington, at the National School in Ramsbottom.

The Halmot Court and Court Baron for the Manor of Ightenhill, at the Court House in Burnley.

The Halmot Courts and Courts Baron for the Manor of Colne, and Forest of Trawden, at the Court House in Colne.

The Halmot Court and Court Baron for the Forest of Pendle, at the Court House in Higham.

The Audit is afterwards holden at Clitheroe Castle.

[2] The reeves, or bailiffs: see p. 284.

The several halmot courts before mentioned are commonly kept twice in the year, (to wit) within a month after Easter and within a month after Michaelmas, but may be by the custom kept oftener if need require, and have been kept at all times in the year.

The Court of Wapentake of Blackburn parish is kept every three weeks, at which court all those wapentake copyholders receive their admittances and have all their transactions concerning their copyhold lands and not elsewhere.

The said halmot courts have power by their custom to try all kinds of real actions as at the common law in form and nature of all kinds of writs there, and these are to be tried within all the manors (saving Tottington), a jury of twenty-four copyholders to be returned by the greaves, out of every manor a certain number, and in the manor of Tottington by twelve within their own manor, and in Wapentake likewise by twelve of their own copyholders.

The said halmot courts have likewise power by their custom to hold plea of any sum whatsoever in all kinds of actions and are not limited.

A copyholder of the Newhold or Forest cannot be empanneled and sworn upon a jury of the Oldhold, nor on the contrary, although they be all of one manor.

If a copyholder be presented by the homage for wrongful withholding of lands, &c. from another, the steward or his deputy may give time at his discretion for a traverse to be entered thereupon, and if the person presented do not enter his traverse within the time limited to be tried the next court, and sufficient pledges within the same manor, and hold to answer for the mesne profits, the steward may grant his warrant to the greave to give possession of the same lands to him from whom they were withholden.

If a copyholder have been in quiet possession of lands by the space of three years and upwards, no presentment lieth against him for wrongful withholding of the same lands, but the party grieved may bring his action for the same.

If a copyholder be disturbed in his quiet possession of any lands, ways, or privileges which he enjoyeth and hath quietly enjoyed for the space of three years past, the steward may grant his warrant to the greave to keep him in quiet possession thereof till the next court, and afterwards as he shall see cause.

If any copyholder or other person shall resist the greave in the execution of any of the warrants abovesaid or of any other warrant to him directed by the steward, the steward or his deputy may commit such persons to the castle of Clitheroe, there to be and remain till their submission.

Copyhold lands are surrendered by the rod, and may be surrendered in open court in the hands of the lord by the steward or his deputy, or out of court a surrender may be received by the steward or his deputy or greave or by a copyholder of the same manor where the lands that are surrendered do lye.

A surrender may be received by a copyholder of the same manor where the surrendered lands do lye or by the steward or his deputy or greave, otherwise the surrender is void.

A surrender may be kept in the hands of a customary tenant unpresentable till the court day, if all the parties concerned therein do agree thereunto, but if the said customary tenant be required to present the same surrender at the first or second court and he refuse or neglect so to do he is to be presented and amerced.

If a surrender be not presented into the court at the third court day (or before) it afterwards becomes void, except the customary tenant who received the same die or go out of the county before the third court day, in such cases the surrender may after it shall be found be brought in the court and be presented by the homage although the third court day be past, and such surrender is in force.

If a copyholder who receiveth a surrender do keep the same in his hands unpresented past the third court day, or doth cancel or lose the same or wilfully denieth to present the same, and being presented by the homage, in this case he forfeiteth his copyhold lands to the lord of the manor.

A copyholder may by the custom surrender his copyhold lands to another for warranty and security of monies or any other condition, which being performed before the third court day, such conditional surrender may be countermanded and cancelled without any danger to the customary tenant who received it.

Copyhold lands within the said honor cannot be entailed, and if any more than one use be expressed in a surrender it is void; but a copyholder may surrender his lands to one, two, or more feoffees or trustees, and the uses may be declared in an intent or schedule annexed to the same surrender, or by the last will and testament of the surrenderor, or by any other his act to which the surrender hath relation, and the *cesti que use* hath only an equitable estate in the same lands.

If a *cesti que use* in copyhold lands be capable or liable to do suit and service at court, may they receive a surrender? They may.

If a copyholder surrender his lands to another, and he dieth before his admittance, his next heir is to be admitted thereunto after he be found and presented by the homage.

If a copyholder die seized of copyhold lands, his heir at the next court is to be presented by the homage and admitted thereunto, and to pay unto the lord of the manor a fine, and they do defend according to the course of common law.

The wife of a copyholder who dieth seized of copyhold lands is dowable of a fourth part thereof for her life, and may bring her action for the same in the halmot court in the nature of a writ of dower.

The husband may surrender immediately to the use of the wife, or the wife to the use of the husband.

If a copyholder surrender lands to another for life or years, he to whom the surrender is made may assign over the same land by will or any other act without surrender during the same term.

If a surrender be presented into the court, and the person to whose use the surrender is made come not to receive his admittance, after three solemn proclamations made at three several courts, he is to be amerced.

A copyholder may by the custom surrender his copyhold lands by an attorney.

A copyholder may demise his lands for one year, and no longer without a surrender; if he let it longer without surrender, he is to be presented and amerced.

After three proclamations be made at one and the same court, he to whom the surrender is made is to be admitted by the steward or his deputy, and if on the same proclamation any person come to forbid and enter his claim to the same lands, the person to whose use the surrender is made is to find a pledge (to wit) a copyholder of the same manor, and hold the mean profits of the same lands in case he that forbids shall recover the same.

If any person shall enter such forbid or claim, he is to bring his action for the same lands within three courts, or otherwise the same forbid or claim shall be void.

If any forbid or claim be granted in open court, it only debars him who granted the same and not any after him.

Every copyholder on his admittance is to pay to the lord of the manor one year's ancient rent for the same land and no more for a fine.

A copyholder (by the custom) may be tenant by the courtesy of England, in like manner as of a freehold inheritance at the common law.

1. A tenant in copyhold for one, two, or three lives may (for prevention of occupancy) assign his term without surrender; but the assignee, or, for want thereof, the occupant must pay a fine to the lord, and so must he that takes bankrupt lands. According to the statute of Eliz. 30, ch. 1.

2. If a copyholder in the court be called and returned to be sworn of the homage, and refuseth to be sworn without shewing to the court any lawful and reasonable excuse, he forfeiteth his copyhold land until he shall submit and pay a reasonable fine as the court shall amerce.

3. 'Tis said that if a copyholder purchase land it will descend first to the heirs of the father's side and then to the heirs of the mother's side.

4. If a copyholder (to wit) tenant for life or years or tenant in fee simple or tail, commit waste voluntary or permissive, that this waste is a forfeiture of the copyhold tenements so wasted, during their respective estates in the same, until such time as the same shall be put into sufficient repair, and such forfeiture will bring a new fine to the lord upon the new admitted.

5. If a thief steal goods and by strict pursuit leaveth the goods within the manor, that the said goods (as waifs) belong to the lord of the manor.

6. If a copyholder be outlawed for any criminal offence, as murder, felony, or the like, the same maketh a forfeiture, but the lord is not to have benefit until presentment be made by the homage.

7. If any person come to untimely death without fault of any reasonable creature, the cause of his death is a deodand, and belongs to the lord of the manor.

8. If a tenant (by copy) surrender generally into the hands of the lord, and it doth not appear who shall have the land nor to whose use the surrender is made, then the lord shall be seized to his own use.

9. A tenant hath right to all wood, timber, and underwoods, slate mines, flags, and free power to get the same for his own use, or to sell the same within the manor for repairing the housing within the same, but not to sell the same to strangers or such as dwell out of the manor.

10. The heir of a copyholder is not liable to pay debts upon judgment, obligation, or any other debt; and that if the lord enter into statute or take a wife, and after the land falls into the lord's hand by surrender, forfeiture, or otherwise, his land whilst it is in his lord's hands is liable to the charge; but if he grant it again to the tenant according to the custom, the copyholder shall hold his estate discharged because he is in by custom which is paramount the grant.

11. An heir of copyhold land is heir before admittance and hath power to enter in the lands and take the profits thereof, to punish trespassors and to defend his possession, but cannot bring a real plaint before his admittance.

12. Where a father hath a son and a daughter by one venter and son by another, the possession of the brother, upon death of his father (though his brother die before admittance) will make his sister heir, and the land would escheat to the lord rather [than] the son by the second venter should take as heir to the first brother or sister; and before admittance the right heir may sell, the purchaser paying a double fine to the lord.

13. The tenant paying his rents and performing his services is no more tenant at will (*by the decree or late act made for confirmation thereof*), is free from arbitrary impositions, and only liable to pay his rents, &c. and observance of the customs aforesaid.

The last thirteen rules were laid down amongst many others in the manor court of survey at Slaidburn in the year 1662.

(This document has been communicated to the present edition of this work by Capt. Grimshaw, of Grange, late of Burnley. It has been submitted by the Editors to Mr. Dixon Robinson, the present Chief Steward of the Honor, who has had the kindness to peruse it, and to examine the archives under his care, but he states that no such Customs are upon record. So far as the Editors are informed, the Customs of the Honor of Clitheroe have not hitherto appeared in any book, but they were printed (differing in various particulars from the present copy) on loose sheets, at Bury, in 1793.)

PENDLE FOREST.

The Forest of Pendle was so called from the celebrated mountain of that name, over the long declivity of which it extended. The name of this mountain is an instance of the gradual operation of language upon the names of natural permanent objects. Having been originally denominated *Pen* or the head, its first appellation becoming insignificant the Saxons superadded *hull*, and *Penhull* was its orthography probably before the Conquest; but the latter syllable in turn lost its meaning by being melted down into *Pendle*; and the modern "hill" was once more superadded, to design the nature of the object. The perpendicular elevation of this mountain, after many attempts and notwithstanding the facility of obtaining a base line from the sea, has never been exactly ascertained;[1] but it is an enormous mass of matter, extending in a long ridge from N.E. to S.W. and on the S.E. side forming a noble boundary to the forest, which stretches in a long but interrupted descent of nearly five miles to the Water of Pendle, a barren and dreary tract excepting on the verge of the latter, which is warm and fertile.[2]

A Paper written by Mr. Charles Townley, and directed by him to Richard Townley, Esq. the Philosopher.—*From Addenda to the Third Edition.*

On August the 18th, 1669, between nine and ten o'clock in the morning, there issued out of the north-west side of Pendle Hill a great quantity of water, the particulars of which eruption, as I received them from a gentleman living hard by, are these: the water continued running for about two hours. It came in that quantity and so suddenly that it made a breast of a yard high, not unlike (as the gentleman expressed it) to the eager at Roan in Normandy or Ouse in Yorkshire. It grew unfordable in so short a space that two going to church on horseback, the one having passed the place where it took its course, the other being a little behind, could not pass this sudden torrent. It endangered breaking down a mill-dam, came into several houses in Worston (a village at the foot of the hill), so that several things swam in them. It issued out at five or six several places, one of which was considerably bigger than the rest, and brought with it nothing else but stone, gravel, and earth. He moreover told that the greatest of these six places closed up again, and that the water was black like unto moss pits: and, lastly, that fifty or sixty years[3] ago there happened an eruption much greater than this, so that it much endamaged the adjacent country, and made two cloughs or dingles, which to this day are called Burst or (in our Lancashire dialect) Brast Cloughs.

Thus far this gentleman related—what follows take from myself. Going since this to see what I could of this accident, I found nothing that did contradict the abovesaid relation. What I observed more, con-

[1] [According to the Ordnance survey the height is 1,831 feet above the level of the sea.]

[2] I knew not whether it be worth while to relate, that the gloomy enthusiast George Fox professed to have received his first illuminations on the top of Pendle. *Vide* Lesley's Snake in the Grass. ["As we travelled on (from Bradford) we came near a very great and high hill, called Pendle Hill, and I was moved of the Lord to go to the top of it; which I did with much ado, it was so very steep and high. When I was come to the top of this hill, I saw the sea bordering upon Lancashire: and from the top of this hill the Lord let me see in what places he had a great people to be gathered. As I went down I found a spring of water in the side of the hill, [probably Robin Hood's well in Downham Moor,] with which I refreshed myself; having eaten and drunk but little in several days before." (Fox, Journal. London, 1694, vol. i. p. 72.) The spring here alluded to is called George Fox's Well to this day. Note in 7th Edition, by Wilson Armistead, vol. i. p. 121.]

[3] Probably the eruption mentioned by Camden.

cerning this and other eruptions is that, passing under the N.E. end, commonly called the Butt end of Pendle, I saw several breaches in the side thereof, at several distances from the top. From these stones mixed with earth had been tumbled down, and lay in such a confused order as if they had been brought thither by such a like eruption as this last; and, inquiring of a country fellow who was our guide, he confirmed the conjecture, and told us these breakings out of water were very frequent, so that he wondered we took so much pains to go and see this late one. I went to look amongst the rubbish of stone and earth of one of these breaches to see if I could find anything like ore, but could find nothing. Having passed the end of the hill and coming to the other side, we after a short time discovered the aforementioned six breaches, of which two seemed to be very near the top. I went only to the biggest of the breaches, in which I observed these particulars: the water had taken away the soil, which was about two feet deep, and bared the rock between twenty and thirty yards in breadth, and downward a considerable deal more. It appeared evidently that the water came from between the swarth and the rock, for at the top of the breach we saw several holes whereat the water had issued forth; others were closed up with the fall of the earth. Wheresoever the water had taken away two feet deep of the earth the rock appeared among the rubbish. I found nothing that could be supposed to come out of the bowels of the hill, but only such stones as might be loose on the rock amongst the earth that covered it. This is what I observed in the breach, which for bigness was most remarkable, and presume I should have found nothing worth notice in the lesser ones. Though the noise of this eruption was so great that I thought it worth my pains to inquire further into it, yet in all these particulars I find nothing worthy of wonder, or what may not easily be accounted for. The colour of the water, its coming down to the place where it breaks forth between the rock and earth, with that other particular of its bringing nothing along but stones and earth, are evident signs that it hath not its origin from the very bowels of the mountain, but that it is only rain-water collected first in the moss-pits, of which the top of the hill (being a great and considerable plain) is full, shrunk down into some receptacle fit to contain it, until at last, by its weight or some other cause, it finds a passage to the side of the hill, and then away between the rock and swarth until it break the latter and violently rush out. The great eruption mentioned to have happened so many years ago perhaps is that taken notice of by Camden in his *Britannia*, p. 613. "Verum hic mons damni quid subjecto agro jampridem intulit, aquarum vim eructans, et certissimo pluviæ indicio, quoties ejus vertex nebula vestitur, maxime insignis est."

I know not whether it may not be worth notice that, going to the top of the hill and observing a considerable part thereof, especially towards the skirts where turfs had been gotten, I found that the rock reached within a yard or two of the highest part. Considering this with what I observed of the mentioned breach and several other places, I think it is very probable that the whole mountain, great as it is, is one continued rock, and it may be a question whether all other hills be so or no; but this I leave to further inquiry.

The whole extent of it cannot be estimated at less than 25 miles or 16,000 statute acres, which as early as the great Inquisition in 1311 were divided into eleven vaccaries, each of which paid 10*s*. In the commission of Henry VII. already referred to these vaccaries were denominated as follow:—

West Close and Hunterholme	XLVI*s*. VIII*d*.
Heigham Boothe	LXVI*s*. VIII*d*.
Newelawnde	XXVI*s*. VIII*d*.
Bareley Boothe	LXXIX*s*. IV*d*.
Heigham Close *olim* Nether-heigham	XXVI*s*. VIII*d*.
Overgouldeshey and Nethergouldeshey	IV*l*. XVI*s*. VIII*d*.

Feelie Close	xxvis. viiid.
Old Lawnde	xxvis. viiid.
Whitley Carre	xxs.
Over Barrowforde and Nether Barrowforde	ivl. iiis. ivd.
Over Rougley and Nether Rougley, *alias* Rougley Boothes . . .	ivl. vis. viiid.
Haweboothe and Whitley in Haboothe	lvs.
Redhalowes	xiiis. ivd.

Of these Filly Close is the flower of the forest,[1] and Reedley-hallows crosses the Pendle Water, and extends nearly to Burnley.

Besides these, I find also the vaccary of Admergill, granted 20th Rich. II. (1395-6) to William son of John de Radcliffe. (Townley MSS.)

Admergill is undoubtedly called *qu.* Ald-Mere-Gill, the Gill or Gully which formed the old boundary of the parish towards Barnoldswick. Here were lately found 117 pennies of Edward I. and John Baliol, King of Scotland.

On 26 Feb. 2 Edw. IV. 1462 William Leylond received a grant of herbage and pasture of Newland with the forest of Penhull, late in the tenure of Thomas Haryngton, esq. at a yearly rent of 106*s.* 8*d.*; of Higham Close, late in the tenure of John Dyneley, at £4 13*s.* 4*d.*; of Higham (both late in the tenure of Mr. Cawchope and Miles Parker) at 10 marks; of West Close (late in the tenure of John Croukshawe) at 113*s.* 4*d.* (Duchy of Lanc. xxv. X. 1 a.)

On 12th May following the same person had a grant "a festo Sancti Michaelis ultimo preterito usquo proximum adventum Consilii nostri in partibus illis," of the herbage and pasture of Overbarrowe Forde and Netherbarrowe Forde, of Overroghlegh and Netherroghlegh, of Barleboth, and of Oldeland with Little Blakwode, in the Forest of Pendle, and several pastures and vaccaries in the Forests of Trawden, Rossendale, and Accrington at the rent of £114 7*s.* a-year. (Ibid.)

5 Edw. IV. 14 July, 1464. A lease for twelve years to William Nutter, Christofer Baudewyn, and Peter Jakeson of two pastures called Overroughlegh and Netherroughlegh, *sufficiente pastura et pascua pro feris dicti domini Regis reservata.* (Ibid.)

5 Edw. IV. 21 Nov. 1464. Lease for twelve years to Richard Halstede and Ric. Foldes of the fourth part of the herbage of Rydelehalghs within the forest of Penhulle; rent 50*s.* 1*d.* "Et iidem firmarii salvabunt et dimittent tantam et talem pasturam pro feris domini Regis qualis et quanta in dicta quarta parte perantea solebat salvari et dimitti. Et feras dicti domini Regis in foresta predicta non interficient neque destruent aliquo modo." (Ibid.)

6 Edw. IV. 10 July, 1465. Lease for seven years to William Leylond of the herbage and pasture of Neuland for 106*s.* 8*d.* a-year, of Higham Close for £4 13*s.* 4*d.*, of Highamboth for 10 marks, of West Close for 113*s.* 4*d.*

7 Edw. IV. 22 June, 1466. A similar lease of the same pastures at the same rents was granted to William Leylond and also the herbage and pasture of Nethergoldeshagh and of Overgoldeshagh, "cum lez Cragges," at £8 6*s.* 8*d.* and Redeleghagh £9 6*s.* 8*d.*

7 Edw. IV. 22 June, 1466. A lease for ten years to William Leylond of the herbage and pasture of Overbarrowforde and Netherbarrowforde, of Overroghlegh and Netherroghlegh, of Barleboth, of Whithawboth and Hawboth, and of Oldeland cum parva Blakwode in the forest of Penhull, together with other pastures and vaccaries in Trawden, Rossendale, and Accrington forests, for £108 7*s.* and 100*s.* more *de incremento.*

[1] [So named after the fillies there kept: see the account of the royal haras, or *equitium*, under Ightenhill hereafter.]

8 Edw. IV. 20 May, 1467. Lease for twenty years to John Sotehill of a pasture called Felyclose, rent fourteen marks sterling.

11 Edw. IV. 26 Feb. 1471. Lease for twenty years to Hugh Gartside of the herbage and pasture of Westclose at the yearly rent of £5 13*s*. 4*d*., of Hegham Bothe at £6 13*s*. 4*d*., of Hegham Close at £4 13*s*. 4*d*., of Le Newe Launde at £5 6*s*. 8*d*., and of Fellyclose £9 6*s*. 8*d*. (Duchy of Lancaster, xxv. X. 2 a.)

1 Rich. III. 20 Mar. 1484. Lease to Hugh Garthside and his son Nicholas for seven years from Michaelmas last past of Overrughley and Netherrughley at £8 a-year rent. Herbage and pasture of Higham Bothe at £6 13*s*. 4*d*., ditto of Higham Close at £4 13*s*. 4*d*., ditto of West Close at £5 6*s*. 8*d*., and the vaccary of Bareley Both at £5. (Duchy of Lanc. Reg. t. Rich. III. f. 87.)

NEWCHURCH IN PENDLE.

Towards the end of Henry VIII.'s reign a chapel was erected here by the inhabitants the five booths of Gouldshaw, Bareley, Whitley, Roughlee, and Ouldlawnde, of which the sentence of consecration by John Bird, the first Bishop of Chester, bears date Oct. 1, 1544, dedicating it to St. Mary, and decreeing, "That all y[e] fruits, oblations, and proventions of the saide chappel should go to y[e] support of a fit chaplaine for celebratyng divine service, and for repayring y[e] saide chappel, without contradiction or reclamation of the vicar of Whalley, and saving the rights of the rectory." Townley MSS. 4, 2.[1]

[In the instrument of consecration the bishop exonerated the vicar of Whalley *a quacunque cura et regimine* in the district belonging to this chapel. He prohibited also the curate of the Castle Chapel at Clitheroe from officiating here. *MS. Marginal note by Dr. Whitaker.*]

The chapel has been recently rebuilt, but the original tower remains.[2]

[1] Besides these booths, which constitute the chapelry of New Church, some parts of the forest to the west, as Heyhouses, are within the chapelry of Padiham; and some to the east, as Barrowford, within that of Colne. But Reedly Hallowes, Filly Close, New Laund, and Wheatly Carr, together with Ightenhill Park, having been allotted to no chapelry, are considered as still belonging to the Castle Parish : in consequence of which, their inhabitants marry at Clitheroe.

[2] [The lower portion of the tower is the only part of the Chapel that has any claim to antiquity. The nave was entirely rebuilt in 1740. The plan consists of nave, north aisle, tower, and small vestry. The north aisle is separated from the nave by a range of six arches supported on classical pillars. There are galleries to north side and west end, the latter containing a small organ.

The tower (which has been almost entirely rebuilt within living memory) is square and low, with simple window openings and embattled parapet. It contains one bell. In its walls are inserted two stones, bearing the dates 1653 and 1712. To the nave has been added a massive stone porch of classic design with bold rusticated masonry. The church was repewed in 1855, when the battlement on the tower was renewed. There are no monuments worth mentioning. Earliest tombstone 1651. W. A. W.]

In the neighbourhood of Newchurch in Pendle was found, several years ago, a stone mallet, with a perforation for the handle. This is inserted as the only remain of British art, in stone, ever discovered within the parish. (From Addenda to Third edition, p. 522.)

HEYHOUSES.

The first village which arose in Pendle was Heyhouses, of whose origin the following account is given. There was, it seems, a portion of the forest upon which the freeholders and customary tenants of the eight following towns, viz. Merley, Penhulton, Wiswall, Read, Simonstone, Padiham, Downham, and Worston, claimed right of common. There was also a laudable custom for commissioners of the Crown to make periodical circuits over the royal demesnes to inquire into encroachments and other abuses. In the 29th Hen. VI. I find that Rauf (Holden) Abbot of Whalley, with the charterers and customers of these towns, held a meeting at Pendle Cross, where they entered into several resolutions in most barbarous old English, of which the following is the substance: "That their entertayning lies from Croybrig to Cleg yate and so to Padiham towne end," &c. Next follow several resolutions to abate encroachments, and afterwards the same persons preferred a bill before the Commissioners of Edward IV. against "Ric. Radclyffe sqyer for makeyng a town upon a tenement called ye Heyhouses where he had no right without the Kynges staff." This might be wrong, but the commissioners probably thought, "Quod fieri non debuit, factum valet," for the obnoxious town has subsisted ever since.

IN the earlier part of the seventeenth century a scene of pretended witchcraft was exhibited in this Forest, which, from the high rank of the parties who interposed rather than from any thing to distinguish it from stories of a similar kind which abounded in that credulous age, seems entitled to a distinct narration. In or about the year of 1633,[1] a a number of poor and ignorant people, inhabitants of Pendle Forest or the neighbourhood, were apprehended upon the evidence of one Edmund Robinson, a boy, whose deposition, taken before two neighbouring magistrates, is here subjoined:—

THE EXAMINATION OF EDMUND ROBINSON, son of Edm. Robinson, of Pendle Forest, mason, taken at Padiham before Richard Shuttleworth and John Starkie, esqs. two of his Majesty's justices of the peace within the county of Lancaster, 10th Feb. A.D. 1633:

Who informeth upon oath (beeinge examined concerninge the greate meetings of the witches), and saith that upon All Saints Day last past, hee, this informer, beeinge with one Henry Parker, a neare doore

[1] This story made so much noise, that in the following year, 1634, was acted and published a play entitled *The Witches of Lancaster*, which has been applied by Mr. Steevens to the illustration of Shakespeare. Johnson's and Steevens's Shakespeare, vol. ix. p. 483, &c. The term has since been transferred to a gentler species of fascination, which my fair countrywomen still continue to exert in full force, without any apprehension of the County Magistrates, or even of the King in Council.—Permit me to add, that a certain reviewer has accused me of inattention, in having passed over a narrative of pretended witchcraft, which was supposed to have taken place in the house of Mr. Starkie, A.D. 1592, and is adverted to in Harsnet's *Detection of Popish Imposture*. I was perfectly aware of the circumstance; but the reviewer was not aware that it happened at a considerable distance from the parish of Whalley. [The attention of the Chetham Society was directed to this subject in one of their earliest volumes, entitled "The wonderful Discoverie of Witches in the Countie of Lancaster, with the Arraignment and Trial of 19 notorious Witches: by Thomas Potts:" originally printed in 1613, edited, with an Introduction and Notes, by James Crossley, Esq. 1845, pp. lxxx. 184, 52.

neighbor to him in Wheatley Lane, desyred the said Parker to give him leave to get some bulloes,[1] which hee did. In which tyme of getting bulloes hee sawe two greyhounds, viz. a blacke and a browne one, came running over the next field towards him, he verily thinkinge the one of them to bee Mr. Nutter's and the other to bee Mr. Robinson's, the said Mr. Nutter and Mr. Robinson havinge then such like; and the said greyhounds came to him and fawned on him, they havinge about theire necks either of them a coller, and to either of which collers was tyed a stringe, which collers, as this informer affirmeth, did shine like gould, and hee thinkinge that some either of Mr. Nutter's or Mr. Robinson's family should have followed them, but seeinge noe body to followe them, he tooke the said greyhounds thinkinge to hunt with them, and presently a hare rise very neare before him, at the sight whereof he cryed, "Loo! loo!" but the dogges would not run. Whereupon, beeinge very angry, he tooke them, and, with the strings that were at theire collars, tyed either of them to a little bush on the next hedge, and, with a rod that hee had in his hand, hee bett them, and in stede of the blacke greyhound, one Dickonson's wife stoode up (a neighbr) whom this informer knoweth, and in steade of the browne greyhound a litle boy whom this informer knoweth not. At which sight this informer, beeinge affraid, indevoured to run away: but, beeinge stayed by the woman, viz. by Dickonson's wife, shee put her hand into her pocket and pulled out a peace of silver much like to a faire shillinge, and offered to give him to hould his tongue, and not to tell, whiche hee refused, sayinge, "Nay, thou art a witch!" Whereupon shee put her hand into her pocket againe and pulled out a stringe like unto a bridle that gingled, which shee put upon the litle boyes heade that stood up in the browne greyhound's steade, whereupon the said boy stood up a white horse. Then immediately the said Dickonson wife tooke this informer before her upon the said horse, and carried him to a new house called Hoarestones, beinge about a quarter of a mile off, whither when they were comme, there were divers persons about the doore, and hee sawe divers others cominge rideinge upon horses of severall colours towards the said house, which tyed theire horses to a hedge neare to the sed house, and which persons went into the sed house to the number of three-score or thereabouts, as this informer thinketh, where they had a fyer and meate roastinge, and some other meate stirringe in the house, whereof a yonge woman, whom hee this informer knoweth not, gave him flesh and breade upon a trencher and drinke in a glasse, which, after the first taste, hee refused, and would have noe more, and said it was nought, and presently after, seeinge diverse of the company goinge to a barn neare adioyneinge, hee followed after, and there hee sawe sixe of them kneelinge, and pullinge at sixe severall roapes which were fastened or tyed to ye toppe of the house, at or with which pullinge came then in this informer's sight flesh smoakeinge, butter in lumps, and milke as it were syleinge from the said roapes, all which fell into basons whiche were placed under the saide roapes; and after that these sixe had done there came other sixe which did likewise, and duringe all the tyme of theire so pullinge they made such foule faces that feared this informer, soe as hee was glad to steale out and run home, whom when they wanted some of theire company came runninge after him neare to a place in a highway called Boggard Hole, where this informer met two horsemen, at the sight whereof the sed persons left followinge him, and the foremost of which persons yt followed him hee knoweth to bee one Loynd's wife, which said wife, together with one Dickonson wife and one Jenet Davies, he hath seene at severall tymes in a croft or close adioninge to his father's house, whiche put him in a greate feare. And further this informer saith upon Thursday after New Yeares Day last past, he sawe the said Loynd's wife sittinge upon a crosse peece of wood, beeinge within the chimney of his father's dwellinge house, and hee, callinge to her, said "Come downe, thou Loynd's wife!"

"It is rather strange (remarks Mr. Crossley) that Dr. Whitaker, to whom local superstitions were always matters of the strongest interest, and welcome as manna to the sojourners in the wilderness, should have been ignorant, not merely of Master Potts's discovery, but even of the fact of this trial of the witches in 1612:" and that notwithstanding the pamphlet had been already reprinted in the Somers Collection of Tracts.]

[1] [Wild plums.]

and imediately the said Loynd's wife went up out of his sight. And further this informer saith y^t after hee was comme from ye company aforesed to his father's house, beeinge towards eveninge, his father bad him goe fetch home two kyne to seale, and in the way, in a field called the Ollers, hee chaneed to hap upon a boy who began to quarrell with him, and they fought soe together till this informer had his eares made very bloody by fightinge, and, lookinge downe, hee saw the boy had a cloven foote, at which sight hee was affraid, and ran away to seek the kyne; and in the way hee sawe a light like a lanthorne, towards which he made hast, supposinge it to bee carried by some of Mr. Robinson's people, but, when hee came to the place hee onley found a woman standinge on a bridge, whom, when hee sawe her, he knewe to bee Loynd wife, and, knowinge her, he turned backe againe, and immediatly hee met with ye aforesed boy, from whom he offered to run, which boy gave him a blow on the back, which caus'd him to cry. And hee farther saith, y^t when hee was in the barne he sawe three women take three pictures from off the beame, in the which pictures many thornes, or such like things sticked, and y^t Loynd wife tooke one of the said pictures downe, but thother two women y^t tooke thother two pictures downe hee knoweth not. And beeinge further asked, what persons were at ye meetinge aforesed, hee nominated these persons hereafter mentioned: viz. Dickonson wife, Henry Priestley wife and her sone, Alice Hargreaves widdowe, Jennet Davies, Wm. Davies, uxor Hen. Jacks and her sone John, James Hargreaves of Marsden, Miles wife of Dicks, James wife, Saunders *sicut creditur*, Lawrence wife of Saunders, Loynd wife, Buys wife of Barrowford, one Holgate and his wife *sicut creditur*, Little Robin wife of Leonard's of the West Closse.

Edmund Robinson of Pendle, father of ye s^d Edmunde Robinson, the aforesaid informer, upon oath saith, that upon All Saints' Day he sent his sone, the aforesed informer, to fetch home two kyne to seale, and saith y^t hee thought his sone stayed longer than he should have done, went to seeke him; and in seekinge him, heard him cry very pitifully; and found him soe afraid and distracted, y^t hee neither knew his father, nor did know where he was, and so continued very neare a quarter of an hower before he came to himselfe: and he tould this informer, his father, all the particular passages y^t are before declared in the said Edmund Robinson his sone's information.[1]

Upon such evidence, these poor creatures were committed to Lancaster Castle for trial, not greatly to the honour either of the understanding or humanity of the magistrates: for surely the statute of witchcraft did not bind them to commit, upon any evidence, or upon none, or to shut their eyes against apparent malice and imposture. On their trials they had the misfortune of falling into the hands of a jury equally ignorant or prejudiced, who found seventeen of them guilty. The judge, however, whose name I have not learned, very properly respited the convicts, and reported the case to the King in council. They were next remitted to the Bishop of Chester (Bridgeman), who, certifying his opinion of the case, whatever it was, four of the party, Margaret Johnson, Francis Dicconson, Mary Spencer, and the wife of one of the Hargreaves', were sent for to London, and examined, first by the King's physicians and surgeons, and afterwards by Charles the First in person.

A stranger scene can scarcely be conceived; and it is not easy to imagine, whether the untaught manners, rude dialect, and uncouth appearance of these poor foresters would more astonish the King; or his dignity of person and manners, together with the splendid

[1] This copy of the deposition differs very materially from that of Webster, and is undoubtedly more accurate, particularly in the proper names; which, to a Lancashire ear, authenticate themselves. [Another copy, together with the examination of Margaret Johnson, has been printed in Baines's Lancashire from the Harl. MS. 6854.]

scene with which they were surrounded, would overwhelm them. The end, however, of the business was, that strong presumptions appeared of the boy having been suborned to accuse them falsely, and they were accordingly dismissed. The boy afterwards confessed that he was suborned.

After all this, how must the reader be surprised to find, that one of the women had actually confessed the fact with which she stood so injuriously charged. This was unknown to Webster, the original relater of the story; but appears from a paper in the Bodleian Library, Dodsworth MSS. vol. lxi. p. 47, which is here given.

The Confession of Margret Johnson.

That betwixt seaven and eight yeares since, shee beinge in her owne house in Marsden, in a greate passion of anger and discontent, and withall pressed with some want, there appeared unto her a spirit or devill in ye proportion or similitude of a man, apparelled in a suite of blacke, tyed about with silk points, who offered y^t^ if shee would give him her soule hee would supply all her wants, and bringe to her whatsoever shee did neede; and at her appointment would, in revenge, either kill or hurt whom or what shee desyred, weare it man or beast. And saith, y^t^ after a solicitation or two shee contracted and covenanted with ye said devill for her soule. And y^t^ ye said devill or spirit badde her call him by the name of Mamilian. And when shee would have him to doe any thinge for her, call in Mamilian, and hee would bee ready to doe her will. And saith, y^t^ in all her talke or conference shee calleth her said devill, Mamil my God. Shee further saith, y^t^ ye said Mamilian, her devill, (by her consent) did abuse and defile her body by committinge wicked uncleannesse together. And saith, y^t^ shee was not at the greate meetings at Hoarestones, at the forest of Pendle, upon All-Saints Day, where . But saith y^t^ shee was at a second meetinge ye Sunday next after All-Saints Day, at the place aforesaid, where there was, at y^t^ tyme, between 30 and 40 witches, who did all ride to the said meetinge, and the end of theire said meeting was to consult for the killinge and hurtinge of men and beasts. And y^t^ besides theire particular familiars or spirits, there was one greate or grand devill, or spirit, more eminent than the rest. And if any desyre to have a greate and more wonderfull devill, whereby they may have more power to hurt, they may have one such. And sayth, y^t^ such witches as have sharp bones given by the devill to pricke them, have no pappes or dugges whereon theire devil may sucke; but theire devill receiveth bloud from the place, pricked with the bone; and they are more grand witches than any y^t^ have marks. Shee allsoe saith, y^t^ if a witch have but one marke, shee hath but one spirit; if two, then two spirits; if three, yet but two spirits. And saith, y^t^ theire spirits usually have knowledge of theire bodies. And being desyred to name such as shee knewe to be witches, shee named, &c. And if they would torment a man, they bid theire spirit goe and torm^t^ him in any particular place. And y^t^ Good Friday is one constant day for a yearely generall meetinge of witches; and y^t^ on Good Friday last they had a meetinge neare Pendle water-syde. Shee alsoe saith, that men witches usually have women spirits, and women witches men spirits. And theire devill or spirit gives them notice of theire meetinge, and tells them the place where it must bee. And saith, if they desyre to be in any place upon a sodaine, theire devill or spirit will, upon a rodde, dogge, or any thing els, presently convey them thither; yea, into any roome of a man's house. But shee saith it is not the substance of theire bodies, but theire spirit assumeth such form and shape as goe into such rooms. Shee also saith, y^t^ ye devill (after he begins to sucke) will make a pappe or dugge in a shorte tyme, and the matter which hee sucks is blood. And saith y^t^ theire devills can cause foule weather and storms, and soe did at theire meetings. Shee alsoe saith, y^t^ when her devill did come to sucke her pappe, hee usually came to her in ye liknes of a cat, sometymes of one colour, and sometymes of an other. And yt since this trouble befell her, her spirit hath left her, and shee never sawe him since.

What account can be given of so strange a conduct? That an accused person, without torture, which will often compel the sufferer, for present ease, to utter truth or falsehood indifferently, as it may answer the purpose, should confess a capital crime, of which she knew herself innocent, when the effects of such a confession would be nearly equivalent to a conviction! It is not impossible, that in persons of weak understandings, depressed and affrighted almost to distraction, the strong persuasion of their guilt, which they observe in all about them, may gradually produce an imagination that they really possess diabolical powers, and have had diabolical communications, which they have not.

On the whole:—Of the system of witchcraft, the real defect is not in theory but in evidence. A possibility that the bodies of men may sometimes be given up to infernal agency is no more to be denied than that their souls should be exposed to infernal illusions: that such appearances should be exhibited in one age and withdrawn in another is equally the case with miracles: that they do not extend to all countries is common to them and to revelation itself. But every modern instance of supposed witchcraft which I have read of is discredited either by the apparent fraud or folly of the witnesses. Were I to behold with my own eyes such circumstances as have often been related, or were they to be reported to me by a philosophical observer of perfect integrity upon the evidence of his senses, I know not upon what principles I could refuse my assent to the conclusion, that they were really the effects of diabolical power.[1]

The boundaries of Pendle Forest, contiguous to those of Bernoldswick, had been perambulated by the first Henry de Lacy, in person, on the day when he delivered possession of that village to the monks; and they are thus described:—

Henricus de Lacy de divisis inter Bernolswic et forestam suam.

Omnibus Sancte Matris ecclesie filiis presentibus et futuris Henricus de Laci Salutem. Sciatis has esse rectas divisas inter Bernolswic et forestam meam de Blakeburnscire, quas ego et homines mei perambulavimus ea die qua tradidi Bernolswic cum omnibus appendiciis suis Monachis ordinis Cistercienсis, ad abbatiam construendam, et predictam Bernolswic per has easdem divisas perpetuo possidendam eisdem Monachis, assignavi scilicet per rivum qui vocatur Blakebroc et ita sursum ultra Moram in directum usque ad Gailmers, et ita in directum usque ad capitem de Clessaghe, et ita in transversum Montem qui vocatur Blacho, et ita usque ad Oxegile, et ita per Oxegile sursum usque ad Dukedelawe qui vocatur Alaine Sete et ad Pikedelawe, usque ad antiquum fossatum inter Midhop et Colredene. Et ideo ne inter Monachos et heredes meos possit de eisdem divisis aliqua in posterum oriri contentio, hanc cartam dedi eis in testimonium predictarum divisarum. Teste. (Coucher of Kirkstall, in the Duchy Papers, Class XI. No. 7, fol. 54.)

[1] That these opinions may not be accused of leaning too much to the doctrines of exploded superstition, I will take leave to refer my readers to the following sentiment of a great and enlightened modern Divine:—"That for anything we know, he (the devil) may (still) operate in the way of possession, I do not see on what certain grounds any man can deny."—Bp. Hurd's Sermons, vol. iii. p. 239.

The words *antiquum fossatum* (old dike), when referred to the reign of Stephen, prove how early the forests were bounded by these *haiæ dominicales*. In the perambulation of Bowland repeated mention is made of paling and dykes, where strong natural boundaries were wanting; and the forest of Rossendale was divided from Cliviger by a *fossatum* yet remaining, called the Old Dyke.

These boundaries seem to have been nearly forgotten: and it is remarkable, that not one of these ancient names appears in the perambulation of the parish of Whalley, of which the antiquity is uncertain, but which cannot be later than the reign of Edward III. as it is found in the Coucher Book of Abbot Lyndlay.

On this account Henry de Lacy the second had encroached on the property of the monks at Kirkstall, and his successors in the Honor of Clitheroe seemed disposed to maintain the wrong. This gave rise to a suit between that house and Queen Isabella, which produced the following inquisition (7 Edw. III.):—"The jurors find, that Henry de Lacy, Earl of Lincoln, violently took away 840 acres of moor and pasture, parcel of the commons of Bernoldswick, val. 35*s*. per annum and no more; that is, an halfpenny per acre, *quia nullum extat ibi alium proficuum capiendum, nisi pastura frisca pro grossis animalibus inde pascendis et debilis existit.*" It was accordingly restored to the proper owners. During the time of this suit, it appears that William de Tatham was keeper, and Ric. de Merclesden master-forester of Blackburnshire.[1]

In the Inquisition of 1311, the pannage of Pendle was found to be sometimes of no value, but *communibus annis* worth 6*s*. 8*d*. This is precisely the case at present, as acorns sometimes ripen, and sometimes do not.

I find, from the rolls of Clitheroe, 17 Hen. VIII. that there were certain grounds called FENCE,[2] within the vaccaries of Sabden,[3] West Close,[4] and Higham, upon which "the herde of the stagges, always before the deforesting, had their several being;" and doubts having arisen with respect to the right of the tenants to the said lands, it is decreed that they shall pass and endure to the said tenants as part of the said vaccaries.

[1] Mon. Ang. vol. i. p. 858, &c. [A list of the Master Foresters of Blackburnshire will be found hereafter.]

[2] [In 1836 a church was erected at Fence, around which within a circle of a mile and a half was then a population of 2,000. Its cost, 1,000*l*. was raised by subscription, and 1,000*l*. was given as an endowment by Mrs. Greenwood. Consecrated Oct. 6, 1837.]

[3] ["I was born and lived at Bank, close to Fence, until I went to school; and at that time Sabden was understood to extend between Sabden Fold and Sabden Hall; but now, as Sabden Bridge (which is at the bottom of the dale) has increased, that village is often called Sabden, and the old Sabden is nearly deserted."—J. GRIMSHAW, 1870. "Et de liij s. iiij d. de firma de Sapdenhey sic dimissa Thome de Radclif per litteras domini Johannis nuper ducis Lancastrie patentes, tenenda secundum consuetudinem Manerii etc. et reparandum per eundem domos prout in eisdem litteris plenius continetur." (Computus Collectorum herbagii de Blakebourneshire (1422-3.) Duchy of Lanc. Class XXIX Bundle 220. Clitheroe 1 and 2 Hen. VI.)]

[4] [There is a place called West Close in Higham, with West Close Booth, to the south of Higham, while Fence Gate is to the north-east.—J. GRIMSHAW.]

IGHTENHILL PARK.

Separated from the forest of Pendle by the Calder, is Ightenhill Park,[1] another of the demesnes of Clitheroe Castle, which, though never taken as a portion of the forest, may, from its contiguity to it, most properly be noticed here. The ancient orthography of this word is Hightenhull; of which, though the meaning is sufficiently clear, the propriety is not very apparent; for it is, in fact, a soft and gentle swell of ground, rising from a curvature of the Calder, to no very considerable height, but commanding some very pleasing views to the north and west. Within this park was a very ancient manor-house of the Lacies, which was certainly in existence as early as the 22nd Henry II. or 1176,[2] as appears from a grant of lands in Tottington, given at Hightenhull in that year, the earliest date, excepting one, I have ever met with in any of our charters. There is a tradition in the neighbourhood, that the house was abandoned by the family in consequence of the last male heir having been killed by a fall from a window. This is merely an echo of the genuine account already given, concerning the untimely death of the heir of Henry de Lacy at Pontefract or Denbigh; and is only mentioned here to show how long traditions of real events may be propagated, and how seldom they are found, when traced to their sources, entirely destitute of foundation, however they may have been corrupted.

This park, with its appurtenances, is valued in the great Inquisition of 1311 :—

Hightenhull, one capital messuage worth yearly, besides reprises .	*nil.*
8 acres in demesne	ij s. viij d.
1 acre of meadow	xij d.
A park, in circuit one league and half (*leuca*), the agistment [and herbage] of which is worth	xl s.
52 acres and 2 roods demised to tenants at will . . .	l s. v d.
Halmot of the same, together with a certain revenue (*proficuum*) called Thisteltakes[3]	xl s.
	vj l. xiv s. ij d.

The *leuca* or league (*vide* Spelman *in voce*) was extremely variable. That of Domes-

[1] In the Inquisition of Survey for the Rectory of Whalley, immediately before the foundation of the abbey, Ightenhill is included in the chapelry of Brunley.

[2] [See hereafter, under Tottington. The true date of 22 Hen. II. instead of 22 Hen. III. is restored in the text, according to Dr. Whitaker's note in his last edition, p. 228. A charter of Edmund de Lacy is dated at Ightenhill on Sunday next after the nativity of the blessed virgin Mary in 1251. Coucher Book, (Chetham Soc.) p. 77.]

[3] In the manor of Halton, also belonging to the Lacies, was a revenue (*proficuum*) called *Thistletake.* This has been understood to mean a payment exacted by lords of manors, for the depasturing of drove-beasts upon their

day Book was 1,000 geometrical paces: the French league was twice the former; and this I conceive to have been the measure intended here.

[*Pur encloser le park de Ighteny ll.*

(From the Register of John Duke of Lancaster, temp. Ric. II. f. 25.)

Johan, &c. A nostre trescher et bien ame Chief Gardein de nostre Chace de Penyll ou a son lieutenant saluz. Nous vous mandons qe par lavys et assent de nostre seneschal deniz nostre Duchee de Lancastre facez faire enclore nostre park de Ightenyll' deinz nostre Chaee oue fosse quicwode et petit hegge desouz en le meliour manere qe vous verrez qe soit affaire pur nostre honour et profit, et a tout le bon hast qe ce faire purra, entendent qe nous avons escrit a nostre Receivour de celles parties pur faire paiement de les coustages par temoignautz de vous et lun de vous. Et ce ne lessez. Et cestes noz lettres vous en serront garrant. Done, etc. a nostre Manoir de la Sauvoye le xxi jour de Feverer, lan, &c. tierz. (21 Feb. 3 Rich. II. 1380.)

Pur paier les costaiges pur lenclosure de le Park de Ightenille et autre.

Johan, etc. A nostre trescher et bien ame Clerk Sire William de Horneby nostre Receivour deniz nostre Duchee a Lancastre et aillour saluz. Nous vous mandens qe par lavys et assent de nostre trescher et bien ame monser Nicole de Haryngton Chief Gardein de nostre Forest de Quernemore faciez carier touz les keynes[1] et maerisme queux sont coupez pur nostre oeps deniz nostre dit Forest a nostre Chastel de Lancastre, et illeoqes faces ordener pur le bone et sauve garde de ycelles tanque vous eveiez autre mandement de nous, et des costages resonable queux vous issint ferrez nous volons qe le tesmoignance du dit monser Nicole et par cestes vous eveiez du allouance en voz acontes. Et outre ce qe vous mandons qe par survieue et ordenance de nostre seneschal de Lanc. et del Chief Gardein de nostre Chace de Penille faciez paier les coustages pur encloser nostre Park de Ightenill ove fosse et quiewode et petit hegge desous selonc leur devise. Et des coustages resonable queux vous issent ferrez nous volons qe par le tesmoignance de eux ou lun de eux vous eveiez due allouance en voz acontes. Done, etc., a nostre Manoir de la Sauvoye le xxi jour de Feverer, lan, etc. tierz. (The same day as the former.)]

In the 21st Richard II. I met with a John le Parcour de Hightenhull. This was merely a name of office, but gradually became hereditary; and I suspect, from several circumstances, that the Parkers of Extwisle, could their descent be traced to its source, would terminate in a keeper of Ightenhill.

In the earlier part of the reign of Henry VIII. this park was in lease to the Townley family; for, in the court-rolls at Clitheroe, A. 14° of that reign, is an inquisition of survey, taken at the instance of Sir John Townley, knt. in order to certify to the King's council the state in which the manor-house was then found. And, as this ancient mansion, which was sometimes probably a royal residence, is now destroyed to the foundation, it will not be uninteresting to enumerate, from this record, the names of its principal apartments,

commons, even if they stayed to crop a thistle. Dr. Pegge reads the word *Tresseltake*, and understands it to be a payment made to the lord for every hog placed upon the tressel for slaughter: very improbably.

[1] [*Kanes*, oakes, Kelham, Norman Dict.]

and to ascertain the precise state of dilapidation and decay to which they were reduced, even at that early period.

Juratores dicunt, quod magna aula et meremium *(the timbers of the roof)* ruit et prosternetur ad terram, et magna pars illius inde asportatur. Item dicunt, quod magna camera ad finem aulæ ex occid. parte simili modo ut supradict. est. Item quod coquina et domus pincernæ et le pantree deformentur. Item domus fornac. in simili modo ut sup. Item dicunt quod magnum oreum[1] simili modo ut sup. est. Item quod longa camera ad finem aulæ ex occid. ruit et prosternetur. Item, quod domus custodis parci adhuc exist. stans et desuper contect. cum tegul. et later. voc. sclait-tons, et quod hostia et fenestræ illius asportatæ sunt, et veresimile est cadere. Item quod Capella[2] ibm. adhuc existens, stans simili modo. Item stabulum simili modo, et in captione sive destructione meremii sive lapidum domorum p'dict. Johannes Townley cul. non est invent.

The park of Ightenhill continued to be held by Sir Richard Townley 4 Edw. VI. and by John Townley, esq. to about the 35th Eliz. when Sir Richard Shuttleworth grants a lease of lands in Ightenhill Park, reciting and confirming the conditions granted in the former lease by John Townley, esq. There was little difficulty, at that time, for a rising lawyer to displace an obnoxious recusant. *O si angulus ille!* must frequently have been the wish of the Gawthorp family, when they beheld that fair domain, which extended almost to their door; and what they thus acquired by lease, they have since converted into a fee simple, excepting merely the site of the manor-house, which could not be alienated without a transfer or an extinction of the manor. For it must be remembered that Ightenhill is one of the factitious manors within the parish, which have grouped together several of the original ones, for the convenience of holding courts; and it consists of Ightenhill *mag.* and *parv.*, Burnley, Habergham Eaves, Padiham, Marsden, Briercliffe, and Heyhouses.

[At Ightenhill there was a considerable Royal *equitium*, or establishment for the breeding of horses, maintained in connection with another in the park of the Hay near the castle of Knaresborough, regarding which the following extracts from the records of the King's Remembrancer in the Exchequer will be found highly curious:—

In the compotus Menaldi Brocas, custodis quorundum magnorum Equorum et Pullanorum Regis in partibus borealibus, for 61 days from 2 Sept. to 2 Nov. 9 Edw. III. 1335, among the forty-two horses in his charge he names i niger de Hightenhille, i niger cum uno pede (forefoot) albo. (Exchequer, Q. R. Equitium Regis $\frac{3}{7}$.)

In his compotus 2 Nov. 9 Edw. III. to Michaelmas following written "die Sabbato secundo die Decembr. Anno x" (2 Dec. 1336) several Ightenhill horses are named.

Ces sount les nouns des chivals queux Manaut de Brocas resceust de Johan Brocas le secunde jour de

[1] For *horreum*, the great barn, see *oreum*, in Du Cange.

[2] From the *Compotus* of Whalley Abbey, A.D. 1536, it appears that the Chapel in the manor-house of Ightenhill was then remaining; for, after an enumeration of the chapels within the castle-parish, follows this entry:—*Ightenhill Park de perq. capellani.*—See p. 116, note.

Novembre Lan de regne le Roy Edward tierce apres le conquest neusme, cest a savoir . . . . . une Morell de Itinhill, ... une Morell ad une pee blank de Itinhill.

October 1, Anno x. Johan Brokays received from Manaut Brocais x chivals, cest a savoir une Morell de Itinhill, une pee blank derere, une Morell de Itinhill, une Grisel de Hitenhill, une grisel bausan de Hitenhill, deux Morell de Makesfeld, etc.

Ses sont les noms des chivals que Johan de Brucquas resceust de Manaut de Brocas le primer jour Decembre lan de sus dit, se est assaver, i bayant de Histenhell, etc. (Equicium Regis $\frac{347}{24}$.)

COMPOTUS Edmundi de Thedmersshe de equicio Regis in partibus borialibus et de receptis et expensis suis factis circa custodia ejusdem equicii a festo Sancti Michaelis anno xv Regis Edwardi tercii post conquestum finiente usque ad festum Sancti Michaelis proximum sequens, videlicet de anno xvj. (After the titles Knaresb. parco de Haywara, Equicium de Plumtonlande, parco de Haye in foresta de Knaresb.)

EQUICIUM DE IGHTENHILL. *Jumenta.*—Idem respondit de xxxv jumentis de equicio Regis de Ightenhill de remanentibus compoti sui anni precedentis, quorum vj nigra, ij sor, vij bay, v ferrantz bauzan, iij ferrantz pomele, iij nigra bauzan, i sor grisele, i sor bauzan, i Powys cum duobus pedibus posteris albis, i grisel, i brounbay, i nigra cum stella, i lyard et ij lyard bauzan. Et de vij jumentis de adjunccione pultrellarum, quarum ij grisel, ij lyard cum stella, ij nigra et i liard. Summa xlij jumenta. Et remanent—

Pullani. Idem respondit de viij pullanis etatis trium annorum et dimidii equicii predicti de remanentibus, quorum ij grisel, ij grisel cum stella, ij bay cum stellis, i grisel bausan, et i niger cum stella. Quos computat tractatos ad domandum inter magnos equos Regis, de quibus dictus Edmundus respondit in compoto suo de eisdem equis.

Item respondit de v pullanis etatis duorum annorum et dimidii, quorum iij grisel et ij nigri. Et remanent etatis iij annorum et dimidii.

Item respondit de iij pullanis etatis unius anni et dimidii equicii predicti, quorum i lyard, i grisel cum stella, et i niger. Et remanent etatis ij ann. et di.

Item respondit de vj pullanis equicii predicti de illis xj pullanis remanentibus de exitu in compoto suo anni precedentis, quorum iij grisel, i bay, i niger, i sor. Summa vj pullani. Et remanent etatis unius anni et dimidii.

Pultrelle. Item de xj pultrellis diverse etatis equicii predicti de remanentibus, quarum ij grisel, ij lyard cum stellis, ij nigre, et i lyard etatis trium annorum et dimidii, i lyard, ij nigre et i sore bauzan etatis duorum annorum et dimidii.

Inde computat in adjunccione supra cum jumentis vij pultrellas sicut supra patet. Et remanent iiij pultrelle, quarum i lyard, ij nigre, et i sore bauzan, etatis trium annorum et dimidii.

Item respondit de ij pultrellis etatis unius anni et dimidii equicii predicti de remanentibus, quarum i sore et i lyard. Et remanent etatis ij annorum et dimidii.

Item respondit de v pultrellis equicii predicti de illis xj pultrellis remanentibus de exitu in computo suo anni precedentis, quarum i nigra, i bay, ij grisel, et i dun. Et remanent etatis unius anni et dimidii.

Pulli de exitu. Item de xiiij pullis diversi sexus et coloris de exitu predictorum jumentorum hoc anno, et non de pluribus quia residuum dictorum jumentorum sterilia erant (*sic*) hoc anno. Inde in decima soluta i pullum. Et remanent xiij pulli diversi sexus et coloris.

Empcio feni et avene. Item computat in feno lx acras prati emptas in parco de Ightenhill pro sustentacione predictorum jumentorum et pullanorum per tempus hujus computi iiij li. x s. precium acre xviij d.

Et in xxvj quarteriis avene emptis in ciiij thravis[1] garbarum, quarum singule iiij thrave fecit per estimacionem i quarteriam avene xxx s. iiij d. precium quarterie xiiij d.

De cariagio nichil hic quia per plaustr. Regis.

Summa vj li. iv d.

[1] See p. 180.

Vadii. Item computat in vadiis unius hominis custodientis equicium predictum a predicto festo Sancti Michaelis anno predicto, usque festum Sancti Michaelis proxime sequens, per ccclxv dies xlv s. vij d. ō. cap. per diem i d. et ob.

Et in vadiis ipsius Edmundi pro custodio ejusdem equicii et equiciorum de Knaresb. et Plumtonlande per idem tempus, xij li. iij s. iiij d. cap. per diem viij d. Summa xiij li. viij s. xj d. ō.

Summa totalis expensarum xx li. ix s. ob.

Fenum et avena. Item respondit de feno lx acrarum prati et xxxvj quarteriis in cxliij thravis garbarum avene receptis de supra-empcione. Et totum computatur in sustentacione predictorum jumentorum et pullanorum per tempus hujus computi. Et est quietus.

Summa totalis expensarum super equicium predictum xlj li. xiij s. ix d. ō.

Sed subtractis xxiiij li. xviij s. xj d. ō. q^a^ quos deliberavit de remanenti computi precedentis sui jussu Receptoris, Remanent de superplusagio xvj li. xiij s. ix d. ō. q^a^.

COMPUTUS prefati Edmundi de exitu herbagii parcorum Regis de la Haye, Haywra, Ditton, et parvi parci subtus Castrum in foresta de Knaresb. in Com. Ebor., parci Regis de Ightenhill cum tribus clausis eidem parco pertinentibus videlicet Westclose, Hegham et Fylyclose in Com. Lanc., et parci Regis de Macclesfeld in Com. Cestr., a festo Sancti Michaelis anno xv° finiente usque festum Sancti Michaelis proxime sequens videlicet de anno xvj°.

PARCUS DE IGHTENHILL.—*Recepta pasture.* Idem respondit de liij s. iiij d. de herbagio et pastura in le Westclose pertinente parco de Ightenhill sic dimisso ad firmam pro toto anno ultra sustentacionem equicii Regis in dicto clauso.

Et de xl s. de consimili firma in quodam clauso vocato Fylyclos ultra sustentacionem ejusdem equicii per tempus isti computi.

Et de Liiij s. de agistamento lv bestiarum in parco predicto tempore estivali, quarum videlicet Lii quelibet ad xij d. et iij quelibet ad viij d.

Et de iiij li. xix s. vj d. de agistamento iiij^xx^ xi bestiarum agistatarum in clauso de Hegham tempore predicto, quarum xviij bestie quelibet ad xviij d. lxxj quelibet ad xij d. et iij quelibet ad vj d.

Et de xxx s. ix d. de agistamento xxviij bestiarum in quodam clauso vocato Roell (*i.e.* Royle) tempore predicto, quarum xxiiij quelibet ad xij d. iii quelibet ad vj d. et i ad iij d.

Et de xxvij s. ij d. o' de agistamento cxlj bestiarum in parco predicto et clausis de Hegham et Fylyclos agistatarum tempore yeme, quarum v bestie quelibet ad iiij d., lxix quelibet ad iij d., xxij quelibet ad ij d., xxj quelibet ad j d. ō, xxiiij quelibet ad j d. Summa xiiij li. xix s. ij d. ō.

Fenum venditum. Idem respondit de iiij li. x s. de feno lx acr. prati vendito pro sustentacione equicii Regis ibidem per tempus predictum, precio acre xviij d. Summa iiij li. x s.

Summa reddituum xix li. ix s. ix d. ō.

EXPENSE.—*Decima.* Idem computat in decima soluta Rectori ecclesie de Clyderhowe pro pastura, herbagio et agistamento in parco et clausis predictis supra vendicium xxix s. xj d. ō. q^a^.

Summa xxix s. xj d. ō. q^a^.

Claustura. Idem computat in C perticatis haye circa clausos de Hegham, Fylyclos, et Rowel per diversa loca fracte et prostrate reficiendis et emendandis per tempus predictum iiij s. ij d. pro perticata ō.

Et in xxviij perticatis haye circa le Midelzerd similiter reparandis per idem tempus xiiij d. pro perticata ō.

Et in xxxij perticatis haye circa quoddam clausum prati vocatum Stodmerhalgh similiter per idem tempus emendandis xvj d. pro perticata ō.

Et in xlv perticatis novi palicii circa parcum predictum similiter per idem tempus faciendis vij s. vj d. pro perticata ij d.

Et solut. ij hominibus pro coopertura ij domorum feni et emendacione iij helm., ex convencione facta eis in grosso viij s. viij d. Summa xxij s. x d.

Falcacio prati. Idem computat in lx acris prati in parco predicto in quodam loco vocato Stodmerhalgh falcatis per tempus predictum xxv s. pro acra v d.

Et in herba inde spargenda, feno colligando, levando, et in pratis cassando x s. pro acra ij d.

Et in conduccione ij hominum per iiij dies pro tassacione feni in domis ibidem xvj d. cuilibet per diem ij d. Summa xxxvj s. iiij d.

Vadia. Item in vadiis unius parcarii custodientis parcum predictum et clausa predicta a predicto festo Sancti Michaelis dicto anno xv° finiente usque festum Sancti Michaelis proxime sequens per ccclxv dies xlv s. vij d. ō. capientis per diem j d. ō.

Et in vadiis unius hominis continue morantis ad parcum predictum pro veteri palicio cum fractum fuerit emendando et sustinendo, et unius hominis euntis ad plaustrum Regis ibidem pro palicii meremio ad idem, spinis pro haiis ejusdem parci et feno cariandis, ac custodientis viij boves pro plaustro predicto per idem tempus lxv s. x d. cuilibet per diem j d.

Et in stipendio dicti plaustrarii per idem tempus iiij s. vj d. Sm^a^ cx s. xj d. ob.

Summa expensarum x li. j d. q^a^. Et debet ix li. ix s. viij d. q^a^.

Fenum. Idem respondit de feno lxv acr. prati de remanenti compoti sui anni precedentis.

Et de feno lx acr. prati falc. per tempus hujus compoti.

Inde in sustentacione viij boum Regis fenum v acr. prati. Et in vendicione feni lx acr. prati. Et remanet fenum lx acr. prati.

Boves. Idem respondit de viij bobus de rem. computi sui anni precedentis. Et remanent.

Plaustrum. Idem respondit de uno plaustro de rem. computi sui anni precedentis. Et remanet.

(Exchequer, Queen's Remembrancer. *Equicium Regis* $\frac{35}{16}$.)

Part of the computus of Edmund de Thedmersh in the following year, 16–17 Edw. III. when he delivered the horses in his charge to Roger de Normanville his successor, several of whose rolls of account are extant.

EQUICIUM DE IGHTENHILL.—*Jumenta.* Idem respondit computans de xlij jumentis de equicio Regis de Ightenhill de remanenti computi sui anni precedentis, quorum viij nigra, ij sore, iij ferrantz pomele, vij bay, v ferrantz bauzan, iij nigra bauzan, i sore grisel, i sor bauzan, i Powys cum duobus pedibus posteris albis, iij grisels, i braunbay, i nigra cum stella, ij lyard, ij lyard bauzan, et ij lyard cum stellis.

Et de iiij jumentis de adjunccione pultrellarum, quarum i lyard, ij nigra et i sore bauzan.

Summa xlvj jumenta. E quibus—

Idem computat in morina[1] iij jumenta, quorum i nigra bauzan iij die Januarii, i nigra bauzan x° die ejusdem mensis, et i nigra bauzan iiij^to^ die Febr.

Et liberavit Duci Cornubie[2] iiij jumenta per breve Regis indentatum, quorum i ferrant pomele, i sorbausan, i nigra, i brounbay. Et Rogero de Normanville, xxxj jumenta quorum ix nigra, ij sor, ij ferrantz pomele, vij bay, v ferrantz bausan, i sor grisel, i powys cum duobus pedibus posteris albis, iij grisel, i nigra cum stella, iij lyard, ij lyard bausan, ij lyard cum stellis, et j sorbausan, per indenturam. Et est quietus.

Pullani masculi. Item respondit de v pullanis masculis etatis trium annorum et dimidii de remanentibus, quorum iij grisel et ij nigri. Et tractantur ad domandum inter magnos equos Regis, de quibus idem Edmundus respondit in computo suo de eisdem equis. Et est quietus.

Item respondit de iij pullanis masculis etatis duorum annorum et dimidii de rem. quorum i lyard, i grisel cum stella, et i niger. Et liberavit prefato Will. de Fremelesworth etatis trium annorum et dimidii per indenturam.

[1] These mares had died in a murrain.

[2] The Black Prince.

Item respondit de vi pullanis masculis etatis unius anni et dimidii de remanent. quorum iij grisel, i bay, i niger et i sor. Et liberavit prefato W. etatis duorum annorum et dimidii. Et est quietus.

Item respondit de vi pullanis masculis de illis xij pullis rem. de exitu in computo suo anni precedentis, quorum i grisel cum stella, ij grisels, i niger bausan cum uno pede postero albo, i grisel bauzan cum iiij^or pedibus albis, et i bay. Summa vi pullani masculi. Et liberavit Rogero de Normanvill etatis unius anni et dimidii per indenturam. Et est quietus.

Pultrelle. Item respondit de iij pultrellis etatis trium annorum et dimidii de rem. quarum i lyard, ij nigre, et i sore bauzan. Et adjunguntur supra cum Jumentis. Et est quietus.

Item respondit de ij pultrellis etatis duorum annorum et dimidii de rem. quarum i sore et lyard. Inde in morina i pultrella sore iij die Decembr. Et liberavit Rogero de Normanville i pultrellam lyard etatis trium annorum et dimidii. Et est quietus.

Item respondit de v pultrellis etatis unius anni et dimidii de rem. quarum i nigra, i bay, ij grisels, et i dun. Et liberavit prefato Rogero etatis duorum annorum et dimidii per indenturam. Et est quietus.

Item respondit de vi pultrellis de predictis xij pullis rem. de exitu in computo suo anni precedentis, quarum iij grisel cum stellis, i bay, et ij grisel. Et liberavit prefato Rogero etatis unius anni et dimidii per indenturam. Et est quietus.

Pulli de exitu. Item respondit de xv pullis de exitu predictorum Jumentorum hoc anno. Et liberavit Rogero de Normanville videlicet xi masculos et iiij femineas diversorum colorum per indenturam. Et est quietus. (Exchequer. Q. R. Equicium Regis [illegible].)

From the Receiver's Compotus, 1 and 2 Hen. VI. (Duchy of Lanc. Cl. xxix. Bundle 220.)

Et solutis Johanni Parker paliciatori parci de Ightenhull sic conducto per Senescallum loci videlicet ad sustentandum vetus palicium parci predicti per totum circuitum ejusdem cum fossato ejusdem hoc anno, et ad purgandum cxx rodas cujusdam veteris fossati quod ducit circa parcum predictum, cum corroboracione dicti palicii, sumptibus ipsius Johannis, quas purgavit, et alia profecta per sacramentum ipsius Johannis et per testimonium Senescalli prout allocatum est in computo precedente	xv s.
Et solutis eidem Johanni pro nova factura de lij rod. fossati quod ducit circa parcum ibidem cum albis spinis in duabus cursubus plantatis, roda ad v d.	xxi s.

Receiver's Compotus, 3 and 4 Hen. VI. (1426.)

Custus reparacionis domorum Manerii de Ightenhull.

Jacobo del Hogh pro carpentria Coquine et Granarii ibidem ex convencione facta in grosso ultra cibaria, etc.	xiij s. viij d.
Johanni Herne pro cariacione iij rod. et quart. lignorum ad idem opus . .	xi s. vi d.
Pro cibario Carpentarii tempore factionis domorum predictorum . . .	xiij s. viij d.
Stephano le Couper et Will'o Caterynson pro cariacione maeremii ad idem opus . .	ij s.
Will'o de Henden lucracione xxxviij plaustratarum de *sclatston* cum cariagio earundem .	xliij s. iiij d.
Roberto Maude pro coopertura x rod. et purgacione Coquine et aliarum domorum ibidem	iij s. iiij d.
Whithed pro factura murorum lapid. ibidem	xi s. xd.
Pro muris Coquine predicte	ix s.
Henrico Gyour pro cariacione earundem plaustratarum	vi s.
Johanni Wilson pro lucracione zabuli et factura de morter' ibidem	iv s. iv d.
Roberto Maude pro M^l *lathes* emptis ad idem opus	x s. v d.
Johanni Smythe pro iiij^ml de *stonbrodes* et c *spykynges* emptis ad idem opus . . .	vj s. vd.
Johanni Parker et Johanni Smyth pro M^l et cccc de *stonbrodes* vi^c et dimidio de *spykynges* .	v s. ij d.
Johanni Wilson pro labore suo per ii dies	iiij d.

Johanni Smyth pro factura *des bandes* ad fenestram ibidem	ij s. iiij d.
Eidem Johanni pro vi petris ferri emptis pro diversis ferramentis inde faciendis . .	iiij s.
Johanni Mercer pro xvi quartereis calceti emptis ad idem opus cum cariagio ejusdem . .	xvi s.
Roberto Couper pro factura tabellarum ibidem	ix d.
Johanni Wilson pro servicio dato tempore levacionis et exaltacionis grossi maeremii ibidem .	vi d.
Roberto Maude pro victu duorum hominum per unum diem	iiij d.
Will' Haworth pro emendacione *des sparres* ibidem	ij d.
Johanni Smyth pro factura *des hokes* fenestre ibidem	xij d.
Johanni Colynson pro *pargettynges* murorum Granarii ibidem	xiij d.
Thome Maude pro vi^c de *stonbrodes* emptis ad idem opus	x d.
Et in rewardo facto Jacobo Banastre pro supervisu et ordinacione dictorum operum in convencione facto per Auditorem et Receptorem	xiij. iiij d.
Summa	xiij li. iij s. vi d.

(Compotus of Thomas Urswyk, Rec. of Clitheroe, 3 & 4 Hen. VI. Duchy of Lanc. Class xxix. Bundle 220.)

From Receiver's Account, 3 & 4 Edw. IV.

Reparacione et emendacione Manerii de Ightenhill	vi li. xvij s. xi d.
. . . . Palicii de Ightenhill	xxx s. iiij d.

(Duchy of Lanc. Class xxix. Bundle 221.)

Parkers of Ightenhill.

9 Mar. 1400, 1 Hen. IV. Warrant to the Receiver of the County of Lancaster to pay to John Parker, Parker of Ightenhill, his wages appertenant to the office. Duchy Register, Vol. 15, f. 63 b.

Johannes Parker fil. Joh. Parker parcarius parci de Ightenhull, appointed by patent, 1 Mar. 4 Hen. V. 1416. He occurs as "the younger Parker of Ightenhill" 13 Feb. 1423 (Ibid. f. 79); also in the Receiver's Accounts of 1-2 Hen. VI. and 3-4 Hen. VI. He had a son Richard.

Johannes Talbot, succeeded by
Carolus Belfeld, 19 July, 1 Edw. IV. 1461.
Alexander Butirworth, 7 Nov. 1 Edw. IV. 1461.
Johannes Talbot occurs 22 Edw. IV. 1482-3.
(Harl. MS. 433, f. 317.)

Rob. Ryssheton "valettus Garderobe cum dilectissimo filio nostro principi," on the death of John Talbot. 26 Oct. 18 Hen. VII. (1502). Register, f. 32.]

Of the Chases within Blackburnshire: the next is

TRAWDEN;

so called probably qu. Trough-den, the hollow or excavated valley, stretching from the summit of Boolsworth to Colne Water, about four miles, and from the boundary of Briercliffe nearly to Emot, about three. It may therefore be estimated, allowing for irregularities in the outline, at ten square miles, or 6,400 statute acres. At the time of the great Inquisition of 1311, it consisted of five booths or vaccaries: the agistment of each was valued at ten shillings.

[*Foresters of Trawden.*

William Nutter, 12 Feb. 1423, to be Master Forester, with a grant of 2*d.* a day (Register, Hen. VI. pt. 1, f. 26.)

John Whitched Forestarius, appointed by patent 5 Dec. 1 Edw. IV. 1461, died 9 Aug. 1464.

William Nutter, Custos Chacee de Trauden, succeeded by

John Hunter, patent 6 March, 3 Edw. IV. 1463, wages 2*d.* a day.]

In the commission of approvement, 22nd Hen. VII. these were reduced to three; namely,

		IMPROVED RENTS.
Berdshaie Booth, of which the old rent paid by John Hartley, Jeffrey Hartley, and other ould tenants was	x l. xiii s. iii d.	xx mks.
Over and Nether Wycoller, old rent paid by Peirs[1] Foldes, Piers Hartley, and other ould tenants .	iiii l. xiii s. iv d.	vi l.
Wynewall	vi l.	viii l. xiii s. iv d.

A very moderate advance for the latter years of Henry VII.

The name of Berdshaghbooth is now become obsolete, and is lost in that of Trawden proper. To these has since been added Emot Moore, a more recent improvement, which pays 1*l.* 5*s.* 1*d.*; and as the last improved rents of Henry VII. were fixed and rendered perpetual by the decree of James I. the whole forest now pays 29*l.* 5*s.* 1*d.*

The next, and most extensive of the chaces, is Rossendale; which, including Brandwood, Cohope, and Lench, originally members of it, though in the parishes of Rochdale and Bury, cannot contain less than twenty-four square miles, or 15,360 statute acres.[2] I was once inclined to deduce this word from the British *rhos,* a bottom; but the following etymology, for which I am indebted to Baxter (*vid.* Gloss. in voc. *Carnovacæ*) is much more appropriate. *Pagus iste, de Russeo puto graminum colore, Rossen dicitur, nam ejusmodi ericeum pascuum Britannorum vulgo Rhos dicitur.* If there was a circumstance about the place which would strike the observation of the first colonists above every other, it must have been the brown and dreary hue of its native herbage, which the labours of three centuries have not been able to overcome.

Within this chace, in the neighbourhood of Broadclough, are the remains of an entrenchment called The Dykes, to which no tradition is annexed that may serve to ascertain either its antiquity, or the end it was designed to answer. It is cut out from the gentle slope of a rising ground, in one direction, nearly parallel to the horizon, for more than 600 yards in length, not exactly in a right line, but following the little curvatures of the surface. In one part of the line, for about 100 yards, it appears to have been levelled; and in another, where it crosses a clough, is not very distinct: but more than 100 yards of the line exhibit a trench eighteen yards broad in the bottom, and of proportionate depth:—a most gigantic, and at the same time almost inexplicable work,[3] as it

[1] Ancestor of the ancient family of the Foldes's of Trawden, still resident in that place. The estate of the Hartley's passed, by marriage, to the Cunliffes of Hollins in Accrington, and is now the property of Henry Owen Cunliffe, Esq.

[2] [*A History of the Forest of Rossendale,* by Thomas Newbigging, Member of the Historic Society of Lancashire and Cheshire: with a chapter on the Geology of Rossendale by Captain Aitken, J.P., Vice-President of the Manchester Geological Society, and Observations on the Botany of the District, by Abraham Stansfield, President of the Todmorden Botanical Society, has been published in 1868. Rossendale is now essentially a manufacturing valley, and for its modern history the reader must be referred to that work, and to the particulars derived from it in the new edition of Baines's Lancashire, vol. ii. pp. 44 *et seq.*]

[3] [Mr. Newbigging (Hist. of the Forest of Rossendale, p. 10) states that the dyke is 11 or 12 feet high in the deepest part; that it extends from the farm called Dykes House to the edge of Whitaker's Clough,—not continuously,

could only have been intended for some military purpose; and yet, in its present state, must have been altogether useless as a fortification: for, though it would have defended a great army in front, yet their flanks might have been turned with the greatest ease, and the whole might have been destroyed in their trenches, from the high grounds which immediately command it. On the whole, I am inclined to think it one side of a vast British camp, which was intended to have been carried round the crown of the hill; but for some reason, never to be recovered by us, was left in its present unfinished and useless state. Abating for the herbage with which it is covered, the present appearance of it is precisely that of an unfinished modern canal, though much deeper and wider in its dimensions.

At the time of the great Inquisition in 1311, here were eleven vaccaries (or *loci vaccarum*, as they are called), of which the herbage is valued at ten shillings each. These were increased, in later times, to nineteen, including the laund or park of Musbury.

The following are the names of the booths, together with the advanced rent [1] of each, as settled under the commission 22nd Henry VII. which was afterwards perpetuated and confirmed by the decree of James I.

Gamulside	IV l.	Dedqueneclough	X l. II s. VII d.
Dunnockshawe	II l. III s. IV d.	Wolfenden Boothe [3]	IV l. XVII s. II d.ob
Love Clough	V l.	Tunstead	V l. XII s.
Goodshawe	V l. VI s. VIId.qu	Lenches	IV l. VI s. VIII d.
Crawshaweboothe	X l. IV s.	Cowhope	V l. XIII s. IV d.ob
Constablelee	V l.	Newhall Heye	VII l. XIII s. IV d.
Rawstonstall [2]	(*deest*).	Oakenheade Woode [4]	IX l. IX s. II d.ob

however, for much of the centre is levelled. He differs from Dr. Whitaker and Mr. T. T. Wilkinson (Lanc. and Cheshire Hist. Soc. Transactions, ix. 21, 42), as to its being an unfinished work, suggesting that the rising ground in the rear and extremities was protected by strong natural defences of trees and underwood. The tenant of the farm on which the dyke is situated has frequently dug to the depth of six, eight, and even ten feet, and has always found the soil "loose and intermixed with sticks and bark."]

[1] My copy of the decree of Henry VII. being defective in the end, I am not able to state the ancient rents of Rossendale and Accrington. [See hereafter most of these vaccaries mentioned among the leases described from the Duchy records.]

[2] Of which the old orthography was *Routandstall*, and the adjoining clough *Routandclough*, from the Saxon hputan, *strepere*, the brawling brook.

[3] [Reparacione et emendacione logii de Wolfanden, vijs. viijd. Compotus of Receiver of Clitheroe, 3 and 4 Edw. IV. Duchy of Lanc. Cl. xxix, Bundle 221.]

[4] [Adam de Balochawe granted to Henry de Lacy a messuage and 16 acres of land near Oakenhead, by the following charter:—Universis Christi fidelibus presens scriptum visuris vel audituris, Adam de Balochawe salutem in domino. Noveritis me remisisse et omnino quietumclamasse pro me et heredibus meis domino Henrico de Lascy Comiti Lincoln' et Constabulario Cestrie totum jus et clameum quod habui aut aliquo modo habere potui in uno messuagio et sexdecim acris terre cum pertinenciis in foresta de Roscindal apud Hokenhevedd. Ita quod nec ego nec heredes mei nec aliquis nomine nostro aliquod jus vel clameum in dictis messuagio et sexdecim acris terre cum pertinenciis exigere vel vendicare poterimus imperpetuum. In cujus rei testimonium huic scripto sigillum meum apposui. Testibus dominis Roberto Banestre, Henrico de Lee, Johanne Biron, Adam de Bury, militibus, Henrico de Clayton, Alexandro de Keverdal, Willelmo del Hacking, Rogero de Middleton, Adam de Prestwyche, Willelmo de Hopwode et aliis. Great Cowcher of the Duchy, vol. i. 78 b. Lancaster Carta Clxxv.]

Musbury	xiii l. i s. viii d.	Wolfenden	xiii l. v s. i d.
Hoddlesden[1]	ix l. xix s. xi d.	Henheads	xiii s.
Bacope	xi l. xvi s. viii d.		

We will now endeavour to collect what can be retrieved concerning the vaccaries; and, first, of the Park of Musbury, so called qu. Moorbyrig, the hill of moss, from Moor, the Saxo-Danish genitive of Moor;[2] a brown conical hill on the confines of Rossendale and Tottington, anciently inclosed as a lawnd for the lord's deer.

[In a list of charters found at Pontefract Castle, r. Edw. II. occurs—"Musbury. Item carta Lodowici de Geraville facta eidem Johanni [de Lacy], etc. de tota terra de Musbury cum pertinenciis."]

Custody of the herbage of Musbury[3] was granted to James de Radcliffe by John of Ghent, 18 Rich. II. and there were several renewals to the same family.[4]

The first mention of Rossendale, by name, is in the memorable story of Liwlphus, dean of Whalley, who, at a place called Ledmesgreve, cut off the tail of a wolf in hunting.[5] The ordinary period allowed by chronologers to human life, together with the number of deans in succession from Liwlphus to those whose æra is ascertained, will carry up this event to Canute, in whose charter of the forest we have seen that the existence of this animal in England, though contrary to the vulgar tradition, is expressly referred to.

[1] In the Inq. of 1311, Hoddlesden is neither included in Rossendale nor Accrington.

[2] *Vide* Dr. Hickes ap. Thoresby's Duc. p. 267.

[In 1850 a handsome church was erected at Musbury, of which Mr. Shellard of Manchester was the architect. The site was given by William Turner, esq. of Flaxmoss House, whose body was the first interred there, March 27, 1852, two days after the consecration.]

[3] Here are three small subdivisions of the hamlet, called Ugden, Musden, and Holden; of which the first is called the "Trippet," or third part of Ugden; the only instance which I know of the subdivision of a hamlet—but it claims the rights of a constablewick.

[4] Concessio per literas patentes 2 Hen. V. Ric. Radcliffe de Radcliffe de uno parco vocato Musbury Park, habendum ad term. 20 annor. reddendo viij li. vj s. viij d. et vj s. viij d. de incremento. (Last edition, p. 236, from Towneley MSS.) 16 June 2 Edw. IV. a lease to Jac. Radcliffe arm. of the herbage and pasture parci de Musbury at viij li. x s. for 16 years from Michaelmas last past; and of Hudelsden vaccary for 16 years at 10 marks a year. (Chancery Rolls, Duchy Off. Class 25 x. 1 a.) 20 Oct. 7 Edw. IV. 1467. Lease to Galfridus Warton, arm. for 20 years of the herbage and pannage of Musbury Park, rent 8*l.* 10*s.* "et predictus Galfridus reparabit et sustentabit palicium, sepes et fossatum dicti parci per totum circuitum ejusdem sumptibus suis propriis expensis durante termino predicto." (Ibid.) It was ordered by a decree dated 1 Mar. 19 Edw. IV. (1480), "that no fees nor wages are to be paid to any officer of Musbury Parke, as by Act of Parliament no fees nor wages shall be paid for any office as nedeth nat dayly exercise, and that also in our said parke there is no game to kepe." (Register, f. 59 b.)

Parkers of Musbury.

Nic. Brounlawe. Patent dated 24 May, 1 Hen. V.

Nic. de Brunlawe, 17 Feb. 1423, confirmation or reappointment by Henry VI.

John Barlow, who was succeeded by

John Cay. Patent 24 May, 3 Edw. IV. Occurs 1 and 2 Ric. III. in the Receiver of Clitheroe's Compotus.

Laurence Maderer, appointed by patent 1 Oct. 1 Hen. VII. 1485.

9 Edw. IV. a lease to Richard Radcliffe for twenty years at the rent of viij li. vj s. viij d. and renewed for the like term. (Last edit. from Towneley MSS.)

[5] See before, p. 74.

The first part of this tract which was inclosed and planted with inhabitants was Brandwood,[1] which was granted by Roger de Lacy, about the year 1200, to the abbot and convent of Stanlaw, in the same charter which conveys to them four oxgangs of land in Recedham.

Dedi etiam eis in foresta mea pasturam illam quæ dicitur Brendwude, ad eorum animalia pascenda, per divisas subnotatas, scilicet a Goresichelache usque Cuhopeheued, et sic sicut Cohope descendit in Yrewil, et sic [per] Yrewil usque Fulebacope,[2] deinde ascendendo usque Saltergat, et sic usque Hamstalesclowe, et sic usque Denesgreue,[3] et sic per transitum muse[4] usque Cumbeheph ad Gorsichelache: habebunt autem predicti monachi in pastura illa C. vaccas cum exitu duorum annorum; et si animalia ibi habuero, eorum animalia pascent et ibunt in latum et in longum ubicunque mea pascunt et vadunt, *&c.* Testibus, Turgisio abb. de Kirkstal, Ric. de Cestria, Eustach. de Cestria, fratribus meis, *etc.*

And in the 18th Edw. III. a suit which R. de Radcliffe, Master Forester of Pendle, brought against the abbot and convent of Whalley, for puture of the foresters, which certainly was not reserved by the grantor in the former charter, according to the usual form, *salva foresta mea*, produced this curious account of the first population of Brandwood :—

Inveniunt juratores quod temp. Reg. Johan. non erat in prædicta placea de Brandwode aliquod manerium nec aliqua mansio, immo fuit vastum, non edificatum neq. cultum, et fuit parcella p'dictæ forestæ de Penhull; et dicitur quod tempore regis Henrici proavi regis nunc quidam abbas qui tunc fuit primus construxit et edificavit domos in p'dicto vasto de Brandwode, et magnam partem vasti includi fecit, quod nunc vocatur Manerium de Brandwode.

In this instance alone Rossendale appears included within the chace of Pendle.

Again, John de Lacy, son of Roger, by charter directed to his foresters and bailiffs, grants to the abbot and convent of Stanlaw licence "falcandi fænum in foresta mea de Rossyndale, ad sustentanda in yeme averia sua quæ illic habent."[5]

We are not to suppose that this charter has any reference to inclosed and cultivated meadows, but that it was merely a permission to cut and carry away the native herbage of the forest; which, as it was probably much understocked either with deer or cattle, would afford some moist and level spots of luxuriant vegetation.

This representation will give a modern farmer very low ideas of the husbandry of the thirteenth century in the forests; but, in truth, the vast quantities of sheep and cattle

[1] [It has been remarked: "The etymology is obvious. Brent-wood, firewood from the forest; *brent* for burnt, and *brenning* for burning, being still provincialisms in the neighbourhood." Coucher Book, Chetham Soc. p. 153. It is probable that the name arose from a wood burnt by some memorable conflagration, as Pontefract was named from its broken bridge. There is in Essex, in the parish of South Weald, a Brentwood, which, being on a high road, grew into a considerable market town.]

[2] Probably miswritten for *Futebacope*, or *Bacop Foot*. [See note in p. 320.]

[3] Which I suspect to be an error of the writer for the *Lenesgreve*, or *Ledmesgreve*, of Liwlphus. [This conjecture is contradicted by a tracing of the original charter, which is preserved in the Author's copy of the last edition (at p. 436), and which is now followed in the text; and also by the copy entered in the Cartulary, as printed by the Chetham Society. *Denesgreue* might possibly be a greve, or boundary-ditch, of the ancient deans of Whalley: although, in ordinary acceptance, a *dene* is simply a valley.]

[4] But more probably *Moræ*—unless *Musæ* be meant for *Moss*. [See under Billington a grant of turbary to the Abbey of Whalley "*in musea et mora mea.*"]

[5] [Cartulary, Chetham Soc. edit. p. 154.]

which were anciently slaughtered at the approach of winter prove a general inattention to the important article of winter-fodder throughout the kingdom at that period.

The abbots of Stanlaw set an example of inclosure and improvement which had no followers during three centuries; for, in the 3rd Hen. VIII. the inhabitants of the several vaccaries within Rossendale describe themselves as consisting of no more than 80 souls, or about one family to a booth.

This and some other interesting facts,[1] with respect to the progressive population of Rossendale, appear from a decree of the commissioners of pious uses, 4th Edw. VI. which recites a petition of the inhabitants, stating—"That forty-four years before, or thereabouts, (referring to the date of Henry VII.'s commission of improvement,) the forest of Rossendale was replenished only or chiefly with foresters and keepers of the deer; but upon representation to King Henry VII. and afterwards to King Henry VIII. that if the deer were taken away, the forest was likely to come to some good purpose, the said forest was disforested and granted, demised and let forth in divers sorts, some for a term of years, some by copy of court-roll; so that, whereas before that time was nothing else but deer and other savage and wild beasts, there is since, by industry of the inhabitants, grown to be very fertile ground, well replenished with people. And forasmuch as the Castle Church of Clitheroe, being their parish church, is distant twelve miles from the said forest, and the ways very foul, painful, and perilous, and the country in the winter season is so extremely and vehemently cold, that infants borne to church are in great peril of their lives, and the aged and impotent people, and women great with child, not able to travel so far to hear the word of God, and the dead corpses there like to remain unburied at such times for want of carriage, till such time as great annoyance doth grow thereby: the premises considered, the inhabitants of the said forest, about thirty-eight years past (1512), or thereabouts, at their proper costs made a chapel of ease[2] in the said forest; since the disforesting of which, from eighty persons in the forest there are grown to 1,000, young and old." A remarkable increase, but more than equalled in later times.

At the same time (3 Hen. VIII.) one Lettice Jackson, widow, vested in feoffees certain lands situated in different parts of Rossendale, for the use of the New Church of our Saviour in Rossendale, which the commissioners of chantries,[3] either from their inconsiderable value at that time, or for some other reason which we are not acquainted with, forbore to seize upon (an instance of forbearance never practised by them in any other case), and decreed that Laurence Ashworth should hold and occupy the place of parson of the said church.

[1] This circumstance, together with the peculiar dialect of Rossendale, so different from the rest of the parish of Whalley, so similar to that of the adjacent district of Brandwood, proves to me, beyond a doubt, that the population of Rossendale was a colony from Brandwood. The small number of surnames in this tract proves, if any proof were wanting, its recent colonization.

[2] [In the will of Sir George Gregory, priest, of Rossendayle, 1548, quoted by the editor of *Notitia Cestriensis*, this is called "ye Sedenayse chappell in Rossendayle," and there is still on the north of the village a high ground called the Seeton-heys, from which that name was evidently derived.]

[3] [Newchurch was not a Chantry, but a Chapel of Ease to the Castle Church of Clitheroe, and therefore the Chantry Commissioners had no power to divert the pious gift of Lettice Jackson.—Note by Canon Raines in *Notitia Cestriensis*.]

These lands, though some part of them appears to have been lost by the neglect, or something worse than neglect, of the feoffees, were valued in the latter end of the last century but one at 50*l.* per annum [1]; and form the endowment of the chapel, the most valuable curacy in the patronage of the Vicar of Whalley. Its value occasioned, as we have already seen,[2] a long contest for the patronage, betwixt Dr. Keene, then Bishop of Chester, and Mr. Johnson, the Vicar of Whalley, grounded on a decree of the chancellor of the duchy, 4 Edw. VI. that the ordinary should appoint a minister: but as the original decree could not be found in the registry at Chester, or elsewhere, the vicar presented as of common right, and the ordinary was compelled to license his antagonist's presentee.

[The following is a catalogue of the incumbents of this church:—

George Gregory, ob. 1548; his will and inventory are printed in *Lanc. and Chesh. Wills and Inventories*, (Chetham Soc. ii. 199).

Laurence Ashworth, 1548.

James Kershaw,[3] licensed Sept. 1, 1598.

William Horrox clericus, sacri Dei verbi predicator apud Newchurch in Rossendall. (Lanc. MSS. xxii. 80.) Died 1641.

Robert Dewhurst occurs 1650. By the Lambeth Inquisition of that year it is found that the chapel of Newchurch in Rossendale is parochial, the chapelry consisting of Dedwen Clough, Tunsted, Woolfenden Booth, and part of Wolfenden and Bakcop, which contain in all 300 families desiring to be made a parish: that the minister received no allowance but what was paid by the inhabitants. (Lamb. MSS. 912.)

Mr. Jonas Browne, 1660.

Thomas Saunders, clerk, licensed to this curacy Sept. 5, 1662. His successor has given this account of him in the church register: "Tho. Saunders presbyter, Christi Dñi nostri servus humilis, honestis moribus præditus, ecclesiæ Anglicanæ pastor vigilans, artium bonarum studiosus, in hac gente rustica Rossendaliæ per spatium 33 annorum plus minus commoratus est. Qui per varios casus longo tempore jactatus deinde in patriam suam nativam Com. Cest. decessit. Et ipsa hora in qua domum suam ingressus est, placide inter familiares expiravit. Sepultus apud Mag. Budworth, 9° die Nov. 1695.

Thomas Leigh, B.A. Nov. 29, 1695.

John Welsh, licensed Nov. 5, 1730 (formerly at Todmorden); died after 1762.

John Sherrock, A.M. Feb. 1767.

Nicholas Rigby Baldwin, A.M. 1802; ob. Nov. 1824.

Philip Abbot, 1825, res. 1833; died 1852. Writing Master at Clitheroe School.

Edward Burrow, 1833.

John Bartholomew Phillips, A.M. 1850.]

The original chapel of the 3rd Henry VIII. having been calculated only for the slender population of that period, was pulled down, and the present church erected upon its site in 1561. It is a very decent structure, with a nave, side ailes, choir, and tower, but without any sepulchral memorials of importance.[4]

[1] [They were valued at 40*l.* per ann. in 1718, a case then pending in the Duchy Chamber; and in 1724 the Chancellor of the Duchy, with Lord Chief Justice King and Mr. Reeves as assessors, decreed the lands in question, being by estimation 150 statute acres, to the Church, with mean profits and costs. *Notitia Cestriensis*, ii. 341.]

[2] See before, p. 215.

[3] [James Kershay, Curat of Rossendale and Scholemaster, was excused appearance at the Bishop's visitation of Blackburn deanery 1609. He was still Minister of Newchurche in Rossendale, 2 Nov. 1622. Lanc. MSS. vol. xxii.

To one of this family there is a gravestone in the churchyard thus inscribed: "In memory of John Kershaw of Wolfenden Booth Fold, the beneficent donor of the estates situated in Heald, in Bacup Booth, for the benefit of New Church School. He was buried the 1st of February 1701, at the age of 85 years. Anne Kershaw his wife was buried 4th January, 1709. They lived long beloved, and dy'd bewailed, And two estates upon our School entail'd." The Schoolhouse was finished in 1711, and rebuilt in 1829-30. *Notitia Cestriensis*, ii. 342, 343.]

[4] [Again rebuilt in 1824-25: see Baines's Lancashire, 1870, ii. 46.]

Not thirty years after the erection of Newchurch arose a Chapel of Ease, high up in the forest at GOODSHAW, a proof of the rapid increase of population, for by deed of covenant[1] dated Dec. 16, 32 Hen. VIII. it was condescended and agreed between, &c. &c. that "they should found, edifie, and build one chapel in the honour of God, our blessed Lady, and all Saints, in a certain place within the forest of Rossendale named Morrell height, for the easement of the said parties and of their neighbours the inhabitants of Crawshaw Booth, Gambleside, Goodshaw, and Loveclough, and all other the King's liege people which shall be disposed to hear mass and other divine service in the said chapel."

A very humble edifice was erected accordingly; and, growing ruinous a few years ago, was replaced by another not much more ornamental.[2]

By the Lambeth Inquisition of 1650, it was found that the chapel of Goodshaw was not parochial; that the chapelry consisted of seventy families; no minister or maintenance; but a house and backyard, value 10*s.* and that they desire to be made a parish.

In the course of the last century the manufacturing village of BACOPE,[3] within this forest, increased from seven or eight families to 306 houses, and 1,426 souls, of which it was found to consist by an accurate enumeration in October 1798. In consequence of this rapid increase of population, a spacious and handsome chapel was erected by the very laudable zeal of some of the principal inhabitants, in the year 1788, and consecrated by Dr. Cleaver, then Bishop of Chester, August 16th in that year.

On the ridge of the hill, which forms the north-east boundary of Rossendale, are considerable remains of the Haia Dominicalis, now called the Old Dyke; within this, but in a piece of ground, though anciently included in the forest, now by prescription belonging to Cliviger, is the real source of the Irewell.[4] Of this rich and useful stream the Historian of Manchester, b. 1, c. 7, informs us, "That it wells gently from a double fountain near the upper part of an hill between Broadclough and Holme in Rossendale; that it carries its waters on the western side of Maneenion, and was therefore denominated Ir Gaeil, Irwell, Irwill, or the Western Torrent." A more accurate acquaintance with the face of the country, and with the dialect of its inhabitants, compels me to differ from the learned antiquary both in his statement of facts, and in his conjectures on this subject: for, in the first place, Holme, as I have reason to know, is not in Rossendale, but in Cliviger; and, secondly, the only genuine source of this river is at the foot of Dirplay Hill, once within the forest, but now in Cliviger, as above stated, where it flows from a copious

[1] [Mr. Newbigging, at p. 134 of his *History of Rossendale*, has printed this document at length. Its date is in the 32d Hen. VIII. (not 35 as given by Whitaker). The said Chapel was to be in length 16 cloth-yards, in wideness 7 cloth-yards, the walls in height 3 cloth-yards, with two doors of hewn stones and three windows of hewn stones,—"to be timbered accordingly, and to be made, thached, and finished afore the feast of Mari Mawdlin next."]

[2] [Again rebuilt 1829: see Baines's Lancashire, 1870, ii. 52.]

[3] Qu. Bay-cop, the cop or hillock where the deer stood at bay? [This etymology is less probable than Beck-hope, the valley of the beck or brook, and if Fulebacope (see p. 317) was the original name, it was the valley of the full beck. Bacup is now a large town, the church dilapidated, and about to be rebuilt: see its modern history in Baines, 1870, ii. 48.]

[4] Irwel (saith Harrison), a notable water, "riseth above Bacop, and goeth thence to Rossendale, and in the way to Aytonfield it taketh in a water from Haselden. After this confluence it goeth to Newhall, Brandlesam, and Bury, and above Ratcliffe joineth with the Rache, a fayre stream."

fountain universally known by the name Erewell. Not far beneath however rises another spring called Whitewell, which, after a course of several miles, unites with the principa stream, and these, I suppose, constitute together the double fountain of which Mr Whitaker was told.

And with respect to the etymology of the word, I fear we must be contented to deduce it from a nearer and less venerable source than the British language, for Ere in the semi-Saxon dialect of this neighbourhood is *hoar* used as a substantive; and very high grounds which are often grey with sleet or hoar-frost while the meadows and pastures beneath remain unsprinkled are said to be in the Ere. Now this remark is strikingly verified in Derplay Hill, which many times in every winter presents an hoary head while the low lands of Rossendale retain their native brown. Erewell therefore is the spring in the Ere. The neighbouring Whitewell probably derives its name from the same circumstance, and the very next elevation north-west of Derplay-hill, in ancient charters (for the present coarse orthography of the word rests on no authority) is styled Hor or Horelaw.

Irwell is first mentioned in the charter of Brandwood [1] by Roger de Lacy about the year 1200, and should any future litigation arise in which the name of this stream is involved a reference to that authentic document would determine its real course.

The great increase of population both here and over the whole chace of Rossendale is solely to be ascribed to the woollen manufactory, which appears to have been attracted hither by the smallness of the estates into which the country was distributed, not sufficient to support the owners or employ their dependants; by the plenty and cheapness of coal; and, above all, by the great abundance and rapid descent of the streams, of which almost every foot of fall is employed in working mills; so well have art and industry compensated for blessings which had been denied by nature.

Last among the chaces of Blackburnshire is ACCRINGTON, sometimes considered as a member of Rossendale, but more anciently as an independent portion of the demesnes of Clitheroe.

At the time of the great Inquisition in 1311, here was a capital messuage—*val. nihil;* in demesne, XXX acres, x s.; demised to tenants at will, CVI½ acres, and half a rood at 4*d*. an acre, Cxv s. vj d.; four vaccaries, at x s. each, ij li.: one water-mill, j li.; total, v li. v s. vj d. In consequence of a deficiency in my copy of the commission of Henry VII. I am not able to give the names of these vaccaries, or the improved rents paid severally by each; but the whole sum, as settled under that commission and paid at present, is 33*l*. 4*s*. 2¾*d*.

However, by a lease (date uncertain) the vaccary of Antley, in the forest of Rossendale, was granted to John Rushton for ten years. Towneley MSS. g. 13.

[Et de cvj s. viij d. de Johanne Ruyssheton pro firma vaccarie de Antley sic sibi dimissa per Senescallum predictum ad terminum predictum (10 years) solutis, etc. (terminis Pasche et Michaelis) hoc anno quinto,

[1] See p. 317.

que quidem vaccaria onerari solebat nisi ad iiij li. iij s. iiij d. (Compotus Collectorum herbagii de Blakbourne-shire, 1 and 2 Hen. VI. Duchy of Lanc. Class xxix. Bundle 220.)

The lease had been made by Roger Flour, Chief Steward of the North, five years before, that is, in 6 Hen. V. It began 29 Sept. 1417.

By a lease dated 20 Mar. 1 Ric. III. 1484, the vaccary of Anteley was granted to Hugh Garthside and his son Nicholas for seven years from Michaelmas last past, at 6*l.* a-year rent and Lufelough rent 60*s.* *prout ultimus firmarius et 20s. ultra.* (Duchy of Lancaster, Register t. Ric. III. f. 87.)

Et de iiij d. de novo reddito pro minere lapidi ferr' invent' in Acryngton sic dimisso Galfrido Russyngton tenendo sibi et assignatis suis ut in Rotulo Curie de anno secundo Regis Ed. IIIIti. (Compotus of the Master Forester of Blackburnshire, 11 and 12 Edw. IV. Duchy of Lanc. Class xxix. Bundle 220.)]

Having now considered the four Chaces of Blackburnshire particularly, it may be proper to attend to a few circumstances recorded in the great Inquisition of 1311 as common to them all :

The winter agistment and herbage of Trawden, Penhull, Rossendall, Heddesdene, and Romesgreve, was found to be worth . . .	i li.	ix s.	viii d.
Summer agistment of the same	ij li.		
Profits of the sale of hay, viz. for every cart-load mown and carried away i d. comm. ann.		vi s.	viij d.
Profits of old wood, charcoal, &c. sold for the use of iron forges, comm. ann.		ix s.	iv d.
	iv li.	v s.	viij d.[1]

With respect to these statements of ancient economy, the following observations occur:

1st. The profit of winter agistment must have arisen principally from sheep, which in most countries require a change of air and herbage at different seasons of the year, and in the mountainous parts of Lancashire must necessarily be withdrawn from the high grounds in winter, yet cannot be trusted to meadows or very fertile plains: lower grounds, therefore, comparatively barren, must be sought out for their winter habitation; and such were the more sheltered parts of the forests.

2nd. The smallness of the profits arising from wood and charcoal proves that the native forests were in a great measure decayed in 1311, for, if we multiply the sum of 9*s.* 1*d.* so as to bring it to the present standard, much more advantage would be made of the old wood, &c. grown upon the same grounds at present.

But, perhaps, a demand for these articles might be wanting.

[1] [The following is the original text of these items:—Pannagium de Penhill aliquando valet, aliquando nichil valet, et ideo communibus annis extenditur ad vi s. viij d. Agistamentum herbagii yemalis de Troweden, Rossindale, Penhill et Romesgrave valet per annum xxix s. viij d. Agistamentum herbagii estivalis in eisdem locis valet xl s. quolibet anno. De proficuo feni venditi in eisdem videlicet de quolibet falcante levante et asportante i carrucam feni, summa communibus annis vi s. viij d. Item proficuum Minere ferri de veteri bosca sustentata et annuatim vend. in eisdem forestis, communibus annis ix s. iiij d.—Summa iiij li. xij s. iiij d.]

THE MANOR OF TOTTINGTON.

Another member of the Honor of Clitheroe, which belongs not indeed to the demesnes and forests of Blackburnshire, but, as it never formed a part of the original parish of Whalley, has no claim to any other place in this account, and may, therefore, most properly be considered here on account of its contiguity to Rossendale. And as this district has no other than a feudal connection with the Honor of Clitheroe, it will be considered principally in that relation.

I have said that Tottington belonged not to the forests, and, in strictness of language, it did not, yet in the very first charter in which the name is found Robert de Lacy grants certain lands abutting upon "Pilgrim-crosse-slack in Foresta de Tottington. Dat. ap. Ightenhill,[1] 22 Hen. II. Test. Galf. Dec. de Whalley." Thus Saddleworth is called a forest,[2] and for the same reason only, viz. that both were dreary and uncultivated tracts, rejected or overlooked at the first distribution of property, and therefore fallen, as lands unclaimed, into the hands of the lords.

Tottington, however, had another and better claim to the name of forest, for I find that Roger de Montbegon gave to the priory of Monk Bretton, in the county of York, the pasture of Holecombe, reserving to himself the wild beasts, and pasture for his cattle within certain bounds. By a second charter, about 1236, he grants all Holecombe: and by a third, *totam forestam de Holecombe,* thereby releasing the reservation of his first grant.[3] By a fourth charter, the same grantor conveys to the said priory three acres of meadow near Pilgrim-crosse-chahe,[4] which seems to countenance an opinion that this was a resting-place of the pilgrims (see under WHALLEY ABBEY), and that they had a chapel here for their devotions.

[The charters of Roger de Montbegon are highly curious and important from the names contained in their boundaries.

[1] *Vide supra,* (p. 306) under Ightenhill. [The name of John de Lacy is now altered to Robert in accordance with Dr. Whitaker's note in his last edition, p. 228. The word "slack" is probably still incorrect: see note [4].

Charters found at Pontefract Castle in the reign of Edward II. a roll among the Duchy papers Class xxv. A, 9. *Toteynton.* Carta Henrici de Middleton per quam dedit Johanni de Lascy Comiti Lincolnie et Constabulario Cestric, et heredibus suis in feodo, totam terram suam in Totyngton cum omnibus pertinenciis suis.

Item carta Regis Henrici confirmans donacionem predictam.

Item carta Will'i fil. Hug. de Haselum per quam quiete clamavit domine Margarete de Lasci et heredibus suis quatuor acras terre in foresta de Totynton.]

[2] *Vide* cart. W. de Stapleton, under Rochdale.

[3] [The charter itself now printed from the coucher of Monkbretton shows that the reservation was retained.]

[4] [Dr. Whitaker printed this "Pilgrim crosse-charche," which he suggested was an error for *churche;* but it more probably meant a *shaw*, or wood. It follows that his theory of a pilgrims' church or chapel standing near the cross is imaginary.]

Carta Rogeri de Monte Begonis.

Omnibus sancte matris Ecclesie filiis ad quos presens scriptum pervenerit, Rogerus de Monte Begonis salutem. Noverit universitas vestra me divine pietatis intuitu dedisse et concessisse, et hac presenti carta mea confirmasse Deo et ecclesie Sancte Marie Magdalene de Bretton et monachis ibidem Deo servientibus totam forestam meam que vocatur Holecumbam, videlicet boscum et planum intus et extra sine ullo retenimento, per istas divisas subscriptas, scilicet quantum foresta mea se extendit versus Querendonam in longitudine et latitudine, et ascendendo per divisas foreste mee usque ad Langschauet,[1] et de Langschauet usque ad Aldenehevet, et de Aldene hevet extranverso usque Arkilishou,[2] et inde per medium Arkilishou versus ad Pilgrimscroschahe, et inde descendendo versus ad viam que ducit per medium Tyteleshou, sequendo predictam viam usque ad Titeleshou broc, et inde versus occidentem sequendo semitam que dicitur semita latronum usque Salterbrigge, et de Salterbrigge usque viam de Oskelei. Tenenda et habenda omnia que sunt infra divisas prescriptas tam super terram quam subtus, et de omnibus predictis pro voluntate faciendum et utenda sua, libere, quiete, pacifice et honorifice sicut puram et perpetuam elemosinam. Salva tamen venacione et salvis nisis[3] mihi et heredibus meis infra predictas divisas. Preterea dedi et concessi eisdem monachis totam pasturam foreste mee et sustentacionem plenariam averiis suis de bosco infra divisas subscriptas videlicet de Caldwelt hevet[4] versus in aquam de Þrewil,[5] sequendo Caldwellsic, et inde sequendo Þrewil versus Titeleshoubroc, et inde ascendendo per Titelishou broc usque ad viam que ducit per medium Titeleshou, et inde sequendo predictam viam versus ad Caldewell'hevet. Salva tamen hominibus de Totington comuna quam antiquitus habere solebant. Preterea dedi et concessi predictis monachis tres acras de prato sub Arkilhou juxta Pilgrimcroschahe, et licebit eisdem monachis circa illud pratum[6] sepem facere vel fossatum prout voluerint. Et sciendum est quod prenominati monachi debent communicare ubique cum hominibus de Totington. Et si averia predictorum monachorum prenominatas divisas transgredierint predicti monachi inde non debent causari nec homines eorum nec pastores, sed predicta averia debent reduci inter proprias divisas predictorum monachorum sine calumpnia alicujus vel molestia. Ista omnia prenominata sicut prescripta simul dedi et concessi predictis monachis in puram et perpetuam elemosinam pro salute anime mee et uxoris mee et patris mei et matris mee et Johannis Malherbe fratris mei et antecessorum et successorum meorum. Ita tamen quod nullus ballivus meus seu serviens sive forestarius meus vel heredum meorum vel assignatorum meorum vel assignatorum heredum meorum inquietabit vel molestabit nec gravabit predictos monachos nec homines eorum nec pastores nec averia eorum in nullis rebus, nec in cibis nisi ex mera liberalitate eis conferre voluerunt. Quare volo et firmiter precipio ut prenominati monachi habeant et teneant et possideant omnia prenominata sicut suprascripta sunt in puram et perpetuam elemosinam tam libere tam pacifice tam honorifice et integre quam aliqua elemosina melius et liberius dari poterit vel teneri vel possideri in tota Anglia. Et ego prefatus Rogerus et heredes mei vel assignati mei vel assignati heredum meorum omnia prenominata sicut prescripta sunt predictis monachis sicut puram et perpetuam elemosinam contra omnes homines warantizabimus et defendemus in perpetuum. Hiis Testibus, domino Will' fil. W. etc. (Lansd. MS. 405, f. 43 b.)

[1] In the Monasticon Anglicanum, (1st edit. p. 662, edit. 1825, v. p. 138,) will be found still another charter of Roger de Montbegon de Foresta de Helecombe different from any of the three now printed, for it had different witnesses, beginning with Eudo de Lungvilers. In it Langshauet is written Langschahevet, *i. e.* the head of the long shaw: which confirms the meaning now assigned to Pilgrim's cross *schahe* or shaw.

[2] Harcles Hill, which is 1,216ft. high.

[3] Young falcons taken from the nest. [4] *i. e.* the head of the cold well. [5] *i. e.* the Irwell.

[6] —Et singulis annis sepes eis facere licebit circa illud pratum, et circa pratum suum apud Haderleies, prout voluerint. Preterea licebit illis habere edificia sua ubi Henricus Luggejambe mansit vel alibi versus Querendonam ubi voluerint. Licebit eisdem illam terram excolere ad victualia pastorum suorum circa domum in qua dictus Henricus mansit. Charter in the Monasticon.

(2). *Confirmacio [Rogeri] de Monte Begonis.*

Omnibus sancte matris Ecclesie filiis ad quos presens scriptum pervenerit, tam presentibus quam futuris, Rogerus de Monte Begon sal. Noverit universitas vestra me divine pietatis intuitu dedisse et concessisse et hac presenti carta mea confirmasse Deo et sancte Marie Magdalene de Bretton et monachis ibidem Deo servientibus totam Holcumbam, videlicet boscum et planum intus et extra, per istas divisas, scilicet de Holcumbhevet usque ad supercilium montis de Arkeleshow versus Aledeneheuet, et de Arkellhou versus Tyteleshougate, et de Titeleshougate usque Caldewellhevet, et de Caldewellhevet usque in Irewil, sicut rivulus currit, cum omni libera communione ad Totintun pertinente ex una parte, et ex altera parte de Holcumbe versus Querendune in longitudine et latitudine quantum forestum meum extendit, salva tamen venacione mea, et salvis nisis meis infra prenominatas divisas, pro salute anime mee et uxoris mee et Johannis Malherbe fratris mei et antecessorum et successorum meorum, in puram et perpetuam elemosinam. Ita tamen quod nullus Ballivus neque serviens neque forestarius meus vel heredum meorum inquietabit vel molestabit homines vel pastores eorum in aliquibus rebus nec in cibis nisi ex mera liberalitate conferre voluerint. Quare volo et firmiter principio ut prenominati monachi prenominatam elemosinam teneant et possideant, libere et quiete, pacifice et honorifice, sicut aliqua elemosina melius et liberius tenetur in tota Anglia. Ego vero prenominatus Rogerus et heredes mei predictam elemosinam prenominatis monachis contra omnes homines warantizabimus in perpetuum. Hiis Testibus, Will'o fil. Will', et cetera.

(3). *Carta Rogeri de Monte Begonis.*

Omnibus sancte matris Ecclesie filiis ad quos presens scriptum pervenerit Rogerus de Monte Begon salutem eternam in Domino. Noverit universitas vestra me dedisse et concessisse et hac presenti carta mea confirmasse Deo et sancte Marie Magdalene de Bretton et Monachis ibidem Deo servientibus pasturam meam de Holecumba cum pertinenciis in puram et perpetuam elemosinam, salvis bestiis et avibus meis, et ad avaria sua pascenda per istas divisas scilicet de Holecumba usque ad supercilium montis de Arkeleshou, at ab Arkeleshou in[de] descendendo usque ad viam que se extendit per medium Tutelleshou versus villam de Totington. Ita quod predicta averia non debent excedere predictas divisas, et si forte excesserint non tamen inde causabuntur, sed libere servientibus monachorum deliberabuntur si capta fuerint. Si autem averia hominum meorum vel aliorum prefatam pasturam ingressa fuerint servientes monachorum ea imparcabunt nec ea dimittent quousque satisfiat eis de ingressu illicito suo. Hanc autem donacionem Ego Rogerus et heredes mei warantizabimus predictis monachis contra omnes homines imperpetuum. Hiis testibus, Johanne Malherbe, etc.

In the reign of Richard III. the estate of the monks of Mount Bretton was annexed to the Duchy of Lancaster, and the King granted to the Priory in exchange the advowson of Darton in Yorkshire by the following charter:

Rex omnibus, etc. salutem. Sciatis quod nos per avisiamentum consilii nostri et in recompensacionem cujusdam Foreste sive pasture vulgariter nuncupate Holcombe in com. Lancastrie que jam in manibus nostris existit ut parcellum Ducatus nostri Lancastrie, et que ad Priorem et Conventum Monasterii beate Marie Magdalene de Monkebretton et successores suos pertinere deberet, prout per inspeccionem diversarum cartarum Rogeri de Monte Begoñ predecessoribus predicti nunc Prioris confectarum plenius apparet, et pro aliis diversis consideracionibus et convencionibus inter nos et prefatum Priorem et Conventum Monasterii beate Marie Magdalene predicte indentatis, de gracia nostra speciali dedimus, concessimus et per presentes damus et concessimus Priori Domus et Ecclesie beate Marie Magdalene de Monkebretton et ejusdem loci Conventui et successoribus suis Advocacionem sive patronatum Ecclesie parochialis de

Derton in Com. Ebor. et Ebor. dioecessis predicte parcelle Ducatus nostri Lancastrie predicti Honoris de Pountfreit, habendam et tenendam advocacionem sive patronatum predictam prefatis Priori et Conventui et successoribus suis in recompensacionem predictam absque aliquo fine seu feodo inde ad opus nostrum quovismodo capiendo, faciendo seu solvendo, eo quod expressa mencio de vero valore annuo premissorum aut de aliis donis sive concessionibus eisdem Priori et Conventui per nos ante hec tempora factis in presentibus minime facta existit, aut aliquo statuto actu ordinacione permissione sive restitucione inde in contrarium facto, edito, ordinato sive promisso non obstante. In cujus rei, etc. Dat. etc. apud London. viij° die Februarii Anno etc. primo. (8 Feb. 1 Rich. III. 1484.) Duch. Lanc. Class xi., No. 20, f. 11.]

Where this cross and chapel stood, or whether the latter were on the site of the present chapel of HOLCOMBE, I am not informed;[1] but of the last, tradition reports that it was once a prison, and an adjoining eminence the place of execution belonging to it.[2] It is, indeed, not improbable that the Lacies, or the Montbegons, who were mesne lords of Tottington under them, might have a local jurisdiction here extending to capital offences.

The composition of the word Holcombe is one instance, among many, of the combination of two or more syllables of local names, expressing the same idea in different and successive languages. Thus *Cwm* in British, and Hol in Saxon, both denote a bottom. The lands granted by Montbegon to the priory of Monkbretton were, with an immense quantity of others, re-granted to John Braddyll,[3] of Whalley, gent. the great dealer in this unsafe commodity, by letters patent of Henry VIII. dated March 23, anno regni 36, under the description of "omnes illas terras, &c. jacent. in Holcame, al. dict. Holcome et Tottington, com. Lanc. nuper Prioratui de Monkbretton, com. Ebor. dudum spectantes."

I have once seen it styled (Towneley MSS.) the Honor of Tottington, an appellation to which, though holding of the superior Honor of Clitheroe, it seems entitled, from the number and opulence of the manors dependent upon itself; for to the court of Tottington the Earl of Derby owes suit and service for his manor of Bury; Lord Suffield for the manor of Middleton; Sir Thomas Horton for Chatterton, and the Lever family for Alkerington.

In the great Inquisition of 1311 Tottington is thus described:—

TOTTINGTON IN SALFORDSCHIRE.—A capital messuage	vj s.
C acr. demised to tenants at will at iiij d. per acre	xxxiij s. iv d.
viij oxgangs, demised in like manner iij s. each	xxij s.
The park of Musbirry[4]	xiij s. iv d.
A separate pasture	x s.
Water Mill	xx s.

[1] [Whewell Cross or Pilgrim's Cross will be found in the Ordnance Map upon Holcombe Moor. Its height is 1,200 feet above the sea.]

[A new church at Holcombe was consecrated by the Bishop of Manchester, April 8, 1853.]

[2] A grant of the furca or gallows within Tottington was obtained by Edmund de Lacy from Henry III. Towneley MSS.

[3] (Braddyll MSS. No. 57.)

[4] *Vide* Rossendale [p. 316], to which it was afterwards annexed.

Profits of Court estimated at	xx s.
Sir Henry de Bury[1] held of the Earl the manor of Bury as one knight's fee, with suit of court at Totyngton.	
Roger de Middleton held the manor of Middleton for one knight's fee, and suit to the said court.	
Henry de Trafford, for Chadreden, with its appurtenances, one knight's fee.	
Adam de Prestwich, for Alkrington, one fourth part of a knight's fee.	
Henry de Bury, for half the manor of Shotlesworth	xij d.
Richard de Radcliffe for xx acres in Tottington	jii s.
Roger de Chatterton[2] xij acres pro homagio et i lb. comyni prec. . .	i d. ob.
Robert de Bradeschagh, a free pasture in the said town . . .	xij d.
Summa . .	vj li. vi s. iij d. ob.

Such, then, is the manor, honor, or forest of Tottington,[3] which stretches about five miles on the banks of the Irwell, and far up the sides of the adjoining hills, from Elton southward, to the great opening into the parish of Whalley northward, a tract approximating in soil and climate to the Appennine of Lancashire, and upon which its warm and wealthy feudatories of Bury, Middleton, Chatterton, and Alkerington, if ever they remember their dependence at all, will probably look upward with contempt.

[1] In the 9th Edw. IV. a licence was granted to Thomas Pilkinton, to kernel and embattle his manor-house of Bury. (Towneley MSS. G. 13.) This was the old manerial residence of the Burys, and afterwards of the Pilkintons, upon the attainder of the last of whom it was granted to Thomas Earl of Derby. The remains of the moat, which are still visible, were mistaken by Mr. Percival for a Roman station; for which he has been very properly corrected by the historian of Manchester.

[2] [Et de i d. ob. de firma Galfridi de Chaderton pro Shillingbotham pro i libra Cymini. Compotus terrarum Hen. de Lacy, 23-24 Edw. I. 1294.]

[3] The Greenhalghs of Brandlesome were hereditary bailiffs of Tottington. MS. pen. C. Chadwick, Ar.

[*Baillivi et Prepositi de Tottington.*

Henr. Nathawe, prep. 1—4 Hen. VI.

Thurstan Bothe, prep. 31—32 Hen. VI., 36—37 Hen. VI. 1 Edw. IV.

Joh. de Grenehalgh, prep. 1—4 Hen. VI. 31—32 Hen. VI.

Edmund Grenehalgh, prep. 36—37 Hen. VI. 11—12 Edw. IV. 1—2 Ric. III.

Will'mus Leylond, 3—4 Edw. IV.

Henr' Bury, 9 Edw. IV.

Henr' Wode, 11—12 Edw. IV.

Christ' Bothe, 1—2 Ric. III.

Tho' Nuttall, prep. 9—10 Eliz.

Franciscus Gartside deputatus Thomas Grenehaughe ar. ballivi 9—10 Eliz.]

BOWLAND.

Having now surveyed the Forest of Blackburnshire and its sub-divisions, it remains that we turn northward, where we shall find another of the demesnes of Clitheroe, a forest till very lately "peopled with its old inhabitants."

Bowland is undoubtedly so denominated as having been famous in the Saxon times for the exercise of archery. The first mention of the word is in the Status de Blackburnshire, which evidently refers it to a period as early as the foundation of the Deanery of Whalley. The circumstances relating to its ecclesiastical history will be noticed below. It was undoubtedly a member of that great fee which the Conqueror bestowed upon Roger de Poitou, and was by him granted either to Ilbert or Robert de Lacy; but thus much is certain, that Robert de Lacy obtained from Henry I. a grant of Boeland, which he had before held of Roger de Poitou, to be henceforward held of the King in capite.[1] Thus it appears that this portion of the demesnes of Clitheroe Castle was held under a title distinct from that of the Honor itself.

The whole tract of country vulgarly called Bowland, and consisting of the parishes of Slaidburn and Mitton, together with the forest, is now equally a member of the fee or honor of Clitheroe, and was equally comprehended within the original parish of Whalley: the two former, however, were separated at an early period from their mother church, and at the time of the Domesday survey were taken as portions of the manor of Grindleton, as they have since been of Slaidburn. But the Forest of Bowland, in the strict sense, was in its civil relation included, from its first acquirement by the Lacies, in the demesnes of the castle, and subject to the court of Woodmote alone, and in its ecclesiastical was always a portion of the extra-parochial tract called the Castle Parish, and uniformly paid tythes to the abbey of Whalley, after the annexation of the chapel of St. Michael in Castro.

The knowlege of this distinction is so nearly lost, and the precise boundaries of the forest so ill ascertained, that circumstances may be foreseen in which it would answer even a legal purpose to have retraced them with a reference to original authorities. First, then, the following passage from the Status de Blackburnshire, of the vigilant and learned abbot Lyndlay:—

Memorandum quod quondam erat in Bouland quedam capella, que *Brenand chapelle* dicebatur, que quidem Capella tunc pertinens erat ad ecclesiam parochialem de Whalleye. Unde omnes Decani predicte ecclesie invenerunt capellanum cotidie sumptibus suis ibidem celebrantem. Et quia illo tempore nullimoda sepultura ibidem habebatur, corpora mortuorum totius foreste de Bouland deferebantur apud Whalleye,[2] et fuerunt ibidem tradita sepulture, tanquam ad ecclesiam tunc matricem. Et tunc temporis omnes decimationes tam majores tam minores totius foreste de Bouland, scilicet de Brenand, del Tregh, ubi illi de

[1] Dugd. Bar. vol. i. p. 99. "Ex autographo nup. in Cast. de Pontefract."

[2] This was before the foundation of the castle or church of Clitheroe.

Whytlidale nunc habitant, et del Sikes, de Harden, de Stapelhaw, Thorniholme, Grishurste et de Bathirarghes sicut le Frythebroke descendit usque in aquam de Hodre predicte ecclesie de Whalley penitus solvebantur, unde locus adhuc à multis cognoscitur ubi predicta capella fuit situata. (The sequel will be found under Slaidburn.) Addit. MS. 10,374, f. 126 b.

A perambulation[1] of the Forest of Bowland, dated Whalley, 1483, will completely ascertain the boundaries, so far as the ancient names are now intelligible. It was made in consequence of the great suit for tithes between Christopher Parsons, Rector of Slaidburn, and the abbot and convent: but it refers to a much older perambulation in the time of Abbot Lyndley and Henry Duke of Lancaster, which explains the expression of "the Duke's ground" or lands.

Universis sancte Matris Ecclesie filiis Jacobus Stanley,[2] Archidiaconus Cestrie, Sal^{m}. Noveritis nos inspexisse Registrum Abbatis et Conventus Monasterii Beate Marie de Whalleye, in hec verba:—

Mem^{m} de Terminis et Bundis Capelle S'cti Michaelis Archangeli in Castro de Cliderhow, annexe et unite ecclesie parochiali de Whalleye, notatis et determinatis per Dom. Johem Lyndlay, S. T. P. quondam Abb̄tem Monasterii Beate Marie de Whalleye predict. et Dom. Thom. Halton quondam rectorem ecclesie parochialis de Slaydburn.

Imp^{s}. Rawcrosse and Newhay-head, bounding upon the parish of Slaydburn, and from Newhay-head following westward unto Longshaw, and from Longshaw unto Grypden-head, and following upp the Oaken-clough unto the height of Kyteholme, and from Kyteholme to Fyldynge Clough Head, then to the Desn[3] clough head, and so to water of Hoder; then following upp the water of Hoder to the departynge between the Duke's ground called Thorniholme and Hamerton lands, and so unto the water of Hoder, and so following water of Hoder into Longden water, and from thens following the meares betwixt Borholme and the Stotclose unto the Red syke; then following upp the Red syke to the height of Todridge; soe following Todridge as heaven water deales unto the head of Brandslacke brooke, bounding upon the parish of Chippin, and so from Brandslacke brooke unto the head of Threapleigh unto Paycocke clough; then to Chippin brooke; soe following Chippin brooke to the park yeate of Laygram at Chippin brooke; so following from the park yeate the brooke to the head of Hudefeld; soe from the head of Hudefeld to the pale; so following from the pale to the lands of Startivant; so following the said lands to Chippin brook; so to foot of water of Lowde; so unto water of Hoder bounding on parish of Mitton; so following Hoder unto Wyerburne foot; so following Wyerburne to head of Bashall Parke; so following lands of Bashall and the Duke's lands to Newhahouse, and from Newhahouse following the devise of the lordship of Bashall and the Duke's land to head of New-hay; so ensuing the Woodward Scoore to north end of Whitston Cliffe, as heaven water deales: so following said Woodward Scoore from head of Whitstonecliffe to the Wolfstanbanke as heaven water deales; so the height of Stiversten line (*sic*) Swarthaw as heaven water deales; and so to well in the north end of Stiversten; so following the well streame from the north end of Stiversten to the Champon dyke upon the parish of Slaydburne aforesaid; so following Champon Dyke to Fellbrig water; also following upp Harrop dyke to the height of Helden hill as heaven water deales; so to Brynhill pyke as heaven water deales; and so from Brynhill pyke to Whitstoncliff, and so to Ravencross aforesaid.

[1] *Vide* Coucher Book at Whalley, and Towneley MSS. G. 26.

[2] Afterwards Bishop of Ely.

[3] Qu. Dene?

The following is of the earlier part of the seventeenth century:—

The oute bounderies of the forrest of Bowland—how farr and into what places doth the same extend, and upon what lords' landes doth the same bound and border:—

Beginning at the lowe end of Graddell, next adjoining to a certayn place called Grange, and soe along after a river called Hodder, leading to Cross of Greate, which bounds north-east upon the lordship of Horneby, as heaven-water deales, and from thence to Croasdale and Whitledale, and part of Brennand North, which bounds upon said lp̄ of Horneby, as heaven-water deales.

The rest is from Brennand, and bounds upon the farmers of Tarnebrooke, and so to a place called Ughtersik, as Harrington ditch leads, lying over the west end of Millhouse, and soe as heaven-water leades over the Threape Hawe to the stone in the Trough, that divides Yorkshire from Lancashire.

And from thence west from Sykes, which bounds upon Marshay, Hathernwaite, Catshay, Calder, Bleasdale, Fairsnape, Blindhurst, and Woolfhall, as heaven-water divides, and from thence down brooke called Dobson Brooke to Chippin Brooke, and soe all along after, by the ende of Chippin towne, and about 16 roodes downe brooke of Chippin, and soe lineally to Red Banke.

And from thence all along the lands of Richard Marsden, of the pale which bounds part upon Mr. Yates his grounds, the lordship of Thorneley, and lordship of Braidley Hall.

And from thence to after the grounds of Clem. Towlson, bounding upon the lordship of Braidley Hall aforesaid.

Then after, and all along the grounds of Rob. Rawthmell, bounding upon Mr. Shereburne lordship and Mr. Sunderland lordship.

Thence to Wyrdburne Foot, Browsholme, and Newhay, bounds upon the lordship of Bashall.

Thence over comon called Whitstonecliffe, Bradford Moore, and Grinleton Moore, which boundes south upon lordship of Waddington, and the coppie-houlders of Bradford and Grinleton, parcel of manor of Slaydburne.

And, lastlie, thence to the Vaccary of Harrope, within forest of Bolland, which bounds upon south-east side of lordship of Boulton.

Next is the Survey of this Forest during the great Usurpation:

Ebor. et Lanc.—Chacea de Bolland.

A Survey of the Chace of Bolland, part of the possessions of Charles Stewart, the late King, of which he was seized as in right of the Duchy of Lancaster; but now settled on trustees, for the use of the Com'onwealth of England. 12th Oct. 1652.

The Chace of Bolland was held of the Crowne, as parcel of tho Duchy of Lancaster, by several tenants on lease: but now, for moste part, said landes are held in fee-farme, being sold to the respective tenants by King James and King Charles, as appears by diverse letters patents.

Leaseholders within said Chace, in all 15, holding among them 8,429 acres, 2 roods, 28 perches. Of these, part, Brennand, contained 1,713; another part, 1,145; and a third, held by Rob. Parker, esq. 929. Whitendale, held by Rob. Sherburne, esq. alone contained 3,693 acres.

Out of these leases were excepted all woods, underwoods, mines, and quarries; also, sufficient pasture for the wild beasts. These leaseholds were all the lands in Bowland which had not been granted in fee-farm by the Crown.

The whole township of the Forest of Bowland then contained 64 tenements.

The officers belonging to this forest were, a Bow-bearer and chief Steward. By the steward are yearly kept two swainmotes, a woodmote court, two courts leet, and two courts baren, to which the inhabitants of Bolland do suit and service, in which all such as felled anie wood without lycens, or killed anie deere, were fyned; also, all actions under 40*s*. were tryed.

The profit of which fynes and amerciaments estimated to be worth 1*l*. Other casual profit, as waiffs, estrays, felons' goods, deodands, amount, com^{s} a^{s}, to 3*l*.

Other officers of the Chace are, 12 keepers for the deere,[1] both red and fallow.

The several tenants, as well lease holders as fee-farmers, are bound to suffer the deere to goo unmolested into their several grounds: they are also fyned, if anie, without lycens, keep anie dogg bigger than will go through a stirupe,[2] to hunt the deere out of the corne.

There are of redd deere of all sortes; viz. staggs, hyndes, and calves, 20; which we value to be worth 20*l*.; and of fallow deere, 40; which wee value to be worth 20*l*.

	£	*s*.	*d*.
Present rent of leaseholds	30	4	0
Perquisites of courts and casul^{s}	4	0	0
Value of herbage of deere	28	10	0
Sum total of present rents and profits	62	14	0
Sum total of improvements *per an.*	428	6	5
Value of wood *per an.*	52	0	0
Radholme Parke was surveyed by the Com^{s} aforesaid, but the return not made in time. Rental	16	0	0
	£559	0	5

Some additional evidence, to the present purpose, is contained in an inquisition taken at Skipton, A.D. 1577.[3]

Juratores dicunt, &c. quod Newton in Bowland, Knolmere, Stanemarrow, Grand Battirge infra villam de Newton, Slaitburne, Woodhouse, Highfield, Grinleton, Bradford, Waddington, Mitton, Bashall, Crook, Withgill sunt infra cur. vis. franc. pleg. Dñæ Reginæ de Slaydburne, et infra Wap. de Staynecliffe; et quod Grangeæ seu terræ dominicales de Edisforth, Esington, Hamerton, Rishtonmere, Harden, Staplehocke, Thorneholme, Betrax, Harrop, Nether Carr, Over Browsholme, Birholme, Troughe, et Sikes, Lee al. Leehouse, Whittledale, Brennand, Le Lees, Swinehurst, Gradale, Newhay Past. et Radholme Parke sunt infra forestam D'næ Reginæ de Bowland et infr. cur. woodmote infr. for. p'dict. tent. apud Whytewell.

Harrop, Countess Flat, near Slaidburn, part of Burholme, and Browsholme, are within the parish of Whalley; and the same part of Burholme, with Browsholme and Little Bowland, constitute the chapelry of Whitewell.

More particularly it appears, from Sir Raphe Assheton's Tithing Book in 1676, that the tithery of Bowland consisted of Browsholme, Newhey, Radholme, Burholme, Thorniholme, Farrick House, Fence, Dinkley Green, Lickhurst, Over and Lower Grafton Lee, Lees and Wardsleys, Legram, Harrop, and Burnslack. At this time the tithery of Bow-

[1] That is, there were twelve keepers of sixty deer. The stock had evidently been wasted in that period of anarchy.

[2] [See the gauge represented in the Plate.]

[3] Towneley MSS. G. 16.

land consisted of about 72 families; at least, so many families paid Easter dues, &c. in that year.

At the time of the Domesday Survey the boundaries of the Forest, as distinct from the tract of country popularly called Bowland, do not appear to have been accurately traced; for the greater part of the villages mentioned above, whether within the forest or without, were considered as dependent upon the manor of Grinleton, which is now become dependent upon Slaidburn. This will appear from the following transcript of that ancient and authentic record, so far as it relates to these places:—

> M̄. In Gretlintone habet Comes Tosti iiii car. t're ad gld.
>
> In Bradeforde [ii car.], Widiton [ii car.], Baschelf [iii car.], Mitune [iiii car.], Hameretone [ii car.], Slateborne [iiii car.], Badresbi [ii car.], Neutone [iiii car.], Bogeuurde [ii car.], Esintune [iii car.], Radun [ii car.], Sotelie [iii car.], ha' t're adjacent in Gretlintone.

These were surveyed under the lands of Roger of Poitou, and were held under him by Earl Tosti, who was soon to give place to the Lacies. Of these villages, Bogworthe and Sotelie, so far as I know, have entirely perished; and Radun, or Radholme, is only remembered as a lawnd; so that we have here what never occurs in the forests of Blackburnshire, an instance of depopulation, whether active or otherwise, previous to the proper afforesting of the country.

Bowland,[1] though principally inclosed, is still ranged by herds of deer,[2] under the jurisdiction of a master forester; here, in allusion to the name of the forest,[3] called the

[1] One custom, in letting the great sheep-farms in the higher parts of Bowland, deserves to be mentioned, as I do not know that it prevails anywhere else. It is this: that the flock, often consisting of 2,000 sheep, or more, is the property of the lord, and delivered to the tenant by a schedule, subject to the condition of delivering up an equal number, of the same quality, at the expiration of the term. Thus the tenant is merely usufructuary of his own stock. The practice was familiar to the Roman law, and seems to have arisen from the difficulty of procuring tenants who were able to stock farms of such extent.

I have met with the following miscellaneous facts relating to this Forest.

16 Edw. II. The bailiwick of Bowland is granted to Ed. de Dacre, p. 1. m. 15, 17.

20 Edw. II. The bailiwick of the Chace of Bowland is granted to Ric. de Spaldington (Tower Records, 20 Edw. II. m. 5), and again in 1 Edw. III.

22 Edw. III. A grant of free chace in Bowland to Isabella, queen dowager.

9th of Henry VI. [1493-4] is a grant of a vaccary called Batterax, for 32 *vaccæ*, one bull, and their issue, both at summer-pasture, and hay, for the rent of lxs. to John Harrison and Thomas Hammerton.

And, at the same time, a grant of half the vaccary of Hardon to Robert del Shaw.

Also, a pardon to Thomas de Radcliffe for transgressions in the forest of Bowland, 16 Hen. VII. [1500-1].—Townl. MSS.

[2] [This was written in or before 1800 (appearing in Dr. Whitaker's first edition, p. 207). In p. 335 hereafter will be found a postscript written after 1805.]

[3] This title was not peculiar to the keeper of Bowland; for in the church of Blakesley, co. Northampton, I find the following epitaph:—"Hic jacet Matth. Sweetenham portator arcus et armiger Regis Henr. IV. Mccccxvi."—Gough's Sepulchral Monuments, vol. ii. [There were one or more officers termed bowbearers in several of the royal forests, according to Harl. MSS. 240. They were usually of inferior rank to the keeper of the forest or forester. In the forest of Galtres in Yorkshire the bowbearer and collector of the attachment moneys received a yearly fee of 8*l.* 16*s.* In Longstrother were a keeper of the forest, whose fee was 4*l.* 6*s.* 8*d.*, a bowbearer with a fee of cs., and

J. Basire. sculp.

This View of Whitewell and the Keeper's Lodge in the Forest of BOWLAND, is humbly Dedicated to His Grace Henry Duke of Buccleuch, by his obedient Servant.

Bow-bearer, who has under him an inferior keeper. The former office is now held by Thomas Lister Parker, Esq. as it has long been by his ancestors. Here have been two lawnds or inclosures for the deer,[1] Radholme Laund and Lathgram Park.[2] [The latter was disparked by a decree dated 2 March, 1 and 2 Phil. and Mary, 1556.[3]]

The following is a copy of one of the letters patent by which the office of [Master Forester[4]] of Bowland [with the appointment of all inferior offices] was anciently held.

Ricardus (3tius) D. G. Rex Ang. et Fr. et Dñs Hib. omn', &c. Sciatis quod nos in consideratione veri et fidelis servitii quod perdilectus miles pro corp. nr̃o Jacobus Harrington nobis antea impendit et impendere intendit in futuro: Dedimus et conc' ei officia Mag̃ri Forestarii, Senescallorum, Balliv^{m}, Forestar^{m}, et *le Drivers* foreste ñre de Bowland, in com' Ebor. et Lanc. Habend. occupand. et gaudend. offic. p̃d' p̃fat. Jacobo per se, vel dep^{m} suum, vel dep^{s} suos sufficientes, a festo Sc̃i Mich. Archang. ult. p̃terito durante vita sua, pcipiend' in et pro occupatione officiorum p̃dict' sum̃am xx et i lib. et xd. in recompensatione certarum puturarum, quas dicti officiarii ñri temp. pgenitorum ñrorum usitat. et consuet. fuerunt habere et percipere de diversis tenentibus et inhabitantibus ñris infra comitatus p̃'dict. et forestam pro suorum feodis et vadiis, ultra x M. annuatim ab antiquo debit. et consuet. pro feod. dict. Mag^{r} forestar. Dat. sub sigillo Ducatus, apud London, 16 Feb. A. R. 2do. [1485.]

The beautiful river Hodder, famous for its umber, rising near the Cross of Grete, and passing through the parish of Slaidburn, intersects the forest, and forms by its deep and fringed banks the only ornamental scenery of a tract otherwise bleak and barren. On one of these is the little Chapel of WHITEWELL,[5] together with an inn, the court-house of Bowland, and undoubtedly a very ancient resting-place for travellers journeying from Lancaster to Clitheroe or Whalley. The landscape here is charming. The Hodder, brawling at a great depth beneath the Chapel, washes the foot of a tall conical knoll, covered with oaks to its top, and is soon lost in overshadowing woods beneath. But it is for the pencil, and not the pen, to do justice to this scene. On the opposite hill, and near the keeper's house, are the remains of a small encampment, which have been supposed to be Roman; but they

two foresters who had 40*s*. each. In Westmarshe in Cumberland the clerke and keeper of the forest received 66*s*. 8*d*. and two bowbearers had a fee of 106*s*. 2*d*. between them. The bowbearer of Bishopsdale and Coverdale had a fee of 40*s*., while the forester of Bishopsdale received 4*l*. 11*s*., and the forester of Coverdale 10*s*. In Agilgarth dale was a bowbearer with a fee of 40*s*., and four foresters whose "fee amongst them" was 46*s*. 7*d*. In Wensleydale the bowbearer had 20*s*. "De Archeariis, qui portabunt arcum Regis, unus quisque v d. in die, et alii Archerii tantundem." Liber Niger Scaccarii (edit. Hearne), p. 359.]

[1] "Up̃ towards the hills by Grenehaugh (Castle) be three forests of *redde* deere, Wyresdale, Bouland, and Blesdale; they be partly woody, partly hethye." Leland, vol. iii. p. 92. The last stags in Bowland were destroyed within the memory of the present keeper, a fine old forester of more than fourscore. [See passage in the text, p. 335].

[2] [Some extracts from ancient rolls of account relating to both these parks are now appended hereafter, pp. 347, 349; with lists of the Parkers, pp. 356, 357.]

[3] [Duchy of Lanc. Class XI. No. 23, fol. 136 b.]

[4] [See the List of Master Foresters hereafter, p. 355.]

[5] [This appears to have formed part of an ancient manor house, under the title of "the manor of Whitewell," as remarked by Dr. Whitaker in his Third Edition, p. 527*. In the reign of Henry VI. its houses were repaired, at the costs detailed in the rolls of account printed hereafter. The kitchen of the manor was covered with slatestone brought from Marsden, but the chapel with thatch only: see p. 351.]

are too inconsiderable to justify any conjecture about them. At no great distance a cairn of stones was opened, and found to contain a sort of kistvaen, and a skeleton. It is singular that neither of these remains have been noticed by Rauthmell, a diligent and accurate investigator of the Roman antiquities of his own neighbourhood; but, as he was minister of Whitewell,[1] he could scarcely be ignorant of this incampment, and may therefore be presumed not to have thought it Roman.

On an adjoining height was discovered a quarry and manufactory of querns, or portable millstones; of which, though probably introduced by the Roman soldiers into Britain, the use appears to have continued among us till after the Norman Conquest.

The little Chapel of Whitewell, from the style of its east window and of the woodwork within, appears to have been erected in the reign of Henry VII.[2] This is confirmed by the accounts of Whalley Abbey; for, in the Computus of the fifteenth year of Abbot Paslew, or 1521, a charge is made by the bursars of xs. paid *Capellano de Whytewell;* and in that of the seventh year of Abbot Holden, or 1478, no mention is made of this payment.[3] After the demolition of the chapel of St. Michael in the Castle, the remaining revenue of that chapel was settled upon Whitewell.[4] In this chapel on a marble monument is this inscription:

[1] [" Richard Rauthmell was born at Little Bowland, and baptized at Chipping, where he was also interred. He was educated at St. John's college, Cambridge, where he took the degree of A.B. 1713, and was in 17— presented to the perpetual curacy of Whitewell, which he held to the time of his death. He is said to have been a lively and entertaining man, which made his company always acceptable at Browsholme and at Barrow; and he well repaid the hospitalities of the latter place by a dedication (dated Bolland, March 24, 1738-9, to his patron Robert Fenwick, esq.) in which, though his style in general was rough and coarse, he touched some topics of adulation with a delicate and skilful hand."—Dr. Whitaker, in his *History of Richmondshire*, i. 266; where full particulars will be found of Rauthmell's *Antiquitates Bremetonacenses*, a work on the Roman antiquities of Overborough, or *Bremetonacæ*, already mentioned at p. 41 of the present volume.]

[2] I suspect this chapel to have been a monument of the piety of our forefathers, in accommodating travellers, upon roads where there were no churches, with the means of late and early devotion. To the same motive are to be ascribed the chapels formerly erected on the piers of bridges.—"Prayers and provender hinder no journeys," said the devout and excellent Herbert, a maxim of which the former part is now entirely forgotten. [Whitewell Chapel, serving for the township of Great Bolland in Yorkshire, in which county it stands, as well as for that of Little Bolland in Lancashire, has been already mentioned in p. 60 by our Author, as "a little oratory of the humblest class, without cemetery or inclosure:" and it is stated in Bishop Gastrell's *Notitia Cestriensis* that it would not hold above 200 persons. "This chapel was rebuilt in the year 1817, and consecrated by Dr. George Henry Law, Bishop of Chester, July 10, 1818, on which occasion the sermon was preached by the author of this work. To this chapel belongs a very large and old chalice of beaten silver, which from a Memorandum at Whalley I find to have been delivered by Sir Ralph Assheton, A.D. 1694, as a legacy from Archbishop Tillotson. But it must even then have been of considerable antiquity." (MS. note by Dr. Whitaker.) The sermon, preached in troublous times, from the words "Sound an alarm," Joel ii. 1, was published by its author.]

[3] Its æra might be ascertained more exactly were any Compotus extant in that interval.

[4] [In 1724, "Certified 6*l*., paid by Abp. of Canterbury; no other profits. This 6*l*. does properly belong to Castle Chapel in Clitheroe, and is given to Curate of Clitheroe for preaching here once a month." Robert Parker of Carlton in 1717 gave lands worth 400*l*. towards the augmentation of this chapel, which lands were in 1724 let for 19*l*. per ann. He gave also house-rent in Clitheroe of 34*s*. per ann. and the governors of Queen Anne's Bounty granted 200*l*. in 1724. Value in 1834, 88*l*. *Not. Cestr.* edit. Raines, ii. 346. In 1650 there had been no minister here, nor provision for one: see the return in p. 219.]

To the memory of Mr. Edmund Butler, younger son of Alexander Butler, of Kirkland, Esq., and of Elizabeth his wife, daughter of Thomas Parker of Browsholme, Esq., who being on a visit to Browsholme, after a few days' illness, died the 27th of September 1757, in the 58th year of his age, and was at his own request buried in this chapel. His nephew Alex. Butler, Esq., as a testimony of his respect and friendship, and of that regard that his family must ever owe to his memory, hath erected this monument, in the year of our Lord 1767.

Not far from Burholm Bridge are the vestiges of another and more ancient place of worship; but I know not whether there is any tradition of the chapel of Brennand, mentioned by Abbot Lyndley as only remembered by its site in the time of Edward III.

The following Commission, dated 7 Rich. II. [1383-4] was directed to inquire into certain offences and disturbances committed within these forests.

Rex, &c. Dilectis et fidelibus suis Waltero Urswic ar., Rad. de Radcliffe, Rob. Urswic, Ad. Skillicorn, Rob. de Blakeburn, &c. Quia datum est nobis intelligi quod quidam malefactores et pacis perturbatores liberas chaceas nostras de Bowland, Pendle, Rossendel, Trawden, et Tottington vi et armis intraverunt, &c. Ideo vobis mandamus per inquisitionem factam transgressionum prædictarum auditis et terminatis, &c. &c.

The following is an appointment, by the Trustees under the will of Henry V. [of the joint successors of] Sir John Stanley [in the offices of] Master Forester, &c. of [certain portions of] the Forests of Blackburnshire. It is taken from Dr. Cuerden's MS. and in some places almost illegible.

Hen. Arch's[1] et feoffati, &c. Omnibus, &c. Sciatis quod cum Johannes Stanley miles, per literas patentes . . . . . hab. officia capitalis Forestarii Forestarum de Pennyl et Rosendale, et Tomerden (evidently a mistake for Trawden), in Blackburnshire, et Staurarii et Senescalli ibidem, ac officium Senescalli maneriorum de Totyngton, et Ratchdale, et Penwortham, quoad nobis placuerit: Nos ad instanciam sereniss. principis et Dni nostri Regis, nunc nobis fact. ac consider" boni et laudabilis servitii tam præfato nuper regi quam Dno nunc regi per dilectum . . . . dedimus . . . . offici . . . . pro termino vite Dom . . . . et alterius eorum. 7 Nov. 16 Regni 1437.

With respect to Bowland, one circumstance only remains to be told: viz. that in the year 1805 a fine herd of wild deer, the last vestige of feudal superiority in the domains of the Lacies, were destroyed. The loss, however, of these ancient ornaments of the forest has been in some measure compensated by the late improvements of the house and grounds at Browsholme, by the taste of the present owner. Of these improvements it is no small praise, in this age of experiment and innovation, to say, that while they have produced some splendid modern apartments, the shell of a venerable mansion has been left entire.

[1] Archbishop Chicheley.

BROWSHOLME.

On an elevated situation in the forest is the ancient house of Browsholme, for more than three centuries the residence of a family who derive both their name and arms from the office of Parker, or park-keeper. Browsholme is a large house of red stone, with a centre, two wings, and a small façade in front, of that species which was peculiar to the reigns of Elizabeth and James I.[1]

In 1603 Charles Blount, Earl of Devonshire, sold to Thomas Parker, Esquire, of Over Browsholme, "all that messuage, tenement, and one pasture within the Forest of Bowland, in the county of York, called Nether Brookesholme, which premises were late parcel of the Duchy of Lancaster." Hereupon the present mansion was erected, or materially enlarged;[2] and the grounds were laid out, in the formal fashion of the times. In front was a bowling-green, inclosed by a high wall and iron gates, over which was this inscription—

NEMO HANC EXTRAT PORTAM QUI VIOLAT ÆQUUM.

The house had two wings, and was in the form of a half H. The doorway, surmounted with pillars of three orders of architecture, is not exactly in the centre, having three windows on one side and two only on the other. The interior space was in one room, called the Hall, in extent 68 feet long, 23 wide, and 12 high: its roof a fine example of the good beams and timbers then used for floors and ceilings. There were two large fire-places, and some plain massy oaken tables, the reliques of old English hospitality. The principal staircase went out of this hall, and was curiously carved in oak. The west wing contained the principal drawing-room, 30 feet long by 22 wide and 15 high; the principal bed-room; the staircase; and, at the top of all, the Chapel. In the east wing were the offices, below; on the second floor a room called the Oak Drawing-room, very richly carved in oak wainscot;[3] and a great many lodging-rooms; and at top the old library. In the middle of the last century, Edward Parker, Esq. divided the hall, making one part the Dining-room, and the other a Library.[4] The former portion (now again the Hall) is wainscoted with very fine old oak taken from the ancient house of the Kenyons at Parkhead, and presented to Mr. Lister Parker by James Taylor, Esq. in 1809; the chimney-piece bears the arms of the Towneleys of Hapton Tower, to whom it originally belonged.

[1] [The description of Browsholme, following this paragraph, though additional to the former edition, is in the main from Dr. Whitaker's own pen, derived from the *Description of Browsholme*, mentioned in the next page.]

[2] Whether the family removed at this or an earlier period from Higher Browsholme, of which the foundations are now barely discoverable, I do not know.

[3] [The Oak Drawing Room was thoroughly restored about the year 1866, under the direction of Mr. Shaw of Saddleworth. The wainscot is divided into panels by boldly carved mouldings, and is continued to the ceiling, having an elaborate frieze ornament and enriched cornice. A new arched chimney-piece, wrought in stone, presents on either side the richly panelled pilasters so frequent in the Elizabethan style. During the progress of the works an unsightly ceiling was removed. Its length is now broken by a single carved beam. W. A. W.]

[4] [The panelling of the Library is of curious construction, its compartments being framed diagonally, bearing a close resemblance to the wainscot in the dining room at Towneley Hall. W. A. W.]

BROWSHOLME.

Drawn by Wm. Turner A.

Engraved by James Basire.

Ab antiqua prosapia oriundo, antiquarum virtutum, spe, votis multorum æmulo futuro THOMÆ LISTER PARKER ARM:
Protoforestario de Bowland hanc tabulam sum[p]tibus ejus ære incisam D.D.D. T.D. Whitaker.

Drawn by J. Buckler. Engraved by J. Stow.

South East View of Browsholme Hall Yorkshire.

THE SEAT OF THOMAS LISTER PARKER, ESQ.

Mr. Lister Parker[1] commenced his alterations in 1804; when he removed the stables which had been erected directly in front of the house by his grandfather, and levelled the old bowling-green. In 1805 he rebuilt the west wing, with the same materials, and on the same space, as to the exterior; but within with a new drawing-room, measuring 36 feet by 24, and 16 high; and other apartments. A new dining-room was subsequently attached to the side of the same wing (as seen in the accompanying view by Buckler). In 1806 the lodge was erected:[2] its archway came from Ingleton, co. York, as also did the old font; the arms over the door from Waddington Hall; the image of a saint from Whalley Abbey. The approach was then made from Bashall Moor, on the east side of the house, and a new approach from the west by the garden. The pool of water that had been commenced in 1803, was finished in 1807, when four acres of Bashall Moor, adjoining the water, were planted; and to these were added thirty acres more in the year 1813. These improvements were carried out under the superintendence of Mr. Wyatt, afterwards

[1] [Mr. Thomas Lister Parker received the early part of his education at the Grammar-school of Clitheroe, as a pupil of the learned Thomas Wilson, B.D.; and became (as his father had been) a fellow commoner of Christ college, Cambridge. Inheriting a large estate on attaining his majority, he enjoyed the advantages of the highest society, and was honoured with the notice of the Prince of Wales and Duke of Clarence. He was elected F.S.A. in 1801, and soon after F.R.S. His historical and antiquarian tastes led him at an early period to cultivate an intimate acquaintance with Mr. Charles Towneley, with Dr. Whitaker, with Dr. Watson the Bishop of Landaff, with his old master Mr. Wilson, with the Hebers, Currers, and other distinguished and intellectual families in the North of England: whilst, in the metropolis, he became the friend of West, Turner, Northcote, Romney, and other artists, to some of whom he was a generous, and to others a munificent, patron: evincing a sound perception and justness of criticism on works of art, which made his advice to be often sought. He was guardian to Sir John Leycester, afterwards Lord de Tabley, and assisted him in selecting his valuable gallery of paintings. The productions of his own pencil in his many portfolios were careful and elaborate drawings of exquisite landscapes, ancient ruins, fine edifices, and curious specimens of mediæval art. He was unfortunately lavish in his expenditure, which brought him into difficulties, and for the last few years of his life he resided mostly at the Star inn in Deansgate, Manchester, where he died on the 2nd March, 1858, at the age of 78. Mr. Canon Raines has printed some of Mr. Lister Parker's letters in his Life of Wilson of Clitheroe, 1858, vol. xlv. Chetham Soc. Series, 4to.—See further particulars in the *Gentleman's Magazine* for April 1858, p. 447. There are two portraits of Mr. Lister Parker by Northcote.

In 1815 Mr. Lister Parker, with the assistance of Dr. Whitaker, printed privately a "*Description of Browsholme Hall*, in the West Riding of the County of York; and of the Parish of Waddington, in the same county: also a Collection of Letters, from original manuscripts, in the reigns of Charles I. and II. and James II. in the possession of Thomas Lister Parker, Esq. of Browsholme Hall," 4to. pp. 130, of which the original papers occupy 106. It is illustrated with many etchings, made by Mr. John Chessell Buckler, then a young draughtsman, and afterwards an eminent architect. The book is described and a list of its numerous engravings given in Upcott's British Topography, p. 1408.]

[2] [This entrance lodge displays a combination of architectural fragments of various dates and from various places—both Ecclesiastical and Domestic. The arched gateway is decorated with Elizabethan scrolls and finials, and shields of arms. On the lintel of the gatehouse door are the initials of Thomas Parker with the date of 1682. Above this is a finely-carved panel, containing the arms of Parker, with deeply-relieved mantlings, and a scroll with the motto, "NEC FLUCTU, NEC FLATU MOVETUR." In the gable is placed a figure of a saint, said to have originally formed part of the decorations of Whalley Abbey. This can only be accounted for under the relaxed discipline of the Cistercians, for their early rules strictly forbade the use of sculptured representations of the human form in their conventual buildings. There are many quaint carvings and other interesting relics built into the walls of this singular structure, and close by is the bowl of an ancient octagonal font, showing no ornaments sufficient to indicate its date. W. A. WADDINGTON.]

Sir Jeffry Wyatville. Mr. Lister Parker sold the estate in the year 1824 to his cousin Thomas Parker, Esq. who, dying without issue in 1832, devised Browsholme to his nephew Thomas Goulbourne Parker, Esq. (See the annexed Pedigree).

Here is a good old library, a large miscellaneous collection of ancient coins, and a valuable assemblage of MSS. relating principally to the antiquities of the neighbourhood, to which this history is much indebted: these are monuments of the intelligence and curiosity of the family. Another relic, preserved with religious reverence, attests their devotion:—it is a skull, said to have been employed by a former owner, in the private exercises of religion, as a monitor of death; and it is polished, by frequent attrition, to a surface resembling coarse ivory. But the most valuable relic preserved at Browsholme is the original seal of the Commonwealth for the approbation of ministers.[1] It is of very massy silver; and is inscribed—THE SEALE FOR APPROBATION OF MINISTERS. The device is an open book, inscribed—THE WORD OF GOD, surrounded by two branches of palm. The workmanship is good, but I could scarcely venture to ascribe it to Simon.[2]

On a piece of needle-work [3] in the house, but copied probably from an original upon board, are the following lines:

I PRAY GOD BLESSE THE LIFE OF MASTER
EDMVND PARKER AND HIS WIFE AND ALL
THE CHILDREN THAT WITH HIM WONN
ES FIVE DAVGHTERS AND SEAVEN SONNES.
ANNO DOMINI (*Shield of Parker*) 1450.
NEC FLVCTV NEC FLATV MOVETVR.

The dining-room is adorned with some of the best works of Northcote. The house also contains many paintings by the best Flemish masters, besides two fine specimens of Gainsborough and Wilson.[4]

The original head of Velasquez's pupil, by himself, is esteemed one of the best portraits of that master ever brought to England. Among the portraits is one of a Parker, in the reign of Charles II. with the insignia of Bowbearer of Bowland, viz. a staff tipped with a buck's head, in his hand, and a bugle-horn at his girdle. (As engraved in the accompanying Plate.)

The hall, 40 feet long, is furnished with antiquities: such as the Ribchester inscription

[1] See Calamy's Continuation [8vo. 1727], vol. i. p. 462, where there is an engraving of another seal [used in] 1659, with the same inscription; but instead of the palm-branches and open book the latter has a plain cross. [Dr. Whitaker wrote without due comparison: the seals have not the same inscription, nor were made for the same purpose, though a correspondent one. The seal published by Calamy was, THE SEALE FOR APPROBATION OF PUBLICK PREACHERS.]

[2] [This seal is now in the possession of F. H. Fawkes, esq. of Farnley, near Otley.]

[3] [This needlework is represented in the accompanying Plate. Its date, 1450, was probably an accidental error for 1540, as shown by the character of the letters, and by the name of Edmund Parker; see the Pedigree.]

[4] [A list of the pictures in 1815 will be found in the Description of Browsholme, p. 8. There is now no work of Gainsborough, but the dining-room contains some portraits by Vandyck.]

EDWARD PARKER ESQ.R in the Costume of Bowbearer of Bowland Circ 1690.

Legionary Stone from Ribchester now at Browsholme

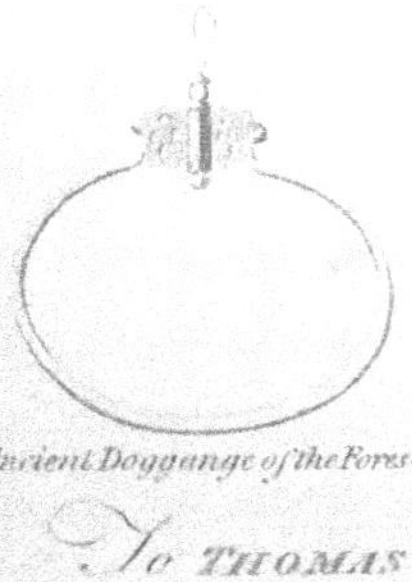

Ancient Doggange of the Forest

Ancient Wooden Tankard at Browsholme

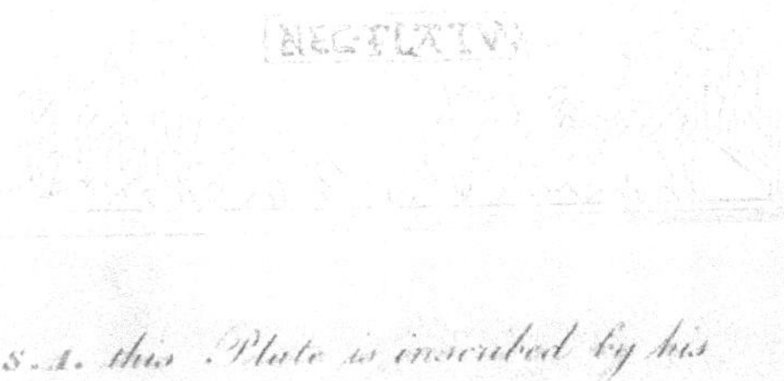

To THOMAS LISTER PARKER ESQ.R F.S.A. *this Plate is inscribed by his*

of the xxth legion,[1] celts, fibulæ, different pieces of armour, and particularly a small spur[2] found in the apartment called King Henry the Sixth's at Waddington Hall. Among the rest is a complete suit of buff, worn by the head of the family—a sufferer for his loyalty in the great rebellion. The papers of the family contain many curious and original documents of those times. The staircase-window is rich in painted glass. The only vestige of the forest laws yet preserved here (and that too now become useless) is the stirrup through which every dog, excepting those belonging to the lords, must be able to pass. (Also engraved in the Plate.)

That the office of Bowbearer was held by the family as early as 1591 appears from the first of the following warrants, which are now remaining among their papers:

After my hartie cōmendacōns. Theso shalbe to will and require you to delyver, or cause to be delyv̄ed, to my verie good Lord, Will'm bushop of Chester,[3] or to ye bearer hereof in his name, my fee stagge of this season to be had w^th^in her Maj^ties^ forrest of Bowland; and this my lr̄e shal be your sufficient warr^t^ and discharge.

Great Bartholomewes, this xxvjth of June. Ant' Mildmaye.

To ye M^r^ of her Maties game within the forrest of Bowland; and to his Deputie or Deputes there.

By the Kinge.

Trusty and Welbeloved, Wee greete yow well: willinge and cōmandinge yow that ye im̄ediately upon the seight hereof doe deliver or cause to be delivered unto ye bearer hereof one fatt bucke of this season towards the better furnishinge of our dyet for our President and Councell in the North: And this shalbe yor sufficient Warrant in that behalf. Given under our Signet at our City of York the eight day of Julie the ninth yeare of our reigne [1611].

And by his Councell.

(*Signed*) Fr. Boynton.
Ch. Hales. W. Ellis.
W. Gee.

To the Maister of our Game, Bowbearer, keeper, and all other our officers and their deputie or deputies within ye Forrest of Bolland, and to every of them.

To show the state of this country during the civil wars, I select two letters of protection; one from a notorious sequestrator, the other from a gallant royalist.

For the Col^s^ and Lieu^t^ Col^s^ within Craven these.

Noble Gentlemen, I could desire to move you in the behalfe of Mr. Edward Parker, of Broosome, that you would be pleased to take notice of his house, and give order to the officers and souldiers of your regiments, that they plunder not, nor violently take away, any his goods, without your privities; for truly the proñess of souldiers sometimes to cōmit some insolencies w^t^out comand from their supiors is the cause of my writing at this time; hoping hereby, through your care, to preuent a future evill, in all thankfullness I shall acknowledge (besides the great obligation you putt on Mr. Parker) myselfe to bee

Your much obliged, Ric. Shuttleworthe.

Gawthrop, 13 *February* 1644.

[1] [Engraved in the Plate, and before described in p. 30. It is now in the British Museum.]

[2] [The spur attributed to King Henry the Sixth has been stolen.]

[3] Chadderton. The fee-stag was due to Sir Anthony Mildmay as Chancellor of the Duchy.

These are to intreat all officers and souldiers of the Scottish armie, and to require all officers and souldiers of the English armie under my comaund, that they forbeare to take or trouble the pson of Edward Parker, of Brousholme, esquire, or to plunder his goods, or anie other hurt or damage to doe unto him in his estate.

This 8th day of August, *anno Dom.* 1648. Tho. Tyldesley.

This was only ten days before the battle of Preston.

The following specimen of old local poetry has been lately discovered among the papers at Browsholme. It is given with some abridgments and corrections.

A Balade of Maryage.

In yonder wode there is a dene,
  Wher I myselfe was late reposyng,
Wher blossomes in ther prime have bene,
  And flowers faire ther colors losyng;
A love of myne I chaunced to meete,
  Wch causid me too longe to tarye,
And then of hym I did entrete,
  To tell me when he thought to marye.

If thou wilt not my secrete tel,
  Ne bruite abrode in Whalley parish,
And swere to kepe my counsel wel,
  I will declare mye daye of marriage.
* * * * * *

When Somer's heate wyl drie noe myre,
  And Wynter's rain noe longer patter;
When leade wyl melt withouten fyre,
  And beare brades[1] doe nede noe water;
When Downham stones[2] with diamond ringes,
  And cockles be with perles compared;
When golde is made of gray-goose winges;
  Then wyl mie love and I bee maryed.

When buck and harte in Hoder lies,
  And graylings on the fells are bredyng;
When muscles grow on everie tree,
  And swannes on everie rock are fedyng;
When mountains are by men removyd,
  And Ribble back to Horton caryed,
Or Pendle hill grows silk above;
  Then, etc.

When moore or mosse doe saffron yelde,
  And becke and sike ren downe with honie;
When sugar growes in every fielde,
  And clerkes wyl take no bribe of monie;
When men in Bowlande dyeth here
  And at Jerusalem bee buryed;
Or when the Sunne dothe ryse at noone;
  Then, etc.

Now farewel, frende, yf it bee soe,
  And thys thy once expected wedyng;
For neither I, nor none of my kinn,
  Wyl ev'r nede to loke for bidyng.
I swere and vow, yf this bee trowe,
  And thou of such an evyl carryage,
If I shoulde lyve ten thousande yere,
  I'd never more expecte thie maryage.

[1] Bear, that is, coarse barley, or bigg as it is sometimes called, is said, in old English and modern Scottish, to be *brair'd* or *brade*, when its leaves first shoot above the ground. Rain is, of course, indispensable to the *brair'd* of bear and all other grain. (This explanation of the line in the text, not at first understood by Dr. Whitaker, was supplied to him by Walter Scott, and printed in the Addenda to the last Edition, p. *523.)

[2] At Downham is found a species of crystals, usually called *Downham diamonds*, which in lustre equal Bristol stones.

Pedigree

OF

PARKER OF BROWSHOLME.

Arms: Vert, a chevron between three stag's heads caboshed or.
Crest: A stag trippant proper.
Motto: NEC FLUCTU NEC FLATU MOVETUR.

Extract from a letter of Chief Justice Sir Thomas Parker to Ralph Thoresby, of Leeds, 22nd Nov. 1711.

"The family of the Parkers which you are bestowing your labor upon is not allyed to mine in the manner you suppose, but yet with more tyes than one. I think you mention Bridgett [really Elizabeth] a daughter of that family to have been marryed to James Carryer of Helpston, and to have had a daughter whom you suppose to have been my mother. That daughter was marryed to my father's eldest brother, and by him had issue one son, George, who lives now at Park-Hall in Stafford-shire, a very sober religious man, and one of the best Justices of the Peace in England, and serves his Queen and Country with great application in that office. I believe you said another sister Jeanett marryed to another Carryer. I think his name was Robert. [It was Richard: see the Pedigree.] He was brother of James. That Jeanett had issue by him Robert Carryer, who was father of my wife, and left issue no son, and only two daughters, besides my wife, who is named after her Grandmother.

" * * * Pray give my service to Mr. Parker [of Browsholme], and tell him that I am very proud of my relation to his family, which has furnished me with two so very near to me, the one the best and faithfullest friend and the other the best wife in the world." *(Description of Browsholme Hall, &c. 4to.* 1815. *Page* 32.)

PARKER, OF BROWSHOLME.

Robert Parker, of Browsholme, in the Forest of Bolland, co. York.

.... Redmayne, a younger son of Redmayne, of Thornton, in Ewcross, co. Lancaster. = Elizabeth, dau. and heir of Robert Parker.

Edmund Parker, of Browsholme aforesaid, younger son of Parker, of Horrockford, aº 19 Hen. VIII. (1528). = Jennet, dau. and heir of .... Redmayne and Elizabeth Parker.

Jenet, wife of Thomas Sherborne, of Ribleton, co. Lanc. esq.

Robert Parker, of Browsholme, esq. 1591. = Elizabeth, dau. of Edmund Chaderton, of Nuthurst, and sister of William Chaderton, Bishop of Lincoln, who died in 1608.

Elizabeth, wife of Leonard ... of Goosnargh, co. Lanc. (See Fishwick's *History of Goosnargh*, 1871, p. 185.)

Edmund Parker, eldest son, died unmarried; drowned at Cambridge.

Thomas Parker, of Browsholme aforesaid, esq. Bowbearer of the forest of Bolland, in the duchy of Lancaster. = Bridget, dau. and coheir of James Tempest, es... in Craven, son of Leonard, 3d son of Roger T... of Broughton; died 4 Oct. 1610.

Robert Parker, eldest son, born 23 Sept. 1591; ob. s.p.

James Parker, 2d son, born 6 Feb. 1598; died 20 Jan. 1599.

Edward Parker, of Browsholme, esq. eldest surviving son and heir, born 3d Aug. 1602; died 1667. His will dated 5 June and proved 7 Sept. in that year; bur. at Waddington. = Mary, dau. of Richard Sunderland, of High Sunderland, co. York, esq. by Mary his wife, 6th dau. of Sir Richard Saltonstall, knt. lord mayor of London, and Susanna his wife, dau. of Thomas Poyntz, of North Ockendon in Essex, esq.; mar. 28 Jan. 1629; died 16 Jan. 1673.

Roger Parker, M.A. 4th son, born 30 Oct. 1603.

Richard Parker, 5th son, born 28 Jan. 1604; ob. s.p.

William Parker, M.A. rector of Tetford, co. Lincoln; born 28 Mar. 1608. = ... dau. of ...

Nicholas Parker, of Wirksworth, co. Derby, born 20 Sept. 1610.

Thomas Parker, of Browsholme, esq. son and heir, bapt. at Waddington 1 May, 1631. Executor to the will of his father in 1667. His own will dated 7 July, 1695. = Margaret, 5th dau. of Radcliffe Ashton, of Cuerdale, co. Lanc. esq. brother of Sir Ralph Ashton, of Whalley, bt.; bapt. at Lowchurch 17 July, 1627. (*Note*.)

Robert Parker, of Carlton in Craven, and of Marley Hall, esq. 2nd son, bapt. at Waddington 23 June, 1633; co-executor of his father's will 1667; living 1695. = Jane, dau. of William Rookes, of Esholt, co. York, living 1720.

Edw. Parker, of Gray's Inn, esq. barrister-at-law; bapt. at Waddington 1st May, 1636; living 1669. = Anne, dau. of John Boteler, of Kirkland, co. Lanc.

Three sons.

Richard Parker, bapt. at Waddington 14 Nov. 1637; died 15 June, 1639.

Roger Parker, bapt. at Waddington 20 Jan. 1638; mar. and had issue.

M... 17... ...

Catherine, dau. and heir of Henry Bourne, of Ingleton Hall, esq. 1st wife. = Edward Parker, of Browsholme, esq. son and heir, justice of the peace for the county of York, born 1 Jan. 1658, died 11 July, 1721. = Jane, 4th dau. of John Parker, of Extwistle, bur. at Waddington 6 Feb. 1721.

Elizabeth, wife of Alexander Butler, of Kirkland, co. Lanc.

Robert Parker, 2nd son, three years' old aº 1665; bought the estate of Alkincoats; died 10 Nov. 1714. = Eli... of ... W... of ... sto...

Thomas Parker, of Browsholme, esq. son and heir, bapt. at Waddington 17 Oct. 1689; died in 1728 without issue, leaving his estate at Ingleton, &c. to his half-brother John Parker, of Browsholme, esq.

John Parker, of London, and afterwards of Browsholme, esq. Bowbearer of the forest of Bolland; born 11 June, 1695; died 28 March, 1754; buried at Waddington. = Elizabeth, dau. of Henry Southouse, of Mansden, co. Essex, esq.

Edward Parker, of London, admn. to wife Elizabeth, 3 Feb. 1731; had issue Thomas and Edward.

Robert Parker, bapt. at Waddington 6 Nov. 1693; died unmar.

Mary, bapt. at Waddington ... 1696; died young.

Margaret, bapt. at Waddi... 8 Mar. 1708; died young.

Jane, wife of .... Southou...

Elizabeth, wife of George To... of Skipwith, co. York.

King Edward the First, died 3rd July, 1307.

Humphry de Bohun, Earl of Hereford and Essex. = Elizabeth, dau. of King Edward.

William de Bohun, Earl of Northampton. = Elizabeth, sister and coheir of Giles Lord Badlesmere.

Richard Earl of Arundel and Surrey, ob. 21 Ric. II. = Elizabeth, dau. of William Earl of Northampton.

Sir Robert Goushill, knt. = Elizabeth, eldest dau. of Richard Earl of Arundel.

Thomas Stanley, Lord Stanley, Comptroller of the Household, ob. 37 Hen. VI. = Joan, eldest dau. of Sir Robert Goushill.

Sir John Savage, of Clifton, knt. = Katherine, dau. of Thomas Lord Stanley.

Thomas Leigh, of Adlington, co. of Chester, esq. = Katherine, dau. of Sir John Savage.

William Hulton, of the Park, co. Lanc. esq. ob. 1556. = Elizabeth, dau. of Thomas Leigh, of Adlington, esq.

Adam Hulton, of the Park, esq. ob. aº 15 Eliz. (*Note*.) = Clemence, 5th dau. of Sir Wm. Norris, of Speke, knt.; living a widow 1572.

William Hulton, of the Park, esq. son and heir. = Margaret, dau. and coheir of ... Kighley.

Adam Hulton, of the Park, esq. eldest son and heir. = Alice, dau. and heir of .... Bagnley, of Manchester.

William Hulton, of the Park, esq. ob. 1623. = Katherine, dau. of Robert Hyde, of Norbury, esq.

Adam Hulton, of the Park, esq. died in 1652. = Grace, only dau. of Edmund Haworth, of Haworth, gent.

William Hulton, of the Park, esq. died 27th May, 1694. = Anne, only child and heir of W. Jessop, esq. M.P. for Stafford.

Jessop Hulton, of the Park, esq. ob. circa 1725. = Mary, dau. of William Haselden.

Thomas Lister, of Gisburne Park, co. York, esq. ob. 1761. = Beatrix, dau. of Jessop Hulton, esq.; died in 1774.

Edward Parker, of Browsholme, esq. only son and heir, bowbearer of the forest of Bolland, born 1730; died 22 Dec. 1794, aged 64; bur. at Waddington. = Barbara, dau. and coheir of Sir William Fleming, of Rydal Hall, co. Westmerland, Bart.; mar. at Lancaster 1750; died 23 April, 1813; bur. at Waddington.

John Parker, of Browsholme, esq. son and heir, Bowbearer of the forest of Bolland, sometime Fellow Commoner of Christ Coll. Camb. M.P. for Clitheroe; died 25 May, 1797, aged 42; bur. at Waddington 10 June. = Beatrix, dau. of Thomas Lister, of Gisburne Park, co. York, esq. and sister of Thomas 1st Lord Ribblesdale; born 25 Nov. 1749; mar. at Giggleswick, co. York, 1778; died 10 May, 1807, bur. at Waddington.

Edward Parker, died young.

1. Thomas Lister Parker, esq. son and heir, Bowbearer of the forest of Bolland, born 27 and bapt. at Giggleswick 29 Sept. 1779; died unmar. 2 March, 1858, buried at Waddington.

2. Edward Parker, esq. 2d son, born 3nd Nov. 1780; bapt. at Giggleswick 15th July, 1781; died 17 Dec. 1828. = Isabella, dau. of Rev. J. Strode, of Hatfield, Herts; mar. 1813.

Isabella-Beatrix, born July 1814; died unmar. 2nd Aug. 1844.

3. Reverend John Fleming Parker, M.A. b. at Marshfield 17th April, 1782; bapt. at Giggleswick 5th June, 1785; mar. Dec. 1817; died 26 Nov. 1862. = Hon. Catherine Lister, dau. of Thos. 1st Lord Ribblesdale, and widow of James Skurray Day, esq. of Burnett, co. Somers.

Thomas-Lister, d. 1 Aug. 1852, s.p.

John, d. 13 April, 1845.

Catherine, d. 10 Dec. 1841.

Frederick, d. 7 Dec. 1841.

4. Charles Robert Parker, born at York 4 April, 1783; bapt. at Giggleswick 1st Nov. 1785; d. s.p.

5. Henry Parker, born at York 6th April, 1784; bpt. at Giggleswick 1785; Major 53d regt.; died at Cuddalore, E.I. Admin. 3d Jan. 1824. = Anne, dau. of John Maclean, of Galway in Ireland; mar. there in May, 1808.

Thomas Lister Parker, born 1809; died s.p.

6. Rev. William Parker, vicar of Waddington and afterwards of Skipwith; bapt. at Giggleswick 5 June, 1785; died s.p. 24th Sept. 1848; J.P. and D.L. York East Riding.

7. Septimus, b... at Giggleswick 27 April, 17... bur. there 23 ... 1792.

8. Octavius, b... at Giggleswick 13th; bur. 27 Aug. 1790.

(*Note*.) Another line in which the Royal Descent of this family may be traced is from Adam Hulton and Clemence his wife, through their daughter Margaret the wife of Richard Ashton of Downham, esq. father of Radcliffe Ashton of Cuerdale, who by his wife Elizabeth Hide had issue Margaret, married to Thomas Parker of Browsholme, esq. Through this line the present family preserves its Royal Descent. Mrs. Margaret Parker died at Browsholme 12 Sept. 1710, and was buried at Waddington.

…ger Parker, D.D. 2nd son, 14 years precentor of Lincoln; …ted Dean of Lincoln 29 Nov. and installed 13 Dec. 1613; …1 29 Aug. 1629, aged 71; bur. in the cathedral. M. I. = Alice, da. of . . Pont, survived her husb. and erected a monument to his memory in the cathedral of Lincoln.

William Parker, D.D. rector of Blisland, co. Cornwall, 1601, archdeacon of Cornwall; bur. at Warleggan 1631. = Jane, dau. of . . . . Panchard, of Wilts; bur. at Blisland 22 Nov. 1625.

…hard Carr…r, of …rksworth, … of Derby, …metime …llow of …s John's …llege, …mbridge. = Jennet, dau. of Thomas Parker, esq. born 3 Feb. 1593; mar. Aug. 1612.

George Parker, of Parkhall, co. Stafford, esq. 1663. = Grace, dau. of Hugh Bateman, of Hartington, co. Derby.

James Carryer, of Helpston, c. Northampton, 2nd husband. = Elizabeth, dau. of Thomas Parker, esq. born 2 Aug. 1595. = Henry Slinger, of Catlow, m. 23 April, 1612; died 20 Aug. following, 1st husb.

Jane, born 28 Nov. 1596; died 33 April following.

Captain Thomas Whittingham, slain at Newbury 1643, ex parte Regis. = Anne, born 8 Oct. 1606; mar. 14th Feb. 1624. = John Conrade Molanus, a German, 2nd husband.

James Parker, son and heir, 30 years old in 1620; died at Warleggan 1680. = Katherine, eldest dau. of Sir Richard Buller, of Shillington, Cornwall, knt.; mar. at St. Stephen's, Saltash, 31 Dec. 1616; died at Warleggan aº 1686, aged 86.

William Parker, 2nd son, rector of St. Feock, Cornwall, 28 years old in 1620; died unmar.

Robert Carryer. = Elizabeth, dau. of . . . .

Thomas Parker, 2nd son. = Anne, dau. of Robert Venables, of Antrobus, co. Chester.

William Parker, son and heir, aged 41 years in 1663. = Bridget, dau. of James Carryer, of Helpston.

William. James. Robert. Anthony. Richard. Francis. George. John. Rowland. 3 children still-born. Jane, living unm. 1705, aged 67. Katherine, two years old in 1620.

See pedigree in *Maclean's* History of the Deanery of Trigg *Cornwall*, parish of Blisland, 1868, p. 68.

Alice, bapt. at St. Stephen's in Saltash, 28 May, 1625; mar. at Warleggan 19th Oct. 1641; died at St. Neot's 1666. = George Smith, of Warleggan, Cornwall; died and was buried at St. Neot's in said county 1656.

Jennet Carryer. = Sir Thomas Parker, Earl of Macclesfield, Lord Chief Justice.

George Parker, of Parkhill co. Stafford, esq.

John Anstis, of Duloe and Lunna in St. Neot's, Cornwall. = Mary, dau. and coheir.

Catherine.

Thomas Parker, esq. eldest son, in the commission of the peace, born 7 Dec. 1696; died at Alkincoats 16 Dec. 1774. = Alice, widow of Henry Lonsdale, of High Riley, and only child and heiress of John Blakey, of Lanehead, co. of Lanc.; died at Alkincoats 21 April, 1737.

Robert Parker, of London, 2nd son, twice married, and had issue, Edward, Thomas and John Watts, who died unmar. and Elizabeth, mar. to Dr. Ramsden, Master of the Charterhouse.

Edward Parker, 3rd son, died at Alkincoats; bpt. at Colne 13 Apr. 1701; bur. there 27 March, 1754.

John Anstis, of Duloe aforesaid, and of the Middle Temple, London, esq. Garter Principal King of Arms, &c.; died at Mortlake, Surrey, Mar. 4, 1743-4; bu. at Duloe March 23. = Elizabeth, dau. and heir of Richard Cudlipp, of Tavistock, merchant; d. 1750.

See Maclean's Blisland, *ubi supra.*

Elizabeth, only dau. named in the will of her father 1753 and 1754; bur. at Colne 2 Dec. 1781. = Robert Parker, of Alkincoats, esq. bapt. at Colne 9 March, 1720; mar. 1 Oct. 1751; bur. at Colne 12 May, 1758.

Thomas, born 8 Aug. 1723; died 23 March, 1740.

Betty, born 16 Aug. 1728; died 16 Oct. following.

Thomas Parker, of Alkincoats, J.P. and D.L.; born 20 April, 1754; died 27 April, 1819. = Betty, only dau. and heiress of Edward Parker, of Newton Hall, co. York, by Elizabeth, dau. and heiress of John Goulborne, of Manchester, mar. 4 May, 1778; died 8 Nov. 1808.

Robert Parker, died unmarried 1805.

John Toulson Parker, esq. born 21 March, 1755; died 2 Oct. 1822. = Esther Arthur, dau. of John Arthur Worsop, of Howden, co. York, esq. mar. 19 July, 1804; died 24 June, 1837.

…rt, …h. … … … Thomas Parker, of Alkincoats and Newton Hall, formerly a Capt. in the Royal Horse Guards Blue, J.P. and D.L. He purchased Browsholme from his cousin Thomas Lister Parker in 1820; died s.p. 22 April, 1832. = Mary, dau. of William Molyneux, of Liverpool; mar. 6th May, 1824; died 22d May, 1838.

Edward Parker, formerly of Selby, co. York, solicitor, and afterwards of Browsholme and Alkincoats, J.P. and D.L.; born 18th July, 1786; died 22nd May, 1865. = Ellen, only child of Ambrose William Barcroft, of Noyna, co. Lanc.; mar. 4th July, 1816.

Robert Parker, Lieut. 76 Regt; died at Walcheren 2nd Sept. 1809 unmarried.

John Parker, born 29 March, 1791, mar. 29 Nov. 1821 Ann Edmondson of Coates Hall, co. York, d. 4 Jan. 1830; she died 2 Sept. 1851, leaving issue, 1. Thomas of the Heaning near Newton in Bowland, b. 9 Nov. 1826; 2. Richard, died unmar. 14 Feb. 1856; and Elizabeth, mar. 30 Dec. 1856 to Rixon Ellingthorpe, esq. of Shorrock Hey, near Blackburn; died 1869, s.p.

Elizabeth, mar. Capt. John Atherton; died 14 Feb. 1842.

Ellen, died 19th Dec. 1802.

John Arthur Parker. Thomas, died an infant. Richard, twin with Thomas.

Sarah-Mauleverer. Frances-Mauleverer. Mary-Mauleverer.

…e-Barcroft … Captain …, of Foot; …3th April, … J.P. and … died un… … Jan. 1830.

Thomas-Goulbourne Parker, now of Browsholme and Alkincoats, M.A. of Lincoln's Inn and the Middle Temple, barrister-at-law, J.P. and D.L. Major 5th Royal Lancashire Militia; born 4th Aug. 1818. = Mary Ann, elder dau. and coheiress of John Francis Carr, of Carr Lodge, Horbury, co. York; mar. 28 Nov. 1845.

Edward Parker, M.A. St. Peter's College, Camb. Rector of Waddington, county York; born 14th Nov. 1821; mar. 24 Oct. 1850. = Catherine, dau. of Jas. Neville, of Beardwood, co. Lanc. by his wife Helen, dau. of Thomas Hargreaves, of Oak Hill.

Robert John Parker, of Selby, co. York, a solicitor; born 13th Jan. 1823.

Elizabeth Agatha.

Ellen Barcroft, wife of Lieut.-Colonel Duncan Campbell, Major 90 Light Infant; she died 11th Nov. 1865.

Barbara Phœbe, wife of Nicholas England, of Southfield House, co. Lanc.

Mary-Martha, died 20th Dec. 1833.

William Barc… bo. 25 Feb. 1… died 1 Dec. 1…

James Willia… d. 18 Sept. 18…

Septimus, die… 12 July, 183…

…ard …er, … …ept. …

John-William-Robinson Parker, born 6 Oct. 1857.

Thomas-Goulbourne Parker, born 27 Dec. 1859.

Ellen, wife of Malcolm-Nugent-Ross Davenport, Capt. 5th Lanc. Militia, son of Major Trevor Davenport, and grandson of Rear-Admiral Sir Salusbury Davenport, K.C.H. C.B.

Mary-Barbara-Beatrix. Alice-Isabel. Margaret-Anne. Harriet-Maria, deceased.

Charles-Edward-Neville, bo. 12 Dec. 1852. Robert-James-Neville, bo. 25 May, 1854. Reginald-Barcroft, bo. 9 Oct. 1855.

Arthur-Henry, bo. Dec. 1861. Francis-Ambrose, bo. 22 Nov. 1863. Ernest-Neville, bo. 26 Nov. 1868.

Sybil-Catherine. Phœbe-Ellen. Everilda.

A few particulars only remain to be added with respect to the forests and demesnes of Blackburnshire in general.

The records of this extensive district, now remaining at Clitheroe Castle, contain little which is either curious or ancient. This is accounted for from a return of Richard Assheton and Edward Braddyll, Esqrs. to a commission directed to them out of the Duchy Court, anno 22 Elizabeth, to inquire into the state of the records at this place. They say that the most ancient rolls, some of the reign of Edward III. and others without date, having been kept upon a damp floor, were become almost illegible; but that of those which remained in a tolerably perfect state, a schedule, beginning with the rolls of Henry VII. had been made by their directions, and the rolls themselves deposited within closets in an upper room under three locks and keys.

During the great usurpation, after the murder of Charles I. the four forests of Blackburnshire were sold under an ordinance of the Commons in Parliament, intituled "An Act for the Sale of all Honours, Manors, &c. belonging to the late King, Queen, and Prince," to Adam Baynes, of Knowsthorp, Esq. for the sum of 6,853*l.* 16*s.* 1*d.* together with the rents, royalties, and profits of the Halmot Courts. This transaction bore date April 16, 1651.

In January of the same year the free wapontake courts of Clitheroe and Blackburnshire, excepting the forests, were alienated to one Jeremy Whitworth. On this occasion a doubt arose whether Colne, Ightenhill, Accrington, and Tottington were really distinct manors; and in a case submitted to Sir Orlando Bridgeman, it was stated that either in the reign of Henry VI. or Edward IV. (the original record, I suppose, having rotted away on the damp floor), a decree had been made, that, to avoid an inconvenient concourse of people at the Castle, courts should be holden twice every year at Burnley, Colne, Accrington, &c. But, whatever might have been the date of the decree, it appears, from the *Custumale* already given, that courts had been holden at the first of these places much earlier; and Bridgeman thought the usage sufficient to constitute them so many distinct, though not independent, manors.

During all this time, the old account between the Crown and the copyholders remained unsettled. An agreement had been made between the two parties, in the reign of James I. that forty years old rent should be paid for the confirmation and settlement of these lands: one moiety on the passing decrees for that purpose in the Duchy Court, and the other within one month after they were confirmed by act of parliament.

Decrees for all the manors and estates thus compounded for were passed, and the first moiety paid, before the death of King James. In the 5th of Charles I. the remaining moiety was assigned to Sir Allen Apsley, for the satisfaction of debts contracted in victualling the Navy. In the 16th of this reign a bill of confirmation passed both Houses of Parliament; but, on account of the distractions then beginning in the kingdom, did not receive the royal assent. In the year 1650, however, Sir Allen Apsley obtained from the governing powers an ordinance to confirm the decrees, and to compel the copyholders to pay the remaining moiety; with a heavy penalty of 5*l.* per diem, on default of payment, after the 1st of September then following. Several of the copyholders failed in providing their quotas; which occasioned a general deficiency of payment, according to the act. This alarmed the wiser and more wealthy of the parties concerned; who paid the whole moiety, together with a great overplus, *nomine pœnæ*, amounting in all to 4,833*l.*; and thus the affair slept till the Restoration: soon after which, namely, in 1661, a general act of confirmation was passed.[1] And on this foundation rest all the titles to wapontake or copyhold lands of the new tenure, in Blackburnshire.

By the same act the forests were attached to the adjoining manors; as, *ex. gr.* Trawden to Colne, Pendle to Ightenhill, and Rossendale, with Accrington, to the manor of Accrington-Vetus. These two last-mentioned forests constitute what is called Accrington Newhold.

[1] ["An Act for confirming the Copyhold Estates of divers of His Majesty's Copyhold Tenants within the Honour of Clitherow, in the County Palatine of Lancaster, parcel of the Duchy of Lancaster, according unto severall decrees in the court of Duchy Chamber of the said county palatine." Private Acts 14 Charles II. 1662.]

DOCUMENTS RELATIVE TO THE FORESTS.

BOWLAND.

A Warrant of John of Ghent, Duke of Lancaster, to Sir Wauter Ursewyke, Chief Forester of Bowland, to deliver as much venison to the gentry of the neighbourhood as could be conveniently spared:—Johan *etc.* a nostre bien ame Monser Wanter Wrsewyke nostre chief Forestier de Bouland saluz. Nous voulons et vous mandons que faces prendre de nostre savagyn deinz nostre chace de Bouland attant come vous semblera que pur nostre profit soit affaire, et faces bailler as gentz du pays la entour ou vous semblera meulz que soit affaire pur nostre profit et sauvacione de nostre sauvagyn illoeques. Et cestes *etc.* Done a nostre Chastel de Knaresburghe le xv jour de Septembre. (15 Sept. 48 Edw. III. 1374.) (Regist. temp. Edw. III. f. 209.)

A Warrant to the Storer of Bowland to sell nine colts:—Pur vendre neof Coltes. Johan, par la grace de Dieu Roy de Castielle et de Leon, Duc de Lancastre. A nostre cher et bien ame William atte Lee nostre Storour deinz Bouland saluz. Nous vous mandons que par lavys et survieue de nostre tresame Clerc Sire William de Horneby facez vendre neof nos Coltes esceantz de nostre harase deinz vostre garde, a quel lieu et quanque vous mieux semblera pur nostre honour et profit, et meismes les deniers facez liverer au dit Sire William nostre Receivour illoeques en due numere. Et cestes noz lettres vous en serront garrant. Done, *etc.* a nostre Chastel de Pountfreit le xxvii jour de Juylle lan de reyne nostre tresredote seignur le Roy Richard second puis le Conquest quint. (27 July, 5 Ric. II. 1381.) (Duchy of Lanc. Class xi. Register t. Ric. II. f. 51.)

Warrant to deliver six oaks fit for building:—Pur Thomas Talbot, esquer. Johan, *etc.* A nostre tresame Bacheler monser Wautier Ursewyk Chief Gardein de nostre Chace de Bouland saluz. Nous vous mandons que a nostre bien ame Thomas Talbote facez liverer sys cheisnes convenable pur merisme, queux nous lui avons octroiez de nostre doune apprendre deinz vostre baillie susdite. Et cestes noz lettres vous en serront garrant. Done, *etc.* a Leicestre le primer jour d' Augst, *etc.* seisme. (1 Aug. 6 Ric. II. 1382.) (Ibid. f. 62.)

Compotus Henrici de Worsley Instauratoris de Bowlande, from Michaelmas 1 Hen. VI. to Michaelmas 2 Hen. VI.[1]

Sclatbournewarde.—Idem respondit de xl s. de herbagio de Crossedale sic dimisso Ricardo Hoghton filio Henrici Hoghton militis ut patet per extractam Rogeri Flore Capitalis Senescalli super compotum ostensam et examinatam, et antea reddere solebat nisi xiij s. iiij d.

Et de liij s. iiij d. de firma vaccarie de Brennande sic dimissa Henrico Hoghton militi ad terminum vite sue per litteras Regis patentes datas apud Pontemfractum primo die Julii anno regni regis Henrici quinti secundo.

Et de c s. de firma vaccarie de Hieghoke et Randolfboth sic dimissa hoc anno et non plus quia Abbas de Kyrkstall habet communem pasturam in eisdem.

Et de lxvi s. viij d. de vaccaria in Whytledale sic dimissa predicto Henrico Hoghton per litteras patentes supradictas.

Et de cvi s. viij d. de vaccaria de Trogh et Sykes sic dimissa Thome Bonde ad terminum vite sue per litteras domini Regis patentes datas apud Westmonasterium xxiij die Marcii anno regni regis Henrici quinti secundo.

[1] According to this Compotus the Forest of Bowland was divided into four Wards: and it appears that there was a Forester to each Ward. Richard Whitesdale and John Grayson were each appointed to be "one of the four Foresters" in 6 Hen. V. (Register, fol. 67 b.)

Et de liij s. iiij d. de firma de Stotleclose sic dimissa predicto Henrico Hoghton per litteras patentes supradictas.

Et de xx s. de firma medietatis vaccarie de Harden cujus alia medietas instauratur.

E vaccariis de Baterax et Stapilloke nichil quia instaurantur, pro quarum albo responsus est inferius.

Summa xxij li.

Harropwarde.—Et de l s. de firma vaccar. de Harrope et Netylearre sic dimissa predicto Henrico ut supra.

Et de xxvj s. viij d. de firma herbagii de Harrope sic dimissa predicto Henrico ut supra.

Et de iij s. de tenentibus de Chattebourne pro communa pastura habenda in Sclatebourne cum averiis suis tempore estivale ut ex antiquo tempore habere solebant.

Et de ij s. de tenentibus de Sclatebourne pro Overshote quod tenentes de Holden habuerunt cum averiis suis super pasturam dictorum tenencium in Sclatebourne sic eisdem dimissam per senescallum, unde de incremento vid. Summa iiij li. xxd.

Baxsholfwarde.—Et de xxx s. de Newehey sic dimissa predicto Henrico ut supra.

Et de x s. de firma de Thorneholme sic dimissa Henrico Whytedale hoc anno.

Et de xviij s. de firma de Spersmore sic dimissa Nicholao de Swynehirste hoc anno.

Et de viij s. viij d. de firma cujusdam placee vocate Spaldyngtonmoneclose sic dimissa eidem Nicholao.

Et de x s. de herbagio iiij^te partis de Broghseholme cujus alie iij partes instaurantur.

Et de iiij li. de firma cujusdam placee pasture vocate les Leghes sic dimisse hoc anno cum ii placiis extra Baxsholfswarde et viij acris vasti quas Henricus Langtaa nuper tenuit inclusas, antea ad lxvj s. viij d. Ac cujusdam placee vocate Crumbilholme quam Johannes de Threfalle nuper tenuit, antea ad vi s. viij d. sic simul dimisse prefato Henrico ut supra.

Et de xxxiij s. iiij d. de firma de Swynhulhurst sic dimissa hoc anno.

Et de viij li. de herbagio parci de Radom sic dimissi predicto Henrico ut supra.

E iij. partibus de Broghseholme nichil quia instaurantur. Summa xvij li. xs.

Chepynwarde.—Et de xxvi s. viij d. de firma de Wardeslogh cum ij. partibus de Hogekynhey sic dimissa predicto Henrico ut supra.

E Nicolhey, iiij^ta parte de Hogekynhey, Bernardclose, Chepynbroke, Grenelaunde, Laythegryme, et Colston, nichil quia imparcantur infra parcum de Laythegryme.

Et de xij s. de firma de Wyndbulles sic dimissa ipsi computanti ad terminum x annorum hoc anno vj^to per placitum Ricardi Hoghton Chevaler et Thome Urswyk ut patet per extractam Rogeri Flore Capitalis Senescalli super computum Anni vi^ti Regis Henrici v^ti ostensam.

Et de xxxv s. iiij d. de agistamento del Fence hoc anno tempore yemali sic dimisso prefato Henrico ut supra ultra xxxij vaccas Regis de Birholme, xvi vaccas Regis de Harden, et xvi vaccas Regis de Eshenoke.

Et de vi s. viij d. de agistamento yemali dicte defence dimisso per Henricum de Whytledale diversis hominibus a festo sancti Martini infra tempus compoti usque festum Invencionis sancte Crucis tunc proxime sequentem pro xi averiis habendis in eodem fenso per idem tempus, averium ad ij d.

E firma unius domus cum gardino infra parcum de Laythegryme nichil quia obructur et vacat.

Et de xiij li. vi s. viij d. de agistamento parci de Lathegryme sic dimisso Roberto Urswyke militi ad terminum x annorum hoc anno vi^to solvendis terminis Pasche et Michaelis equaliter per placitum de Laurencio de Hamerton et Thome de Urswyke Ricardi del Knolles et Michaelis Levers ut patet per extractam Rogeri Flore Capitalis Senescalli super compotum Anni vi^ti Regis Henrici v^ti ostensam ultra xxxvi. boves dicti domini Regis in yeme pec' ad viij d. eorundem boum in estate durante agistamento pec' ad ix d. xxxviij bovettorum in yeme pecia ad viij d. eorundem bovettorum in estate pecia ad xviij d.

Et de v s. de firma de Accornhirst prope parcum de Laythegryme nuper in eodem incluso sic dimissa hoc anno Ricardo Henryson.

Et de xx s. de firma de Brendlake sic dimissa Johanni Parker filio Elie Parker ad terminum xx annorum per extractam Rogeri Flore Capitalis Senescalli hoc anno iiij^{to}, et antea reddere solebat nisi xvis., et sic de incremento iiijs. per Annum.

Et de vs. de firma cujusdam parcelle pasture vocate Accornhirst incluse ad parcum predictum sic dimisse eidem Ricardo Henryson hoc anno et includit sumptibus suis propriis.

E vjs. viijd. de herbagio del Fence tempore yemali nichil hoc anno quia occupatur cum averiis Regis.

Summa xviijli. xvijs. iiijd.

Vendicio Stauri.—Et de ixli. xs. de xx bobus venditis hoc anno ut extra,[1] precium capitis ixs. vjd.

Et de iiijli. viijs. receptis de xi bobus venditis ut extra, precium capitis viijs.

Et de vijli. xiijs. iiijd. de xx vaccis venditis hoc anno ut extra, precium capitis vijs. viijd.

Et de xxvs. receptis de v vaccis venditis ut extra, precium capitis vs.

Et de ijs. receptis de iij vitulis valde debilibus venditis simul post vitulis non oneratis extra sic venditis in grosso per ipsum computantem. Summa xxijli. xviijs. iiijd.

Lactagium.—Et de xvli. iijs. de lactagio iiij^{xx}x tenerum vaccarum ad v plenas vaccarias et dimidium et octavam partem vaccarie, vacca ad iijs., et xxij. vaccarum anulorum ad dictas v vaccarias et dimidium et ad viij partem vaccarie, computans pro integra vaccaria vacca ad xviijd. et non plus quia medietas vaccarie de Whytledale que nuper instaurata fuit modo est in herbagio ut supra.

Et de ijs. de incremento firme medietatis vaccarie de Lekehirste sic dimisse Johanni Parker filio Elie Parker per extractam Capitalis Senescalli predicti.

Et de xixs. iiijd. de incremento facto per predictum Capitalem Senescallum de diversis vaccariis videlicet de Johanne Parker, Ricardo Parker pro firma vaccarie de Broghisholm, iijs. iiijd., sibi dimisse ad terminum xx annorum; Will'o Swynehulhurst pro dicta vaccaria de Fayrakhous et Graystonlegh, iijs. iiijd. sibi dimissa ad eundem terminum; Johanne Greydale pro alia medietate de Greystonlegh, iiijs., ad eundem terminum; Nicholao Swynhulhurst pro medietate vaccarie de Essheknottes et Denglegrene, iijs. iiijd., ad eundem terminum; Johanne Swynhulhurst pro Birgholme, vs. iiijd., ad eundem terminum, ut patet per extractam Capitalis Senescalli predicti hoc anno iiij^{to}. Summa xvili. iiijs. iiijd.

Summa totalis Recepte cjli. xjs. viijd.

Allocacio firme.—E quibus computat xxs. in allocatione firme superius onerate in titulo de Harropwarde infra summam de xxvis. viijd. de firma herbagii de Harrop nuper dimissi diversis tenentibus de Gryngleton per Capitalem Senescallum, quod quidem herbagium Wodewardi ibidem tenuerunt pro vjs. viijd. per annum nomine rewardi sibi facti pro ministracione officii pro custodia ferarum domini Regis ibidem, etc. eo quod predicti Woodwardi habuerunt dictum herbagium in modo quo prius habuerunt, videlicet pro vjd. viijd. ex consideracione consilii hoc anno ut in annis precedentibus quousque illud rewardi (*sic?*) fuerit pro eisdem ordinatum pro eis alloc. fuit per litteram Will'i Nesshefelde nuper Capitalis Senescalli nuper ducis Lancastrie annotat. in compoto de anno I^{o} quia aliter dictas feras noluit custodire et sic hiis annis allocatur secundum formam allocacionis in compotis annorum precedencium ut superius dictum est, non obstante dimissione dicti herbagii in Harropwarde facta, postea dimissum Ricardo Talbot per litteras domini nuper Ducis patentes ad terminum xxx annorum quod predicti Wodewardi modo non habent virtute dicte dimissionis facte de novo per dominum Regem Henricum quartum Henrico de Hoghtone Chivaler. Summa xxs.

Feoda et vadia.—Et xxxs. iiijd. in vadiis ipsius computantis per annum integrum capientis per diem jd.

Et iiijs. in Salario Clerici ejusdem prout allocatum est in computis precedentibus. Summa xxxiiijs. iiijd.

Summa omnium expensarum liiijs. iiijd. Et debet iiij^{xx}xviijli. xvijs. iiijd. Quas solvit Thome Urswyk Receptori dominorum[2] ibidem super compotum sive indenturam. Et sic recessit.

On the back of the same membrane written from the head downwards, which is very unusual in these accounts, the returns of stock are rendered thus:—

[1] *i. e.* on the back of his compotus.

[2] *i. e.* The executors of King Henry V.

Instauri de Bouland.

Boves.—Infrascriptus Henricus respondit de xxxj bobus receptis de rem. bovett' anni precedentis. Summa xxxj quos computat in vendiccione ut infra. Et nichil remanet.

Tauri.—Et de x tauris receptis de rem. compoti anni precedentis. Summa x.

E quibus computat mortuum in morina hoc anno ut patet per quandam inquisicionem super hunc compotum liberatam i. Summa i. Et remanent ix, unde apud Baterax i. Byrgholme i. Broghisholme i. Greystonlegh ij. Lekhyrste i. Esshenok i. Harden i. Laythegryme i.

Vacce.—Et de clxxv vaccis receptis de rem. compoti anni precedentis.

Et de xxxiij vaccis receptis de adjunccione juvencularum ut inferius. Summa ccxiij.

E quibus computat in morina hoc anno ut patet per eandem inquisicionem iiij.

Et in vendicione ut infra. Summa xxix. Et remanent clxxix, unde Baterax xxxi. Stapillok xvj. Byrgholm xxxj. Brogisholm xx. Greystonlegh xxxij. Lykhyrste xvj. Esschenok xvj. Harden xvj.

Bovetti.—Et de xxxj bovettis receptis de rem. compoti anni precedentis.

Et de xlij bovettis de adjunccione boviculorum ut inferius. Summa lxxiij.

E quibus computat in adjunccione cum bobus ut superius xxxj.

Summa xxxj. Et remanent xlij apud Laythgryme unde i taur'.

Juvence.—De Juvencis non fit mentio hic quia computantur cum vaccis ut superius secundum consuetudinem hujus loci.

Juvenculi.—Et de xxxiij juvenculis receptis de rem. compoti anni precedentis.

Et de xxij de adjunccione vitulorum annalium femineorum ut inferius. Summa lv.

E quibus computat in adjunccione cum vaccis ut superius xxxiij.

Et in morina hoc anno ut patet per eandem inquisicionem i. Summa xxxiiij. Et remanent xxj, unde apud Baterax xij. Stapilok ij. Byrgholm vj. Brogisholm vj. Greystonlegh v. Lekhyrste v. Essbenok iiij. Harden iiij.

Vituli.—Et de lxviij. vitulis annalibus receptis de rem. compoti anni precedentis.

Et de iiij^{xx} receptis de adjunccione vituli de exitu anni precedentis. Summa cxlix.

E quibus computat in adjunccione cum boviculis ut superius xlvj.

Et in adjunccione cum juvenculis ut superius xxij.

Et in morina hoc anno ut patet per eandem inquisicionem vij.

Et in decima data hoc anno viij. Summa iiij^{xx}iij. Et remanent lxvj., unde apud Baterax xiij, unde iij masculi, Stapillok viij. unde iij masculi, Birgholme xj. unde iij masculi, Brogisholme vj. unde iiij masculi, Greystonlegh xiij. unde ix masculi, Lekhirst v. unde iiij masculi, Esshenok v. unde iiij masculi, Harden vj. unde v masculi.

Et de iiij^{xx}j vitulis receptis de rem. compoti anni procedentis.

Et de iiij^{xx}x vitulis de exitu vaccarum supradictarum, et non plures quia iiij^{xx}ix vacce transierunt steriles per sacramentum pastorum. Summa clxxj.

E quibus computat mortuos in morina per inquisicionem predictam iij.

Et in adjunccione cum vitulis annalibus ut superius iiij^{xx}j. Summa iiij^{xx}iiij. Et remanent iiij^{xx}vij. unde apud Baterax xvj. Stapilok viij. Birgholme xvj. Brogisholme x. Graystonlegh xiij. Lekhirste vij. Esshenok viij. Harden viij.

LEAGRIM PARK. (See p. 333.)

Et solvit Ade del Swynhilhirst et Thome de Crumbilholme pro sustentacione palicii per circuitum parci de Laythegryme tam de veteribus quam de novis *palis*, *shoris*, et *raylis* de meremio Regis per convencionem in grosso sic factam per senescallum . . . . xlvj s. viij d.

Et solvit eidem Ade pro sustentacione nove launde infra defensam in Bouland apud le Knottes per convencionem in grosso sic factam per senescallum . . . . . . iij s. iiij d.

Et in pergamino empto pro Rotulis et extractis curie annuatim . . . . . ij s. vj d.

Et solvit pro lucracione ccc *raylis* pro reparacione launde in parco de Laythegryme c ad xij d. iij s.

Et solvit pro cariagio eorundem, c ad xij d. . . . . iij s.

Et solvit cuidam carpentario pro *carpentre* dictorum *raylis* et posicione aliorum veterum *postis* et *raylis* circa dictam laundam per xxx dies per diem iiij d. . . . . . x s.

Et solvit cuidam carpentario pro reparacione domorum logii de Laythegryme per duos dies per diem iiij d. . . . . viij d.

Et solvit pro reparacione parietum dictaram domorum et *daubynge* per duos dies, per diem iiij d. viij d.

Et solvit cuidam tectori pro tectura et coopertura dictarum domorum per x dies, per diem iiij d. . . . . iij s. iiij d.

Compotus of the Master Forester of Bouland 1 and 2 Hen. VI. (Duchy of Lanc. Cl. xxix. Bundle 220.)

Custus logii parci de Lathegryme, xj s.—[viz.]—

Et in stipendio cujusdam carpentarii operantis super emendacionem defecte cum logii parcii ibidem in opere carpentre per iij dies capienti per diem iiij d. . . . . . xij d.

Et in stipendio cujusdam laborarii operantis circa dauburam et *wyndynge* parietum ejusdem per iiij dies capientis per diem iiij d. . . . . xvj d.

Et in stipendio ejusdem operantis super coopertura diversarum domorum ibidem per x dies capientis per diem iiij d. . . . . iij s. iiij d.

Et solutis pro factura porte parci ibidem ex parte boriali ejusdem ex convencione facta per Senescallum in grosso . . . . ij s.

Custus palicii parci ibidem.—Et in stipendio Nicholai Swynhilhirst operantis ibidem in prostracione et fissura quercuum pro *palis* et *rayles* inde fiendis pro factura c dimidii palorum, inde dando pro C^{na} xij d. . . . . xviij d.

Et solutis eidem pro cariagio eorundem a loco ubi succidebantur usque diversa loca necessaria reparacione indigencia, dando pro C^{na} xij d. . . . . xviij d.

Et in stipendio ejusdem operantis circa emendacionem palicii predicti in diversis locis magis defectuosis per xx dies, capienti per diem iiij d. . . . . vj s. viij d.

Et solutis eidem pro palis cadentibus reponendis et iterum firmandis per totum circuitum dicti parci pro una parte ejusdem parci in grosso . . . . vij s. vij d.

Et in stipendio Thome Crumbilholme alterius paliciatoris parci ibidem pro prostracione bosci pro palis inde fiendis cum factura cc palorum, inde dando pro qualiter C^{na} xij d. . . ij s.

Et solutis eidem pro cariagio eorundem usque ibidem, dando pro C^{na} xij d. . . . . ij s.

Et in stipendio ejusdem operantis circa emendacionem palicii predicti in diversis locis defectivis per xx dies, capientis per diem iiij d. . . . . vj s. viij d.

Et solutis eidem pro veteribus palis cadentibus reponendis et iterum firmandis per totum circuitum dicti parci ut pro medietate parci in grosso . . . . vij s. vij d.

Custus fossate ibidem, lv s.—[viz.]

Et solutis Henrico Pemberton pro factura lxvij rodarum nove Fossate, latitudine viij pedum et profunditate iiij pedum et dimidii, plantate cum albis spinis in iij cursibus de novo factis ex parte boriali parci ibidem, roda ad viij d. . . . . xliiij s.

Et solutis Ricardo Swynhilhirst pro factura lxvj rodarum palicii positi super dictam fossatam tam de veteribus palis quam de novis, roda ad ij d. . . . . . . xj s.

Custus laundee in parco ibidem, v s. iiij d:—[viz.]

Et in stipendio cujusdam laboravii operantis in prostracione bosci pro *rayles* inde fiendis pro laundea de Laythgryme cum factura C *rayles* inde . . . . xij d.

Et solutis eidem pro cariagio eorundem a loco ubi succidebantur usque ibidem . . xij d.

Et in stipendio Ricardi Swynhilhirst carpentarii operantis circa emendacionem palicii predicti per x dies, capientis per diem iiij d. . . . . iij s. iiij d.

Compotus of the Master Forester of Bouland, 13 & 14 Hen VI. Duchy of Lancastèr, Class xxix. Bundle 220.

Custus palicii parci de Laythegryme.—Et in denariis solutis Will'o Swynhilhurst pro prostracione et factura de ccc de *palesbord* ac cariagio earundem pro una medietate parci de Laythegryme, Centena ad ij s. . . . . vj s.

Et in stipendio ejusdem operantis super facturam palicii predicti per lxj dies, capientis per diem iiij d. . . . . xx s. iiij d.

Et solutis eidem Will'mo pro palis cadentibus reponendis et interim firmandis per totum circuitum dicti parci ut pro dicta medietate ejusdem in grosso . . . . . . xv s. ij d.

Et solutis pro factura unius porte de novo ex parte orientali parci predicti, cum cariagio macremii ad idem, ut patet per billam . . . . vj s.

Custus logii parci de Lathegryme.—Et in stipendio Edwardi Crumbelholm operantis super emendacionem diversorum defectuum logii ibidem in opere carpentre per i diem . . vj d.

Et in stipendio Alexandri Huntyngdene operantis super dauburam diversorum parietum Logii predicti per ij dies, capientis per diem iiij d. . . . . viij d.

Et in stipendio Ricardi Boys operantis super falcacione cirporum pro *thak* inde fiendo pro coopertura logii predicti per ij dies, capientis per diem vj d. . . . . . xij d.

Et solutis pro cariagio cirporum predictorum, precium cariagii i d. . . . . . vj d.

Et in stipendio dicti Alexandri operantis super tecturam diversarum domorum infra logium predictum per x dies, capientis per diem iiij d. . . . . iiij s. iiij d.

Et in stipendio Thome Penhulton servientis sibi per x dies, capientis per diem iij d. . ij s vj d.

Et in stipendio ejusdem operantis super *le Riddyng* dictarum domorum per viij dies, capientis per diem iiij d. . . . . ij s. iiij d.

Custus Fossate de Lathegryme.—Et solutis Ricardo Merseden et sociis suis operantibus super facturam Clx[me] rodarum nove Fossate in circuitu parci ibidem latitudinis viij pedum et profunditatis iiij pedum dimidii plantate cum spinis albis in iij cursibus, capienti pro qualibet roda viij d. . . . . cvj s. viij d.

Et solutis Edwardo Crumbelholme pro factura clx[me] rodarum palicii positi super dictam Fossatam tam de veteribus palis quam de novis, roda ad ij d. . . . . . xxvj s. viij d.

Custus landee infra parcum ibidem.—Et solutis Edwardo Crumbelholme pro prostracione de lx *palesbord* pro emendatione de *les pailes* laundee infra parcum ibidem in grosso . . vj d.

Et in stipendio ejusdem Ed'i operantis super facturam de *lez pynnes* ad idem per unum diem iiij d.

Et solutis Alexandro Huntyngden carianti dictos *palesbordes* in grosso . . . . vj d.

Et in stipendio Ricardi Boys operantis super facturam del *railes* in circuitu landee predicte per x dies, capientis per diem iiij d. . . . . iij s. iiij d.

Compotus of the Master Forester of Bouland, 18 and 19 Hen. VI. Duchy of Lanc. Class xxix. Bundle 220.

Reparaciones.—Et in diversis custubus et expensis per Robertum Hoghton parcarium de Laythgryme factis et appositis super reparacionem logii infra parcum predictum, ut in falcasione iij s. iiij d., et cariagio corundem iij s., vadiis unius coopertoris iiij s., et serviencium suorum vj s., vadiis unius carpentarii et unius daubatoris conductorum ad emendandos muros ejusdem logii ij s., necnon emendacione unius gurgitis ij s., in eodem parco acceiam nova factura unius tenementi vocati Wyndshilles in grosso xiij s. iiij d., ut patet per billam de parcellis inter memoranda compoti hujus anni remanentem . . . . xxxiij s. viij d.

Et in quadam convencione facta per Senescallum, Auditorem et Receptorem cum eodem parcario quod ipse pro lxxiij s. iiij d. per annum sustentabit et reparabit totum et integrum palicium dicti parci et *lez Railes* lande ejusdem in omnibus operibus novis et veteribus que ad paliciatorem aliquo modo pertinent, sicut pater suus prius fecit, videlicet per predictum tempus hujus compoti . . . . lxx s. iiij d.

Compotus of the Master Forester of Bouland, 36 and 37 Hen. VI. Duchy of Lanc. Class xxix. Bundle 220.

RADHOLME PARK. (See p. 333.)

Et in diversis custubus misis et expensis factis et appositis circa reparacione domorum logee de Radom hoc anno, videlicet—

Solutis cuidam homini falcanti cirpos per iiij^or^ dies, capienti per diem vj d. . . . ij s.

Et solutis pro collectione dictorum cirporum . . . . viij d.

Et solutis pro cariagio iiij^or^ plaustrorum dictorum cirporum, plaustrum ad ij d . . . viij d.

Et solutis cuidam tectori per iiij^or^ dies, capienti per diem iiij^or^ d. . . . . xvj d.

Et solutis cuidam servienti dicti tectoris per iiij^a^ dies, capienti per diem ij d. . . viij d.

Et solutis cuidam homini pro muracione parietum dictarum domorum per iij dies, capienti per diem iiij d. . . . . xij d.

Et solutis per carpentria dictarum domorum per ij dies, cap. per diem iiij d. . . viij d.

Clitheroe, Receiver's Compotus 2 and 3 Hen. VI. Duchy of Lanc. Class xxix. Bundle 220.

Custus logii parci de Radom, xix s.—[viz.]—

Et in stipendio Nicholai Swynhillhirst carpentarii pro emendacione defectuum logii ibidem per unum diem . . . . vj d.

Et in stipendio Nicholai Turnour operantis super dauburam et *Wyndynges* diversorum defectuum logii ibidem per xij dies, capientis per diem iiij d. . . . . iiij s.

Et in stipendio Ed'i Huetson coopertoris operantis super cooperturam ejusdem per xij dies, capientis per diem iiij d. . . . . iiij s.

Et in stipendio servientis sui operantis in consimili per xij dies, capientis per diem iiij d. . iiij s.

Et in stipendio Nicholai Turnour falcantis cirpos pro *thak* ad idem inde fiendo per vj dies, capientis per diem vj d. . . . . iij s.

Et solutis pro rastracione corundem in grosso . . . . . . xij d.

Et in cariagio x carectarum ejusdem *thak* usque dictum logium, precium cariagii iij d. . ij s. vj d.

Custus palicii parci de Radom, lij s. x d.—[viz.]—

Et in stipendio Nicholai Swynhillhirst paliciatori pro prostracione bosci pro palis inde fiendis pro emendacione palicii parci de Radom cum factura ccclx palorum inde, dando pro qualiter c^{na} xij d. . . . . iij s. vj d.

Et solutis eidem pro cariagio eorundem a loco ubi succidebantur usque diversa loca necessaria reparacione indigencia, pro qualiter c^{na} xij d. . . . . iij s. vj d.

Et in stipendio ejusdem operantis circa emendacionem palicii predicti in diversis locis magis defectivis per iiij dies, capientis per diem iiij d. . . . . xviij s.

Et solutis Thome Turnour paliciatori pro prostracione macremii pro hujusmodi palis ac factura ccc palorum inde, dando pro qualiter c^{na} xij d. . . . . . . iij s.

Et solutis eidem pro cariagio eorundem a loco ubi succidebantur usque diversa loca necessaria reparacione indigencia, dando pro qualiter c^{na} xij d. . . . . . . vj s. viij d.

Et solutis Nicholao Swynhillhirst pro palis veteribus cadentibus reponendis et interim firmandis per totum circuitum dicti palicii ut pro uno quarterio ejusdem parci in grosso . . vij s. vij d.

Et solutis Thome Turnour pro hujusmodi palis cadentibus reponendis et interim firmandis per totum circuitum dicti palicii ut pro secundo quarterio ejusdem parci in grosso . . vij s. vij d.

Custus Fossate parci ibidem, lxx s.—[viz.]—

Et solutis pro factura iiij^{xx} iiij rodarum nove Fossate latitudine viij pedum et profunditate iiij pedum et dimidii cum plantacione cum albis spinis in iij cursibus ex parte [*vacat*] parci de Radom, roda ad viij d. . . . . lvj s.

Et solutis pro factura iiij^{xx} iiij rodarum palicii positi super dictam fossatam tam de veteribus palis quam novis, roda ad ij d. . . . . xiiij s.

Custus laundearum infra parcum et extra, xxvij s. viij d.—[viz.]—

Et solutis Roberto Parker pro prostracione et factura ccc palorum pro emendacione palicii laundee infra parcum ibidem, dando pro qualiter C^{na} xij d. . . . . . iij s.

Et solutis eidem pro cariagio eorundem, C ad xij d. . . . . . iij s.

Et in stipendio Nicholai Swynhillhirst et Nicholai Turnour operantum super emendacionem et facturam del *rayles* dicte laundee per xxv dies, utroque capienti per diem iiij d. . . . xvj s. viij d.

[*Newlaunde.*]—Et solutis Thome Turnour pro prostracione C palorum pro emendacione palicii nove laundee parci ibidem cum factura eorundem . . . . . . xij d.

Et in cariagio eorundem usque ibidem in grosso . . . . . . xij d.

Et in stipendio ejusdem operantis super emendacionem et facturam dicti palicii per ix dies, capientis per diem iij d. . . . . iij s.

Computus of the Master Forester of Bouland, 13 14 Hen. VI. Duchy of Lanc. Class xxxix. Bundle 220.

Custus palicii parci de Radom.—Et in denariis solutis Nicholao Swynlehurst paliciatori pro prostracione bosci pro palis inde fiendis ad unam medietatem parci de Radom pro emendacione ejusdem palicii ac factura ccc *palesbord* inde, dando pro C^{na} xij d. . . . . . iij s.

Et solutis eidem pro cariagio eorundem a loco ubi succidebantur usque diversa loca necessaria reparacione indigencia, dando pro qualiter C^{na} xij d. . . . . . iij s.

Et in stipendio ejusdem operantis super emendacionem palicii predicti in diversis locis magis defectivis per xxv dies, capientis per diem iiij d. . . . . . . viij s. iiij d.

Et in denariis solutis Thome Turnour paliciatori pro prostracione bosci pro palis inde fiendis ad alteram medietatem parci de Radom pro emendacione ejusdem palicii, ac factura ccc *palesbord* inde, dando pro C^{na} xij d. . . . . iij s.

Et solutis pro cariagio a loco ubi sneeidebantur usque diversa loca reparacione indigencia, dando pro qualibet Centena xij d. . . . . iij s.

Et in stipendio ejusdem operantis circa emendacionem palicii predicti in diversis locis magis defectuosis per xxiiij dies, capientis per diem iiij d. . . . . . . viij s.

Et solutis Nicholao Swynhilhurst pro palis veteribus cadentibus reponendis et interim firmandis per totum circuitum dicti palicii, ut pro uno quarterio ejusdem parci in grosso . vij s. vij d.

Et solutis Thome Turnour pro hujusmodi palis cadentibus reponendis et interim firmandis per totum circuitum dicti palicii ut pro secundo quarterio ejusdem parci in grosso . . vij. s. vij d.

Custus fossate parci de Radom.—Et solutis pro factura xl rod. nove Fossate, latitudinis viij pedum et profunditatis iiij pedum dimidii, cum albis spinis in iij cursibus ex parte boriali parci predicti, roda ad viij d. . . . . xxvj s. viiij d.

Et solutis pro factura xj rodarum palicii positi super dictam Fossatam tam de veteribus palis quam de novis, roda ad ij d. . . . . vj s. viij d.

Custus logii parci de Radom.—Et in stipendio Nicholai Turnour operantis super facturam et dauburam parietum diversarum domorum logii ibidem per iij dies, capientis per diem iiij d. . xij d.

Et solutis Edwardo Ryder operanti super falcacionem cirporum pro *thak* inde fiendo pro coopertura dicti logii per iij dies, capienti per diem vj d. . . . . . . xviij d.

Et solutis pro rastracione corundem cirporum per iij dies capienti per diem iij d. . ix d.

Et solutis pro caragio viij plaustratorum de *thak* usque dictum logium precium plaustrate iiij d. . . . . viij s.

Et in stipendio Edwardi Henetsen operantis super cooperturam diversarum domorum ibidem per octo dies, capientis per diem iiij d. . . . . ij s. viij d.

Et in stipendio cujusdam hominis servientis eidem per idem tempus, precium per diem iiij d. ij s. viij d.

Et in stipendio cujusdam hominis operantis super *le Ryggyng* dictarum domorum per ij dies capienti per diem iiij d. . . . . viij d.

Custos laundearum infra parcum.—Et in denariis solutis Thome Turnour pro prostracione et factura C palesbord pro emendacione de *lez pailes* laundee infra parcum ibidem . . . xij d.

Et solutis eidem pro cariagio earundem . . . . xij d.

Et in stipendio Nicholai Turnour operantis super emendacionem et facturam *dez Railes* dicte laundee per viij dies, capientis per diem iiij d. . . . . ij s. viij d.

Computus of the Master Forester of Bowland, 18 and 19 Hen. VI. Duchy of Lanc. Class xxij. Bundle 220.

Manor House of Whitewell. (See p. 333.)

Custus reparacionis diversarum domorum infra Manerium del Whitwell. (1 *and* 2 *Hen. VI.*)

Et in diversis custubus misis et expensis factis et appositis circa reparacionem diversarum domorum infra Manerium de Whitwell hoc anno, videlicet:—

Solutis Nicholao de Swynelhirst pro successione maremii in bosco et *postyngs* ejusdem cum carpentria Coquine et aliarum domorum ibidem per xxxiij dies, capienti per diem iiij d. . . xj s. iiij d.

Et solutis Roberto de Mitton pro cariagio vij plaustratarum maeremii, plaustrata ad iiij d. . ij s. iiij d.

Et solutis Johanni del Legh pro falcacione cirporum pro coopertura Capelle et aliarum domorum ibidem per iiij^{or} dies, capienti per diem vj d. . . . . . . ij s.

Et solutis pro cariagio viij plaustratarum cirporum plaustrata ad ij d. . . . . xvj d.

Et solutis Johanni Rudde pro coopertura dicte Capelle et aliarum domorum predictarum per xj dies, capienti per diem iiij d. . . . . iij s. viij d.

Et solutis cuidam servienti pro tractatione et portacione cirporum predictorum per xj dies capienti per diem iiij d. . . . . iij s. viij d.

Et solutis Johanni Rudde et Thome Turnour pro depositione veteris tecture Coquine predicte et cariacione ejusdem abinde ex convencione in grosso . . . . . . xvj d.

Et solut. Willielmo de Handon pro lucracione lxvj plaustratarum de *sclatston* apud Merseden pro coopertura dicte Coquine, capienti pro plaustrata vj d. . . . . . xxxiij s.

Et solutis pro *baterynges* earundem *sclatstone*, plaustrata ad iij d. . . . . xvj s. vj d.

Et solutis Ed. de Duedale et aliis pro cariagia lxvj plaustratarum de *sclatston* de Merseden usque le Whitwell, plaustrata ad xvj d. . . . . iiij li. viij s.

Et solutis pro DM. (5,000) de *Stanbredes*, M[1] ad xv d. . . . . . . vj s. iij d.

Et solutis pro viij[c] de *Spykynges* . . . . xvj d.

Et solutis Ricardo Sclater pro coopertura vij rodarum i quarterii coquine predicte cum dictis petris lapid. roda ad v s. vj d. . . . . xxxixs. xd. ob.

Et solutis pro lucracione mosse pro coopertura dicte Coquine ex convencione facta in grosso per Senescallum . . . . ij s. iiij d.

(Duchy of Lanc. Class xxix. Bundle 220, Clitheroe. Receivers' Account, 1 and 2 Hen. VI.)

Custus Manerii de Whytwelle, xxxvij s. v d.—(13 & 14 Hen. VI.)

Et in stipendio Willielmi Swynhilhirst operantis super prostracionem maeremii pro quadam nova camera juxta capellam Manerii de Whitwell inde fienda, per x dies, capientis per diem vj d. v s.

Et solutis pro cariagio viij carectarum ejusdem maeremii, precium cariagii vj d. . . iiij s.

Et in stipendio dicti Willielmi Carpentarii operantis super facturam ejusdem per xiij dies, capientis per diem v d. . . . . vj s. vj d.

Et in stipendio unius laborarii pro falcacione cirporum pro *thak* inde fiend. pro coopertura ejusdem domus per iij dies, capientis per diem vj d. . . . . . . xviij d.

Et in stipendio unius laborarii operantis super rastracionem ejusdem per iij dies, capientis per diem ij d. . . . . vj d.

Et in cariagio viij carectarum inde usque ibidem, precium cariagii iiij d. . . . ij s. viij d.

Et in stipendio unius cooportoris operantis super cooporturam ejusdem per vj dies, capientis per diem iv d. . . . . ij s.

Et in stipendio servientis sui operantis in consimili per vj dies, capientis per diem iiij d. . ij s.

Et solutis cuidam laborario pro prostracione virgarum vocatarum *spelles*, *temples*, et *wythes* ad idem per unum diem . . . . iiij d.

Et in stipendio dicti Willielmi Swynhilhirst operantis super emendacionem defectuum diversarum domorum ibidem per v dies, capientis per diem vj d. . . . . . ij s. vj d.

Et in stipendio cujusdam laborarii operantis tam super daubaram et *beemsillynge* dicte camere quam emendacionem defectuum Aule ibidem per xviij dies, capientis per diem iiij d. . vj s.

Et solutis pro factura et emendacione gutture circumquaque Aulam ibidem per ij dies, capienti per diem iiij d. . . . . viij d.

Et solutis pro M[1]C clavis vocatis *lathnailles* emptis ad idem . . . . . xxj d.

Et solutis pro iij seris et iij *dorbandes* emptis ad idem . . . . . xx d.

Et solutis pro C clavis vocatis *spikinges* emptis ad idem . . . . . iiij d.

(Comp. of Master Forester of Bouland, 13 & 14 Hen. VI. Duchy of Lancaster, Class xxix. Bundle 220.)

The repairs of the manor-house at Whitewell are mentioned in the accounts of various other years in the reigns of Henry VI. and Edward IV., and in the following entry it is termed a lodge :—

Et in diversis custubus et expensis per ipsum Computantem hoc anno factis et appositis super reparacione et emendacione logei de Whitwell xiij s. iiij d.

(Compotus of the Master Forester of Bowland, 11 & 12 Edw. IV. Duchy of Lanc. Class xxix. Bundle 221.)

Leases of the Vaccaries in the Forest of Rossendale. (See p. 315.)

The first two of these leases are given by Dr. Whitaker (3rd edition, p. 222). The others have been collected for this edition from the Duchy of Lancaster Records.

5 Hen. V. To John Booth, of Barton, Esq. the vaccary of Bacope, and a certain pasture called Newhall-hey, for the term of ten years, *ita quod p'dict. Jo. Booth et assignati non interficient neque destruent aliquas feras bestias infra forestam prædictam.*—Townl. MSS. g. 17.

To James de Greenhalgh, Dedquene Cloghe, in the minority of Henry VI. year uncertain.—Test. Humph. Duc. Glocestr. cust. Angl., apud Lancastr.

26 Feb. 2 Edw. IV. 1463. To Wm. Leylond the vaccary of Tunstedes with *le settynges* of Soclogh, late in the tenure of Margaret Remesbothome, rent 76*s.* 8*d.* and the vaccary of Godeshagh, late in the tenure of Roger Pyllyng, rent 73*s.* 4*d.* (Duch. Lanc. xxv. xi. a.)

12 May, 3 Edw. IV. 1463. To William Leylond, until the Council of the Duchy should come into those parts, the vaccary of Rowtanstall *cum pertinenciis*, the vaccary of Constabullegh with a close called Okenhewode, the herbage and pasture of Crawshawboth, Lufelugh, Grimshed, and of Bacopbothe and Horleyhed, with other vaccaries and pastures in the forests of Pendle and Trawden,[1] for 113*l.* 7*s.* a year. (Ibid.)

29 June, 5 Edw. IV. 1465. To James Radeclyf, esq. the vaccary of Hodulsden for 14 years at 10 marks a year. (Ibid.)

9 Nov. 5 Edw. IV. To Ric. Barton, of Middleton, arm. and Rad. Barton his son, a messuage with a vaccary called Wolfandenboth for 12 years, rent 6*l.* (Ibid.)

7 Mar. 6 Edw. IV. 1466. To John Pilkyngton and Thomas Pilkyngton, arm. for 20 years, the vaccary called Constablelegh, a pasture called Okinwodhed, rent 10*l.*, and a pasture called Newhalhey at the same rent Richard Barton paid. (Ibid.)

10 July, 6 Edw. IV. 1466. To William Leylond, for 7 years, the vaccary of Tunstedes, &c. (as in 1463.)

22 June, 7 Edw. IV. 1467. To Ralph Barton and W. Barton, for 12 years, Wolfandenboth, Dedequeneclogh, the pasture called Lenches, with half of another pasture called Newhalhey adjacent, rent 14*l.* 13*s.* 4*d.* (Ibid.)

22 June, 7 Edw. IV. 1467. To William Leylond, for 10 years, the vaccaries of Rowtanstall and Constabullegh with the close called Okenhewode, the herbage and pasture of Crawshawboth, Lufelough, Prymerosdyk, Gamulshed, Bacopbothe, and Horleyhede, with other vaccaries and pastures in the other forests for 108*l.* 7*s.* a year old rent and 100*s.* increase. (Ibid.)

[1] In this lease to William Leyland were included the herbage and pasture of Overbarrowe Forde and Netherbaroforde, Overroghlegh and Netherroghley, Barleboth, Whialboth and Hawboth, and Oldeland cum parva Blakwode in the forest of Pendle; the vaccary of Berdshawboth, with pasture of Overwycoller, Nethwycoller, and parcel of Wyndwall, in the forest of Trowden; and the vaccaries of Anteley, Berbyrley, Cowhouse, and Baxtonden, and the pasture of Newland in Acryngton, in the forest of Acryngton. Various other leases to the same person, in Pendle Forest, have been already described in p. 298.

6 July, 8 Edw. IV. 1468. For 20 years to John Pylkyngton *Armigero pro Corpore domini Regis,* and Thomas Pylkyngton, Esq. Constablegh, Okenwodehed, and Newhalhey, *nuper in tenura Richardi Barton.* The rent of Okenwodehed 10*l.* that of Newhalhey as much as the said Richard paid.

16 Feb. 8 Edw. IV. 1469. To James Radclyf, Esq. and John Radclyf, his son and heir, the vaccary of Hudelsdon, for 10 years, rent 10 marks et 4*d. de incremento.* (Ibid.)

Bowland.—Survey of Woods, 31 May, 1610.

	£	*s.*	*d.*
Bolland Forest held by Lease.			
John Swinglhurst hathe of Carbige land on grounde called the Fence conteyninge 30 acres, which grounde is fitt to be in Coppice.			
There is of underwood belonging to dyvers tenauntes lyinge northe and southe, 400 loades at xij d. the loade	020	00	00
Richard Swinglhurst hathe in the lands of Saplinges 10, at ij d. the peece, xx d. Of underwoodes 40 lodes, at xij d. the lode, xl s. .	002	01	08
John Parker, of Saplinges 30, at xviij d. the peece	002	05	00
Leonard Holmes, of underwood 100 lode, at xij d. ye lode	005	00	00
The saide Holme hathe 40 acres, being carbye land, which at the lordes pleasure maye be coppised and lyethe fit for the game.			
John Crumlholme, of Timber Trees 3, woorthe ij li. . . . . . Of Ashe 3, woorthe xx s. ye peece, iij li. . . . . Of Elmes 2, woorthe xx s. . . . . . . Of decayed Trees 4, woorthe xxv s.	007	05	00
Mr. Swinglehurst, of Saplinges 30, at ij s. the peece, iij li. . . . . . Of Ashe 60, at xviij d. a peece, iiij li x s. . . . . Of Underwoode 120 loade, at xij d. ye lode, vj li. . . . Fitt for Coppices 30 Acres	013	10	00
John Parker, of Underwood 40 loade	002	00	00
Summe of Timber Trees 82, lvij li. . . . . . Of Saplinges 740, xlviij li. . . . . . Of decaied Trees 066, vj li. x s. v d. . . . . . Of Underwood 2,860, cxlv li.	256	10	05

There is 100 acres fitt for coppis and very necessary bothe for increase of Timber, the benefitt of the country, and alsoe for the preservinge of his Magesties Deere.

The full title is—

> A survey of all his Maties woodes: bothe of Forests, Parkes, and Chases, and also other woods either held be lease, Coppie, or lives, Court-role or customary Tenaunte right within the Counties of Lancaster and Chester, belonginge unto the Duchy of Lancaster, taken the last daie of Maie, A^o 1610: by us, Robert Treswell and Abraham Allen, Commissioners appointed for the same, together with the perticular names of the Tenaunts nowe in possession therof; and the number, quality, and Value of Trees, Coppis, and Underwoods to them belonginge, as hereafter ensueth. (A paper book, 14 folios 4to. and 3 maps.) (Duchy of Lancaster, Class xix. No. 11, f. 11.)

Master Foresters of Blackburnshire.

Robert de Dalton, "custos boscorum et chacearum Isabelle Regine Anglie matris nostre carissime in Blackburnshire," reign of Edw. II. (Lansd. 559, f. 49 b.), date of charter 26 June 1339. See Great Mearley.

Richard de Merclesden, "capitalis forestarius ipsius Regine de Blakeburnshire." (Inquisitio de Bernoldswick, 7 Edw. III. 1334, Mon. Angl. V. 532.) *not Edw. II. as printed Hist. Whall. 3 Ed. p.* 218. Occurs 16 Oct. 4 Edw. III. (Great Coucher, vol. i. f. 71 b.)

William de Swynywat, "nuper custodem boscorum et chaceo Isabelle regine Anglie," during the forfeiture of Thomas Earl of Lancaster. (Lansd. 559, f. 50.)

Richard de Radcliffe. Patent 13 June 46 Edw. III. 1374. (Register of John D. of Lanc. t. Edw. III. f. 153.) On 10 Oct. 49 Edw. III. 1375, John of Gaunt granted a pension of 20 marks per annum to Richard, son of William de Radclif, on having surrendered the office of Master Forester of Blackburnshire. (Ibid. f. 97.)

Walter Urswyk, 15 Apr., 3 Ric. II. 1380, to be Chief Warden of the Chaces of Traweden, Penhull, Rossingdale, Totyngton, and Hodelesden. (Duch. Reg.)

Henry Hoghton, Chivaler, 25 Oct. 1402, to be Chief Forester of Pennyll, Rossendale and Trawden in Blackburnshire, and Storer and Seneseall of Blackburnshire, and Seneseall of Rochedale and Totyngton. (Reg. Hen. IV. f. 100 b.) He occurs in 1436. (Receiver's Acct. 3 and 4 Hen. VI. 1436.)

Richard Neville, Earl of Salisbury, Pat. 18 Feb. 11 Hen. VI. 1433. Richard Neville Earl of Salisbury was beheaded at Pontefract after the battle of Wakefield, fought 30 Dec. 1460. In 1441 Tho. Radcliffe, mil. was his deputy. A warrant was addressed to him by the King 1 Mar. 18 Edw. IV. 1479, as Steward of oure Forestes of Quernemore, Wyresdale, Blesdale, Mirescogh, Fulwode, Penhull, Trawden, Rossendale and Acrington, desiring that he would cause the officers of the courts and swainmotes to make livery of the estreats, 11 and 12 Edw. IV. 1471-72. (Min. Accounts.)

Thomas Lord Stanley occurs as Master Forester of Blackburnshire, 1 and 2 Ric. III. 1483-4. (Receivers' Accounts.)

Richard Ratcliffe, Esq. of Clitheroe, who died 13 Hen. VII. is said by Dr. Whitaker in the Pedigree of Ratcliffe of Clitheroe to have been Master Forester, but he was probably a Deputy.

Thomas Stanley, 4 May, 20 Hen. VII. 1505, to be Master Forester of Penhull, Rossyngdale, Trowden, Blesedale, Mirescough, Blakeburnshire, and Amounderness.

The revenue collected by the Master Forester diminished steadily as the forests were leased in vaccaries and pastures: 2 and 3 Hen. VI. the amount paid to the Receiver was only 21*s.* 9*d.*, next year 40*s.* 8*d.*, but in 13 and 14 Hen. VI. it fell to 2*s.* 7*d.*, and 18 and 19 Hen. VI. to 10*d.* Thenceforward the Compotus of the Master Forester presented a deficit, which had to be met by payments made by the Receiver: 31 and 34 Hen. VI. it was 31*s.*, 36 and 37, 67*s.* 11*d.*, 3 and 4 Edw. IV. 41*s.* 11*d.*, 11 and 12 Edw. IV. 64*s.* 6*d.*, 1 and 2 Ric. III. 100*s.* 10*d.* In the 11 and 12 Edw. IV. the total revenue was 62*s.* 8*d.*, and the expenses were 6*l.* 2*s.* 2*d.* These expenses of course ceased when foresters ceased to be appointed. In 5 and 6 Eliz. the revenue was 64*s.*, nearly all new rents derived from mines. The Compotus of the Officium Magistri forestarii de Blackburneshire was made in that year by the Receiver of Clitheroe, Richard Asheton, Esq. as Forester.

Master Foresters of Bowland.

Walter Urswyk to be Chief Forester of Bouland and Rybburnsdale, 30 June, 46 Edw. III. 1372. John of Gaunt addressed him, 15 Ap., 3 Ric. II. 1380, as "Chief Gardein de noz Chaces de Trawden, Penhull, Rossingdale, Totyngton, et Heddesdon."

Henry de Hoghton, knight, Pat. 5 Ap., 1 Hen. V. 1413, Register, f. 4.

Thomas de Hoghton occurs in the Receiver's Compotus, 1 and 2, and 2 and 3 Hen. VI. 1423-4.

Thomas Tunstall, Receiver's Compotus, 3 and 4 Hen. VI. 1425.

William Assheton, Chr. was succeeded by

Richard Nevyle, Earl of Salisbury, Patent, 18 Feb., 12 Hen. VI. 1434. Occurs in Ministers' Accounts, 36 and 37 Hen. VI. 1458. He was beheaded in 1461.

Richard Nevile, Earl of Warwick, with whose Deputy in 3 and 4 Edw. IV. was

Jac. Haryngton, mil. who made the Compotus as Master Forester in 11 and 12 Edw. 1471-2 (the Earl of Warwick was slain at the Battle of Barnet, 14 Ap. 1471,) and in 1 and 2 Ric. III. 1484-5, as deputy of

Richard Duke of Gloucester, Patent dated 4 July, 11 Edw. IV., 1471.

James Harryngton, "miles pro corpore nostro," Patent, 16 Feb., 2 Ric. III., 1485, to the office of Master Forester and all the inferior offices within the forest: see this already printed at length in p. 333.

Edward Stanley, knt. to be "Magister Forestarius foresti de Bouland et Custos sive parcarius de parci de Quernemore." Date 6 Dec., 10 Hen. VII. 1494. (Reg. Hen. VII. f. 20.)

Richard Tempest, "miles pro corpore nostro," to have the same offices "immediate post mortem E. Stanley" (who died 6 Apr. 1523). Dat. 7 June, 11 Hen. VIII. 1519, Reg. Hen. VIII. f. 46 b, 47.)

Thomas Clifford, miles, to be "Senescallus forestariorum nostrorum de Bowland et Quernemore, et Magister forestarius forestarum predictarum, et deductus ferarum in forestis predictis, vacant. per mortem sive forisfacturam Ric. Tempest, mil." (Reg. Hen. VIII. f. 85.) 10 Feb., 17 Hen. VIII. 1526.

Arthur Darcy to be "Senescallus Forestarum de Bowland et Quernemore, et Magister Forestarius, etc." as above on the death of Clifford, and also to be Seneschall of Blackburnshire, 26 June, 35 Hen. VIII. 1543. (Reg. f. 179.)

Thomas Talbot, succeeded by

Richard Shierburne, mil. Patent, 16 Nov., 3 and 4 Ph. and Mar. 1556. (Ministers' Accounts.) Occurs 9 and 10 Eliz. (Ibid.)

Richard Haryngton, arm. to be Senescall, Master Forester and Master of the game in Bowland and Quernemore and Parker of Radome. 36 Eliz. 1593-4.

Ric. Houghton, miles, et Gilbertus, ar., filius ejus, to the same offices in Bowland and Quernemore, also Master Forester and Master of the Game of Myrescough, Master Forester of Amounderness and Bleasedale, and seneschal of the domains and manors of Amounderness. 1 Jac. I. 1603-4.

Henry Brogden (Sir Gilbert Hoghton died 1647) to be "Senescallus Foreste de Bowland et Magister Forestarius diete Foreste, necnon custos parci de Radome aliter Radham." 18 Aug. 1660.

PARKERS OF RADHOLME.

Robert Mitton, to be Parker, 6 June, 1 Hen. V. 1413. (Regist. f. 7).

Robert Parker, Patent, 20 Oct., 13 Hen. VI. 1434.

Robert Chatburne, Pat. 16 Feb., 16 Hen. VI. 1438. Occurs 36 and 37 Hen. VI. 1459.

Robert Haryngton, appointed by Edward IV. occurs 3 and 4 Edw. IV. 1464, and 1 and 2 Ric. III. 1485.

Edward Stanley, "unus militum pro corpore nostro," appointed Parker of Lathgryme and Radeham, 16 Dec., 3 Hen. VII. 1487. (Register, f. 25.)

Henry Akers, "unus garcionum promptuarii nostri," appointed 2 April, 14 Hen. VIII. 1523, "post mortem Ed. Stanley, militis, domini de Montegle modo defuncti." (Registrar, f. 62 b.)

Thomas Holcroft, miles.

Richard Sherburne, "officio custodis parci nostri de Radome prout Tho. Holcroft, mil. defunctus habuit." 10 Nov., 5 and 6 Phil. and Mary, 1558. (Register, f. 18 b.)

Richard Shireburne, mil. Pat. 4 Mar., 1 Eliz. 1559.

Richard Haryngton, ar. appointed 36 Eliz. 1593-4.

Henry Brogden to be "Custos parci de Radome aliter Radham," 18 Aug. 1660.

PARKERS OF LATHEGRYME.

Richard de Hoghton, appointed 20 Ap. 1410, confirmed 6 Jan. 1413, 1 Hen. IV. and 17 Feb., 1423, 1 Hen. VI.

Robert Hoghton, Patent dated 21 Nov., 25 Hen. VI., 1446.

Robert Radclyff,[1] Patent dated 6 Dec., 1 Edw. IV., 1461.

Richard Shirbourne, Pat. 4 May, 13 Edw. IV., 1473.

Edward Stanley, "unus militum pro corpore nostro," to be Parker of Lathegryme and Radeham, 16 Dec., 3 Hen. VII. 1487.

Roger Bek, "unus valettorum hostiar. Camere nostre," 26 Ap., 15 Hen. VIII. 1523, post mort. E. Stanley.

Thomas Houghton, ar. 20 Nov., 1 and 2 Phil. and Mary, 1551, vac. per mort. Rog. Bek.

Lathegryme was disparked by patent dated 2 Mar., 1556, 2-3 Phil. et Mar. (Register f. 156b.)

[CLIDERHOWE OFFICIUM RECEPTORIS. Compotus Thome Domini Stanley Receptoris domini Regis ibidem a festo Sancti Michaelis Anno tercio Regis Edwardi iiij^{ti} usque idem Festum Sancti Michaelis extunc proxime sequentem Anno ejusdem Regis quarto scilicet per unum annum integrum. (Duchy of Lancaster. Class xxix. Bundle 221, Honor of Clitheroe, Receiver's Account, 3 & 4 Edw. IV. 29 Sep. 1463 to 29 Sep. 1464.)][2]

The Freehold and ancient Copyhold or Wapontake Rents are—

Ightenhull	lx li. iv s. iv d. ob.
Colne	xxxj li. xix d.
Penhulton	vj li. xi s. iij d.
Worston	vj li. ix s. iv d.
Chatburne	xvij li. xiiij s. iv d. q^{a}.
Acryngton	xij li. ix s. ix d. ob.
Haselyngden	ix li. vij s. iv½ d.
Perquisita Curiarum, from the pleas and perquisites in the Halmot Courts held at Ightenhull, Colne, Chatburn, Penhulton, Worston, et Acryngton	xl s. viij d.
Wapontagium de Cliderhow	lxiij li. iij s. vij d. ob.
Officium Mag. Forestarii de Bowland. Receptis de Jacobo Harrington milite, deputato Ric. Nevile com. Warwick Magistri Forestarii ibidem	xxxiiij li. ij s. vj d. q^{a}.
Officium Magistri Forestarii de Blakbournshire. De aliquibus denarii summis receptis de Magistro Forestario ibidem videlicet per predictum tempus hujus anni non respondit eo quod reprise ejusdem excedunt valorem per xlj s. xj d.	summa *nulla*.
Man. de Todington [recept' de Will'mo Leylond, prepos' ibid.]	xxxij li. iij d. q^{a}.
Ballia ib'm. [Rec' de Edmundo Grenehalgh ballivo ibidem]	xix s. ix d.

[1] 6 July, 6 Edw. IV. 1466. Lease to Robert Radclyf Armigero, for 7 years of the pasture vocate Accornhurst infra parcam nostram de Laythegrime, rent 13*s.* 4*d.* Duchy of Lancaster, Class xxv. (Chancery Roll, xi. a. No. 106.)

[2] [This is the document of which Dr. Whitaker gave a less complete abstract in the Addenda to his Third Edition, pp. *523 *et seq.* The Lord Stanley rendered this account as Receiver of Clitheroe, not as "Master Forester and Chief Steward" as there stated by Dr. Whitaker.]

Manerium de Rachedale; de receptis de Joh. Pilkington, arm. Firmario ib'm. de firma sua	xviij li. vj s. viij d.
Firma pasture in Blackburnshire.	
De xxxix li. x s. xj d. ob. receptis de diversis personis subscriptis pro firmis certarum terrarum, pratorum et pasturarum ibidem sicut eis ab antiquo demissis per annum:[1] viz.	
Nic. Shotilworth, pro Coppethursthey	vj s. vj d. ob.
In Pendle:	
Tenentes de Padeham, pro Shapedenbanke	ij s.
Roberto Banastre, pro iij acris prati apud Blakehey . .	iij s.
Eodem Roberto pro Ric. Hargreves	xij d.
Johanne Hardegreves de Lomeshagh pro v acris vasti juxta Colne	xxij d.
De eodem Johanne pro v acris de vasti	xxij d.
Roberto Blakehey	ij s. x d.
Gilberto Legh pro una acra vasti	iiij d.
Joh. Legh de Lyverode pro dimidio acre vasti . . .	ij d.
Heredibus Laurens del Eghes pro una acra dim. vasti . .	ij d.
Jo. Legh de Lyverode pro dimidia acra vasti . . .	ij d.
Ricardo filio Thome Radclyff Militis pro Shapedenhey (Heyhouses)	liij s. iv d.
Eodem Ricardo, pro xl acris terre in Parva Redelegh . .	xiij s. iv d.
Wm. Leylond, pro firma herbagii et pasture de le Westelose nuper in tenura Johannis Crokshawe	cxiij s. iv d.
Eodem Will'mo, pro Highamboth nuper in tenura Will'i Cowhope et Milonis Parker	vj li. xiij s. iv d.
Eodem Will'mo, pro le Newland nuper in tenura Thome Haryngton, arm.	cvj s. viij d.
Eodem Will'mo, pro Barleyboth nuper in tenura Roberti Banastre	cxiij s. iv d.
Edmundo Parker.	iij s. xj d.
Jacobo Walton pro eodem Edmundo	iij s. v d.
Christofero Parker pro le Carrehey	xx s. v d.
Johanne Clerk pro Roberto Both.	ij s.
Thoma Emmotz jun.	xxij d.
Will'mo Emmotz filio ejusdem Thome	xxij d.
In Rossendale:	
Tenentibus de Alden	xvj s.

[1] These articles relate to lands, not of the ancient Wapontake tenure, but demised to various tenants, at an indefinite period, before the date of the Compotus. The next class, comprising most of the launds and vaccaries of the Forests, had been let out on leases for the term of seven years each, a very few years before this time; but most, if not all of them, were already approved, and, what is remarkable, were almost all relet at reduced rents, in this year. But it appears, from another item in this roll, that "plures dictarum clausurarum de novo approvamento incluse sunt per Rogerum Floure nuper capitalem senescallum Ducatus Lancastrensis." This, and consequently the origin of the Vaccaries, or inclosures, within the forests, must be ascribed to the reign of Henry VI.; for Floure, whoever he was, is described as "nuper Senescallus." [Roger Floure was appointed Chief Steward of the North by Patent dated 1 Dec. 1413. Reg. t. Hen. V. f. 23.] Moreover it must be observed that all these were demised at rack-rents.

Jacobo Radcliff de Radclyff, pro parco de Musbury . .	viij li. x s.
Et de Her's Tho' Holden, pro Ugden et Mugden[1] . .	xv s.
Et[2] de clv li. xv s. iv d. receptis de diversis personis subscriptis pro firma certorum terrarum pratorum et pasturarum terris ibidem sic eis demissis per Henr. Sotehill deputatum Ricardi comitis Warwick Senescalli Domini Regis Ducatus sui Lancastrie, ibidem existentem cum aliis de consilio Ducatus predicti apud Clyderhow, mense Augusti anno xxxvij^mo Regis Hen. VI^ti. pro termino vij annorum, hoc anno sexto, vid.	
IN PENDLE:	
De W. Leylond, pro firma herbagii et pasture de Heghamelose nuper ad cvj s. viij d.	iiij li. xiij s. iiij d.
Eodem Will'o, Ric' Robinson, Joh. Natter et Ric. Feldyng pro Nethirgoldshagh et Overgoldshagh cum lez Craggez[2] nuper ad ix li. xj s. viij d.	viij li. vj s. viij d.
Joh. Pilkyngton, pro parco de Ightenhull nuper ad xxj li. vj s. viij d.	xx li. vj s. viij d.
Joh. Sotehill, arm. pro le Felyclose[3] nuper ad x li. xiij s. iiij d. .	ix li. vj s. viij d.
W. Leylond, pro le Oldelaunde et Parva Blakewode . .	lxij s.
Barnardo Shotilesworth, pro Wheteleyearre nuper ad cxiij s. iiij d.	cvj s. viij d.
Eodem W. pro vaccaria de Overbarowforth, nuper ad c^s .	iv li.
Eodem W. pro Nethirbarowforth nuper ad cxiij s. iiij d. .	iv li. vj s. viij d.
Eodem W. pro iij messuagiis et pastura de Haweboth nuper ad liij s. iiij d.	xlviij s. iiij d.
Eodem W. pro Whitehaweboth nuper ad lvj s. viij d. . .	lj s. viij d.
Jo. Redehalgh, pro Whateleyford nuper ad xvj s. . .	x s.
Tho. D'no Stanley et Wm. Layland, pro Redelegh Halowez nuper ad ix li. xvj s. viij d.	ix li. vj s. viij d.
In TRAWDEN:	
De eodem Wil. pro vac. de Berdshaughboth[4] . . .	x li. xiij s. iv d.
Eod. W. pro vac. de Overwicoller' et Nethirwycoller cum parcello prati nuper parcelli de Wynewall, nuper ad vj li. . .	lxvj s. viij d.
Eodem W. pro vaccaria de Wynewall	vj li. xiij s. iv d.
Laur. Lister, pro piscaria aque de Colne, nuper ad iij s. iv d.[3] .	xx d.
In ROSSENDALE:	
Ric. Barton, pro Newhalley[5]	viij li.
Joh. Harregroves, et Gilberto Risshton pro Henhades et Frerehull[6] nuper ad vj s. viij d.	iij s. iv d.
Eodum W. pro vaccaria de Cowehous[7]	vj li.
Eodem W. pro vaccaria de Routonestall	x li.
Eodem W. pro vaccaria de Constabullegh, et uno clauso vocato Okenhevedwod	x li.

[1] Musbury, Ugden, and Mugden are in Rossendale.

[2] [Et les Cragges in Penhull prope Goldes que reddere solebat per annum xiij s. iiij . . . . . xx s. Compotus Collectorum herbagii de Blakebournshire, 1—2 Hen. VI.]

[3] These are within Pendle.

[4] All these are within Trawden.

[5] In Tottington.

[6] In Rossendale.

[7] *Qu.* De Cowhope. [No: see p. 353, note.]

Ric. Barton pro vaccar. de Dedewhenclogh . . .	vj li.
Dicto Will. Leylond pro vac. de Wolfandenboth nuper ad vj li. xiij s. iiij d.	vj li.
Eodem W. pro vac. de Gamelleshoved nuper ad lxxiij s. iiij d. .	ij li. i s. viij d.
Eodem W. pro vacc. de Bacopboth et Horeleyheved nuper ad ix li. v s. iiij d.	viij li.
Eod. W. pro vaccario de Tunstedez cum le Settynges de Soclogh	iij li. xv s. viij d.
Et de xliv li. vj s. viij d. ob. rec. de diversis personis subscriptis, videlicet, de	
Jacobo Radclyff de Radcliffe pro Hodelesden[1] . . .	vj li. xiij s. iiij d.
Hen. Grymeshagh pro Roberto Grymeshagh pro le Newhey in Hodelesden	vij s. viij d.
Edmundo Waddington pro Ikecornehurst . . .	xvj s. ij d.
W. Rilley	ij d.
Rad. Cowhope pro Nethirbalshaghfeld'	ij s. iv d.
Joh. Elston pro Overbalshaghfeld'	vj s. iij d. q^a^.

These are in Accrington and Rossendale. In this compotus Accrington is considered as part of Rossendale Forest, and not as a separate Forest.

Rad. Mersshden pro Crokshaghenedez . . .	iij s.
Eodem Rad. pro Rad. Cowhop'	xij d.
Hered' Mathei Kendon	xxj d. q^a^.
W. Leylond pro vaccar. de Highriley	vj li. iij s. iiij d.
W. Rilley et Rog. Rilley pro Fernhalgh	xxxv s.
Dicto W. Leylond pro vac. de Antley.	vj li.
Eodem W. pro le Newelaunde in Acryngton . . .	xj s.
Eodem W. pro vac. de Baxstonden	c s.
Eodem W. pro Crawshawboth	vj li.
Eodem W. pro vac. de Godeshagh	lxxiij s. iiij d.
Eodem W. pro vac. de Luffecloch	ix s.
Eodem W. pro vac. de Prymrossyke	xxvj s. viij d.
Et Roberto Both Milite pro Rowelosewode . . .	xvj s. viij d.
Summa . . .	ccxxxix li. xiij s.

Firma Pasture de Bowland	cj li. iij d.
Out of the particulars of which I shall only select—	
De Ric. Parker, sen. pro ij partibus de Broghezholme . .	lxv s. vj d.
Et Joh. Parker, sen. pro tercia parte ejusdem . . .	xxxiij s.
Summa totalis omnis per Compota Ministrorum .	D iiij^xx^ li. vj s. x d. ob. q^a^.

[1] Either in Accrington or in the Graveship, not the Forest of Rossendale. [In these accounts Accrington and Huddlesden are considered as belonging to Rossendale Forest.] William Leyland, whose name is so often mentioned, had been Deputy Steward probably by favour of Lord Stanley, whose neighbour he must have been, and had availed himself of his situation in procuring leases of very large tracts of forest land lately converted into vaccaries.

In the former Compotus no rents are charged for Mines, but in that of the 12th Edward IV. are these particulars:—

De firma minere Carbonum maritimorum in Padyham et Brodehede in villa de Penhull sic dim' Rog' Cokshote et sociis suis per annum xx s.

Et de firma carb. marit. in Colne [1] et Trawden sic dim' Laur' Lyster ad terminum annorum vj s. viij d.

E firma minere de *Sclatestones* [2] apud Longfordlonghede in villa de Marcheden que nuper dimittitur pro xx d. per annum hoc anno non respondit eo quod nullus illud conducere voluit. Set de xx d. de firma minere de *Sclatstone* apud Acryngton in duobus locis sic dimissa hoc anno.

The following miscellaneous particulars are extracted from a later roll [Ministers' Accounts 11-12 Edw. IV.] on the same subject, dated anno 12 of the same reign:—

Et de viij d. de novo redditu ij acrarum de vasto D'ni Regis jacent. super Clivacher More in Dirplegrenyng sic dimiss. Rob'to Whiteacre de le Holmes. [From the Compotus of the Bailiffs of the Wapentake.]

In vadiis iiij^or *Moredrivarum*, in Penhull ij, Rossendale i, Trawden i, custodiencium feras extra Chaceam tam in com. Ebor. quam in com. Lancast', eo quod null. exire volebant, ne per malefactoribus capiantur, quolibet pro sept. vj d. prout allocata est in computis precedentibus, xii s.

Et in stipendio i hominis custodientis feras Dom. Regis apud Estmore x s. Rossendale iv s. ii d. et Trawden x s. ac unius hominis apud Toddington in auxilio quatuor prediet. Moredrivar' eo quod iidem Moredrivar' non sufficiunt feras predictas (defendere) sine auxilio eorundem hominum, prout allocata est in computis precedentibus in solvac. ferme Forest' prediet' . . . . . xxviij s. ii d. in solvac' ferme.

In denar. solut. pro sustentatione fossat. et sepium Nove Laund in Penhull per totum circuitum, xx s. Et in sustent. vj Fald. vj s.

Et solut. forestar. de Penhull pro prostratione ramorum temp. yemali ad sustentationem ferarum, hoc anno iij s. iiij d.

Et Forest' de Rossendale pro cons. prostratione ramorum temp. yemali pro ferarum sustentacione ibidem hoc anno vj s. viij d.

At three pence per diem thirty days were thus employed, which proves at once that there was much wood and many deer. [These were customary payments, and do not vary from 1 Hen. VI.]

Venditio cropporum. Nec respondit de precio cropp. ramorum sive cortice quercuum prostratarum tam pro reparacione palicii, quam ventus prostravit in Penhull, Rossendale, et Trewden, eo quod null' hujusmodi ibidem prostrat. fuerunt. Nec respondit de melle et cera silvestre ibidem hoc anno, eo quod nullum hujusmodi ibidem acciderat per idem tempus. Nec de suet' prisone ibidem hoc anno, eo quod null' suet' ibidem acciderat, nec alique persone ibidem arrestate fuerunt per idem tempus.

Hence it is evident that there were gaols in the forests, to which trespassers against the forest laws were summarily committed. [This item probably refers to the gaol of Clitheroe Castle.] The word *sueta* probably was meant to express some ancient gaol fee demanded on commitment.

Another article, which respects the conveyance of rents from Clitheroe to London, is extremely curious. One pound in every hundred was allowed to the steward as a kind of insurance. The whole was packed up in canvas bags, and two shillings *per diem* were allowed for fifteen days *in eundo, morando, et redeundo*, during the conveyance.

[1] A coal mine was wrought at Colne in the latter end of Edward the Third's reign (Compotus of Bolton, in History of Craven) otherwise I should have fixed this as the original date of that pursuit since become so general and so lucrative in this district. [Colne. De x s. de carbonibus Marinis in Trahden. Compotus terrarum Henr. de Lacy, 23—24 Edw. I.)

[2] Slatestones were now evidently beginning to supersede the primitive covering of thatch.

Solut. Abb'ti de Salley, pro quadam lampade ardente coram summo Altare in Ecclesia de Salley de Elemosina Johannis Lacy, vjs. viijd.[1]

The last extract which I shall produce from these rolls will prove that great improvements in Clitheroe Castle and in the manor houses, &c. within Blackburnshire, took place under the active reign of Richard the Third (anno regni 2°.)

In diversis custubus (costs) et expensis factis per ipsum Computantem hoc anno factis et appositis super reparacionem et emendacionem diversarum domorum et camerarum infra Castrum de Clyderhowe, xxivl. vis. viijd. Maneriorum de Ightenhull, xxxs. ijd. Whytewell et parcorum, logiorum et paliceorum eorundem, &c. S. tot. cxijl. ivs. vd.

Another document relating to the Forests, as it is extremely curious in itself, will satisfactorily explain the subject of Puture Rents within those districts.

To oure right trustie and well-beloved Father the Erle of Derbie, George Stanley, Knt. Lord Strange, Sir Henrie Halsall, Knt. Sir Jhon Towneley, Sir Ric. Sherburne, Knt. &c.

Whereas of olde use and custome the Forsters and Kepers of oure Forests of Penhull, Rossingdale, Accerington, and Trawden, have hadde of verie right and dutie at certayne tymes and daies meate and drinke[2] of the tenants therin and adjoining, the which is now called Puture, otherwise Forster Fee, as is sett forth in a boke, in which boke it also apperith, that for divers displesours and annoyances that ye seide Forsters comitted agaynst ye seide tenants, ther wyves, and servaunts, ye seide tenaunts made complaynt to our progenitors Dukes of Lancaster, wherupon ye seide tenaunts bounde themselves, their heyres, and tenures, to our progenitours, to pay for tyme being yerely xijl. xiijs. ivd. to seide Forsters towards ther wages, and in recompence of ther meat and drinke called Forster Fee; ye which was paid to ye 1st yeare of King Edward IVth, in which yere, by lab^r^ and meanes made wth hym, ye seide Puture was putt in respite, soe that cxixl. vis. viijd. is now in respite, w^ch^, if it shold be longer delayed, would turn to our disherison, and ye utter destruction of oure For^st^, for lack of kepyng: wherfor wee will and desire, and nathless charge youe, and anie five of youe, to call before youe as well our tenaunts nowe in being within ye seide Forests, as other most ancient persons adjoining as ye in your discretioun shall think most convenient, and enquire which of ye seide tenaunts ought to pay ye seide Duties, and what some every one of y^m^, after ye old usage and custome ther, and therupon to compel them, and every of them, to paye ye seide some, and for default to distreyn them and ther tenures, and for utter refusing therof to seaze on ther tenures imediately, and admyt such other persons as will bee content to paye ye s^d^ Duties.

This Commission, which is strongly tinctured by the avarice and severity of Henry VII. is followed by a certificate that the tenants of Bowland were accustomed to pay a Puture of xxil. — xd. per annum, which was regularly continued to 2d of Richard III. and that the whole sum respited and due amounted to ccclvijl. xiijs. ijd. too large an amount to be overlooked by his successor. Dated March 9, a. r. H. VII. 17°.

[1] [*Annuitas.* Et in ann. redd. solut. Henrico Darci militi ut pro redditu per progenitorem domine Regine concess. Abbati et Conventui de Salley pro lampade coram summo Altare et postea Ant. Darcy et heredibus suis dat. per pat. 28 Mar. 27 Hen. VIII. . . . vi s. viij d.—Receiver's Account, 9-10 Eliz.]

[2] [These services of meat and drink are paralleled by the coyne and livery and other exactions which were very customary in Ireland: upon which see a copious memoir in *The Topographer and Genealogist*, vol. iii. 1858.]

END OF VOLUME I.